B⚭nd4Ireland

Tricia Daniels

Intractable Souls

Book1 in the Bound4Ireland Series

Sometimes the one you need, is exactly the one you want…
You only have to choose to believe.

Tricia Daniels

Editing by Barren Acres Editing
Cover Design by SC Brown Design

Acknowledgements

Miss you Dad, with all my heart.

To my sons, who tolerated the missed dinners, the messy house and did their own laundry (Even before I started writing). You are beyond a doubt the best thing to ever happen in my life. And to my Mom, for ignoring my moods and loving me unconditionally, even when I wasn't at my best.

To all my friends and cousins who put up with the endless tears, laughter and anxiety. I love you all from the West Coast to the East Coast and everyone close to home.

Prologue

Ireland, September 1923. The gentle breeze brings along with it, the aroma of crisp fall air and fragrant green apples from the nearby orchard. Sunshine cloaks the chill in the air on the first day of the brand new school year. The sound of laughter and children playing fills the country schoolyard. Younger boys rush around roughhousing, while the girls in their pinafores gather on the other side of yard.

Over on the grass, the older boys organize a game of rounders, an Irish game similar to American baseball. The girls hover close by, whispering and giggling about the older boys; in particular, the two who have taken charge of the game, Owen Jamison and his brother, Liam. After all, their father owns half the nearby town, so no one would dare question their authority.

The Jamison family can afford the finer things in these times, but their father insists that the boys work in either the factory or the stables, wherever they're needed. Hard work and a healthy appetite over the summer have turned them into two very handsome, well-toned, muscular young men. Something that has not gone unnoticed among the girls.

The Jamison brothers proclaim themselves as captains, choosing their teams from the scruffy bunch of hopefuls standing in front of them. Getting down to the final two, Owen scrutinizes them closely. It's a tough choice. The blacksmith's son, whose one eye always seems to be pointing in the opposite direction of the other; or the new, rather small, fragile looking boy. There's something strange about the boy that Owen can't seem to put his finger on. Squinting, he looks back and forth between them. "New boy, you're with me." He flashes his brother a triumphant grin, when he hears him groan in discontent.

Seán, the redheaded boy with all the freckles snickers at the new boy, making fun of his ill-fitting clothes and the fact that he's not wearing any shoes.

"He throws like a girl," Seán shouts, holding his stomach in laughter. Owen warns him to stop several times, but the teasing continues throughout the entire game. Silently the new boy glares at him with something wicked brewing in his eyes.

The score is close, making Owen's competitive nature bubble to the surface. The bases are loaded and the new boy is up to bat. Doubting his abilities, Owen's muscles tense. Liam's team relaxes and starts to chirp him, certain that they have no worries.

"Easy out!" someone hollers from the outfield. "Everybody move in."

The first two pitches are low and wide. Owen stands along the first base line, his arms crossed and his stance widened with anxiety. Stepping away from rock that marks the makeshift home plate, the new boy looks over at Owen, nods his head and grins.

On the next pitch, he leans in and swings. The cracking sound, as he connects with the ball, echoes across the field. Faster than a greyhound, he rounds the bases, chasing the other runners as they try to get home. All the boys stand frozen, their heads looking upward at the ball that is long gone, over the fence, and into the nearby farmer's field. Liam's mouth hangs open, as defeat greets him through his brother's victorious eyes and devilish smirk.

The school bell rings, signaling the end of the game. Cursing under his breath, Liam and the rest of the boys head toward the schoolhouse. Stopping to put on his shoes, the new boy lags behind. Owen is just entering the doorway when he hears the redheaded farm boy's teasing again. He shakes his head. Preparing to take his seat, he hears the piercing sound of girls screaming and the boys start to chant, "FIGHT! FIGHT!"

Owen, being one of the older, stronger boys, shoulders past everyone to get to the action. Through the dusty cloud of dirt that's thrown up from the scuffle, he finds Seán, flat on his back. Holding him down, the new boy unleashes a few quick punches, causing his nose to bleed. Owen crosses his arms in front of him, feeling a small amount of satisfaction that the obnoxious farm boy is getting what he deserves. When the teacher screeches for it to stop, she looks to Owen, giving him a silent plea to step in and break up the fight.

Wrapping his thickset biceps around the small boy from behind, Owen lifts him with little effort and pulls him away. Trying to break free with all his might, the boy makes Owen tighten his grip around him. A strange expression washes over his face as he drags the boy off to the side. *What the? Something is not quite right.*

Liam pulls Seán to his feet. Brushing off the dirt, he mutters one last insult. Rage rushes through the new boy like a wild fire. Lunging for the redhead again, he struggles to get free of the muscular cage that has him trapped. Owen pulls him back and restrains him, holding his small body firmly against his chest. As the boy struggles beneath him, Owen notices something very wrong and confusion crosses his face again.

Demanding that they return to school, the teacher raises an unimpressed eyebrow at the new boy as they reach the bottom of the stairs. Owen grabs the boy's elbow; pulling him around the side of the building, where no one can see or hear. "Is there something you want to tell me?"

"No!" He looks down at the ground, avoiding eye contact.

Owen shakes his head. "Hmmm." Stepping forward, he stands directly in front of the boy. Lifting his hand, he lightly brushes it across the newcomer's chest. Raising his eyebrows, Owen's expression confirms his suspicions. There may be many things that Owen doesn't know about the world around him, but he most certainly knows the difference between boys and girls. Underneath these loose fitting boy's clothes, there is definitely a girl, a curvy, voluptuous girl, at that! Gently brushing his thumb across the swell of her breast, he watches her face turn red. Her chest rises and falls with a sharp intake of breath. Owen becomes aroused by her reaction to him. Pressing his finger under her chin, he forces her to look up into his meadow green eyes. A ghost of a smile haunts his face. "Are you sure?" Reaching up he removes her cap, letting her long curls fall to her shoulders and gives her a playful boyish grin.

Closing her eyes, she lets out a heavy breath. Owen runs his fingers through her hair, smoothing through the tangles and pulling it forward. "Now why would you want to hide such beautiful hair?"

Shrugging, she forces herself to look up at him, her hazel eyes locked to his. He stares at her for a long time with a strange, unsettling smile on his face. "You know, girls aren't supposed to run around in bare feet and play rounders with the boys."

"I know." Frozen where she stands, she wishes he would take his hand off her breast and back up a bit. His muscular body is way too close. She can't think straight while he's touching her.

"You've got one hell of a swing," chuckling, he moves his hand from her breast and scratches his head, looking at her curiously. "How does a girl, no bigger than a jack rabbit, hit a ball like that?"

"Just because I'm a girl doesn't mean I can't hit a ball," she challenges.

"True. Girls shouldn't be starting fights with boys, either."

She grits her teeth and folds her arms in front of her. "He made me angry."

Owen laughs, "What's your name?"

Unsure as to why she feels nervous around him, she looks away. "Elizabeth O'Connor."

Handing her back her hat, he grins. "Well, Elizabeth O'Connor, my name is Owen Jamison, and I have a feeling that you and I are going to be really good friends."

Owen was right. He and Elizabeth become inseparable. Wherever Elizabeth finds herself, Owen is by her side. Liam often teases his brother about it; taunting him by singing childish rhymes about boys and girls kissing. It earns him more than a few ass kickings, usually from Elizabeth.

Their most treasured time together is sitting underneath the large tree in the front yard;, taking turns reading aloud from a book he's chosen from his father's library. They are perfect for each other, equals in every way. Best friends. The universe has brought them together for a reason.

Winter makes it difficult to spend time together, but Owen finds ways to be with her, whenever he can. He doesn't feel complete when they're apart. When spring arrives, it finds Elizabeth transformed into a beautiful, feminine, young woman. Brushing her hair and leaving it down across her shoulders, she even wears dresses and shoes.

Sunny days are spent together laying in the meadow, talking about their dreams; or walking along the river holding hands and feeding the birds. Owen is silently aware of the changes in Elizabeth and the subtle shift taking place in their relationship. Elizabeth, well, she feels her friendship grow into something that feels a lot like love.

As the end of the school year nears, the senior students prepare for the graduation celebration. It's the social event of the year. All the girls are aflutter about it. All the girls, except for Elizabeth O'Connor. She's brought it up a few times with Owen, but he really doesn't seem interested in talking about it. If Owen isn't interested in attending, then she won't go either.

Staying after class, Owen helps the teacher with a few chores. Hearing a loud ruckus from outside, he looks up to see Liam appear at the doorway, winded. "You better come quick."

Moving toward the doorway, Owen shows his concern. "What's going on?"

"It's your girl. She's gotten herself into another brawl."

Owen curses and takes off quickly toward the crowd. Pushing his way through the cheering group of onlookers, he finds Elizabeth scuffling with one of the girls. Immediately he intervenes. "Elizabeth!" Grabbing her, he pulls her to the side, almost tossing her. Stepping in front of her, he stalls her attack. She struggles to catch her breath, while her hands tremble from the adrenaline that's pulsing through her veins like a violent storm. "What's going on?" he demands.

With teeth clenched tightly and murder in her eyes, she can't speak. Grabbing her by the arm, he tugs her forcefully to the side of the building and away from the crowd. "Would you calm down and tell me what happened?"

Elizabeth closes her eyes, embarrassed to tell him the source of her fury. "That girl has been telling everyone that YOU are escorting her to graduation." Looking up, she waits for his denial and sees regret in his eyes. She feels a sharp jab straight into her heart. "Owen? Are you?"

4

Stepping forward he wipes a small trickle of blood from her lip with his thumb. "Well, she asked me if I would escort her." His voice is quiet, calm. In complete contrast to the rage that's boiling inside Elizabeth right now.

Devastated by what she hears, her hands clench tightly into fists at her side. "And what did you say?"

"I said I'd think about it." Taking another step forward, he closes the rest of the distance between them.

Her body tenses as she takes a deep breath. "You said you'd think about it?" Her disbelief resonates in her tone.

"Yes."

A perfectly executed right cross connects with his jaw and snaps his head back. Grimacing, he shakes his head and spits out a small amount of blood. Wiping his mouth on his sleeve, he tries to figure out just what the ever-loving hell is going on. She stares at him, her hands trembling at her side. Before he can say anything, she takes off running, disappearing around the building. Cursing, he starts after her, colliding with his brother as he rounds the corner.

"Hey, what the hell's going on? She looks pretty upset."

"I'll explain later. I have to catch up to her. Cover for me at home, will ya?" Taking off in a fast run, Owen doesn't wait for an answer.

"Elizabeth! Wait!" he hollers angrily, as he quickly closes the distance between them.

"Go away!" She tries to hold back the tears. "I don't want to talk to you." Angry, exhausted and completely heartbroken she starts to slow down. Needing to rest, she heads toward their favorite tree at the fork in the road. Pulling off her shoes while she walks, she throws them angrily at the thick base of the trunk.

Closing the gap quickly, he grabs her arm as she reaches the shade of the tree. "Christ, would you wait? I want to talk to you." Spinning her around, he stands frozen at the sight of the tears that have begun to slowly trail down her cheeks. "You're crying?" Emotion hits him hard in the chest. "Why are you crying?" Something inside him tightens in knots. Lifting his hand to her face, he tenderly wipes away the tears and searches for something in her eyes.

Her heart thumps quickly at his gentle touch, pounding in her chest like a hammer. Looking away, she denies him the answer to the question that his eyes are asking.

"Liz? Talk to me." Suddenly things become very clear, very real, very overwhelming. Feelings ache in his chest, making every muscle tense as his heart beats with an ardor that he's been trying to hide for a very long time. He didn't know, until this moment, that it was love.

Pulling her arm out of his grip, Elizabeth walks toward the trunk of the tree, tired and angry, "Well, I'm not crying over you, if that's what you think."

Impulsively, Owen grabs her and turns her around. She gasps as he presses his hard muscular body against her. "Kiss me," he demands.

5

"No!" She pushes against his chest, stubbornly trying to pry herself away. "Liz. Please, kiss me." He needs to explore this feeling.

"NO!"

Frustrated, he lets out a sigh and shakes his head. "I'm not going to take her to graduation."

She stills and looks up at him through those beautiful hazel eyes. "You're not?"

He sees hope start to shimmer there. "No, I'm not."

"Why not?" she asks suspiciously. She stops struggling, reluctantly letting him reel her in. Biting at her lip, she nervously waits for his answer.

Owen gentles his hold and wraps his arms around her, slowly pulling her into his body. Brushing her hair away from her face, he runs his fingers down her cheek and locks his gaze to hers. "Because, I'm in love with *you*. Somehow, I just know that we're meant to be together. I've felt it since the first day of school. It's like you've always been the other half of me."

Swooping down, he lowers his mouth to hers. Slanting over it, he waits for a refusal that doesn't come. At the press of his lips, she opens to him, slowly parting her lips and letting his tongue slide in. Soft, warm and gentle, his tongue explores her mouth as their bodies melt into one. Relaxing into his kiss, she surrenders completely, letting him sink deeper into her mouth as he swallows the sounds of her moans.

Pulling away for a quick breath, Elizabeth brushes her trembling fingers across his cheek and then returns to him, smashing her mouth against his. Her tongue searches for his, making the bulge in his pants throb and harden, as she tangles them together with an unchained desire.

Something profound happens between them on this day, something almost ethereal. What started as friendship, blossomed into love. Best friends became lovers. With that long awaited first kiss, they awaken entangled souls. Nothing will ever be the same. Eternity will always be theirs.

Chapter One

A small green finch hovers over the foliage just outside the window of Olivia James' office. Its small black wings flutter sprightly, as it surveys the bushes for a steady branch to land on. Olivia watches, mesmerized by the movement of the emerald green leaves as they dance rhythmically in the gentle breeze. The heat of the sun blazes through the window, reaching for her like the warm hands of a lover trying to seduce her. Until today, it seemed as if spring would never arrive and end her long, restless winter.

The sound of a slamming truck door frightens the tiny bird into flight. Frowning, Olivia looks over at the offending vehicle that interrupted what had been, up to then, a peaceful afternoon. In less than an instant, a flurry of activity takes place in the garden outside her window. The sound of buzzing lawnmowers and humming leaf blowers wielded by a well-tanned grounds maintenance crew, offers her a completely different sort of distraction.

Her eyes are drawn to a stunningly handsome blond who yanks his shirt over his head as he makes his way over to trim the shaggy boxwood shrub outside her window. Perspiration starts to glisten on his skin as he snips the branches into a well-manicured square and then steps back to check his work. Olivia's eyes wander, admiring his broad shoulders and magnificent chest. Thankful for tinted windows, she lets her eyes trail, shamelessly, down the sea of rippling washboard abs.

She bites at her lip, marveling at the way his shorts hang loosely at his hips. When he moves to work on the next garden, he leaves her with a greatly appreciated view of his backside. She fans herself with the purple file folder from her desk, jumping when a voice at the door startles her.

"Keep staring out the window and you'll have nothing to do this afternoon," Rachel jokes from the doorway. Olivia smiles, trying to hide her embarrassment.

"What are you up to?" Rachel asks, narrowing her eyes.

"Nothing, I was just reviewing the *Johnson* proposal." She shows her the purple folder in her hand, snickering at the irony.

"Yeah, right." On her way behind the desk she leans forward straining her neck to see exactly what Olivia had been enjoying out the window. "Yes, I can see that you were *reviewing* something."

Olivia blushes. "What do you want?"

"The one on the left," Rachel teases. "Unless you've already called dibs."

"Rachel! Stop it!" Olivia scolds.

"Honestly? When are you going to stop punishing yourself and get back out there and find yourself a man?"

"I've answered that question many times. Never!" Her tone warns Rachel not continue on this topic.

"Okay. I get it… but seriously, every woman has needs. Maybe you should consider a friend with benefits," she nods toward the window, "or two!"

Olivia starts to protest and looks up to meet her friend's incredulous stare. "Really?" Rachel gestures toward the blond as he wanders back to the truck, "You're actually going to try and tell me that you were looking at *that* and not thinking about him between your legs?"

Olivia watches him throw a grass trimmer into the back of the truck and then lift himself to sit on the open tailgate. Reaching for a bottle of water, he empties half of it into his mouth and then dumps the rest onto his head. As he shakes the excess water out of his hair, it trickles down his chest.

"I hate you." Her face turns red and she begins to smile.

Rachel laughs, "Girlfriend, we need to get you back into the world of the living."

Olivia shakes her head in frustration and changes the subject. "Okay…seriously, back to work. What did you want?"

Rachel rolls her eyes at her friend's refusal to finish the discussion, "I need a favor. I need you to go to Scott's soccer game tonight. Cheer him on and then drive him home."

"Where are you going to be?" Olivia asks curiously. "It's not like you to miss your husband's games."

"I have a very early meeting out of town tomorrow. The opportunity has presented itself to leave tonight and stay at a lovely little hotel for a couple of days." After receiving no response, she gives Olivia a pointed stare. "A lovely little hotel with a spa and a masseuse… compliments of the company!" Rachel blinks her eyes rapidly and smiles.

Glancing out the window, Olivia watches as the sexy blond pulls his shirt back on over his rippling muscles. "Okay, fine!"

Rachel launches into a celebration dance that looks a lot like something out of a Charlie Brown cartoon.

A smile, one that would make the Cheshire cat proud, spreads across Olivia's face. "Is there anything else you'd like me to take care of while you're out of town?"

Rachel gasps, "Olivia James!" Her nostrils flare as her eyes narrow. "You had better keep your horny hands off my man!" She folds her arms in front of her and shifts her weight to one foot.

Olivia laughs, but her words are sincere, "I'm teasing! For heaven's sakes, Rach, Scott is like a brother to me."

Rachel physically relaxes, the corners of her mouth slowly curling into a smile. They've been best friends since college. It was a bonus that they had both received job offers, right after graduation, from Dunn and McLellan. Accepting a position with the rapidly growing IT consulting firm put her and Scott, her fiancé at the time, in Olivia's hometown.

Turning, Rachel starts to walk back to her own office. "We're going to finish that other conversation, eventually," she warns, her voice trailing off. "You need a man."

Leaning back in her chair, Olivia glances out the window just in time to see the truck pull out of the parking lot. Her shoulders slump in disappointment.

Before she knows it, the silence is broken by the sound of coworkers bidding each other a good night. She stands at Rachel's open door, listening as she tries to smooth over a situation on the phone. Olivia stifles a giggle when Rachel looks up and crosses her eyes in frustration. Putting her hand over the mouthpiece of the phone, she holds it a few inches away from her face. "Game starts at six. Don't be late," she whispers, "and wear something pretty."

Glancing at her watch, Olivia drops her purse just inside the door of her tiny, little townhouse. Heading upstairs she wonders why she needs to wear something pretty to a soccer game. Opening the closet, she stands in front of it, scratching her head. Tugging on a pair of black denim shorts, and her favorite pink t-shirt, she glances at the mirror, checking to make sure that her breasts are in just the right place.

Her thick, dark brown hair, hangs a few inches below her shoulders. The curse of unruly natural curls is a challenge everyday. It's sticking up everywhere at the moment and there's no time to fix it. Twisting it at the back of her head, she swishes it upward, into a rather impressive looking messy bun. Cutting it kind of close, she hurries down the stairs and grabs her keys.

Arriving at the field a few minutes late, she's surprised that the game hasn't started yet. Putting the car into park, she feels a sudden sense of anxiety crawl through her as the hair on the back of her neck stands on end. Nervously, she scans the parking lot for any sign of *him*. The ex-boyfriend: the man who put her in the hospital with multiple injuries, almost three years ago. The police confirmed that he left town shortly after. To her knowledge, he's never returned, but it's a habit she can't seem to shake. Getting out of the car, she leans against the hood and breathes in the fresh air, letting it wash away some of the anxiety.

"Watch out!"

She winces as a soccer ball narrowly misses her head and bounces into the space between two cars.

"It's customary to warn someone *before* the ball is about to hit them," she snarls. Squinting into the sun, she tries to identify the man who just launched a rocket in her direction. His brown hair hangs about an inch below his ears, held back out of his striking meadow green eyes by a sweatband. His jaw follows a hard edge right down to his perfectly rounded chin. The few days' growth of facial hair is well trimmed, making him look almost elegant, yet rugged and purely male. She has the most peculiar feeling that she's met him somewhere before. Her heart thumps inside her chest with an unexpected exuberance. She's lost for a moment, taken off guard by its odd response to him.

"Will ya fetch the ball for me?" A playful smile appears on his face.

Something tells her that she shouldn't trust that smile at all. *Fetch the ball?* Taking a moment to process the words spoken, with an unmistakable Irish accent, she decides she's unimpressed. She tosses the ball in his direction, trying to ignore his stunning good looks, and the rock hard muscular body that's not very well hidden under the flimsy fabric of his uniform.

"I'm sorry I've upset you, Beautiful." He catches it with ease and gives her a panty melting, come-and-get-me-smile.

Butterflies spring to life inside her. He has her full attention now! What is it about men with accents? Something in that smile makes Olivia's breasts swell in arousal, as her nipples become involuntarily hard beneath her t-shirt. A boyish smirk curls at the edges of his lips as his gaze slides down her neck and across her chest. The wicked sparkle in those meadow green eyes is a clear indication that he's noticed her reaction to him.

"No worries." Surprised by her own reply, she stares at him for several seconds. A warm flush of pink colors her face, and she wonders what's wrong with her for the second time today.

"Maybe you'll let me make it up to you?" He grins, his confidence evident in his puffed out chest and masculine stance. "After I single handedly win this football game."

"Thanks, but I don't think so." Olivia walks away, disgusted at his arrogance. *Gah! All men are the same.* Olivia stares straight ahead as she passes the gaggle of girlfriends and wives, pretending that she doesn't know that they are whispering about her. As the sexy stranger returns to the field, she's thankful that they turn their attention to the powerful Irish soccer god. Mystery man has certainly developed himself quite a fan club. Warming up on the sideline, he shamelessly flirts with them all. She's appalled at their schoolgirl reactions. He probably thinks he can say anything with that accent and it will get him laid. She thinks he's positively obnoxious. Certainly, *she* would never fall for his charm. *Keep telling yourself that.*

Scott waves to her from the field, sprinting back and forth and stretching out his muscles. She's thankful that this tall and rugged man saved her best friend from near social destruction back in college. Still, she teases him about having the skinniest chicken legs she has ever seen; often commenting on how it's a miracle that he manages to get through a game without one of them snapping like a dry twig.

"Where's Rachel?"

"She didn't call you?"

Looking confused, he shakes his head NO.

"She went out of town for a few days on business." Unfolding her lawn chair, she plops herself down, giving herself a good view of the field. She's actually looking forward to this, now that she's here. She'll just ignore the whispering and occasional look of pity that passes her way.

The whistle blows and the game begins. White and blue shirts run back and forth on the field; she's immediately impressed with the new guy's soccer abilities. Like watching the leaves dancing in the breeze outside her office window, she feels mesmerized. She's painfully aware that she can't take her eyes off him. He's strong, yet graceful in his movements, dominating when the ball is at his feet. Oh, how she loves a dominant man. She scowls at herself. *Where did that thought come from?*

She tries hard to ignore it, but the whispering and giggling beside her catches her attention. In an attempt to hear what they're saying, she leans as far as she can to her left, trying not to make it look too obvious that she's eavesdropping. She can't hear the entire conversation, but she makes out the words… Irish, single, work, and Scott.

Suddenly her attempt at being inconspicuous is destroyed as she leans a little too far to the side, and the chair starts to tip. In slow motion, it balances on two legs for what seems like forever, before toppling to the side, taking her with it. Helpless to stop its descent, she hits the ground hard.

In less than a split second, a pair of strong, Irish arms helps her to her feet. Pressed against six feet of hard, well-defined muscle, the smell of his cologne, and the feel of his body once again seem confusingly familiar. When her hands brush across his powerful biceps, he flexes in response to her touch. Electricity sizzles through her veins, giving every nerve ending a little jolt as she looks up into his eyes. The intensity of his stare, the overwhelming feeling of being surrounded by his masculine presence, makes warmth and dampness surge between her legs.

"Are you okay?" He checks her over from head to toe. There's a moment of silence, as all the women on the sideline look at her in shock.

"Yes, I'm fine." Who is she kidding? She's not fine. Horrified by her body's reaction to him, she wishes she could disappear.

"Seems the soccer pitch is a dangerous place for you tonight," he teases, releasing her from his grasp.

Too embarrassed to look at him, she brushes off the dirt and frowns. "Apparently."

"You're bleeding." He points to a gash on her thigh.

She hadn't noticed until he mentioned it. The only thing she has noticed is her thundering pulse every time he touches her. "It's nothing. I'm fine." Not handling the sight of blood well, especially her own, she ignores it to keep from freaking out. Annoyed, that her hair is now awkwardly hanging from the back of her head, she pulls out the clip and lets the full length of the large, thick curls fall against her shoulders.

When she glances up at him through alluring hazel eyes, he feels like he's in the middle of a slow motion movie moment. He holds her gaze, captivated by her beauty. She's the most stunning woman he's ever seen. The need to have her hits him hard in the gut, like he's just been run over by a truck. In a medieval attempt to impress her, he picks up her chair and sets it upright, dramatically wiggling it back and forth to make sure it's sturdy and on flat ground. "Your throne is now secure, m'lady." He brushes the grass off the seat and motions for her to sit.

Scott appears from behind them. "Olivia, are you okay?"

She nods, wishing that the focus would shift to somebody else right now.

"Don't worry, Scotty. I've got everything under control." Ignoring Scott's annoyed look, he pats him on the back.

Two simple words, *under control,* saturated in sin and sex, when spoken with his thick Irish brogue, make her thighs squeeze together.

Steering Scott back toward the game, the Irish soccer god turns to wink at her over his shoulder. Witnessing the gesture, Scott turns to her, looking furious. She has a strong feeling that his mood isn't because Rachel has gone out of town. In fact, she's positive that's not the reason, at all. Something else is going on.

Returning to her chair, she takes a reluctant look to her left. The whispering and giggling is, once again, about her. She sighs. This is certainly not the return to the social scene she envisioned. *Please, let this game be over soon.*

Finally, a rather loud whistle grants her wish and she stands to fold up her chair.

Scott makes his way across the field in a hurry, grabbing Olivia's chair as he passes. "Let's go!" He keeps moving, trying to usher her quickly to the car.

"Don't you want to change your shoes?" Puzzled by his bizarre behavior, she runs to keep up with his long legs. "Scott? What's the hurry?" She cringes as the open cut on her thigh rubs on the edge of her jean shorts.

Opening the car door, Scott tosses both his bag and the chair into the back seat.

"Are you going to tell me what's going on?" she asks, digging the keys out of her pocket.

"Nope! Just drive."

Before she can shift into reverse, there's a sudden knocking on the passenger side window. Scott closes his eyes, "Why couldn't you just drive like I asked you to?" Growling, he rolls down his window.

Olivia looks around Scott to see the Irishman staring in at them. His hair, lightly tousled by the evening wind and now slightly damp from perspiration, curls deliciously around his ears.

"Scotty! I think you forgot to introduce me to your friend."

"No, actually. I didn't forget. I wasn't going to introduce you to my friend."

Olivia is dumbfounded by Scott's behavior.

"Well, that's a shame. I think you should." He smiles as he leans in so he can see Olivia.

"Why?" Scott's tone is flippant, making Olivia feel nervous.

"Well… because I think she's lovely." He extends his hand to her. "Ethan O'Connell," he offers. "Football player extraordinaire and rescuer of pretty girls."

Scott's jaw clenches in anger as Ethan leans across him through the window.

Still unimpressed by his arrogance, Olivia takes his hand and gives it a shake. She pulls away quickly, attempting to ignore the feelings that ripple through her when he touches her. "Olivia James… pretty girl who can look after herself."

Chapter Two

Scott gives her a sideways glance. He's pleased at her rebuttal, but concerned about the unspoken words that seemed to pass between her and his teammate, just now.

"All right, then." Ethan smiles, capturing her attention with his eyes. In the fading sunlight, they're the color of jade. Vivid yellow highlights trail off into thin jagged lines like lightening, warning her that there's something dangerous there. "Make that... rescuer of pretty girls, who've fallen victim to vicious, unprovoked chair attacks."

Olivia fights the appeal of his boyish grin. Annoyed at her temptation, she begins to wonder if he really thinks that every girl will fall for his cheesy flirting, just because he has an Irish accent. She's just about to put him in his place, when a car pulls up behind them and honks.

A bleached blond, with fake boobs, yells out the window, "Ethan! Let's go!"

Ethan turns and acknowledges her briefly, then leans back in through Scott's window. "Will I see you at the bar, Olivia James?"

She looks at Scott, taking her cue from the way he adamantly shakes his head. "Sorry, Mr. O'Connell. I'm afraid you won't." she answers politely.

"Well, then another time soon, I hope," he tries to say, as Scott rolls up the window.

"Seriously, Scott?" she scolds.

Heading toward the road, the silence between them is driving her crazy. She can't take the tension any longer. "So are you going to tell me what that was all about?"

"Nope." Scott stares out the window avoiding eye contact with her.

"Did I do something wrong?"

"Nope."

This isn't going so well. She decides to change direction. "So… how do you know Ethan?"

Scott finally looks at her, his jaw clenched. "Olivia, let it go, please."

Oh, that struck a nerve. "Let what go? I'm just curious. What's wrong with you today?"

Scott's expression turns dark as his tone gets more serious, "Forget about him, Olivia. He's trouble."

Having learned how to avoid conflict as a necessary survival skill, Olivia says nothing. Silence remains between them until she pulls into Scott's driveway and puts the car in park. "Do you want me to come in and make you some dinner?"

"No thanks, I ate before the game." Swinging open the door, he gets out of the car and grabs his stuff from the back seat.

"Oh, okay." She frowns, wondering what it is about Ethan that has him so upset. He's obviously not going to tell her, and she's sure not going to push him for information when he's in this mood.

Scott waves to her from the porch steps, feeling guilty about his behavior. She didn't seem to like Ethan anyway, but he doesn't want to take any chances. Once she's out of sight, he slams the door closed behind him and digs his cell phone out of his soccer bag. Looking briefly at the number of missed calls, he dials his wife's number.

"Hello!" she answers cheerfully. "Do you miss me?" Sitting at the desk in her hotel room, Rachel runs her hairbrush through her recently coiffed hair. Admiring the new strawberry blond color in the mirror, she thinks it suits her pale complexion and dark blue eyes perfectly.

Scott makes no effort to hide how annoyed he is with her. "Why didn't you tell me that you were going out of town?"

"It was a last minute thing. I'm sorry. I left you a message. Didn't Olivia come to the game?"

"Yes, she was there." His footsteps pound heavily on the hardwood as he heads down the hallway.

"Awesome!"

His voice becomes a low, frustrated growl, "What do you mean awesome? What were you thinking?"

Rachel wrinkles her nose. There's no point in even trying to hide her intentions from her husband. She takes a breath and comes clean. "I was thinking that she and Ethan might hit it off."

"Are you out of your mind?" He blurts out in anger, "Rachel… Ethan is my *boss!*"

"He's *also* your friend. Why are you so upset about this?" Unaffected by his angry tone, Rachel climbs into the oversize bed and falls back against the abundant pile of pillows, trying not to be swallowed by them.

Scott tries to remain calm. "Do you remember what happened the last time I introduced Olivia to someone?"

"I hardly think that will be an issue." Finally, she understands his concern. "Is that why you didn't want me to tell Olivia that he was going to be staying with us?"

"Rachel, you don't know him at all!" he yells, feeling stressed.

"Seriously, Scott? I think you need to relax."

Scott rakes his fingers through his short, black hair and takes a deep breath. "Rachel, Honey. Please stay out of it. She doesn't even like him."

Despite his efforts, she's not paying any attention to him. "So, did you introduce them?"

"Did I introduce them?" He's shocked that she's still pursuing this conversation. "No! I didn't introduce them... I didn't have to! The minute she stepped out of the car, he was drawn to her like a moth to a flame."

"Really?" She ignores the frustration in his voice. "What was she wearing?" Excited, she bounces on the bed.

"Are you kidding me? Are you listening to me at all?" He paces heavily on the ceramic kitchen floor.

"Stop with all the negative thoughts," she snaps. "You're going to undo all the positive energy I got at the spa this afternoon!"

Scott has heard rumors that an indiscretion in Ethan's personal life is the reason he's been sent to the Canadian office, to avoid the press and publicity. "Rachel, please trust me," he pleads, angry that she's dismissing his concern as a moment of over-exaggerated drama. "I don't want him anywhere near Olivia."

"Scott, I have to go. I have another call."

"I don't believe you. Don't hang up on me again. Rachel?" The dial tone hums loudly, as he holds the phone away from his ear, looking at the receiver in frustration.

Olivia is happy to be home, and finally, off her feet. Her thoughts race back and forth between the sexy men outside her office window and the evening's events at the field. Taking out her cell phone, she sends Rachel a text.

From Olivia: There's something wrong with Scott.
From Rachel: That's not a secret lol.
From Olivia: I mean he's angry about something.
From Rachel: I know. Just ignore him.

That's it? That's all she's going to say? Olivia heads to the kitchen with the dirty dishes from a few lonely dinners in front of the TV. She grimaces as she smashes her foot on a box of paperwork on the floor in the hall. Stretching as far as she can on her tippy toes, she tries to put the box back on the shelf in the cupboard. A searing pain reminds her of the cut on her thigh. With one final push, the box twists sideways, knocking an old photo album off the edge and sending it crashing to the floor. Jumping, she tries to avoid it from hitting her toes. She looks down to see that the front cover has fallen open, revealing a picture of her and Sam.

Sadness stirs inside her when she picks up the album. She studies the picture as she walks to the living room. Sitting sideways in the oversized chair, she tucks her legs underneath her, as she lays the album open on the armrest. She stops at a picture of her and Sam together with Rachel and Scott, on the night of her twenty-seventh birthday. Everyone looks so happy posing for the camera and holding up their beer.

That was the night that he told her that he loved her for the first time. Emotions start to bubble and churn inside her as she continues to turn the pages. At first, it's a reminder of a happier time and she manages a slight smile. In every picture, his arms are wrapped around her, holding her close. She likes those memories, but flipping forward in the album her smile fades. Pictures taken later in the year show a noticeable change in his body language. His eyes are dark and serious; he no longer looks at her with adoration. His expression is often stony and troubled. She wonders why she didn't notice it at the time. Maybe, it was because she thought she was in love with him. She's often troubled by the thought that she will likely never know what happened to cause such a drastic change in his behavior.

Her thoughts are interrupted by a phone call. "Hello."

"Hi! Is everything okay? I've had the strangest feeling all day, that I should call."

Olivia's eyes start to well up with tears. Only a sister would pick up a distress signal from half way across the country. She and her sister have always had a very strong connection; similar to the bond between twins, even though Megan is three years older. Hearing her voice gives those emotions the encouragement they need to finally bubble to the surface. She tries to hide them from her, but her sniffling gives her away.

"Olivia? Are you okay?"

"Yes, I'm fine. I've just been feeling really emotional these past few days." She wipes her nose with a tissue. "Hormones, I guess."

"Maybe you should go see a doctor?"

"No, that's not necessary." She starts to laugh through the tears. "I know what's wrong with me. It's nothing a doctor can help with."

"Ah… I see. Sounds like it's time to get out of that house and start dating again."

"Geez, you sound like Rachel."

"Well, Rachel is right. You need to start looking after *you*. When you start getting out and doing things again, your soul will begin to heal. You need to increase your vibrations in the universe."

Olivia smiles. She's all about her logical mind. Her sister is all about the universe and self-healing. Sometimes, she finds it hard not to tease Megan about her spiritual side, even though she does adore her for it.

"Yes. You're right, Megan… I need to increase my vibrations, all right. Now would be a good time to buy stock in Duracell." She smiles at her joke, knowing that her sister is probably speechless.

Ignoring it all together, Megan's tone turns serious, "Olivia? Have you been with a man since Sam?"

"No," her answer is void of emotion.

"Sweetheart, why not?"

"How could I possibly?" The tears well up in her eyes, threatening to flow again.

Megan's heart aches for her sister. The anguish in Olivia's voice is almost too much to bear. Everyday she lives with the guilt that her husband's job forced them to move to the East Coast, taking her away when Olivia needed her the most.

"I know that it's hard to trust again. Is there someone you feel safe with, that you could be with? Someone to help ease you back into the game?"

"You mean someone to have sex with?"

"Yes, someone you're comfortable with. Someone that you could have an intimate relationship with, where *you* can control the limits?"

"I don't know. I haven't given it much thought."

"What about your friend, Noah?"

"Noah? He's a dear friend, but we don't have that kind of relationship. I mean, we've had a few naughty conversations over email, but we've never taken it past that."

"Do you trust him?" Megan feels a spark of hope.

"Yes, I've known him for a very long time. He would never hurt me, if that's what you're asking. I'm not sure he would be interested in more."

"How do you know for sure? Maybe he's totally in to you. Call him. Offer him more. You control what you want and don't want, until you feel comfortable. It's a chance to look after your needs, both emotional and physical, in a safe and caring environment."

"Oh, Megan." Only her sister, with many years of counseling experience and the desire to solve all the world's problems, would think of it that way. Olivia likes the idea because it's a logical solution. It's brilliant, in fact. It sounds much more appealing than Rachel's advice to find a fuck buddy. There's only one problem. "I'm not sure if I can bring myself to talk to him about that," she confesses.

"Why not? You're a strong, confident woman. Since when are you afraid to ask for something that you want?"

Olivia stares down at the album and traces her finger around the edges of the photo of her and Sam. "I used to be that woman. I'm not anymore."

"Olivia, I'm so sorry…"

Olivia cuts her off there. "I know."

"I wish I could…"

"Megan, STOP!"

There's a brief silence and then a muffled voice. "Sweetie, I have to go. Come visit me soon! That's an order, not a request."

"Okay, I'll try to get there soon. I promise."

"Promise me something else?"

Olivia hesitates, knowing better than to make promises before she even knows what they are, especially to her sister. "Ummm, maybe… tell me first."

"Promise me that you'll call Noah as soon as I hang up. Ask him over for dinner. Talk to him about your needs."

"Okay, I'll call him."

"I'll call you later in the week when things aren't so crazy around here. Sending big hugs!"

"Hugs and kisses back." She prepares to hang up when she suddenly feels a huge wave of anxiety. "Megan?"

"Yes?"

"Megan, I miss you sooooo much!" her voice cracks.

"I miss you, too! Baby Sister, please believe me… you did absolutely nothing to deserve what happened to you."

"I know. I love you." Giving her sister the answer that she needs to hear, she hangs up the phone. Maybe one day she'll believe it, but that day isn't today.

Keeping her promise, she dials Noah's number, and holds her breath when it starts to ring. She has no idea what she's going to say to him. *Hey, do you want to fuck?* just doesn't sound very appropriate. On the third ring, he answers.

"Ello… Darling," Noah puts on his most exaggerated British accent, just to make her laugh.

"Hi," Olivia tries to sound happy, but she doesn't do a very good job of hiding her emotional exhaustion.

Sensing something in her voice, he drops the accent, concerned. "Olivia, what's wrong?"

Feeling unnerved, she tries to pull herself together quickly. What was she thinking, dialing his number without a plan? How exactly is she going to approach the subject? Pacing nervously back to the kitchen, she bangs her leg on the doorframe. "Ouch!"

"Olivia?"

"Sorry." She panics and starts to ramble, "The chair fell, and my leg is cut and it's bleeding."

"Are you okay? Do you need to go to the hospital? I'll be right there."

"No, I don't need to go to the hospital." Brilliantly, a plan unfolds. "It's not life threatening but you know me and blood. I hate to ask, but could you pop over and help me get it cleaned up and bandaged?" She closes her eyes in shame. How desperate was that?

"Sure, I'll be right there."

"Ummm, Noah?"

"What?"

"Can you bring some bandages? I don't have any."

Hanging up the phone, she walks over to the door and unlocks it. Noah lives on the next street over, so when he says he'll be right there, he's not kidding. She can already see him coming up the street, his silhouette unmistakably tall and broad through the shoulders. When he passes under the gentle glow of the streetlight, she can see his short, jet-black hair.

She sighs, thinking about the crush she had on him when they first met. Noah has the kind of charisma that makes all the girls swoon. In fact, beautiful women are his specialty. Olivia considers herself a small town girl, lacking the style and polish of the women that keep Noah Thompson company. She begins to worry that this is a bad idea. Noah put her in the friend zone a long time ago, never offering her anything more. Why would he be interested in adding *benefits* to their friendship now?

In mere minutes, he's standing at the door, flashing his million-dollar smile, as he holds up the first-aid kit he's brought with him. Geez, she's so caught up in his dreamy good looks, she almost forgot about that. Standing aside, she lets him in and leans in for a hello kiss as he passes. Shrugging out of his leather jacket, he throws it over the back of the chair. "Come on, then… let's get you fixed up." Crouching down, he lifts the bottom of her shorts and lets out a long, drawn out whistle. "Now that's nasty. Do you want the good news or the bad news first?"

Olivia starts to feel a little nervous. "The bad news I guess."

"Well, it's not really a cut, more of a gouge. Something took a chunk of skin right out of your thigh."

"Ew… stop it, I think I'm going to barf now." She holds her stomach and tries not to fall over. "What's the good news?"

"The good news is that I can't get to it, so you need to take your pants off." He looks up at her and smiles.

"That's good news?" She scowls at him.

"Well, its good news for me." He shrugs playfully.

Olivia rolls her eyes and unzips her shorts, letting them drop to the floor. He's seen her in a bikini for heaven's sake, so there isn't much difference standing there in her underwear.

Noah squeezes a large amount of antibiotic first-aid cream on his finger and roughly applies it over the torn flesh. She jumps as he roughly pokes at her.

"Ouch!"

"Sorry." Pressing firmly on the gauze pad, he sticks it in place.

"AH! Holy crap, Noah! Do you have to be so rough?"

"Stay still and don't look down." Leaning forward, he wipes the dried blood off her leg with an alcohol wipe, and discards it quickly out of sight. Reaching down, she runs her hand through his inky black hair as he applies one last piece of tape.

"Okay, all done."

Olivia's eyes follow as he stands. At six-foot-two, he's a giant standing beside her.

"How does it feel?"

"Truthfully? It feels worse than before you started. You aren't exactly gentle."

"Sorry, I'm a veterinarian," he chuckles. "As far as humans are concerned, I guess I'm more of a *spiritual healer*." Closing the first-aid kit, he places it by his jacket. "You sounded pretty upset when you called. What's going on?"

"It's been kind of a rough day," she admits.

Looking down, Noah sees the open photo album and turns to face her.

"Why is this out?" He walks toward her waiting for an answer but she only shrugs.

He snaps it closed and puts it down on the table, "Come here, you," he sighs, wrapping his arms around her in a nurturing embrace. His lips press gently on the top of her head. "How about I hang out and watch TV for awhile?" Taking her hand, he leads her into the living room. Plopping down on the couch with a thud, he pulls her down beside him.

Olivia begins to think about her sister's advice and tucks in under his arm for a cuddle. Leaning her head against his chest, she nuzzles her cheek against him. When he tilts his head down and returns her affection, she moves her hand to his thigh. In a very intimate gesture, she begins to gently caress him with her thumb and fingertips. She feels him take a quick breath and hold it as she accidently brushes across the bulge starting to form in his pants.

Olivia has fantasized about Noah, so many times, over the years when she pleasured herself. Finally, here he is, sitting beside her, live and in person with a semi hard-on forming in his pants. So why on God's green earth, is she suddenly thinking about Ethan O'Connell's rather impressive package? It was difficult not to notice, with the way his shorts clung tightly around it, but it was absolutely impossible to ignore when he pressed it up against her. *STOP IT!* Why is she thinking about that guy?

Noah traces his fingertips lightly up and down her side. When she wiggles a little closer to him, his thumb brushes across her sensitive breast. His chest tightens, and she can feel his heartbeat faster against her cheek.

Her excitement is underwhelming. Her nipples don't even harden in response to his touch, until she thinks about Ethan's green eyes and sensual lips. Then, they harden into taut pebbles as she imagines Ethan's tempting lips muttering dirty words in that sexy Irish accent, while his warm, wet tongue teases her. Heat rushes through her body. *These thoughts just need to stop!*

She obviously needs to look after this aching need, and soon. She lifts her chin to look at the handsome man sitting beside her. Noah is the solution… focus on Noah! But Noah is focused on the TV. Why won't he look at her? She wants him to lower his lips to hers and claim her in a passionate kiss, but it looks like she'll have to make the first move. Pressing a tender kiss on his neck, then another, she nibbles a little trail toward his chin. She feels his excitement start to grow, and hope stirs inside her. Before she can continue any further he picks up the remote and turns off the TV. Pressing his lips to the top of her head, he whispers, "I need to go now."

NOOO! Quick, think of something! Before she can protest, he's on his feet and across the room, sliding into his jacket and reaching for the door. Confused, she follows him. Is he running because of what she was doing?

"Thank you for coming over, Noah." She desperately thinks of a way to stop him.

"You don't think I'd miss the opportunity to get into the pants of the prettiest girl on the block, do you?" He looks at her with sheer affection and touches his finger to the end of her nose. "YOU… need to be more careful."

Why are you leaving? "Noah, can I ask you a question?"

"Yes," he answers, reluctantly.

Here goes nothing. "Why do you think you and I have never…?" she pauses, thinking for the right words. "What I'm trying to say is that… *we* are friends."

Curious where this is going he stops and listens to her. "Yes, we are."

"Well, I'm wondering if… I mean why, we have never been… *more?*"

"More?" He quirks an eyebrow at her, stunned.

Olivia is a beautiful girl, one that any man would jump at the opportunity to have, Noah Thompson included. Having thought that she put him in the friend zone a long time ago, he works hard at squashing his desires for her when they arise.

"Please don't make me say it… you know what I'm talking about." She blushes and looks down, pretending to study some mysterious spot on the black ceramic tiles.

Grinning, he puts his finger under her chin, lifting her gaze to his. "Because you've never asked for *more*." Turning the knob, he pulls the door open.

She wonders if it's just that simple. Was that all she had to do was ask? "I'm asking now," her intentions spill out of her mouth, leaving no room for misinterpretation. He stops and turns to look at her, a faint smile on his lips.

"I want more," she mumbles nervously. "If… if you want that, too." She holds on to hope as she looks up at his expression of amusement.

"Okay," he agrees quickly, wanting to get her into his bed before she changes her mind.

"Can we do it on Friday?" she asks anxiously.

Noah laughs, "In a hurry are you?"

"I'm extremely… umm… err… restless. Should we have dinner first?" Fidgeting uncomfortably, she shifts her weight from side to side.

"Good idea, we'll need our strength."

Now he's definitely making fun of her. Rolling her eyes, she moves in for their usual goodbye kiss. This time her lips brush gently against his and then hover closely, waiting. Leaning in, he claims a second kiss with more passion than he's ever given her before. She feels him start to swell against her hip.

Olivia pulls away, feeling nothing. She tries to blame nervousness as the reason. There's no way she'll admit to herself that it's because she's had a particular annoying Irishman on her mind all night.

"I'll text or call you and let you know what time I can get off work." Noah holds her hand as he backs away.

"Okay. Where will we go for dinner?"

"You decide and let me know when I call." When he's backed far enough away so that only their fingertips still touch, he takes one further step back; releasing her, he lets her hand drop heavily to her side. He smiles. "Good night, Olivia."

"Good night. I'll see you on Friday," She feels a small sense of victory as she watches him swagger up the street, out of the luminous glow of the streetlights, and into the darkness. Closing the door, she secures the lock, then turns and leans against it feeling lightheaded. She's unsure if it's the excitement, or the fact that it's now 11 p.m. and she hasn't had anything to eat. More than likely, it's because she just thought about Ethan O'Connell. She pushes that thought out of her head quickly.

Climbing into bed, her mind is racing. Still fighting to deny her attraction to the sexy Irishman, warmth rushes over her skin, as she recalls her body's reaction to his touch. She's appalled at its betrayal. She tries to focus on Friday, planning her outfit and where they'll go for dinner. Instead, she finds herself drifting into sleep with the thought of Ethan's strong, well-developed muscles pressed against her.

Chapter Three

Strong hands slide down her body feeling every dip and curve. Her heart pounds in her chest as they grasp her wrists firmly and slowly lift them, pinning them over her head. Teeth nip and nibble along her neck, marking her as his own. His hips press against her, adjusting his position, as the heavy weight of his body holds her in place. She gasps as he enters her, tightening around him. Growling, he holds still, throbbing and lengthening inside her. Rolling his hips he sets a delicious rhythm driving her toward ecstasy.

Shadows hide his face from her. She blinks and tries to focus on him, desperately trying to see him clearly. She feels a strong connection to him, and yet, no matter how hard she tries, his identity remains unknown. Releasing her hands, he braces himself on either side of her, pushing in harder and forcing her legs wider to accept the width of his hips. Determined movements and panting breaths signal his release. Writhing beneath him, she moans, meeting his every thrust and pushing him over the edge. Through the shadows she stares into familiar eyes and inexplicably feels his love. Thrusting one last time he leans forward, his breath burning against her ear as he whispers it. Her name. She doesn't recognize it as hers at first, but she knows the sound of it as it brushes sweetly across his lips.

Friday morning arrives as her cell phone comes to life, blasting out an alarm. Its brassy discordant ringtone repeats itself in an unrelenting manner. Without opening her eyes Olivia searches blindly, trying to find it amongst the pillows and blankets. Finally getting her hands on it, she peeks at the time through one eye and turns it off.

Thoughts of a certain, smoking hot Irishman woke her several times during the night. She rolls out of bed, still tired, and feeling more than just a little *edgy*. Pushing unwanted thoughts of him out of her head, she stands in front of the bedroom closet. Trying to focus on her rendezvous with Noah, she fusses over what to wear. Finally, she chooses a black chiffon dress with a simple A-line design. The very revealing neckline makes her feel feminine, despite her tomboy tendencies. It's also just the right length to hide the hideous wound on her leg.

After showering and tending to some personal landscaping, she decides to use the flat iron to straighten the curls out of her hair. She thinks it gives her a much more alluring appearance. Today, she's feeling very seductive. Sliding on her black patent leather high heels, she admires her appearance in the mirrored closet door. *Perfect.*

On the way through the backyard, the sounds of the mourning doves welcome her to the garden. She wishes she could stay and enjoy their hospitality, but she's in a rush to stop at the local coffee shop to buy her breakfast. A small, green finch sits on the fence; watching her make her way to the car. Studying it as she passes, she wonders if it could possibly be the same one that sat outside her office window yesterday. She's certain it must be. She's never seen a green finch before; it seems unusual that she would see two different ones a few days apart. It seems even more unlikely that he would travel from her work, several blocks away, to be casually sitting on her fence. Yesterday, she didn't notice the white patch of feathers on its chest. The two black scrolled marks in the center almost touch at the top and bottom, forming the outline of a heart. She's a beautiful little bird, Olivia acknowledges. She finds its presence almost comforting. *Weird.*

Her old, worn out, *vintage* Mustang coughs and sputters as she makes her way up the street to the coffee shop. The drive-thru line up is backed up around the parking lot and out on to the road. She mutters her frustration, hating the thought of going inside and standing in line. It doesn't look like she has much choice this morning. She's too hungry to wait until lunchtime to eat, but she'll be late if she stays where she is. When a spot opens up by the door, she ditches out of the drive-thru lane and parks. Getting out of the car and heading for the door, she forgets, briefly, that she's wearing heels. She adjusts her steps to a smaller, more ladylike walk. She's definitely much more comfortable in her Converse high-tops.

Approaching the building, she's aware that there's a man walking behind her. She's surprised when he suddenly rushes past to open the door for her. She smiles at him. "Thank you." *Wow, that's never happened before.*

He nods and smiles. "You're welcome."

Every other time she's seen him in the morning he's let the door close behind him pretending he doesn't see her. There's a lecture here about how men shouldn't reserve their manners just for the pretty girls, but she lets it go. In the reflection of the glass door, she can see him checking her out as she walks past him through the doorway. His acknowledgement makes her hopeful that Noah will like what he sees, as well.

There are only a few people in line. She's happy that coming inside, although an inconvenience, was a good choice. Ordering her usual, she digs through her purse looking for her wallet. Suddenly, she becomes aware of a man standing at her side, intruding on her transaction. A strong masculine hand slides a five-dollar bill across the counter in front of her.

"Please... allow me."

She doesn't have to look up to know that it's Ethan O'Connell. The Irish accent and the shiver that runs through her body give him away.

Feeling irritated that he's invaded her space, she turns him down, "Thank you, but you don't need to do that." She makes a huge mistake turning to look at him. His piercing green eyes and warm, friendly smile, instantly make her forget that she's annoyed. *How does he do that?*

Ethan's eyes wander her body from head to toe, admiring her figure in that black dress. He nods once and grins, indicating his approval. Entertaining a little fantasy in his mind, he has to fight the urge to back her up against the counter. He'd like nothing better than to press his body against her soft, alluring curves and taste those tempting lips. A warm flush spreads across her skin as if she can read his mind. She forces herself to tear her eyes away from his penetrating gaze. Her reaction strengthens the *want* already growing deep inside him, causing his muscles to tense and flex.

"I want to and I'm used to getting the things I want." He pushes the money toward the cashier.

Olivia begins to feel uneasy about the lack of space he's left between them. She tries to back up, but someone standing behind her halts her escape.

Sensing her resistance, he puts his large hand on top of hers, pressing it against the counter and stopping her. Leaning in closer he gestures to the cashier to accept the money he's offered.

Olivia tries to ignore the sudden electricity that passes between them while he traps her hand under his, pinning her involuntarily where she stands. Ignoring it, however, is not an easy task, since his chest is now pressed up against her shoulder. Breathing in his intoxicating cologne, she recalls the feeling of being pressed against his hard muscles.

Reluctantly, she lifts her eyes to meet his gaze. His green eyes are breathtakingly bright against the contrast of his royal blue dress shirt. She watches as he rolls the sleeves away from his wrists, exposing powerful forearms and large masculine hands. She's certain they'll adequately cover the soft swell of her breasts and feel like heaven against her skin. *What the? Now, she's definitely heading down a dangerous path.*

Ethan's hair is slicked back to give the appearance of a shorter style and his thin beard is neatly groomed. He looks every bit the successful business executive. She imagines how the girls in his office must swoon over how seriously hot his ass looks in his dark grey dress pants. She closes her eyes and groans. *Holy Moly! This is going from bad to worse! Why did she just check out his ass?*

He tips his head to the side looking at her in a questioning manner. "You aren't going to fight me on this are you?" He teases her with a playful smile that she finds both sexy and annoying. *FOCUS!* She tries again to move, but he presses harder, flattening her hand underneath his. He has no intention of releasing her until she gives in.

Looking down at his hand on top of hers brings back memories of a man who used his strength to intimidate her. A fearful stillness settles into her. Yet, the warmth of Ethan's skin and the closeness of his body makes her feel sheltered and secure. Confusing emotions rush through her mind, as she experiences both fear and arousal at the same time.

"No, I guess I'm not." She gives in to him, not wanting to cause a scene and eager to put some distance between them. She senses his dominance and knows that she would, too easily, fall under his command. Her body's reaction to him is definitely proof of that. In order to put an end to this ridiculous exchange, she smiles politely at him, accepting his offer. She tries to pull her hand from underneath his as she feels him start to lighten his hold.

"Good." He releases her hand completely but doesn't break eye contact. "It's the least I can do, since you've allowed me to start my morning with such a breathtaking vision. Everything else in my day will be dull in comparison to your lovely smile."

Unpleasant and threatening memories are quickly forgotten as Olivia is drawn, unknowingly, into his charm. *Who talks like that?* Even the cashier blushes as she counts out his change and passes it to him. Olivia gives him another smile. It's hard not to. "Thank you, Ethan."

Ethan orders two coffees making her scan the room behind him, looking for the girl that he left with the other evening. She notices the long line that has formed while they debated over who was paying, but he seems to be alone.

Her eyes dart back to the two police officers standing in line. She's always had a thing for men in uniform. Ethan smiles at her, noticing her distraction. Leaning over he whispers in her ear, "I own a pair of handcuffs, if that's your thing."

Olivia gasps, her body tensing. He's purposely trying to get a reaction from her now. She does everything within her power not to give him the satisfaction of seeing her squirm. She refuses to play this game with him. Walking confidently, toward the door, with Ethan at her side, she meets with the jealous looks of more than a few women waiting in line.

The officers smile her way, checking her out as she passes. She glances over at them and blushes a shade of scarlet. When she returns her attention to Ethan, he smirks as he winks at her. Utter embarrassment and his enthralling boyish smile are the only things that keep her from poking him right in the eye. *Gah! How annoying!*

Using his shoulder, Ethan pushes the door and stands against it, holding it open for her. Parked beside her, right outside the door, is Scott's car. Sitting behind the wheel Scott looks at them together as they exit and hangs his head down in defeat. "Great... just great." He knew he should have kept driving when he recognized her car. He shakes his head as she waves an exaggerated hello.

"Hi!"

Scott looks at her from head to toe and raises a brow. "A little over dressed for work today, aren't you?"

She smiles, "Yes, well… I have a date tonight after work."

Ethan stiffens where he stands. *Oh, Hell no!* His fantasy doesn't include sharing her with other men. There may have been a time back in university when he entertained such things, but he would never consider that with her. He's not sharing Olivia James with any other man. *Never!*

"You like?" She gives a little twirl showing off her dress as it dances around her.

Ethan takes in every inch of her body and expresses his pleasure, "*I* definitely like!" If she only knew the wicked, nasty things he wants to do to her. He's half hard thinking about it. A ghost of a grin slants across his lips and then disappears.

Olivia tries to ignore him but her eyes glance over. Involuntarily, her body warms under his appreciative gaze.

Scott looks at Ethan feeling a little nervous. "A date? Who is the lucky guy?" *Please, not Ethan. Please, NOT Ethan he repeats in his mind.*

"Noah Thompson." She blushes as she says his name aloud, feeling as if she's somehow revealed her intentions for the evening. Starting toward her car, her eyes dart quickly to Ethan, one last time. She can't help but notice that he looks annoyed.

Passing the coffees to Scott, Ethan quickly makes his way to her car, holding her off while he opens her car door. "Nice ride."

"Thanks." Olivia likes all the attention she's getting today. She'll have to wear this dress more often. Slipping behind the wheel as ladylike as she can, she makes sure that her dress is neatly tucked underneath her. She winces as the edge of the seat rubs painfully against the sore on her thigh.

After closing the door he leans down to her eye level and speaks to her through the open window, "I thought your leg was okay?" His previously playful mood is now solemn and his smile has faded into a much more serious expression.

"Well, it seems that I may have under estimated the damage. Apparently something sharp on the chair gouged out the Panama Canal in my thigh." She tries to make light of it but he doesn't smile.

"Olivia, you shouldn't mess around with tissue damage like that. Make an appointment with your doctor and have it checked out." His voice takes on an imperious tone that she finds rude and insulting. Yet, warmth blooms inside her and spreads outward. *Sweet Jesus, help me.*

Despite that warmth, anger brews inside her. "I am an adult, if you hadn't noticed. I'm capable of determining when I need to see a doctor." She looks straight at him contemplating saying something extremely unladylike.

His only response is a long intimidating stare. His jaw line tenses and it looks like he wants to say something. His mood sets off warning bells in her head.

For the second time this morning she feels the need to put some space between them.

"Ethan, I need to get to work," she finally manages to say.

"Is Noah your boyfriend?" He waits for her reply without breaking his stare, making her feel like she's under interrogation.

"WHAT? No!" She looks away from him when she answers, fighting the anger that's starting to rise in her. Closing her eyes, she forces herself to turn back and look straight at him. "And *that* is really none of your business." She's proud of herself for speaking her mind. She learned to keep her mouth shut and avoid all conflict around her ex-boyfriend, Sam. However, it's another self-preservation habit that she's trying to break.

Ethan struggles with the decision to hold his tongue. He knows how to handle difficult women and Olivia is no different. He senses that her tenacious, stubborn disposition is just an act to protect herself from men like him: confident and in control. Something inexplicable happened the first time he saw her. Intense feelings stirred inside him, like nothing he's ever felt or experienced before. He's determined to have her, explore these feelings and find a way to explain them. So, he'll concede to her this time, in hopes to gain her trust.

He nods his head in agreement, "You're right, it's none of my business." Standing upright, he takes a step back, allowing her to pull out of the parking spot. Watching as she leaves, he grins as he comments aloud to himself, "But I fully intend to make it my business, Miss James."

Finally at a safe distance, Olivia exhales, trying to expel some of the emotional energy zinging around inside her like the positive electric charge of a proton. She pulls into work just a few short blocks away, deciding that she's going to put Ethan O'Connell out of her mind. Today is all about her and Noah; she'll focus all her energy on that.

Ethan jumps in the passenger side of Scott's car. "Let's go, Scotty. We're going to be late."

Scott looks at him and scowls. "Seriously?"

Ethan tries to convey an austere maturity, "I'm the boss, Scott. I never joke about things like that." They look at each other and burst into laughter. "And on the way, you'll enlighten me by sharing everything you know about Olivia James."

"Ha! You're funny." Scott pulls out onto the road with no intentions of indulging Ethan's newest challenge.

"I'm not joking. Do you know this guy that she's having dinner with tonight?"

"Yes, and you do too. He plays soccer." Scott stops himself, knowing that he's probably said too much already. It's definitely not a good idea to let Ethan know that Noah is the guy that pissed him off during their last game. So much so, that he took a swing at him.

"Hmmm, I don't recognize the name."

Desperate to get off the topic, Scott throws out a random fact. "Did you know that dueling is legal in Paraguay as long as both parties are registered blood donors?"

Ethan scowls at him. "Good to know, in case I'm ever challenged to a duel in Paraguay." Not falling for Scott's diversion tactics, he continues, "Now tell me about Olivia or you're fired."

It's going to be a long ride into the city. Ethan is persistent, if nothing else. Scott thinks hard about his answer. "Well, let's see… she's thirty. She's Rachel's best friend and they work at the same company."

"What does she like?"

"She likes puppies, pizza and long walks on the beach," Scott tries not to laugh; assuming Ethan won't get his cliché reference.

"I see… what doesn't she like?"

Scott takes advantage of their friendship to give his boss a little ego jab. "Apparently, she doesn't like… **YOU.**"

Ethan's mood is anything but jovial at the moment. "Why do you think that is?" He's curious. He's just met her, so he certainly hasn't done anything to offend her. *Yet!*

Scott sees an opportunity to try and discourage him and takes it. "She hasn't dated a man in three years. I think she might like girls… if you know what I mean."

Ethan narrows his eyes. "Are you trying to tell me Olivia is a lesbian?"

It does sound a little outrageous and Rachel will probably kill him, but he says it anyway, "That's entirely possible."

Thirty minutes later Scott pulls into the parking garage of the high-rise office building downtown. Both men get out of the car, grab their suit jackets and briefcases, and head for the elevator. Their footsteps echo as they make their way through the structure that's lit dimly with florescent lights. Standing near the door, an older woman waits. Her silver hair and eccentric clothing make her look suspiciously out of place there.

"I thought security is supposed to keep the crazies and panhandlers out of here?" Ethan looks at Scott with concern when she starts to approach them.

"They usually do." Scott reaches into his pocket for his wallet, expecting her to be looking for a handout.

Without breaking her stare, she stops in front of them. Smiling, she locks eyes with Ethan and speaks only to him. She ignores Scott and his wallet all together.

"It's about time you got here. What took you so long, boy? We've been waiting a long time for you," her voice is warm and friendly… almost familiar.

The hair stands up on the back of Ethan's neck. Looking at Scott awkwardly, he freezes, not knowing what to say.

"Why are you looking so lost, child? You know why you're here," she insists.

Scott and Ethan exchange nervous looks. They're stuck where they stand. Scott discreetly takes out his phone and texts security, giving Ethan a silent nod to indicate that they're on their way.

Her smile is warm and friendly. It's hard for Ethan to fathom that she's completely insane, which she obviously is. "I don't know, actually. Why am I here?" Ethan has no clue what to do, other than play along until security arrives.

Reaching up, she touches his cheek with her cold hands. "Your soul senses her." Fear glazes across her tired grey eyes. "You better find her quickly, boy. I sense that she's in danger."

Ethan's muscles tense, and his stomach squeezes into knots. He has no idea who or what she's talking about.

The door slams heavily, and she turns to see the uniformed security guards heading her way. Looking back at Ethan, she drops her hand to her side and smiles. Pushing in between Ethan and Scott, she heads toward the exit. Rushing toward them, security calls out, forcing Scott and Ethan to step out of the way, as they pursue her. Turning to watch the commotion, the men are shocked to see the officers standing a few feet behind them, one of them scratching his head. The elderly, silver haired woman… GONE!

Reaching the elevator, they wait silently for the door to open. "What the hell was that?" Scott finally asks.

Ethan doesn't look at him. It was a bizarre and awkward experience. "I have no idea, but don't tell anybody about it and we'll just pretend it didn't happen."

"Deal." When the door slides open, both men step in and turn. They watch the security guards wandering through the parking structure searching for the silver haired woman between parked cars, neither one of them wanting to admit that she simply vanished into thin air.

When the elevator door closes, Ethan puts his case on the floor, between his feet. Producing a tie from his jacket pocket he pulls it over his head, adjusts the knot and smoothes the front to make sure it lies flat.

Scott sends a text to his wife, asking her when she'll be back in town. He tries to think of a way to tell her that he may have just wrongfully *outed* Olivia. Maybe not telling her would be easier.

Ethan rolls down his sleeves and buttons the cuffs. He hasn't said a word to Scott since they entered the elevator. As they near the top floor of the penthouse office, Scott breaks the silence.

"Ethan, about Olivia…" he rushes his comment, wanting to get it out in the open before they officially begin work. "You have no intentions of dropping it, do you?" When Ethan O'Connell decides he wants something, he doesn't give up. In addition, he's a ruthless negotiator and Scott has seen him absolutely lose his mind in a fit of rage, if things don't go his way. That's NOT the kind of guy he wants Olivia to be around, *ever again*!

Ethan slides his suit jacket over his broad shoulders, leaving it undone. "NOT A CHANCE!"

He steps out of the elevator with Scott right behind him.

"I didn't think so." His hopes deflate. He has no idea how he's going to discourage Ethan AND deal with his meddling wife.

The bright neon blue Aurora Technologies logo stands out proud on the wall of steel grey behind the busty blonde at the reception desk. "Good morning, Mr. O'Connell," she greets him with a smile and a handful of phone messages.

"Thank you, Hannah." He notices the low cut blouse she's wearing today, no doubt, to try and get his attention. Her voluptuous, tempting cleavage has done that successfully. He immediately draws his gaze back up to her eyes. "Have I told you what a pleasure it is that you're the first person I see every morning?"

She blushes. "Thank you, Mr. O'Connell."

Walking down the long corridor adorned with awards and acclamations, Scott matches his pace beside him. "You're a human resources nightmare. Do you know that?"

Ethan laughs, "Probably, but did you see those tits?"

Scott cringes. "My point proven." They stop outside Scott's office while he unlocks the door. "I have no idea how you do it." He opens the door and drops his stuff on the floor. Spinning the chair around, he sits down and pulls it up against the desk.

Standing at the doorway Ethan responds, "What do you mean you don't know how I do it? I'm irresistible to women… well, except for your friend Olivia, apparently."

Scott silently mouths the word, "LES…BI…AN." Forming each syllable dramatically. "Just saying…you shouldn't waste your time."

Ethan looks at his watch. "My office at 10 a.m. I want to see the updates on the project you're working on."

"You got it, boss!" Scott spins his chair around and answers the ringing phone behind him. Ethan leaves him to his call, making his way to the huge corner office at the end of the hall. Windows line both the east and south walls, giving a fantastic view of both the city and the lakeshore. The modern décor of his office reflects the company's devotion to new technology and future ideas. Ethan takes a few moments to admire the architecture of the historic buildings around him. At times, he finds the contrast between old and new inspiring. He ignores the phone's continual ringing and the constant notification sounds of incoming emails. As usual, his business day arrives like a bull in a china shop, but today he's not thinking about any of the projects on the go at Aurora Technologies. Today he's thinking about Olivia James.

Chapter Four

The morning drags on for poor Olivia, making her feel like it will never end. Minutes feel like hours, as the afternoon ticks on just as slowly. Checking her phone repeatedly, she waits for a message from Noah, but there's no word. She almost jumps out of her chair when she finally receives an incoming email. Clicking on the inbox icon, she's shocked!

Good afternoon Olivia,
I hope you've had a great day! Mine, as predicted, has been extremely dull compared to your lovely smile. I was hoping that you would allow me to enjoy it again this evening.

Ethan O'Connell
SVP International Sales and Marketing
Aurora Technologies

Aurora Technologies? Well, that explains a lot. Of course, Scott doesn't want his boss hanging around. Why didn't he just tell her that yesterday?

Hi, Ethan. My day has been fine, thank you for asking. As I mentioned this morning, I have a date this evening. How did you get my email?

Olivia James
Business Solutions Specialist
Dunn & McLellan IT Consulting

Immediately a reply bounces back. She's extremely annoyed that, on top of their morning encounter, Ethan appears to be a stalker, as well. What makes him think that it's okay to send her emails?

To: Olivia James

It's not rocket science, Olivia. Any teenager can figure it out. I only needed to know where you worked. Blow off that Noah guy and let me take you to dinner instead.

Olivia sighs. She had worked hard at putting him out of her mind. She can't deny that she felt a compelling attraction to him this morning, until the sexy and charming Irishman turned psychotic control freak in a short walk to the parking lot. She couldn't handle a man like that in her life again.

To: Ethan O'Connell

Mr. O'Connell, I thank you again for breakfast this morning. However, Noah is a good man who treats me well and I'm looking forward to enjoying his company. I won't be having dinner with you tonight or any other night.

From his downtown office, Ethan reads the last email and leans way back in his chair. Running his fingers through his hair, he smoothes it back behind his ears and lets out a frustrated breath. Olivia is proving to be quite a challenge, but he knows that eventually she'll reveal her weakness. Ethan's business success is largely due to his ability to negotiate. Everybody has weaknesses. Ethan always finds them; he just needs to be patient. Leaning forward with his elbow on the desk, he rests his chin in his hand, in a pensive gesture, thinking of a response. Grinning, he quickly types a reply with such enthusiasm that the tapping on the keyboard sounds like pounding rain. He hits send and sits back in his chair, waiting.

To: Olivia James

Olivia, I am disheartened by your refusal to see me again. I'm concerned, not for the lack of physical nourishment required to sustain life; but rather for my soul that will endure an arduous fast, if deprived of your exquisiteness. I beg you not to torment me with such a cruel punishment.

OH BOY! His poetic words easily disarm her. She has to remind herself that they're *just words*. Words he's probably spoken to every woman he's tried to seduce. She knows men like Ethan O'Connell; he's definitely not a '*committed to one woman*' kind of guy. She needs to put an end to this, once and for all.

To: Ethan O'Connell

I know what you're hungry for, Mr. O'Connell. I'm sure you'll find suitable company for "dining" among your many admirers. "I" am not one of them.

Ethan smiles when he reads her response. He's rarely come across a woman without insecurities. She's just revealed one of hers.

Finding his persistence and arrogance infuriating, Olivia hesitates when she receives his next reply. She wishes that she could ignore him all together, but unfortunately, curiosity has gotten the better of her. She has to know what he said.

To: Olivia James

Then I'll have to change that Miss James. Call the doctor. NOW!

Putting her hands over her face, she growls as she turns red hot with anger. Gahhhhhhhhh!

Rachel bursts into her office, startling the hell out of her, "You have a date? What the hell? Why am I just hearing about it *now* and from Scott?"

"Hi! Welcome back!" Olivia tries to disarm her with a friendly smile.

"Nice try, James. Spill it. Who are you having dinner with?" Rachel isn't good at hiding that she's extremely annoyed.

"Scott didn't tell you?"

"He said he didn't want to tell me, that I should hear it from you. SO… out with it!"

"Geez, I figured you'd come home in a much better mood."

"I was in a good mood, until I found out that my best friend is going on her first date in three years, and she didn't bother to tell me about it." She folds her arms in disgust.

"I'm sorry." Olivia pouts, hoping for forgiveness. "Noah stopped by to help me bandage my thigh, and one thing led to another and… well, I guess, it was me who asked him out."

"NOAH THOMPSON?" Rachel is dumbfounded. He wouldn't be her choice for a date with her best friend. He's let Olivia down so many times before, and for some reason, she always forgives him. She's never really understood why.

"I know! I'm sorry. He left and I started feeling a little woozy so I went to bed. And then yesterday was insanely busy," she pauses a moment, realizing that her excuses are only making Rachel more annoyed. "So… It's crazy, right? Me and Noah?" She holds her stomach, still not feeling that great.

"I thought that was a lost cause after all these years? And what happened to your thigh that he had to bandage it?"

"Well, that's a long story. I fell out of my chair at the soccer game and took a chunk out of it."

"How the heck did you do that?" Rachel starts to laugh. "Did anyone get video? Wait... I'm going to check YouTube."

"Dear God, I hope not!" Olivia panics and starts to type YouTube into the search engine on her computer.

"Will you give me some details already?" Rachel asks with growing impatience. "You look gorgeous! Where are you going?"

"I don't know, yet. I'm supposed to pick somewhere. He said he would call me to let me know what time he's going to finish work. I was thinking Indian food. What do you think?"

"I think it sounds wonderful. The only place Scott takes me for dinner these days is the drive-thru window."

"I'm getting a little antsy. I thought I would've heard from him by now. I don't want to text him and look like one of those needy girls." She wrinkles her nose. If only he knew just how *needy* she really is.

"Well, it's almost 5 p.m., so maybe you should. As soon as you get home, I want all the details. And don't make me chase you! I've got to get home to my husband, apparently he missed me."

"Aw, that's so cute." Olivia powers off her computer and picks up her purse.

"You'd think so, but my bet is that he probably hasn't eaten since I left or he's out of clean underwear."

Rachel gives her a quick hug before they part ways in the parking lot. Olivia gets in her car, but she just doesn't want to go home. After taking a long look at her phone, she types a message.

From Olivia: Hey, what time do you want to meet for dinner?

She has a strange feeling that she's being brushed off, but she spends the next couple of minutes freshening up her makeup anyway. She gets that feeling often with Noah. It's the reason she's always felt that she isn't quite good enough for him.

Assuming that he must be really busy or he's forgotten, she decides to head home. Pulling into the driveway, she checks her phone one last time. Still nothing. Her women's intuition starts tingling, like Spidey sense. On a hunch, she backs up and slowly rounds the corner onto the next street and finds his car parked in the laneway.

He must have forgotten. With a huge sense of relief, she drives around to the front of the house and parks at the curb. She can see him through the window moving back and forth between the kitchen and the living room. Feeling rather silly spying on him, she takes out her phone and texts him again.

From Olivia: Did you forget about me? I'm starving!

She watches through the window as he walks over to the table, and picks up his phone. He types something then puts it back down. Her phone beeps instantly and she smiles as she opens his message.

From Noah: Sorry babe. Stuck at work. We'll have to do it another time.

Olivia looks at the message, puzzled. She blinks her eyes a few times, making sure that they're focused properly, and that she hasn't misread it. Why would he lie to her? Looking back at the window, she receives her answer. His arms stretch out in front of him as a tall blonde steps into his embrace. She had been standing behind the curtain that obstructed part of her view. Olivia's heart is crushed, as she watches Noah claim another woman's lips in a very passionate kiss.

Trying to fight the bitter sting of rejection, Olivia ambles up the pathway to her back door. The key sticks in the lock causing a struggle to get it open. Wiggling it back and forth, she tries to coax the lock to line up properly. It always seems to stick at the most inconvenient times. Tonight she's tired, upset, and in no mood to be challenged by a stubborn door. Taking a breath, she pulls the knob toward her as far as she can, and gives the key one more twist. Finally, it clicks!

Heading straight to her room she grabs her favorite pink kitten fleece pajamas and tosses them on the bed. Catching her reflection in the mirrored closet doors, she stops to stare at herself in her dress. She pulls at the material around the waist, smoothing it around her hips and trying to reduce the appearance of her curves. *Is that the reason Noah brushed her off?* She sighs as she pulls the dress over her head and discards it on the floor.

Grabbing a pillow and a blanket, she heads back downstairs. Throwing them on the couch, she prepares to sleep there. She does this many nights, when she can't bear to sleep in her bedroom. Nightmares seldom find her downstairs, so the couch has become a warm, familiar place.

Tears stream down her face. She wipes at them with the back of her hand, wondering why she's crying. She should've known better, this isn't the first time that Noah has brushed her off for a pretty blonde.

Standing at the stove, heating up a can of soup, she realizes as she stirs the noodles in a continuous circle, that she doesn't really have an appetite. Running her hand across her forehead, she's concerned that she feels a little feverish. That would explain why she feels very tired. Perhaps a quiet night on the couch is what the universe had in mind. Turning off the stove, she leaves the soup in the pot, no longer having the stomach for it.

Curling up on the couch, she pulls the blanket over her aching muscles. Her feet stick out the bottom and she wiggles her toes in the cool air. As far back as she can remember she hasn't been able to handle the restriction of tucked in blankets. Exhausted, she surrenders to the fever and fades off to sleep.

At the Headwaters Bar and Grill, Rachel, Scott and Ethan are seated for dinner. This is the place to go in town, if you want a good meal and evening entertainment. Tonight there's a live band during the dinner hour, followed by the best DJ from the nearby city. The place is standing room only on Friday and Saturday nights. This Friday night is no exception.

"I love this place," Ethan says, with his mouth half full of food. "I should buy it." Looking around the room at its rich dark wood trim and country character, he gives it serious consideration.

Scott laughs.

"Are you joking?" Rachel looks at him with interest.

"No, not at all," he says, as he swallows and wipes his mouth. "It reminds me of home."

"Sweet." Rachel looks at Scott with raised eyebrows.

The DJ takes over, pumping up the bass. Over the next couple of hours, the room fills to capacity. Drinks flow freely at the table; the alcohol making Rachel very talkative.

Ethan's obsession for Olivia consumes his thoughts. He looks at his watch, thinking about her on a date with another man. It makes his stomach twist in uncomfortable knots. When Scott excuses himself to go to the bathroom, Ethan interrupts Rachel's rambling, hoping that she's much more forthcoming with information than Scott is. "Tell me about Olivia."

Rachel is delighted in Ethan's interest. "My poor, sweet friend, Olivia," she begins. "She's had more than her fair share of assholes. A string of bad relationships, actually."

"Ah, well that explains a lot." Ethan picks up his glass and downs the last mouthful.

"She's barely left her house in three years, except to work. She's still a little... umm... skittish around men." Rachel starts feeling a little protective of her best friend. "She deserves a good man."

"Yes, she certainly does." He reflects on her words a moment, understanding that there's an unvoiced warning in them.

Rachel has a strong feeling that Ethan is exactly what Olivia needs. Against her husband's wishes, she'll continue to try to steer them towards each other.

"If someone wanted to get close to her, they would have to take things really slow," she cautions him, "and be patient. It would be like trying to catch a frightened rabbit."

Ethan leans back in his chair and wipes his mouth with a napkin. "So, she isn't a lesbian?"

Rachel chokes on her drink and almost sends it shooting out her nose. "Oh my God! NO! Where did you get an idea like that?"

"Scott," he answers in a nonchalant manner.

"I'm going to kill him." Rachel puts her hands over her face and growls, "Ethan, you need to know that Olivia's last boyfriend hurt her in more ways than just breaking her heart. And... well... Scott introduced them, so he feels responsible for what happened."

Ethan rubs his hand over his whiskers. "What exactly happened?" He wants to know. He needs to know. It will give him a better idea on how to handle her.

When Scott arrives back from the bathroom, he's met with the icy stare of his wife. Concerned, he pulls out his chair and sits down. "What did I miss?"

Rachel pounces on him. "You told Ethan that Olivia was a lesbian?"

Scott panics. "Um, well... what I said was that it was entirely possible."

Her temper explodes and a liquor-fueled argument ensues. Ethan gets up and goes to the bar, safely out of range. When he returns, Scott is gone and Rachel stands with her arms crossed in front of her angrily. "Where's Scott?" he asks, alarmed

"He left." She pushes the chair back from the table and gets to her feet. "Order me another drink. I'm going to dance."

Chapter Five

The phone rings and startles Olivia out of a sound sleep. She tilts the phone so she can see the display and then sits straight up, alarmed. It's after midnight! There's only one reason Rachel would be calling.

"Hello?"

"Hi, Olivia. This is Ethan. I'm sorry to bother you so late, but Rachel asked me to call you."

She can hear muffled music in the background and her heart starts to beat quickly. "Is she okay?"

"Yes, sorry I didn't mean to alarm you. We're at the Headwaters Bar. She's had a bit too much to drink."

"Where's Scott?"

"They had a fight and he left. I've been calling the house but he's not answering. I was going to call a cab but I can't find my wallet. I hate to ask you to come out this late... if it was just me I'd walk, but I'm sure Rachel wouldn't make it."

Olivia is already on her feet and putting on her shoes. "I'll be right there."

When she gets there, they aren't waiting outside. She tries to cover up her red, tear swollen eyes before she heads in. She's never had another female friend that could down the booze like Rachel. She's alarmed at the thought that she may still be drinking. She can drink most of the men she knows under the table. It was something that she would have accomplished in college, if Scott hadn't found her when he did.

Olivia makes her way through the crowd, her heart beating in time with the loud rhythm of the bass. She finds Rachel dancing up a storm on the floor. Continuing to scan the room, she finds Ethan close by, dancing with a redhead in an extremely short skirt. Her eyes are stuck to him for a few moments. He has perfect rhythm and dance moves that would set any woman's panties on fire.

Everything else about him is absolute sexual perfection, why not this, too? If he moves like that in the bedroom, it's no wonder all the girls on the dance floor are competing for his attention.

Olivia starts to feel a little warm as she watches him spreading himself around the dance floor, attentively looking after all the women who join him. It only confirms her thought, that he's not a one-woman kind of guy.

Rachel sees Olivia across the room and squeals as she stumbles toward her. In an act of chivalry, Ethan abandons his harem and grabs for Rachel's arm, supporting her while she finds her footing.

"Something on the floor tripped me," she explains in a drunken slur.

"Yes, I saw that." A small grin spreads across his lips.

When they reach Olivia, Rachel throws her arms around her in a very forceful hug.

"Thank you for coming!" she screams in her ear, so she can be heard over the music.

"Whoa!" Olivia leans away from the strong smell of alcohol on her breath. "Have you got everything? I'm taking you home now." She tries to prop her upright so she's not leaning so heavily on her.

Leaning forward, Rachel shouts in her ear again, "This is Ireland!" She waves her hand in his direction.

Olivia laughs and looks over at him. "Ireland, huh? You know that's going to stick, right?"

Ethan smiles, his eyes reflecting the flashing lights of the dance floor. As far as he's concerned, she can call him anything she wants, as long as it's his name she's screaming when he's buried deep inside her, making her come repeatedly.

"No, no. That's not right. This is *Ethan*," Rachel corrects herself, her legs wobbling. "He *is* Irish!"

Ethan steps in to help support her, chuckling out loud.

"Yes, I know. We've met," Olivia says loudly over the music. Trying to steer her toward the door, she glances over at Ethan and smiles. "Let's get her to the car before she drops."

With strained effort, they finally get her through the bar and into the waiting car, out front.

Ethan buckles Rachel safely into the passenger side of Olivia's '64 Mustang and climbs into the back seat. Olivia isn't interested in small talk. She just wants to get back home to bed. "I can drop you off first, if you like, where do you live?"

Ethan stares at her, feeling a little awkward. "I've been staying with Scott and Rachel for the last month."

Olivia remains expressionless. Without a word, she just drives. How is it that he's been there a month and she had no idea? It's obviously another effort by

Scott to keep them from meeting. She'll deal with the two of them, once she's feeling better and has the strength to kick some ass.

Rachel is asleep within moments in the front seat, her body slouching forward. Nothing, but Ethan's strong hand on her shoulder, is keeping her from smashing her head on the dashboard. In a hurry to get her home, Olivia turns the corner a little too quickly, causing Rachel's limp body to swing heavily to the side. Olivia puts her hand over her mouth, as Rachel's head hits the side window with a thud.

"Oh my God! Rachel, I'm sorry." Reaching over, she tries to steady her. It's a difficult task since she's out cold, and her head is wobbling from her neck as if it's dead weight. Pursing her lips together, Olivia tries to contain her laughter. When she looks back at Ethan and she sees that he's snickering, she can't hold it back. Their eyes connect and something passes between them. The sound of their laughter somehow strengthens their connection. For a brief moment, Olivia's heart beats with an ardor that she's never experienced before. Taking a deep breath, she pushes it aside, refusing to acknowledge it.

When they arrive, Ethan gets Rachel out of the car and steers her to the front door. Olivia pushes it open quickly and stands aside, letting them pass. He stops at the bottom of the stairs and looks over at Olivia. "I'm thinking that's not happening."

"Not under her own power, anyway." With her and Ethan on either side, they manage to get her up the stairs and to the bedroom. Olivia tips her backward onto the bed, slipping her shoes off before covering her with the blanket. On the other side of the bed, Scott is passed out cold, completely unaware of their intrusion. Ethan shakes his head. "Must be bloody nice to sleep that soundly."

Heading back downstairs, Olivia suddenly realizes that she's left Rachel's stuff in the car. "I'll be right back. I need to get her purse." A sharp searing pain in her thigh forces her to stop dead and take a deep breath.

"What's wrong?" Ethan watches her movements with concern.

Not wanting another lecture about making a doctor's appointment, she lies, "Nothing." She takes a small step and carefully tries to bear some weight on her leg.

He crosses his arms and wrinkles his brow. "You're a terrible liar. Sit down." He motions toward the bench in the front hall. "I'll get the stuff out of the car."

When Olivia keeps moving toward the door, Ethan quickly steps up behind her. "Olivia." He reaches for her arm as his voice takes on a much more commanding tone, "I said, I'll get the stuff out of the car."

"It's okay. I can get it myself." She's determined to be as stubborn as he is persistent. When he firmly takes hold of her elbow, he makes her heart race. Stopping, she turns, her eyes returning his steely glare.

Ethan has already given in to her once today. It's not going to happen again! His tone is firm, militant, "SIT DOWN!"

Olivia's legs bend obediently under his command, her head bowing down. With her eyes to the floor, she makes no further objections.

Aroused by her compliance, Ethan stands over her. His heartbeat races as he throbs and grows, straining against the unforgiving fabric of his jeans. If only he could give in to his desires and take her, right here, right now! Feeling like he needs her to lift her gaze and present her lips, he fights the urge to grasp her hair, and twist it around his fingers. Nothing would be sweeter than to claim her mouth in a forceful kiss until she surrenders the rest of her body. There's no questioning it, she will submit to him.

Rachel's earlier warning stops him. He swallows his desire in a heavy lump, exhaling a torrent breath of air, and forcing himself to walk away. "Thank you. Was that so hard?" he growls in frustration, his hard cock twitching inside his pants without promise of release.

Olivia says nothing as he opens the door and heads out to the car. Once he's out of sight, she puts her hands over her face, appalled at her reaction. *What just happened?* This is how it starts every time. She just can't seem to stop herself from making the same mistake; it's as if she's hardwired to submit to dominant men.

When Ethan returns a few seconds later, Rachel's purse slips out of his hands, spilling all her stuff onto the floor in front of Olivia. Thankful for the opportunity to move from the bench, Olivia drops to her knees on the floor to pick everything up.

Ethan groans. The sight of her, on her knees in front of him, isn't helping to discourage his erection.

Olivia looks down at a black leather wallet that's flipped open to expose Ethan's driver's license.

"Is that my wallet? What's it doing in Rachel's purse?" he asks surprised.

"Knowing Rachel, I'd say we're victims of a little meddling." She shrugs as she passes it to him.

"What do you mean?" Ethan furrows his brow, confused.

"I think she was looking for a way to make sure I had no overnight guest."

"I see." It occurs to him just how sneaky and manipulating women can be. "She took my wallet so that you'd have to come pick us up?"

"Exactly. Effectively ending my date."

Suddenly, there's a huge thud from upstairs. They can tell from the sound, and the cursing that follows, that Rachel has fallen out of bed. Olivia stands up alarmed, limping painfully to the bottom of the stairs. "Rachel?" she hollers.

A muffled voice yells, "I'M OKAY!"

Olivia puts her hand over her mouth to stifle her laughter. "Poor thing is going to be black and blue tomorrow and won't remember a thing." She's sympathetic, but she continues to chuckle in amusement.

Feeling tired, she zips up her hoodie and heads toward the door with Ethan right behind her.

On the way to the car, she tries desperately not to limp at all. Ethan places his hand on the small of her back, guiding her, as they walk. His touch is so warm and soothing that she forgets about her earlier upset. She must be exhausted. She can't think of any other reason to explain why she finds herself wanting to be near him for a short while longer. She surprises herself when they reach the car and she stops to lean back against the hood, staring at him.

Ethan moves to her side, eager to be close to her. The thought of her earlier submission is still on his mind; the remainder of his erection is a noticeable outline in his pants. "Thank you for coming out in the middle of the night to get us home safe."

Olivia smiles. "Yeah… well, it's not the first time I've had to pick her drunken ass up."

The air around them starts to crackle with excitement as he positions himself as close to her as he can get. This time she's certain that he feels the connection, too.

His body tenses against her as he presses his semi hard-on against her hip. "So… how was your date?" He has to know, it's been chewing at him all night.

The truth stabs at her, making her feel wounded all over again. There's no way she's going to let Ethan see her upset. "It was just fine, thank you."

Ethan can't stop himself. He slowly raises his hand to the back of her head, gently taking hold of the elastic band that's holding her ponytail.

Butterflies take flight in her stomach with the anticipation of his touch. Slowly and carefully, he pulls the elastic out. Using his fingers to comb through her hair, he lets it fall softly across her neck.

What the ever-loving-fuck?

Ethan draws in an appreciative breath at the sight of her curls, making his hard chest expands against her side. As he brushes the hair from her shoulder, he lowers his mouth to whisper in her ear, "Did you kiss him?" There's an emulous tone to his question.

"What?" Olivia inhales his cologne and feels unnerved by the feelings that stir inside her. He continues to twirl the soft tendrils of her long hair around his fingers. When he occasionally brushes the tips of them across her neck and shoulder, it makes it hard for her to think or breathe.

"Did you kiss him?" he repeats in a demanding tone. The muscles in his shoulder grow tense while he waits for her reply.

Olivia is distracted by the warmth of his breath on her skin. He's close, again. *Too close!* The evidence of her attraction rolls through her body, confirming that his authority influences her. She hates that he senses it. Turning away from him, she looks up at the stars, jiggling her knees nervously. She doesn't want to tell him what really happened. He's gotten so far into her head, right now, that she can't even think of a lie.

Unfortunately for Olivia, a man doesn't grow up with three sisters and not learn how to read female body language. He knows something has upset her. He changes gears from controlling into caring. "Hey, what happened?" He raises his hand to her face and with one finger, tucks a loose piece of hair behind her ear.

That one tender gesture, somehow, erases her ability to control the communication between her brain and her mouth. She blurts out the truth, "He cancelled." She's instantly filled with regret and her shoulders slouch. *Why did she tell him that?*

Ethan tries not to rejoice at that news, since he tried to convince her to brush Noah off. Instead, he positions himself as a caring friend, trying to gain her trust. "Is that why you were crying?" he asks softly, his lips dangerously close to her neck.

She doesn't answer, only slightly shrugs her shoulders, but it's as good as an admission.

"Why did he cancel?"

"Well… funny thing," she begins, "I was going to ask him why, but I couldn't." Her hands fidget with the cuffs of her hoodie.

Ethan reaches down and holds them still in one of his large strong hands. "Why is that?"

The muscles in her stomach tighten, as he brings the other hand up, lightly brushing his fingertips up and down her arm. The night air is cool against her skin but she doesn't feel it at all. She tries to convince herself that it's the fever and not Ethan that has her feeling like she's on fire. "His mouth was full." She looks up into Ethan's gorgeous green eyes. Even in the dark of night, they look like a summer meadow, all warm and inviting. She resists the urge to brush her fingers over the few days' growth of facial hair, letting it prickle roughly against the soft skin on the pads of her fingertips. Her stomach fills with butterflies at the thought.

"Full?" He looks at her in confusion. "What do you mean his mouth was *full?*"

Olivia takes a short breath as she speaks the painful words, "*Full* with the tongue of the blonde he was kissing." Her tone is sarcastic, bitter. Saying it out loud gives her the strength she needs to move away from him. Knowing that a relationship of any kind with Ethan O'Connell would surely be a disaster, she slides off the hood and starts toward the side of the car.

Ethan grabs for her wrist, stopping her in her tracks. "Olivia, wait."

Her body stiffens as her dream flashes quickly through her mind. *Hands wrapped firmly around her wrists. Her name, flowing delicately from his lips, as if he's said it a million times before.* She keeps her eyes down. If she were to look into those wickedly sexy, Irish eyes, she'd be done. "I should go."

Feeling the intense anxiety in her body language, Ethan reluctantly releases her. Reaching past her, he grasps the handle, and pulls it open. When she gets in, he closes the door then gently knocks on the window with his knuckle.

Against her better judgment, she opens it to hear what he has to say.

"Olivia, that guy is douche-bag."

She stares straight ahead at the steering wheel, trying to gain control of her thoughts.

Ethan reaches through the window and brushes the hair out of her eyes. He frowns as he gently skims his thumb across her cheek. The expression on her face looks as if his touch has caused her physical pain. He feels sick at heart when she moves to the side withdrawing from his touch.

"Don't," she pleads, letting out a heavy breath.

"Olivia, please," Ethan attempts to calm her. "I know you feel it, too." He reaches for her again.

"Don't," she repeats shaking her head. "You and I… it's never going to happen."

Once again, Olivia James leaves him standing alone, watching as she drives away. It doesn't matter what she says. Now, more than ever, he's determined to possess her. His desire is stronger than the gravitational pull. As she disappears in the distance, his thoughts are focused only on her. *Always running away from me, Miss James. We're going to put a stop to that.*

When Olivia gets home, she returns to her spot on the couch. She tries to settle, finding it extremely difficult to rest comfortably, with the throbbing pain in her leg. This whole *friends with benefits* thing is a bad idea. Maybe, when she talks to the doctor, she should take her sister's advice and have her hormones checked. Maybe there's some imbalance that would explain her unwanted reaction to Ethan O'Connell. Suddenly she receives an incoming text message. "What now?" she groans.

From Ethan: Hi, it's Ethan. I'm checking to make sure you got home safe.

What the hell? He must have taken her number out of Rachel's phone when he called her from the bar. *Geez, he has incredible nerve.*

From Olivia: Yes, I'm home safely. pls don't worry about me. I'm Ok.
From Ethan: Ur NOT OK! I noticed you feel feverish. Go see a Dr 2moro or I'll come get you and take U there myself. FORCIBLY if need be.

Is he joking? She's known this guy for all of a week. What has she done to make him feel he has any right to be concerned? She frowns. *Who is she kidding?* He sensed the *submissive* in her the moment she stepped out of the car; now he's hunting her like a predator. God help her, she's not entirely sure that she wants to get away.

From Olivia: Seriously?
From Ethan: Seriously! Over my shoulder kicking and screaming if necessary!
From Olivia: It's a good thing that you don't know where I live.
From Ethan: 333 Oak Tree Lane

Well, she can't say she's surprised. He managed to get both her email and her cell phone number the same day without her permission. He certainly is persistent. That's precisely the problem... controlling AND persistent is a dangerous combination for her.

From Olivia: Ok stalker boy, put the junior spy kit away. I have an appt 2moro a.m.
From Ethan: Thank U, Miss James. :)

Olivia shakes her head as she tosses her phone onto the arm of the couch and covers her exhausted body with the blanket. One minute he has her submitting in the front hallway of somebody else's home. The next minute he's sending smiley faces. Thoughts of Ethan linger in her mind as she tries to drift off to sleep, just as they have every night since she met him.

Chapter Six

In the morning, Olivia drags her aching body off the couch and forces herself to drive into the city. It's one of the few clinics that has hours on a Saturday, and as always, they are way behind schedule. She sits impatiently in the waiting room feeling lethargic and woozy. The skin on her thigh is on fire, making her fidget uncomfortably. When her phone beeps, indicating that there's a new text message, she's glad for the distraction. She sighs out loud when she see's Ethan's name.

From Ethan: What time do you see the doctor?
From Olivia: Geez Ireland. Don't you know how to take a hint?
From Ethan: Do I strike you as the kind of guy who is easily discouraged? WHAT TIME????

She stares at the screen, ready to type him a nasty reply, when she realizes that she's smiling. As frustrating as he is, there's just something about having him fuss and worry over her that makes her feel…normal. As twisted as that seems, she desperately needs to feel normal. So maybe, she won't give him a hard time today.

From Olivia: I'm here now. They're so far behind I'm more likely to die here of old age than an infection.
From Ethan: I hope that's not the case. I am somewhat disappointed. I was looking forward to throwing you over my shoulder. Then you can't run away from me.

Olivia reads his reply and gets butterflies. *Damn him.* That is one sexy thought; her body folded over one of those rock hard shoulders, as he holds her tightly with his beefy biceps to keep her from falling. She shudders, thinking about the few extra pounds she's gained over the winter. That thought paints an unpleasant picture in her mind.

From Olivia: I'm too heavy. You'll hurt your back trying to lift me. Then how will you attract pretty girls if you can't play soccer?

She hits sends and gets a little nervous. So much for not giving him a hard time today.
Ethan replies immediately.

From Ethan: YOU are the only pretty girl I'm interested in. I don't like it when you put yourself down. Don't do it again.

What? She types her reply just as the receptionist calls her name. If she's trying to discourage him, then this was clearly a bad choice.

From Olivia: Yes sir, I'm sorry

Her face flushes red in an unwelcome response as she hits send. The thought of his large, muscular body standing over her when she knelt in front of him last night, makes her heart flutter.

Entering the tiny exam room behind the nurse, she briefs her on the reason for her visit. As per her instructions, Olivia strips from the waist down and covers herself with a paper blanket. Her cell phone beeps from her pants pocket on the floor. Her pulse quickens as she thinks about her last message to Ethan and wonders about his reply. She blushes awkwardly when the doctor comes in and interrupts her thoughts.

He's all business and gets right to the point.

"So you have a cut that's not healing?"

"Yes, it wasn't a clean cut. Something dug into my leg. I've been feverish and sick to my stomach, as well."

"Let's have a look." He pulls on a pair of gloves and snaps them at the wrist as he adjusts the fit. Lifting the paper blanket, he makes a few concerning sounds as he evaluates the wound.

Olivia is still thinking about Ethan's broad shoulders and muscular stomach, the edgy, commanding tone in his voice; the rock hard erection that he purposely pressed against her so that she couldn't ignore it. Doh! Stop thinking about that!

"Miss James?" the doctor repeats, impatiently.

"Oh, I'm sorry. What did you say?"

"I've taken a swab to have the lab evaluate it. I've written you two prescriptions for antibiotics. I'm not sure which one you'll need until I get the results back, so I want you to take both until then. I've also prescribed an antibiotic cream."

She takes the papers out of his hand and folds them as she sits up on the table.

"Is there anything else?" he asks, seemingly in a rush.

Olivia's cell phone beeps loudly reminding her of Ethan's reply. She thinks about how his hard, warm body felt against her, and the brush of his hand across her cheek, as he tucked her hair behind her ear. Completely flushed, she turns her attention back to the doctor. "Well actually, I think it might be time to start back on birth control."

He looks up at her over the top of his bifocals. "Very well," he says as he grabs a new pair of gloves. "Lie back down and wiggle to the end. I'll check under the hood and make sure everything's in order."

A clear head is required for the video conference Ethan is about to join. The thoughts he's having about Olivia, right now, are more than distracting. He puts his phone away after his last reply. He needs to get through this call without an aching hard-on straining inside his jeans. He keeps the entire floor of Aurora Technologies in darkness except for his office. Leaving the blinds open, he lets the sunshine warm the room with a delicate light. Selecting a play list of soothing jazz music, he attempts to create a calm atmosphere. Looking at his watch, he turns on his laptop and prepares for his video conference. He's driven all the way into the city today, to have some privacy and collect his thoughts. Within minutes, he's joined online by his assistant, John McCabe, who is currently at the head office in Ireland.

"Mr. O'Connell," he greets him, in a much more formal manner than usual.

"John. How are you?" Ethan finds his voice comforting, and for the first time he feels a little homesick.

"I'm well, Ethan. Thank you for asking."

John was the head of security with Aurora Technologies when Ethan was promoted to Senior Vice President of International Sales. Ethan's dedication and drive to succeed put him in the office twenty-four seven, making John his only companion on many long evenings. Despite Ethan being ten years his junior, they formed a friendship and John became one of the few people Ethan could trust.

John's insights, in both business and his personal life, continue to be invaluable to him. John often teases Ethan, saying that he's a brilliant young man who lacks nothing but a little *life* experience, and at times, more self-control. It was no surprise to anyone when Ethan hired McCabe away from the company to be his own personal assistant and bodyguard. It was a wise move on his part, since he was a young mustang full of energy and passion; still is at times. Although, a few years have settled him some, he still has an incredible knack for attracting women with extremely jealous boyfriends.

Admittedly, John's maturity and military discipline kept Ethan in line and out of jail on more than one occasion. If only he had been around *that* night. Ethan starts to feel a little on edge. "Is everyone there?"

"Yes, sir, the company lawyers are with me now. We've arranged for the best representation for you."

"Well that's brilliant, considering that it's a load of bullocks. I DIDN'T DO ANYTHING!" His voice is riddled with frustration. He extends and flexes his fingers, trying to keep them from clenching into tightly formed fists.

"I believe you. But it's her word against yours."

One of the lawyers chimes in, "Mr. O'Connell, Jessica Keane has some pretty compelling evidence."

Ethan looks down at his cell phone and reads an incoming text from John.

From John: Calm your temper Ethan. Don't give them any reason to believe you're capable of the things she's accusing you of.

Twisting his neck to try to release some of the tension there, Ethan forces himself to relax.

A very professional sounding woman introduces herself, moving in front of the camera so she can be seen, "Ethan, my name is Shannon Quinn. I'll be handling your case." She's a stunning blonde, in her early to mid thirties, with bright blue eyes that look too kind and gentle.

Ethan takes note and straightens his posture. He's been told that Shannon Quinn is the best in her field. He's impressed that she's developed such a successful career and reputation as a lawyer, at such a young age. Lawyers are all old, wrinkled, argumentative people, right? Not this woman, she's stunning. The legal team may refer to her as a "bulldog" in court, but there's something about Miss Quinn, that's very… personable.

"I'm curious," Shannon begins. "What reason would Miss Keane have to say it was you? Why would she lie about it?"

Leaning back in his chair, Ethan runs both his hands through his hair, holding his head for a few minutes before he lowers his arms to his lap and answers.

"Jessica and I were living together; until I found out she was sleeping with another man."

"So this was something that happened in a jealous rage?"

"NO!" He catches himself sliding into an angry tone and clears his throat. "No, I wrote her a note saying that it was over and that I wanted her to move out."

"That's all?"

"Yes, then I went out and got drunk."

"So if it wasn't you, who did it then?"

"I don't know."

"Was she there when you got home from the bar?"

"No, I don't think so." He scratches his head. "I don't know for sure. I told you I was hammered."

"You were that drunk, that you don't know if she was even in the house, but absolutely positive that you didn't do it?"

"Yes, because I could barely stand. The cab driver had to carry me into the house. The last thing I remember is him dropping me on the sofa." Ethan's stress is now evident in his voice.

Shannon turns to one of the young men sitting beside her. "See if you can track down the cab driver and confirm that no one else was in the house when he took Ethan home." Turning back to the video screen, she adjusts the camera. "Okay, so you don't remember seeing her after you left her the note. Let's assume for the moment that she came home, saw the note and left. When was the next time you saw or heard from her?"

"A few weeks later."

"Who made the initial contact?"

Ethan sighs, "She contacted me after I cut her off financially."

"I see, so you were still supporting her until then?" One of Shannon's assistants is taking notes on his laptop. The loud tapping of the keys is starting to grind on Ethan's nerves. He holds the back of his neck trying to squeeze out the tension.

"Yes, I gave her a few weeks to find a place to stay and get a job, and then I cancelled the credit card and closed the line of credit that I opened for her."

Shannon looks to another one of her associates and assigns him a task, "I want the transaction records on the accounts that Mr. O'Connell paid for and the cancellation information." She turns her attention back to Ethan. "What did she say?"

"I didn't return her call. For two weeks, I didn't hear a single word from her until I cut her off. Obviously, she missed my money… not me."

She looks to the man on her right again. "Get your hands on her phone records. I want to know when that phone call was made and what date she went to the newspaper." Everybody is scrambling, making notes and searching for things in their briefcases. "I think that's all for today, Ethan."

"So, what now?" he asks, trying to wrap his head around everything that's happening.

Shannon flips through the documents in front of her. "My recommendation is that we hire an investigator to find out as much as we can about her whereabouts that night. Hopefully, we can get to the bottom of it quickly."

One of the associates interrupts, "The Garda may request that you return to Ireland. They'll be conducting their own investigation eventually, and Ethan, you should know that you could be charged with assault."

"Do you really think it'll get to that? I didn't do it! This is ridiculous!" His hand lands heavily on the desk in front of him.

"Ethan, we believe that you didn't do it," Shannon assures him. "We just need to prove it. Ideally, we need to find the person who did. Otherwise, it does come down to her word against yours. If you think of anything or anyone that might help us then please contact us right away."

Ethan rubs his hands over his face in disbelief. "Unbelievable." He shakes his head. "I can't believe she would do this. Why go public weeks after it supposedly happened and then file the police report a month after that?"

Miss Quinn adjusts the camera so she's back in view. "We had the same thought. We think she's after money. When you didn't return her calls, she made her public accusation hoping you would contact her and offer her money to be quiet. When you didn't do that either, she escalated it to the police."

Ethan harshly exhales the breath he was holding. Finally starting to feel more like himself, he takes control. "I want this resolved as quickly as possible."

"It's not our intention to drag this out. As long as you're cooperative and available to the investigation team, we should have some answers soon. Until then, I feel it necessary to remind you, as your lawyer, that you need to stay out of trouble and don't discuss this matter with anyone. Don't post anything about it on any social media, Facebook, Twitter or otherwise."

"Fine. You know how to get a hold of me."

Shannon Quinn closes her file folder and stuffs it into her briefcase. "I'll hire an investigator first thing Monday morning. We'll be in touch." She stands and leaves the room with an entourage of assistants following behind.

When Ethan hears the door close he calls out, "John? You still there?"

"Yes, I'm here."

"Is everyone gone?"

"Yes, it's just me now."

"How the hell did everything get so screwed up, John?" His voice strains in defeat.

"I believe Shannon is on the right track. Miss Keane's agenda is money."

"Well, I'm very inclined to pay whatever she wants to put an end to this."

"That would be a bad idea at this point," John advises.

"As always, you're right. I wish I had listened to you, John." Regret is visible on his face.

"Me too, my friend. I had a bad feeling about that woman, right from the beginning." He tried to warn Ethan a few times, but let it go when Ethan ignored his concern. It's a decision he's regretted a thousand times in the past three months. He wishes now, that he made him listen. "Ethan."

"Yes?"

"It's good to hear your voice, you're missed here."

Ethan smiles. "Don't get all mushy on me, McCabe."

John raises his eyebrows and smirks as he leans in closer to the video screen. "I meant by all the young ladies… I don't miss you. You're a pain in the arse."

Ethan laughs, "I can always count on you for the truth, my friend."

"Yes, sir, that's why you pay me the big bucks."

"Go home enjoy the rest of your weekend." Ethan packs up the stuff on his desk. "I might need you to come to Canada for a week or two. I need your help with a few personal deals I'm working on."

"Can't your Canadian assistant handle things for you?" There's an unusual apprehension in John's voice.

"Not as well as you. I'd just feel more comfortable if you were here."

"Very well," he concedes. "Let me know when you want me to arrive and I'll make the necessary arrangements." He looks into the camera with a serious expression. "Ethan, stay focused, keep a level head and stay out of trouble. Would you at least try to stay away from women until after this is resolved?"

Ethan thinks about Olivia and grins. "That might be easier said than done."

John closes his eyes and shakes his head. "Dear God! Already? Don't tell me anymore, I don't want to know.

Chapter Seven

Olivia reaches her car and cringes at the creaking sound it makes when she opens the door. She says a little prayer as she turns the key, "Please start… Please start." The engine shows its age by making a loud wheezing noise, like an elderly man trying to walk up hill. "Come on, girl… you can do it!" The engine responds with an optimistic cough and a sputter. Taking a deep breath Olivia releases the key and closes her eyes. On the third try the old girl muscles up the gumption and her engine rumbles to life. "Yes!" Olivia throws her hands in the air in celebration.

Feeling a little flushed, she rolls down the window, letting the wind blow through her hair; the sun is bright and the fresh air feels good. As she hits the highway, she presses hard on the accelerator and hits an exhilarating speed. Cranking the volume on the radio, she sings at the top of her voice.

Suddenly, she hears a thud as something bounces off the car visor and drops onto her chest. *That was odd.* She raises her hand to brush it off, but whatever it was seems to be gone. Olivia turns her attention back to her song when suddenly; she feels movement inside her shirt. She screams, searching her bra for the June bug that's taking a casual stroll through her cleavage. It wanders around inside her bra, violating her with its scratchy little feet and antennae as it goes. It's HUGE! She doesn't understand how it's possible that she just can't seem to get her hand on it.

Swerving back and forth all over the road she decides that she needs to pull over. When she comes to a complete stop, she jumps out of the car and rounds the hood onto the shoulder in a hurry; her hand still in her shirt searching in distress. Finally, she gets a hold of one of its scurrying little bug legs. In one quick motion, she yanks the largest beetle she has ever seen out of her bra. "Ew! Ew! Ew!" She launches it into the air as she jumps up and down.

A loud pop comes from the engine of her car; it sputters, and then dies. "Nooooooooooo!" She leans through the window and turns the key, but nothing. Lifting the hood, she stands there looking at its inner workings, hoping to receive divine intervention. Perspiration forms on her brow and her eyes start to feel heavy. Her stomach flips and twists. She's thankful that she hasn't eaten today, because it certainly would come back up, right now.

Slamming the hood down in sheer frustration, she watches as a silver car pulls up and stops behind her. The cavalry has arrived! The door opens and out gets an extremely sexy Ethan O'Connell. Divine intervention, indeed! Her breath hitches at the sight of him as she recalls his last reply, *"Good girl, I suspected you were a woman who does what she's told."*

"Having troubles?" He grins as he walks toward her.

That charming smile isn't going to work today. She just wants to get home. She's not interested in anything else he's offering. "What are you doing here?"

"I had to go into the office this morning for a conference call. Looks like it's a good thing I did or you'd be stuck here."

"I would have gotten her started, eventually." She's offended by his comment, and the fact that he thinks she needs to be rescued. Maybe she did, but she thinks it's rude that he makes assumptions about her.

Her eyes skim down his body, noticing that he's wearing jeans and a tight fitting t-shirt that clings to his chest, showing off its impressive definition. A rush of hormones causes heat to wash over her body. "A little under dressed for the office, aren't you?" She tries not to stare.

The look in his eyes and the slight smirk on his face, tells her that he's well aware of her perusal. He's amused at her continual attempt to deny her attraction.

"It's Saturday, Olivia. There was nobody there but me. Get your stuff and I'll take you home." It's an order, not a request, but she's feeling far too sick to argue with him.

He's about to pull back into traffic when she reaches out, grabbing his arm. "Wait! We can't just leave her here on the side of the road."

"Maybe if you're lucky, somebody will steal it."

"My dad left me that car," she says upset. "It was his pride and joy and the only thing I have left of his."

Ethan feels horrible. That look of disappointment is something he would never like to see again. There should never be anything other than complete joy and happiness on her beautiful face. He desperately wants to be the source of her rapture.

"Forgive me, Olivia. I'll look after it." He takes his cell phone out of his pocket, "Hey, it's me. Do you have a mechanic in town? Do you trust him? Can you arrange for someone to come and tow Olivia's car there? It's off on the shoulder on the 410 Highway, just past the Sandalwood exit. Then call John, or that other guy, you know the one that looks like a sloth. Have him arrange for her to get one of the cars from the sales fleet. I want it dropped off at her house today, if possible, no later than tomorrow morning. Yes, that's fine… thanks."

When he ends his call, Olivia stares at him, completely offended.

"What's wrong?" he asks, picking up on her hostility.

"So you think its okay to just take over and make decisions for other people?" She crosses her arms in front of her.

Ethan pulls out into traffic and looks at her confused. "What are you talking about?"

"Did it ever occur to you, that maybe, I can't afford to pay someone to fix my car?"

He didn't consider that, actually, he just took control like he always does. "Olivia, if you're short of money then I'll pay to get it fixed. I can't stand the thought of you driving around in an unsafe vehicle. I won't allow it. That car is a death trap."

He won't allow it? WTF? That only antagonizes her more. Not to mention that she knows from experience that financial dependence is just another way to control someone. She refuses to go through that again. "Well, it's not your job to look after me," she snaps, just about to lose it.

"Soon enough, you'll figure out that there's no point in arguing with me," he says, dismissing her anger.

Olivia's on the verge of giving him a piece of her mind; like she's intended to do several times, since the first time she met him. "You know, just because you are the Senior Vice President of a successful company doesn't mean you can snap your fingers and make your employees, or anyone else, jump anytime you want."

Ethan is working hard at controlling his temper. His jaw clenches as his voice takes on a defensive tone, "I'm not sure why you're so upset with me. I'm trying to do something nice for you." His Irish accent becomes more defined as his anger escalates. No woman has ever raised her voice at Ethan O'Connell. He's not quite sure how to handle it.

"You just called one of your employees on a Saturday and asked them to look after something that's personal business. MINE, I might add!" she yells at him.

"You are way too quick to judge me, Miss James." He shakes his head annoyed.

"I could hear the conversation. I heard you order someone to look after getting my car fixed." Furious, she turns her body and faces out the window.

Ethan scratches his head, frustrated at her reaction. "What the…? Olivia, that was Scott. I didn't call a staff member and give them orders on a Saturday. I called a friend and asked for help." He glances over at her. "And just for the record… John, my *personal assistant* is a twenty-four seven gig that *I* pay for, not the company. If he's unhappy with the terms of his contract, he's free at any time to find another job." Extremely annoyed at her accusations, his jaw stiffens as he glances at her. *Bloody woman!*

Starting to feel a little motion sickness, Olivia reaches into her purse for a something to settle her stomach. She pulls out the handful of prescriptions. Feeling embarrassed that she needs to ask for his help after what she just said, she holds them up to show him. "I need to get these filled."

"No problem, I'll take you." He hesitates, not able to hide the agitation in his tone. "Or do I need to ask you if it's okay first?"

She decides not to reply. It's much safer for her to keep her mouth shut and rest her eyes for the rest of the drive.

Still tense from their conversation Ethan pulls up in front of the drug store, and decides to stay in the car. As Olivia passes around the front hood, he watches her, mumbling about difficult women in general. His eyes are drawn down to her blood-soaked sweat pants. Calling out her name, he gets out of the car, and jogs to catch up with her.

Beginning to feel dizzy, Olivia puts her hand against the side of the building to steady herself. Ethan reaches her just in time and braces her against his body.

"You okay?"

"Yes, I'm fine," she says embarrassed. "I guess it's all the poking and prodding he did today."

"It's bleeding again." He motions down to her sweatpants.

Olivia twists to look back at the blood that's starting to soak through and shivers. "Great." Making her way to the prescription counter, with a concerned Irishman hovering close by, she hands in her prescriptions and leans against the counter for support.

"Will you be picking these up later?" the pharmacist asks.

Before she can open her mouth, Ethan answers for her, "No, we'll wait."

Olivia rolls her eyes at him. Shaking her head, she makes her way over to a chair and sits down. When the pharmacist finally calls her name, she wearily makes her way to the counter. She listens as he takes the bottles one by one, explaining the dosage and tossing them into a bag. When Ethan approaches from behind, listening in on the instructions, Olivia's mood goes from annoyed to extremely grumpy.

"Excuse me," she says to him in an aggravated voice. "Are you at all familiar with the concept of personal space?"

He looks at her intently but doesn't move.

"*YOU* are in *MY* personal space bubble!" She uses exaggerated hand gestures to demonstrate the lack of space between them. When Ethan doesn't back away, she gives up with a heavy sigh, figuring that it's a concept he doesn't grasp, since he did the same thing yesterday at the coffee shop. When the pharmacist is done, Ethan puts a few other first-aid supplies onto the counter and hands the cashier his credit card.

"You don't need to do that," she objects.

Ethan's having a hard time ignoring her abhorrent mood so he retaliates with sarcasm, "What? Let you pay so that you've got nothing to complain about?"

She sighs, wondering how they went so quickly from a playful morning to this. Considering that car repairs are likely to set her savings back quite a bit, and that she's just too exhausted for any more arguments with him, she agrees.

"Fine, go ahead and pay. I was just surprised at your offer. Since, you seem more like the kind of guy that would have his *personal assistant* send flowers than take a general interest yourself." There's a subtle hint of malice in her tone that she immediately wishes she could take it back. She looks up at him nervously, knowing that she deserves whatever his reaction will be.

Ethan glances at her sideways, his mouth set in a grim line. His patience is worn thin by today's inquisition. "I'll have my assistant send flowers to you another time, today you need Band-Aids." The way she challenges him at every turn is exhausting. He's not used to a woman who would question his authority. Suddenly he wishes he had taken the advice from his friend.

However, Ethan is drawn to this particular woman. Despite her censure, he doubts he can stay away. "And since you're clearly not feeling well, I'll forgive your contentious behavior today." He establishes eye contact, warning her with an arctic glare, "Just so we're clear, when I say I'm paying for something… it's not up for discussion." He slides his credit card back into his wallet and stuffs it back into his pocket.

Oh shit. He's angry. She wilts a little, feeling the sudden desire to avoid any conflict with him. When she gets back into the car, the onset of the fever consumes her. She closes her eyes, and sits in silence the rest of the drive.

When Ethan delivers her safely home, she decides an apology is in order. "Thank you, Ethan. I'm sorry I was in a grumpy mood today. I really do appreciate you helping me out and not leaving me stranded." She looks at him confused when he gets out of the car, and walks beside her toward the house.

"You don't honestly think I'm going to leave until I make sure *that* is properly dressed." He points down to the bloodstain on her pants.

Wow! She can't believe how overbearing he is. He can't seem to go more than half an hour without saying something to make her angry. She doesn't want his help, she certainly didn't ask for it. "What makes you think that I'm letting YOU into my house?"

"I saw your face the night it happened and again when you got out of the car. I'm thinking you're not entirely comfortable dealing with the blood." Confident that she'll give in, he continues to follow her toward the door.

The thought makes her woozy. "Especially my own." Putting her key in the lock, she scowls when it sticks. "Still, you can't just assume you're welcome in my house, and that you can bully me into doing things your way."

"Is that what I'm doing? Bullying you?" Amused, he places his hand on the door and gives it a firm push, forcing it open.

Olivia shrugs, trying to gauge his mood. "Well, kind of."

"Okay. Here's the deal. I'll come in and make sure that this is bandaged properly." He runs his hand gently up her thigh and then holds her hip. "And then, I promise I'll leave, if that's what you want."

Oh, no you don't! He's not going to distract her with those little sensual touches and that boyish grin that says, *'trust me, I'm a good guy'.* She's seen a side of him today that proves that she was right about there being something dangerous in those eyes. She's not falling for dark and mysterious, ever again.

Ethan grins at her hesitation, already knowing that she's going to give in. He patiently waits while she considers his offer, as if she would refuse him. *Ridiculous!*

Olivia finds herself looking at his lips and the sexy way they curl at the corners. His eyes have softened; that controlling look, that was there just a short while ago, is gone. He squeezes her hip, gently reminding her that he's still touching her.

Olivia would like to send him on his way, never to see him again. She knows he's right; there's no way that she can look after changing the bandages herself. She's certainly not going to ask Noah over again. She pries his hand off her hip, giving him a defiant look. Standing aside, she lets him in. "Let's get this over with." She's not falling for his charm today; she just wants to get into bed and go to sleep. Alone!

"Okay, good. Take your pants off."

"What?" Startled at his request, her heartbeat kicks up a notch.

"Take your pants off." He smiles knowing that he's caught her off guard. "Unless you'd like me to put the bandages on the outside of your pants?" He makes his way to the sink and washes his hands.

"Of course not," she says, bothered by his teasing, "this is the second time this week I've taken off my pants for someone in this living room."

"Really, now?" Kneeling in front of her, he looks up at her and raises his eyebrows. "That's interesting. And who else have you taken your pants off for?"

"Noah. He came over the night it happened."

Not feeling bashful at all in her fevered state, she hooks her thumbs on the waistband of her sweat pants and yanks them down off her hips. When she reaches the spot where dried blood has stuck them against the wound, searing pain pulls at her skin. "Ow!"

Ethan reacts quickly. "Wait, wait, wait!"

She lets go and puts her hands over her face as he runs his finger around the pant leg, gently prying the blood-stiffened fabric off her leg.

Easing them down the rest of the way, he's careful not to brush against the raw flesh of her thigh. "There. Are you okay?"

She looks down to see a trail of fresh blood running down her leg and becomes frantic. "NO! I'm not okay! Get the blood off me, Ethan. Hurry!" Her hands start to tremble.

"It's okay, Olivia. Relax." Comforting her comes naturally; like he's done it all his life, "There was just one little spot where the pants were stuck and the bleeding has already stopped. Your doctor did a horrible job of dressing this." He hates seeing her upset. As he cleans the blood from her skin, he decides she needs a little distraction. "Nice panties." Gently caressing along the tender bit of skin where her thigh meets her butt cheek, he looks up to meet her eyes with a mischievous smile. "Pink is my favorite color. Were you thinking about me when you put these on this morning?"

Olivia is certain that he has no reason to be anywhere near where he's currently lingering, and a different kind of tension stirs deep inside her. Her stomach muscles tighten as his hand grazes tenderly across her inner thigh. "Odd as it seems, Ireland, I don't think about you when I'm putting my panties on." She looks away, finding the gaze of his green eyes and his Irish charm, just a little too potent in her weakened state.

"Ah, only when you take them off, then." He smirks, reaching for the waterproof tape.

She stares straight ahead, strategically NOT saying aloud all the things that she would like to say to him, right now. However, the change of direction in the conversation is extremely welcome, considering the angry tension that's been between them for the past hour and a half.

"Open your legs," he demands, as he gently nudges them, prying them far enough apart to apply the adhesive.

Olivia's heart starts to race as she shifts her weight, giving him a little more space to work as he wraps it around her leg. Sliding his free hand against her inner thigh, he smoothes the tape down, making sure it sticks.

His mouth is only a few inches away from the throbbing that's started to occur between her legs. Inhaling deeply, she holds her breath, trying to deny the desire that start to coil tighter inside her. The same desire that makes her want to thrust her hips forward against his lips and encourage him to take action.

"Brilliant! I knew you were the kind of girl who does what she's told." His licentious Irish accent is delivered in the warmth of his breath across the skin of her inner thigh. He's dangerously close to being extremely intimate with her. The slightest advancement in his hand, and he'll discover that her pink panties are now very wet.

She begins to feel dizzy, and she's certain that it's not the fever. It's Ethan. She's afraid to speak; for fear that he'll sense the burning ache that he's ignited deep inside her. As if he's missed the way that her body has reacted to him. It's anything but subtle.

Getting to his feet, he takes a good long look at her body on the way up, showing his appreciation with a dirty little smirk. "All done. You can put your pants back on. Or leave them off if you like. I don't mind."

"Nice try. You're done?" She hides her disappointment as his hands move away from her body, leaving her feeling almost abandoned.

"Why are you surprised?" Walking into the bathroom, he cleans his hands.

"Well, because it hurt a lot when Noah did it." She walks over to the laundry basket on the couch and grabs another pair of sweat pants from the top of the pile.

Ethan returns to the room, drying his hand on a small towel. He stands completely still, admiring one last look of her pink panties. "I can guarantee that I have a much better bedside manner than your friend Noah." From across the room he becomes aroused as he watches her step into her pants and pull them up over her hips. He has to fight the urge to bound across the room, grab her, tug them back down, and get between her legs. *Brilliant idea!* He'd like to get between those legs for pleasure this time, exploring every inch of her pussy. *Need* starts to grow deep inside him. He thinks about his mouth on her and imagines just how sweet she'll taste on his tongue. He'll learn to recognize the little sounds that she makes when he's doing something she likes. Then, he'll do those things to her until she screams his name, coming harder than any other man has ever made her come before. His body responds by sending all the blood in his veins straight to his groin.

"But then, you've likely had more practice playing doctor with all your girls." *Oh crap! She didn't mean to say that aloud.* She turns away from him pretending to fold laundry and avoiding eye contact.

Her comment ruins his little fantasy, making him shake his head. Staring at her, knowing that this is her insecurity talking again, he moves across the room toward her. It amused him at first, but now he's offended at her continual suggestion that he's some kind of playboy. He's not like that anymore. "Olivia, there are no other girls," he says with a stern voice, as he moves in behind her.

She senses him closing the space between them and her spine straightens.

Nuzzling his forehead against her temple, he whispers in her ear, "Do you want me to stay and play doctor with *you?*"

Scorching heat washes over her, as she feels his hot breath in her ear and his firm chest pressed up against her back.

He senses his effect on her. He holds her hips squeezing them with his hands, holding her in place while he gently sways with her; rubbing his growing erection against the crease at the top of her buttocks. "I could give you a very…thorough… examination," he whispers, in a low rough voice.

Betrayed by her body, once again, she's both speechless and breathless. *How is it possible to become that aroused by somebody that you find so aggravating?* Ethan's touch sets her every nerve ablaze as his hands move across her body. The ache between her legs is begging not to be ignored any longer.

Her breathing comes in short excited breaths, making her feel weak. She's just about to give into him when logic takes over. She needs to stay in control. Something she's sure that Ethan O'Connell won't allow. She doubts that she has the emotional stability to handle his dark controlling moods. The struggle between mind and body ends with a victory for her logical side. She struggles to breathe in enough air, so that she can speak. Swallowing hard she forces out her request, "You promised to leave once you were done. I'd like you to leave."

Ethan's body goes stiff against her. Dropping his hands to his sides, he backs away, frustrated by her capricious behavior. "Okay, if that's what you want. I don't do non-consensual." He's never had to. Not once has any woman, that he set his sights on, told him *no*.

He knows that she also feels the very strong attraction; she wants him as much as he wants her. It occurs to him that he could force the *submissive* card, but this is a bad time to gamble and be wrong. He regrets that he didn't press Rachel to tell him what happened to her. His mind races with questions he wants answers to. Right now, she's saying no. So he'll leave.

Olivia watches as he picks up his keys and puts on his shoes. She's already wishing she could take back her rejection. He looks miserable. As he starts down the stairs toward the door, she calls his name, "Ethan."

With his patience completely spent and at the brink of emotional exhaustion, he ignores her. This time, it's him that needs to put some space between them. He feels his anger building and knows that any further discussion with her will coax it to the surface.

"Ethan, please wait." She stands at the top of the stairs, feeling dizzy.

Hesitating briefly, he flashes her a look that's dark and unforgiving then opens the door and leaves.

Chapter Eight

That look haunts her for the rest of the night and she struggles to put it out of her mind. She was the one who sent him away; now she's hoping he'll call. Thinking about her dreams, she wonders if they're the reason she's developed such intense feelings for him in such a short period of time. Sitting with her cell phone in hand, she fights the urge to call him. When it rings, she jumps.

"Hello?" Without looking at the caller ID she anxiously answers it.

"Hi!"

"Oh. Hi, Megan." The disappointment is evident in her voice.

"Gee, don't sound so excited to hear from me."

"I'm sorry. Of course I'm happy to hear from you." Looking up at the wall clock, Olivia squints. "It's late there. Is everything okay?"

"Yes, I just got everyone into bed and Rick is asleep on the couch. I was wondering how things went with Noah."

"Don't ask."

"Oh, no, what happened? Tell me that you talked to him."

"Yes, I did."

"And he said no?" Megan says shocked. Turning to her husband, she whispers, "It's Olivia, go back to sleep."

"No, he said, YES."

"I'm confused, what happened?" Megan grabs the cordless phone and moves to the kitchen.

"We made plans to go out for dinner last night, but he blew me off for a pretty little blonde with long legs and fake boobs."

"Oh, honey, I'm so sorry."

"It's okay." She tries to make it sound like she's not upset, but her sister knows better.

"You sound tired, have you been sleeping?" Megan holds the phone to her ear with her shoulder while she drops the dinner dishes into the sink and begins to wash them.

"Actually, don't laugh, but the other day I tipped out of my chair and cut my leg. I went to the doctor today and it's infected. He's given me a couple of different antibiotics to take, but I'm still feeling miserable."

Megan tries to unsuccessfully stifle her laughter, "You fell out of your chair?"

"I said don't laugh," Olivia says dryly.

"Sorry," Megan offers, regretting her lack of restraint. "So, who were you hoping to hear from tonight? It certainly wasn't me."

Olivia hesitates, not sure if she wants to discuss Ethan with her sister.

"Was it a man?" When Olivia doesn't answer, she knows the answer. "It *is* a man! What's his name? Where did you meet him?" She can barely contain her excitement.

"Whoa! Relax, girl! His name is Ethan. He's Scott's boss. But there's nothing going on between us. He's actually the most frustrating man I've ever met."

"Then, why were you disappointed when it wasn't him on the phone?" Finishing the dishes Megan pulls the plug and lets the water drain.

"I don't know… we had an argument earlier and I felt bad how things were left." Feeling chilly, Olivia wraps the blanket from the couch around her and shivers.

"So you just want to be friends, then?" Megan can't let it go.

"Yes. I mean no… I guess so." She exhales a very heavy sigh.

"Sweetheart, why are you so conflicted? What's really going on?"

"I don't know. I'm so confused."

"About what?"

"My feelings for him." Olivia fluffs the throw pillow, and lies down.

"How do you feel about him?" Megan dries her hands and settles comfortably at the kitchen table with a cup of tea.

"It's hard to explain. I'm definitely attracted to him. He's beyond super hot."

"Well, that doesn't sound so horrible."

"I know but, one minute he's so sweet and charming, and the next minute, he goes all Michael Collins on me."

"Who?"

"Michael Collins," Olivia sighs. "He was one of the leaders of the IRA in the early 1900's."

"Oh, okay. I'm not sure I get it."

"He can be very *controlling*. Argumentative at times."

"And that scares you because you're trying to regain control of your life."
It suddenly becomes clear to Megan.

"Yes, exactly. He has the most beautiful green eyes I've ever seen. Yet,
there's just something in them that warns me that he has a dark side."

"Do you think he'd hurt you? If you think he's at all capable of that, then
you need to stay away from him," Megan warns.

"When I'm around him I feel very safe, like I've known him forever. It's
really kind of strange. But he makes me extremely nervous and I guess that's
what's so confusing. My brain and my heart are always in conflict. It's like trying
to force together the opposite ends of two magnets and it's exhausting."

"Maybe you're confusing the good nervous with the bad one."

"I don't know. I'm…. afraid."

"Olivia, you've been through a very traumatic experience, just take things
slow." The baby's cries can be heard in the background. "I need to go, the baby is
awake. He's teething, poor little guy."

"Okay, give him a hug and kiss for me."

"I will. Before I go, I want to know what you're going to do about
Ethan."

"I have no idea. I asked him to leave tonight. Then regretted it the minute
he closed the door behind him. I guess I'll just have to take one day at a time and
see what happens."

"Call me anytime if you want to talk! I'll check in with you in a few days
to see how you're feeling."

"Okay, love you."

"Love you too! Good night."

Olivia's eyes become heavy as she makes herself more comfortable on the
couch. Laying in the dark, she thinks about Ethan's abrupt mood changes and
wonders if she's responsible for turning sweet, loving men into monsters. She
places her phone on the cushion beside her, just in case he calls. As her eyes
become heavy, she sees the bag of medicine sitting unopened on the table. She
needs to take those before she falls asleep. If she could just get back up, she'd do
that.

Olivia's sleep is continually interrupted by dreams where she seems to be
magically teleported back in time. She's been having the same recurring dreams
for several weeks now. They linger in her mind with remarkable clarity, yet the
people and places are unfamiliar to her. The only thing she's absolutely sure of is
that she's the beautiful woman with the long chestnut hair and flowing curls.
When she wakes she vaguely remembers the man, who is unmistakably her lover.
She has such strong feelings for him, even though his face always seems to be
hidden in the shadows.

Olivia's disrupted sleep is aggravated by the fact that she didn't take the
antibiotics last night. Over the past several hours, the fever consumes her as the

infection spreads. Tossing and turning uncomfortably on the couch, she's soaked in perspiration, yet chilled to the bone and shivering.

Opening her eyes briefly, she sees her little green, feathered friend sitting in the windowsill. Looking in at her, it taps its beak against the glass. Olivia can barely lift her head off the pillow, but she manages to reach up and close the blinds, blocking out both the sun and the worried little bird.

The morning passes as Olivia fades in and out of consciousness. She manages, only once, to force her weary body to get up and take the medication. It's a pointless effort since not even water will stay down at this point. Her body is exhausted, making her arms feel heavy, like they're encased in cement. When she picks up her phone to call Rachel it slips from her hand, hitting the floor. Losing her battle to the fever she drifts back to sleep.

Lying in bed Ethan is awake, replaying the past week in his mind. He needs to find the strength to put Olivia James out of his mind. It's not an easy task. Especially considering, that it's her that waltzes with him through his dreams, even before he met her. He doesn't understand how it's possible, but he recognized her the minute she stepped out of her car. Since then, she's the last thing he thinks about when he falls asleep, and the first thing he thinks about when he opens his eyes. His dick gets hard just thinking about her beautiful rounded breasts and the curve of her hips. He's going to have to dig down deep to find the strength to stay away from her.

Ethan spends the morning and part of the early afternoon reviewing proposals for the upcoming week. That fails to prevent him from thinking about Olivia James, even after he's stroked himself to release. He decides a rigorous work out is in order, if he's going to get her out of his head.

Rachel calls Olivia several times during the day. Concerned that she still can't reach her, she decides she should check on her in person. The last time Olivia didn't return her calls, she found her nearly dead in a pool of blood. Those memories play in her mind as she unlocks the door and lets herself in.

She hasn't been gone long when Scott calls her cell phone. "Hey, how's Olivia? Is everything okay?"

"She's not in good shape, Scott!" The anxiety is evident in Rachel's voice.

"What's going on?"

"She's lying on the couch, barely conscious. I'm freaking out here! I've tried to wake her up a few times, but she refuses to let me take her to the hospital. I don't know what to do."

"Hang on Rach, I'm going to get Ethan."

"Okay…. why?" She waits, listening to Scott's heavy footsteps on the stairs.

When he doesn't find Ethan in his room he calls out to him. Scott searches until he hears the sound of the treadmill in the basement. "Um... okay, Rachel listen... Ethan doesn't like people to know this, but he took a couple of years of medical school before he switched to business. He still works part time with the emergency medical response team in Ireland." Reaching the bottom of the stairs, he motions for Ethan to take off his headphones.

"What's going on?" he puffs between breaths.

Scott hands him the phone, "It's Rachel. She needs to talk to you about Olivia."

Ethan shakes his head and pushes the phone away. "No, I'm done talking about her. Besides, Olivia has made it perfectly clear that she doesn't want me around." Putting his headphones back on, he continues to run.

Scott reaches over and shuts off the machine. Angrily, Ethan pulls off his headphones and glares at him. "What the hell are you doing? I said, I don't want to hear any more about her. Isn't that what you wanted?"

Aggravated, Scott hands the phone to him again. "Olivia is really sick. Rachel is over there, right now, and she thinks there's something seriously wrong."

The thought of Olivia being in distress alarms him, more than he would like to admit. It makes it hard to refuse Scott's request. Stepping off the treadmill, he wipes the sweat from his face with a towel and reluctantly takes the phone. "Rachel, what's going on?"

"I don't know, she hasn't returned any of my calls since last night. She's just lying on the couch. I can't keep her awake. Even now and then she opens her eyes and closes them again. She's burning up, Ethan. I'm really worried."

"How high is her fever?" he asks, heading upstairs.

"I don't know!" Rachel bites at him in frustration. "How am I supposed to know?"

"There's a thermometer in the medicine cabinet in the main floor bathroom, Rach," he says calmly, having seen it there the day before. He waits while she looks.

"I found it, but I have no idea how to use it." She pushes buttons and the led display lights up and flashes. The drug store bag on the table catches her attention. "Ethan, is she supposed to be taking this medication?"

Ethan leans against the wall and puts on his shoes. "I'm on my way. Rachel, listen to me... if anything happens before I get there... anything that doesn't seem right, then call an ambulance, immediately. Don't hesitate and don't give Olivia a choice."

Stuffing his wallet into his pocket, he hands the phone back to Scott. As he opens the door, Scott hands him a container of food.

"Make sure my wife eats, please." He puts the phone back up to his ear. "Rachel, I'm sending you some food, Honey."

"Scott, tell Ethan to hurry. I'm really worried and I'm not good with this stuff," her voice vibrates with the sound of threatening tears.

"Sweetheart, don't worry. Ethan will be there in just a few minutes. He'll know what to do."

Scott puts his phone in his pocket and follows Ethan out the door. "You do know what to do. Don't you?"

Ethan turns and pauses before giving Scott a reassuring nod. "I'll take good care of her."

Chapter Nine

Ethan jumps over the flower garden and sprints to the car. In record time, he's rounding the corner into the parking space at the back of Olivia's house. When he bounds through the back door, he startles Rachel and halts her frantic pacing.

"Thank God, you're here!"

"Has she opened her eyes, yet?"

"Just briefly, then she's out of it again."

Ethan stands at the side of the couch looking down at her. Something hidden in his memories haunts him, making him swallow hard. Flashing Rachel a concerned look he gently brushes the back of his hand on Olivia's forehead, trying to gauge the fever. Kneeling on the floor beside her, he wipes the perspiration from her brow before brushing her damp hair away from her face. "Olivia," he coaxes. Trying to rouse her, he nudges her lightly, but she doesn't respond. "Pass me the thermometer, Rach."

Rachel holds it one way and then turns it the other way, trying to figure out how it works. "See? This is why I don't want kids." She walks over and hands it to Ethan. "I'd never be able to figure this thing out."

Ethan smirks as he guides the end of the digital thermometer into Olivia's ear.

Rachel makes a face. "I would never have thought to put that in there."

Ethan feels the tension in every muscle of his body, watching Olivia lay there, looking so helpless. He almost lost his youngest sister, Kaylie, to a high fever when she was just a small child. It's something that he'll never forget. His stomach tightens with anxiety. When the thermometer finally beeps, he anxiously looks at the digital display. "Christ, Rachel. It's 105! How long has it been this high?" Alarmed, he quickly gets to his feet and looks over at her for an answer.

"I... I don't know. I just got here an hour ago, so at least that long."

"Shit!" Ethan rubs his head, "We have to get the fever down or she could start to seizure." Looking around the main floor of the tiny townhome, he glances at the stairs and then back to Olivia on the couch. Then he looks over at Rachel, "Take her clothes off," he instructs, "leave on her bra and panties." He starts up the stairs, taking them two at a time. The sound of running water comes from the upstairs bathroom.

Rachel follows his instructions, willing to try anything to get the fever down. When she tries to sit her up so she can get her undressed, Olivia opens her eyes. "Olivia? Honey are you okay?"

She shakes her head NO and then closes her eyes again.

"Olivia! I need to know if you've been taking your medication." Rachel tries again to get a response, "Olivia!"

Olivia's eyes open very slowly, trying to focus.

"Did you take your antibiotics? Have you taken any Tylenol?"

"I tried, but I threw them up." Moaning as if she's in pain, she closes her eyes again. "I dreamed Ethan was here. It was a nice dream."

The sound of running water stops and Ethan reappears downstairs.

"She woke up long enough to tell me that she tried to take the meds but she kept throwing them back up."

Ethan frowns. "That means the infection is getting worse."

"What do we do?" Rachel asks, panicked.

"I want to get this fever down first, and then I'll get the meds into her." He walks over to where she's laying on the couch. Thoughts of her in nothing but her underwear are usually arousing. At the moment, there's nothing remotely enticing about it. It's agony for him to see her in this frail condition. He scoops his arms underneath her, lifting her into them. As he carries her up the stairs, her eyes open.

Olivia stares at him and smiles. "You're here? My Prince... you've come to rescue me."

Ethan smiles in amusement and glances over at Rachel. "Hallucinations from the fever, obviously. I can honestly say I've never been called a prince before."

Rachel laughs as she follows him up the stairs. Ethan pushes through the bathroom door with Olivia still in his arms. The small space forces Rachel to stand in the doorway. When Ethan attempts to lower Olivia into the bathtub, he's halted by her sudden high-pitched squeal. She wraps her arms around his neck in a death grip! She's holding so tight that he can't breathe and his eyes open wide with the lack of oxygen. "It's okay, Olivia. It's just a bath." He tries to loosen her grip. "Olivia, let go."

"Put me down!" she screams. "Put me down!"

Needing air, Ethan reluctantly complies.

She releases her grip from around his neck as her feet hit the floor. Her weak legs do their best to support her.

"Olivia, we need to get your fever down. Please get into the bathtub," Rachel pleads from the doorway.

Olivia wobbles, as if she's had too much to drink, and Ethan reaches for her; trying to give her some support. She giggles when she sees her reflection in the mirror. "Where are my clothes?" Tipping forward, she lands against him, her hands rubbing across his chest. "Is my handsome Prince going to join me in the bathtub?"

Rachel's mouth falls open in shock, "Olivia! Geez!"

Ethan takes both of her hands in his and removes them from his chest. Holding them up to his mouth, he gives them a little kiss.

"Perhaps another time, Princess. Let's get you in the water and get that fever down."

"No! No! No! No! No!" She shakes her head. "I'm not getting in there, unless you get in there with me."

"Olivia, stop being difficult." Frustrated, he glances over at Rachel in the doorway, "Help me out here would you, Rachel?"

Rachel thinks about it for a moment. With her hand on the doorknob, she shakes her head, "I don't care what it takes, Ireland. Do whatever you've got to do to get her in that bathtub." With that, she slams the door closed, leaving them alone.

Ethan is stunned at what Rachel is suggesting. Speechless, he looks down at Olivia as she tugs at his shirt, trying to rid him of it. Rachel is right. The only thing that's important right now is getting Olivia into that bathtub and getting the fever down. He wipes away the beads of perspiration that run down the sides of her temples, with a gentle hand. He considers it briefly and rubs his hand against his jaw, not believing what he's about to do. Lifting his arms over his head, he allows her to pull his shirt off.

Now bare-chested, the jet-black tribal tattoo on his left shoulder is exposed. Olivia smiles at her victory; admiring the dark ink by brushing her fingertips over it, tracing the intricate Celtic design. "I like this," she whispers.

Ethan's muscles flex beneath her touch, inspiring an erection.

Olivia turns her attention to the silver chain that hangs around his neck. At the bottom of it, a masculine silver cross sits just above his well-defined pectorals. A gift from his mother, reminding him that he was raised to be a good Irish Catholic boy, a fact that he's seriously struggling with right now.

"And I like you," she continues, as she picks up the shiny pendant and runs her fingers over the raised pattern. Leaning into his chest, she rests her cheek against his skin, with a deep sigh. Skimming her hands down his sides, she rubs over his hardening shaft, as she moves to undo his belt buckle.

Ethan jumps and grabs her hands. "Jesus! Woman!" he growls. He's never going to be able to keep his shit together if she's going to be doing stuff like that.

Pouting at him, her eyes close as her weak knees finally surrender. He grabs her just in time, lifting her into his arms. Laying her head against his chest, she whispers, "Please."

Ethan can feel the heat from the fever burning against his bare skin. She's on fire! Closing his eyes, he lets out a loud sigh, acknowledging what he has to do. "Olivia I'm going to put you down in the water and then I'm going to get in behind you."

This time, she doesn't protest as he lowers her into the tub. The water gently ripples around her, rising up to cover her curves.

"How did I get myself into this?" he groans out loud. "McCabe would definitely *not* approve." Undoing his pants, he drops them to the floor and steps out of them.

Olivia looks up and smiles, watching as he climbs into the tub behind her, still wearing his boxers. The minute he's seated, she wiggles back so that she's between his legs and fully resting against his chest.

Arching her back slightly, she reaches behind to unlatch her bra. In one swift movement she removes it, tossing it to the bathroom floor. Taking his hands from his side she intertwines her fingers with his, pulling his arms around her waist; wrapping him completely around her body.

Ethan closes his eyes, trying to calm his thoughts. Holding his breath, he attempts to stop his semi hard-on from becoming a full-blown erection. He steadies his movements and tries to regain his composure. Looking up at the ceiling, he whispers, "Lord, you have an awful lot of faith in me… and a very cruel sense of humor."

He reaches for a cloth and washes the tepid water over her skin. When she rubs her hands up and down his thighs, he does his best to ignore the feelings that start to stir inside him. In the past few days, he's often thought about how it would feel to have her hands on him. He's half hard thinking about it now.

Being this close to her slowly dissolves his self-control. When he moves the cloth gently across her stomach, his thumbs brush across her breasts making her nipples become hard and responsive.

Cooing, Olivia lets her knees fall to the side, allowing him access to her inner thighs. She grabs his hand, steering it down between her legs. In this very intimate moment, she moans. Ethan holds his breath, unable to prevent his already rigid shaft from thickening further.

Lying beneath her, he can feel her heart start to race and the quickening of her breath. His hands skim across the material of her panties, as she encourages him further. Ethan can't ignore his arousal anymore; his raging hard-on presses against her back.

Forgetting why he's there, he slowly draws his hand back toward her stomach, moving her panties ever so slightly to the side. His fingers tease across her as he goes.

When he moves his hand away from her, it leaves her *wanting*. Without hesitation, she pushes his hand back down between her legs, this time sliding it underneath the waistband of her panties and across her clean-shaven pussy.

It feels smooth and soft under his touch. He groans his approval, grazing his fingertips along the outer folds. Consenting to his advances, Olivia lifts her hips, pressing her clit against the palm of his hand, encouraging him to take action. She nuzzles her cheek against his chest and moans, "This is the best dream ever."

Her words jolt him back to reality like a slap across the face. This is wrong, very wrong. Cursing, he stops his hand abruptly, before it reaches the spot she's longing for him to touch.

"Please," she whispers, her tone desperate and pleading as she tries to push him forward.

Ethan somehow finds the strength to pull his hand away, "Sorry, Love. Not today." He presses his lips against the back of her head in a kiss. In an effort to put some distance between their bodies, he forces her to sit up. Using the cloth to wet her hair, he wrings out the water so that it trickles down her back. He'll make her beg him to touch her again, one day soon. Now that he knows how she feels about him, he won't stop until she submits.

The cooling water makes her shiver. Ethan lets out a sigh of relief, eager to get out of this situation while he's still able to control himself. "Okay, Princess, bath time is over." He steps out of the tub and quickly wraps a towel around himself, just as Rachel knocks on the door.

"You okay in there?"

"Yes, just getting out. Can you take Olivia and get her dressed?"

Rachel pushes the door open an inch and tries to peek in, "Are you decent?"

"Yes, I'm good." Reaching down, he puts his arms around Olivia and helps her to her feet. Wrapping a towel around her, he lifts her out of the tub and steers her toward the door. Rachel stares at Olivia's discarded bra on the floor. She crosses her arms and squints her eyes at Ethan in an icy glare.

Ethan puts his hands up in the air in a convincing confession. "I was a perfect gentleman. Honest."

The cool air makes Olivia a little more lucid as Rachel walks her to her room to get dressed. Ethan runs downstairs and grabs his grey sweat pants out of his gym bag. As he discards his wet boxers, a loud argument erupts from the bedroom. He heads upstairs commando style, to check on Rachel's progress. Standing in the doorway, he smiles as he watches Rachel trying to wrestle a t-shirt on over her head, with no success.

Olivia fights her. "I want to go back downstairs!" she yells as she slaps at Rachel's hands.

Rachel throws her hands up in the air out of frustration. "Fine! I give up." She throws the t-shirt onto the bed and turns to walk away. She glares at Ethan standing in the doorway, chuckling.

"She's all yours!" she snarls, as she pushes past him into the hallway. He can't hear everything that she's ranting about as she stomps down the stairs, except the words "*stubborn*" and "*impossible*." Those words are crystal clear.

Olivia sits placidly on the side of the bed, her eyes down, looking at the floor. Ethan squats down in front of her, trying to ignore the fact that he's a short distance from her bare breasts. He can't help but fantasize about sucking one of those beautiful pink nipples into his mouth. He's always been a breast man and hers are the most beautiful he's seen: large, soft, and curvy. He imagines just how delicious they would taste. There goes his dick again.

"What's the matter, Olivia?" He tries not to growl, pushing his desires to the back of his mind.

"I don't like this room. Bad things happened and I don't want to stay here."

Ethan's intrigued. "What happened to you here, Princess?"

Looking haunted, she remains still. That look bothers him; he has to know what happened to her. John would agree that tonight isn't the night to push her, so he decides that he'll let it go, for now. He brushes the hair out of her eyes and frowns. Standing, he picks up the shirt that Rachel abandoned on the side of the bed. "Put on your shirt and I'll take you downstairs." She grabs it from him and pulls it over her head. "That's a good girl." He rubs his hand along the side of her cheek. "Can you walk?"

"I don't feel very good." Putting her hands over her face, she tries to hide the tears in her eyes. His heart feels heavy. He wishes he could make her forget about all the bad things that happened here. If she would give him a chance, he'd do everything he could to heal her body, heart, and soul. He's only known her a few days, but she's been in his dreams for as long as he can remember. He just knows, somehow, that he's the man that's meant to take care of her.

When she fails to get to her feet, he carries her back downstairs to the couch. Rachel is sitting at the table, eating her dinner. Ethan smiles at her when she raises her eyebrows and rolls her eyes at him. Reaching for the thermometer, he puts it in Olivia's ear. The beep comes quickly this time. "100. That's good news."

Dumping the antibiotics into his hand, he passes them to her with a glass of water. Sitting up, she washes them down with one gulp, and then lies back down. Within seconds, she's on her feet, dashing for the washroom. Without even thinking twice about it, Ethan follows her in, holding her hair back. When it finally stops, Ethan wipes the tears from Olivia's eyes and helps steady her as she heads into the other room.

"That's so disgusting," she says, with a sour look on her face.

Ethan looks over at Rachel, who's abandoned her dinner and is looking a little green herself. Getting to her feet, she follows Olivia to the couch. Holding the blanket, she lets her get settled and then covers her up.

"Rachel, why don't you go home? I don't have any meetings tomorrow so I can stay with her."

In the corner of the living room, there's a small cabinet with a hutch. Obviously, it had been meticulously handcrafted a long time ago. It's the kind of furniture that's passed down through generations, a place to keep safe one's most special treasures. He knows what he's looking for. *His* Nana always kept them in the middle drawer. He pulls it open and smiles. Taking one out, he breaks the left over candy cane from Christmas, into little pieces. Sitting on the side of the couch, he holds a small piece to her lips, "Here, Olivia. This will help." Looking across the room, he waits for an answer. "Rachel?"

"Are you sure?" She feels guilty for even thinking about leaving.

Ethan gives her a serious look. "Rachel, I raised three sisters. I know how to look after a sick girl."

"Yeah, but this one is pretty fricken stubborn."

Olivia fights with the blanket that Rachel has tucked around her. Instinctively, Ethan reaches down and frees her feet. Her struggling stops; she wiggles her toes, and then drifts back to sleep.

"I'm pretty sure I can handle her." He smiles, as he watches her settle.

Rachel notices the way he looks at her best friend. That look says it all; she doubts there's anything that could tear him away. Feeling that she was denied the *caregiver* gene, she knows that Olivia will be in much better hands with Ethan. He obviously knows what her needs are. Again, she entertains the thought that *he* just might be the answer to her prayers. A look of relief washes over her face. "Thank you, Ethan." She throws her arms around him in an appreciative hug, then wanders over to the couch and kisses Olivia on the cheek.

Slowly, Olivia opens her eyes. "Hi, Rachel, I'm sick."

"Yes, I know. Olivia, I'm leaving now." She ignores Olivia's frown. "Ethan is going to stay with you, okay?"

She smiles, her voice very groggy, "My Prince, Ethan?"

Sitting on the stairs Ethan tries to hide his amusement. He shrugs his shoulders and holds his hands out conceding defeat. "Guilty as charged."

"I'm not even going to go there." Rachel shakes her head, returning her attention to Olivia. "Olivia...I love you... but you better do what Ethan tells you or I'll kick your ass."

Ethan closes the door behind Rachel and clears the two stairs to the living room in one jump. Olivia is resting peacefully, for the moment, he watches her from a few feet away. Even as frail and ill as she is, he still thinks she's the most beautiful woman he's ever seen. He hates to take his eyes off her, but he needs to get the meds into her as soon as possible.

After taking the bag of ice out of the freezer, he searches the drawers, finally finding a small hammer. He shakes his head at how delicate it is, for a tool. He grasps the pink handle, glad that there's no one there to see him. It's hard to look manly smashing ice with a pink hammer.

Taking a bowl of crushed ice with him, he sits on the floor in front of her, and settles in for a very long night.

The pill bottles bulge in his pocket giving him an uncomfortable reminder. Olivia is sleeping so peacefully at the moment that he hates to wake her. "Olivia." She opens her eyes when he whispers her name. "You need to take your medicine."

She shakes her head and closes her eyes. "I can't. I'll be sick."

"Not this time, baby girl. I know a trick. We need to keep your fever down."

Ethan thinks back to his childhood in Ireland and a very sick sister. Kaylie was only a year and a half old when she became so sick that she couldn't even keep water down. She became severely dehydrated, making the fever even more dangerous. Ethan tried everything, but ice chips were the only thing that worked.

Olivia opens her eyes again and tries to focus on him.

"Trust me."

When he gently presses an ice chip against them, she parts her lips, allowing him to slide it in to her mouth. Her eyes are tired and heavy; she struggles to open them. He dumps two of the anti-nausea pills into his hand. "Olivia, I'm going to put a few ice chips in your mouth and I want you to chew them just a little... but don't swallow. Okay? He waits for her confirmation, "Do you understand? Chew but don't swallow."

She nods and opens her eyes slowly. "Or Rachel will kick my ass."

Ethan smiles at how completely adorable she is, even when she's this sick. "Here they come." He pops a few ice chunks into her mouth and she chews as instructed. She opens her mouth to show him. "Good girl, I'm going to put the pills in your mouth now and I want you to swallow them right away, okay? Don't chew them." Quickly he pops the two anti-nausea pills onto the crushed ice in her mouth. "Swallow." He gently pushes on her chin with his finger forcing her lips together.

She does as she's told and they seem to go down easy, letting Ethan relax a little; until she speaks, "You're lucky, Ireland. I don't usually swallow."

Lord have mercy! Why does everything between them, end up being sexual in nature? His stomach muscles tighten and his dick starts to come to life.

Smirking, he traces his fingers over her lips. If that's true, it's something he intends to change. "We'll see about that, Princess."

There's nothing to do now but wait. Forty-five minutes pass and Olivia hasn't been sick. The anti-nausea medication has had plenty of time to start working. Ethan walks to the kitchen and gets more ice from the freezer. When he returns, he finds her sitting up on the couch. "Olivia?" Concern creases his brow. "You okay?"

"Yes."

"Are you going to be sick?" He moves to sit beside her.

"No."

That's a relief. "You need to take the rest of your medicine." He takes it out of his pocket and reads the dosage instructions, then sets cell phone alarm to go off in four-hour intervals.

"Do you want to do it yourself?" She takes the bowl from him and picks up a few chunks of ice. He holds out his open hand with the two pills. "Take one at a time. Okay?"

Olivia throws the ice chips in her mouth, crunches them a few times, and then grabs for one of the pills. Swallowing it, she opens her mouth and sticks out her tongue, showing him that it's gone. "Do I win immunity?"

Ethan can't resist her sense of humor. Playfully touching the end of her nose with his finger, he smiles. "Not yet, Princess. One more to go."

Her hand heavily drops back into the bowl of ice and she scoops up a few more pieces. Tossing them in her mouth she quickly grabs the last pill and tosses it into her mouth... then chews.

"Olivia!" He's not quick enough to stop her; he cringes as he watches her finally swallow.

Coughing, she desperately tries to get rid of the bitter taste in her mouth. Tears form in her eyes. "It burns."

Ethan grabs ice from the bowl and pushes it into her mouth, "Here, keep chewing ice." He shoves a few pieces past her lips. "Not one for following instructions, are you, Miss James?"

She sticks her tongue out at him. He can't hide his amusement. "Watch it, now," he warns. "I might just bite that." He offers her one more piece of ice and she turns her head rejecting it.

"No more. I'm okay."

He drops it back in the bowl and takes it out of her hands. "Lie down and rest," he coaxes.

She frowns at him. "I want to sit up for a little while. My back hurts."

"Probably a muscle spasm from all that throwing up."

She holds the aching spot and winces.

"Lay down and I'll rub it for you." He grabs one of the throw pillows from the back of the couch and puts it on his lap. Without hesitation, she lies down, resting her head on the pillow. Her muscles tense and twist, as he applies expert hands. Almost immediately, she feels relief as he kneads the spasm into submission. He feels her body relax and slows his movement to a gentle caress.

Olivia reaches for the remote and switches to the cartoon channel, and catches the final few minutes of Scooby Doo. "And I would have gotten away with it too... if it wasn't for you meddling kids," she laughs.

Ethan takes the remote away from her. "Rest now," he demands. Closing her eyes, she settles into a comfortable position.

Just as she's about to drift off, she whispers his name, "Ethan?" She jolts upwards so she's sitting again.

Her actions alarm him. "What's wrong?"

Her eyes grow wide and her expression fearful. "Are you going to be here when I wake up?"

He breathes out a sigh of relief, "Yes, I'll be here." He leans forward, places his lips on her forehead in a gentle reassuring kiss, and lingers there enjoying the intimacy.

"You need to be here to save me," she whispers.

Still intrigued by the seemingly tragic events of her past, he leans back to look at her. "Save you from what?" What horrible thing has happened to this poor girl that it stalks her in her sleep, making her terrified of her own bedroom?

"The monster that hurts me in my dreams," she admits in a childlike confession.

Ah... so there *is* a monster. The thought angers him, making tension grow in his shoulders. Gripped by her vulnerability, he reaches out and strokes her hair, tucking the stray pieces behind her ear. It's a comforting gesture that's become so second nature to him that he doesn't even realize he's doing it anymore. He presses his lips against her forehead, needing to protect her. He can't explain why, but it feels like he's done it all his life.

"You're safe with me. I won't let anything hurt you."

Olivia believes him; he can see it in her eyes, even though they're dark and heavily burdened from the fever. The specks of gold are not their usual sparkling hue, but he intimately knows the love and trust in those hazel eyes. Taking her hand, he lifts it to his mouth, kissing it in a heroic gesture. It's the last thing she remembers as she leans into him and drifts back to sleep.

Chapter Ten

The sun warms Olivia's face, waking her slowly. She's vaguely aware that she's lying on the couch. Moaning in discomfort, she rubs her stiff and sore neck.

Barely able to lift her head, she turns in the direction of his voice as it registers in her thoughts. Ethan is sitting at the table with his cell phone to his ear and his laptop open. She can tell from his tone that he's tending to business.

Noticing that she's awake, he ends his call. Walking toward the couch, he smiles. "Good morning, how are you feeling?"

Sitting up, she tilts her neck from side to side, trying to ease the stiffness. "I actually feel a lot better." She has little recollection of the past day. Her eyes follow him as he sits beside her, like an old friend. Feeling shy, she pulls the blanket up and over her body hiding her breasts. He places the back of his hand against her forehead to check for fever, smiling as he brushes his fingers down her cheek. "Good."

Feeling a little awkward, she wonders why he seems so comfortable with such an intimate gesture. "Have you been here all night?"

"Yes. You were running a dangerously high fever and someone needed to make sure you took your meds."

"I remember. I kept throwing them up." Embarrassed she adjusts the blanket again, pulling it upward.

It suddenly occurs to him that she's a little fuzzy on the details. "It's okay; I found a way to get them into you." He smiles wickedly.

Olivia looks down at his hand on her thigh and starts to panic.

"Every FOUR hours to be precise." Unable to resist teasing her, he nods and winks. When she covers her face with her hands, groaning, he nudges her playfully with his shoulder. "Relax, Princess. Nothing happened. I slept on the floor and when the alarm went off, I woke you up to take your meds."

She exhales a huge sigh of relief and relaxes.

Ethan heads back to the table to answer an incoming email. Leaving her wondering about the new nickname... *Princess?*

"Was Rachel here?" she asks, trying to jar her memories.

"Yes. She was concerned when she couldn't reach you on the phone. When she called me you were in pretty rough shape." He peeks at her over the edge of the laptop.

"I remember her saying something about kicking my ass." Frowning she gets to her feet and makes her way to the bathroom on weak legs. Ethan stands quickly and holds out his hand in support. She reluctantly takes it.

"Yes, that's right. She said you needed to do what I told you or she was going to kick your ass." He smiles as he pushes open the bathroom door and starts to follow her in.

Where the heck does he think he's going? Turning, Olivia presses her hand on his chest and stops him. "Ummm, that's as far as you go, Ireland!" she growls, as she slams the door in his face.

Ethan leans against the door. "That's not what you said last night!"

"I don't believe you!" she hollers back. *What exactly happened last night?* Reality and dreams are all jumbled together. Brief images of him standing in the bathroom, shirtless, come to her mind. Her face begins to flush and then horror strikes her. Did she have a bath with Ethan? That couldn't have been real, could it?

When she opens the door, he moves to help her. "It's okay. I'm fine, thank you." She makes solid, steady steps back across the room. "Did you really sleep on the floor?"

"Yes." He can't resist making her squirm, "Well... part of the evening I sat on the couch with your head in my lap."

Getting wise to his teasing, she decides that she's not taking the bait this time. He gets too much satisfaction out of trying to get a reaction out of her, and she needs to put a stop to it. "How did I get into my pajamas?"

"Rachel helped you before she left." Well, that's partly true.

Her face starts to flush as she asks the question that's really on her mind, "Did you and I take a bath together?"

Ethan sits straight up and looks at her, considering all that could go wrong if he tells her the truth. Closing the laptop, he opts for a lie, "Of course not." He stares at her, gauging her reaction.

She returns his stare, not quite sure if she believes him, "So then, how did you get my fever down?"

It takes quick thinking on his part. "Ice chips."

"Ice what?"

"Ice chips. I sat up all night feeding you ice chips. I was worried about you becoming dehydrated."

"And every four hours you woke up to make sure I took my meds?"

"Of course, someone had to look after you, Olivia. It's not a big deal, really. I offered to stay because I wanted to be here."

What man does that? Not many men she knows would stay up all night with a sick woman. Especially, one who usually goes out of her way to give him a hard time.

"What time is it now?" She lies back down on the couch and struggles with the blanket that's half tucked underneath her. Walking over, he eases it out from under her, and covers her body.

"3 p.m."

"What?" She's alarmed. "Don't you have to go to work?"

"Relax... I'm the boss. Remember? I can work from home for a couple of days, if I want. Mine or yours, it makes no difference."

"Wait... a couple of days? What day is it?" She reaches for her cell phone, which he's thoughtfully charged for her. "It's Tuesday," he answers, before she can check.

"Oh my God!" She's shocked! "I've been out of it for three days?"

Ethan puts his hand on her shoulder to calm her.

"You were a very sick girl."

"And you stayed with me the whole time?" She starts to get a little emotional; that speaks volumes about this man's dedication.

He nods his head and tries to lighten the mood. "Yes, and you were an absolute pain in the ass."

Olivia looks up at him through tired eyes and smiles. "You've done so much. You don't need to stay any longer." Deep down she kind of likes having him here. She feels strangely connected to him now, but she'll never admit that to him. "I feel like I'm taking advantage of you."

"Not at all." He smiles. The lightening yellow lines in his eyes sparkle with mischief. "But if you'd like to take advantage of me, I wouldn't stop you."

She groans. She was just starting to like him, too. What is it about men that makes them ruin everything by talking? She rolls her eyes. "That's not going to happen."

He crouches down so that he's at eye level with her. "Now, that's a shame." He takes hold of the blankets edge, pulling it up and over her shoulders. With the same caring and tenderness as the night before, he strokes her hair before planting a kiss on her forehead. Warmth runs through her body as his lips linger there; stirring in her a nervous tingling that makes her heart beat to a new rhythm. That is, until her brain steps in and takes back control.

"Hey, Ireland."

"Yes?"

"If you kiss me again, I'll punch you right in the nose."

Ethan lets out a loud laugh. "Well, you're back to your old self, I see. I'm glad you're feeling better. I'll be over there doing some work at a safe distance. Let me know if you need anything. Maybe you should try to eat and drink soon."

She makes a face at the repulsive thought.

Ethan chuckles. "Okay. Later then." He reaches to touch her, withdrawing his hand as he remembers her warning. As he walks back to the table, she opens her eyes and watches him cross the room. Every move this man makes is with an alluring confidence. She hates to admit that she finds him extremely sexy. Pushing the thought out of her mind, she drifts back off to sleep.

Ethan answers a few emails and make a few quick calls about a business deal he's negotiating. It will cement his presence in the community and he's very excited about it. He loves this little suburban town, with its rolling hills and lush green countryside. In many ways, it reminds him of home. He puts his shrewd negotiation skills to work. "Not a penny more. The deal closes before the end of the month or my offer expires."

Over on the couch, Olivia's dreams are in high definition and X-rated. She lets out a small moan. Ethan leans around the laptop to see if she's okay. "I have to go. Do the job I'm paying you for, or you'll find yourself looking for another one."

The voice on the other end of the phone begins to protest but Ethan disconnects the call; his attention is focused on Olivia. Still sound asleep, she moans again and rolls onto her side. Thinking she's experiencing discomfort, Ethan picks up the bottle of Tylenol and moves to sit on the side of the couch. It only takes him a second to realize what's going on.

Olivia is having one of her recurring dreams of the mysterious man who's the center of her world and *lover extraordinaire*. Like the others, this dream is shockingly clear in detail. Squirming, she rubs her legs together, clenching and trying to appease the ache there. Pushing her hips forward, her hands grip the corners of the pillowcase and hold on tight. When she moans out Ethan's name in a sensual manner, his dick hardens with amazing swiftness.

He squeezes the Tylenol bottle tightly in his hand, nearly crushing it. "Damn! That's hot."

Olivia eyelashes flutter opens and looks at him; taking a moment to decipher what's real and what's a dream. She blinks her eyes rapidly, making sure she's awake. "Hi," she says softly.

"Hi, yourself. Did you have a good sleep?"

"Yes, actually." She stretches out her muscles and sits up, wondering why he's looking at her with a strange sort of smile. It looks like he knows a secret he's busting to share.

Ethan adjusts the erection in his pants as he heads to the kitchen to get her a glass of water. On his way back, Olivia's eyes skim over every inch of his body, recalling her dream: the feel of his rock solid chest against hers, his lips skimming across her body, his thick hard cock inside her. Her eyes stop there, noticing his pants straining from his arousal. *Oh my! Why does he have a hard-on?*

A disturbing thought forms in her mind. Is it possible that Ethan is the man in her dreams, who's hidden by the shadows? Is that even possible? Is that the strange connection she has with him? The reason that she's drawn to him? It doesn't really matter, now that her brain has made the connection, she certainly can't have him hanging around. She'd never be able to maintain control. Now that she's feeling well, he'll likely return to all the other women in his life, she rationalizes. She's confused about why that thought makes her sad. Reaching for her phone she texts Rachel.

From Olivia: How could you leave me here with Ethan?
From Rachel: Hey! I'm glad you're feeling better! Trust me you're better off with him than me.
From Olivia: I doubt that.
From Rachel: Scott says Ethan took a year or two of medical school before he switched to business. I on the other hand couldn't figure out how to work the thermometer.
From Olivia: Ethan was a med student?
From Rachel: Apparently. Scott says he doesn't like people to know that.
From Olivia: When are you coming back?
From Rachel: In about an hour why? Everything ok?
From Olivia: Yes, just come back ok?

When Ethan rushes back into the room to answer his phone, the strange way she looks at him, stops him in his tracks. "What?" He lets the call go to voicemail, since he's much more curious about what's on her mind.

"You were going to be a doctor?"

"Hardly, I took one year of pre-med." He sits beside her and raises an eyebrow, curious about how she found out.

Intrigued, she looks at him with bright eyes, wanting to hear more about his life. "Why did you quit?"

Ethan hesitates, not sure that he wants to share the details of his childhood. "When I was a child the family business was struggling. My mom was forced to work with my dad at the office. I was left to look after my three sisters." He adjusts the way he's sitting, still feeling a little bit uncomfortable.

"You have three sisters? You're the only boy?" she asks, somewhat surprised.

"Yes."

That doesn't sound right to her. "You don't have a brother?"

"No."

A look of bewilderment glosses over her face, making him narrow his eyes in an inquisitive manner. "What's going on in that mind of yours?"

She tries to hide her embarrassment. "Nothing. I was just wondering." She can't exactly blurt out the reason for her confusion. She's not even convinced that he is the man in her dreams. Shaking her head quickly, she tries to jiggle that thought loose. "Are you the youngest or the oldest?

I'm the oldest." Ethan squirms uncomfortably, starting to feel a little vulnerable. "My youngest sister, Kaylie, was very premature, such a tiny little thing, no bigger than a ladybug, and always so sick. She almost died from the complications of a high fever when she was a little over a year old." Ethan was just a child himself, at the time. His father had moved them into a cold, cramped country home until the business started making money. Poor little Kaylie lay shivering in the bed she shared with two other sisters.

Olivia listens, watching him closely, as he tries to hide his emotion behind a masculine veil.

"I would never have forgiven myself if she had died on my watch." He looks off into the distance avoiding eye contact with her.

Feeling a great amount of compassion for him, Olivia sits up and leans her head against his shoulder. He hesitates a moment, before putting his arms around her. When she sighs and squeezes him tightly, he tucks her in under his arm and presses her snuggly against the hard muscles of his chest. He feels tightness in his stomach. He's not sure if it's because he's talking about his past or if it's being this close to her.

"No parent should ever place that much responsibility on a child, Ethan," Olivia says sympathetically, reaching for his hand.

"They had no choice." He shrugs his shoulders. "I spent my teenage years looking after bumps and scrapes, broken bones and broken hearts. When I finished high school, I thought that's what I wanted to do. Fix people."

When she starts to caress his hand with her thumb, he nuzzles his chin against her head. Her touch is so warm, so tender; it stirs something inside him. It always feels like there's an electric charge running through his body when she's near. He stops talking and soothes himself by matching the rhythm of her breathing.

"So you took a year of pre-med, then what?" she continues to pry.

"Like I said, my parents were struggling financially. I had to work in order to put myself through school. I took odd jobs wherever I could and ended up in a small sales office working on commission. That's where I learned that I had a gift for business."

"Wow!" She hangs on his every word, fascinated.

"That's when I changed focus. After my first year, the company I was working for was so impressed with my grades that they paid my full scholarship, so I could pursue my business degree. Then they hired me full time."

"Really? Was that at Aurora?"

He looks down as she intertwines her fingers with his, holding his hand. That electricity zings through his bloodstream, making him feel warm. "Yes, at Aurora. I owe them everything and I almost screwed it up." He starts to tense. He shouldn't have brought that up, now she's sure to have questions. "But that's enough about me. It's a boring story really."

"Do you regret not being a doctor?"

"No, not really. I'm really good at what I do. I've made money and been able to help my parents. I still work with the emergency response team… or I do, when I'm in Ireland. I've applied here to work as part of the volunteer emergency and rescue team, but I haven't heard back from them, yet."

"What are your sister's names?"

"Madison is the oldest; she's two years younger than me and then McKenna. Kaylie is the youngest. I was 14 when she was born. My mom thought she was going through menopause, so that pregnancy was a shock to my parents."

"I would guess so!" Olivia is touched by the vulnerability Ethan shows while he shares his life with her.

"Kaylie was a twin," he offers, not knowing why he suddenly has the urge to tell her everything. That's something that he never even shared with Jessica. He becomes nervous when he realizes that this woman wields a lot of power over him; too much, he worries. He's never wanted to share the details of his life with someone before. It's making him feel more than a little unnerved.

"Was?"

"Yes, my mother was very sick during the pregnancy and had complications that caused her to go into labor before she was full term. Kaylie's twin, Katelyn, died shortly after they were born; she went into distress. The hospital wasn't equipped to deal with the needs of a baby that premature. It was really tough on the family. So you can understand how horrible it would have been if we had lost Kaylie as well."

The door swings open, startling them both. Rachel stops dead at the sight of them cuddling on the couch. Olivia sits straight up, when Rachel flashes her a look that basically says; *what the heck are you doing?*

Olivia pulls her hand away from his. "You're lucky, Ireland. Reinforcements have arrived."

"I guess I can leave now." Looking disappointed, he heads to the table and gathers up his stuff. Rachel asks for the update on the medication routine as he makes his way to the door.

"Did she do what she was told?"

Ethan gives her a wicked grin. "Yes, every four hours… she did *exactly* what I told her to do."

The words are no sooner out of his mouth, when he's hit square in the face with a cushion from the couch, lobbed at him by an extremely perturbed Olivia.

"You wish, Ireland!"

Ethan snickers and tosses the cushion to Rachel. "I think that's my cue to leave."

"Don't let the door hit you in the ass," Olivia growls from the couch.

Ethan gets Rachel's attention, nodding his head in the direction of the door. "What's up?" she asks, concerned as she follows him out the door.

"She doesn't remember much about the last couple of nights. I thought it was best not to tell her."

"Really? She doesn't remember?"

"No. She has vague memories of the bath and she's asked a few questions, but I kind of played it off as if it was just a dream induced by the fever."

"Good call," Rachel agrees.

"So, I'll leave her in your hands and get on my way. Please make sure she eats something." Ethan looks dejected. Rachel wonders if it's because he's had no sleep for two nights, or if it's because he doesn't want to leave. She holds out her arms for a hug to thank him for all he's done.

When he's gone, Rachel stands in front of Olivia, demanding an explanation. "Okay, seriously? What's going on with you?"

"Nothing." She pretends that she doesn't know what Rachel's talking about.

"Don't give me that crap, lady. First, you beg me not to leave you here with him. Then I get here and you're cuddling on the couch together. THEN not two seconds later you're throwing things at him and being rude."

Olivia gets defensive, "I wasn't rude."

"Yes, you were. Ethan has been here for two days looking after you, and you're no picnic, let me tell you. Instead of thanking him, you tell him not to let the door hit him in the ass?" Rachel scolds her and Olivia realizes that she probably deserves it.

"I can't help it. He makes me so angry."

Rachel sits beside her. "Did you ever think that maybe he makes you angry because you actually *like* him?"

"Don't be ridiculous!" Olivia snaps.

"Whatever… if you didn't care about him, you wouldn't let him get you so riled up."

Olivia thinks about it for a moment and frowns. "Things would never work out between us."

"Why?"

"I don't know… he's rude… and bossy. Girls fall all over him and his, *'look at me I'm Irish'* accent," she pauses, "besides he doesn't strike me as the kind of guy who'd be happy to settle down with one girl."

Rachel looks at her in astonishment. "Really? That's the best you've got? I think you should give him a chance. He's smart and successful and an extremely sexy man. Scott says he's taken quite an interest in you. He said that you're the most beautiful woman he's ever seen." She pokes Olivia playfully in the arm. "Just get to know him a little better before you kick him to the curb. Okay?"

Look at her friend, being all sincere in pleading Ethan's case. "I don't think that's going to happen, Rach. Every time I talk to him, he says something so ridiculous that it makes me want to stomp REALLY HARD on his toes."

Rachel laughs.

Olivia's drawn in for a moment. "Did he really tell Scott that he thinks I'm beautiful?"

Rachel celebrates inside. There's hope after all. Now all she has to do is keep her away from Noah.

"Yup, that's what he told Scott." Rachel heads for the kitchen. "Ethan says you need to eat, so I'm going to make you some soup."

Olivia's head is spinning. She doesn't know what to think anymore. Just a few days ago, she had decided that there was something dangerous about him, and that she needed to stay away. Now she's seen a very different side of him, one that's tender, kind, and gentle. She looks to see if Rachel is out of sight, then picks up her phone and sends him a text.

From Olivia: Hey, thank you for looking after me. Sorry about the pillow to the face ☹
From Ethan: No worries Beautiful. I'm glad you're feeling better.

Ethan gets back to Scott and Rachel's house and tosses his bag on the floor in his room. Stepping into the shower, he lets the warm water rain down onto his sore and aching muscles. He hadn't realized just how tired he is. Thoughts of Olivia linger in his mind as he rinses the lather from his hair. When he's finished his shower, he props up the pillows on the bed and settles in. Powering up his laptop he works on business reports until his eyes are tired and sore. Closing them tightly, he pinches the bridge of his nose trying to relieve some of the pressure.

Ethan leans his head back against the wall with a thud and sighs. Thinking about Olivia again, his erection tents his boxers; it doesn't matter how hard he tries to put her out of his mind. He'll have to figure out what he's going to do about her. He can't ignore the fact that he's been dreaming about her since he arrived here in Canada. The minute she got out of her car at that soccer game, it was as if she walked right out of his dreams. He didn't understand it. Didn't want to. All he knows, right now, is that after being with her the past few days, staying away from her is no longer an option. He can't. He won't.

Chapter Eleven

"What are you doing?"

"I'm opening the door." She glances at him with a strange look and then understands his frustration. "I'm sorry."

"Can you just learn to be patient? I'll get the door for you."

"I'm just used to doing stuff for myself." She shrugs. Letting go of the handle, she steps to the side.

"You're **my** girl. You deserve to be treated like a lady and I intend to do so." He holds the door open, admiring her as she blushes. As she brushes past him, he gently skims his hand across her hip. She looks up into his green eyes and holds his gaze. The mischievous grin that forms on his lips makes her heart beat faster. She steps further into the room, trying to put a little space between them.

"I like this one," she declares, running her hand along the side of the muscular thoroughbred.

"You have good taste."

His body presses up against her from behind. Strong masculine hands grip her hips and then travel around her. Her body responds to his touch, as he firmly pulls her back against his chest.

"Owen," she says through shallow breaths, "what if somebody comes in?"

He slides her top off her shoulder, exposing the skin there. "They'll have to leave. I have no intentions of sharing you."

"OWEN!" she protests, but her struggling only makes him hold on tighter.

Lowering his lips to her shoulder he growls, "You smell so good." He nips at her skin making her gasp. Trailing kisses across her shoulder and along her neck, he feels her surrender. That's the moment that gives him the most satisfaction... the surrender.

He loosens his grip so she can turn in his arms. Lips smash together in desire, hungry and passionate. She parts her lips, letting him in and allowing him to completely consume her.

His hands explore her body, making her ache with desire. Lifting her in his arms, he carries her to a well-hidden corner and lowers her gently to the ground. A clean pile of straw aids their comfort, but she's not thinking about that right now. All she's thinking about is the man who has laid her there. The man, who is about to take what's his. If he doesn't do it soon, she feels like she'll go out of her mind.

His hands work quickly on pearl buttons and when he has them mastered, cool air washes over her skin. His lips surround her sensitive nipple, drawing it into his mouth and closing around it. Nipping the hardened bud, he makes her squirm beneath him.

"Please," she begs.

Grasping the hem of her skirt, he pulls it upward, exposing her. A firm strong hand travel across her thigh and between her legs. "Since you asked so nicely, Princess." Pulling her panties to the side, he slides his hand across her and moans, "Wet and warm and smooth as silk." Desire takes over. Grasping her panties, he pulls them off. Unzipping his trousers and tugging them down, he settles between her thighs. The wide head of his cock, rubs against her, teasing. The anticipation is driving her wild... one small thrust of his hips and he'll finally be inside her...

Olivia wakes from her dream, feeling overheated. She wipes the perspiration from her brow and fans her face, trying to cool herself down. It has nothing to do with the fever. It's been several days since the stubborn infection knocked her off her feet.

Wandering around the house, feeling restless and bored, she decides to call Rachel. "Hey, I've got to get out of this house. I'm going crazy."

"Don't you dare even think about coming to work on a Monday, if you don't have to!"

The same small brick townhouse that has kept her safe for the last three years now feels like a prison. "Honestly, Rachel. I can't stand being stuck here another minute."

"Well, don't come in here for heaven's sake. It's bad enough that you insist on working from home. Scott said they dropped your car off this morning, why don't you go for a drive and get some air? Maybe do some retail therapy?"

Olivia opens the door to the back yard and sees her car in the driveway. There's an envelope on the back porch and based on the lump in it, she assumes it holds the keys. "That's actually a pretty good idea. Do you want to go with me?" Fumbling to open the package, she dumps the keys into her hand.

"Sorry, sweetie. I'm stuck here," Shuffling papers on her desk, Rachel becomes a little distracted.

"You suck!"

"I love you, too, but I've gotta go."

The phone goes silent and Olivia knows that Rachel has hung up. Something Rachel is known to do when she's finished with a conversation. Olivia heads upstairs and looks at herself in the bathroom mirror. Being sick sure makes a girl ugly. Yuck! She makes a face as she reaches over and turns on the shower.

The water is warm and soothing; the soapy bubbles smell so good. Closing her eyes, she lets the tension melt away from her body.

Putting on something pretty makes her feel like a new woman, strong and healthy. Grabbing her keys, she heads out the back door into the sunshine. The flutter of wings startle her as they whiz past her head and land on the fleet car parked beside her Mustang. Olivia watches as the little green bird hops frantically back and forth on the hood of the silver grey car, chattering at her.

"Are you trying to tell me something?"

The original Twilight Turquoise paint of her Mustang sparkles in the sunlight. She's eager to take her for a drive. She reaches to unlock the driver's side door when she realizes that the key in her hand is for the other car. The little green bird watches her intently from the hood of the car that's on loan to her from Aurora Tech. It's almost as if it knew the whole time that Olivia was holding the wrong keys in her hand.

"You're starting to creep me out, you know that, bird?"

As she digs through her purse for the right keys, she has a thought. Returning the car to Aurora Tech today would provide the possibility of running into Ethan. She can't deny that they developed a deeper connection, while he nursed her back to health. She would certainly never admit it to him, but she misses him; especially after this morning's dream.

Olivia climbs into the driver's seat of the Aurora fleet car and calls Scott's cell phone. As the call is being connected, the little bird pecks a few times at the windshield and then flies away. She scratches her head, watching it find a spot close by in the tree.

"Hey! How are you feeling?"

"A hundred percent thanks, Scott! Are you coming home at the regular time today?"

"I think so, unless the Senior Vice President of International Sales has other plans for me. He's annoying like that sometimes," he laughs. "Why? What's going on?"

"I need to get out of this house. I was thinking that I could drive to Toronto, return the fleet car, and then maybe do some shopping downtown until you're done work. Do you mind bringing me home?"

"No, I don't mind, but Olivia... Ethan will freak when he finds out you brought the car back. He's already asked me to make the arrangements for someone to pick it up."

"Now you don't have to. And you might be afraid of your boss, but I'm NOT!" she adds.

Scott's tone gets serious, "Well, maybe you should be."

"I'm coming anyway. I'll see you soon."

"Fine. Have reception notify me when you get here." He knows there's no point in arguing with her.

"Will do. Bye."

Scott looks up at a coworker who has wandered into his office, with some papers to be signed. "The freaking women in my life are determined to drive me crazy."

An hour later, Olivia pulls into the only downtown lot that still has available parking. It's a short walk to Aurora Technologies, and she could use the exercise and fresh air. Well, as fresh as the air gets in a big city. As she rounds the corner onto the main street, her eyes follow the majestic, Toronto high-rise office building from ground to skyline. WOW! Walking toward it in awe, her eyes are drawn down a small pathway that leads to a rustic wooden door, discreetly tucked in between its renovated neighbors. The weathered, dark green and burgundy trim has obviously hidden itself from any threat of modernization. The window is decorated with beads, baubles, and an amateurish hand painted sign: "Eva Storm - Psychic. Palm & Tarot Card Readings."

The hairs on the back of her neck stand up as the door flies open and a woman, dressed with a gypsy like appearance, heads straight for her. Her long, silver hair blows in the breeze, leaving it tousled and looking unkempt.

She stops, reaching out to takes Olivia's hands in hers and gives them a squeeze. They feel weathered and boney, like brittle twigs on a fallen tree. Her long fingers delicately brush across Olivia's cheeks while she studies her face for what seems like forever.

Strangers push past them, making their way along the busy city street, oblivious to their presence in the middle of the walkway. Olivia is frozen, staring back at the woman she presumes is the psychic. Several talismans are strung around her neck and large ornate rings decorate her fingers. Her face, pale and wrinkled, shows her age; but her eyes sparkle with a youthful appearance as a smile starts to form across her bright red lips.

"It IS you, I knew it!" Lowering her hands to her side, she smiles. "Everybody is finally here!" She's delighted and it shows in her expression.

Olivia finally finds her voice, "I think you have me confused with someone else, we've never met before."

"No child, it's YOU. I'd know you anywhere."

Olivia gets nervous and takes a step. "I have to go." Pulling away, she tries to sidestep her, when a frail hand grips her arm to stop her. "He's looking for you," her voice becomes eerie and thick with an Irish accent. "He's very close."

Fear washes over Olivia. She takes a few steps, afraid to turn her back on a woman who is obviously insane. As she puts some distance between them, the woman calls out one last time, "Trust your intuition child... he **WILL** find you... soon."

Olivia takes the elevator on its long journey to the penthouse offices of Aurora Technologies. Her impromptu psychic encounter has left her feeling a little unnerved. The warning, about Sam returning for her, has left her feeling dizzy and slightly nauseated. She pushes that thought out of her mind as the elevator door opens and teleports her to a whole other world.

The receptionist smiles as she approaches. "Hi, welcome to Aurora Technologies. How can I help you?"

Olivia suddenly feels severely underdressed. She's never seen such perfect teeth and beautifully styled, blonde hair. The bright pink lipstick is dull in comparison to the diamond chandelier earrings she's wearing. Her low cut dress looks more like a ball gown than office attire. Olivia is suddenly aware that she's staring. "I'm here to see Scott Parker."

"Whom should I say is here?" She gives her a friendly smile, but Olivia senses the insincerity in it.

"Olivia James."

The receptionist motions Olivia toward the waiting area as she returns to her desk to answer a call. Feeling small and insignificant in this space, Olivia fades into one of the oversized leather chairs. They look to her like they belong in a gentlemen's cigar club rather than an office reception area. A familiar voice rambles off instructions in the hallway. She gets a nervous stomach as she peeks around the large winged back of the chair.

A young man wanders out of an office trying to juggle a stack of heavy papers. Beside him, a very professional looking Ethan O'Connell buttons his perfectly tailored double-breasted suit. It hangs ruggedly off his broad shoulders as he walks, accentuating his very trim muscular waist. Jesus, the man can work a suit. His tanned skin is flawless against the apple green silk dress shirt. His hair is brushed back, falling in soft curls behind his ears. Extremely sexy! She draws in a deep breath, knots starting to tangle in her stomach.

Olivia's sudden onset of nerves gets worse, making her wish that she had given this more thought. Maybe he won't see her. She could just leave and ask Scott to meet her downstairs.

Suddenly a conference room door opens, its occupants filling the hallway. Amongst all the commotion, she's met with polite smiles and greetings as they pass; despite the fact that she tries to shrink further out of sight and blend into her surroundings.

Ethan senses her presence immediately and eagerly searches the room. Whether it's the pheromones, or the subtle smell of her perfume that alerts him of her presence, he doesn't know. The burning desire that coils deep inside his stomach when she's near is an indisputable sign. His face lights up, when he spots her across the foyer.

As he nears her, the intensity of his green eyes set the fluttering butterflies in her stomach into a frenzy. An intense, tingly warmth washes over her body. She can keep trying to deny it, but it's clear that she has it bad for Ethan O'Connell.

As he walks past the large wooden desk in the foyer, on a direct path toward her, the receptionist calls his name, "Mr. O'Connell!"

His eyes locked to Olivia's, he continues toward her. Not to be ignored, the receptionist pursues him with eagerness. Getting to her feet, Olivia looks past him to see her scowling and heading around the oversized desk toward them.

"Hi." There's something quiet and almost shy in her greeting. His commanding presence is overwhelmingly strong when he's in his element.

"Hey! You look like you're feeling a lot better." Ethan reaches out in a manner that suggests he's going to pull her in for a hug. The receptionist who's now standing right beside him interrupts him.

"Mr. O'Connell," she persists.

He refuses to acknowledge her, making Olivia feel a little embarrassed for stealing away his attention. The persistent receptionist, Hannah, stands tall and puffs out her chest. Olivia gets her first full view of this magazine perfect woman. Long, lean legs leading up to what can't be anymore than a size two waist and the largest breasts she's ever seen. Olivia looks down at herself and frowns at her curves.

"Walk with me to my office." He directs his hand toward the hallway to the left, unfazed by Hannah's attempt to get his attention.

Olivia glances at Hannah, wondering how Ethan can be unaffected by her voluptuous presence. "Oh well, I shouldn't really," she replies, noting Hannah's disapproving look.

Pressing his hand on the small of her back, he begins to gently guide her down the corridor. He turns to the receptionist who's now looking extremely bothered by his dismissal. "Hannah, please hold all my calls."

"But, Mr. O'Connell..." Ethan shoots her a warning look that immediately halts her, "Yes, sir, I'll hold all your calls." She returns to her post with a very sour look on her face.

Olivia is glad to see that she's not the only woman who *falls in line* with one look from Ethan O'Connell. She assumes that he probably has that effect on all women. Finding Hannah's behavior a little odd for an employee, she leans in and whispers, "I think she's pouting."

Ethan leans in and whispers back, "Don't worry, she'll get over it. She always does."

She always does? What does that mean? Olivia glances back for one last look at her; jealousy nibbling at her. Trying not to think about Ethan keeping company with a female employee, she turns her attention to the art along the hallway. When he ushers her into his office, she's immediately drawn to the window view and walks directly to it.

"Do you like it?"

Ethan pours her a glass of water from a pitcher filled with freshly crushed ice and lemon slices. Hannah's handiwork no doubt. Why does the thought of this woman claw at her? When Ethan joins her at the window, she takes the glass out of his hand and returns her gaze to the overwhelming view of the city. "It's beautiful."

Olivia glances at him, meeting with his ardent stare as she tips the glass to her lips. Stepping closer, Ethan takes the glass out of her hand, and puts it down on the windowsill. "*You* are beautiful. I could gaze into your eyes forever. They promise me all kinds of wonderful things. I feel lost in them and to be perfectly honest with you, I don't want to be rescued."

Olivia takes a quick breath and tries to hide her blush. "Always so poetic, Mr. O'Connell." She takes the opportunity to turn his game against him. "Tell me…does your receptionist fall for your sweet talk?" She walks away leaving him standing alone at the window.

"My receptionist?" He smirks and watches her lean back against the edge of his desk. He's pleased at the jealousy in her tone. It's proof that she does have feelings for him.

"Yes, your receptionist. Have you kissed her?" She fans her hand out in front of her, admiring her bright red nail polish.

"What?" He knows she's teasing him. Mocking the conversation they had about her date with Noah, and turning his little jealous inquisition against him.

"Have... you... kissed... her?" She looks up, raising her eyebrows in a taunting manner. "It's not a difficult question, Mr. O'Connell." She fights hard to keep from smiling.

Unbuttoning his jacket, Ethan shrugs it off his shoulders, and hangs it over the arm of a chair. Finding her performance entertaining, a radiating grin forms on his lips. He loosens his perfectly knotted tie and releases the button beneath it. "No, I haven't kissed her. And before you go any further with this line of questioning… I don't sleep with my staff." He undoes the cuffs of his shirt, rolling them back one fold at a time, exposing his forearms.

Watching him meticulously smooth out each crease, in what seems to be a compulsive behavior, makes the hair stand up on the back of her neck. A nervous chill moves through her. It's a gesture she recognizes as a sign that he means business, though she's not entirely sure how she knows that.

"Hmmm, I don't think that I believe you."

Her playful manner kick starts a rush of testosterone that Ethan can't ignore. "Well, that's your prerogative, Olivia. I assure you that it's true." His smile fades as he prowls toward her like a hungry lion stalking his prey. He places his hands on either side of her, trapping her there.

Denying her any space, he moves in closer, pinning her between his desk and his rock hard body. Olivia's heartbeat kicks up a notch, her body reacting with a surge of heat. Afraid she doesn't have the will to fight him, she plans her escape. "I really should go find Scott. He'll be waiting for me."

"You're here to see Scott?" Ethan leans back so he can look at her, feeling wounded. Olivia can see it in his eyes. She tries to move her body so that her sensitive breasts are no longer pressed against him.

"Yes, well… kind of. My car is fixed so I was returning the fleet car. I'm going to do some shopping this afternoon and then Scott is going to drive me home."

Ethan's mood swings from playful to petulant in a split second. "You drove all the way to the city to return the fleet car? Why would you do that?" he snarls at her. "I was having someone arrange to pick it up." There's no hiding the annoyance in his voice. Scott was right. He's pissed!

Olivia shrugs her shoulders. "Don't be mad. I'm just used to doing things for myself." Ethan stands up straight, releasing her from his muscled cage. Moving to the other side of the desk, he growls audibly. Picking up the phone, he pounds one of the buttons and waits. "Please let Mr. Parker know that I'll take Miss James home myself." He hangs up, looking extremely pleased with himself.

Olivia's mouth drops open in disbelief. "Really? What makes you think that I want to go home with you?" She folds her arms in front of her, annoyed.

"Not home. I have an errand to run and I'd like you to go with me."

Ignoring her obvious objection to him taking control, he picks up the phone again. "Clear my afternoon, I'm leaving for the day." He glances over at her as he hangs up the phone.

"Can you do that?" She's impressed by his position of authority. Ethan in charge is definitely a huge turn on for her. It's a fact that's becoming increasing hard to ignore.

"I just did." Ethan is used to getting everything he wants; and he wants Olivia. He'll do anything to have her.

"What are we going to do?"

"Shop for my new car. Give me two minutes and then we'll go."

Ethan emerges from the private bathroom, wearing a pair of jeans and a casual plaid cotton shirt.

She wonders if he could ever look anything but fantastic. His beard is no more than a few days' worth of growth, neatly trimmed, and traces his hard jaw line down to his perfect chin. She likes how it conveys his masculinity. Without it, he would look too… pretty. His boundless swagger has definitely won her over, despite her best efforts to resist him. She tries to distract herself from thoughts that are causing her face to turn red. If he notices her admiring him, it would certainly go straight to his head.

"So what's wrong with the car you have now?"

He takes his wallet and keys out of his desk drawer, putting them in his pocket. "It's not mine. It's a fleet car, as well. Since it looks like I'm going to be sticking around for awhile, I thought I'd buy myself something a little more… stylish."

"Sounds like fun. What did you have in mind?" Olivia has just a little bit of a fetish for fast cars.

"I'm not sure. I thought we could take a few out for a test drive."

"Can I pick?"

Ethan laughs, "Pick what? The color?"

"No... the car. I know a lot more about cars than you think." She crosses her arms in front of her offended by his comment.

"Well then, I guess this is your chance to impress me." He opens his office door and stands against the frame, forcing her to brush against him on her way out. She knows that he's done it on purpose. Giving him a daring look as she turns sideways and slides fully against his body, she draws from him a deep raspy growl, as her breasts brush against the taut muscles of his chest.

As they reach the foyer, the receptionist once again throws herself at him as they head for the elevator. "Are you leaving for the day, Mr. O'Connell? Is there anything I can do for you this afternoon?"

"No, thank you, Hannah." He pushes the elevator button and waits, rubbing Olivia's back with a nurturing touch; a touch that she's missed the past few days. Olivia feels angry eyes burning into her from behind, as she gets into the elevator. She looks over her shoulder at Hannah as the get in the elevator. If looks could kill then she'd most certainly be dead.

As the heavy steel doors begin to close, Hannah yells again, "Anything at all, I'd be happy to..."

In the privacy of the elevator, Olivia looks at Ethan and makes a face. "Amazing!"

"What do you mean?" he asks curiously.

"That she doesn't tip over when she stands up. Honestly how does she support those things?"

"What things?" He knows that his best defense here is to play dumb.

"Seriously? Her boobs!"

"Oh, I hadn't noticed." He tries not to smile.

She rolls his eyes at him. "Whatever, like I'm supposed to believe that?"

It's a long way down and Olivia starts to fidget uncomfortably. As they stop to pick up a few more people, she begins to look visibly distressed. Ethan reaches out and touches his hand to her hip making her jump. "Are you okay?" he asks with concern.

She takes a few short breaths. "Yes, sorry. I get a little anxious in elevators. I'm okay until people start getting in and then I start to panic."

"Claustrophobia? I hear it's common in elevators."

Unsure on how to explain herself, she makes a face. "Yeah, but it's kind of strange. I've never had problems before. It just started a few months ago." She shrugs. "I have no idea why."

"We can get off on the next floor and wait if you want." His need to protect her is instinctive.

"No... I'm okay, I'm wearing my big girl pants today. And besides I need to learn how to deal."

When the door opens again, a few more people join them. Ethan moves in front of her, shielding her from the crowd and impressing her with his chivalry.

The valet has his car waiting for them at the front door. Ethan tips him generously. "Thank you Mr. O'Connell. Have a nice afternoon, sir."

As they pull away from the front of the building, Olivia stares nervously at the small psychic shop, remembering her warning. *He will find you!* Fear grips her by the throat making her swallow hard and shiver.

While Ethan maneuvers them through the busy city streets heading for the highway, Olivia takes a long look at him. She's never met any Irish men before; she wonders if they're all as handsome as he is. Who in their right mind leaves Ireland to live in the little hick town in Dufferin County? It's an hour from anywhere for activities and sightseeing. Well, it's an hour away from any form of excitement really. She's intrigued now. "So, why are you here? In Canada, I mean."

He glances at her from the corner of his eye while trying to concentrate on driving. "The Board of Directors felt I needed a change of scenery."

"Oh." She figures from his tone that it's not something he wants to discuss, so she decides not to press him for more information. This is the first time they've spent time together, when she's actually enjoying his company. The conversation is light and playful. She hasn't felt this happy in a long time.

When his phone rings, he looks at the display and hits the hands free button. "O'Connell."

"Mr. O'Connell, your offer has been accepted."

"That's good news." Ethan is pleased. "Contact my assistant to schedule a time for you to come in with the paperwork. When do I take possession?"

"Immediately, sir. I can give you the keys as soon as you sign the paperwork and advance the money."

"Very well, we'll do that tomorrow."

"Yes, sir."

He hits the end button and disconnects his call then hits speed dial. His call is answered on the first ring, "McCabe."

"Hey, when is the next flight?"

"There's one that gets into the Toronto airport on Wednesday morning. There are still a few seats available to book."

"Nothing sooner?" Ethan is eager for John to join him as soon as possible.

"The only other flight leaves this evening but it has a stop over somewhere in the Far East that requires I take a two day journey by alpaca to the connecting flight," he jokes.

Olivia laughs out loud and there's dead silence for a few moments. Ethan smirks knowing what's probably going through John's mind right now.

"We're not alone, Ethan?" John's voice takes on a cautious tone.

"Sorry, John. No, we're not alone." He might as well get it over with, since he'll meet her soon anyway.

"John McCabe this is Olivia James."

"Hi, John," she says loudly.

"Hello, Miss James. Ethan can I assume your urgent need to have me there means that things have worked out as planned?"

"Yes, and I would really like you here as soon as possible."

"I'm packed and ready to leave. Will you be sending the car for me on Wednesday morning or should I learn how to ride an alpaca?"

The humor in his voice reveals to Olivia that John and Ethan must have more than a business relationship. Ethan wouldn't tolerate that kind of behavior from an employee. Scott is very careful to mind his P's and Q's around him, even when they aren't in the office.

The smile on Ethan's face confirms her assumption is correct. "It's very tempting… but Wednesday is fine."

"See you then."

"Travel safe, old man." Ethan disconnects the call before John can retaliate and embarrass him in front of Olivia.

She waits for him to elaborate on the conversation that he's allowed her to overhear, but when he fails to do so, she finally asks, "Good news, I assume? Are you going to tell me?"

"Oh, sorry. I think its good news. You're looking at the new owner of the Headwaters Bar and Grill." He can't hold back a proud smile as he says it, turning his head to watch her expression.

Olivia is pleasantly surprised. "What? Seriously?"

"Yes, seriously."

Chapter Twelve

Arriving in Dufferin County, they turn down the road where all the auto dealers are.

"We should have probably looked in the city. You won't find any Lamborghini's out here," Olivia teases.

Ethan raises an eyebrow in a quizzical manner. "And what makes you think I can afford a Lamborghini?"

"Hello? Despite the fact that I've just learned you have personally purchased a bar, I've also just seen your office. I don't have to *assume* you're ridiculously rich," she laughs.

Ethan shakes his head in amusement. "Not even close. I'm afraid I'm nowhere near a financial genius. I closed a few business deals early in my career that landed me huge bonuses. I invested wisely. I don't make an obscene amount of money, just enough to live comfortably and buy the things I want without having to worry."

Olivia nods her approval. "That's pretty awesome, Mr. O'Connell!"

Ethan is shocked and he looks at her with wide eyes. "No way! Have I finally impressed you, Miss James?"

She rolls her eyes and grins. "Don't let it go to your head. I'm sure you'll do something to spoil it soon."

Shaking his head, he chuckles, "No doubt. You're a tough crowd to please."

They spend the next couple of hours walking through import car dealerships, getting in and out of cars and listening to the well-rehearsed sales pitches of the staff. The last stop is the only high-end dealer in town. Ethan is immediately drawn to one of their top of the line models.

Olivia lets the salesman jump through all the hoops and patiently tags along on the test drive. When they get back into the boring grey company car, Olivia is bored.

"You've been awfully quiet for someone who claims to know something about cars. Do you like that one?" His Irish accent grows thicker when he's excited.

Olivia has been itching to get a few thoughts off her chest and since he's asked. "It's ok, for a girl's car."

Ethan looks at her, confused. "A girl's car?"

"Yes, it looks like a girl's car, all little, curvy and squishy. It's... cute. But then... if the hair fits." She pauses, avoiding his stare, knowing this could turn into a playful conversation or an all out argument.

Ethan raises an eyebrow. "Are you saying that you don't like my hair or that you don't like the car?"

She purses her lips tightly together and says nothing. "I see," he finishes. "You don't like either, then?" Ethan pays close attention to her body language, trying to determine if she's teasing him or not.

"I didn't say that," she chuckles.

Her laughter is a welcome sound, putting to rest the anxiety he's experiencing. "I thought North American girls loved men with long hair?"

"Yes, we do. If they're wielding a sword and slaying dragons."

Her sarcasm amuses him. "Well then, if you don't like any of my choices what would you suggest?"

"Well, I've never been too impressed with performance *imports*." She smirks.

Ethan catches on, loving the challenge. "Well, perhaps you've just never given one a chance." He raises his eyebrows, flirting competently.

"I definitely prefer North American muscle," she declares in a matter of fact manner.

Ethan smirks. If she insists on playing this game, his Irish sense of humor will prove to be a worthy opponent. "Is that so?" Ethan turns the car into the next row of dealers.

Olivia becomes downright cheeky. "Yes it is. While imports make many promises about their performance. It's the North American muscle that always comes through... with a Good. Hard. Ride!"

She returns his stare with a ballsy confidence that makes his dick twitch. Jesus! This woman seriously turns him on. "Well then, I'm always up for a good hard ride. Convince me. Where will we start? I'm guessing we're heading for the Mustangs?"

Olivia scowls at him and then snickers. "Now you're just talking crazy, Ireland. You're not cool enough to drive a Mustang."

Ethan takes a good long look at her. He grins when he realizes that he hasn't thought about the office, work, or the nasty investigation back in Ireland all day. He can't remember the last time he felt this *happy*. It's definitely because of Olivia James. At first, he had thought his attraction to her was just physical, that his need was of a sexual nature. That's not the case at all. The curve of her hips and her full soft breasts get his pulse racing, that's true. He fantasizes about how good it would feel to sink deep inside her and lose himself in her softness, but that's not what's drawing him to her. He's starting to feel something for her. Something deep down inside that he can't explain. He wants to protect her, know everything about her, to take care of her, to be with her always. He wants to be to be the one to make her smile.

When they enter the next showroom from the side door, Ethan sees nothing spectacular, just normal looking family sedans. He wonders what she has up her sleeve as he follows her to the far side. They're met part way by a salesman who looks very tired and stressed.

"Hello, again. You've brought a friend, I see." He holds out his hand.

Ethan shakes it and looks at Olivia inquisitively.

"This is Jim, salesman of the month." She points over to his picture mounted on the nearby wall.

Ethan follows her lead. "Congratulations."

Jim is still shaking Ethan's hand vigorously. "Thank you." He turns to Olivia. "Are we here to visit again, or are we considering something else?"

Ethan tries to follow the conversation, but obviously these two have a past.

"Actually Jim, my friend Mr. O'Connell, **SVP of INTERNATIONAL Sales for Aurora Technologies**, is looking to purchase something with a lot of power and style."

Jim nods his head. "Is that so?" He finally lets go of Ethan's hand.

Ethan shrugs. "Apparently so, Jim." He glances over at Olivia and raises a brow. She bites her lip, trying not to laugh.

"Well, right this way, then. I assume we're taking a look at Olivia's favorite?"

Ethan chuckles, "That would be my guess, as well." When he glances over at her, she's batting her eyelashes, giving him the most seductive smile. It takes enormous restraint on his part not to grab her, smash his body against her, and kiss her lips. Growling, he curses under his breath.

"What?" she asks innocently.

"One day…" he whispers.

"Is that a threat, Mr. O'Connell?"

"No, Olivia, it's a promise."

The chemistry between them is strong today. Olivia tries to mask the excitement that races through her at that promise, but she's unsuccessful. Ethan knows exactly how she's feeling, she can tell by the look of satisfaction on his face.

They follow Jim, as he makes his way to the far side of the show room, through a narrow walkway into another room. Bright lights and fancy displays adorn this room. It's obviously where they keep the *expensive* cars. Olivia walks over to the brand new Challenger SRT Hellcat; running her hand along it, as if she was caressing a lover.

Jim jumps through all the hoops, spouting specifications, gas mileage, engine power, and performance points. Ethan watches Olivia with curiosity, unable to tear away his gaze.

"I'm sure Olivia could give you all the finer points, she has them memorized. Would you like to take it for a test drive? I'll go get the dealer plates."

Olivia leans back against the door and looks at Ethan. Even standing on the other side of the room, he can't help but notice that she's glowing. He gets a warm, tingly, tight feeling in his stomach that spreads outward to every nerve ending in his body. Good Lord, what is it about this woman?

Within seconds, Jim is back with the dealer plates and the key fob. Olivia opens the passenger door, flips the seat forward and begins to climb in the back seat.

"You can sit in the front, Miss James. I won't be going with you," Jim pipes up.

Ethan is a little shocked. He's never known a dealership to send out a car on a test drive without the accompanying salesmen. "You won't?"

"No, sir, I've driven with Miss James before and if you drive anything like her, there's not a snowball's chance in hell that I'm getting in that car."

Perplexed by Jim's comments Ethan glances over at Olivia and notices her blush.

"Now, Jim, I've said I'm sorry at least a thousand times." Olivia says feeling a little embarrassed.

Jim bangs his hand on the roof twice. "All good to go. Don't be gone long, we'll be closing soon."

Pulling out of the showroom and into the parking lot, Ethan can't stand it any longer. "So, you and Jim have some history, do you?"

"No, not really. He came with me on a test drive once." She couldn't stop smiling if she tried, but decides not to elaborate on the details.

"Are you going to tell me what happened?"

"Nope, not a chance."

Ethan grins and pulls out onto the road, cautiously testing the steering and control. He speeds up and slows down taking his time, getting to know the clutch and all her sweet spots. The interior is lush and luxuriously comfortable, molded perfectly for them side by side. For the first time in hours, she looks at him; really looks at him. Something happened when she was sick, something that profoundly connected her to him on an intimate level. She doesn't know how much longer she can continue to fight him, or even if she wants to. How will she ever deal with all the other women in his life? She doubts he'd ever give up his bachelor lifestyle.

Ethan notices her staring. "So you like this one do you?"

"Yes, but I think the Z4 is more for you." She watches his facial expressions as he changes gears and checks his rear view mirror for approaching traffic.

"Why do you say that?"

"Because, not only do you look like a girl… but you also drive like one!"

"You're hilarious today." He reaches over and playfully pokes at her and tries to tickle her as she squeals in laughter.

"No, seriously," she pants through her giggles. "I think you might actually have ovaries."

Ethan puts his hand back on the shifter and gears down, pulling over onto the shoulder and stops. "Alright then, miss 'I know a little something about cars'… you drive, then." He undoes his seat belt and jumps out.

"Seriously?" She's out her door and around the front in seconds.

Grabbing her as she passes, he slows her for a second, his touch stoking a fire inside her. "Just get us back in one piece."

Olivia jumps into the driver's seat, adjusts the position, and mirrors. Reaching into her purse, she finds an elastic band and pulls her long hair back into a ponytail, "Can I use your sunglasses?" When he hands over the aviator style sunglasses, she puts them on and looks at him with a very seductive smile. "Sexy?"

"Very sexy." His mind wanders. Lure you into the backseat and fuck you, kind of sexy. *Calm yourself, O'Connell!*

"Hold on!" she warns.

"What?"

Tires squeal as she jolts into first gear, hitting the gas hard. The force pushes Ethan back against his seat. Olivia grins; feeling pleased that for the first time she has some power over him. Heading south among the slow moving traffic, she signals toward the highway. A very nervous Ethan is starting to regret his decision,

"Are we supposed to take it on the highway?" he asks, in a tensed Irish brogue.

"Of course! They want us to check her out." She merges safely into the southbound traffic and turns on the radio. The volume vibrates the dashboard. No longer able to contain herself, she finds an opening between cars, shifts gears and is gone! In and out of traffic, she puts that car through its paces with expert maneuvering and precision shifting.

Finally relaxing, Ethan loosens his grip on the door handle and begins to enjoy the ride. Becoming even more intrigued with her, he wishes they could just drive off somewhere together, forgetting about everything and everyone else.

Olivia finds her exit and gets off the highway, taking the country road that loops back toward the dealership. The Challenger caresses the sharp curves in the road and takes every hill with ease. The tires grip the asphalt, staying their course as she pushes speed and steering to its limits. Finally, they're led back toward the dealer. When Olivia pulls over to shoulder to change places with him, there are no spoken words as they pass, only the look of desire and passion. The chemistry in the air is electric, but neither of them makes a move to act on it, heightening the anticipation.

When they pull into the lot, Jim is waiting for them outside. "Well, what did you think?"

"Let's talk in your office, Jim." Ethan rushes around and opens Olivia's door.

Olivia is like an excited child waiting for Christmas morning. Jim heads toward his office with Ethan following behind. He takes Olivia by the elbow and slows her. "Olivia, negotiations are my *thing*. When we begin to talk about money, don't say a word."

When she nods her understanding, he allows her to enter before himself. Jim has started piling paperwork on his desk. "Let's start with the model."

Ethan defers. "Olivia?"

She sits at the desk with eager anticipation. "SRT Hellcat"

Jim looks over at Ethan for his approval. Ethan nods. "Now there's a surprise."

"6 speed manual," she adds. "6.2L Supercharged Hemi V8" This time she looks for Ethan's approval.

Ethan raises his eyebrows. "Seven-hundred and seven is a lot of horsepower. You're not concerned about reducing my carbon footprint?"

She shakes her head sheepishly, knowing that she should. There's just something about the additional power the V8 provides that she has to have. Or… that Ethan should have. She bites her lip and gives him a hopeful smile.

He grins at her reaction. "Okay, then."

Jim hands Ethan a page of options and accessories to review. Ethan hands it Olivia with a pen. "Pick what you want Baby, you know better than I do."

Olivia wonders if he's really going to let her build this car for him. He did say that he could afford the things he wants. *Did he just call me Baby?* Stomach flip. She grins and makes short work of the list, checking all the appropriate boxes for the best performance options. She hands the list back to Ethan who raises his eyebrows and nods in appreciation of her choices as he reads it. "Impressive, but do I really need that stereo system?"

She nods her head, hoping he'll agree. She went for broke, but expects that he'll veto a few of her choices. He reads further down the list and hums in appreciation, "Nice call on the rims."

Olivia is gleaming when Ethan hands the list to Jim who peruses it quickly and whistles. "Your girl sure knows what she wants, Mr. O'Connell."

Ethan grins. "Yes, she does and I'm sure it's going to be very expensive." He glances adoringly in her direction, making her feel off balance.

His girl? It's alarming how much Olivia likes the way that sounds. A little more than a week ago, she couldn't stand to be in the same room as him. She knows she's heading into dangerous territory, but for the moment, she lets him lead her there.

Jim starts to bang numbers into the calculator adding options and accessories. She glances over at the number and suddenly feels very overwhelmed. Poor Ethan. What has she gotten him in to? Jim is eager to close the deal on this big-ticket item, she can tell. "I just need to know what color."

Ethan looks over at Olivia. "Well? What's it going to be?"

"Orange! With dual black center stripes." She waits nervously for an objection. When Ethan looks at her with amusement, she shrugs.

Jim flips through the glossy sales brochures. "I'm not sure this model comes in orange anymore."

"The lady would like orange, Jim."

There's that authoritative tone: the one that makes her stomach feel funny; the one that lets everyone know that Ethan O'Connell means business. Apparently, he'll not be denied what he wants in any facet of his life. Desirous feelings stir deep inside her, making her squirm uncomfortably in her chair. Ethan gives her a half smile. She wonders if he knows what's going on inside her pants. *Of course he does!*

Her eyes dart back and forth between the two men, waiting for someone to speak. Jim taps his pen nervously on the desk, his stare locked in a power struggle with Ethan. He needs this sale. The four growing children in the family picture behind him tell the story. Ethan has already figured it out. Sensing the deal is about to go sour, Jim becomes very accommodating and breaks the silence, "Of course, we'll look into it for you."

Ethan picks up one of Jim's business cards and slides it into his shirt pocket. Taking out his wallet, he gets out one of his own, flips it over and writes something on the back of it. Jim pulls a large document out of a folder on his desk. "We just need to fill out the finance paperwork."

Ethan very confidently picks up the sheet of options and accessories and places his business card on top of it. Lining it up in the top corner, he picks up the stapler off the desk and attaches them together. "Finance papers won't be necessary, Jim." He puts the papers back down on the desk in front of him. "I'll be paying cash, and that's what I'll be paying."

With that, he turns to Olivia and holds out his hand. "We're done here."

Damn that's hot! She has a brief fantasy of wrestling him to the ground and having her way with him right there, or maybe inside the car! Jim can watch if he wants, she really doesn't care. All she can think about is getting Ethan in between her legs and finally putting an end to the relentless throbbing there. She blushes at the thought as she takes his hand and follows him out of the office.

A rather stunned salesman finally speaks, "Mr. O'Connell, I think you've made a mistake. I couldn't possibly sell you this car for this price."

Olivia begins to feel anxious. "Ethan? Should we go back and renegotiate?"

He squeezes her hand in a reassuring manner. "Don't say a word. Just keep walking."

Ethan pulls into the lane behind her house and parks. "Thank you for coming with me today. It was quite an experience." The corner of his mouth begins to curl into a smile.

"Are you referring to the car shopping itself or my test drive?" For Olivia, everything they did today was quite an experience.

"Ah, well the test drive was an adventure on its own."

"Yes… well, I like my music loud… my cars fast and my men in…" She halts herself and looks over at him, horrified at her near admission.

Ethan gives her a knowing look as he finishes her sentence, "in control?"

She puts her hands to her face embarrassed. "I can't believe I almost said that out loud." She's become so comfortable with his companionship today, the words just popped out of her mouth.

Ethan gives her a cocky grin. "Don't be embarrassed, Olivia. That wasn't a secret."

Humiliation and shame wash over her. "I should go inside, now." She tries to get out of there quickly, to avoid an awkward conversation that she doesn't want to have.

Needing to find a way to spend more time with her, he reaches over and puts his hands on her knee; stalling her. "Don't run away, I want to ask you something."

Olivia looks down at his hand on her thigh. The electricity travels through her like a closed circuit, making her nerves tingle with his touch. Taking a deep breath, she looks into those dangerously green, bedroom eyes and waits.

"I need to start looking for a permanent place to live. I'm going to book some appointments to go look at apartments. Would you go with me?"

"You want me to go with you? To look at apartments?"

"Yes, why do you sound so surprised? You were a great help shopping for a car. Why not an apartment?"

"Is this apartment for you to live in?"

"Yes, of course. That's an odd question." He looks at her perplexed.

"Not really odd. You could be looking for an apartment for a girlfriend that's coming over from Ireland to be with you."

"There is no girlfriend." He's exhausted at the number of times he needs to reaffirm that. "So, will you go with me?"

"I suppose," she says apprehensively. On the way to the door, she glances back at him several times, questioning her strength and ability to continue to resist him. Maybe she should consider changing her mind.

Ethan waits until she's inside safely, feeling pleased at the knowledge that she's drawn to him when he takes control. Olivia will soon discover that he's more competent in his seduction skills than he is at negotiation, and he *always* gets his way in negotiation.

Olivia puts her phone down on the table and plops herself down on the couch with a very large glass of wine. Drinking half way through the glass in just a few minutes, she's already feeling a little buzz. Turning on the radio, she heads back into the kitchen to grab the bottle. Standing at the counter, flipping through mail, she becomes aware of the lyrics of the song playing. Is it just the wine or does every song that's played in the past ten minutes have explicit lyrics about sex? She changes the station several times and can't find one that doesn't. The wine helps encourage the hormones that she's wrestling, making her even more painfully aware of her needs. Taking another large swallow of her wine, she wonders about Ethan. *Butterflies!*

Grabbing her laptop, she opens Facebook and types in his name. She's not surprised to find security locked down tight. She sighs in disappointment. Her hand subconsciously moves the mouse over the button, "add as friend." Why is she doing this? Being with Ethan would be a mistake, right?

She takes another huge mouth full of wine as her finger right clicks on the mouse, sending the request. Already regretting what she's done, she tips the bottle and refills her glass.

Within seconds, she receives his acknowledgement and an update that reads, "Olivia James is now friends with Ethan O'Connell."

Ethan is running on the treadmill in the basement, smiling at his victory. Tucking his phone back in his pocket, he ramps up the speed.

Now that she has access to his profile page, Olivia creeps through his information. She's shocked that the majority of his 797 followers are women. His relationship status says, "single," but his timeline is crowded with comments and posts from his many flirting female admirers. Olivia rolls her eyes at how cheesy some of them are. She closes the page, deciding that she really doesn't want to know about all the other women in his life.

With the wine weighing heavily on her eyelids, she heads upstairs. She stands, staring at her bed for several minutes. Taking a deep breath she climbs in and lies back, trying to get comfortable. Staring at the ceiling, for what seems like forever, she thinks about Ethan. Feeling empty, after spending an incredible day with him she picks up her phone, sending him a message.

From Olivia: Goodnight Ethan

Ethan has finished his workout and is sitting out on the patio, in the dark. Staring at the stars, he's thinking about Olivia James. When he gets her message, he's filled with a nervous excitement that he's never felt before.

From Ethan: Goodnight Princess. Sweet dreams.
From Olivia: I keep meaning to ask you why you started calling me Princess.
From Ethan: It was something you talked about when you were sick.
From Olivia: How embarrassing.
From Ethan: Does it bother you?
From Olivia: No, I was just curious. Good night.
From Ethan: Bonne nuit mon cher. Vous êtes dans ma pensée. Je rêve de votre yeux nuit et jour.

Holy shit! He speaks French? Of course he does, she thinks, mocking herself for being surprised. She knows that Aurora Technologies has an office in France because Scott has had to go there. Being the SVP of International Sales would surely require Ethan to know the language.

French is an official language of Canada, but she only studied it until high school. She loved it and wanted to continue, but dropped the university course in favor of another subject. A decision she has always regretted. The thought of him whispering sweet nothings into her ear in French, makes her insides burn with desire; something she might admit to him some day. But not today…

From Olivia: My French is a little rusty. Did you just say that my nuts are beautiful and that you are attracted to squirrels? And then something about egg yolks that I'm certain I don't want to know about.

Ethan shakes his head and laughs. He's in so much trouble with this woman. She makes him think of nothing else but her. Now, he finds himself thinking about sharing the rest of his life with her. *Dangerous thoughts!* Thoughts that he never expected to have. EVER! Wanting to hear her voice one last time before he goes to sleep, he hits dial. She answers instantly, laughing into the phone.

"Not even close," he says, trying to suppress his laughter. "But then, I'm pretty sure you're just messing with me again."

"Me? Messing with you?" she feigns innocence.

The night air is cool and damp, making his voice raspy, "I said… good night, beautiful. You're in my thoughts. I dream of your eyes, night and day."

Olivia takes a deep breath. Reading it in French was pretty sexy; hearing him say it in English, in that low sensual tone with his Irish accent, is so much more. She's not even sure if there's a word that exists to accurately describe the feeling that makes her experience the simultaneous stomach flip, heart flutter, and wet panties.

It seems like forever before she can find her voice. "Good night, Ethan," she finally says still trying to hide the way he affects her.

"Good night, Olivia." He grins from ear to ear. She's not hiding a thing. He's getting under her skin. He can tell.

Chapter Thirteen

Olivia spends her morning chatting with concerned coworkers, who stop by to see how she's feeling. She's thrilled to be back to work, finally. Since she insisted on working from home, her backlog is at a minimum, giving her time to settle back in slowly.

Rachel shoots into her office with a couple of files and hands them to her. "Hey, slacker! Welcome back."

"Thanks! What are these?" Flipping open the files, she starts reading through the papers.

"It's a conundrum," Rachel laughs.

"Thanks, that tells me absolutely nothing." She scowls at her and then raises her eyebrows waiting for her to elaborate.

"Trent was working on this one, and he's come to an impasse. The client has some specific needs regarding their accounting procedures. He couldn't find a business solution with the software they purchased."

"AND?"

"AND… the big boss is confident that you can resolve the problem."

Olivia sighs. "Okay, leave it with me and I'll look at it."

"You'll need to call the client and find out exactly what their needs are. The only feedback we got from them was that Trent was a moron."

Olivia shakes her head. "Oh great, I love projects that start out with smoothing over someone else's mess."

"Thank you!" Rachel she sings, already half way out the door as she says it.

Olivia has a brilliant mind for problem solving and a stubborn determination that settles for nothing less than success. Unfortunately, that makes her the go to girl for all the difficult problems. Rachel has begged her many times to start up her own consulting business, but Olivia likes working with the clients.

Helping them find solutions for their business is what she does best. It's what she finds most fulfilling about her career. Unlike Ethan, she's not interested in sitting in an office at the south end of the building overseeing operations and negotiating contracts.

The city of Toronto skyline is reflected in the glass exterior of the high-rise office building that's home to the Canadian branch of Aurora Technologies. Ethan waits impatiently in the reception area for the elevator to make its way to the penthouse floor. When the heavy metal doors finally open, John McCabe strolls out dragging his luggage. Ethan stares at him and looks at his watch. "It's about bloody time."

John pulls his luggage off to the side and out of the way, "If you missed me that much then you should have picked me up yourself."

Both men break into a smile and throw their arms around each other, patting the other on the back in a masculine embrace. Ethan pulls away. "It's good to see you. I have a lot of things that I need your help with. I've set up an office for you across from mine."

Unaware of her presence, Ethan turns and bumps into Hannah. He reaches out to grab for her as she topples. "Hannah, I'm so sorry."

Trying to regain her balance, she throws her weight forward and lands against him. There's an awkward moment as she clings to his chest longer than necessary.

"Are you okay?" Ethan pries her away, as he waits for her answer.

Standing back on her own two feet, she smoothes her dress and adjusts her breasts. John's eyes open wide as he glances over at Ethan. He's doing his best to look anywhere but at her chest.

"Yes, I'm fine. I'm sorry. I shouldn't have snuck up on you like that. I just wanted to see if there was anything I could do for your friend." She glances over at John, giving him a seductive smile.

"Thank you, but we're fine." Ethan crosses his arms and waits for John to break his stare. As they make their way to his office, John glances back at her for another look. Standing in the middle of the hallway, she raises her hand, wiggling her fingers at him in a flirty wave.

When they're far enough down the hallway, John looks at Ethan and smiles. "How do you concentrate on work with that around all day?"

Ethan shrugs his indifference. "Easy. She's not my type."

There's nothing in his tone that suggests that he's joking but John laughs. "Who are you kidding? She's *exactly* your type."

Swinging open his office door, Ethan lets John enter first. "Not anymore."

Sitting down on the couch, John leans back, resting his arms along the top. He watches as Ethan sits behind his desk and adjusts his laptop so they can see each other. "And I suppose Olivia James is your type?"

Ethan smiles when he hears her name. John sighs in disappointment. "Jesus, I know that look."

A reminder pops up on Ethan's laptop and he looks down at his watch. "Conference call. Close the door."

John pushes the door closed then sits opposite of Ethan at the desk. "I read the preliminary report from the investigator on the plane. What did you think?"

Ethan shrugs as he logs in to the video meeting with the lawyers. "I haven't had a chance to read it."

"Well, it might have been a good idea to do that before today's meeting," he criticizes.

Ignoring him, Ethan turns his attention to his phone. He can't stop thinking about Olivia since John mentioned her name.

From Ethan: **I'm taking you out for coffee tonight after soccer.**
From Olivia: **Well, that's kind of bossy.**
From Ethan: **and your point is?**
From Olivia: **I'm not going on a date with you.**
From Ethan: **Ok then, it's not a date… it's a beverage. You do get thirsty don't you?**
From Olivia: **No.**
From Ethan: **Did you have other plans?**
From Olivia: **Does it matter?**
From Ethan: **No.**
From Olivia: **Some things never change.**
From Ethan: **Be there at 7.**
From Olivia: **I'll think about it.**

"ETHAN!"

Ethan looks up when John yells at him, demanding his full attention, "You need to prepare yourself. They're going to ask you some tough questions today. Ones you're not going to like. For God's sake control your temper."

The sound of Shannon Quinn's voice comes over the speakers, "Hello. Mr. O'Connell? Are you there?"

Hitting the videoconference button, he activates the video cam. "Yes, Mr. McCabe and I are here."

"Good. I met with investigators yesterday to see what they've found out so far. I need to ask you some questions as a result of their findings. Ethan, this is a difficult question but I have to ask… and I need you to answer me honestly."

"Okay." Ethan looks nervously at John.

"Do you consider yourself to have a temper?"

Ethan sighs and squirms in his chair. "Yes, I suppose. No more than any other man," he adds.

"Fair enough. Is it true you're a boxer?"

"Yes. I mean no… not really. I box at the gym, only as a way to keep fit. I don't participate in matches or anything."

Shannon's questions start coming at a rapid pace. "Have you ever hit Jessica Keane in anger?"

"NO!" Ethan starts to perspire under this line of questioning, making John worry.

"Did you ever get a little too rough and hurt her unintentionally?"

Leaning forward, Ethan positions himself squarely in front of the video camera, "NO!"

"What about during sex?"

Whoa! Ethan hesitates, weighing his answer carefully. "Is she saying that?" Getting to his feet, he paces behind his chair. Raking his fingers through his hair, he utters barely audible curses.

The awkward silence is broken by the sound of shuffling papers as Shannon Quinn lifts her head and looks straight into the video cam. Ethan tries not to completely lose it when she holds up pictures of his alleged crime. When she lowers the pictures from view, he sits back in his chair and looks into the faces of his long distance audience.

"I didn't do that." His jaw clenches tightly, despite his efforts to stay calm.

"I'll email you a copy of the actual police report. We received a copy of it this morning." Looking down at her phone, she touches the screen several times before looking back up. "You should have it shortly."

Ethan's phone beeps as her email arrives in his inbox. He opens it and begins to read, his mouth falling open in disgust.

"I can't believe this malarkey." He puts his phone down with a loud bang. John glares at him reminding him that he needs to control his outbursts.

Shannon continues her questioning, "According to the investigator, Reese Wilson is the man that Miss Keane had the affair with. Do you know who he is?"

Ethan picks up his pen and taps it nervously on his desk. "You could say that."

"How?"

Ethan inhales deeply and looks to John for strength. "We grew up together. Until that night, he was my best friend."

"Did you know it was him that she was having the affair with?"

"Yes." The heartbreak over his friend's betrayal can be heard in Ethan's voice. John wishes there was something he could do to end this nightmare for his friend.

Shannon's voice takes on a soft tone, "I'm so sorry, that must have made it harder."

Ethan ignores her sympathy. "Is there anything else?"

"At the moment both Miss Keane and Mr. Wilson are refusing to meet with our investigator."

Ethan throws his hands up in the air in frustration. "Of course they are."

"We're looking into her credit card and debit receipts, and anything else that might give us an idea of where she was that night."

Ethan sits back in his chair and looks at his watch. "Keep me posted. I'm due at another appointment shortly, so if there's nothing else for today, I need to go."

John scowls at him from the other side of the desk.

Shannon forces a smile and nods. "Very well. I think we're done for today."

"Thank you, Miss Quinn." Ethan disconnects the call and catches John's staring. "How do you think that went?"

John shakes his head and narrows his eyes at him. "Just fine, I suppose. What other appointment do you have? There's nothing on your schedule."

Ethan hands papers to John. "I have some things to do before I see Olivia tonight. And YOU... are going to start working on the official grand opening of the bar. I want you to go over there this afternoon and take a look around. That..." he points at the paperwork, "is the list of tentative arrangements that I've made. I'd like your opinion before we confirm anything."

John takes a quick look at the list.

"I want you to stay in Dufferin County so you're closer to the bar. There's a hotel nearby. Grab your suitcase. I need you to drop me off somewhere first."

"And so it begins." John grins as he picks up his briefcase and stuffs Ethan's notes into it.

Olivia waves at them as she approaches the soccer field.

Scott looks like he's going to be physically ill when he sees her. "What's she doing here?"

Rachel shrugs. "I have no idea. She never mentioned she was coming. What's wrong?"

Scott puts his hand to his forehead. "We're playing Noah's team tonight."

"So?" She makes a face, not understanding the reason for his anxiety.

"We're playing **Noah's** team tonight," he repeats in frustration. "Do you not remember what happened between Noah and Ethan at the last game?"

Rachel panics, "Oh Crap! I'll see if I can convince her to leave."

Scott thinks about it and shakes his head. "No, don't. Maybe she should witness the anger he's capable of."

As Olivia reaches them, Scott drops the conversation and welcomes her with a hug. "Hey! What a nice surprise. I didn't know you were coming."

"What else would I do on a Wednesday night?" She smiles. "Actually, Ethan invited me... or should I say he *ordered* me. He wants to take me out for coffee afterward." Olivia observes Scott and Rachel exchanging a nervous glance. "What? It's NOT a date. It's a beverage."

"Nothing," Rachel says innocently. "So you and Ireland are friends now?"

Olivia contemplates it for a few seconds. "The jury is still out on that one."

Scott turns away angrily and heads out onto the field. Olivia senses the tension. "Rachel? Is everything okay? With you and Scott, I mean."

Rachel frowns, not offering an explanation. "I'm sorry." Olivia continues, "I've just noticed that you're both a little out of sorts, lately. I was just wondering if you guys were having some problems?"

"Scott really wants to start a family," Rachel begins, feeling uncomfortable. "I'm just not sure I'm cut out for parenthood. It's not like I had any role models in that area." She shrugs, looking a little embarrassed. "It's causing a little tension."

Olivia puts her arms around her in a supportive hug. Scott is the only other person who knows that Rachel's mother left when she was only two years old. Devastated and unable to cope with the pressures of being a single parent, her father suffered a severe emotional breakdown. When he was deemed incapable of caring for her, Rachel was removed from the home. For years, she was moved from foster home to foster home; all good people, adequately clean and safe places to grow up, but she never really found *family* or a solid female role model.

"You would be an awesome mother," Olivia reassures with a tight squeeze.

"But what if I'm not? What If I break it? The idea absolutely terrifies me."

"It?" Olivia laughs, "People don't generally break babies, Rach. And you won't be in it alone. Scott will be an awesome dad and you have me to help."

Rachel pulls away, still looking unsettled.

"Okay, I'm not going to hound you about it. I'll support whatever your decision is. But, Rachel… Scott really wants a family. If you've decided that you don't want the same, then you're going to have to make some really tough decisions."

"I know." It's not the first time she's thought about that. Scott loves her so completely, despite her social shortcomings. She didn't think she knew how to love until he found her and taught her how. It would be unfair of her to stick around when having children is something that he wants so badly. "I have two choices." She frowns. "Leave my husband or have a baby."

The sound of a roaring car engine catches their attention. "Who is that?" Olivia stretches her neck, her curiosity piquing.

Rachel stands on her tiptoes, trying to get a better look through the already parked cars. She shrugs her shoulders. "I have no idea. I've never seen that car around here before."

The driver steps out and into view. His dark grey v-neck fits snugly against well-defined pectoral muscles. So well defined, they can be seen from a couple hundred feet away. Rachel raises her eyebrows in appreciation, "Whoever he is… he's HOT!"

Olivia isn't interested. She has a certain dream dwelling, Irish man on her mind.

Rachel stares at the stranger, shamelessly, admiring his body as he walks towards the field. There's something very familiar about him and it suddenly hits her. "Umm." She nudges Olivia. "You're not going to believe this."

"What?" She turns to notice Rachel's astonished look.

"That," she nods in his direction, "is Ethan."

Chapter Fourteen

"WHAT?" Shocked, Olivia's head whips back toward the parking lot. The rest of his appearance aside, she'd know that walk anywhere. Her heart skips a beat. Tipping his sunglasses to the top of his head, he gives her a panty-melting smile.

It is Ethan... curls all gone, hair shaved short and spiked at the front. His beard has been trimmed to a thinner, well-manicured line, outlining his jaw and revealing the dimple on his chin. She's glad it's not gone completely. She's fantasized many times, about how the scruff would feel brushed along the tender skin of her inner thigh. When he reaches them, Olivia's blood is burning so hot with desire that she's staring and speechless. Even Rachel is in awe.

"Well, Miss James? Do I look enough like a boy for you now?" His Irish accent is thick and dripping with a raw masculinity. There is nothing sexier.

She stumbles with words, "I...You...WOW!" She stops rambling when she notices the amusement on his face. "You're cleverly disguised as a responsible adult," she finally says.

"That I am." He grins.

"Well, you're secret is safe with me." Her teasing is met with a sharp elbow in the side. "Ouch!" She gives Rachel a disgruntled look. "He knows I'm only joking, geez." She blushes when she looks up at him, "You look very handsome." That's an understatement. He looks HOT! Jaw dropping, pulse thrumming, panty wetting hotness!

"I'm glad you approve." He holds up the key fob and nods toward the car. "Will you watch my new ride for me?" Olivia tries to keep her heart from beating out of her chest when a van backs up, revealing the bright orange Challenger Hellcat with dual black stripes.

"You got the Challenger!" She takes the key fob out of his hands as he leans in and gives her a quick kiss on her cheek. Once again, he's made her the center of attention, and she hates him for it. Now, she has to avoid making eye contact with everyone, so she doesn't see the glares of hatred.

Rachel's eyes open wide in surprise. When she gets the chance, she leans in close whispering, "Ummm, what exactly has happened between you two in the last week?"

Fidgeting with the key fob, Olivia blushes. "Nothing. Honest."

Ethan gets his uniform out of his bag and drops it on the ground beside them. Her witty banter is rendered silent as he strips off his shirt, revealing the bare, smooth skin of his chest and the dark ink of his tattoo. His silver chain and cross reflect in the sunlight, drawing her attention to his rock hard pectorals. *Mercy Sakes!* Standing in the middle of the soccer pitch, he's a magnificent sculpture on display. Every muscle is carved to perfection, as if in stone. There's not a woman there that isn't enjoying the view.

Suddenly, without warning, Ethan grabs his athletic pants on both sides of the waistband. In one swift movement, he lowers them to the ground. Olivia is dumbfounded that he just dropped his pants, without any modesty at all, in full view of every woman there.

Knowing exactly what kind of fantasies seeing his body conjures up in a girl's mind, she suddenly has the urge to claw out their eyes. Nope, she doesn't like the idea of them seeing his body at all. Peeking at him through her peripheral vision, she repeats to herself, "Don't look… don't look!"

Screw it! Turning, she takes a good long look at him, wearing nothing but his Under Armor sportswear; all bare-chested and muscly. When he steps into his shorts and straightens, pulling them up over his hips, he turns to catch her looking and grins. She tries to hide the quickening of her breath, as lust sweeps across her skin like a warm breeze.

Rachel doesn't filter her thoughts and leans in to whisper in her ear, "Holy crap! If you're crazy enough to pass that up, I'm interested."

Olivia's eyes narrow as she glares at her. "You're married."

"I am?"

Olivia is giving her the, *'that's not funny' look*, when strong arms swoop in and encircle her from behind. Wrapping her in an extremely intimate embrace, they pull her back against a tall body and rock hard chest. In contrast, very soft lips come at her from the side, biting at her neck, and nibbling their way up to her ear. She knows that it's Noah. No one else would greet her with such a brash display of affection, unannounced. Leaning into him, she breathes in his delicious sporty scent and completely forgets how he broke her heart just a few days before.

As Ethan watches another man wrap himself around the girl that he wants, his body tenses. Without breaking his stare, he tugs at his shoelaces so harshly that it's a miracle that he doesn't break them. Rachel nervously watches his reaction, concerned there may be a fight before the game even starts. From the field she see's Scott expression and she knows that he's stressing over the same thing.

"Are you upset with me for missing our date the other night?" Noah asks, nuzzling against her cheek.

"Sort of." She doesn't tell him that she knows why he ditched her. Lord knows that she should push him away and give him a piece of her mind, but she won't. That's the way their relationship has always worked. She *always* forgives him.

A few feet away, Ethan looks up at Rachel and captures her attention. "Tell me that asshole is *not* Noah Thompson." His words are laced with acid. When he gets to his feet, he meets Rachel's nervous expression.

"Sorry, Ethan." She slightly cringes, worrying about his reaction. "Yes, that's Noah."

Ethan curses, glaring at him with murder in his eyes.

Noah hears the cursing and feels the heat of his stare burning through him. Glancing over, he gives Ethan a hardened look, but says nothing. Taking Olivia by the hand, Noah walks her along with him to the opposing team's bench. "Tell me there isn't anything going on between you and that guy," he says, when they're safely on the other side of the field.

"Who?" Olivia turns to see Ethan's intense and unsettled stare as he tucks his jersey into his shorts. "Ethan? He's a just a friend." Yet, she can't seem to tear her gaze away from him.

Noah lifts her hand to his mouth and kisses it. "Could have fooled me. He's looking like he'd like to kill me, right now. Promise me you'll be careful around that one," he says with concern. "He has a bad temper and a very short fuse."

The referee blows his whistle. Olivia glances over at Ethan before giving Noah a kiss on the cheek. Nodding her head, she acknowledges Noah's warning then hurries to the other side of the pitch to watch the game.

Ethan watches them from the field, his anger building. He's had many women in his life but he's never felt like this. Watching another man touch Olivia makes his stomach twist. His chest feels like a semi truck has just backed up on it. The torment he experienced watching her kiss him, forces him to admit to himself, that it's more than just a physical attraction that he has for her. He cares for her. The day he spent alone with her, made him feel happier than he's felt in a very long time. He wants more days like that one. He wants her in his life. More than that, he needs to be the *only* man in hers.

Olivia gets back to Rachel before the referee begins the game. Right from the start, the game is very aggressive. The whistle blows every few minutes for fouls. Ethan is very vocal at criticizing the referee's calls. It's only twenty minutes into the game and he's already received a warning. Rachel and Olivia glance at each other with an awkward silence.

Ethan pushes forward hard, determined to get a goal. His efforts thwarted by an extremely competent Noah, playing defensive fullback. He whisks the ball away from Ethan's feet, causing him to trip and fall.

Olivia covers her eyes. "Oh God, I can't look."

Ethan screams at the referee, wanting a foul to be called. Noah holds out his hand to help him up but Ethan rejects it, cursing as he gets to his feet on his own. The rest of the first half follows suit with tempers flaring on both sides and still no score. The tension on the field is making Olivia uncomfortable and Rachel senses her anxiety.

"You okay?"

"Fine, I guess."

"Olivia, I should have warned you."

"About what?" She turns to look at her, curiously.

"Ethan and Noah. The last time they played against each other there were a few… um… brawls."

"Fights?" Olivia is shocked. "They got into fights?"

"Yes, and I just want to prepare you, because judging from the way this game is going so far, I think we might get a glimpse of that nasty Irish temper Scott has been warning me about." Rachel now regrets not listening to her husband.

"Oh, I guess that's what Noah was talking about, too." She can feel the tension crawl through her shoulders as she watches him.

"Yes, and to be honest, that's the reason why Scott didn't want him around you." Rachel feels so much better getting that off her chest. At that moment, Ethan loses what little self-control he has left, just as predicted.

Olivia watches in horror as he goes after Noah, shoving him in anger. Noah holds his ground as teammates try to keep them apart. She cringes as Ethan takes a swing that catches Noah square on the chin.

"Oh my God, I just want this game to be over." Putting her hands over her face, she tries to block out what's happening.

Rachel shakes her head. "Well, you're about to get your wish. Ethan just got thrown out of the game."

Ethan storms across the field peeling his shirt off as he walks and uses it to wipe the sweat off his face. Seeing the tattoo on his left shoulder, she's hit with a stunning recollection of events; a collage of memories past and present. She sees Ethan and her, alone and naked in the bathtub; his arms wrapped around her like a guardian angel. She recalls the feel of his chest against her back and his lips against her neck. She remembers that tattoo, and how soft the skin was under her fingers as she traced its pattern along the hard muscle of his shoulder.

Then she remembers a different place and time, a small dark cabin somewhere in the past. Awakening nestled in the crook of his arm, with her face nuzzled into his neck; her breathing matching his in perfect unison. Both images leave her with the overwhelming feeling of safety and love. Quickly, she rises to her feet.

Rachel becomes frightened for her friend. "Olivia? Are you okay?"

"Yes. I just remembered something." She can't take her eyes off him, "I mean, I think it's a memory. Maybe it was a dream. I don't know." She grabs her purse and swings it over her shoulder.

Rachel gets even more nervous. "What are you doing?"

Picking up Ethan's bag, she glances over at Rachel with a strange look.

"You're leaving with him?" Rachel gasps. She's certain that's not a good idea.

Olivia watches him as he nears. She should be afraid of him and she knows it, but she's not. She looks back at Rachel. "Believe me... I'm just as surprised as you are."

"Don't go with him," Rachel begs. "What about Noah?"

Olivia looks at Noah who's staring at her from the other side of the field. "I'll check in on him later."

Reaching the sideline, Ethan kicks off his cleats and is distracted for a few seconds while putting on his shoes. Olivia uses the opportunity to put her hand to her lips, blowing a kiss across the field to Noah. He holds his hands out in a questioning gesture as she mouths the words, "I'm sorry."

Clutching the key fob tightly in her fist Olivia hands Ethan his bag. Following him silently to the car, she leaves Rachel flabbergasted that she'd go anywhere near him after witnessing his behavior.

Rushing to keep up, she forgets about the proximity sensor and the doors automatically unlock as she nears. Good thing, because Ethan is not exactly in a patient mood. He swings open the door and tosses his stuff in the backseat, with the force of a child-like temper tantrum. As she rounds the hood of the car toward the passenger side door, Ethan comes around the back and meets her. "What are you doing?" he yells, as she reaches for the handle.

Olivia jumps and steps back embarrassed. She had assumed that he still wanted her to go with him. She looks up at him wanting to apologize, but she stalls when she sees the anger on his face.

"You'll never open a car door for yourself as long as I'm around," he growls.

"Oh." She stands back, allowing him to open the door, then climbs in apprehensively. Thinking this might be a bad idea after all, her hand readies on the handle, in case she needs to escape.

Ethan takes his place in the driver's seat, his anger not yet subdued. With his foot on the brake, he starts the engine with a press of the button. Holding the key fob tightly in her hand, she notices a small cut on the edge of his eyebrow that's starting to swell. Proof that Noah got in at least one good shot.

"Are you hurt?" Her voice is a little shaky, not sure of his reaction. "Do you want me to drive?"

"No, I'm fine." Suddenly his mood lightens. "You're certainly eager to get your hands on my stick shift." He smirks and raises his eyebrows in jest, but it does little to ease her anxiety.

Her phone beeps, making her jump.

From Noah: please don't leave with him.
From Olivia: relax. I'm safe. We are just going to have a coffee.

Ethan notices the look on her face. "Let me guess… that was Rachel."

Does she dare tell him the truth? "No, it's Noah. He just wants to make sure I'm safe."

Ethan shakes his head. "I have no idea what you see in that guy."

Ethan's phone beeps. He smiles and looks at Olivia. "Mine's from Rachel." He hands her the phone so she can read it.

From Rachel: Just so you know. If you upset Olivia in ANY way, Scott will kick your ass.

"Oh, for Pete's sake! What's wrong with everybody?" Olivia asks.

Ethan grins and types a quick reply.

From Ethan: I don't doubt that. Olivia will always be safe with me.

On the way to the coffee shop, Olivia vents about how her friends are too overprotective.

"You're lucky to have friends that care about you that much."

There's a strange regret in Ethan's voice that leaves Olivia wondering. "You must have friends that care about you?"

Ethan's face takes on a sullen expression, remembering something hurtful. "I thought I did back home, but I was wrong."

Feeling sad, she puts her hand on his knee, giving it a reassuring squeeze. His expression softens with a gentle smile, as he places his hand on top of hers caressing it softly, enjoying their connection as he drives. He wants to feel this connection all the time. He has to have it.

Ethan impresses her at the coffee shop by remembering how she drinks her coffee and ordering for her. The cashier totals the bill and Olivia unzips her purse and reaches for her wallet. When she looks up, Ethan is staring at her.

"We're not going to have this argument again, are we?"

She looks at him with fawn like eyes, wide and bright; a soft brown that he's never seen in them before. Her long eyelashes flutter nervously. "You bought last time. It's my turn."

"Not a chance." He turns to the cashier and starts to get his wallet out of his pocket.

His dismissive tone makes all her pent up anxiety manifest in a fit of anger.

"Excuse me, but just who do you think you are?"

Ethan's head jolts sideways looking unimpressed. "I'll pay."

"How about you don't make decisions for me." Not backing down, her voice gets louder.

"Olivia… Don't. I'm not in the mood." Ethan turns to face her, with a strong warning in his look.

"Neither am I. If I want to buy my own damn coffee, then I will." She takes her wallet out of her purse, slamming it down on the counter with no intention of giving in.

Ethan growls when he realizes that he needs to give her this one. In a way, it's somewhat refreshing to have a woman challenge him. "Okay then, have it your way." He puts his wallet back in his pocket and stands out of the way so she can pay.

Looking extremely uncomfortable the cashier looks between them. "Is there anything else?"

Ethan shakes his head no. "That's everything," Olivia advises, as she unlatches her change purse and looks up at the cashier.

"$3.70, please."

Horror strikes Olivia, as she stares down. Beside her, Ethan has noticed the look on her face and peeks into her completely empty wallet. Leaning on the counter with his hand on his chin, he takes great pleasure in her failure.

"What's wrong?"

"Uh, I forgot I emptied my change out this morning and I guess my debit card is in my car." She's so embarrassed.

Ethan knows it's wrong, but seeing her squirm makes him grin from ear to ear.

"It's not funny," she says angrily at his reaction.

"Of course not." He digs his wallet back out of his pocket. Taking out a five-dollar bill, he hands it to her. "Here, I'll LOAN you some money, so you can buy yourself a coffee." He can't hold off his smile.

Snapping it out of his hand, she passes it to the cashier. When he flashes his boyish smile, she suddenly sees the humor behind it and tries not to laugh. "You're so annoying, Ireland." She shakes her head.

Chuckling, he flirts with the girls behind the counter as he waits for their order. He indulges them in playful conversation, as if he could ever resist. "Can we get those 'to go' please."

Olivia stares at him perplexed. Not because he's flirting, but because the entire time he talks to them there's absolutely no sign of his Irish accent.

When he turns his attention back to Olivia, she asks him, "Are we leaving?"

"Yes, let's go back to your place. It's getting chilly and I don't want you getting sick again.

She makes a face at him. "Okay, Mom."

He shakes his finger at her. "You best behave yourself, Princess. I'm not above giving you a spanking." In fact, he would love nothing better.

"I wouldn't try it, if I were you." She tries to hide her excitement; wondering what will happen when he realizes that she has deep desires for his kinky promises. All the more reason NOT to date him. Despite her efforts to discourage him, he persists.

"Luckily, you're not me." The golden highlights in his eyes threaten to keep his promises.

Olivia is thankful that it's a quick drive to her house since she's now picturing herself, bent over his knee with her skirt pulled up to her waist; her panties pulled down, just enough, to give him access to her bare ass.

She squirms uncomfortably along the way, willing him to drive faster. The minute he pulls into the driveway, she jumps out of the car, making him curse at her for not waiting. Once inside she turns on the stereo trying to distract herself. Turning, she finds him sitting on the couch watching her curiously with that sexy smile. Deciding that it's not a good idea to sit beside him, she turns sharply toward the chair and settles in. His grin widens, knowing why she made that choice.

The curiosity is killing her. She can't ignore it any more, "Hey, Ireland, can I ask you something?"

"Of course." There's no hesitation in his response. She wouldn't be the first woman to ask him a question that he doesn't want to answer. Regardless, he always will.

"Inside the coffee shop, when you were talking to those girls… why didn't you have an accent?"

He didn't think she had noticed and he jokes, "Ah, well I didn't want to lead the poor girls on. Speaking without my Irish accent makes me *less attractive* to women."

"Really?" She can't help herself. "Because I would think that your personality would have the same effect."

"Olivia, you wound me with your harsh words." He holds his right hand to his heart and pouts.

She pouts back at him, mocking him, "Awww. I'm sure you'll get over it, Pumpkin."

A small purple bruise is starting to show on his eyelid, just below the cut. The dry blood and swelling cause her a little concern. "Do you want some ice for that eye?"

"No, I'm fine." He shrugs, as if it isn't a big deal at all.

The bruising brings back memories of the marks she used to hide, making her feel a little unsettled. Anxiety starts to creep through her body and up into her shoulders, as she recalls tonight's event. No longer able to avoid her thoughts, she rattles out her words in an overwrought tone, "I can't handle physical violence!"

Startled by her outburst, Ethan looks at her, curious about her confession. "Okay."

She looks down, avoiding eye contact. "I can't be around you if you're going to be getting into fights and punching my friends," she blurts out nervously, twisting her hands in her lap.

He assumes that her present reaction has to do with the *monster* she talked about when she was sick. There's obviously violence in her past. Ethan regrets that his actions tonight have made her feel threatened and unsafe. That's the last thing he wants, but he couldn't stand seeing Noah touching her. He watches her as she sips her coffee, still avoiding eye contact. A sick feeling rolls in his stomach at the thought of his temper ruining any chance of having her in his life. He needs to fix it.

The need to put her at ease is strong, making him move toward her. When she still refuses to look at him, he kneels in front of her, taking her hands in his; stilling their nervous fidgeting. "Hey." He caresses her hands in his, rubbing his thumbs along them until she finally lifts her eyes to his. "Okay, I understand. I'm sorry," his voice is calm and reassuring. Leaning his forehead against hers, he makes everything in the world disappear for just a few moments. "No more fights with Noah."

"Promise?" She's hopeful, since he appears to be a man of his word. She doesn't really know him all that well, but there's definitely some kind of connection between them. There's something in her heart that inexplicably draws her to him, despite the warnings about his temper.

Ethan lets out a frustrated sigh, "I promise. It won't be easy because I hate that prick, but I'll do it for you."

There's sincerity in his voice. She leans back so she can see his face. "Do you get into fights often?"

"Way too often, when I was younger." He shrugs. "Luckily, I trained at McGuire's." He notices that she's looking extremely uncomfortable with his answer. Getting to his feet, he pulls on her hand and then drags her over the couch. When he sits, he tugs her down beside him.

"Is that some kind of martial arts training center?" she asks, curiously.

He takes his last mouthful of coffee and puts the cup down on the end table. "No… it's a bar. In Ireland."

"Oh." She fidgets, still finding it hard to stifle the nagging anxiety growing inside her. "Tough crowd?"

"Yeah, and that's just the women." He's joking of course, but he can tell it's not well received.

It takes a moment for her to find the humor in his answer. A smirk starts to curl on her lips, drawing a sigh of relief from Ethan.

Their moment is interrupted as his phone vibrates. Looking at the display, he sees that it's John and asks Olivia to excuse him as he answers.

"Yeah, what's up?" Ethan looks at his watch. "Okay, I'll meet you there in ten minutes."

Ending his call, he looks at Olivia and frowns. "I'm sorry, but I have to go." He walks to the door and puts on his shoes. By the time he stands up, she's pulled herself together and is standing beside him.

"Good night, Ethan. Thank you for loaning me money for coffee." She rolls her eyes, feeling pretty foolish again.

"No worries, Beautiful. I assume you'll be paying me back in sexual favors?" His eyes sparkle and that charming grin spreads across his mouth; begging her to press her lips against it. She's tempted, very tempted, but her brain keeps going back to his temper, warning her to keep her distance and stay cautious.

"Don't hold your breath, Ireland." Reaching for the knob, she opens the door to let him out.

Ethan makes his move before she has the chance to mount a defense. Stepping toward her, he presses his warm body against her, lowering his mouth to her ear, "It would be worth holding my breath for your kiss." As he slowly pulls away, he brushes his warm lips along her cheek toward her mouth; hovering so close that she can almost taste him. The promise of his warm lips and wet probing tongue makes her ache with anticipation. Closing her eyes, she waits for his touch, willing him to put an end to her torment. Instead, she hears the door close. He's left her standing there alone, wanting, desiring him. She pulls aside the curtain that hangs over the small glass window in the wooden door and watches him walk through the garden. As he gets to the gate he turns, knowing that she's watching and smiles. Trust her to stumble upon a man who is a master at seduction.

Once she sees the taillights of his car travel out of the laneway, she makes a quick call to Noah, who doesn't answer. She leaves a message saying that she hopes he's not badly hurt and that she's sorry. Heading for the shower, she feels both restless and anxious. The running water doesn't help her relax. Her mind is still jumbled with a thousand thoughts. All of them compliments of Ethan O'Connell. She wishes she could just go back a few weeks, to that day in the office and refuse Rachel's request to pick up Scott. Things would be so much less stressful now; but it would also be a lot less exciting. The house phone rings several times. Wrapping a towel around herself, she hurries to get to it in time. "Hello."

"It's me. Are you okay?"

"Yes, Rachel, I'm fine."

"He didn't lose his temper or do anything stupid?" Rachel sounds aggravated. Olivia suspects that Scott has probably been talking in her ear all night, about how she should have kept her from going with him.

"No! By the time we got to the car it was over with. We actually had a lovely visit over coffee." Well, that wasn't exactly the truth, but if Rachel starts fussing over her like Scott does, she'll never get any peace. "Will you please tell Scott that I said to stop worrying? I'm fine. I don't think that Ethan is a threat to me. Even with his temper."

Rachel starts hollering into the background, "Honey! Olivia said Ethan is not a threat, she's fine and you should stop stressing." She puts her mouth back to the phone. "You're absolutely sure?"

"Yes, I'm very sure."

There's some rustling on the phone and then Rachel whispers, "Did he kiss you?"

Olivia laughs aloud, "Are you hiding in the closet again, so Scott can't hear?"

"Maybe. Tell me! Did he kiss you? I have to know. Oh my God, he looked hot tonight!"

Olivia is shocked. "Easy girl! He didn't kiss me but he was definitely thinking about it."

"I knew it! There's something going on between you two!" She's yelling in a whisper and Olivia chuckles in amusement.

"NO! Honestly, Rachel, I think you need to spend some much needed cuddle time with your husband. You're way too interested in what's going on in my life." She hears a loud creak and more muffled sounds followed by Scott's voice.

"What in the hell are you doing sitting in the closet?" The confusion in his voice is comical.

"Busted! Got to go." The phone goes dead and Olivia spends the next few minutes smiling, extremely glad for the comic relief.

Chapter Fifteen

Getting into his car, Ethan gets McCabe on the phone. "I'm on my way. Meet me in the hotel bar and order me something to eat. I'm starving."

A few minutes later, he rolls into the parking lot. Women stare as he makes his way through the lobby. His confident stride and broad shoulders are an aphrodisiac to those susceptible to the pheromones of such a stunningly handsome and masculine man. Ethan doesn't notice them at all; the only thing on his mind, other than Olivia James, is what John has ordered him for dinner.

It takes Ethan a moment to locate John in the dark bar. He's sitting at a small table in the back of the room, with documents spread out on the table and a pen in hand. Ethan's steak dinner arrives as he reaches the table.

"Brilliant!" Putting the first forkful into his mouth, he nods his head in approval.

John stares at him with his mouth slightly open, wanting to ask for an explanation, but not saying a word.

Ethan looks up at him and scowls as he swallows. "What's the matter with you?"

"Did Miss James do that to you?" John points at the swollen gash on his brow.

Ethan shovels another forkful of steak into his mouth and chews, making John wait for an answer, "Don't be ridiculous."

"What happened then?"

"I had a little mishap at soccer." Ethan continues to ravage his food like a hungry animal, keeping his head down to avoid the disapproving look of John McCabe.

John leans forward, resting his forearm on the table. "By mishap, do you mean fight?"

Ethan shrugs. "It was just two guys working some stuff out on the pitch. Nothing serious."

John bites his tongue as the waitress clears Ethan's empty plate from the table then slides some documents in front of him.

Taking the pen out of his hand, Ethan scribbles his signature on the dotted line and hands it back.

"Tomorrow, I need you at the bar all day." Ethan establishes full eye contact for the first time since he sat down. "There will be contractors coming by to give estimates on some renovations and a new sign."

"Okay."

"That reminds me." Ethan pulls his phone out of his pocket and types Olivia a message.

From Ethan: Don't forget that you promised you'd go with me to look at an apartment tomorrow. I'll pick you up at eight.

Sleep eludes Olivia most of the night, confusion being the culprit of her restlessness. She struggles to make sense of the memories that flashed through her mind at the field. It seems reasonable that they could be dreams she had when she was running a fever. With dreams like that who wouldn't want to run a fever? Nevertheless, if they were just dreams, why does she have such vivid memories of how his skin felt under her touch? Why does she remember the warmth of being surrounded by his large masculine body?

It's very unlikely that she conjured up those feelings out of the blue, right? If something happened between them, then why doesn't she remember? Why would he lie about it? He may be an arrogant ass, with a childlike temper when he doesn't get his way, but he doesn't strike her as the kind of guy who would take advantage of a woman when she's not in her right mind. Or is he? What does she really know about him? She thought she knew Sam well. *Sam!* The name makes her feel nauseated. Is it possible that lying beneath all that sexy Irish charm there's a darkness lurking inside Ethan, too? She's felt his dominance. Responded to his authority. Witnessed his temper. His dark, dangerous mood swings have already set off warning bells. Yet, there's some kind of inexplicable force that draws her to him, assuring her that he'd never hurt her. He's here to *save* her. Somehow, she just knows it to be true. *Confusing.*

Rolling over, she tries to untangle the blanket and get comfortable. Her eyes feel heavy but her brain just won't relax. Visions of the silver haired psychic begin to haunt her as she tries to force herself into sleep. Opening her eyes, she looks around the room, having the strangest feeling that she's being watched. Eva's words roll around in her mind, making her feel unsettled. *He's looking for you. He will find you.* Is he here now? Is that the eerie feeling she's experiencing? Olivia gets out of bed and checks the windows and doors, making sure they're locked tight. On her way back to bed she decides to turn on several lights, so the house is not in complete darkness. It's silly, but it makes her feel better.

Climbing back into bed she turns the TV on; turning up the volume just enough to drown out all the little noises that houses make. Every little thud and creak will have her nerves raw by morning, for sure.

When she closes her eyes, finally drifting off to sleep, she thinks about the cabin: the small wooden shack in the middle of a heavily treed forest. The one she saw so clearly in her mind, as Ethan walked toward her after being thrown out of the game.

Why is she thinking about this place? It's not a place that she knows; in fact, she's positive that she's never been there before. Why is it that, in her mind, she sees herself there with Ethan? The memory brought to her with amazing detail; Ethan moving to lie on top of her on a small single bed in a dark, cold room. A thin red blanket is tousled on the floor. The only source of light is the full moon through the window. She can feel the weight of his body on top of her as he makes love to her gently, innocently, like it's her first time. She experiences the intense emotion, as if she's right there in the moment. Every kiss, every thrust of his body, marks her for eternity, leaving his fingerprints on her soul.

Olivia opens her eyes and stares at the ceiling for a long while, unsettled and more than a little restless. That's it! Enough is enough! She's going to ask Ethan to take care of her needs. There's no denying that her body burns with an insatiable desire whenever he's near.

Sitting straight up, she throws her legs over the side of the bed. Not so fast girl! She takes a deep breath and tries to slow her thoughts, reasoning that if he holds that much power over her, he could also steal her heart and smash it into a million pieces. If she's completely honest with herself, that thought terrifies her more than his wicked temper. She'll have to come up with a solution.

A few blocks away, Ethan tosses and turns for hours, before getting out of bed. Pacing the floor, he checks his phone constantly. He's sent her at least a dozen text messages and called twice. He's beyond feeling stressed, trying to figure out why she's not answering. Looking at his watch, he considers getting in the car and driving over there.

She was very upset about the fight between him and Noah. Maybe she's still concerned about his temper. Jesus! His fucking Irish temper has always been one of his demons. It's the source of all his problems back home; now, it's going to screw up everything here, as well. It's always been the one thing that he can't seem to control. If he wants Olivia to be in his life, then he'll have to find a way to curb it. He'll talk to John about it in the morning and figure it out. For now, maybe he needs a good work out until he's too exhausted to think.

After getting very little sleep, Olivia is almost late for work. Frantically, she searches through her purse for her phone. When she can't find it, she hits the floor on her hands and knees, searching under the couch and the chairs. Thoroughly frustrated, she grabs her keys and heads for her car, accepting the fact that she'll just have to survive the day without it.

On the way through town she notices the Challenger parked outside the bar; it's an odd sight since Ethan and Scott are usually well on their way into the city by now. As she passes, it occurs to her that the last time she remembers using her phone was on the way to the coffee shop. Wondering if it fell out of her pocket in his car, she checks her watch and decides that she has time to stop. Screeching to a halt along the curb, she rushes to the front door and pushes it open in a hurried manner. "Hello?" she calls out.

Expecting to see Ethan emerge from the back office, she's startled when the door swings open and a tall handsome stranger with dark hair appears.

"Hello, did we have an appointment this morning?"

Olivia's face starts to flush. "No, I'm sorry to bother you." Confusion is evident in her voice, "I… I was looking for Ethan."

"Ah. Let me guess… Olivia James?" He walks toward her with a confident swagger, smiling brighter than the afternoon sun.

Suddenly Olivia feels a little shy. "Yes."

He extends his hand. "John McCabe. We spoke briefly last week."

Olivia relaxes and shakes his hand, taking in a deep appreciative breath of his cologne. She didn't think it was possible for anyone to smell better than Ethan does, but John McCabe is a very close second. "It's nice to meet you. I hope you had a safe and 'alpaca' free flight," she teases.

"Yes, thank you." John smiles, revealing the small wrinkles around his bright blue eyes; evidence of his age and the years of long, tireless hours of service. There's a subtle appearance of grey mingling throughout the short, black, silky strands of hair. He's much more distinguished than she expected for a personal assistant. John McCabe is every bit as handsome and charming as Ethan, just older.

"I'm sorry to bother you. Is Ethan here?"

"You're no bother at all. And you're much prettier than the big hairy contractor that was here at 7 a.m. I'm afraid Ethan isn't here."

Olivia feels disappointment wash over her. "Oh. His car is out front."

John quickly offers an explanation, "Yes, he had a business lunch today with some important clients and we thought it a better idea that we switch vehicles instead of him trying to cram them into his car." He takes on a look of amusement. "Which, by the way, I understand was your doing."

"Yes, I guess it was." She grins. Olivia likes the idea of having John to herself for a few minutes. Despite knowing that she's going to be late for work, she decides that she'll try to take advantage of it. "Have you known Ethan long?"

John raises an eyebrow, apprehensive about what he suspects is coming, "Yes, I've known him for several years."

"Can I ask you a few things about him?"

He knew it. Crossing his arms, he leans back against one of the booths. "Well, I'm not entirely sure that would be appropriate. If there's something you need to know you should ask Ethan. You'll find he's very forthcoming with the truth."

"Please," she persists, "I just need to know about his temper and his tendency to get into fights." Feeling a little embarrassed for putting him on the spot she reaches out, touching his arm.

John stares at her for a long while. The despair on her face and his earlier conversation with Ethan convinces him that he should answer, "Ethan used to have a tendency to get into fights, when he was younger. He's a very passionate man, as I'm sure you've already discovered. He's come a long way in learning to control his temper."

"Not far enough, unfortunately." She frowns.

John nods his head in acknowledgement. "You're referring to the fight at the game last night?"

"Yes. He hit one of my friends." There's something different about John's accent. Curiosity hijacks her thoughts for a moment. "Why does your accent sound different from Ethan's?"

John laughs, "We're from different regions of Ireland." They're interrupted by the loud exchange of foul language between a couple of workers, in the back of the bar. John looks agitated. "Excuse me a minute."

When he disappears around the back, Olivia takes a minute to admire the transformation taking place in her favorite hangout. The stained glass panels being installed between booths proudly display Celtic symbols in a rich frosted glass. They provide some privacy but allow a gentle light to shine through. She thinks they're perfect and very elegant.

When John reappears, Olivia notices for the first time, his incredible body; tall and beefy, his chest and biceps bulge with muscular definition. "Please accept my apologies. Some men have no class at all. Where were we?"

"We were talking about Ethan's temper." She forces her eyes away from his chest, hoping he hasn't noticed her staring.

"Right." John rubs his hand on his chin while he thinks about his words, "My employer would be furious if he knew I talked to you about this, but I can tell you're concerned. Ethan is not perfect." He holds his hand up to halt her interruption, while a wry smile forms on his lips. "I know it's hard to believe, but it's true." He chuckles, "He loses his temper *often* without warning and sometimes reacts without thinking about the consequences. Sometimes… he's downright bossy and rude."

Olivia nods in agreement. "You obviously know your boss, very well."

"Yes, but here's the key to handling him. Don't let him intimidate you."

She squints her eyes, trying to focus on what John's trying to say. Everything Ethan does intimidates her. How could she possibly avoid that?

He notices her distressed look. "Olivia, he's a brilliant man, but he's still *just a man*. One who doesn't respond to subtle cues and hints. He only understands open and honest communication. You'll have to tell him *clearly* what your needs are."

Olivia thinks for a moment about her needs and she sighs heavily, "That's easier said than done."

"Open and honest," he assures her. "I know that can be a difficult thing to do sometimes but trust me, if he likes you as much as I think he does, he won't disappoint you."

She does find some comfort in his advice, noting there does seem to be some truth to it. Yesterday, Ethan seemed oblivious to how his behavior made her feel until she blurted it out blatantly, later in the evening. "Thank you, John." She manages a warm smile. "I can see why Ethan considers you a friend."

John lets out a half chuckle as he moves to the door, holding it for one of the contractors as he maneuvers in supplies. "You're very welcome. But if anyone asks… this conversation never happened." He waits for her to nod her acknowledgement and then looks at his watch. "Why were looking for him this morning?"

Olivia had almost forgotten. "OH! My phone! I can't find my phone and I thought maybe it fell out of my pocket in his car."

"Ah, well that I can help you with." He pulls the key fob out of his pocket and holds it in the air. Olivia grins and follows him outside. John swings open the car door and searches the floor. When he stands, he holds up the phone for her to see. He raises is eyebrows when he gets a look at the message notifications. "Fifteen missed messages from Ethan last night," he announces. "Well, Miss James, seems like you have quite a hold on my friend." He passes her the phone, but when she tries to take it from him, he holds it firmly, forcing her to look up at him. "Be patient with him, Olivia. He's going to make mistakes. Probably a lot of them."

Chapter Sixteen

Olivia thinks about John's advice all the way to work. She's so deep into her thoughts that she doesn't even notice Rachel as she walks past her office. Sitting at her desk, she absentmindedly starts up her computer. When she looks up, Rachel is standing at her door, looking at her watch.

"Awesome! The afternoon shift is here," Rachel says in a sarcastic tone.

It takes Olivia a minute to slide out of her fog. "I'm sorry," she lies. "I had car trouble."

Rachel notices her friend's distress. "Is everything okay?"

Olivia tries to snap herself out of it. "Yes. Yes, everything's okay. Sorry, I'm just a little distracted this morning."

Rachel stands sternly with her arms crossed in front of her, "Olivia, are you sure Ethan didn't do anything stupid last night?"

"NO! Everything's fine." Olivia takes on a defensive tone, "We're going to be fine."

"WE? As in, *you* and *Ethan*? Together?"

Olivia gets flustered. Did she just admit that out loud? "Yes. Maybe. I don't know." She puts her hands over her face. "God! He gets me so worked up, I can't think straight."

Rachel's expression softens and she tries to hide a smile. "Well, well… It looks like someone has a crush on our sexy little Irish boy," she teases.

Olivia closes her eyes tight and groans, "Really? What is this? High school? Go away!"

Rachel laughs, "Okay, I'll leave you alone to get your work done and figure out what you're going to wear tonight. I hear you're going to look at apartments together." Snickering, she takes a step back and reaches for the door handle.

Olivia's eyes shoot wide open and she grabs her phone and scrolls through his messages. "Oh my God! I forgot!"

Rachel closes the door on her way out. "Have fun!" She stops and sticks her head back in. "And I want all the details."

As the door closes with a snap, the phone rings. Olivia jumps and reaches for it, not noticing the display reads Aurora Tech. A young man's voice greets her, "Good morning, Miss James. Please hold a moment for Mr. O'Connell." Before she can say anything, he's gone and there's a brief moment of music while she's on hold.

"Olivia, is everything alright?"

There's concern in his voice and it makes her heart start to flutter. "Yes, I'm fine. I…"

"Good," he interrupts in a curt tone, "Why haven't you answered my messages?"

"I'm sorry, I…"

Impatiently, he cuts her off again, "I've been worried sick."

"I couldn't call because…"

"I didn't sleep at all last night." Catching the tone in his own voice, he leans back in his chair and tries to get control of his anxiety.

Gaaaah! That's the last straw! He's not the only one that didn't get any sleep. Olivia's way too tired to deal with this shit. "Stop interrupting me!" She growls at him angrily, "Then maybe I can tell you! Geez! Why are you harassing me, anyway? Don't you have to get ready for a lunch with important clients?" She gasps! Oh no! She's not supposed to know that.

There's dead silence on the phone and she closes her eyes waiting for that Irish temper to erupt.

Ethan is no longer sitting back in his chair calmly. His entire body leans forward, sitting on the edge of his seat, fingers digging into the arms with white-knuckle force. He refrains from shouting angrily, although that would be his usual reaction. He's been thinking about what she said last night; worrying that her inability to handle violence is the reason she's been avoiding him. John's advice this morning was to prove to her that he can control his temper. He forces himself, with tremendous effort, to push his angry tension aside and answer her in a tone that's calm and steady, "How did you know about that?"

Olivia cringes knowing that this isn't going to go over well. "I met John McCabe, this morning."

Ethan's face turns red and the nerve on his temple starts to spasm. Keeping calm is extremely difficult. He's unable to hold back his sarcasm, "I see. Did you two meet over breakfast to discuss my schedule for the day?"

"No! I couldn't find my phone. When I drove past the bar, I noticed the Challenger there and I wondered if it had fallen out of my pocket, last night. I stopped to check. That's all!"

"And that's when you and Mr. McCabe decided to discuss my schedule?" There's still a bite to his tone that he's unable to hide as he taps his pen against his desk repeatedly.

"No, Ethan! It wasn't like that. Stop being an ass!" Immediately, she slaps her hand over her mouth. *Did she just say that out loud?*

His tapping stops abruptly. Olivia thinks she hears him growl something under his breath. She tries not to be intimidated but she finds it hard to swallow. "He only told me that, to explain why you and he had switched cars. Please don't be upset with him. It's my fault."

There's a long torturous silence before Ethan speaks, "Did you find your phone?"

Olivia's confused. Where's the temper everyone is warning her about? What's going on? "Yes. John checked for me and it somehow ended up under the front seat. I'm so sorry, that's the reason I couldn't answer your messages. *You* had my phone."

"I was worried." He was terrified actually, that he'd lost her before he even had a chance to have her.

There's a strange vulnerability in his voice and it makes her stomach flutter. "About what?"

"At first, I was worried that death trap you call a car had broken down again. It drove me insane thinking about you being stranded somewhere alone and unsafe." He's not sure why he makes his next confession, "Then, I worried that you were upset with me. I thought maybe you weren't talking to me because you were angry with me about the fight at the game."

The torment in his voice makes Olivia's heart start to throb. "Ethan. No."

"Not hearing from you for either of those reasons would not be acceptable to me, Olivia. Especially the second one."

He doesn't sound at all like the bossy, in control Ethan O'Connell that she knows and has been repeatedly warned about. "Stop," she says softly, not allowing him to drag her into one of those emotional girlie reactions that she hates so much. "It was only because of the phone. I just got to the office and was in the middle of sending you a message when you called."

Ethan flexes his fingers and relaxes. Leaning back in his chair he begins to feel more at ease. "I'm glad everything's okay. Do you still want to go with me tonight to look at an apartment?"

"Yes, of course I'll still go. You're going to pick me up at the house at 8 p.m. right?" She lifts her voice a bit trying to lighten the mood.

"Is that okay? If it's not, I can reschedule the appointment at a more convenient time for you."

"No, that works fine for me, I'll see you then." Scratching her head, Olivia wonders why it feels like she's just climbed down the rabbit hole.

"I'll see you then."

There's still something tense in his tone and she desperately wants to change it. "Ethan." She stops him from hanging up, but she's not exactly sure what it is that she wants to say.

"Yes?"

She searches her brain for a reason to draw out a finished conversation. "Have a nice day. I hope things go well with your important clients," she says cheerfully, trying to end the conversation with a little levity. "I'll be thinking about you." She slaps her hand to her forehead feeling foolish.

A happier tone returns to his voice, "I like the idea of that. You... thinking of me. I can't wait to see you tonight." Ethan hangs up and digs his cell phone out of his jacket pocket to send John a message.

From Ethan: Something you'd like to tell me about a visitor you had this morning, McCabe?

Dressed in the prettiest flowered cotton dress, Olivia chooses comfortable flat shoes this time, wanting to avoid the challenge of high heels tonight. She's decided, with much deliberation today, that she'll take John McCabe's advice. She'll tell Ethan, open and honestly, what her needs are. The thought scares her a little. She's still unsure how she can meet her physical needs without developing any emotional attachments to him. She's not ready to involve her heart, any time soon. In fact, she's not entirely sure if she can ever trust someone with her heart, ever again. She'll have to give it some thought. The one thing she knows for sure, is that the thought of him touching her sets her whole body on fire. At 7:30 p.m. Ethan knocks on the front door.

Olivia glows when she sees him. "You're early."

"Yes, well... I have an extreme intolerance to tardiness." Butterflies whirl around in her stomach when he tries to disguise a smile with a serious expression. "Good to know. Luckily, I'm ready to go."

When she gets to the front entrance, Ethan moves to stand in the doorway with his hands on each side of the frame, stopping her from exiting. Looking up at him, with those sparking hazel eyes, she gives him the most beautiful smile, sending his heartbeat into a hurried rhythm.

"You look beautiful tonight," he says seductively. Staring at her full sensual lips, he thinks about them on his body. Oh, the places they would go! The things that they would do! His dick twitches, as he takes a deep slow breath in. Jesus, there's no controlling it. The minute she's anywhere near him, the damn thing has a mind of its own.

"Thank you, Ethan. I was hoping to run into my favorite guy this evening."

Ethan recognizes the playful tone in her voice and he's intrigued. "And who might that be?" Standing aside, he lets her exit, and then pulls the door closed behind her.

"Oh, I think you might know him. He's the most handsome and charming man I've ever met. And my knees get weak when I hear his sexy Irish accent." She can't resist giving him a hard time. Biting her lip, she waits for his reaction.

"Is that right?" Smiling, he places his hand on her back to steady her down the front porch steps and escorts her the rest of the way to the car.

"Yes, his name is John McCabe. Do you know him?" Ethan stiffens beside her for a moment, making her nervous. When she peeks up at him, she finds him smiling as he opens the car door. *Thank God!*

When he gets in behind the wheel, he glances over at her, taking a moment to appreciate her beauty. "Yes, I do know him. Luckily for him, he's way too old for you or he might find himself in the unemployment line, as of tomorrow." Her smile makes his heart beat loudly in his chest, pumping blood straight down into his dick. Holy shit this woman is potent! He has no idea how much longer he'll be able to keep his hands off her.

Ten minutes later, he pulls up to the front of a rather old, brick apartment building. "Wait," he says, as he jumps out to get her door. Olivia's phone beeps several times on the walk to the front door. "Your friends are very demanding," he muses.

"Oh, wait a minute, *my* friends? Remind me, who's living with them?" she snorts.

Ethan shakes his head from side to side, comically mimicking her words, stopping only when she looks at him.

She raises her eyebrows at him. "Seriously?" She tries not to chuckle as she stops in front of the elevator and pushes the button. "How immature!"

Ethan grins from ear to ear. "Well, that's why we're here to look at this apartment, so I can move out of Mom and Dad's house and have sexy dance parties." He grabs her hips and twirls her around. In a failed attempt to dip her in a graceful manner, he almost drops her. When the elevator door opens, she squeals as he quickly stands her upright.

There's a sparkle in Ethan's eyes that makes Olivia feel settled. They may have had a rough start at things, but she knows that she's making the right decision with what's she's going to suggest tonight.

Ethan pushes his way in to the elevator, as people push their way out. Olivia moves to the side to get out of the way. Sticking her head inside, she whispers, "Hello? Is the coast clear?" In an over exaggerated sigh of relief she quickly steps in, speeding up her entrance as the door starts to close.

Ethan adores her smile. Oh, how he loves playful Olivia. He can't get enough of her. He pushes the button for the fifteenth floor, but for some strange reason, the elevator starts to descend. Olivia looks at him in confusion. "Uh oh, we're taking a trip to the dark underworld first," she whispers.

As the elevator stops abruptly, Olivia tips forward and reaches for him to steady herself. Sliding her hand slowly from his shoulder down to his chest, she lingers against him, remembering the first day they met. His mouth is dangerously close. It prompts her to think about how soft and sweet his lips look. She's tempted to lean forward and press her lips to them. The small purple bruise on his eye distracts her. Pouting, she rubs her thumb across the healing cut on his brow. Standing on her tippy toes, she gives his injury a gentle kiss.

Ethan's chest rises and falls in reaction to her touch. The sexual tension between them right now is unbearable. He reaches for her, swooping down for her lips as the elevator stops abruptly. The doors open, revealing another mob about to encroach on their privacy.

Olivia turns to face the crowd as they push in around her, edging her breathing into short erratic pants. Feeling space starting to disappear, she desperately tries to control her irrational fear and retreats into the corner, toward Ethan.

When Ethan's back is against the wall and he can move no further, he puts his hands firmly on her hips and guides her back against his rock hard chest. He can feel the tension in her body. "I've got you," he whispers in her ear, as his arms wrap around her in a protective embrace.

As the elevator begins its journey, delivering its residents to the safety of their homes, Olivia relaxes. She begins to feel an amazing calmness in his arms. She doesn't stop him when he caresses her, from her hips to the sides of her breasts, creating a heated connection between them. She doesn't want him to stop. As the elevator repeatedly stops and starts, with jerky movements, she can feel the hard brass button on his jeans rubbing against her backside.

Leaning his head in, Ethan rests his chin on her shoulder, before lifting his cheek to rub against hers. Slowly he massages his whiskers across the very sensitive skin of her neck and downward, stopping only to place a small tender kiss on her shoulder. "Are you okay?"

Olivia nods her head, trying to ignore the searing heat his lips are leaving behind and her, now wet, panties.

Taking in a slow deep breath, Ethan moves his lips back to her ear and whispers, "You smell so delicious."

Heat bursts through her veins making her squeeze her thighs together. Trying to soothe the gnawing need between her legs she moves her hips in a gentle motion, rubbing her bottom against him. Through the thin material of her dress, she feels the beginning of his erection. He moans softly, growing firmer and pressing the button of his jeans against her bottom as she continues to lightly sway.

After the elevator empties, Ethan exercises incredible restraint on the rest of the journey. Thinking about business, politics, war and foreign affairs… anything to get his mind off how badly he wants to lift her dress and fuck her against the elevator wall. By the time they reach the fifteenth floor, his hard-on has finally subsided.

The building manager meets them at the door and walks them through, what Olivia's father always referred to, as a *two-dollar tour*. The place is small and stuffy. Although there is a strong smell of disinfecting cleaners, it's worn out appearance makes it look filthy. Surely, it hasn't had a fresh coat of paint in many years; the floors are scuffed beyond anything a good scrubbing would revive.

Olivia decides to keep her opinions to herself about the apartment, since this was not her decision to make. She hopes that he'll find this place unacceptable since she can't fathom the idea of spending any time with him here. That's assuming, of course, that he's interested in what she's going to propose to him tonight.

There's not much to see: one bedroom, one bathroom, a living room and a small kitchen. Suddenly the tour is done. Ethan follows the manager down a narrow hallway. Her mousey-grey hair is pulled back out of her face with an elastic band. Tired eyes tell a story of way too many long days at work. "Two more couples are coming tonight so you better make your mind up fast," she says in a dry, harsh voice.

Ethan suddenly looks a little awkward and lost for words. Olivia smirks, amused by this rare sight.

"Well, I think," he pauses, "I think we'll just have to take our chances. Won't we, Sweetheart?" Reaching down Ethan clasps Olivia's hand, making her heart flutter. Years of role-playing have made him a pretty good actor when he needs to be. "We have a few other places to look at yet."

"Yes, you're right, Honey," she adds putting on a serious face. "But we'll be in touch." She extends her hand out to the manager and shakes it quickly.

"Suit yourself," she answers in an indifferent tone.

Ethan keeps a firm grasp on Olivia's hand as they make their way down the hallway to the elevator. Comforted by his, strangely familiar, possessive behavior, she makes no effort to pull away. When they're a fair distance down the hall, Olivia can't hold it in anymore and tries to hush the sound of her snickering. Shaking his head and trying not to laugh himself, Ethan ushers her into the elevator. When the door closes, providing them some privacy, he begins to think about the feelings that stirred inside him on the way up. In an attempt to protect her, from himself, he pushes the button for the ground floor and heads for the opposite corner. "That place was horrible," he gasps as the door closes.

"Truly dreadful," Olivia adds, twisting her curls around her finger. She starts to hum a pleasant tune and sways with the melody.

Raising one eyebrow, Ethan takes on a look of bewilderment. "Are you humming Shostakovich's Second Waltz?"

"I have NO IDEA." She shrugs, "Last night I dreamt about beautiful women in long flowing ball gowns waltzing around a grand ballroom." She holds out the bottom of her dress and side steps back and forth, imitating their movements. "That music is stuck in my head now."

"I see." Ethan leans back against the wall and crosses his legs at the ankle, watching her with an amused smile.

Olivia starts feeling a little embarrassed. "That sounded strange didn't it?"

Ethan shakes his head. "Not at all." What's strange is that he had the same dream last night. Dressed in tails, he keeps her in hold. She surrenders to his lead. The orchestra plays Shostakovich's waltz. Her long ball gown flows around her, as he dances her effortlessly across the floor. It's as if they're alone in the room. Everything was in such clear, vivid detail. He has such strong emotions attached to these dreams he's been having, but he can't bring himself to tell her about them, just yet.

Feeling a little sheepish, Olivia looks down to the floor. "Sorry, I usually wait until I know someone better before I unleash the *crazy*." She nervously taps her foot against the wall avoiding his grin. There's an awkward silence between them as he continues to stare at her from the other side of the elevator.

"Soooooo…" She stops dramatically, deciding not to finish her thoughts.

Squinting his eyes, he tries to figure out what's going on in her head. With curiosity evident in his voice, he asks, "Soooo what?"

"So… is that the reason you're all the way over there?"

Ethan raises his eyebrows. "Because you're crazy?" Enchanted by her demure behavior, he shakes his head and chuckles, "No. Not at all."

She peeks over at him coyly, barely lifting her head. "Why then?"

"Well, you see… I have this problem."

Olivia is immediately haunted by her post-traumatic stress. Thoughts roll through her mind at lightning speed. She knows that she's not an easy girl to love. She can't blame him for not wanting to get involved with her bullshit. She carries an awful lot of baggage, compliments of her ex. "I get it. It's okay."

"You get what?"

Finding it hard to hide the disappointment on her face, she looks away from him.

Ethan can't tolerate the distance between them anymore and crosses the empty space in one stride to get to her. "Apparently…" he whispers; his Irish accent soft and sensual. "When I'm close to you, I'm prone to inappropriate behavior."

The excitement building inside her is whirling like a cyclone, sucking in all the energy that surrounds them. The tension is almost unbearable as he reaches for her. Again, their journey ends as the elevator door pops open.

On the way to the car, Olivia's hormones start screaming at her! She has to do something. Her head and her heart begin negotiations. Ethan waits until she's buckled in safely before he closes the door. As he rounds the hood of the car, she watches his perfectly silhouetted physique in the moonlight.

She thinks about running her hands all over every glorious muscle as he opens the door and slides in beside her.

"Do you want to go to the bar for a bit before I take you home?" he asks, "Scott and Rachel are there and it would be a shame to waste that beautiful dress just on me."

"Sure," the word almost sticks in her throat. What she really wants is for him to take her somewhere and fuck this unrelenting ache out of her. She struggles with what's on her mind while Ethan drives out of the maze of a parking lot and toward the main road. This time both her head and heart lose the battle to a vagina urgently in need of some loving. "Ethan… I need to tell you something," she blurts out anxiously.

"Sure." He's calm and casual, unaware of what's about to hit him.

"In the elevator a few minutes ago…"

"Yes." He glances at her quickly and then turns his eyes back to the road.

"Well, what if I told you," she swallows hard, "that I WANT to do *inappropriate* things with you?"

Chapter Seventeen

Ethan gears down the Challenger and pulls into a spot at the back of the lot. Putting it in park, he turns off the key and turns to look at her. "You what?" Completely stunned by her words, he needs her to repeat herself. He couldn't possibly have heard her correctly.

Now isn't the time to feel bashful; the throbbing between her legs begs her to put an end to the torture. His incisive expression makes her nervous; she's afraid for a moment that she'll back down. "I want to come to an arrangement about sex." She fidgets anxiously, twisting her fingers unable to still them in her lap.

"An *arrangement?*" Ethan can't decide if he's amused or appalled. "What kind of an arrangement did you have in mind?"

Not being able to read the expression on his face makes Olivia even more anxious. "One where we have sex." *One where you don't break my heart.* She can feel the radiating heat from her cheeks, "If we mutually agree on it," she adds.

Lifting her hand to his mouth, he kisses the back of it. A somewhat evil looking smirk forms on his lips in. "You'll never tell me *no*, Princess."

Olivia surmises that he's probably right about that, but she hates it when he's so arrogant. "We'll see about that."

Ethan humors her, "I've already told you that I don't do non-consensual. Is that all?" He twirls her hair around his finger in such a sweet and tender gesture that she almost forgets the solution she came up with last night. *No intimacy. Just sex. Protect your heart.*

"No kissing." She knows, without a doubt that the minute his lips touch hers, she'll be done: helpless, defenseless, even. There would be no staying in control, no turning back, just inevitable and utter heartbreak when it's over.

"No kissing? How can you have sex without kissing?" He stops twisting her hair and furrows his brow.

144

Olivia stares at his lips and the very sexy way they curl at the edges when he smiles at her. She imagines they'd be *oh so wicked* on her body. She definitely didn't think that through very well, at all. "Okay... No kissing on the mouth."

Ethan laughs. Then, it dawns on him. "Oh, you're serious?"

"Yes, I'm very serious. No kissing on the mouth and no cuddling."

"What? You're messing with me, right?"

"Ethan, I need to keep it physical only: no emotional attachments, no relationship, and no dating." *Way to take control girl! Her sister would be proud.*

Ethan's expression becomes pensive. "Sounds like every man's dream." He pauses, scratching his head; then suddenly looks frustrated. "So, why does it bother me?

He knows why it bothers him. This was exactly what he wanted at the beginning. He had to drag her along, protesting for the most part; then he seduced her the rest of way. *But now?* Now, he feels more than just physical desire for her. This is no longer just about his dick. There's no denying that he'd love to spread her out and sink into her fast and hard, punishing her for making him wait so long to have her body. How can he expose her to his dark sexual desires and drag her through his impending allegations of abuse? After spending all this time chasing her, he can't believe that he's going to try to discourage her.

There's no way to ease into the subject, so he lays it all out in the open. "Olivia, you don't know what you're asking me for. My sexual desires are nowhere near conservative."

Already suspecting that, Olivia stares at him with confidence. "I know."

This isn't going to be easy. Looking straight ahead, Ethan puts both hands on the steering wheel. Squeezing it tightly, he attempts to work out the anxiety that he's starting to feel. "I like to play games. Role play."

Olivia's mouth goes dry, making her words stick in her throat. She raises her shoulders in a small shrug. "Me, too. Well, I've never done that, but I've always wanted to." Her face turns red, but she maintains eye contact.

Ethan becomes excited by her beautiful blush. His reaction is stalled when he recalls her admission of past violence. How could she possibly cope with his dirty thoughts and the kinky things he wants to do to her? "I don't think you fully understand," he says harshly.

Ethan's former best friend, Reese Wilson, is a dominant male, actively immersed in the BDSM lifestyle. Ethan attended events with him on several occasions. Most of the time, he only observed and learned. Hardcore punishment scenes just aren't Ethan's thing. Ethan's vice is control. To him there's nothing more beautiful than a woman letting go of herself; completely submitting to him. Surrendering her body for his pleasure. It's a gift that he worships, but hasn't actively sought out in some time. Olivia brings out those desires in him.

How do you bring that up to a woman who's a victim of violence, without scaring the living shit out of her? Olivia jumps when he drops his hand heavily on the console, confirming his fear. She's frightened of him. Looking for guidance, he lifts his eyes to the heavens and stares at the roof of the car. After a long period of reflection, he exhales a deep breath and places his hand on her thigh. Looking into her imploring eyes, he agonizes over his next confession. He knows that he has to be honest with her. "I would never hurt you. I'm not into torture or pain… but sometimes," he hesitates, "Sometimes, I'll need to dominate you sexually. I will take complete control. I'll expect you to submit. I'll demand it." Gently he moves his hand up and down her thigh, skimming across her skin tenderly with his fingertips.

The searing heat of his touch drives Olivia wild, making her heart pound against her chest. She's one giant ball of sexual arousal. She's certain that if he was to move his hand a little further north… she would orgasm, instantly.

She's confident now, beyond a doubt, that she's made the right decision. Ethan is meant to be the one. Trying to reassure him that she fully understands and accepts what he's telling her, she confesses her own secret desires, "I want that, too. I have fantasies of reluctance and resistance. But then, I'm sure you figured that out already. We're not so different in our desires, Ethan. I can handle it, just maybe not all the time."

Her answer sends a scalding thrill through his body. Is it possible that he's finally met the perfect girl for him? He'll have to work really hard at not fucking this up. Pressing his finger under her chin, he gently forces her to raise her gaze and look at him. "Are you sure this is what you want?"

Olivia nods and tries to look away from his indomitable stare.

"Don't turn away. Look at me. You're saying that you want to fuck me… but you don't want to date me… or kiss me?" Can he live with that as long as he gets the rest of her body? His body is pulsing with energy right now: anger, shame, anxiety… arousal.

Olivia feels embarrassed suddenly. When he says it like that, it doesn't sound like such a great idea. *Don't let him intimidate you,* she repeats to herself. *Protect your heart.* "Yes, that's what I'm saying."

Scratching his head, he frowns; disgusted with himself for even considering it. She's an incredible woman, sexy and smart… the kind of girl that a guy wants to marry and have babies with. Why is he thinking about leading her down the dark path of his desire? She says that she can handle it, but his intuition tells him otherwise. *Leave the girl alone!*

Ethan doesn't say another word as he starts the car. Pulling out onto the road, he heads toward the bar without giving her an answer. He clenches his jaw angrily, thinking that he could lose her if he doesn't agree to what she's asking of him. *Bloody hell!*

Olivia hopes the darkness of the night hides the embarrassment on her face. "So, I guess this discussion is over then? I take it you're not interested."

This is the last thing Ethan ever expected from Olivia James and everything he's been hoping for. He's not going to give up the chance to have her, not now, not after dreaming about her for months. There's a reason the universe has brought them together. He'll find a way to make it work. Take things slow, not push her too quickly into his kink zone. Maybe her arrangement is not such a bad idea.

"Are you on birth control?"

Olivia turns her head sharply to look at him, surprised by his question. "Yes, I just started, so for the first month we should use condoms, as well." *Geez, could you sound any more desperate, James?*

"The *first* month? Are you planning on long term fucking with no obligations?"

His tone is harsh, leaving her feeling lost. "I don't know… I guess. Until you get bored with me." She still doesn't fully comprehend why he sounds so angry.

Ethan shakes his head to show that he's not impressed with her comment. "I've never had sex without using condoms, but I've recently been tested and cleared of any STD's. You?"

She hadn't even thought of that. The way that he throws it out there is so callous, she suddenly feels like she's negotiating some form of prostitution. Now she feels uncomfortable. "Yes, I'm clear. I haven't been with anyone in three years, but I asked the doctor to run the tests anyway."

"*Three years?*" He curses under his breath, then says nothing, as if the gears in his brain have seized.

His long, pregnant pause leaves Olivia nervous and wishing that she could turn back the clock and forget the whole thing.

"When do you want to start this agreement?" His tone has softened, some, but he still sounds apprehensive.

"As soon as you agree." Olivia is still fidgeting, totally confused.

Ethan turns into the parking lot of the Headwaters Bar and Grill. The anticipation is agony for her as she mindlessly reaches for the door handle.

Ethan flashes her a warning look, growling impatiently, "WAIT! Dammit!"

Crap! She keeps forgetting. Stopping abruptly, she lets her hand fall to her lap and waits.

When he opens her car door and extends his hand to her, she's no longer capable of waiting for an answer. "Ethan, do you want to do this or should I just forget the whole thing?"

Without missing a beat, he answers, "I accept your agreement." His tone is cold and emotionless.

It's as if they've just struck a business deal. Then, she supposes that it pretty much is one.

When Olivia puts her hand in his, he pulls it gently, helping her to her feet and then directly into his arms. Wrapping his arms around her, he pulls her close to him. He's waited for this moment for what seems like forever. He lowers his lips to hers, leaving only millimeters separating them. Hovering there, he torments her. "I reserve the right to renegotiate terms at any time," he whispers gently against her mouth. "Agreed?"

He's so close she can almost taste him. Preoccupied with how warm his breath is against her lips, she almost forgets to breathe. "Yes, agreed." She's already regretting the '*no kissing on the lips rule*' and she's certain that's his intent.

Inside, Ethan leans in, so he can be heard over the loud music.

"Shall we go find Scott and Rachel?"

The lights flash on and off with the bass of her favorite dance song and Olivia is feeling the groove. "No... I saw them at the bar when we came in. I want to go dance." She's seen Ethan dance. He has some of the smoothest moves she's seen from a man on the dance floor. Feeling a brand new confidence around him, she wants to show him a few moves of her own.

Ethan is intrigued and grins. "Okay then, lead the way." *God she's beautiful and now she's mine.* Well, sort of.

Jason Derulo sings... Olivia heads into the crowd and onto the dance floor with Ethan following closely behind. Turning to face him, she finds the rhythm, swaying her hips from side-to-side.

Ethan joins in, moving around her on the floor.

Olivia eliminates the space between them. Pressing herself against him, she moves to the music in a very seductive manner. Lifting her arms in the air, she lets the beat wash over her.

Ethan puts his hands on her hips, holding her against his body, as the chorus pulses its rhythm. She can feel every muscle in his stomach ripple as he moves against her. They move perfectly together, as if they've been dance partners forever. His body predicting her every step, surrounding her in a possessive manner, making sure everybody knows they're together.

Scott watches them from the bar, taking a big swig of his beer to calm his nerves. Tapping Rachel on the shoulder, he tries to bring it to her attention, "Honey... Olivia is here. Have you seen her?"

Rachel is talking to other friends, her back to him. She turns her head slightly to answer. "No, I haven't seen her yet. She's probably sitting in a corner somewhere reading a book," she chuckles.

"Ummm... no, she's not!" Scott puts both hands on Rachel's shoulders and spins her around to face the dance floor.

"Holy shit!" Rachel's eyes open wide in shock.

"Yup, that's what I thought, too."

When the song ends, the slow, sexy introduction to a very provocative song begins to play. Ethan wraps his arms around her from behind. Olivia lets him take control. Every beat of the music becomes very sensual as he caresses her with a gentle rhythm. She matches his movement, leaning her head back to rest beneath his chin. Ethan presses his lips to the side of her temple, breathing hot and heavy in her ear. Gripping her hips, he anchors her against him. Rolling his hips, he strokes himself into her. It's fully clothed sex on the dance floor and everyone is watching.

Running his hands down her arms, he grasps her hands. Lifting them over her head, he twists her, spinning her around to face him. When he releases her, her hands fall against his chest.

Becoming lost in the sensuality of the music, Olivia rubs her palms across his body, finding her way to his strong muscular shoulders. Ethan's hands skim down her sides and over her hips and further. She doesn't stop him when he dangerously glides along the bottom of her dress. On the next swaying movement, he pulls her toward him, so that her body is firmly against his growing erection.

Even through his jeans, Olivia can feel the rigid outline of his hardening shaft. The swelling head presses against her, makes the sensitive knot of nerves between her legs begins to ache.

Ethan relentlessly rubs against her with every movement. Every touch, every stroke, fuelling her desire. When she lets out a small breathy moan in his ear, Ethan feels his control start to wane. Leaning into her neck he whispers, "Follow me." Turning her around, he edges her forward.

"Ethan?"

Leaning in, he whispers into her ear, "You need to be fucked. And I'm going to fuck you, right now." He takes his place at her side, holding her elbow and guiding her to the back of the bar.

Every nerve and muscle between Olivia's legs clench and tense. Finally!

Ethan leads her to a large, heavy wooden door; a brass nameplate dons the word, "MANAGER." Olivia hesitates as Ethan pushes open the door and pulls her inside. Spinning her around and stepping forward, he forces her to step backward until she can't go any farther. Olivia's heart races at an unhealthy rhythm when the door snaps shut behind her.

Pinning her against the door, Ethan moves his hand above her head and slides the lock across, preventing any unwanted interruptions. When he's certain that it's secure, he slides his hand down and cups her breast in his hand. Twisting her sensitive nipple, he makes her body keen.

"Should we do this in here?" She squirms beneath him, trying to line up their bodies.

Busying both hands with her sensitive breasts, Ethan nibbles down the side of her neck. In between bites, he answers, "Luckily the owner is a personal friend of mine." Within seconds, he's found his way inside her dress and has his hands on bare breasts. Teasing her, he keeps her nipples hard and taut. Every nerve ignites with an insatiable desire that makes her body start to tremble. She moans when he presses his hard, steel rod against her, making her feel the thickness.

No longer able to curb her desire, Olivia runs her hands down his chest to the waistband of his pants and starts to undo his black leather belt. She's fumbling with it, trying to unlatch it when she has a strange flashback of struggling with the same buckle.

Ethan lifts his head when she suddenly stops. "What's wrong?"

She looks at him confused. "I'm having a weird kind of déjà vu."

Ethan thinks about the night he had to do whatever was necessary to get her in the bathtub and get her fever down. Keeping eye contact the entire time, he reaches down and undoes the buckle for her. "Don't be ridiculous. I'd remember if you'd been in my pants before."

With his belt now undone, Olivia slides down his zipper, letting his cock spring free. She runs her hand along him from tip to base, becoming concerned about the large size of it.

Grabbing her hand, he stops her. "Wait here, don't move." Taking a step back, he takes a long appreciative look at her body, before he turns and walks over to the desk. Opening the bottom drawer, he takes out a condom and holds it up for her to see. Olivia watches with eager anticipation from her spot at the door. It doesn't occur to her to move. She's been told not to.

"You and the owner must be really good friends," she muses when he returns to her. Grabbing a belt loop on each side, she pulls his pants down quickly.

Stepping out of them, he kicks them to the side. Opening the package, he rolls it over his shaft as she watches, getting her first full look at his impressive size. When he's ready, he presses his hard muscled chest against her. Lifting her dress, he gets a hold of her underwear, and roughly yanks them down. He has no thoughts of tender moments or romantic gestures, only a desire to sink his cock deep inside her. He's been thinking about it for weeks; stroking himself often to the thought of how good she would feel. He can't wait any longer.

Olivia gasps for air as he lifts her suddenly, forcing her back against the door so hard that her feet lift off the ground. Sliding his hands under her ass, he supports her until she wraps her legs around him. Sliding his cock along her opening, he pushes into her impatiently.

Olivia winces, and then tenses, forcing him to slow down his penetration. It's been *three years* for her. In his haste to get inside her, he'd forgotten. Taking in a deep breath, he tries to calm himself. Pushing in a few inches at a time, he groans as he slows his approach. He knows that he's not going to last long with her squeezing around him so tightly. He wasn't expecting her to be so… impenetrable. Despite his lust, and the incredible feeling of being inside her, he lifts his head and looks into her eyes. "You feel amazing, Baby. Are you okay?" He stalls his movements, waiting for her answer; praying that she gives him the green light to continue.

Not wanting him to stop, Olivia tries to hide her discomfort. "Yes I'm fine. Just fuck me." She arches her back, forcing her hips toward him and sinking him in further.

Ethan has no regard for subtlety at this moment, his control waning a long time ago.

His dick twitches inside her, lengthening further and pleading for release. *Want* will no longer be ignored. "My pleasure," he growls. Freeing her breasts from the top of her dress, he lowers his mouth and sucks a pink tender nipple into it. Desire takes over, and he begins pumping himself into her tight pussy with a heavy rhythm.

Knowing that she needs this, Olivia tries to hide any sign of the anguish that's starting to build inside her. "Harder," she begs, as her body twitches with desire. His every touch makes her groan. The burning need inside her squeezes around him, making her ignore the uncomfortable fullness caused by his girth. This is exactly what she needs!

The heavy thud of his flesh against hers echoes in her ears. Without warning, the weight of his body makes Olivia feel claustrophobic. The intense passion she's feeling is lost to feelings of distress. *Please no. Just a few more minutes.* She tries to talk herself through it but she can't focus on the pleasure any more; she's unable to enjoy the feel of his mouth on her breasts or his hands as they explore her body. The intensity of her anxiety is so overwhelming that she holds her breath. All she can feel is the intense pounding between her legs and the feeling that she's going to lose consciousness at any minute. She wants to ask him to stop, but she's aware that he's about to reach his release. She refuses to deny him that. Not a chance! She wanted this so badly that she asked him for it. Now, she grimaces, just wanting it to be over.

Completely oblivious to her anxiety, Ethan grunts, emptying himself into her with one last needy thrust. He's fully aware that she didn't finish. Not on his watch, he won't allow it. Still inside her, he pauses to catch his breath, and then continues; he has no intention in stopping until he's given her pleasure.

Putting her hands against his chest, Olivia tries to push him away. "Ethan, stop."

"Not until you to come for me," he whispers through labored breath.

She can't take anymore. The sensitivity of her swollen clit is almost painful. "I did," she lies.

Ethan doesn't believe her for a single moment. Groaning, he runs his hands over her body, heightening his arousal. "I want more."

Her body goes rigid when he starts to lengthen inside her again. "Ethan! Stop! I can't." Her hands push against his chest. "I can't!"

Her strained, frightened voice makes him stop immediately and gently withdraw. Nuzzling his way up her neck and across her jawbone, he's about to claim her lips in a kiss, when she turns her head. He barely manages to contain his frustration. "Okay. I'm sorry."

Olivia forces herself to breathe, closing her eyes, as he lowers her feet to the ground.

Chapter Eighteen

When Ethan returns from freshening up, Olivia is gone. He leaves his office to look for her in the bar. Standing like a soldier, Scott waits for him.

"Did you see where Olivia went?" he asks, ignoring Scott's militant look.

"She left." Scott folds his arms in front of him, extremely pissed off.

"What?" Ethan asks confused, "Why did she leave? *How* did she leave? She came here with me."

Scott raises his eyebrows at him. "You tell *me* why she left. Rachel said it looked like she was crying. She went after her to make sure she's okay."

Ethan looks alarmed, "Crying? I don't understand. Everything was fine just a minute ago."

Olivia heads straight for the first cab parked at the curb. John McCabe glances up to see her, and rushes to open the cab door. "Good evening, Miss James."

Avoiding eye contact, Olivia nods, trying to hide that she's upset. It doesn't matter; John senses it anyway.

"Is everything okay?"

Olivia reaches into her purse for her wallet, and pulls out her panties. She stuffed them in there quickly in her haste to leave. Scrunching them into a ball, she hides them in her clenched fist. She ignores Rachel's plea to wait.

"Yes, everything's fine, John. Here." She holds out her hand. "Please make sure your boss gets these."

Looking apprehensive, John holds out his hand. Olivia drops the balled up undergarment into it and then slams the cab door closed. As the cab drives away, John unfolds the material and holds up her panties. Reaching his side, mortified, Rachel puts her hands over her face.

Shoving them into his pocket, John shakes his head, exhaling harshly. He's afraid to know what kind of trouble his friend has gotten himself into now.

Extremely angry, Rachel heads back inside. She fights the urge to wrap her hands around Ethan's neck when he walks toward her.

"Where's Olivia?"

"In a cab on her way home." She glares at him. "What part of take things slow and be patient, didn't you understand?" She punches him in the arm. "Dumbass!"

Ethan looks lost. "You think I did something to upset her? She was the one who…" He pauses, starting to put everything together. The way her body suddenly went rigid when he touched her; the look of desire that turned to despair, as he claimed her. Lying about having an orgasm.

"Shit!" Ethan looks horrified. Raking his hands through his hair, he begins to pose a question. "Rachel, was she R…," he pauses, not able to bring himself to say the words. Unfortunately, he doesn't have to; the tears forming in Rachel's eyes confirm it. Closing his eyes, his shoulders slouch, letting his hands fall heavily at his side. "FUCK!"

Rachel pushes past him, into the comforting embrace of her husband. Scott looks over at Ethan with an angry stare. "Christ, O'Connell! Can't you keep your dick in your pants?"

Ethan has his phone in his hand, repeatedly hitting redial. "She's not answering. I'm going over there."

Rachel turns to look at him and sniffles, "Do you really think that's a good idea?"

"I have to make sure she's okay." He gets his keys out of his pocket, "You might find it hard to believe but I care about the girl." He directs his frustration at Rachel. "For fucks sake, Rachel. You should have told me."

Scott's eyes meet his in a hard stare. "Watch it O'Connell! That's my wife you're talking to."

Ethan twists his neck, trying to release the tension in it. "You're right. I'm sorry."

Rachel tries to settle her husband. "It's okay, Scott. He's right. I should have told him." Rachel wishes she had told him. She realizes now that she pretty much sent him on a suicide mission. Now, Olivia is upset and Scott is going to be livid that she ignored his warning.

"GO!" She sends Ethan on his way. "Make sure she's okay."

John is busy trying to defuse an argument between two men who've had too much to drink. When Ethan flies out the front door, he calls after him, "Ethan? Where are you going?"

He hurries to the car. "I need to see Olivia!"

"Ethan, wait! I need to talk to you." He summons one of the other security guards to stand between the two combative men.

"Tomorrow," Ethan yells out the open window as he pulls away.

Rachel suddenly has a bad feeling about Ethan going over there, unannounced. She decides she should send Olivia a warning by text.

From Rachel: Don't be mad. Ethan is on his way there.

Sitting on the couch in the dark, Olivia tries to decide how she feels about what just happened.

From Olivia: Did you tell him about Sam?
From Rachel: No, but he knows something upset you.

She should have known he wouldn't just let her leave. He wouldn't know that she was upset unless Rachel said something. She sighs, it doesn't matter much now; he'll be there soon.

She splashes cool water on her face and quickly brushes her hair. Determined not to show him any signs of vulnerability, she squashes her emotions deep down inside. She never wants him to know how scarred and broken her past has left her.

Ethan is furious with himself. He knew he was making a mistake when he agreed to her *arrangement.* His intuition warned him that she was lying when she said she could handle it. He ignored it to fulfill his need for her. The two-block drive to her townhouse feels like it takes forever. Making his way through the backyard, he prepares himself to find her in an extremely fragile emotional condition. He turns the handle and pushes the door open. "Olivia? It's Ethan."

She's done a great job pulling herself together. "Come in." She waits for him at the top of the stairs. "Back for more already?"

Ethan blinks his eyes in shock. "No, I came to check on you. I was worried."

"I'm fine," she assures him.

"Why the fuck was your door not locked? Do you have any idea how dangerous that is?"

"Please, sit down." Ignoring his last comment, she motions to the couch. "Do you want a drink?"

"No thanks." Sitting, Ethan searches her face for some kind of clue to her behavior. Her eyes are a little red and her eyeliner is slightly smudged, but she appears to be *okay.*

"Why did you leave like that?"

Olivia would prefer that her past remains completely hidden from him, but it's too late. He knows; she can see it written all over his face. She refuses to allow him to show up and pity her; or protect her… or whatever the reason is that he's come.

She stares at his muscular body. It makes her painfully aware that her earlier desire has yet to be sated. She can't think of a better way to avoid having *this* conversation with him than getting him between her legs again. She remembers her sister's advice. *Take Control.* Making her way over to where he's sitting, she stands in front of him.

"I'm fine." Without hesitation, she drops one knee to the edge of the couch beside him. Throwing her other leg over top of him, she straddles his lap. She runs her hands across his chest and lowers her mouth to kiss his neck; stopping every once in awhile, to suck a little bit of tender skin into her mouth and nibbling.

Her unexpected behavior has Ethan momentarily paralyzed beneath her. His body responds immediately. Struggling to remember why he's there, he grabs her hands and stops their movement. "Olivia! Stop."

Olivia leans back and looks him in the eye. "I don't want to stop."

"We need to talk about what happened at the bar."

Protective walls ten feet high and three feet thick guard her emotions. "I don't need to talk, I'm fine." Her demeanor is determined, almost defiant. She adjusts her position, moving her knees forward, so that they press against his hips. Rolling her body, she rubs herself over his lengthening cock.

Releasing her, Ethan lets his hands fall heavily to his sides. "Stop saying that. You're not fine." His chest heaves with his obvious arousal and he fights the urge to touch her.

One by one, Olivia unbuttons his shirt. When she's done, she runs her fingertips across his bare chest, sliding the shirt to the side and off his shoulders. His tattoo is now in sight and she lowers her lips, kissing along its dark outline.

Ethan growls as he rids himself of his shirt altogether. When he leans back, he pulls her with him so she's lying against his chest; her breasts crushed against him. As she grasps his hands and moves them to her hips, he whispers his warning, "Olivia, if I touch you right now, I don't think I'll be able to stop myself."

The thought makes her stomach squeeze. She encourages him further, guiding his hands to her thighs. Moving her hips forward, she continues to masturbate herself against the head of his cock, her arousal saturating the material of his jeans. Ethan doesn't move, still struggling with his conscience.

Growing impatient, Olivia pushes his hands further up her thighs, under the dress. He exhales harshly as the warm, soft feel of her flesh brushes across the palm of his hands. When his cock throbs and pulses painfully in his pants, he realizes that he's unprepared. Condom or not, he can't fight it anymore; his control is almost completely dissolved. Ethan takes control, running his hands along her thighs with a hungry desire. Grasping them, he pulls her hips forward so she's firmly pressed against his cock. Caressing the smooth warm skin across her back, he moans. Making his way down to her bottom, he cups her ass cheeks and squeezes them firmly. It's then that he realizes his hands have met with bare skin. Alarmed, his body stiffens beneath her, as he pulls back enough so he can see her face. "Where are your panties?" he growls harshly.

Olivia moans as his hands continue to explore her. "I left them behind."

In one fluid movement, he grabs the bottom of her dress, stripping it off over her head. His eyes trail down her, now completely naked, body. "You took a cab home without wearing any underwear?" His voice hits a hard tone, but he's quickly distracted by the full view of her breasts as she leans forward, brushing them across his lips.

Olivia is lost in the sensation between her legs. It gains strength, as his hand slides across her wet swollen folds. A delicious pleasure builds inside her when he finds her most sensitive spot with the pad of his thumb. Moving with expertise, he rubs her with just the right pressure. She finally answers through panted breaths, "Yes."

As he takes her breast in his mouth, he teases her nipple with his tongue, "We'll talk about that later," he growls against her sensitive skin. Right now, he just wants to get this perfect pink flesh into his mouth.

Leaning back, Olivia undoes his pants. Lifting his hips slightly, he guides them down to his thighs, giving her full access to his painfully hard erection.

Running her hands through his hair, she lifts her hips as he adjusts his position underneath her. She doesn't care that he's not protected. She wants to feel his cock inside her, naked, nothing between them. She wants that more than anything else, right now. When she lowers herself, she can feel him in place, pushing against her, about to enter.

She's ready for him. She'll control what she wants and what she doesn't. She'll no longer be anybody's victim. She lets him slide in, sheathing him completely with her body.

It's even tighter this way and she gasps slightly at the feeling of being stretched so wide. She's never been with a man who's so long and thick. Without a condom on, the raw feel of him against her causes an amazing friction that only ratchets up her desire.

Ethan tries to slow her movements. "Go slow, Baby. I don't want you to hurt yourself."

Olivia tightens her muscles and squeezes him as she lifts her hips, forcing him to come to the edge of withdrawal. With both hands on her hips, he guides her back down and buries himself deeper inside her.

Olivia purrs her pleasure, "Oh God, YES!"

That's all the encouragement he needs. Lifting her, he gets to his feet, stepping out of his pants as they slide to the floor. Getting to his knees, he lowers her to the carpet.

Still inside her, he pushes himself in further as he lays her down, meeting the end of her. This time Ethan goes slowly, careful not to overpower her. His balls land heavily against her bottom, stimulating the sensitive nerves there.

Olivia takes a deep breath, enjoying the new sensation, "Oh, Ethan… Oh!" Running her hands all over his body, she feels every taut muscle, every ounce of glorious male flesh. It's far better than she'd ever imagined. Rolling her hips in small circles on his inward strokes, she forces his pelvic bone to brush across her clit. The continuous and deliberate pressure makes the tiny knot of nerves swell.

Ethan wants to finally possess those full sensual lips, to hell with the rules. He lifts himself, supporting his weight on his forearms. Moving his lips to hers, he claims them for a few moments, before she turns her head and offers him her neck. He growls his displeasure. "We're going to talk about that later, as well," he warns, as he lowers his mouth to nibble along her collarbone.

Moving downward, he finds her very sensitive nipple, and tongues it gently before gently sucking it completely into his mouth. Taking the other taut nub between his thumb and forefinger, he gives it a little twist as he tugs on it.

His touch fuels the fire already burning strong between her legs. She desperately calls out his name, wanting him to deepen his thrusts.

Ethan lowers his body, pressing her bare breasts against his chest. Filling her with every inch of himself, he finally meets her needs. The sensation is too much for Olivia and the ripples of a small orgasm begin to pulse through her, building in intensity. Ethan arches his back, holding himself over her. Lowering his forehead to hers, he holds her gaze. Not for a single moment does he abandon her eyes. It's the most intimate thing she's ever experienced.

Ethan adjusts his weight above her, stroking into her with hard, slow thrusts. His skin becomes damp with perspiration, making his body glisten above her.

Olivia lifts her hips to meet his. The sound of rushing blood in her ears is all Olivia can hear. Her body stiffens as anxiety once again takes hold of her, pulling her into a dark place and erasing all promises of pleasure.

Ethan grunts as he pounds himself against her, his release near. Turning her attention to his pleasure, she digs her fingers into the flesh of his ass, pulling him forward. His balls draw tight and she knows that with a few more thrusts he's going to come, *hard.*

Pleasure builds and thrums from his core, spreading outward. Somehow, through all the glorious sensations rushing through his body, he has the presence of mind to remember that he's not wearing a condom. "Shit!" he curses. He withdraws harshly, taking himself in hand. Giving himself the last few strokes he needs, he explodes; spreading warm spurts of cum all over her stomach.

When he's done, he nuzzles against her neck and gently rolls to the side freeing her from the weight of his body. "Were you going to stop me?" he asks through panted breaths.

Olivia runs her hand through his damp hair. "I meant to," she whispers. Exhausted, she stretches, trying to relax the muscles in her legs. She lets out a small groan of discomfort; there's not a single bit of her that isn't feeling strained.

"Baby? Are you okay?" He's alarmed. "Olivia, I'm so sorry."

"For what?"

"You didn't come again. Let me make it right for you." He slides his hand down between her legs.

She winces, feeling chaffed, sore, and far too sensitive. Grabbing his hand, she stops him. Putting her finger to his mouth she shushes him, "Shhhhh. I did come and I'm just fine. I'm just a little sore. It's been a long time for me." She moves her head against his chest, caressing him with her hands. Cuddling was against the original set of rules, but she really doesn't care now. In fact, she's willing to let that rule fall by the way side. She needs to be close to him now.

Ethan wraps his arms around her and holds her tightly, guilt haunting him. She's lying to him again; he knows it. He doesn't understand why but he'll let it go, for now. "I shouldn't have forced you at the bar." His hands rub apologetically up and down her back.

"Ethan, I was a willing participant. You didn't force me to do anything."

"But afterward, you were upset. I was too rough." He strokes her hair in a loving and nurturing gesture that seems to make him feel better. "Rachel said..."

She interrupts him, "I'm fine. I just needed to sort some stuff out in my head. And I really don't want to talk about it anymore." Sitting up, she pulls away from him. Avoiding his eyes, she grabs her dress off the floor and tugs it back over her head.

Leaning on his elbows, he props himself up. "Okay then... let's talk about you leaving the bar and taking a cab home without your panties."

"Let's not." She shrugs her shoulders, nonchalantly; trying to make it seem like it's not a big deal.

However, Ethan is agitated; it's a HUGE deal to him. His domineering nature won't permit him to let things like that go. He sits straight up so he can look her straight in the eyes. "Do you have any idea how dangerous that is?" His voice is no longer tender and loving, as it was a few moments ago. His body language changes; his expression becomes harsh as he chastises her, "You could have bumped into any one of those drunken assholes on the way out of the bar. What if the cab driver noticed while you were getting into his car? Jesus, Olivia! He could have locked you in and driven you out to some remote area..." His blood starts to boil just thinking about it.

Olivia gets defensive, "But I didn't bump into anybody and the driver didn't see anything."

"But he could have. And then I get here and you haven't even locked the doors to the house," he scolds her like a child. "You put yourself in a very dangerous situation."

She hadn't thought about that when she left. She only wanted to put some distance between them. She looks down, avoiding the harshness of his stare. "I'm sorry."

Ethan lifts his hand to her face, forcing her to look at him as he brushes his thumb across her pouting lip. His words slightly soften but his expression is still hard and intimidating. "If anybody hurt you, Baby Girl... I swear to Christ I'd come unglued!"

The tormented expression on his face, confirms that he's telling the truth. His words are overwhelming. She gets a heavy feeling in her chest as her heart fights the feelings starting to build. She stares at him, trying to figure out what it is about him that gets her all tied up into knots. Especially considering the short time that they've known each other. She's going to have a difficult time trying to stay in control of this relationship, if that's even possible.

Ethan's hard tone diminishes. He leans forward, kissing her on the forehead, feeling her anxiety as his lips touch her. "Okay then." He takes a deep calming breath. "So, let's just agree that from now on..." He taps her on the nose. "*You* will wear underpants at *all times* when you're out in public." His words are playful but stringent at the same time.

Olivia manages a somewhat forced smile. How does he do that? How does he go from dark and controlling to warm and fuzzy within seconds? It makes her feel uneasy and yet, oddly aroused. Still, he's had some good points about her safety.

Then, it dawns on her. The way she felt at the field when all the women were enjoying the view of his body. "Okay... It's a deal." She gets to her feet and starts to walk toward the bathroom, safely out of range and making sure that she gets in the last word. "AND... *you,*" she says, pointing at him for dramatic effect, "will no longer be dropping your pants at the soccer field so all the girls can gawk at you." She gives him back one of his own, *I mean business* looks. Closing the door behind her, she smiles, pleased at her counter request.

Ethan smiles at her rebuttal. He had no idea that had upset her, but he likes that she feels jealous and just a tad possessive. It's further proof that she does have feelings for him. She's not submitting completely to him yet, but she is submitting. If she needs to feel that she has some control in this relationship then he's willing to let her. Especially, if it means she'll start to drop her guard and let him in to her life.

When she returns to the room, he reaches for her as she walks toward him, pulling her into a warm embrace. His stomach gets all jittery as he holds her there. This is where she belongs, in *his* arms. He doesn't want to let her go. "I can stay if you like. John can handle things at the bar."

Olivia has often wished that she was one of those girls that had long sexy legs that went on forever, adding a few more inches to her height. Snuggling against Ethan's chest, she considers his offer. She's thankful, for the first time ever, for genetics and her mere five foot four inches of height. She tucks her head perfectly in under his chin. It feels good… it feels right. She worries about how quickly she could develop feelings for him… how could she not? Hell, it's happening already. She'll be devastated when he leaves. There's no doubt in her mind that he'll leave. He's too suave and charming to be a *one-woman* man. As much as she wishes she could lie all night in his arms, she knows that she has to stick to the plan. "No, you need to go. Staying over is against the rules of our arrangement," she says, in a very businesslike tone and it irks him.

"Olivia, listen… about these rules."

Before he can utter another word, she becomes distressed and interrupts him, "You'll follow the rules won't you, Ethan?" Her body goes rigid in his arms. "Please… promise me, you'll follow the rules."

Clenching his jaw, he looks toward the ceiling, mumbling something she thinks is a prayer for strength. "Please," she pleads one last time.

Against his own desires, he agrees, "Okay, okay… I promise." Feeling resentful of her demands, he releases her and heads for the door.

Following him to the stairs, she struggles with what to say, "Goodnight, Ethan. Thank you."

He looks at her with an injured expression that conveys his discontent. "Thank you for what? Fucking you?"

Embarrassed by the apparent stupidity of her remark her face flushes. "I guess."

He turns the doorknob and opens the door. "You're welcome." He stares at her with an agonizing fury as he lets himself out. Standing just outside the door he stops and waits… angry…conflicted. He shouldn't leave things like this. He was hurt when she rejected his offer to stay. He shouldn't have given her a choice. He should have just told her that he was staying.

Inside, Olivia's bottom lip begins to tremble as a storm of different emotions hits her with all the finesse of gale force winds. Overwrought by their intensity, she sits on the top step, covering her face with her hands, and starts to cry. Still standing just outside the door, Ethan hears her sobs through the open window. You would think with three younger sisters that he'd be immune to the sounds of a woman crying. This is gut-wrenching torture for him! Putting his hand back on the doorknob, he hesitates, listening to her gasp for air between sobs, while trying to catch her breath. Leaning his forehead against the door, he curses before forcing himself to turn and walk away.

Chapter Nineteen

The following morning, more than an hour late and feeling extremely out of sorts, Ethan waits to turn into the parking garage. Agitated, he looks up to see the silver haired woman standing out front of the rustic little storefront. **Eva Storm – Psychic.** Well, that explains a lot; now he knows for certain that she's off her nut. She stares at him, making him feel uneasy. Great. As if he isn't stressed out enough.

On the way to the elevator, he continually looks over his shoulder expecting to find her there. Heading straight to his office, he forgoes his usual morning flirt with Hannah. Dropping his bag heavily on the floor beside his desk. He sits, feeling like a first class asshole for leaving Olivia crying. Ten minutes later, John finds him still sitting in that exact spot, staring out the window, looking crestfallen. Closing the door behind him, John walks to the desk and puts a coffee down in front of him. "Thought you might need that."

"Thanks." Ethan grimaces at its potent taste.

John reaches into his pocket, "Oh, and these, apparently, are for you."

Ethan isn't quite sure what to make of it when John drops the small rolled up ball of fabric on the desk in front of him. He glances up at John as he unfolds Olivia's panties, and holds them up by the corners. "Sweet Jesus," he grumbles, as he stashes them into his bottom desk drawer. The last thing he needs before his conference call is for his dick to get hard.

John fights a smile. "Interesting night?"

Ethan puts his hands over his face, thinking about how good it felt to be deep inside her with nothing between them. Leaning forward, he rests his elbows on the desk, his voice muffled through his fingers, "You have no idea. And NO, I don't want to talk about it. Just dial my father's office and let's get that over with."

John dials the number and hits the speaker option on the phone. Voices are already engaged in a conversation when the connection is made, "Ethan is that you that's just joined? This is Ian Walsh."

"Yes, I'm here." Ethan looks over at John and shrugs his shoulders. He's not surprised that his father has left it to someone else to do the communicating. It's only natural that person is his brother-in-law. "How's McKenna?" Ethan asks, trying to lighten the mood.

"She's well. She misses you. And Kaylie is going right out of her mind with you gone."

Ethan can't wait to put this whole mess behind him, so that he can resume his position from the head office in Ireland. Feeling homesick for his family, he wants to go home.

Ian quickly steers the conversation back to business, taking full control of the meeting. "We've been talking about the Artemis Project."

Sensing that he's about to be blindsided, Ethan's muscles tense. "I've skimmed through the latest update. We're way behind schedule. What's the delay?"

Ian clears his throat in a nervous gesture. "The design and manufacturing engineers are having problems with the criteria set out by the physician you have working on the project."

Ethan sits back in his chair. "Okay, so there must be a solution. The technology is available, why can't we apply it to our prototype?"

A young, quiet voice speaks up, "Sir, this is James, one of the engineers working on this project. The problem is that in order to meet the specifications Dr. Cameron has set out, we need to apply several different types of technology. We're having problems trying to integrate them all with the same software. We keep testing but the failure rate is still extremely high."

A firm commanding voice impatiently interrupts, "In short, we're hemorrhaging money on this project and there's still no light at the end of the tunnel."

Ethan sits up in his chair, as if the school principle has just entered the room. "Hello, Dad."

"Ethan," he acknowledges out of obligatory politeness. His cool tone is evidence of a father and son at odds with one another. "We're recommending that we suspend any further work on this project. We need these resources elsewhere."

"That's not acceptable," Ethan snaps. "There's still money in the allocated budget. Keep working at it. I'll be there in a few weeks and I'll review it then. If we're still getting nowhere at that time, then I'll privately fund the project."

There's a short silence before Aiden O'Connell speaks again, "Ethan, be reasonable. I know this is important to you, but we stand to make little profit on this project to begin with."

"Profit?" Ethan shakes his head, letting out a frustrated chuckle. "It's important to me because it'll save lives, Dad. The lives of premature babies arriving into this world in distress; I don't care about the profit."

Half way across the world, several men sit in an office at O'Connell Industries staring at each other nervously, afraid to speak. None of them brave enough to step between the two O'Connell men that are currently competing for alpha male status.

Ethan stands firm. "We'll continue working on it until I get there. I want to speak with the engineers, ASAP, and get more information. John will set up a meeting." He looks up at John, who is nodding his head and already searching for an appropriate time in Ethan's schedule. "Is there anything else?" Ethan drums his fingers on the desk while he waits for a reply.

Ian finally acknowledges, "No, sir. That was all we wanted to discuss today."

"Very well, good evening, gentlemen." Ethan hits the button on the phone and disconnects the call.

John sits on the other side of the desk sending meeting requests. Ethan watches him, without saying a word. John senses his tension and glances up at him for a second. "Have you eaten?"

Ethan shakes his head no.

"I'll have them send something up." John types furiously into his phone. "I've also sent an email to Dr. Cameron, asking for a time you can speak with him. Maybe he can help shed light on things. Engineers have a tendency to overthink things, maybe they're making it more complicated than it needs to be."

Ethan nods. "Good idea."

John gathers up his stuff, trying to find the courage to bring up what's on his mind. "Ethan, I know you probably don't want to hear this today."

Ethan stops what he's doing and sits back in his chair, giving John his full attention. "But you're going to say it anyway?"

John takes a breath. "It doesn't help things between you and your father when you continually trump his decisions regarding the business."

"You're right, McCabe. I don't want to hear this today," Ethan's frowns, feeling frustrated. "That's the whole purpose of having controlling interest in a company."

"Yes, I understand that. But this wasn't just a business acquisition. You became a partner in your father's business with the intention of helping him out financially during some difficult times."

Ethan becomes impatient. "What's your point?"

"My point is that your dad sweats blood into that business and has done so for many years. He built it from nothing and kept it on its feet through extremely difficult times. Yes, he needed your help financially to grow the business and pay off some debt... but it's still *his* business. Despite the fact that you negotiated controlling interest, I think that once in awhile, where his business is concerned, you should just let him *win*."

Ethan's mouth is pressed in a hard line. Glaring at John, he bites his tongue.

"Your father is an extremely competent business man, Ethan." John looks down, distracted by his phone, "Where do you think you get it from?" Glancing up, he acknowledges the silence that is uncharacteristic of Ethan O'Connell. "Just think about it."

They're interrupted by a loud knock on the door and John opens it to find Scott holding Ethan's breakfast. Scott can tell by looking at Ethan that it hasn't been a good morning, so far. He regrets that he's the one that has to give him bad news. Placing the food down on the corner of the desk, he stands there awkwardly. John instinctively knows that there's something brewing and sits back down

Ethan looks back and forth between the two of them. "What's going on?"

"I was in Taylor's office when he received the call." Scott grimaces as he continues, "It looks like we've lost the Anderson account." Looking nervously over at John, he waits for the proverbial shit to hit the fan.

Ethan's face turns red. *Could this day get any worse?* "How the hell did that happen? We had that one locked up."

John makes his way to the door and closes it to spare the rest of the team from Ethan's yelling.

"I have no idea what happened." Scott continues, "Taylor convinced them to meet with him today before they make any decisions. He's going to their office at 1 p.m. and I think you should be there."

When Ethan looks over at John, he already has an answer. "You have a conference call at 2 p.m. with Miss Quinn. Everything else, I can clear."

Ethan rubs his hand on his forehead, trying to relieve some of the tension. "You stay here and find out if Miss Quinn has any new information. I can't deal with her today."

John nods.

Looking over at Scott with clenched jaws, he gruffly demands, "You'll go with us. Make sure you're familiar with the file and the proposal. Try to find out what the hell happened before we go. I don't like surprises."

Scott acknowledges and turns to leave, ignoring the grumbling and cursing behind him as he closes the door.

Back in Dufferin County, Olivia returns to the office feeling refreshed and successful after spending her Friday meeting with clients. As she makes her way through the foyer, Rachel is suddenly at her side, steering her down the hall.

"I'm glad you're here. I need an update on the O'Connell project," Rachel says, glancing quickly at the nosy receptionist.

The muscles in Olivia's legs are still weary from last night. She has a hard time keeping up with Rachel's brisk pace. "The what?" she asks confused.

"Just keep walking," Rachel whispers.

When they reach Olivia's office, Rachel closes the door behind them. "What the hell happened last night?" Rachel blurts out.

Olivia is shocked. "Shhhh! Everyone will hear you."

Rachel lowers her voice, "What happened at the bar? Did he force you to do something you didn't want to do?"

"What? NO!" Blushing, Olivia bites at her lip trying not to smile.

"Oh my God! At the bar?" Rachel whispers in disbelief.

Olivia nods her head, her face flushing with heat.

"Where?"

"In the office."

"In the office?" Rachel repeats loudly.

Olivia puts her finger to her mouth to remind her to be quiet.

"And again at my house, afterward." Her blushing is barely noticeable past the grin on her face.

"Holy shit! You had sex *twice*?" She pauses for a reality check. "Are you okay?"

Olivia's grin grows a little wider. "Yes, it was my idea. Well… not that we do it in the office, but that we come to an arrangement about sex."

Rachel's eyebrows rise. "An arrangement?"

Olivia scowls. "Ethan said it the same way. Yes, an arrangement; one where two adults with needs, get together and have sex. You do know what century this is, don't you?"

"So then, why were you so upset when you left?" Rachel pauses. "Oh!" She whispers, "Was he bad at it?" She wrinkles her nose in disappointment.

"No, that was definitely not a problem," Olivia laughs, "The man is very good with his body and he certainly knows how to look after mine."

"Why then?" She sits in the chair opposite to Olivia and waits for an answer.

Olivia sighs and purses her lips. She's given that a lot of thought since last night. "I'm not sure. He had me feeling sooooooo good. Then, all of a sudden, I got an overwhelming feeling of impending doom. I kind of freaked out a little." She makes herself perfectly clear, "But it wasn't because I didn't want to be there."

Rachel leans back, looking out the glass office door, to make sure that nobody is lurking near by. "Is he a good kisser? I have to know. He has the most delicious looking, kissable lips I've ever seen."

Olivia shrugs. "I don't know. Kissing is against the rules."

Rachel's mouth falls opens. "What do you mean against the rules?"

Olivia starts to feel very emotional. "I decided that there shouldn't be any kissing."

"Are you nuts?" Rachel blinks rapidly at the absurdity of it.

Olivia starts to feel defensive. "Well, I want to keep it strictly physical. I thought that if I let him kiss me that I might start to develop feelings for him."

"Olivia." Rachel feels horrible for her friend. "That's ridiculous and you know it."

"What if I develop feelings for him? Where does that leave me when he's gone?"

"Why are you so convinced that he's going to leave you? And don't even try to give me that nonsense about him not being the kind of guy that can commit to one girl. Guys that are only interested in one night stands don't spend three days nurturing sick girls back to health."

Olivia puts her thumb to her mouth and nervously chews on the nail. "I've thought about that."

Rachel tries to put her at ease. "Sweetheart, I've seen the way he looks at you. Trust me, he's in it for the long haul."

Olivia's voice cracks, "I just don't get what he sees in me. How could I possibly keep him interested for any length of time?"

"Now I know you're nuts. You're a bright, beautiful, sexy woman."

Olivia squirms uncomfortably and shakes her head, still not convinced.

"I know it's scary, especially after Sam. Life doesn't always bring us relationships that end in *happily ever after*. Don't deny yourself the attention of a man who obviously has feelings for you... even if it's only for a little while. If things don't work out with Ethan, someone else will come along. I promise."

Ethan arrives back at work after failing to save the Anderson account. Through the side window of his closed office door, he can see John sitting with his back to him, still on the conference call with Shannon Quinn. Turning the knob quietly, he pushes the door open, so as not to disrupt them. He's so quiet that John doesn't hear him come in. As Ethan slowly steps into the room, he raises a quizzical brow when he notices that Shannon's voice is unusually casual. He curiously pays attention to the conversation, careful not to alert John of his presence.

"When will you be home?" Shannon asks.

"I don't know. There are many things here to look after. Ethan will be home at the end of the month but he hasn't told me yet, if I'm to accompany him."

"I hope so. I miss you," her voice is soft and sincere, almost sensual.

Ethan figures out exactly what's going on.

"I miss you, too. I'll get home to you just as soon as I can," John promises.

Ethan stands silently at the door, not wanting to interrupt the obviously personal and intimate conversation.

"I should go now." John glances at his watch. "He sent a text a short while ago saying he was on his way back to the office."

Shannon looks disappointed. "Okay. Will you call me before you go to bed?"

John smiles. "As always, I wouldn't be able to sleep if I didn't."

"Good bye, then." Despite her efforts, she can't disguise the sadness in her voice.

As John ends the call, Ethan pushes the door the rest of the way closed making it click as it latches. John turns around to find him standing there staring, with his eyebrows raised. "You and Miss Quinn?"

Extremely uncomfortable, John tries to explain, "Yes, I'm sorry. We shouldn't have been talking about personal things."

Ethan holds up his hand to halt him as he makes his way to this desk. "It's okay, John. I shouldn't have snuck in. Nice catch, old man." He glances over at him trying to make him feel at ease. "How the hell did you manage that?"

"I have no idea. I guess she's defenseless against my charm." A grin forms on John's lips as he glances a contented look Ethan's way.

"No doubt," Ethan agrees. "Now get out. Take the rest of the day off. This day just needs to end."

John grabs his stuff. "You don't have to tell me twice." Stopping as he reaches the door, he turns back to Ethan. "Call me if there's anything you need."

Ethan looks up at him annoyed. "Have I ever not?"

John nods. As the door closes, Ethan pours himself a glass of water and walks over to the window. The overcast sky makes the city look dark and miserable, a perfect reflection of his day. His shoulders and neck are stiff and sore from the tension lingering there. Swirling his glass, the lemons swish around the edge, reminding him of Olivia's visit the day they went shopping for the Challenger. She was very playful in his office that day. Thoughts of her teasing bring a smile to his face, for the first time today. Making his way to his desk, he dials the phone. There's only one thing that's going to make him feel better.

Olivia and Rachel are still talking when the phone rings. Olivia gets nervous as she looks at the display. "It's Ethan."

Rachel gets excited. "Put him on speaker phone!"

"NO!"

"Come on, put him on speaker."

"Absolutely not!" On the third ring, she answers it. When she fails to put it on speaker, Rachel rounds the desk and sticks her head against Olivia's, so she can hear. Olivia rolls her eyes and stops fighting her, turning the phone slightly so they can both hear.

"Hi!" Olivia says enthusiastically.

"Hello, Beautiful," Ethan's voice is seriously sexy. But when he unleashes his full Irish accent, it's almost panty melting, "I've been thinking about you all day."

Olivia takes a deep breath. "I was thinking about you, too." She elbows Rachel when she squirms closer so she can hear. "How's your day been?" she asks politely.

There's a short silence before he answers, "Actually, it's been a very stressful day."

Olivia senses the distress in his voice and it upsets her. "Oh, I'm so sorry to hear that. Is there anything I can do?"

Ethan gets right to the point. "I was wondering if I can see you tonight?"

Judging from the tenderness of her breasts, her period is about to make an appearance. It immediately dampens her excitement. "Oh, well, Ethan I don't know if that's a good idea."

Rachel throws her hand over the mouthpiece of the phone and pulls it away from her face. "Are you insane?" she whispers.

"I'm going to start my period," she says, as she grabs the phone back.

Ethan closes his eyes and clarifies his intentions, "Olivia, I don't want anything from you." He sighs heavily, "It's just been such a crap day and… well… being around you seems to calm my inner turmoil. Let me take you to dinner, coffee… whatever you have time for." His voice is desperate. "I just need to be with you tonight."

Olivia puts her hand over the phone and looks at Rachel in a panic. "How do I say no to that?" she whispers.

Rachel shakes her head. "You don't."

Olivia turns her attention back to Ethan. "Okay, why don't you come by my place after work? I'm making spaghetti for dinner tonight. Then we can watch a movie and chill for a bit."

Ethan's shoulders relax as relief washes over him. "I think that sounds wonderful. Is 6 p.m. okay?"

"That's fine, I'll see you then." She hangs up the phone, panic still evident on her face.

Rachel finds it humorous. "Oh my God, he's so adorable. You calm his inner turmoil?"

Olivia rolls her eyes. "You wouldn't believe some of the things he says. Sometimes I want to pinch him to see if he's real."

"And this is the man that you don't want to kiss?" Rachel shakes her head in disgust.

Olivia flashes her an angry look. "Stop giving me a hard time. I'm just trying to figure things out."

"Fine, but it seems to me that kissing is the best way to calm a man's inner turmoil."

Olivia stares at her not amused. "Go away." She points to the door.

"Okay, I'm going. But you don't have to worry about him putting the moves on you tonight. I've seen you eat spaghetti and it's definitely not a turn on." Rachel smiles as she closes the door behind her. Olivia groans, realizing that she has a point.

Chapter Twenty

When she gets home, Olivia changes into a pair of casual shorts and pulls on a bright red T-shirt, hoping that it'll disguise any spaghetti sauce that she might slop on herself. Bare footed, she heads to the kitchen to start dinner.

When she answers the knock on the door, she finds Ethan standing there, looking extremely fuckable. The faint aroma of his cologne lingers around him and she inhales deeply. She blushes as she remembers every hard line and edge to the muscles on his chest and the dark ink of his tattoo. She tries smiling to hide her nervousness. It's a response she still doesn't understand, since this is a man she's already been extremely intimate with. It frightens her that he makes her feel so off-balance.

"Dinner smells great!" Ethan hands her a bottle of red wine and follows her into the kitchen. "What can I help with?"

Olivia opens the wine and pours a glass, hoping it will help calm her nerves. "Nothing, dinner is ready and the table is set." She dishes him up a hearty helping and hands him the plate. She's heard Rachel complain many times about his voracious appetite. She's pretty sure that doesn't just apply to meals.

Olivia sits across from him at the table. She needs to give herself some space, so she can stop thinking about his hard body pressed against her.

"This is delicious." Ethan twirls his pasta around his fork, getting it to his mouth in an expert manner every time.

Olivia tries to focus on dinner, but all she can think about is the feel of his strong warm hands on her skin. Nervously, she tries to eat without making a mess of herself. So far so good. Finishing her glass of wine, she immediately lifts the bottle and refills her glass. She relaxes, starting to get a little buzz. "So, tell me about your day."

Ethan wipes his mouth on a napkin, "It was miserable, really. Are you sure you want to ruin such a wonderful dinner with the details?"

Olivia smiles. "I'm all ears." Twirling the last bit of her spaghetti, she lifts her fork to her mouth. She thinks she's almost home free when it suddenly slips off her fork and lands on her chest. Using a napkin she quickly tries to wipe the spaghetti sauce that's about to run down between her breasts. When she glances over at Ethan, he's smirking.

"I could help you with that."

Olivia considers his offer, knowing what he has in mind. If he touches her right now, even playfully, dinner would be over. She can't deny the tingling that's been rushing through her body since the moment he stepped through the door. "Thanks, but I've got it. Maybe one day I'll get through a meal without wearing it," she pouts. "Please tell me about your day."

Having finished with his dinner, Ethan takes a deep breath and puts his fork down. "Did you ever have one of those days that's horrible from the minute you opened your eyes?"

Olivia nods. "Unfortunately, yes."

"Well, today was like that for me. It started off with my disciplinary hearing with the football… err… soccer association."

"Because you got a red card for fighting?"

"Yup."

"And?"

"I received a three game suspension."

"I'm so sorry."

"My own fault. I should have controlled my temper." He shrugs. "Then, we lost a huge account that I thought we had in the bag." Picking up his wine, he takes his first small sip. "I don't like losing business."

"Do you know why you lost it?" She starts to clear the table while he talks.

"Money. They received a quote from another company that came in significantly less than ours. We tried to explain to them that the other company was under quoting the charges. Once they've signed on the dotted line, they'll be told that they need to pay additional costs for any design changes. It'll end up costing them well over what our quote is, all-inclusive. But we weren't successful in convincing them."

"That must be extremely frustrating. I run into that all the time in our business, too. Other companies sell bare bones software. The business installs it and finds that it doesn't quite fit their needs. Then, they're charged an arm and a leg for consultants to come up with solutions and $700 a day for tech support to install any upgrades or changes they need. We don't do that at Dunn and McLennan. Our prices are higher out of the gate, but we provide all the other services free of charge, until our client has a product they're happy with." Standing tall, she announces proudly, "That's MY specialty."

"I'm sure that's not your only specialty." Ethan flashes her that boyish grin that leaves her speechless and blushing. Getting to his feet, very pleased with himself, he clears the rest of the table and heads into the kitchen. Olivia stands at the doorway watching in awe, as Ethan fills the sink with soapy water and begins to wash the dishes.

"I'm so sorry about your business deal, Ethan." Moving to his side, she picks up a dishtowel. "Hopefully my spaghetti dinner and the wine helped to ease the pain."

Ethan rinses a plate and hands it to her. "Oh, that's not even the half of it."

"Oh no! There's more?" She puts the last dish in the cupboard and motions to toward the living room. "Come on then, tell me about the rest." Picking up both glasses of wine, Olivia heads to the couch. Ethan follows, with his hand on the small of her back. Sitting beside her, he takes his wine out of her hand and takes a sip before placing it down on coffee table.

"I had to call my father's office today," he begins.

Olivia wrinkles her nose, not fully understanding how that contributed to his bad day.

Ethan rubs his hand over his face, trying to figure out where to begin. "Right, so it's a long story but I'll try to give you the short version. I told you that when I finally started making money, I helped my father's business out financially."

"Yes, I remember." Olivia nods and starts to feel a little light headed. Maybe this wine is going down a little too smoothly.

"Well, I did that by negotiating a partnership. I paid him to become part owner of the business. In doing so, I negotiated fifty-one percent of the business, giving myself controlling interest."

"Okay, I understand so far." Olivia tries hard to follow, not wanting to let on that she has a fuzzy wine brain.

"About a year and a half ago I ran into an old friend I went to medical school with, Dave Cameron. He went on to finish medical school and become an obstetrician. He specializes in premature births and high risk pregnancies."

Olivia downs her last mouthful of wine and puts the empty glass on the coffee table beside his. Grinning, Ethan dumps what's left of his wine into her glass.

"Are you trying to get me drunk?" It's already extremely difficult not to think about his naked body. If she keeps drinking, she won't be held responsible for her own actions.

"Not at all. Don't drink it if you don't want to."

His charming smile rockets her *warm and fuzzy* feelings into *hot and bothered*.

"Like that will ever happen," she laughs, "Carry on. You were telling me about your friend."

"Dave and I got talking. He was telling me that he had approached a small company to develop a piece of equipment for him. It would have the capabilities to provide the obstetrician with the ability to monitor everything, instantly: providing trauma and resuscitative care, eliminating delay times in those precious few moments after the birth. It could possibly save the lives of hundreds of newborns in distress."

"It sounds wonderful." Olivia finds his passion for this subject extremely appealing. She understands why it's so important to him. Technology like that could possibly have saved his sister.

"Yes, I thought so, too. And so, against my father's wishes, I began the acquisition of this small company so I could gain the rights to the design and take over the project. We call it Artemis."

"Artemis? After the Greek goddess?"

"Very good, Miss James, I'm impressed. I like that she's the twin sister of Apollo. She's been referred to as the goddess of many things, but the fact that she was considered by many to be the goddess of childbirth... well, that kind of sealed the deal for me."

"So what happened today with your father that upset you?" She reaches over and touches his hand, finding the warmth of his skin enticing.

Ethan suddenly feels guilty for putting such a dim light on the evening. "I'm sorry. I shouldn't be dumping all this mess on you."

Feeling sympathetic, Olivia brushes her hand along his cheek. Ethan relaxes, gently nuzzling his face against it, soothing himself.

"Ethan, I want to help. You need someone to talk to."

Since the first day he saw her, Ethan has had thoughts about Olivia James that make his dick hard: thoughts of physical pleasure. Today, when he was feeling stressed, all he could think about was being comforted in her arms and surrounded by her softness. He doesn't need just *someone* to talk to; he needs *her*. "My father's office in Ireland called me today. They've been talking about this project amongst themselves. It was delayed because of some design problems. Now they've decided to put the entire project on the back burner."

"Oh, that's too bad. But certainly, they've given it a lot of thought. They must feel it's the right decision."

Ethan tenses, and raises his voice, "You don't understand. Failing is not an option. Not on this project! Not on anything that I do. I *cannot* fail."

"Okay, so step away from it for a few weeks. Then, take a look at it again with fresh eyes." She tries to soothe him, gently stroking her fingertips across the back of his hand. "Maybe hire an outside consultant to come in and review everything. Scott's a brilliant engineer, have you thought about having him take a look at it?"

"That's a brilliant idea." Is it really that simple? He's been stressing about it all day long, and the solution comes from a beautiful woman no more than a foot away. Sitting beside him on the couch, in bare feet and drinking red wine, she looks pretty damn alluring. *Take a deep breath; you promised her you wanted nothing from her tonight.* That was before she touched his hand and before she stroked his cheek. Her perfume smells so sweet, flowery, and feminine. There goes his dick again.

"Come here." She holds open her arms, for him to nuzzle in for a hug.

That's not going to help at all, but he takes full advantage of the opportunity to get closer to her.

Olivia pulls him into her arms, squeezing tightly. The tension leaves his shoulders when he leans his head against her chest. Lightly pressing his lips against the bare skin he sighs, "Do you know what the worst part about that call was?"

"No, what?" She rakes her fingers through his hair, making his dick twitch.

"After I got off the phone with my father, that bloody Irish Jiminy Cricket chirped in my ear all morning.

"Ah, and what words of wisdom did John have for you?" She sensed from the moment that she met John that he wasn't just a friend but also Ethan's outer conscience.

He smiles at her acknowledgement. She's undoubtedly the brightest woman he's ever met. "When they said they were going to suspend the project I got angry and... well, I pulled rank. I told them that they would continue with their work until I had a chance to review the files." He looks at Olivia feeling a little embarrassed. "John feels that even though I have controlling interest in the company, that it's still my father's company and that it would help our relationship some, if I let him run the business and stopped overruling him."

"I see. Sounds like good advice to me. You and your father don't get along?"

Ethan shakes his head. "No, we had a falling out a few months ago. He's barely spoken to me since."

"Oh, I'm sorry." Olivia takes a deep breath. "Well, you sure have had a miserable day, Mr. O'Connell. Tell me what you need? How can I help make it better?"

"Just being here with you makes it better."

She smiles. Pleased that she's discovering that there's so much more to this man than she ever thought possible.

Suddenly Ethan sits straight up, pulling himself away from her, a wicked grin curling on his lips. "There is one thing you can help me with."

She takes another large mouthful of wine. "What's that?"

"It seems that you've been withholding orgasms. Maybe you can help me understand why."

Olivia's stomach jumps up into her chest, as if she's on a roller coaster that's reached the highest peak and is plummeting down the other side. Ethan doesn't take his eyes off her and she can feel them searing right through her.

"You didn't think that I would be that intimate with you and not notice? I felt it. You were almost there, both times, and then for some reason you denied me. Then you lied to me about it, and I want to know why."

"I didn't deny you, I mean… I didn't mean to." Her face turns beet red as the wine takes hold of her tongue and she can't get her thoughts out.

"So you're admitting that you lied to me?"

Feeling ashamed, Olivia lowers her eyes. "Are we really having this conversation?"

Ethan's tone changes, placing his finger under her chin; he guides her eyes back to his. "Yes. Answer me. Why did you chase away your orgasm?"

Don't let him intimidate you, John said. Is he for real? Ethan can sense submissive all over her. Damn it, if he hasn't already figured out that she'll respond to his command.

Finding a moment of bravery, she locks her gaze to his. "I don't know. I wanted to. I… I just can't."

"Yes, you can." He doesn't blink.

"NO… I can't. I start to get too… freaked out," she continues to argue. Reaching over and picking up the glass of wine, she dashes the remaining contents down in one gulp.

Taking the empty glass out of her hand, he puts it on the table. "You can." His voice gets softer, as he lifts her hand to his mouth, pressing his lips against it. "Lie down with me," he coaxes.

This is one of those times that Ethan is grateful that Reese insisted that he learn how to be a responsible Dom: more importantly, how to look after the submissive in his care. He'll show Olivia how to stop fighting, give up control, and just *feel.*

Chapter Twenty-One

Olivia stares at him for quite some time, considering what he's asking. Feeling woozie from the wine, she lays down, turning her body away from him. She rests her head on his arm, feeling the warmth of his chest against her back.

The summer sun is starting to set, leaving the room in darkness. Wrapping his arms around her, he pulls her closer, causing her to panic. "Ethan, I'm just starting my period."

"Are you bleeding yet?" Adjusting his position, he tries to make them both more comfortable.

"No. But…"

"Shhh. It's okay, Olivia. I won't fuck you."

"You won't?" she asks confused.

"It wouldn't bother me at all, but no, not if you're not comfortable with it. I don't need to in order to show you that you're capable of having mind-blowing orgasms. Do you trust me?"

"I have no idea why, but yes, completely." Dear God, what is he going to do? An electric charge zips through her blood stream as she thinks about all possibilities.

"Good. Let's just relax." Relax? Jesus, he's almost going out of his mind being this close to her. How the ever-loving-hell is he going to control himself? His entire body is already thrumming with excitement.

Olivia can't help but feel nervous. "I'm trying. You'd think all that wine would have helped." This whole *'don't let him intimate you'* thing just doesn't seem to work for her.

Ethan moves his mouth to the side of her ear and whispers, "Let me help you then. We'll do it together. Put everything out of your mind. There's absolutely nothing in this world but *you* and *me*. The only thing you're going to think about, for the next little while, is *us*. Do you understand?"

"Yes," she exhales a very long breath in anticipation.

"Good, put everything else out of your mind. Do you feel me behind you? Can you feel the rise and fall of my chest as I breathe?"

"Yes." That's not all she can feel. His growing erection presses against her back, reminding her of how large that impressive package really is. *Oh my!*

Ethan rewards her with a tender kiss on the shoulder. "I want us to breathe in together as one. Can you do that? Can you match your breathing to mine?"

"Yes." She concentrates on the movement of his chest and matches the rhythm.

He trails tender kisses across her shoulder and up her neck. When he breathes heavily into her ear, Olivia begins to crave more of his touch. Only Ethan O'Connell can make something as simple as breathing, feel so erotic.

"Nothing but you and me. And *we* are now *one*," he whispers.

"Yes," Olivia starts to feel squirmy. She knows that she's supposed to '*be relaxed*,' but all she can think about, right now, is forcing her body against his and letting him explore his desires.

"What things are you noticing, right now?"

"I can smell your cologne." *and I notice how hard your dick is!*

"Do you know why I wear cologne?"

"For me?"

"Clever girl. You're catching on. I wear this cologne for you."

His strong arms wrap around her, holding her tightly and making her feel safe. Olivia can see nothing in the darkened room, but the sound of his voice soothes her.

"Every time you smell it, I want you to be reminded of where I have touched you, and how I've made you feel."

Olivia clenches involuntarily, trying to relieve the throbbing ache that's building between her legs.

Ethan moves his hand under her t-shirt, taking her breast in hand. No longer able to contain herself, she pushes her hips back against him.

Ethan moves his mouth against her ear and in a deep primal growl, he warns her, "Be still." He's having a difficult time trying to keep *himself* calm. If she keeps rubbing her ass against his dick, he'll lose it for sure.

"I'm trying." She wiggles restlessly, needing a firmer hand on her breast.

"You have the most beautiful breasts I've ever seen. Thinking about them makes my cock hard. Do you like it when I touch them like this?" Firmly pinching the sensitive nub, he twists. The sensation ripples through her body. She tries to match his breathing, but her heart is pounding in her chest like a jackhammer.

"Yes, please. More!" Twisting her body, she tries to encourage him further. When he refuses to move his large hand to caress her breasts, she whimpers and clenches her legs together, trying to soothe the ache there.

Ethan grins as she struggles. "Woman, I said keep still. Is there something that you need?"

"Yes," she lets out an extremely edgy, frustrated breath.

"Then concentrate on your breathing, Baby." His masculine tone is never harsher than a whisper. Nuzzling his cheek against the back of her head, he soothes her; trying to keep her focused on him. "What do you want?"

"I want you to touch my body. Please, let me feel your skin against mine," she begs.

Grasping the bottom of her t-shirt, he lifts it over her head then discards it on the floor. "As you wish." Starting with the sensitive spot on the back of her shoulder, he kisses and nibbles. Skimming his lips across her body, he varies his attack, making it impossible for her to anticipate his touch.

He lets out a low growl as he unlatches her lace bra and slides it over her shoulder. Olivia shivers, as her bare breasts are exposed to the cool air.

Ethan tugs his shirt over his head and drops it on the floor. When he settles in behind her, she quickly tries to match his breathing again, fearing that she's about to freak out. This is about the time the PTSD induced panic sets in; when things get...*intense*. Determined not to be robbed of pleasure again, she forces herself to focus on his touch: his lips on her skin, his hands on her breasts, his hard chest pressed against her back. She begins to perspire, desire building within her like a generously stoked fire.

Adjusting his position, Ethan's hard, smooth chest skims across her back. When the light trace of hair that begins on his lower abs, brushes against her damp skin, it pushes her into sensory overload.

"I need you to touch me," she pleads, her nerves twitching; craving more.

Ethan grazes her jaw with his teeth, biting at her chin. Kissing his way toward her mouth, he sucks her bottom lip into his. "I need to touch you." Finally putting an end to her torment, he caresses her breast, kneading it beneath his palm. Grasping it firmly he gives the nipple a firm pinch, making her gasp. Abandoning it, he pushes his hand downward, skimming over her stomach. The soft, sensual touch of his fingertips makes her body vibrate with *want,* as he brushes them across the sensitive nerves there.

His torture is relentless. "Do you like the way I touch you?" He guides his hand down between her legs on the outside of her shorts and stops.

"Yes!" She arches her back, hungry for his touch.

Running his hand between her legs, he presses his palm firmly against her. He can tell even through her shorts that she's aroused and extremely wet.

Moaning, she maneuvers herself onto her back and opens her legs, giving him better access.

"But you want more...?"

"Yes, Please... Yes!"

Ethan hooks his thumbs on the waistband of her shorts and lowers them down, just below her thighs. She trembles when his hand slides across her bare skin and between her legs.

Her body arches involuntarily, pressing herself against his touch. "I'm sorry. I can't help it."

"You need to learn how to stay still, Baby." He begins to rub his fingers in gentle circles around her swelling sex. "It's my job to give you pleasure. Trust me to take you there."

When he finally lowers his mouth to her breast, he licks, sucks, and teases with his tongue, drawing from her a low sensual moan. He's not finished yet, not by any means.   He continues to torment her with hot breathy whispers in her ear while he masturbates her.

"Turn back onto your side, facing away from me."

"What? No... Ethan?"

He bites at her neck and presses his mouth against her shoulder, knowing it's her weakness. "Do it."

Olivia does as she's told, shifting to her side and allowing him to press his chest to her back.

He releases her just long enough to lower his shorts. Waiting for him to return his touch, Olivia feels like she's going to lose her mind.

Freed from his pants, Ethan rolls his hips, dragging his heavy cock along her, from the very swollen limit of her sensitive clit to her buttocks.

Olivia is overwhelmed by the feeling. She's never felt this good when anyone else has touched her south of the border. Ethan rubs himself over the sensitive nerves around her anus, occasionally pushing against it. He repeats his movements, stroking from clit to bottom. Threatening to enter her there, takes her arousal to a whole new level.

Olivia grips the cushions tightly with her hands, as his cock presses against her tight virgin bottom; pulsing and wanting.

Ethan moans. Just one firm push of his hips and he'd be in. It would be heaven, he's sure of it.

Olivia's eyes widen in panic. "Ethan!" Her hand swings toward him in an attempt to push him away.

He grabs her wrist and restrains her. "Shhhh."

"Ethan, I don't want to. I'm not comfortable with that."

He groans in disappointment, "Okay, I won't go there." Moving away from her, his cock drops heavily against his leg. "Not tonight, anyway... I'll pleasure you there another time." He nips at her ear playfully, but he's very serious about that promise.

Olivia struggles to swallow. She's never considered having anal sex. She's confused that his promise has ignited an excitement and curiosity in her.

Ethan slides his hand across her opening, moistening his fingers before returning to rub her sensitive clit in a gentle rhythm.

"Ohhh!" Olivia's breathing becomes shallow gasps.

He reads her body with expertise, knowing exactly when to slow his movements and when to press harder and faster. Within moments she's writhing against him, tender and swollen.

"Ethan," she whispers his name, as she feels her orgasm starting to build.

"You feel it now," he groans into her ear

"Yes!"

"Concentrate on the pleasure." Intending to finish business, he varies the pressure and technique until the sensation starts to overcome her.

After a sharp intake of breath, she calls out his name, "Ethan!" She arches her back and rocks her hips, trying to get more pressure from his hand against her clit. The head of his cock rubs against her from behind, sliding across sensitive nerves as he continues to move his body, meeting her needs.

"That's right, Baby. *This* is the only reason I exist. I live, only to bring you pleasure."

She meets her climax as her body shakes violently, convulsing against him. She repeatedly screams out his name in celebration of the pleasure he promised and skillfully delivered.

The sound of his name screamed from her lips, prompts his own release, spreading burst after burst of hot semen over the folds of her warm pussy.

Exhausted, Olivia forces weak muscles to turn and face him and leans against his chest.

Reeling from his own orgasm, Ethan folds his arms around her and pulls her close, pressing his lips to the top of her head. He's the first to break the silence,

"See… I told you that you could."

Olivia smiles, tracing her fingers over his tattoo, "I'd say… and then some. I need a shower."

Ethan props himself on his forearms and watches her cross the floor and up the stairs. Still craving her intimacy, he heads up the stairs, taking them two at a time.

Olivia stands under the warm spray of the shower, aware that he's there. When he pulls back the curtain and steps in, she turns to take a long look at his delicious muscular body. He grins at her boldness when her eyes drop to the large package between his legs. If her brain wasn't still numb from her orgasm, she would find this in violation of their agreement. But when he takes the body wash out of her hands and finishes lathering her up, she can't think of one single reason to protest. When he's done, she returns the favor leaving a trail of soapy bubbles over every inch of him.

Wrapped in each other's arms they stand under the soothing hot water, letting it wash the lather from their bodies. It's an epic fail in Olivia's attempt to restrict intimacy with him. Quite frankly… at the moment, she doesn't care.

Holding out his hand, Ethan helps her step out of the shower. As he holds out a towel and wraps it around her, she starts to smirk.

"You smell like flowers now."

Pulling her close, Ethan nuzzles his chin against the top of her head. Wanting to be close to her for a little longer, he breathes her in. "I really don't care."

What's going on here? This wasn't supposed to happen. Olivia's head takes over, making her pull away from him. "I should get dressed." She starts to back away and then remembers something. "Ethan."

He glances up as he towels the moisture off his well-toned body. Swallowing hard, she stops, staring as he rubs it across his muscled chest and then cinches it around his waist. *Lucky towel.* "I keep forgetting to tell you. You left clothes here when I was sick. I washed them and they're hanging in the closet in the spare room."

He nods, pretending not to be frustrated by the distance she keeps trying to put between them.

When Olivia comes out of her bedroom, she can hear Ethan in the kitchen. Stopping midway down the stairs, she watches him wash the wine glasses. Singing an upbeat and happy song while he works, he's unaware that she's returned.

Her eyes follow the thick grey material of his sweatshirt along his broad muscular shoulders. At their widest point, his powerful back begins to narrow downward, ending at a very trim waist. The elastic of his sweat pants hold snuggly at his hips, the pale grey fleece clings seductively over a round firm ass, perfectly showcased by his powerful, athletic thighs.

Olivia sits on one of the steps and watches him, her heart throbbing. Closing her eyes for a moment, she takes a deep breath and whispers to herself, "I definitely must be dreaming."

Drying his hands on the towel, he turns to find her sitting there watching him. He stops singing, wondering what she's thinking.

"It's getting late, I should get going." He gives her that charming boyish grin that Olivia's certain gets him laid, A LOT.

"Okay" She gets to her feet and follows him. Here they are again, standing at the top of the stairs to the back door, feeling uncomfortable. Why is it so awkward saying goodbye? She doesn't know if she should hug him or shake his hand. Maybe neither? This agreement was supposed to keep things simple, but in a way, it's made things so much more complicated.

Ethan doesn't hesitate; he wraps his arms around her in a snug embrace. "Thank you, for keeping me company tonight."

She smiles, feeling relieved that he took the lead. "I hope you feel better now."

"That would be a good assessment." He grins at the way her face turns red. "Listen, Olivia… I have a really busy weekend and the following week is booked solid with appointments for the grand opening of the club. I'm not sure how much time I'll have for us."

"That's okay. You don't have to spend any time with me. You have important things to look after. I understand." She has no right to be disappointed after setting the terms of her own agreement, but she is and she doesn't hide it well.

Frowning, he brings his hand to the side of her cheek, rubbing his thumb across her bottom lip, "Don't pout, it's killing me. I just meant that if you call me and I don't answer right away, it's because I'm busy. I just didn't want you to think I'm avoiding you."

"Oh." She blushes.

"Next weekend, I'm all yours. I promise." Ethan is defenseless against her glowing radiance. When her heart dances in her chest, her eyes sparkle like starlight. She bites her lip trying to hide her demure smile. She's so beautiful that he almost forgets to breathe. "Jesus, stop looking at me like that or, period or not, I'm coming back in there to fuck you."

Leaning forward, his lips skim softly against hers before she pulls away. He growls in frustration, "Fucking agreement." Shaking his head, he makes his way down the stairs. "I'll try to find time to see you before next Friday, if I can."

Something stops him. He turns to watch her walk down the stairs. Stopping on the bottom step, she puts them at the same eye level. Taking a step toward her, Ethan looks her over from head to toe, admiring her body. "I can't believe the things I put up with so I can be with you, Miss James. You're going to drive me completely insane. I know it."

"Good night, Ethan," she whispers, reaching for him. Running her fingers through his hair, she smoothes out the parts that are still sticking up from his towel drying.

Grabbing her hand, he gives her a warning, "Stop, I'm not joking. If you keep touching me, I **will** take you straight back upstairs. Only this time, you may be punished for teasing me."

Yes, please! "Okay I'm sorry, you better go." She frowns.

Stepping out the doorway, he mutters things she can't make out in his Irish accent. When he's out of site, she steps back inside, locking the door behind her. Leaning against it, she takes a deep breath. A smile spreads across her face from ear to ear. Putting her hand over her heart, she feels it beat loud and happy. She can't remember the last time she felt so full of joy. That's a good thing right? So then, why does the feeling terrify her?

Chapter Twenty-Two

Olivia spends the rest of the weekend on the couch with a hot water bottle and a large bottle of extra strength Midol. Her contact with Ethan has been minimal; other than the few times he's texted to let her know that he's thinking of her. If the truth were told, she's somewhat glad that his busy schedule has given her a break, right now. She's feeling bloated, cranky, and not good company at all. By Sunday night, she's terribly lonely. After making herself a cup of tea, she curls up on the couch and calls her sister.

"Hello."

"Hi! It's me... just checking in."

"Hi! How are you feeling?"

"I'm doing much better, except I've got my period," Olivia complains.

"Ew. Yuck. That's the one thing about being pregnant. I didn't miss that at all."

"How is everything there? Are Rick and the kids okay?"

"Yes, everyone is just fine."

"Good! I haven't heard from you for a while."

"Well, I called to check on you a few weeks ago but you were sick. I talked to your friend."

"Oh? Rachel didn't tell me you called." She's surprised that it would slip Rachel's mind.

"It wasn't Rachel I spoke with. It was Ethan." Megan struggles to bite her tongue, determined not to pry but busting at the seams to know what's going on.

"Oh." Olivia doesn't know why, but she feels a little embarrassed.

"I called at least ten times. I tried your cell phone and the house phone. He finally answered your cell and apologized, saying that he wasn't quite sure who I was. You were so out of it he had to ask you several times before you actually told him."

"Is that all he said?" Olivia wonders just how much her sister knows.

"Pretty much. He said that you had been very ill, but that he was staying with you until you were well and that I shouldn't worry."

"Oh."

"It seemed that you were in good hands." Megan is getting suspicious. Why isn't her sister elaborating on anything?

"Yes. I really was."

"I don't recall you mentioning that he's Irish."

"I probably didn't," Olivia laughs.

"What is it about men with accents?" Megan muses as she lets out a dreamy sigh.

"I know right?"

"The last time we talked, you were feeling a little conflicted about him. Have you worked it out?"

"Well... kind of."

There's something in her voice that only a sister would notice. "Oh my God! You slept with him."

Olivia gets defensive and she's not sure why, "Only twice... but it was on the same day, so it really only counts as once." How ridiculous is that logic?

Olivia hears the creak of the screen door hinge. She knows that Megan has taken the phone outside for privacy.

"I knew it!"

"It really sucks that I can't hide anything from you, do you know that?" Frustration strains Olivia's voice.

"And yet... you still try. So the big question is... are you okay?"

"Yes, I'm fine. It's just a casual relationship. You know? Friends with benefits kind of thing."

"Oh."

"You sound disappointed."

"Sorry. It's just that when I talked to him, he spoke of you with such adoration and caring, that I kind of envisioned him in a more *significant* role."

There's dead silence on the phone and Megan knows there's much more to the story.

"Olivia?"

"Yes?"

"What's really going on?"

She isn't even going to bother trying to deny it. There'd be no point. Megan has always been able to tell when Olivia's world is a little off skew. "I don't know Meg. I feel like I'm ready to move forward, but something keeps stopping me."

"Well, maybe you need to cleanse your chakra. Let all the negative energy drain from your body. You know? Make room for more positive things."

"I think I'm beyond chakra cleaning. Truth is that there's just something about him, something familiar, like I've known him forever. He makes me feel things I never thought I'd feel again... and it's wonderful and exhilarating and then... I panic."

"Hmmm. Sounds exciting and confusing at the same time. So your thoughts are that you'll keep telling yourself that it's just a physical thing, so you won't fall in love with him?"

"Yes! I'm so glad you understand. Rachel thinks I'm nuts, and I was beginning to wonder if she's right."

"So, I take it Ethan is okay with this arrangement then?"

"I think he might be interested in more, but this is all I can offer him, right now."

"Well, it sounds like you are controlling the things you need. I can't really object as long as you feel safe and he treats you well." Megan will make every effort to support her little sister. She has to, now that she's the matriarch of the family.

"And that's why you are my favorite sister!"

"I'm your only sister," she says seriously.

Olivia fights the urge to laugh. "Yes, Megan, I know. It was a joke. Geez... maybe the next time you clean your chakra you should knock some cobwebs off your sense of humor."

"Very funny. When are you coming to visit? The kids ask to see you all the time."

"I'm not really sure. I'm pretty busy at work, right now, and I have some bills I need to pay off. I'll try to figure something out, I promise."

For Olivia, Monday was a day of irrational mood swings and an extreme intolerance to stupid people. She was glad to see it end. Hopefully, her mood today will be a little more pleasant. She opens the blinds and welcomes in the bright morning sunlight. Suddenly she's startled by a loud thud against her office window. Peeking between the slats, she sees nothing out of the ordinary. She returns to her work, engaged in the paperwork in front of her, when there's another loud thud. Olivia opens the blinds to see the little green bird, pecking at the ground for food. It turns and looks at her, its head twisting in jerky robotic movements, and then taking flight, it lands on the branches of the bush outside Olivia's window. It stares at the glass, as if it knows that Olivia is watching. Its tiny wings begin flutter and it hovers, a few inches above the branches before flying forward, straight into the glass.

Olivia jumps and covers her mouth. "Oh my Gosh!" Leaning forward, she looks for it on the ground, fearing that it couldn't possibly have survived such a collision. When it suddenly reappears, she grabs her phone and tries to take a picture. Again, it flies forward hitting the glass a third time. Frightened that it's going to kill itself, Olivia takes off running down the hall and out the front door.

"Shoo!" she yells, flailing her arms. The little green bird sits on the bush, unafraid. "You're the strangest little bird," she whispers, snapping a picture with her phone.

On her way home, Olivia notices Noah's car still outside his office and decides to stop in to see him. He hasn't talked to her since the soccer game. She can use the picture of the little green bird as an excuse to see him. The waiting room is empty. The small space, where the receptionist would normally sit is in darkness. "Hello?" she calls out.

Noah's head pops out of a doorway at the end of the hall, grinning when he sees her. "Hey! Come in."

The smell of antiseptic is so strong it leaves a taste in the back of her throat. "Hi! You're here late."

"I had a few surgeries today and was just checking to make sure everyone was doing well, before I left."

Olivia feels an unpleasant awkwardness between them that she desperately wants to go away. "Noah… are *we* okay?" She frowns at him. "I feel bad about what happened at soccer."

"I can't believe you left with him." Noah turns to lean against the counter and crosses his arms, looking for an explanation.

"I know, I know. I should have stayed with you."

"So why didn't you then?"

Shrugging, she sits down on the nearby stool, using her feet to make it roll on its casters back and forth across the floor. "I really don't know." She plays with all the knobs and gadgets on the equipment around her, avoiding his stare.

"Do you like that guy?" He sure as hell hopes not.

"He's okay," she says with indifference, trying to play it down.

It doesn't work. Noah sees right through her. "Olivia, that guy is dangerous." He quickly turns to organize vials of medication on the counter, trying to hide his frustration.

"He won't hurt me." It's beginning to bother her that she always seems to be defending him.

Noah shakes his head and ignores her statement. "We're going to be getting some thunderstorms at the end of the week. Do you have enough medication?" He glances over at her and waits for her reply.

"Yes, but I'm almost out."

"Okay, you let me know when you need more and I'll look after it."

Olivia remembers the picture. Now would be a really good time to change the subject. "Hey, I know this is a silly question to ask a veterinarian, but how much do you know about birds?"

He furrows his brow. "What kind of birds?"

"Little, green, stalker birds."

Noah tilts his head to the side and looks at her strangely. "Okay, you've lost me."

She laughs, "There's a green bird that I see outside my office window all the time. And now... I see the same bird in my backyard frequently. It's almost as if it follows me. Do birds do that?"

"I've never heard of anything like that. Are you sure it's the same bird?"

"I think so." She scrolls through her phone looking for the picture. "I've never seen a bird like it before. Look." She hands him her phone. "The markings on its chest are pretty unique."

"Huh. I don't recognize it, either." He hands her back her phone. "I'll tell you what, email me the picture and when I get a chance I'll do some research for you."

"Sweet!" She logs into email from her phone and attaches the photo. "Done!"

The continual barking and whining from the back room is starting to get on her nerves. "I don't know how you can listen to that all day."

"I guess I've learned to tune it out."

"Well, it's giving me a headache."

Leaning his back against the counter he crosses his feet at the ankle and grins. "Let's go out for dinner."

Olivia is surprised. "Tonight?"

"Yes, right now. Let's go to Headwaters for dinner, one last time before it changes."

"It's not really changing that much, Noah."

"Yes, it is. The new 'owner' is changing the name to 'Ireland's.' I hate it."

"No, I think you just hate the new owner." She crosses her arms in front of her and leans her head to the side.

"Yup, that's true. So how about it?" He grins from ear to ear, giving her a charming smile.

Olivia takes a good long look at her friend. Tall, dark and handsome, what girl wouldn't want to spend an evening with him? It wasn't that long ago, that she asked him for *more* and now he's finally asking her to dinner. Her mind flashes quickly to Ethan. He's too busy to spend time with her, so what's to stop her from spending time with Noah? Maybe the fact that Ethan will blow a gasket, when he finds out. *Sucks to be him.*

"Well, I don't know. Are you planning on wearing that white lab coat?" She smiles.

"Only if it turns you on." He gives her a cheeky grin. One that would have made her tingle a few weeks ago. Boy, have things have changed since then.

"No, I'm quite certain that wearing it to dinner could be a deal breaker."

"Okay, I'll take it off." He undoes it while she watches and smirks. "Anything else you want me to take off?" Maybe there's still a chance for him to get her into bed.

"Why, Mr. Thompson! Your unexpected, amorous behavior is making me blush."

Noah grins. "Let's go before I try to talk you into staying here and ordering in." He wishes he had that idea several minutes ago; then he wouldn't have to share her with anybody.

At the restaurant, Olivia and Noah sit on opposite sides of one of the newly renovated booths. They pick off each other's plates, just as they've done for years. He has to admit that the new menu is definitely an improvement. As the bar starts to fill up, the atmosphere becomes a little less quaint and the music gets louder.

Recognizing one of the girls at the bar, Olivia strains her neck trying to get a better look. Without a doubt, it's Hannah, receptionist extraordinaire at Aurora Technologies. *Damn!* She looks even better in the evening than she does during the day. How is that even possible? Olivia wonders.

Noah reaches over and touches her hand to get her attention over the noise. "Do you want to get out of here?"

Hell yes! Quick before she's seen. "Yes. I need to go to the ladies room first."

Standing in front of the bathroom mirror, she fixes her hair; pretending she doesn't notice when Hannah walks in and plants herself beside her at the counter. *Crap!* Taking her lipstick out of her purse, Hannah runs it smoothly across her bright red, voluptuous lips and stares at Olivia in the mirror. Washing her hands, Olivia tries to avoid eye contact.

"Where do I know you from?" Hannah asks when Olivia finally lifts her head.

Olivia dries her hands. "I was at your work not that long ago. I'm a friend of Ethan O'Connell's."

Hannah pretends she doesn't remember and then her expression changes. "Right, I remember now. I see you've moved on. Good for you!"

Olivia is confused. "Excuse me?"

"The man in the restaurant, I assume he's your date." She gives her a pity frown. "It's for the best, honey. You're not Ethan's type anyway." She tries to hide her insidious intent behind a polite smile.

Olivia's growing tension conveys a flippant tone, "Enlighten me… just what exactly is Ethan's *type?*"

"Oh, I'm sorry. I've offended you. I'm just saying that Ethan spends his time with girls who, you know… look after themselves." She wrinkles her nose, feeling obligated to let Olivia know she falls short of the standards.

Olivia's face turns red. Had this conversation taken place yesterday, no amount of extra strength Midol would've saved Hannah from a PMS fueled ass kicking. She hates the way she allows her to zero in on her insecurities, hacking away at them, making her feel unworthy and defeated. "Like you?"

"Yes…like me. I'm sure you sensed the sexual tension between us." Hannah puckers her lips and dabs at the edges to remove a few smears.

"So, there's something going on between you two, then?" Olivia's emotions swing dangerously between jealousy and anger.

"I certainly couldn't tell you if there was. The company has strict policies about that." Hannah admires herself in the mirror, then picks up her purse, and heads for the door. Her skirt is so tight that she can barely move her legs. Turning, she smirks in Olivia's direction. "I can tell you one thing… I know how to keep a man like Ethan O'Connell happy."

Olivia almost forgets to breathe when the blonde glances over her shoulder on the way out the door and says, "Don't worry, sweetie, it's not too late for you to find a man. I could give you the number of my personal trainer and you can get to work on those hips."

Oh No! She didn't just go there? Olivia takes a moment to try to calm down before she heads back into the restaurant. When she gets back to the booth, Noah has already paid the bill and is waiting. He's confused by the sudden look of rage on her face.

"You okay?"

"No, I need to get the hell out of here."

"Okay, let's go." Giving her a concerned look, he ushers her to the door.

Olivia doesn't say much in the car on the way back to Noah's office. She's too busy overthinking everything. Despite Ethan's declaration that he doesn't sleep with his staff; she can't help but wonder if he's spent the past few days with Hannah.

When Noah pulls into the parking lot beside her car, Olivia doesn't move to leave. Turning off the key, he finally asks, "Are you going to tell me what happened at the restaurant?"

"No."

"Does it have anything to do with the blonde with the big boobs that followed you to the bathroom?" He tries not to chuckle.

Olivia crosses her arms in front of her. "She works with Ethan. She doesn't like me very much."

"So what happened? You looked like you wanted to rip her to pieces when you came out of there."

"I can't believe I let her get me that riled up. Stupid girl brain."

"Well, it was a nice dinner up until then. It would have been awesome, if the evening ended in a girl on girl death match in the parking lot. Even better, if you were fighting over me."

He finally makes her smile. "Very funny. I bet she fights like a girl. Nothing but scratching and hair pulling."

There's a quiet moment between them and Noah leans over with the clear intention of kissing her. She meets him half way, letting him press his lips against hers. She returns his kiss, reaching for him and running her fingers through his soft black hair. When he pulls away, Olivia feels nothing. For years, she would have given anything for his affection. Now, he's kissing her and she's void of the feelings she used to get. It's Ethan O'Connell's fault, no doubt about it.

Noah smoothes her hair behind her ear with his hand. "Olivia, I've thought about making love to you at least a thousand times over the years."

"Then why didn't you?" Peeking up at him through her lashes, she feels a little vulnerable talking about it.

"Because I was afraid it would ruin our friendship."

"You think it would get weird and awkward after?"

"I don't know, but what if it did? Your friendship means more to me than anything. I don't want to mess that up."

She smiles and nods her head. "I get it, it's not worth it."

"I really want to, though." He *really* wants to.

She lifts her hand to his cheek and smiles. Then, as men tend to do, he ruins a tender moment with an inappropriate thought.

"But feel free to pop over and give me a blow job anytime you want."

Olivia laughs aloud and searches her purse for her keys. Leaning over, she gives him a quick goodbye kiss. "Thank you for dinner. Let's get together again, soon."

Chapter Twenty-Three

Olivia lies on her back staring at the ceiling, unable to sleep. The conversation with Hannah plays repeatedly in her mind. She tries to convince herself that none of it's true. It's a good thing that her relationship with Ethan is only physical, or she might actually feel hurt. Oh, wait. She *is* hurt. Tormented actually. Hannah's words cut her like a knife aimed straight at her heart, leaving behind a jagged tear where trust, hope, and healing had only just begun. Now she feels them slipping away like the slow and constant drip of a leaky tap, taking with them what little self-esteem and confidence she had left.

Olivia rushes into her office, and answers the ringing phone, out of breath, "Good Morning. This is Olivia James."

"Good morning, Olivia James!"

She had almost forgotten how silky and sensual his voice sounds. It's a tone that he reserves only for her. It warms her to the core when she hears it, temporarily chasing away her uncertainty and the unpleasant thoughts from last night.

"Hey!"

"I have good news! I've found a place to live."

"Really?" She's curious. "How did you manage that when you're so busy?"

"Okay, so John found me a place to live," he chuckles.

The sound of his laughter is contagious and it makes her smile. "I thought we'd ruled out all the available apartments in town?"

"It's not an apartment. It's a house, just on the outskirts of town. It's a small little country home on a couple of acres of land and my only neighbors for miles are the four legged kind."

"It sounds lovely." She tries to imagine the type of home Ethan O'Connell would feel comfortable in.

"The place is vacant so I can get possession right away… but the only day the moving company is available to move my stuff there from storage is Saturday… and then there's all the utility hook up people on Friday."

She feels tightness in her chest. "You're blowing me off." There's no question, it's extremely clear.

"I'm sorry; John is going to be out of town for the weekend, so I need to be there."

"Don't they usually do utility hook ups during the day?"

"They said anytime between 8 a.m. and 8 p.m. Then, I need to go to the restaurant, at some point, to check on things there and close."

"Oh, I see." Her stomach churns into tight painful knots, as she imagines him and Hannah sneaking into the boardroom after hours for a little rendezvous.

Her reply makes him feel guilty. "I know I said I was all yours this weekend. I'm sorry."

She feels the weight of heavy, stone walls beginning to form around her, shielding her from the emotions. Protecting her from heartbreak. She had forgotten they were there, since she hadn't needed them until this moment. Once in place, they squeeze her fears and anxiety down to a place where they can be controlled, leaving her the ability to continue functioning with a calm and composed demeanor.

"We can still see each other. You can come by the house and spend time with me there."

"No, it's okay. I'll just see you Saturday night at the BBQ. If you're still going."

"Yes, I'll pick you up and we'll go together."

"No, I think I'd rather just meet you there."

Ethan senses something is wrong. "Liv?"

"Sorry, Ethan, I have another call, I have to go." She hangs up before he can say anything else. Standing perfectly still, her heart squeezes in her chest. What did she just do?

Cursing, he digs his phone out of his pocket and sends her a text.

From Ethan: We must have been disconnected because I'm sure you know that hanging up on me would make me extremely angry. I'll call you this evening, so we can finish our conversation.

When he looks up, John is standing at his desk and looking at him perplexed. "What?" His tone is clipped.

"I'm going to be busy this weekend?" John asks curiously.

"Yes." Ethan is now impatient and angry.

"Okay." This is news to him. "Where am I going to be?"

"You're going to be staying at a hotel downtown Toronto for the weekend."

"Are you going to tell me why, or are we going to keep playing this game?" John stares at him, not intimidated by his mood at all.

Glancing up at him, Ethan gathers up the papers he needs for his next meeting. "I have an appointment on Monday with someone from out of town, but the only flight they could get comes in Friday afternoon. I need you to keep them entertained all weekend. I've got plans."

"Okay. Who am I entertaining?" He's obviously going to make him drag it out of him. John is used to dealing with Ethan's habit of being uncooperative when he's agitated, but he's being particularly challenging today. A result he's certain is due to the phone call he just finished.

Ethan says her name as he passes, "Shannon Quinn."

John stands frozen at the desk.

Ethan waits impatiently at the door. "Let's go, old man! We're going to be late for our meeting."

John walks beside him, as he makes his way down the hall at a brisk pace. "Why is Shannon coming here for a meeting, Ethan?" He's eager to know what's really going on.

Ethan has been feeling terribly guilty for keeping his friend away from the woman he loves, for so long. He certainly wouldn't want word to get out that he has a soft spot for romance. If John insists on asking questions, he'll dodge and deny in order to protect his reputation of being a hardened executive.

"Stop complaining. Miss Quinn is the legal counsel overseeing my case. It's only appropriate that we meet in person, at least once. You need to keep her happily entertained and out of my way until Monday." Ethan stops walking and turns to face him, "Do you have a problem with that, John?"

John grins. "No, sir!"

"Good, I don't want to hear another word about it."

John continues at his side as he resumes his walk to the boardroom. "Thank you Ethan," he says discretely before they enter.

"Don't know what you're talking about." Ignoring John's smile he pushes the door open and steps inside.

Olivia has been on edge since receiving Ethan's text. Every time her phone rings, her stomach fills with nervous anxiety. She needs to find a way to deal with him and quick, not to mention come up with an explanation for her behavior.

Her appetite has been off all day, she's picking at a ham sandwich when he finally calls. Closing her eyes tightly, she gets control of her nervous stomach by the time she answers.

"Hi," she says nervously, not knowing if he's still angry.

"Hi, yourself. Is everything okay?"

"Yes, why wouldn't it be?" she asks calmly.

"You didn't seem yourself this afternoon." Ethan taps his pen on the desk in a restive manner.

"Everything's fine," she lies again, and he knows it.

"Can I explain to you about this weekend?" He desperately wants to tell her that John was not available because he arranged to have his girlfriend flown in for the weekend.

Her stomach begins to tighten and she struggles for a moment. "Ethan, there's really no need to explain. It's none of my business what you do and who you do it with."

"*Who?* What do you mean?" Ethan leans back in his chair, troubled by her lies and bothered by her statement.

"We aren't dating remember? We talked about that as part of our agreement." She doesn't mean for it to happen but her tone gets insolent, "I'm pretty sure you were there."

Ethan sits up in his chair. "Careful," he warns.

Olivia looks to the ceiling and closes her eyes. "I'm sorry, I didn't mean for it to sound like that."

"What did you mean, then?" He hears her sigh heavily through the phone.

"Just that, you don't have to feel bad about not spending time with me. We agreed that sometimes we would get together and have sex. I have no other expectations from you other than that." Her heart aches as she says it. *Lies! All Lies!* This isn't what she wants.

Ethan puts his pen down and tries to massage the tension out of his neck.

Olivia probably should have stopped talking at that point, but something spurs her on. "So, it's okay if you want to go out with other girls. It's perfectly acceptable under our current agreement."

Ethan's temper is starting to flare. "That's ridiculous!"

"Well… you can if you want to."

Ethan is beyond fed up with this agreement. He's on the edge of losing his mind, when there's a knock on his office door. "Olivia, I have to go now, I think it's best that we continue this discussion in person."

"Okay. I'll see you on Saturday, for sure." This time she waits for him to say goodbye before she hangs up.

Peeking through the side window of Ethan's office door, Hannah waits until he waves her in. She brings him a fresh pitcher of ice water with lemons, as she does every day and places it on the corner of his desk.

"Thanks," he says in a low voice, clearly stressed.

Hannah can't resist trying to engage him in conversation. She has something on her mind. "Girl trouble?" she asks, knowing full well that it is; compliments of her little chitchat last night.

Ethan sighs heavily, "How did you know?"

Hannah picks up the pitcher and pours him a glass. "Women's intuition."

Ethan opens up a little. "She's acting strange today, but I don't know why."

Hannah was hoping, when she came in, that she'd have the opportunity to have this discussion with him. "She seemed alright last night."

Ethan's brow creases. "Last night?"

"Yes, I ran into her at Headwaters last night. She was having dinner with a very handsome man."

It takes a moment to sink in, and then it occurs to him. The reason she's insisting that he date other women is that she's obviously dating other men. The thought leaves him feeling a little shaken.

Hannah stands at the side of his desk hoping to console him. "Ethan? Is everything okay?"

He rakes his fingers through his hair. "Yes, I'm fine. Will you excuse me please, Hannah. I have another conference call in a few minutes."

Hannah isn't disappointed. "Oh, of course." She turns to leave, knowing that she's planted a seed in his brain, and *mistrust* grows quickly.

"If you see John, please tell him I need him."

"Yes, I will." She closes the door behind her and turns to see John walking towards her. "He wants to see you," she says softly.

John notes the tension in her stride. "I take it he's not in a particularly good mood?"

She shakes her head no and keeps walking, concealing her smile until she's out of sight.

As John opens the door, an object that's launched across the room in anger, narrowly misses him. "Whoa! What the hell happened in the twenty minutes I was gone?"

"Call the gym and tell them I'm on the way down. Make sure there's somebody ready to spar." Ethan makes his way into the bathroom and changes.

"You're going for a few rounds of boxing… now?" John looks at his watch.

Ethan's jaw is clenched tight. "I need to punch something." The vein in his forehead is jumping. He slips on his black Converse high-tops and ties them tightly.

John raises an eyebrow. "Okay, I'll have Parker sit in on the meeting and give you an update in the morning." He pauses a moment. "Ethan… make sure you don't say stuff like that when Miss Quinn is here."

Ethan shoots him a look as he does up the zipper on his hoodie then shoulders past him into the hallway, leaving him without any further explanation.

Ethan is almost at the gym when John catches up with him. "It's your lucky day."

"What's going on?"

"There's no one at the gym to spar with, so you're stuck with me."

Ethan gives him a half a grin. "Are you sure you're up to it? You're kind of old."

John throws his head back in laughter. "Well, I guess we'll find out, won't we?"

Both men suit up and step into the ring. Moving around each other, they size each other up, but it's Ethan that takes the first swing. John steps back and avoids the blow. Frustrated, Ethan steps in and tries again. This time John blocks and counters with a hard shot to Ethan's stomach. Ethan pretends it was nothing, but the grunt he makes as the air is forced out of him tells a different story. "Is that the best you've got?"

John grins. "I'm just getting started, junior."

Ethan is all youth and power, unleashing one punch after another in a relentless assault. Despite his age, John is fast and is able to block or avoid most of them. John counters a few good shots of his own, landing a quick jab on Ethan's chin, forcing his head to jerk back. Stepping back, he gives Ethan a moment to recover. Ethan opens and closes his jaw, twisting his neck trying to realign everything. A heavy sweat now soaks his clothes and beads on his forehead under the protective headgear.

Ethan comes back at John hard, swinging at him wildly, with unrestrained power. John watches and responds. Ethan continues the same attack repeatedly and within minutes, his energy is spent. His arms, heavy and tired, slow in their assault. Waiting for the perfect moment John delivers one powerful shot that sends Ethan to the floor. HARD.

Offering Ethan his hand, John pulls him to his feet. "You need to learn to harness that power. Boxing isn't much different from soccer. You need to watch your opponent and get to know his habits, then wait patiently for a well-placed shot. Hitting hard and fast only tires you out."

Ethan says nothing. He's been taken to the proverbial woodshed, by a man ten years his senior. He can't deny that it was a well-taught lesson. "So what pissed you off? Or did you suddenly find your stapler offensive?" John unties his gloves, preparing to leave.

"Hannah said that Olivia was at the restaurant last night having dinner with another man."

John looks surprised. "Are you sure? I would be careful believing anything Hannah says. She does have an ulterior motive, after all." He moves to the corner and picks up both water bottles, and tosses one to Ethan.

"What do you mean?" Ethan squirts a generous amount of water in his mouth and then spits it out.

John picks up a towel and wipes the sweat off his face before looking at him in disbelief. "You're joking right? Hannah doesn't want Olivia around. She wants you for herself."

Ethan is surprised. "She does?"

John throws a towel at him. "Christ, how hard did I hit you?"

It's late by the time Ethan showers and walks to his car. His shoulders tense when he sees Eva Storm leaning against it, waiting. He sighs and makes a mental note to have a chat with security. She looks worried today; the kind and gentle expression morphed into a look of anguish and unrest. Unlocking the door with the remote, the blip echoes loudly through the empty space. Eva doesn't wait for him to acknowledge her. She needs to tell him something. "What are you waiting for, child? You need to tell her."

He knows that he should ignore her, but he engages her in conversation. Wrong thing to do with a stalker! "Tell who, what exactly?" He's just plain curious now.

"The one whose fingerprints are on your soul. You must tell her who you are."

A cool breeze blows past them and makes him shudder. Nervously, he looks around for the source of the draft. Eerie! Swinging his bag off his shoulder, he opens the back door to the Challenger and throws it in. When he turns to tell her that he thinks she's bat shit crazy… Yup, *vanished,* again.

Driving home to Dufferin County, he considers stopping at Olivia's and straightening things out. His mind is racing in several different directions; it's been such a strange day. Deciding that it's best to wait until he's not both mentally and physically exhausted, he drives home and finds Rachel sitting on the couch with a cup of tea.

She looks up when he comes in. "Hey."

"Can't sleep?" He puts his bag down on the floor.

She shakes her head no, looking lost and forlorn

"You and Scott still not seeing eye to eye on starting a family?"

Again, she shakes her head no. "I just wish I was as sure as he is that I'd make a good mother."

Ethan sits beside her. "Well, from what I've heard, every woman worries about that."

"I guess." She shrugs, taking a sip of tea and putting her mug down on the coffee table.

"I think you should trust Scott, Rach. He loves you very much and believes you would be a wonderful mother. I've only known you a short while, but I see the way that you care for your friends. And really… the only prerequisite you need to raise a child is the ability to love. You certainly have that."

His words are sincere, for the first time she doesn't feel like motherhood is an impossibility. "Thank you, Ethan. You're right." She relaxes a little and smiles. "So, you've been working late every night. Tough week?"

"Brutal, actually."

Rachel laughs, "Ha! You're lucky you haven't had to deal with Olivia this week. She's been absolutely impossible. I don't know why but she isn't eating. Something's bothering her."

"No kidding. I talked to her today and she hung up on me."

"No way!" It strikes her as kind of humorous, and she giggles, "Part PMS, part starvation."

Ethan suddenly feels agitated. "Someone told me that she was on a date with some guy last night."

Rachel is stunned "What? That's not possible."

"It's true; she was seen at my restaurant having dinner with a man. A very good looking man apparently." He finds it hard, even now, to think about it without feeling a jealous rage starting to brew.

Rachel is still a non-believer. "Ethan, there are only two men, besides yourself, that Olivia would trust enough to go out with. So, it could only have been either Scott or Noah. And Scott was working late with you last night." She pauses, feeling suspicious for a moment. "Wasn't he?"

Ethan reassures her, "Yes, he was. So, it was Noah, then." That doesn't make him feel any better.

Rachel gives him a sympathetic smile. "Hey, trust me. She's done with him."

"I don't get it, then why is she so determined to push me away?"

"She's frightened."

"Rachel, you have to tell me what this Sam guy did to her. Please," he begs.

Rachel sips her tea and thinks for a moment. "It's not really my story to tell, Ethan. However, I think you should know. Olivia had just broken up with someone and was feeling very vulnerable when Scott introduced her to Sam. He had just moved here from the city and had joined the soccer team. They hit it off right away. Olivia fell fast and hard. Things seemed great, and then I started noticing small marks and bruises on her arms and legs. One day she showed up with a split lip and black eye and a non-convincing story about falling."

Ethan listens without interrupting; thinking about what he would do to this man, if he ever crossed his path.

Rachel sighs, "I finally convinced her to leave him. She told him that night that she was breaking it off and… he snapped."

She chokes back the tears, trying to get the rest of the story out. Ethan passes her the box of tissues from the end table. "I found her the next day unconscious on her bed. He had hit her so hard that he split her head open. The mattress was so soaked with blood that I was afraid she was dead." She wipes her nose with the tissue. "We got her to the hospital and they came out to tell us that it took fourteen stitches to close the gash on her skull and that they were keeping her in an induced coma until the swelling went down. Other than that, she had a lot of bruises and a fractured rib, but they were confident she'd be okay." Rachel's tears start streaming down her cheek at an increased pace. Ethan's heart becomes heavy, feeling guilty that he's caused her this upset. "It wasn't until later that the doctor in the emergency department told me that there was overwhelming evidence that he had raped her."

"Jesus Christ!" Ethan can't focus his thoughts. His mind is racing in a million different directions: all different ways he's going to hunt this bastard down and murder him.

Rachel wipes her nose with the back of her hand and takes a deep breath in. "To this day, she denies it."

"What?" Ethan feels sick.

"She denies that he raped her. She says that it was consensual."

"Why would she do that?" It's an irrational thing to do and Ethan struggles to wrap his head around it.

"Scott thinks it's because she can't cope with it. Accepting that he raped her, I mean. The doctors diagnosed her with post traumatic stress disorder."

Ethan blows out a deep breath, "Wow!" Pressing his hands to his temples, he massages the twitching nerves.

Rachel pulls herself together. "I shouldn't have told you. You were so good for her and now you'll probably want nothing to do with her."

"Why would you say that?" Ethan is annoyed. Why does everyone think he's a heartless bastard?

"That's an awful lot of baggage to take on. No one would blame you, least of all Olivia. I think that's why she created your agreement. It gives her the protection she needs by keeping you from getting too close."

"I hate that fucking agreement." He rakes his fingers through his hair in frustration.

"Think of it as a castle wall that she's built around herself. She needs you to start climbing the wall to rescue her."

"If she wants to be rescued, why is she being so difficult?"

"I told you, because she's frightened. She's been hiding in that castle for three years and the world left her alone. You show up and start climbing the wall. You got dangerously close to the top, before she even knew what was happening. Now she's trying to regain control of her fortress by making you comply with the rules. She may not *want* to be rescued… but she *needs* to be."

"I think I understand."

Rachel purses her lips together. "Think of each rule as a section of the wall you need to climb. Each time you dissolve a rule you get closer to the top."

"I don't know, Rachel. She doesn't seem very flexible where the rules are concerned."

"Ah, but she'll give in to you. The minute she packed up and followed you to your car, after you punched Noah in the face…I knew. You're the one she needs. You're the one she wants." Rachel looks at Ethan and grins. "Something tells me that you know **exactly** how to handle her."

"Well, I can tell you one thing; I know exactly which rule is going to go first."

Chapter Twenty-Four

Ethan stands up to his knees in warm, salty ocean water. The force of the crashing waves hits the back of his knees, pushing him forward toward the shore. Holding his hand out, he waits for her to join him. Olivia stands on the beach, just out of reach of the water. She looks like a goddess under the golden glow of the midday sun, the ocean water reflecting in her eyes and making them sparkle. Removing her hairpins, she lets her hair fall loosely to her shoulders, allowing it to blow in the ocean breeze like a banner of silk.

Lifting her face to the sun, she breathes in the fresh ocean air. Holding her arms out at her sides, she lets the wind wash over her. Overwhelmed by her beauty, Ethan stands frozen where he is, incredibly at peace and very much in love. Leaving the water, he joins her on the sand, taking her in his arms and claiming her lips. Lifting her gently off the ground, he spins her, then presses his lips against hers again, before releasing her and letting her slide slowly down the length of his body. When her feet touch the ground, she raises her hands to the sides of his face, holding him as she returns his kiss with an unbridled passion.

As Ethan wakes, he can still feel the warmth of her lips on his. With the last few moments of fleeting sleep, he takes in one last breath of the comforting scent that he encounters only in his dreams. It's a mixture of the crisp ocean air and the sweet smell of her perfume. Now fully awake, he lays there for several minutes, his heart basking in the afterglow of her kiss.

Dressing for his day, he feels a heartbreaking emptiness. He hasn't seen Olivia in a week. What little contact they've had has been brief and indifferent. He thinks about it in the car on his way to the new house. Being away from her feels unnatural and he needs to see her today to make things right.

The garden walkway to the front door of the new house is lush and fragrant with flowering bushes and bright summer flowers. There's a small brown bunny peeking at him from its safe haven, underneath the front porch. Ethan knows already that he's going to love living here. He had a strange sense of déjà vu the first time he saw it. From the outside, its quaint cottage appearance hides the modern upgrades that have taken place inside. The previous owners took meticulous care in making sure that the interior renovations provided modern comforts and style, while maintaining the house's charm and character. It suits Ethan perfectly.

Flipping on the lights, he's glad to see that the electricity has already been switched on. Wandering from room to room, he imagines what it will look like with his stuff here. It's just after 10:30 a.m. when the technician arrives to hook up the Internet. Finally, he can get some work done. Setting up his laptop at the counter, he prepares to send Olivia an email.

To: OIivia James

Why aren't you eating?

Ethan O'Connell
SVP International Sales and Marketing
Aurora Technologies

Olivia sits at her desk and reads his email. Seriously? He hasn't spoken to her in two days and that's what he starts with?

To: Ethan O'Connell

Which one of your spies told you that? As if I didn't know.

Olivia James
Business Solutions Specialist
Dunn & McLellan IT Consulting

Ethan grins. Relieved that things seem to be back to normal.

To: Olivia James

You didn't answer my question

Olivia rolls her eyes, but a smile starts to form on her lips. Oh, how she's missed him. She wouldn't admit it to herself, until just now.

To: Ethan O'Connell

I'm not hungry

That's not a lie. She's had very little appetite since her chat with Hannah. It could be the thought of Ethan and Hannah together, or that Hannah suggested

Olivia was a little too thick around the middle. Either way, food has had no appeal to her.

To: Olivia James

You need to eat. You know this.

Gahhhh! He's going to drive her nuts!

To: Ethan O'Connell

Don't worry. There's still plenty of me to hold on to.

Ethan leans against the counter and reads her reply. Shaking his head, he mumbles under his breath.

To: Olivia James

I'm certain that I've told you before that I don't like it when you say stuff like that about yourself. You are beautiful. Now… please tell me that you brought a lunch today and that you intend to eat.

Olivia does the only thing she can do to settle his mind… lie.

To: Ethan O'Connell

Yes, I did and I do. Now, leave me alone I have work to do.

Ethan knows her a little too well. He has a hunch that she's not telling the truth. His phone rings and he answers it promptly, "O'Connell."

"This is the technician calling to confirm your installation for today. Is someone going to be home?"

"Yes."

"We'll be installing both your land line and your satellite. We'll be there sometime between 4 and 8."

"4 and 8? You can't narrow it down any further than that?"

"No sir. We have several installations booked for this afternoon."

"Okay, I'll be here," Ethan is annoyed. At least he has free time up until 4 p.m. and he knows exactly what he's going to do with it.

To: Olivia James

You're a horrible liar, Miss James and I'm afraid you've left me with no other choice.

Oh, crap.

To: Ethan O'Connell

What are you going to do?

She gets nervous when he doesn't reply.

To: Ethan O'Connell

Ethan?

Ethan has already left the house and is on his way into town. Stopping at the market, he grabs a variety of fruit and two mixed green salads. The delectable smell of homemade bread lures in into the small sandwich shop next-door. He flirts with the woman behind the counter as she makes him two fresh sandwiches and wraps them to go. There's no woman immune to his sense of humor and Irish charm. She slips two brownies into the bag without charging him. He winks at her as he says thank you; making her blush and break into a smile that lasts for a long time after he leaves.

Walking into the office of Dunn and McLellan, he realizes that he doesn't know which one is her office. The receptionist smiles politely at him as he approaches.

"I have lunch for Olivia James," he says, smiling at Diana.

"I'll make sure she gets it." Diana checks him out from head to toe, admiring his exquisite male physique.

Leaning his forearm on the edge of the desk, Ethan gives her a playful smile. "I need to give it to her in person."

She smiles and blushes, a reaction that Ethan so easily draws from women. "I'll call her." Picking up the phone, she dials Olivia's extension. "There is a delivery for you at reception. Can you come down?"

Olivia feels nervous as she gets up from her chair and opens her office door. As she heads down the hallway toward the reception area, his muscular body comes into view.

"Ethan," she whispers. Her heart skips in excitement, making her fight hard to maintain her composure. *Why does he make me so nervous?*

Ethan watches her approach, grinning at her puzzled expression when she looks at the bags he's holding.

"What are you doing here?"

"I've brought you lunch."

Of course he did. She should've known. Olivia looks nervously at the receptionist. She's too busy answering calls and still shamelessly checking out Ethan's ass.

"Thank you, but you didn't have to do that."

"Ah, but I did. And don't think, for even a minute, that I'm leaving without making sure that you eat it. Do you want to go to your office?"

Olivia stares at him, contemplating about what he'd do if she refused, when the smell of fresh bread reaches her. Suddenly she's starving, for both lunch AND Ethan.

"Liv?" Ethan wonders what's going on in her brain. The damn thing always seems to be working overtime.

"Sorry. My office is down here." It seems like a long walk past all the closed office doors, as her coworkers look up in curiosity. "I thought you were stuck at the new house today?"

"I found myself with some free time until the next installation."

"I have to admit it smells really good." She sits in her chair, looking down at the sandwich and salad he's placed in front of her. "Help yourself." He gestures toward the apples, oranges, and brownies that he's unpacked in the middle of the table. Ethan sits in the chair on the opposite side of her desk. This is something new. Ethan seldom sits on the *other* side of a desk.

Olivia reaches for an orange and places it in front of her. Her stomach makes a loud grumbling noise. She looks up to find Ethan staring at her with one eyebrow raised and that damn, annoying, boyish grin. She's embarrassed by her body's basic need for food, and its announcement that it's been lacking. The bread is still warm and she restrains the urge to moan as she takes her first bite. "Thank you, Ethan, this is really good."

"I'm glad you're enjoying it. You have no idea what I had to do to get those brownies." He smirks, when her eyes widen, unsure if he's just joking.

Finished with his meal, Ethan watches her closely; smiling at the adorable way she alternates between sandwich and salad. Reaching across the desk, he picks up her orange and proceeds to peel it. "I wish you would tell me what's upset you, so I can put your mind at ease."

She thinks about it for a minute as she carefully uncovers all the tomatoes in her salad and pushes them off to the side with her fork. "It was just something someone said. I'm over it."

"You don't want to tell me about it?" He's not very optimistic about her willingness to confide in him yet.

Finishing with her orange, he places it down in front of her on a napkin. She looks at it curiously. "Did you just peel my orange?" she teases.

Ethan replies with a quizzical look. "I always peel your oranges; we'd be here forever waiting for you to pick off all the stringy things," he says it so casually that he doesn't even realize what he's said.

Olivia stares at him completely baffled. *You always peel my oranges?* She's never eaten an orange around him before. How did he know about her strange aversion? Most people just eat them but she has an irrational phobia and a compulsion that won't let her eat the orange until she picks off every single last little string. How did he know?

Ethan continues to tidy up, completely unaware of his strange confession. Olivia watches him with a schoolgirl infatuation. She's been craving his body for days and now he's standing right there. Close enough to touch. Close enough to…. Stop! Don't even go there! She shakes her head. What is she thinking? This is her office! *Damn hormones!*

Rachel bursts into her office ignoring the closed door. "Ethan's car is in the parking lot!"

They both freeze and look up at her, startled. Rachel looks back and forth between them feeling ridiculous. "Aaaaaand Ethan's in your office."

Olivia laughs, "Can't put anything past you, Rach."

"Oh no, I'm sorry… I've interrupted something." She starts to feel awkward.

"Only lunch." Ethan holds out the remaining brownie for her.

Olivia appears to be well nourished for the first time in days. Rachel picks up the brownie and sinks her teeth into it, rolling her eyes at its sinful chocolaty taste. "Mmm, this is so good."

She notices the way that Olivia is looking at Ethan. "I'm going to go back to my office and let you guys finish your… lunch." She closes the door behind her.

Olivia brushes the crumbs off her desk, into her hand and discards them in the garbage. Ethan is struck by how the light through the window glistens golden on her face, just like in his dream. He situates himself between her and the desk, half sitting on the edge. Crossing his legs at the ankle, he gives her a disapproving look. "Now… am I going to have to hire someone to follow you around and make sure you eat?"

Olivia looks up at him feeling annoyed. "No."

Taking hold of her hands, Ethan pulls her to her feet. Standing in front of him, every nerve ending in her body awakens. The smell of his cologne makes heat sizzle through her as she remembers why he wears it.

Lifting his hand, he brushes the hair out of her eyes. Being this close to her gives him a tight feeling that twists his muscles into knots. "I'm glad to hear that. There's something I want to ask you." He plays with her hair, twisting her curls around his finger. It's one of his habits that she's quickly growing accustomed to. Although, it's precisely the kind of intimate gesture she was hoping to avoid, she doesn't discourage him.

"Will you be my date for the grand opening of the restaurant?"

Olivia is totally taken off guard. "Me?" Didn't she say something about no dating? It's hard to remember being this close to his body. It's hard to think about anything really, when he's near.

"Yes... *you.*"

The memory of Hannah's words haunt her, she hesitates, very seriously considering saying no.

Ethan's aware that her mind is elsewhere again. It seems to happen a lot. "Olivia?"

There's something about his meadow green eyes that coaxes her back to him. "Well, I guess... but that's only because you'll refuse to take NO for an answer, anyway."

Ethan nods in agreement. "This is true. I'm not fond of that word."

"Do you ALWAYS get your way?"

He smirks in his annoying, Irish, charming way. "Yes, most of the time."

Olivia presses her lips together tightly. "Are you sure that's what you want?"

Ethan scowls at her, trying to figure out what the hell happened to her this week, "Yes, that's what I want. It would make me very happy." He puts his hands on her hips and pulls her forward.

Forgetting that they're in her office, in the middle of the day, Olivia leans her face against his chest. He wraps his arms all the way around her in a warm embrace. She can't stop herself. This is what she's been missing.

"Okay, I'll go. But it's NOT a date."

Ethan hesitates a moment, almost reacting angrily. Before he speaks, he lets out a heavy sigh. "Will you let me pick you up in the limo?"

"Yes."

"You'll stay by my side and be only with me?"

She sighs in frustration, "Yes."

"And you'll let me take you home afterwards and maybe stay for a little while?"

She leans back so she can see his face. "YES!" she says impatiently.

He grins. "Then, you can call it whatever you want." He sways her gently in his arms, breathing in her perfume. "I want you to wear that black dress, the one you were wearing that day at the coffee shop."

She laughs under her breath, "Well, that's pretty much a given."

"What do you mean?"

"I can't afford to buy anything new, until after I get the car repairs paid off."

"I thought you had the money to pay that?" He leans back so he can see her face.

She uses the opportunity to take a step back. She knows that she needs to separate herself from his addictive, muscled body and get back to her workday. "Well, not exactly. They're letting me pay it off in equal payments over the next three months."

Ethan's jaw clenches and he exhales harshly in frustration. "Olivia, I told you that I would pay for it if you didn't have the money."

"Relax, I'm managing."

He shakes his head. "See? I knew you were going to drive me completely crazy."

She grins. "Well…every girl has a talent. I guess that's mine."

Ethan shakes his head. "Great!"

The sarcasm in his tone amuses her. "I need to get back to work. You've been here for over an hour. You're going to get me in trouble." She steers him out the door and down the hall toward reception.

"Just tell your boss that I'm a potential client."

"Uh huh, and you were in my office for almost an hour and a half, why?"

She pushes open the front door and follows him to his car.

"Discussing the *services* I'd like you to provide. Of course." He winks, as he flashes her that irresistible smile.

Maybe it's his cologne or maybe it's the pheromones, bringing out the naughty in her. "If I had blinds on my office door, I would've shown you exactly how well I would *service* you." She locks onto his gaze with a sensual audacity that leaves him speechless and makes his dick spring to life with amazing swiftness.

"Jesus… there's that look again." He unlocks his car door. "I best get on my way before my cock takes control and I wrestle you into the back seat to have my way with you."

She gives him a devilish grin. "Ah, did you read the fine print? There's an extra fee for *out of office* consults."

When she turns to walk away, Ethan grabs her wrist and yanks her toward him. Her body stops against the unmistakable bulge of his semi hard-on. His biceps flex as they wrap around her, preventing her escape. Holding her against his hard chest, he lowers his lip and whispers, "I really missed you this week."

Olivia feels the same way but she can't bring herself to say it. She presses the palm of her hands on his chest. After rubbing them gently across the rigid outlines of his muscles, she pushes herself away. "I have to go." Turning, she walks toward the building, without looking back. Ethan grins as he watches her swing open the door and disappear inside. He's wearing her down. He can tell.

Pulling out of the parking, Ethan decides that he has more than enough time to stop at the auto repair shop on the way. There's a certain matter of an outstanding repair bill that requires his attention.

Olivia stops at Rachel's office and stands at the door with her arms crossed, waiting for Rachel to acknowledge her. When she does, Olivia gives her a look. "Really? You told him that I wasn't eating?"

Rachel cringes. "Geez, yeah. I'm sorry. I didn't mean to tattle on you. We were just talking and he was worried about you and… Do you forgive me?"

Olivia lets her arms relax at her side. "Yeah, I guess so. I can't believe he showed up here with food."

"The brownies were killer. Did you have one?"

Olivia shakes her head no. "I had fruit." Her curiosity piques. "Rachel, did you tell Ethan about my orange peel phobia?"

"No."

"Do you think Scott might have mentioned it to him?"

"I'll ask him, but I doubt it. Men don't talk about that kind of stuff. Why? What's going on?"

"Ethan did the strangest thing today."

Rachel gets excited. "Tell me!"

"We were eating lunch and chatting. He reached over and picked up my orange and peeled it for me."

Rachel looks disappointed. "That's it? That's actually kind of sweet."

"I know, but when I asked him about it he said." She stops, wondering if Rachel is going to think she's nuts.

"What?" Rachel presses her to continue.

"He said that he has *always* peeled my oranges because I take too long trying to pick off all the stringy bits."

Rachel's brow creases. "Really? That is a little strange. But oh my God, he looked so cute!"

Olivia smiles. "Yeah, he did. And he always smells so heavenly."

Rachel laughs, "Well, that's special for you because he didn't smell like that at my house."

Olivia saunters back to her office with absolutely no motivation to continue working. The more she tries to put him out of her mind, the more she thinks about being pressed up against his chest with his strong arms wrapped around her and his hard cock rubbing against her. She's suddenly consumed by the need to have him. It's not the kind of need that will be sated if she were to *take things into her own hands*, so to speak. An idea that's been lurking in the corner of her mind begins to unfold, in the form of a steamy fantasy; one that she's thought about for a very long time. One that allows her to be a very dirty girl.

Chapter Twenty-Five

Holding her breath, Olivia dials his number.

"O'Connell."

"It's me."

"Is everything okay?" Ethan leans on the counter supporting himself on his forearms and shifting his weight onto one hip.

"Do you have to go to the restaurant tonight?"

"Yes. I'm afraid so. Why?"

"I don't want you to go," she spews out, sounding whiny and needy.

He furrows his brow in concern. "What's going on, Liv?"

"I want you to come see me, instead."

"Olivia, are you okay?"

"No. I'm having… um… thoughts." No, that didn't sound desperate at all. She rolls her eyes.

"Thoughts?" A smile forms on his lips. "What kind of thoughts?"

Talking quietly, she looks up to make sure her office door is closed. "Naughty thoughts."

Ethan stands straight up, shocked. "Okay. You've got my attention."

"I'm feeling a little adventurous," she whispers into the phone.

"I'm intrigued." His cock is already hard and he doesn't even know what she has in mind, yet.

Olivia hesitates, "Remember the other night, when you suggested I could pay you back for the coffee with sexual favors?"

Ethan begins to pace across the kitchen floor, his arousal tenting his sweatpants. "Yes, go on."

She can't believe she's having this conversation. "Well, I thought you could come by and," she clears her throat, "*deliver* dinner… and"

She doesn't have to finish her thought. He knows what she's getting at. "Give me five minutes. I'll call you right back." Hanging up abruptly, he leaves her sitting at her desk with her phone in her hand, not quite sure what just happened.

Ethan searches through the records of his incoming calls until he finds the number for the technician that called. He hits dial and waits.

After several rings the technician finally answers, "Hello."

"This is Ethan O'Connell."

"Yes, sir. I still don't know what time we'll be there."

Ethan gets straight to the point. "I'll give you one hundred dollars cash each, if you're done and gone by 5 p.m."

There's a moment of muffled silence as the technician has a few words with his partner.

"Mr. O'Connell, we're just around the corner. We'll see you in a few minutes."

Olivia has a moment of anxiety when Ethan's name shows up on the caller display.

"It looks like I'll be able to accommodate your request, after all."

A delicious tingling starts between her legs. "You can?"

"Yes, I'll meet you at your place at 6 p.m., I still have to go over to the restaurant later on, but we'll have lots of time before then."

"Okay."

There's a knock at Ethan's door. "I've got to go, the technicians are here."

"Ethan, wait! Come to the front door… and don't bring pizza, it's a little too cliché."

Olivia has no idea how she managed to get through the rest of her afternoon. Standing at the mirror, she smiles. Her outfit leaves little to the imagination. It's sexy *and* naughty; perfect for what she has planned. Ethan is going to lose his mind when he sees her.

She's so nervous that when the doorbell rings, she almost jumps out of her skin. Opening the door, she finds Ethan leaning against the porch rail, holding a paper bag with Chinese food.

When he sees her, he jolts upright, like he's been struck by lightening, "Holy mother of all…!"

Olivia blushes. "Come in." She motions to him. "You can put it on the counter."

He takes a long, shameless look at her breasts. Electricity crackles between them as he brushes past her in the doorway. Ethan places the bag on the counter and turns to find her staring at his perfectly taut ass.

"How much do I owe you?"

Ethan buries his hand into his pocket and digs out the receipt. "Seventeen dollars."

"My wallet is right… there." She points to where he's standing. "I'll get it for you."

Ethan doesn't move, making her press up against him. She looks up into his eyes. "Excuse me."

He exhales hard as she leans against his chest, pressing her breasts against him as she reaches for it. When she has her wallet in hand, she takes a step back. She opens all the different compartments, looking through them. Looking up at him, she tucks her hair behind her ears. "I'm afraid I don't have enough money." She tips the wallet toward him so he can see that it's empty, "I guess I forgot to go the bank machine."

In the dim light of the kitchen, he tries to refrain from smiling at her performance. Surveying her body from head to toe, his gaze settles back at her breasts. Damn, she looks sexy tonight! He needs to be inside her. He hopes to hell that he can restrain himself long enough to let her fantasy play out. If she feels like being a dirty girl, who is he to deny her?

"Well, what are we going to do about that?" He stares at her, pretending to be unimpressed. Moving toward her, his movements become somewhat threatening.

Oh he's very good at this game. Olivia fights her instincts to take a step back, away from his overwhelming virility. The air around them is sexually charged. Excitement surges through her body, like it's been infused directly into her veins.

"I could drop by the restaurant tomorrow with the money," she offers, as she drags her fingertips across his chest in a zigzag pattern. The muscles in his stomach tighten as she nears the waistband of his jeans.

Ethan's nostrils flare as she runs her hand over him, on the outside of his jeans. Lowering her eyes, she watches him swell as she traces its outline with her fingers before firmly rubbing her palm on the head of his cock.

Enjoying the sensation, Ethan almost forgets to talk. "No, stopping by tomorrow won't work for me." He blatantly stares at her breasts, as they tease him from underneath the thin sheer blouse. *I need to get my hands on those.*

Putting her hands up against his chest, she stops his advances as he reaches to touch them.

"I don't want you to take back the food. I haven't eaten all day and I'm starving." She looks at him with desperate eyes.

Raising his eyebrows, he peers down at her through eyes so full of sexy wickedness and promise. "I think we can come to an arrangement." The irony isn't lost on him. Grabbing her wrists, he removes her hands from his chest. Freeing himself from their restriction, he can now bring his hand up to her breast. Rubbing it through her blouse, he kneads it roughly, until her nipple goes hard in response.

Brushing the tips of his fingers across her skin, Ethan moves his hand to her throat. She bites her lip in anticipation, as he traces her lip with his index finger. He closes his eyes, breathing in hard and deep, as she closes her mouth around it and gently begins to suck.

Olivia is overcome by lust. Putting both hands on his chest, she pushes him back forcefully, until the counter stops him from moving any further. With an unexpected confidence, she keeps her gaze fixed on his, as she unbuttons his jeans. Sliding the zipper all the way down, she gets a rush from taking complete control. She makes his nerves twitch, as she runs her fingers around the waistband of his jeans, and slowly pries them off his hips. When they fall to the floor, his underwear goes with them, revealing his hardened enthusiasm. Reaching down she takes him in hand, stroking him from tip to base. Squeezing it gently at the crown, she repeats her movements until she hears him let out a low raspy growl.

Kissing his neck and across to his throat, she lifts the bottom of his t-shirt. She trails tender kisses down the center of his bare chest to his navel, then all the way down. Slowly she kneels in front of him on the kitchen floor, looking up at him; wanting to look into his beautiful green eyes when she takes him in her mouth, for the first time.

Without breaking eye contact, she licks the wide crown of his cock. Ethan leans back, his hips pushing forward, as he holds onto the edge of the counter with both hands, groaning. His breathing becomes shallow and ragged, as his already rock hard erection thickens and expands. Stepping out of his jeans, he pushes them off to the side, giving her better access.

Olivia leaves a warm wet trail with her tongue along the length of him, while she works her way to the base and back up to the head. When she reaches the most sensitive spot, she teases him, licking in slow deliberate circles while she pumps him rhythmically with her hand.

Ethan's abs stiffen and his thigh muscles begin to twitch, as he moves his hips forward pushing himself toward her mouth. When his beautiful cock presses against her lips, she takes him in.

"Fuck. Olivia…" he moans her name. She becomes wetter at the sound of it. Reaching down he puts his hand on her head, holding her still and trying to force himself deeper into her mouth.

She resists him, wanting to take her time, unsure that she can take him all in. It really is a magnificent package and his length is daunting, the width equally intimidating. No wonder she was so sore after he fucked her so thoroughly.

Olivia is absolute in her protest. Ethan finally lets her go and runs his fingers through her hair, allowing her to control the depth. When she's ready, she loosens her grip and lets him slide further in her mouth. Moving her head back, she takes a breath then slowly takes him in again. She sets a steady rhythm, controlling the movements and making him growl.

"Fuck, that feels good."

Taking him as far as she can in her mouth, she holds what remains of the shaft in her hand, pumping and sucking, at the same time. He rocks in a gentle rhythm, fucking her mouth, the sensation nearly driving him insane.

Excitement coils deep inside Olivia, knowing that the pleasure pulsing through him is her doing. With her free hand, she reaches down between his legs, and caresses his balls, squeezing and pulling gently on them. Lowering her mouth, she trails her tongue over them, taking them gently, one at a time, into her mouth. She's rewarded with a small burst of precum as she continues stroking and licking. She laps it up, sliding her tongue across the slit and making him moan.

When his balls become heavy and draw up, she runs her hands up the outside of his thighs and around to his ass. Pressing the palm of her hands on his clenched cheeks, she squeezes tightly. Pulling him forward, she makes him hit the furthest possible spot in her throat. It's almost his undoing and she knows it. The muscles in his thighs strain when she does it again.

His knuckles turn white on the edge of the counter. "God. Olivia... stop or I'm going to come."

Leaning back, she lets him slide out of her mouth and land heavily in her hand. Looking down, he watches her lick along the length of his cock one last time.

"Fuck... you were wrong this afternoon, Baby." Reaching down, he brushes his thumb along her jaw.

Getting to her feet, she runs her fingers under his t-shirt, dragging them across the crisp damp hairs on his stomach, making his entire body shudder. "About what?"

Leaning into the nape of her neck, he nibbles and kisses his way toward her shoulder. "About your talent."

"Was that good?" she asks, trying not to smile. Every nerve ending in her body is pulsing with energy. His steely erection, poking against her thigh is still a distraction. "Are we even, now?"

Ethan smirks. "Hell no, I'm not done with you, yet." Grabbing the bottom of her blouse, he tugs it roughly over her head, tossing it to the floor. She arches her back when he runs his hands over the delicate lace of her bra. Her breasts are so sensitive that she's sure he could coax her to orgasm just with the touch of his hands. Sliding his hands under the lace, he rolls her nipples with his fingers, making them hard. She purrs with pleasure between breaths.

Lifting his t-shirt over his head, he tosses it on the floor. Pressing his bare chest against her, he kisses along her throat with building passion. He swiftly rids her of her leggings, stripping them down to her ankles in one movement. His bestial desire unleashed when he gets a look at her matching black lace panties.

"You're so beautiful." Holding her hips, he rubs his erection against her. Lowering his lips to her breasts, he sucks on them, alternating between nipples and making her clench. Sliding his hand between her legs, he rubs her firmly on the outside of the lace. Teasing her, he makes her squirm before he pushes them to the side. With expert precision, he glides his fingers across the swollen folds of her slick sex.

"Ethan," she moans.

"You're so wet for me already." He's pleased with the way she responds to him.

"I was wet the minute you brushed past me in the doorway."

Her admission expedites his need to be inside her. Tucking his arm behind her knees, he lifts her into his arms and carries her, with little effort, to the stairs.

Panic-stricken she grabs at the railing, stopping him in his tracks. "What are you doing?"

Chapter Twenty-Six

Ethan stops abruptly and looks at her perturbed, "I'm taking you upstairs for a good fucking."

She shakes her head. "NO! Not in the bedroom. I… can't."

Alarmed by the fear on her face, he concedes with moderate protest. "You're killing me," he growls, changing direction and placing her down gently on top of the table. He releases her bra, guiding the straps off her shoulders and discarding it on the floor. Lowering his lips to her nipple, he teases it back to a hard peak with his tongue. Taking it into his mouth, he sucks with a hunger that makes the muscles in her lower region tighten in anticipation. Growling, his hands skim over her hips, skillfully ridding her of her panties.

Pushing her knees apart, he forces her to spread open for him. He can't wait to sink into that beautiful smooth, clean-shaven pussy. Wrapping one arm around each leg, he grabs hold of her, lifting her hips slightly off the surface and pulling her forward. Positioning her at the edge of the table, he gives himself full, unrestricted access to her.

Rubbing his hands along her thighs and in between her legs, he watches the expressions of pleasure on her face. Holding his cock against her swollen lips, he rubs it back and forth lubricating himself with her excitement.

Unable to hold back any longer, he aligns himself with her entrance. Holding her hips firmly, he pushes the first rock hard inch of himself into her. In this position, he can see every expression on her beautiful face. Rubbing her clit with the pad of his thumb, he backs out, and then pushes in further this time. When she gasps and winces, still not yet used to his size, it makes his desire burn hotter.

Olivia feels herself stretch around him, trying to absorb his length. When she thinks that he's finally hit the end of her, he gives one last hard thrust, making her cry out.

Olivia desperately wants to touch him, but her position prevents it. She tries to lift her hips, to meet his forward strokes but with her legs against her chest, she can't get any traction or support. She's trapped there unable to move until she finally finds her voice, "Ethan."

He looks up at her curiously, "Yes, Baby?"

"Can we move to the couch? I'm not comfortable here."

He lets her straighten her legs, helping her to sit up, and then lifts her again. Her arms wrap around his neck, to support her, as he moves her quickly to the couch. As he lays her down, he crawls over top of her, his biceps flexing as he supports himself. He's a magnificent specimen of well-honed muscle.

Olivia reaches for him, touching him everywhere that she can. As he lowers himself down on top of her, it feels like heaven to be against his bare chest.

His dick softens slightly with the disruption. Reaching down, she takes him in hand, giving it a few firm strokes. The narrow cushions on the couch feel too restrictive when he kneels between her legs. As he trails his lips across her body, his silver chain skims across her chest. The feeling of it dragging against her sensitive breasts enthralls her. When he runs the tip of his tongue, sensually, across her lips, it sets her on fire and she moans. His chest falls heavy with short breaths. In a very brave move, he attempts to kiss her on the lips. With ninja like swiftness, she pushes her hands against his chest and turns her head to stop him.

"FUCK!" he growls angrily.

Olivia's heart thumps hard against the inside of her chest with the hard tone of his disapproval.   Clenching his jaw, he presses his lips in a firm angry line, and lifts her off the couch. Lowering her to the floor, he gives himself plenty of room to maneuver. Spurred on by frustration, he grabs her wrists and pins them over her head, holding them down so she can't move them. Moving between her legs, he uses his knee, roughly forcing her legs further apart.

Instantly his cock reaches its full potential. In a selfish attempt to meet his need, he slams into her hard. She gasps at the fullness. In a punishing rhythm, he continues tirelessly, every thrust driving them both closer to the finish line. Her breasts jiggle and rub against the bare skin of his chest. He occasionally lowers his mouth and nips at them, making her jump.

Having her hands restricted over her head, catapults her lust into overdrive. She writhes beneath him in pleasure, moving her body to meet his thrusts. *This is exactly what she needed.*

Perspiration dampens her skin as the pulsing waves of pleasure grow in intensity. She's almost ready to explode when she stops moving beneath him and becomes completely still.

Ethan senses the change, a tension slowly creeping in. He knows that he's losing her. The muscles in her legs stiffen and once again, it's gone, her pleasure stolen from her.

Releasing her wrists, he stops thrusting, his cock still pulsing and twitching inside her in protest. Pulling back, he rests on his forearms so he can see her face.

"Hey," he says softly.

Olivia is non-responsive, lost in her subconscious, where something shadowy has grabbed hold of her, pulling her away.

Still panting, Ethan brushes the hair off her forehead, staring at her. "Olivia, look at me."

His voice is little more than a whisper but it echoes through her soul like a lifeline, pulling her back from the edge of darkness. Her hands grab onto him, digging her fingers into his flesh; holding on as if her life depended on it. When she opens her eyes to look at him, she knows that he has sensed what has just happened to her.

"Stay with me," he whispers.

Olivia nods her head and takes a deep, slow breath in through her nose. When she exhales, she synchronizes her breathing with the rise and fall of his chest. Holding his face in her hands, she maintains eye contact. The love she sees in those green Irish eyes saves her, keeping the darkness from coming back for her.

She pushes her hips against him; she encourages him to continue. He follows her lead, moving slowly at first and then growing stronger with his desire. She runs her hands through his hair, pulling at it as she rolls her hips.

Ethan's breathing becomes labored and his movements more precise; each forward stroke is orchestrated to rub against the over-stimulated nerves inside her.

Olivia opens herself to him, giving him all of her, straining to take him all in. Her hands slide down his muscular back and clutch his ass, feeling it flex as he pistons into her. Arching her back, she's consumed by wave after wave of glorious pleasure.

Ethan lowers his head to her throat. Breathing hot and humid against her, he continues to thrust into her with a slower rhythm. "We're safe now, right?"

"Yes, we're safe," she pants.

He pushes himself into her one last time, rolling his hips and groaning as his abs tighten. His body shakes, filling her with a hot rush of semen that seems endless.

Only when her body stops twitching and she relaxes beneath him does he pull out, collapsing against her body. Rolling off her, to relieve her of the weight of his body, he slides his arm under her head and pulls her against him, tucking her into the safety of his chest. They lay there forever, reeling and waiting for their breathing to return to normal. Olivia anchors herself around him, holding on tight and not wanting to let go.

Ethan is concerned, now that he knows what drags her away from him in those moments. The monster in her dreams, recently identified as her ex, Sam. He holds her close, his breath warm in her hair as he presses a kiss to the top of her head. Smoothing her hair, he holds her head against his chest with the other. "Are you okay?" he asks in a tender Irish whisper.

Olivia nods her head enthusiastically. Everything is okay when she's in his arms. After drawing in a deep breath, she lets it out slowly and makes the strangest purring sound, "What kind of cologne are you wearing?"

"Dolce & Gabbana, The One Sport. Why? Do you like it?"

"I love it. It smells like the ocean." She pauses, taking another appreciative breath. "Funny, because last night I dreamed that you and I were at the ocean," she whispers. Nuzzling under his chin, she caresses her hands across his chest and down over the hard slab of muscular abs.

Ethan tenses all over and then holds his breath. Again? This is not the first dream that they've both shared. Why is this happening? How is it possible?

"Ethan?"

"Yes?"

"Is everything okay?" Something's not right. Every muscle in his body went taut, all of a sudden.

"Yes." *Don't say anything. Don't say a damn word. The girl will think you're off your nut.* "It sounds like a lovely dream."

"It was." There was no sex in that dream. Just love. Pure emotion. She wants to feel that way again. She can't stand the thought of being away from him, not even for a moment. She sighs against his chest, "Do you have to leave?"

"Yes. I'm afraid so. John can't be there, so I have to go." He doesn't want to leave either, but he has no other choice tonight, not with John out of commission.

"But neither of you were there on Tuesday night." She holds her breath for a moment, waiting for his reaction.

His jaw clenches as anger flashes through him. "You were there on Tuesday?" Sitting up, he collects their discarded clothing with the long reach of his arm.

"Yes."

"Alone?" It bothers him to ask, when he already knows the answer. Maybe subconsciously, he needs to know if she'll tell him the truth. Passing her clothes to her, he watches her reaction, wondering if she'll lie.

The red hue that colors his face and the ticking nerve on his temple is a good indication that he already knows the truth. "No. I was there with Noah."

Feeling flustered, he gets to his feet, heading into the kitchen to retrieve his pants. Olivia leans back, watching him go; understanding why Diana couldn't take her eyes off him. His perfectly rounded Gluteus Maximus, supported by his strong muscular thighs, is an impeccably powerful conformation. When he turns, she doesn't even pretend to be ashamed of being caught admiring the package between his legs that she often craves.

Ethan asks the question that he really doesn't want to know the answer to, "On a date?"

Olivia can sense his irascibility all the way across the room. "No, not really. He just wanted to have dinner there one last time, before you reopen it as 'Ireland's.' We used to hang out there all the time. I guess you can say that we were there for sentimental reasons."

Ethan returns to the room and finds her still sitting in the middle of the floor. Holding his hand out, he helps her to her feet. She can tell that he's desperately trying to stay calm. His body seems tense now, his expression hardened, evidence of his *inner turmoil.*

Ethan doesn't hide his anxiety very well. "Do you have an *agreement* with Noah?"

"No!" His jealousy niggles at her, giving her a warm jittery feeling. She suddenly realizes that he must have feelings for her, if he feels possessive.

He brushes the hair away from her face, trying to find a way to reconnect with her. "I've seen the way he looks at you. He wants to fuck you."

"WHAT? No he doesn't." Even if he did, that will never happen. She's certain of it now.

"I know that look. I get it every time I think about you." He pulls her into his arms. "I can't stand the thought of him being anywhere near you." Still basking from their recent intimacy, he wants to be close to her but he feels tense and agitated. "Tell me that there's no reason for me to feel jealous of that wanker."

Olivia sighs against his chest, "Ethan, there's no need for you to feel jealous of Noah. He and I are only friends." Odd that he should be jealous, since he's the one that has girls falling all over him wherever he goes.

Ethan wants to believe her, but he's haunted by these feelings of possessiveness. "Do you have *arrangements* with other men that I should know about?" *Stop it! You're going to fuck things up.*

Olivia frowns at him. "Nope, just you. But since you started this conversation..." This is the perfect time to get things out in the open. She hesitates, pulling back so she can see his eyes. "Do you... are you and Hannah..."

Ethan is appalled and halts her questioning, immediately. "Absolutely not." Then it dawns on him. "There's nothing going on between me and that slapper." John's instincts were right about Hannah. "Liv, did Hannah say something? Is that why you've been upset the past few days?"

Licking at her dry lips, Olivia nods in embarrassment. Ethan lets out a harsh breath as he grasps her arms at the elbow, forcing her to step back, so he can see her face. His voice is raspy and angry, "There's nothing going on between her and I. You should have just asked me. Jesus, woman!"

Olivia doesn't answer, just stares at him. Looking into her eyes, he tries to determine if what he sees there are feelings for him that she's trying to hide or his own feelings reflected back at him. It makes his heart ache. Looking to the ceiling, he utters a silent prayer, pulling her back in against his chest and holding her so tightly that it's difficult to breathe.

When it's time for him to leave, she follows him to the door and leans against the stair railing. Putting his foot on the edge of the step to tie his laces, he notices something on her elbow. He reaches for her, lifting her arm gently so he can see to her wound. Closing her eyes, she winces from the pain. Ethan lowers his lips to kiss the graze. In a very loving, nurturing way, he continues kissing his way up her forearm and across the back of her hand, giving each knuckle a tender playful kiss.

When he stops, she opens her eyes to meet his gaze. He frowns at her, his forehead wrinkled with his disapproval. He runs his thumb across her cheek. Giving him a coy smile, she turns her face slightly so that her cheek rests across the palm of his hand. She pauses there for what seems like an eternity when he finally breaks the silence. "You wouldn't get these boo boos if you would let me take you upstairs to make love to you."

"I can't," she whispers into his ear, shaking her head. "I just can't."

"Okay, Baby. I know." Gently rubbing his hands up and down her sides, he attempts to soothe the tension that he just felt creep through her body. Lowering his lips to the top of her head, he dwells there for some time: not pushing, not demanding.

"Promise me that one day you'll tell me what happened."

Olivia shakes her head. "I don't want to. You'll treat me differently, once you know."

Ethan is perturbed by the hurt look on her face. "That's not true. Why would you think that?"

She shrugs. "Everybody treats me different when they find out."

"That's ridiculous. Nothing you could tell me would change the way I feel about you or the way I treat you. So promise me… one day, when you're ready, you'll tell me."

Olivia wants to believe him. His sincerity seems genuine. She feels herself surrounded by his safety. No matter how hard she tries to fight it, she feels like he's somehow imprinted on her soul, almost as if he was her guardian in a past life. Well now, that's just silly. The warmth of his green eyes soothes her and she lets out a slow gently sigh, "One day."

Chapter Twenty-Seven

Saturday morning Olivia putters around the house, catching up on chores. As she comes down the stairs from the second floor, she slows her steps, looking around the room. Everything reminds her of Ethan; the counter where he stood while she knelt in front of him and rocked his world, the table, the couch, the carpet! Confusing feelings quickly throw her off balance. Plopping herself heavily into the chair, she lifts her knees to her chest, her heels resting on the edge of the cushion.

She stares at the blanket and pillows that she's stacked on the arm of the couch, ready for this evening's use. Thank goodness, Ethan couldn't stay with her last night. What would she have done if he had said yes? She gets a little anxious, realizing that eventually she's going to have to face the demons that haunt her bedroom.

Olivia's three-year abstinence didn't just leave her physically wanting. After Sam, she learned how to turn off the part inside her that thrives on intimacy; the human need to connect with others on an emotional level. Ethan has started to fill that space inside her. It's exactly what she wanted to avoid, in order to protect her heart. He instills in her, emotions that make her acutely aware of the emptiness inside her. Even if sometimes that emotion is anger or frustration.

It's clear in her mind this morning that this is the reason she asked him to stay. It's true; he's a man who knows her body so well, that he's completely adept at looking after her physical needs. Last night that wasn't enough for her. It's hard for her to face the truth. She massages her forehead with gentle pressure trying to smooth away the tension.

She thought she had done everything right to avoid this need, but here she is AGAIN - wanting… *desiring* his love, needing it to feel alive and whole. And it's getting stronger. Dumbfounded by how this happened, she rests her elbows on her knees and leans forward, holding her head against the palm of her hands.

She decides that the only way to reign in these emotions is to slow things down. Reinforce the agreement. It's not going to be easy, but she's not eager to repeat the same mistake, so she'll try. *Keep your heart out of it.*

Ethan sleeps in after coming in late from the restaurant. He feels guilty that he didn't go back to Olivia when he was done, but once the kitchen closes, the bar and nightclub atmosphere lingers on. It was nearly 2 a.m. before he could close and lock up. He's glad that the nightclub manager he hired is available to start full time soon. He had to resist the urge to text John several times with questions and things he wanted done. He hopes that John's taking the full opportunity to enjoy his girl, while she's here. For a moment, he feels a great amount of self-satisfaction.

The bed is the only piece of furniture at the house, since he ordered it new and had it delivered it yesterday. He's barely awake when he hears the moving truck roll up. He stays out of the way and lets the movers do their job. When they're done, he inhales deeply, taking in his surroundings. It's not home, but he'll be comfortable here. Sitting on the leather couch, he digs his phone out of his pocket. It's a common occurrence these days for Olivia to cross his mind whenever he has a still moment.

From Ethan: Hey, What time do you want me to pick you up today?
From Olivia: For what?
From Ethan: ?? The BBQ. We're still going, right?
From Olivia: Oh! Yes, but I'm going to go on my own.
From Ethan: Tell me why.
From Olivia: Because it's NOT a date.
From Ethan: What exactly is your issue with going on a date with me?
From Olivia: It's not what we agreed to.
From Ethan: Fine, it's not a date. I can still pick you up and we can go together.
From Olivia: NO!
From Ethan: Olivia, I'm not happy about that and quite frankly I'm getting a little tired of this arrangement bullshit.
From Olivia: Consider this one of those rare times when you don't get your way. You'll live.

Normally that would have sent Ethan into an angry tailspin, but he finds himself smiling. *What has she done to him?* He shakes his head in amusement. Who would have thought that a woman could tame his irascible temper? But this is not just any woman… this is Olivia James. The woman he fell in love with the moment he laid eyes on her. The woman who has been visiting his dreams for months, long before she actually walked into his life. Ethan knows things about her that he can't possibly explain. There's no doubt in his mind, that she's *the one.* Olivia is the one whose fingerprints are on his soul. He knows now, exactly whom the psychic was referring to. Well, if you believe in that sort of thing.

Olivia's phone rings and Rachel's name shows on the display. "Hey!"

"Hi! Do you want us to pick you up for the BBQ?"

"No thanks, Ethan just offered as well, but I think I want to go by myself."

"What? Why?"

"Well, it's the first *party* like thing I've been to in a long time. I just want to make sure that if I start feeling a little freaked out, I can leave without disrupting anybody else's fun."

"Are you still having anxiety attacks?"

"Well, no. I haven't had one for weeks, actually."

"Uh huh… since you met Ethan?"

Olivia thinks about that. "I guess so, what are you getting at?"

"Nothing. Just wondering. Can I ask you a question?"

"Can I stop you?"

"NOPE."

Olivia laughs, "Well, then ask away."

"Why do you give Ethan such a hard time?"

Olivia is confused. "What?"

"You know what. Not letting him kiss you, making him leave after sex. Is it true you won't let him take you upstairs to the bedroom to make love to you?"

Olivia gets defensive and more than a little upset. "He told you all that?"

"Oh my God! It's true?" Rachel is astounded.

Olivia is mortified. "Yes."

"Soooo, where are you doing it then?" Rachel asks, her curiosity getting the better of her.

"The kitchen table, the couch… the floor." Rubbing the rug burn on her elbow, she glances down at the carpet.

Rachel sits wide-eyed in silence. "I'd ask why, but I know the answer. Sweetie, I know that it's difficult for you, but what about Ethan?"

"What do you mean?"

"I mean, how long do you expect him to put up with that? Maybe it's time for you to start thinking about what Ethan needs from *you*."

Olivia can't argue that point. What Rachel says makes sense, so there isn't an argument to be made.

"Just think about it. We'll pick you up at around 4 p.m. End of discussion."

"Geez. Bossy much? I think you've been spending too much time with Ethan."

"Maybe. But we're still going to pick you up."

"Fine! Whatever." She hangs up and texts Ethan.

From Olivia: Change of plans. I'm going with Scott and Rachel. If you're a good boy, I might let you drive me home.

Olivia rolls her eyes, so much for slowing things down. It took all of ten minutes before she caved.

From Ethan: Well then, you can count on me to be a VERY good boy

Laughter echoes over the music and a sea of lawn chairs dots the grass. Ethan works the crowd with a drink in hand, socializing with friends, coworkers, and teammates. No one has to tell him that Olivia has arrived; he feels her presence the moment she gets out of the car. Watching her walk up the dirt path in her flip-flops, he gets a tightness in his stomach that makes him feel warm all over.

Olivia lifts her hand and waves, getting a rush of nervous excitement when she sees him. She knows immediately that she's in trouble.

Meeting them half way, Ethan takes her chair and cooler. Scott and Rachel follow behind. Making sure she has a drink in hand, Ethan keeps her close as they mingle with friends. Olivia's heart swells at the sight of Ethan laughing. He's enjoying an evening away from the stresses of the workweek. Away from all the tension and the rigid business environment, he has a delightful sense of humor. On top of his normal charm, he's very entertaining. She can't remember the last time she enjoyed herself this much.

He hasn't let her out of his sight for a minute. She decides she should give him a little break from her company. Leaning in, she whispers in his ear, "I'm going to go sit down for a bit."

"I'll go with you." Ethan excuses himself from his companions and walks her back to her chair, with his hand on the small of her back. People exchange what they think are discreet glances, but Olivia notices. She knows what they're thinking. *There's THAT girl.*

Scott and Rachel are engaged in a conversation with friends about something. Rachel is holding Scott's hand and leaning in close when he talks to her. Olivia is happy to see the love and adoration return to Rachel's face when she's with her husband. When Rachel glances over at her, they exchange a smile. It's a silent acknowledgement that everything is just fine.

When they get to their chairs, Ethan opens the cooler and exchanges her empty bottle with a new one. "One beer and you're done?" she asks, surprised when he opens himself a bottle of water.

He shrugs. "I'm not much of a drinker, anymore."

Suddenly someone yells his name and launches a soccer ball in his direction. Olivia ducks as it heads straight for her. Ethan throws himself in front of her, stopping it and making the ball drop to the ground.

One of his teammates shouts from the back of the property, "Come show Terry that move."

Ethan flips the ball in the air. After juggling it a few times on his foot, he grabs it with his hands. Not wanting to abandon Olivia, he extends an invitation, "Come watch."

Olivia takes a mouthful of her vodka cooler, "You go, play with your friends. I'm going to sit for awhile and relax."

Moving in behind her, he playfully brushes the hair behind her neck and kisses her tenderly on the shoulder. Feeling all warm and fuzzy, she practically moans. *Damn him!*

"I won't be away long," he whispers in her ear.

The sun surrenders to the horizon, allowing the shadowy twilight to creep in. The band takes their place on the deck that's been converted into a makeshift stage. They've spent tireless hours practicing out in the garage. At the back of the property, a bonfire blazes brightly; the sound of the wood crackles and pops as it burns, echoing in the night.

Olivia sips on her vodka cooler, knowing that she needs to pace herself, since they have a deadly effect on her. In fact, on several *celebratory* occasions, she woke up the next morning without her shoes and bra, with no recollection about how she got home. That was in her younger, carefree days. Now, she's all grown up and determined to make good on her adult obligation of drinking responsibly.

Ethan couldn't have been gone for more than ten minutes, when Olivia feels a hand on her shoulder. She inhales the smell of cologne that's all too familiar. "Noah!" She stands up as he walks around her chair to greet her. "When did you get here?" she asks.

"About half an hour ago. You were busy and I didn't want to interrupt."

He looks so much taller in the dimmed light of dusk. When she stands on her tippy toes and throws her arms around his neck in a friendly hug, she can tell that he's had a few drinks, already.

When Ethan returns, he stops a few steps away, the darkness keeping him hidden from Olivia's view. Jealousy pulses through his body as he watches Noah kiss her on the lips. It was a harmless kiss. Not much more passion than the kind you would give a family member or an old friend; but watching it happen makes Ethan feel like someone has just knocked the wind out of him. *Fucking Noah Thompson!*

Rachel looks up and sees Ethan watching Noah, his hands clenched into tight fists at his side. Obviously, Olivia has no idea that he's there, "Hey Ethan! Can you toss me a water?"

Olivia stiffens. Crap! She pulls herself away from Noah, quickly putting distance between their bodies, "You remember my friend, Noah, right?" She tries not to look panicked as Ethan approaches. She cringes at the stupidity of her question. Of course he remembers Noah, he punched him the face not that long ago. *Ugh!*

The two men nod at each other, neither of them able to hide their malice. Ethan tosses a bottle of water in Rachel's direction; Scott catches it in mid air.

Ethan glances over at Noah. Olivia promised that he has no reason to feel jealous, but he just doesn't trust this guy. He regrets promising that he wouldn't start any more fights with him. Feeling angry and very possessive right now, he has no idea how he's going to push it aside. *CALM YOURSELF!*

"Do you want a beer?" Ethan asks Noah, swallowing his anger.

"Sure" Noah can't help but feel a little cautious. He senses Ethan's malice and the feeling is mutual.

"Are you ready for another one, Olivia?"

She holds up the bottle to show him that it's still three-quarters full. "No, I'm good, thanks." Ethan takes his place by her side, possessively putting his arm around her, pulling her close to his body.

Noah's body tenses. His edged blue eyes show his malevolence. Feeling awkward Olivia gives him a forced smile.

Determined to show her that he's the better man, Ethan apologizes to Noah, "I'm sorry about that scuffle at the game, a few weeks ago."

Olivia's eyes open wide in shock. *What is he doing?*

Noah nods. "I hear you got a three game suspension."

"Yes."

Growing extremely anxious, Olivia takes her phone out of her pocket and texts Rachel.

From Olivia: Rachel HELP!

The cavalry arrives when Rachel and Scott wander over to join them. "Hi, Noah, it's nice to see you. Scott and I were just talking about you."

"You were?" Noah asks curiously.

"Yes, Scott and I were thinking about getting a puppy and we had some questions."

Olivia and Scott exchange a look of surprise. Scott shrugs.

Olivia tries not to laugh as she mouths the words, "I love you guys."

"You don't mind talking shop on your day off, do you?" Rachel asks, as if she's going to give him a choice.

Noah is quite happy to oblige. "Not at all." He sways, and Olivia puts her hand on his shoulder to steady him. "What did you want to know?"

While he's engaged in conversation about his work, Olivia takes the opportunity to sneak away. "Excuse us while you chat." Reaching down, she takes Ethan's hand. "I need to get something to eat."

"I'm glad to see that you're eating." Ethan hands her a hamburger.

"I worked up a bit of an appetite last night." She grins. "But don't worry, I won't go hungry. I have enough Chinese food in my fridge to last a week."

Ethan snuggles up behind her as she peruses the table of salads. "Good, keep your strength up because you're going to need it."

"Oh? And why is that?" She drops a spoonful of potato salad on his plate, trying to hide how his closeness affects her.

"Because you're all I can think about these days. I plan on taking advantage of our agreement, as often as I can."

Olivia raises her eyebrows. "Good to know. Thanks for the warning." She tries to convey indifference, but her insides are a whirling storm of emotions, making goose bumps prickle along her skin.

Ethan leans in, pressing himself against her back. "That's not a warning, Princess. That's a promise. We'll talk later, about revisions I'm going to make to our current agreement."

"Oh, really?" She mocks him. Trying to make him think he has no chance of making any changes, but she's extremely curious about what that might entail.

"Yes, really. If you do remember, my acceptance of your agreement was dependant on being able to renegotiate terms, at any time."

"So, it was." Taking a deep breath of his cologne, she leans back and rests against his hard chest. "What did you have in mind?"

Teasing her, he bites at her earlobe. "Eat first, we'll talk later."

Later in the evening, Noah mingles in the crowd. He keeps his distance, but he never takes his eyes off Olivia. Ethan senses him lurking and keeps her close, intent on sending a clear message that she belongs to him.

Now that the sun has completely set, Rachel runs around in the dark handing out glow sticks. Olivia bends hers, trying to snap it but it limply refuses. Feeling a little buzz from the coolers, she pouts and gives it a little more muscle, making it crack and start to glow.

Standing a few feet away, engaged in conversation, Ethan sees her out of the corner of his eye and turns to capture her gaze. She looks at him helplessly, holding out her hands for him to see that her skin is glowing a bright fluorescent green from a leak in the plastic.

Noticing Noah watching her, from a few feet away, Ethan grins. He decides to send a very ballsy message. Taking the glow stick out of her hands, Ethan squeezes it to find the leak. Using it as a pen, he stakes his claim, writing, "ETHAN'S," boldly across her cleavage in neon green. It's a very effective way to engage Noah in a full-out pissing match.

Noah downs his drink, tossing the empty into a nearby recycle bin. He captures her attention, locking her into a jealous sneer. *What's that look about?* Olivia wonders. Walking straight for them, Noah forcefully pushes between them, bouncing them apart and almost knocking Olivia over.

Ethan immediately reacts, reaching out to grab him. Olivia stands in front of him, stopping him. "Ethan, let it go. He's drunk." Turning around, she leans her back against him, digging her heels in the dirt to get better leverage.

She keeps her eyes on Noah who nonchalantly lifts the lid to his cooler, and then looks over at her. "Would you like a drink while I'm here?"

Furious, Ethan tries to push forward. Olivia digs her heels in harder, giving everything she has to hold him back. "Sure, whatever's cold." She looks back, giving Ethan a look that warns she won't tolerate any interference from him, "Actually Noah, why don't we go into the house and have a talk in private."

Ethan holds her hips tightly, digging his fingers into the soft flesh in protest. "Not a fucking chance that's happening," he growls.

"Ethan, it's okay," she assures him.

"Liv, I don't trust him. I don't want you anywhere near him tonight, it's not safe."

"Funny, I remember him telling me the same thing about you once," she reminds him in a flippant tone. Ethan's body is riddled with tension as he spins her around to face him, his expression warning that she had best be careful what she says next.

Her hands grip his flexing biceps and squeeze them. "Ethan, let me handle it. Please."

Scott and several teammates have sauntered over, casually hovering, just in case there's trouble. Ethan looks into Olivia's eyes, knowing that there's no point in arguing with her. She'll only fight him on it and do what she wants, anyway. "Fine," he surrenders, "but I don't like it." Reluctantly, he lets her leave.

Noah twists the cap off a cooler and wipes the condensation away before he hands it to her. As they walk toward the house together Noah turns, giving Ethan a half smile, as he reaches down and takes hold of Olivia's hand.

With his hands formed into tight fists at his side, Ethan is on the verge of losing it. He takes a step forward, prompting Scott to step in. "Stay out of it. She can handle herself."

Noah holds open the door and follows Olivia into the house.

"ARE YOU OUT OF YOUR MIND?" she turns and yells at him.

Caught off guard, Noah stands staring in a drunken stupor. Olivia can see Ethan watching them through the window, his arms crossed in a very rigid stance. When Noah staggers toward her, she sidesteps him, making him hit the counter with a thud. She grabs him by the shirt and drags him into the other room and out of Ethan's view.

"Noah? What the hell is wrong with you? This bullshit between you and Ethan needs to stop."

"I want you," he announces, his speech slurred from the booze.

Olivia is shocked, "You want me?" She puts her hand to her forehead. "Now you want me? Are you kidding me, right now?"

Noah blinks, the alcohol making his eyes heavy and slow to reopen. "No! I want you. I want to make love to you, just like we talked about."

"Jesus!" Olivia's annoyance quickly turns into anger. "Well, you can't have me, Noah. We decided that it wasn't worth ruining our friendship over. Remember?"

"It's okay. I know you love me." He reaches for her, trying to pull her into an embrace.

Olivia slaps at his hand. "Don't touch me, I'm not kidding."

"You don't mean that." He tries again and she blocks him.

"Oh yes, I do mean it! You have some incredible nerve! For years, I hung around trying to figure out what I had to do to get you to notice me. I would've done anything for your love and attention. I finally had to come right out and ask you for more. I BEGGED you, actually. Every time I tried to make things happen between us, you blew me off for some blonde slut with fake tits."

Noah looks at her with a pathetic, apologetic look on his face. "I didn't know that you knew about her." Trying to make amends, he moves closer. "Olivia, she doesn't mean anything to me."

"Noah, just stop it." Olivia takes a step back. "I know what's going on. Let's be completely honest here. You don't want me; you just don't want Ethan to have me."

"I think we should fuck, and then deal with whatever happens." He continues to move toward her, his body heavy under the influence of alcohol. This time Olivia doesn't get out of the way fast enough. He pins her against the wall.

Wishing that just this once, Ethan would give in to his control freak nature and come looking for her, she struggles beneath Noah, unable to breathe and terrified. She'd scream if she could manage to get enough air into her lungs. Instead, she finds adrenaline-induced strength.

"NO!" She pushes at him, forcing him off and slapping him hard on the face.

Noah holds his cheek and glares at her. "You're a cock teaser. You know that?"

"You're drunk, so I'm going to pretend you didn't just say that."

Off balance, Noah takes a step back and turns, storming out of the room. Olivia follows, practically running to try to catch up with him. "Noah… NOAH!" Angrily she pursues him, her heart racing.

With trembling hands, she grabs his arm as he opens the door. Shrugging his shoulder, he pulls away from her with force. Lurching forward, she trips over the edge of the mat then hits the edge of the door, hard. Noah doesn't even look back.

The adrenaline consumes Olivia for the next few moments. When her hands stop shaking and her breathing returns to normal, she begins to feel the pain from her swelling, throbbing lip. She cringes when she gets a look at it in the bathroom mirror.

Ethan watches Noah stumble out of the door. When Olivia doesn't reappear after a few minutes, he heads in to the house to look for her.

Locking herself in the bathroom, she tries to figure out how she's going to explain this to Ethan. Maybe the swelling will go down and he won't notice. Suddenly there's knocking at the door.

"Olivia?"

Shit! It's Ethan. He's going to completely lose his mind; she's certain of it. *Think quickly.*

She tries to buy herself some time. "I'm okay. I'll be out in a few minutes." With her hands still trembling, she takes her phone out of her pocket to text Scott.

From Olivia: get Noah out of here NOW!

Chapter Twenty-Eight

Ethan bangs heavily on the door. "Olivia?"

"I'm feeling a little sick, too many vodka coolers. I think I might head home."

Her voice sounds strange, nervous, actually. Ethan picks up on it immediately. "What's going on?"

"You should go back out and enjoy the rest of the party, Ethan. I'll call you tomorrow."

Ethan becomes agitated. "You've only had a few drinks, Olivia. Open the door."

Panic hits her as she looks in the mirror at the swelling. It's only getting worse. She pulls her hair forward in a failed attempt to cover it.

Growing impatient, Ethan thrums his fingers on the door. He knows that she's hiding something. "Open the door Liv or I swear I'll kick it down." Her lack of immediate response pushes him over the edge. "NOW!" He turns the knob, trying to force it open.

Olivia jumps. "OKAY! Geez, hang on." Strategically, she turns off the light, hoping he won't see the swelling. Holding her head down, she unlocks the door and turns the knob. The minute it unlatches Ethan impatiently pushes it open, making her jump back out of the way.

"Why is the light off?" He feels his way up the wall searching for the switch.

"I told you, I'm not feeling well."

Finding the switch, he flips on the overhead light. "Do I look stupid?" he asks in an indignant manner.

Squinting as her eyes adjust to the light, she keeps her head down. "Of course not, Ethan." *Way to go girl. Insulting him was probably not a good idea.*

Ethan brushes her hair back so he can see her face. Reaching for her chin, he uses his finger to lift it. When he sees what she's hiding, his body becomes more rigid than hardened steel. He growls through clenched teeth, "I'm gonna kill him." Enraged, his mouth presses into a hard line, and his green eyes get dark with fury. Turning, he reaches for the door handle.

"Ethan, NO! He didn't do this. It was an accident." Grabbing his arm, she holds him tightly, using the weight of her body to push the door closed so he can't leave.

"Really? If he didn't do it then why were you hiding it from me?" His words are sharp and his Irish accent becomes thick. Olivia knows that his temper is on the verge of an angry takeover.

"Because I knew you would overreact, and guess what? YOU ARE OVERREACTING!" Leaning against the door, she effectively blocks his exit.

"Get out of the way!" His commanding glare is a clear warning.

"No, I'm not moving." Her eyes lock with his in a dangerous challenge of power. She needs to buy Scott some time to get Noah out of there. "You can't leave, yet."

Folding his arms in front of him, he raises his eyebrows, "Oh really, and why would that be?" He widens his stance, his body noticeably twitching with rage.

In an act of desperation, she thinks of the only thing that might deter him. Seductively moving toward him, she reaches his chest and rubs her hands across its muscular width. "Because I need you... *here... right now.*" Slowly, Olivia undoes his shirt buttons, starting at the neck.

Ethan's nostrils flare in anger. Ignoring the agony of her swollen, tender lip, Olivia presses her mouth to his neck and kisses him. He softens as she undoes the last button and pulls the sides of the shirt open, exposing his chest. Exhaling harshly, the stiffness in his body retreats. His arms unfold and take their place around her waist.

"I need to be fucked... right now. It can't wait." Olivia's hands massage gently across him, making nerve endings twitch. His muscles tighten as she traces each defined ridge with her finger.

Looking down at her, his expression is somewhere between shocked and amused, "Are you using sex to try and distract me from kicking his ass?" *That's my girl!*

Trying to hide the half smile on her face, she lowers her lips to his nipple and covers it with her mouth. Nipping the hardened pebble with her teeth, she makes him take in a quick breath.

"Is it working?" She reaches down and steers her hand over the rapidly growing bulge in his pants.

"What do you think?" he asks dryly.

Rubbing the palm of her hand over the head of his cock, it swells, becoming harder. On the next upward caress, she traces along the waistband of his pants and runs her finger along the inside. When she undoes the button and slowly starts to lower his zipper, he grabs her hand and stops her.

Looking conflicted, he rubs his hand on the back of his neck. "Don't go any further,"

Olivia looks up at him confused.

"There's no way I'm doing this in the jacks, especially in someone else's home."

"The jacks?" she asks curiously.

"The bathroom," he explains.

"Are you saying NO to sex?" She's shocked and more than a little afraid for Noah. She hopes that Scott has put him in a cab by now.

Ethan shakes his head. As if he would ever say no to sex with her. His body is always on autopilot when she's around.

"I'm saying NOT HERE." He turns the knob to the adjoining door into the master bedroom, testing to see if it's locked.

When the door opens, what started as a distraction grows into a deep gnawing desire that needs satisfying. Olivia follows him into the room and locks the door. Ethan moves to her side. With his hands on her hips, he turns her to face him

"We'll have to be quick, are you ready?"

"Hell, YES!" Heat boils at her core, spreading outward through her veins. Need and desire make her feel an unyielding desperation for his cock.

Olivia pulls her t-shirt over her head and releases her bra. Grabbing her shorts, Ethan roughly pulls them down; letting them hit the floor. Running his hand between her legs, he pushes her panties to the side, rubbing his fingers over the swollen folds of her pussy. He primes her with her own wetness, ensuring she's lubricated enough to take him.

Undoing his pants, he strips them down with an alarming urgency. Shoving her back onto the bed, he pulls at her panties trying to coax them down. When he hears the sound of the material straining and beginning to tear, he abandons his careful efforts. He rips them away with a robust tug, tossing them on the bed beside her.

The sight of them, torn by his need to get inside her, heightens Olivia's arousal. She shifts her weight, rolling her hips desperately against the finger he has slid inside her. Inspired by her response, he slides in a second finger, making her squirm in delight as he pumps them slowly in and out.

When he parts her with his thumbs and kneels between her legs, she moans, knowing what's to come. As his hot, wet tongue slides across the folds of sensitive flesh, she grips the edge of the sheets and bends her knees, inviting him in. He licks her with unrestrained passion, the tip of his tongue occasionally dipping inside her, in a shallow invasion. She wiggles and thrusts, trying to press him in further but he denies her. Closing his mouth around her clit, he draws in soft and long. The compelling suction over the sensitive knot of nerves makes her leg muscles tremble and her knees draw up toward her chest.

"Ethan, please," she begs, "We don't have much time. I need you inside me."

Breaking away from her, he watches her with an uncontrollable lust as she pushes up onto her forearms and uses her feet to push herself further back on the mattress. Putting his knee on the edge of the bed, he crawls over top of her, licking her skin as he travels toward her heavy, swollen breasts. Her knees widen to accept the width of his hips. He quickly takes his place there.

His hard cock weighs heavy on her thigh as he lowers his mouth to surround her sensitive nipple, sucking and licking until she moans. Her chest falls heavy with each exhaled breath, feeling the weight of his body completely pinning her to the bed. Dragging his lips heavily along her neck, he growls in that low raspy *'hurry up and fuck me before I explode'* Irish accent, "Hold on, Baby. It's going to be fast and hard."

Arching his back, he adjusts his position, lowering his hips. The wide crown of his cock slides directly into her with astounding precision. She draws in a deep breath as he begins to pump himself in and out in a vigorous rhythm.

Ethan's forearms press on either side of her head, his face only inches away from hers. His lips part to assist his short panting breaths, hot and humid against her skin. Olivia already feels the pressure building inside her like a storm.

Holding himself back, he refrains from entering her all the way, knowing that it will finish him if he does. Instead, he concentrates on her comfort, her pleasure. Adjusting his angle, he finds the spot inside her that aches for him, making her moan. She lifts her hips to meet his thrusts.

He quickly gets her there. He can feel her pleasure as she begins to tighten around him. His need to release overcomes him. He finally pushes himself all the way to her limit, holding himself there; feeling her cervix against the engorged head of his cock before withdrawing almost completely. Olivia protests, clawing at his back in an effort to pull him back inside her.

He can't steady himself any longer. His words are breathless, desperate, "Olivia, I'm going to come." When he slides all the way back in; he hits her throbbing clit with the pressure she needs to set her off.

"Oh! Oh my God!" Gasping, she tries to muffle the sound of her voice as she becomes completely unraveled. Her orgasm rips through her body, making her shake. Ethan's hips roll forward, pushing him into her one last time. Feeling her quivering pussy around his cock, he hardens and lengthens inside her, pushing out burst after burst of hot semen. Ethan grunts, as his body twitches one last time, ensuring that he's completely emptied himself inside her. When he's completely spent, he falls beside her, his lungs looking for air.

"Holy shit," Olivia whispers.

Ethan chuckles. Their basking moments are interrupted by voices in the hallway, causing Olivia to jump to her feet, searching for her clothes. Quickly she does up her bra and tugs her t-shirt over her head. She picks up her panties forgetting about their misfortune and looks over at Ethan with a scowl.

"What?" he asks, pulling up his pants.

She holds them up by what little is left of them. "What am I going to do with these?"

Ethan laughs, as he buttons up his shirt, "Don't leave them here. I can't imagine poor Pete trying to explain them to his wife."

"Oh my God, I feel a little creepy now. I hope Peter and Gillian don't ever find out what we just did."

"Who's going to tell them? Not me."

Stepping into her shorts, Olivia shrugs as she pulls them up over her hips. "I guess I'm going without." She stuffs them in her pocket. "Just remember that this time… YOU are the reason I'm walking around without any underwear." She stops and reflects for a moment, squinting her eyes, "Actually, *you* were the reason I wasn't wearing underwear last time, as well."

Ethan glances at her sideways. "Nice try, I had nothing to do with that. When I left the room you had fully functional underwear. *You* were the one who chose to leave them behind."

She gives him a sinister grin. "You should have seen the look on John's face."

"I imagine it was much like the look on my face, when he handed them to me in my office, the next day." He tries to hide his amusement.

"So, it doesn't bother you that I won't be wearing any for the rest of the evening?" She knows him so much better than that, but she can't resist teasing him.

"Are you serious?" his Irish accent, hangs heavy on his words. "It's killing me, right now. I'd make you wear mine, if I thought for a minute that you would. Trust me when I tell you that I won't be letting you out of my sight." Opening the door to the hallway, he stands waiting; watching to make sure the coast is clear.

Olivia likes the sound of that. Being held under the watchful eye of a man who's determined to keep her safe. For some reason, he looks even sexier after he's just been freshly fucked.

Olivia's lip begins to throb. Licking at it, she can taste something salty. She touches it with her finger then looks at him in terror. "Ethan!"

Ethan looks back at her, startled by the alarm in her voice.

Olivia holds out her hand showing him the blood. "My lip."

He moves to her quickly. "It's okay, don't panic." Grabbing a tissue from the bedside table, he dabs it gently where the swelling is. "Let me have a look." Pulling her lip out tenderly, he angles it downward, so he can see the inside. "Ah, looks like your tooth punctured the skin on the inside," he assures her. "Don't worry; I know exactly what to do."

Leading her down the hallway to the kitchen, he stands her at the counter. Pressing against her, he reaches up past her head, opening cupboard doors looking for something. The warmth of his body makes her tingle. She's shocked at her arousal so soon after just making love to him. She's not even sure if that's the right phrase to use. It seemed too deeply rooted in carnal need to be considered *making love*. Whatever it is, it follows suit for Ethan O'Connell. Everything the man does is *INTENSE!*

Finally finding the sugar bowl, Ethan scoops a large rounded spoonful. "So are you going to tell me how this happened now? The truth I mean."

"We argued, he walked away and I got mad. When I tried to stop him, I tripped over the edge of the carpet and hit the edge of the door." Her tongue licks at her lip, poking at the wound.

"I see." Ethan studies her face. Her expression will give her away if she's lying. "That sounds like a believable story."

Olivia makes a face. "It's the truth. Can you do something? It hurts and it tastes disgusting."

"Here." Ethan lowers the spoon of sugar to her mouth, acknowledging her inquisitive looks, "Old sports trick." He gently pulls her lip and angles the spoon, firmly pressing the mound of sugar against the broken skin. He holds it there, until it stops the bleeding. When he removes the spoon, it leaves behind a lump of coagulated sugar against the wound. "Just leave it there," he orders, "and keep your tongue away from it." Tossing the spoon into the sink, he looks back at her, waiting for her acknowledgement. When she nods obediently, he winks at her. "There's a good girl."

Olivia relaxes, trusting his healing hands explicitly. She wonders how his life would be different, if he hadn't made the choice to switch career focus.

"Do you ever think that you made a mistake leaving medical school and going into business?"

Ethan looks at her puzzled. "No. Why do you ask?"

She shrugs. "It just seems to come so easily to you. You're a healer. It's in your nature."

"Yes, well I do believe I told you that my bedside manner was exemplary. Besides… you're the only patient I have time for these days."

Smiling, Olivia adjusts the elastic in her ponytail.

"I'm not joking; I've never met anyone clumsier than you."

Olivia glances down at a new text message from Scott.

From Scott: He's gone.

Letting out a relieved sigh, she tucks her phone into her bra.

Ethan's face, once again, takes on a serious appearance. "I take it, that was the *all's clear* message from either Rachel or Scott?"

Olivia's shoulders slouch. "Yes." *Busted!*

"Noah has left." Folding his arms in front of him, he waits for her confirmation.

"Yes." *How does he do that?*

Taking in a long deep breath, he puffs it out in frustration. Olivia lifts her hand to wipe at her lip. Grabbing her wrist, he holds it tightly. "Don't touch it," his commanding tone makes her tingle, again.

She looks at him feeling ashamed. "Did you know that was the plan the whole time?"

Releasing her hand, he moves closer, pressing her against the counter. "You can't hide anything from me, Princess. I know you better than you know yourself." Pressing his cheek to hers he whispers, "You won't be able to keep any secrets. I see you… *completely*." Reaching behind her, he wraps his hand around her hair, pulling on it gently, forcing her head back. Moving his lips within a dangerous distance of hers, he holds her there while he slides the elastic down to the bottom of her ponytail, pulling it all the way out of her hair.

Olivia stands frozen. His aura projects a formidable weight that pins her where she stands, allowing him complete control. Tangling his fingers through her hair, he pulls it forward. The soft curls fall gently, framing her face and brushing the tops of her shoulders. His smile is soft and sensual. "I like it better this way." He tucks the elastic into his pocket then brushes his thumb across her cheek.

Ethan looks at her with a searing intensity that confirms that he can see right through her. There's no doubting it! Starting to feel edgy, Olivia forgets to breathe. Ethan senses the angst that begins to wash over her. Stepping aside and opening the freezer, he breaks their connection.

The screen door opens and their hostess, Gillian, walks into the kitchen. She becomes concerned when she sees Ethan holding an ice cube to Olivia's swollen lip. "Oh no! What happened? Are you okay?"

"She's fine."

Olivia makes a face at him, annoyed that he didn't let her answer for herself. "I tripped. It's nothing serious. The embarrassing part is that I'm sober."

Gillian laughs, "That's probably why. Is there anything you need?"

Ethan answers for her again, wearing an evil grin. "I can assure you that all her needs have been met, but thank you."

Olivia closes her eyes, blushing bright red. When she opens them and glares at him, his lips are pursed tightly together trying not to laugh.

Gillian looks back and forth between them. *What an odd couple.* She shrugs. "Okay! Please be careful, it's awfully dark out there. Let Pete know if there's anything you need." She tops up her glass of wine and heads back outside.

When the door snaps shut, Olivia puts her hands to her face hiding it in shame. "Oh my God, I felt like it was written all over my face." She swats at Ethan playfully. "You didn't help, standing there laughing."

"Relax, she had no idea." He smiles the brightest smile, from ear to delicious Irish ear. Olivia's heart thumps hard in her chest.

Something washes over her; it's a playful, cheeky kind of mood, the one that she normally keeps guarded. Maybe it's the effects of the alcohol; or maybe it's the result of being completely sated… physically and emotionally. She doesn't know and doesn't care. It feels wonderful!

Ethan has only seen playful Olivia twice before; the day she came to his office and in the elevator, the night she proposed her agreement. It puts his mind at rest to know that she's finally starting to trust him enough to let him see the real her. The one she so desperately tries to hide.

"I can't believe I let you seduce me in someone else's bedroom." She stops and stares at him with narrowed eyes, pointing her finger at him, "YOU! What have you done to me? You've corrupted me."

His mouth hangs open and his eyebrows rise. "I seduced *you*? Now, wait a minute…"

Grabbing his hand, Olivia pulls him toward the door smiling devilishly. "Yup, that's my story and I'm sticking to it."

Chapter Twenty-Nine

Ethan follows her outside and over to their chairs. He almost has a heart attack when she bends over the cooler to get another drink. "Whoa!" He moves behind her quickly, trying to shield her.

Olivia stands up straight, unaware of the reason for his anxiety. "What?" She holds up both hands, giving him his choice of beer or water.

"Everyone can see up your shorts when you bend over like that." He chooses the water.

Olivia bends over to return the beer to the cooler.

Ethan growls in frustration, "For Christ's sake… did you hear what I just said?"

"They can see up my shorts, in the dark? I doubt it." She rolls her eyes. She hands him her vodka cooler so he can remove the cap. She could have done it herself, but it's just one of those things that a girl likes her man to do for her sometimes.

Tossing the cap into the recycle bin, he hands the bottle back to her. "Go easy, Baby," he warns, "and if you need something out of the cooler, I'll get it for you. Don't bend over it like that again."

Olivia can see that it's making him tense. She bats her eyelashes at him, trying to make him relax, but it doesn't work.

"I'm not joking." His voice gets stern, "Did you hear me?"

Acknowledging his militant tone, she establishes eye contact. "Yes, I heard you. Let's go over to the fire."

Ethan willingly accepts her outstretched hand, locking his fingers with hers. Olivia doesn't care any more about whose paying attention or what they might be whispering about her.

Standing in front of the glow of the fire, they warm themselves from the chill of the evening air. When the band resumes playing after their brief break,

Ethan and Olivia find themselves alone by the fire. The next tune is a slow, sappy love song and Olivia gets mellow. "I love this song," she says, closing her eyes.

Ethan snuggles up behind her and sways with her, their bodies fitting perfectly together. Singing along with the music in perfect pitch, he serenades her. His smooth voice is so seductive in her ear that it stirs in her very powerful feelings. Even the thundering sound of her pulse seems distant and insignificant.

She melts into his body for support, feeling like her legs have suddenly become boneless. When the song is over, she feels overheated by the combination of the fire and the flame he's ignited inside her.

Ethan whispers in her ear, "Both the moon and I are consumed with jealousy tonight, Olivia. I, due to the attention you gave to an undeserving man,"

Olivia frowns, regretting that choice. "And the moon?" she asks, trying to steer away from conversation about Noah.

"The moon, for failing to compete with your beauty."

Olivia suddenly finds it difficult to breathe. His closeness makes her uneasy. The man has a way of jump-starting her anxiety. She tries to focus on her breathing. Reminding herself that Ethan would never hurt her. Walking away, she tries to hide her sudden onset of vulnerability.

A few feet away, the property boundary is marked with a tree line of tall maples. She leans her back against one of the large trunks, trying to find her balance.

Ethan follows, putting his hand against the trunk just above her head. His body presses against her side making her heartbeat quicker. His incessant stare is daunting, forcing her to look down, trying to avoid it.

Breathing in her perfume, Ethan becomes intoxicated by its sweet, seductive scent. Lifting his free hand, he wraps it around her waist, holding her there. Christ, this woman is so beautiful when she tries to hide the way he affects her.

Ethan presses his mouth against her ear, gently nipping at her lobe. The warmth of his breath against her ear gives her goose bumps. Noticing her reaction, he moves his hand from her side, rubbing up and down her arm trying to warm her. "Are you cold?" The muscles in her stomach tighten and her chest heaves as she inhales quickly.

"No." She shakes her head.

"What then?" He knows what. He just needs to hear her say it.

She looks up at him through alluring hazel eyes. "You."

"What about me?" Is it cruel that he needs her to confess it? Tormenting her by making her say it aloud?

Olivia lowers her eyes again and whispers, "I hate you."

Ethan's hand stills on her arm. Pressing his forehead to the side of her temple he answers, "I don't believe that's true, at all." He slides his hand to her hip, tugging her closer to him.

Olivia bites at her fingernails nervously, covering her mouth. Her stomach twists in anxious knots as she lays out her feelings. "I hate the way you make me feel," she concedes.

Ethan inhales a deep breath, letting it breeze out warm and slow against her ear again. Finally, he gets to the truth. Capturing her hand, he pulls it down, away from her mouth. Not feeling the need to control or overpower her in this moment his voice is gentle, "Look at me."

Trembling with vulnerability, she turns so they're chest to chest. Raising her eyes, she locks his gaze to hers; green to hazel, the soulful energy of their connection, ineffable.

"How do I make you feel?" His heart is beating with a strange wobble, nervous about her answer.

"Frightened." She pauses, swallowing hard. Ashamed at her admission, she exhales as she whispers, "Excited."

"I see."

Lifting her hand to his mouth, he kisses each of her knuckles one at a time. Closing her eyes, Olivia escapes his stare for just a few moments, gathering her thoughts before speaking again, "You make me feel like I've lost control... of my thoughts... my emotions."

"Is that so bad?" Ethan presses her palm to his chest so she can feel the rhythmic beating of his heart. "You're not the only one who feels that way. The moment I saw you, my heart beat your name."

Damn him and his ridiculously romantic side, she's never going to survive it. Her words are laced with fear. "I need to stay in control."

"Why?" When she doesn't answer, his Irish brogue suddenly becomes thick and Irishy. "Sweetheart, you're no more in control of what's happening between us than I am. Whatever this is... it has its own destiny. We can merely follow its path."

"Give in to its force," she adds, knowing that he's stating the truth. It's increasingly hard to fight.

"Yes, bend to its will," he encourages.

Olivia is adrift in his eyes. Lost in his words. Hopelessly held captive under his spell.

Moving his hands to her hips, Ethan pulls her closer. Her nerves tingle with the anticipation of his next move. *Kiss me; just kiss me already.*

This is exactly the opportunity Ethan's been waiting for to kiss her. He's never been more eager to erase that term of the agreement. The faint illumination of the moon lights up her face, reminding him of her swollen lip. She winces as he brushes his thumb gently across it. His heart sinks in disappointment, but he refuses to have their first kiss tainted by the discomfort of a split lip. It's killing him, but he decides it will have to wait.

His hesitation allows Olivia the time she needs to pull herself back to reality. She takes a deep breath and gets her wits about her. Moving back, she gives herself some space. Ethan's heart sinks a little, sad in the knowledge that she still feels she has to pull away. He knows it's to protect herself when she's forced to face her emotions. Grasping for her elbow, he prevents her from moving too far away.

"I just thought of something," she says, feeling overwhelmed. "I brought a bag with pants and a sweatshirt. It's in Scott's car."

"Thank God. I'll go and get them. Wait here."

"Thank you, Ethan,"

"Just promise me that you'll remain upright until I get back." He waits for her acknowledgement. "Olivia?"

"I promise."

There's mischief in her eyes, making him suspicious. It's moments like this that he wonders if she's capable of being an obedient submissive. He's not even sure if he cares anymore. He hurries to find Scott and Rachel. The sooner he can get back to Olivia the better.

"Hey, is your car locked?" he asks when he finds them.

"Yeah. Why?"

"Can I have your keys? Olivia needs her sweatshirt."

Scott tosses them to him and he catches them mid-air. "Thanks. I'll be right back."

"Where is she?" Rachel asks.

"Out back by the fire, staying warm." Rachel gets to her feet and brushes the grass off her backside, "I'm going to talk to her for a minute. I'll be right back."

Scott doesn't want to let go of her hand. "Don't be gone long."

Rachel smiles and leans down to give him a kiss. "I just want to check in on her. Five minutes tops."

"I'll be counting." Releasing her, Scott watches as she walks toward the blazing fire.

Staring at the flames, Olivia is reminded of the sizzling heat that pumps through her veins when Ethan touches her. Her face lights up when she sees Rachel coming to join her.

"Rachel!" She throws her arms around her in a hug.

"Wow, you're certainly happy. What have you and Ethan been doing back here?" she teases. As she pulls herself away she sees Olivia's lip in the light from the fire. "Oh my God! What the hell happened? Did Noah do that?"

Olivia frowns. "Not exactly. We were arguing and then I tripped and fell into the door."

Rachel scowls at her. "Olivia, really? You're not lying to me again, I hope."

"No, trust me. This time I'm telling the truth." She puts her hand to her heart. "Honest."

Rachel shakes her head. "What did Ethan say? I'm surprised he didn't kill him."

"He wanted to. You wouldn't believe what I had to do to distract him while Scott got Noah out of here."

"Oooooh! Is that what was going on? I was wondering. WAIT! What did you do to distract him?"

Olivia smiles, her cheeks blush so brightly that they're visible in the darkness.

"Are you kidding me? You two are unbelievable! Where?"

"You don't want to know," Olivia snickers, as she changes the subject. "It looks like things are pretty steamy between you and Scott tonight."

"Things are great, I feel like we're in love again," she swoons. "You know? I have Ethan to thank for that," she admits.

"Really?" What did he do?"

"He gave me a pep talk last night. He says the sweetest things."

Olivia nods her head in agreement. "He really does. I think I'll let him take me home tonight. I promised him he could, if he was a good boy. And he's been a VERY good boy."

Rachel raises her eyebrows. Before she can get the details, Ethan returns with Olivia's clothes. Rachel nods her head, giving him a knowing smile.

Ethan narrows his eyes suspiciously. "What are you two up to?

"Nothing, I'm going back to my husband." Rachel walks away and turns to look back at them over her shoulder, smirking.

Ethan scratches his head and looks over at Olivia. She tries to look innocent, but fails. Taking the sweatshirt out of his hands, she puts it on. When she's done, she starts to undo the button on her shorts.

"Whoa! What the hell are you doing?" Ethan asks shocked.

"I'm going to change into my sweat pants." She looks at him annoyed.

"Ah, No! Just put them on over top." He is adamant about it.

Olivia makes a sound with her mouth, sucking air against her teeth. "I don't want to, they're uncomfortable," she glances up at him, wrinkling her nose in disgust, "and sticky."

Hearing her say that makes his dick twitch. *Damn thing.* "Well then, go into the house and change." He's dumbfounded that he even has to suggest it. "I'm not even sure why we have to have this conversation."

She challenges him stubbornly and unzips the fly, "Don't be silly, nobody will see." She tucks her thumbs into the waistband, preparing to yank them down.

Ethan has a full out anxiety attack. "Jesus Christ, Woman!" Wrapping his arms around the top of her thighs, he lifts her. Olivia screams. She folds over his shoulder as he moves her away from any possible stream of traffic. Olivia giggles when he sets her down in the darkness behind the garage.

"Here, get changed." He hands her the track pants. "I'll watch to make sure nobody's coming." Turning his back, he keeps an eye out. "Are you determined to drive me crazy?" he asks, arms crossed in frustration. "It's almost like you've made it your personal mission."

Olivia strips down, stepping out of her shorts. She launches them at him, trying to keep quiet as they whiz past the side of his head, and land in front of him.

Ethan shakes his head. "Obviously, the answer is yes." Olivia laughs, as she pulls her long pants up and over her hips.

"Is this what I have to look forward to every time you drink?"

"Maybe." She sneaks up behind him. Wrapping her arms around his waist, she hugs him from behind. "What makes you think that it has anything to do with me drinking?" Standing on her tiptoes, she leans against him, pressing a kiss on the back of his neck.

"Then God help me, because I'm in serious trouble."

Ethan turns to face her, letting her sink into his chest. Her soft body and warmth, soothes the tension from his body.

A mischievous smile spreads across her face. "Do you still want to drive me home?"

Chapter Thirty

Olivia cuts branches from the lilac bushes that outline the garden path. They're in full bloom and fragrant; planted in an alternating pattern of purples and white. Lifting them to her nose, she inhales deeply, considering it one of Mother Nature's biggest crimes that they bloom for such a short period of time.

The garden gets the perfect balance of sunlight and shade, making it a sanctuary to many feathered friends. She's done her best to make them feel comfortable there with feeders and a birdbath that was a loving gift from Ethan. Of course, her friend, the little green bird, sits on the perch of a birdhouse that hangs from the branch of a willow tree. She sings Olivia the most beautiful song.

Entering through the wooden garden gate, Ethan smiles at the sight of her. His cotton shirt unbuttoned all the way and his skin glistening from the heat of the midday sun. Approaching her from behind, he wraps his arms around her. He nibbles on her neck while she arranges her cuttings in a heavy crystal vase to take into the house. Smiling, she leans back against his chest, breathing in the delicious combination of lilacs and him.

Lifting her left hand out in front of them, he admires how the diamond in her wedding ring sparkles in the sunlight. With his heart bursting with the knowledge that she belongs to him for all eternity, he brings her ring to his lips and kisses it. Spinning her around gently, he brushes the loose strands of hair away from her face, so he can see into her beautiful hazel eyes. His hands tenderly hold the sides of her cheeks as he leans in closer, brushing his nose against hers, before softly pressing his lips against her mouth.

When he pulls away, she wraps her arm around his neck to stop him. Pressing her palm against the back of his head, she pulls him forward and forces his mouth against hers. Her fingers splay through his hair, holding him so he can't escape.

Moaning, he deepens the kiss, his tongue parting her lips, licking at her, devouring her mouth. She returns his kiss with equal desire, unable to get enough of him.

Leaning down, he scoops his arm behind the back of her knees, lifting her into his arms, still kissing her possessively. Carrying her into the house and directly into the bedroom, he *sets her down. She quickly tugs his shirt off his shoulders, letting it drop to the floor. Her hands explore broad shoulders and his muscular chest. They spend several minutes kissing and undressing each other, neither of them in a hurry, taking time to play and enjoy the seduction. When she's completely naked, standing in front of him, he reaches behind her and pulls out the pins that hold her hair on top of her head. Her soft, dark brown hair falls to her shoulders. He runs his fingers through the tendrils, pulling them forward and twisting them around his finger, playfully. Laying her back on the bed, he crawls over her, parting her legs with his knee and settling against her. He makes love to her all afternoon, slowly and gently, fulfilling her every need; extinguishing her every desire.*

When her body is exhausted and boneless, unable to take any more, he holds her, smoothing her hair and gazing into her eyes. His kisses never decrease in passion, always cherishing her, as if it's the first time. As he sweeps his thumb along her lips, he whispers to her with unquestionable sincerity, "I love you." With gentle languid movements, he trails sweet kisses down her neck, between her breasts, continuing downward. As his mouth kisses across her belly, swollen with child, he presses his lips against it and whispers, "And I love you, too."

Olivia wakes from her dream still feeling his love so deeply that her heart aches. Her face and pillow are damp from her tears. She brushes her hand across her belly, feeling momentarily disappointed. Mourning her return to reality, her breath skips as she inhales, trying to hold back the sobs. Drying the moisture from her cheeks with the edge of the blanket, she sniffles. In the waking hours, she can stave off these feelings, but at night, in her dreams, she's defenseless.

She's aware that there's an alarming correlation between the amount of time she spends with Ethan and the frequency and intensity of these dreams. However, she's not sure what that means.

Dragging herself off the couch and into the kitchen, she pours herself a cold glass of water from the jug in the fridge then leans against the counter to drink it. She thinks about Ethan's love. He thoroughly and unselfishly tended to her needs last night… more than once. Then, she thinks about the hurt look on his face when she asked him to leave. She imagines that she could have slapped him in the face and it wouldn't have hurt him as much.

Feeling extremely inadequate in her current relationship abilities, she closes her eyes tightly, trying to squeeze away the tears. Pulling herself together, she picks up her car keys and drives into town.

One of her favorite things about this small country community is their main street shops and vendors. Parking at the end of town, she walks along the busy sidewalk, stopping to window-shop along the way. She pauses for a long time, admiring the paintings and stained glass in the window of the art gallery, when something next door catches her eye. On the sidewalk table, just out front of the nature store, is a handmade wooden birdhouse. There are several different ones sitting along side it, some painted to look like hotels, others like two story homes. The one that she's drawn to bears a remarkable resemblance to the home in her dreams, right down to the number of windows and the color of the door. It's not even a home by many standards, more of a cottage.

She walks around with it in hand for several minutes before changing her mind and returning it to the table. She's several shops down the road before she turns around and goes back to buy it. Stopping to sit on a bench for a rest, she stares at it, turning it to look at all sides. It's uncanny really; the only thing missing is the stone pathway through a garden of lilacs… and Ethan.

Olivia sighs. Ethan. She checks her phone for messages from him, but there are none. She's not surprised. In fact, she wouldn't be surprised if she never hears from him again.

When she gets home, she unfolds the stepladder under the tree, wiggling it to make sure it's on solid ground. Holding the birdhouse by the heavy jute string, she climbs to the top step. She searches for a branch that's sturdy enough to hold it. Finding the perfect limb, she leans to reach the small branch, trying to slip the string over it. It's just barely out of her reach. Any normal person would step down off the ladder and move it closer, but not Olivia; she's a rebel. She strains herself, stretching until she's on one foot, leaning as far as she can. The ladder teeters dangerously, two legs lifting off the ground. Olivia's eyes grow wide. She stops moving, aware of what's happening. Dropping the birdhouse to the ground, she tries to grab a branch to steady herself.

Unsuccessful in her efforts, the ladder slowly continues to tip and she's on her way to the ground. Closing her eyes, she prepares for impact.

He reaches her just in time. With one hand firmly on the ladder, he pushes it back onto four legs. The other wraps around her, catching her, as she slides from her perch. She can tell by the familiarity of every hard chiseled muscle, as she slides down his body, that it's Ethan.

With both feet firmly planted on the ground, Olivia opens her eyes and locks them with his. Images of her dream whirl around in her head. She feels like she's all raw emotion, as he holds her safely in his arms. *He's here!* Relief washes over her, putting her earlier fear to rest. But why isn't he saying anything? She moves her arms to his chest, leaning back so she can see him. Unable to read the expression on his face, she worries that he's still angry about last night. She tries to project a calm, somewhat, cool demeanor. "Good timing."

He exhales harshly. It's almost a grunt actually, "What the hell are you doing?"

"Trying to hang my birdhouse." She points to where she tossed it onto the ground. Feeling as if she's a complete idiot, her bottom lip starts to pout.

A smile starts to curl at the edge of his mouth. He rubs his thumb across her brooding bottom lip, taking note that it's no longer swollen. A fact he's glad about, since he has big plans for her lips later. "And are you trying to kill yourself at the same time?"

"NO!" She steps back away from him and scowls as she crosses her arms in front of her. "Well, not on purpose, anyway." She starts to smile as she makes her admission.

Walking over to where she abandoned the birdhouse on the ground, he picks it up, "Why didn't you just call me and ask for help?" Pulling the ladder over a few feet, he climbs it with the birdhouse in hand.

Olivia frowns. "I wasn't entirely sure you would want to see me today." Ethan stops at the top of the ladder and looks down at her, surprised by her answer.

"Why?"

"You looked so upset with me when you left last night." Her heart stings as she thinks about it.

Ethan nods. "I was more than *a little* upset, Olivia. I didn't want to leave." With little effort, he slides the string over a sturdy branch and checks to make sure it's secure. "But I'm not going to stay, if it makes you feel uncomfortable."

Confirming what she already knows makes her feel even worse. "When I didn't hear from you this morning, I just figured you've given up on me." Moisture gathers in the corner of her eyes.

Ethan gets half way down the ladder and stops; alarmed that she's crying. He jumps down, ignoring the bottom two rungs, and moving to her side with an urgent need to comfort her.

"NEVER!" Ethan pulls her into his arms and against his chest, pressing his lips to the top of her head. "I'll *never* give up on you. There's no doubt in my mind that we're meant to be together. Until I've convinced *you* of that, I'll fight hard enough for both of us."

A single tear perches at the corner of her eye, threatening to fall. She wipes at it hoping he doesn't notice.

"I was at the gym this morning," he explains. "I thought I'd give you a chance to rest and catch up on some sleep." Ethan takes a deep breath, inhaling the sweet, alluring scent of her.

"Ethan?" Still in his arms, she looks up through damp eyelashes at the birdhouse.

"Yes?"

Olivia can't believe she's going to ask this question but she's curious. "Does that house look familiar to you?"

"What house?" He releases her and looks curiously around at the adjoining townhomes, before looking back at her for clarity.

"The birdhouse, but not the birdhouse per se." She struggles to find the right words. "The house that the birdhouse is designed to look like." She wrinkles her nose. "Does that make sense?"

He turns to look at it again. *Well, I'll be damned.* It's a long time before he speaks; too long, and it makes her feel uneasy.

"No, I can't say it does." There's an odd sound in his voice. A solemn tone that makes her suspect that he's lying; and he is. He's seen that house many times in his dreams.

Taking her hand, he leads her to the porch. "Does it look familiar to you?" Turning to sit on the step, he reaches for her other hand, positioning her directly in front of him.

Olivia shrugs. "Kind of, but I'm not sure why."

Ethan decides to lead her thoughts a little, without actually disclosing anything. "There were older country homes in Ireland that looked similar to that, but most of them are in ruins or have been torn down and rebuilt."

"Really? In Ireland?" That would explain why her dreams feel like they're in a far away land. She speaks softly; risking the chance that he'll think she's completely nuts. "I think that I've dreamt about it."

Ethan looks down, hiding his eyes from her. It's such an odd thing for him to do that she doesn't know how to react. *What is he hiding?*

When he looks back up, he opens his mouth as if there's something he wants to say. He presses his lips closed tightly and gives his head a little shake. How can he tell her that he dreams about this house, too? This isn't the first time she's mentioned a dream that he's also shared. She barely trusts him now. How would she react, if he told her that he's, somehow, stalking her in her dreams? Deciding to say nothing, he tugs gently on her hands, pulling her forward. Moving his hands to her hips, he directs her between his legs and toward his lap.

Bending her knees, Olivia sits, putting her arm around his neck. His eyes look dark and hooded. Feeling a little concerned and totally off balance by his strange behavior she asks, "Is everything okay?"

Ethan recovers quickly. "No, actually. I came by because I noticed, on my way out last night, that one of your tires looked like it was losing air. It's been bothering me all morning."

"What?" *Why was he checking out her tires at three in the morning?*

Ethan reaches into his pocket and takes out a key fob. "I want you to trade me cars, for the day. So, I can take yours and get it checked out."

Olivia blinks at him a few times, trying to ascertain if he's serious or not. "You want to take my car and have the tires checked?"

"Yes." He drops his hand to her knee, still holding the key fob tightly in his palm.

She starts to chuckle.

"Why is that so funny?" he asks, feeling like he's missed a private joke.

"You've got quite *the inner control freak,*" she laughs, not realizing that he's not laughing with her.

He starts to get defensive, his tone harder, colder, "I won't make excuses for wanting to make sure you're safe. When was the last time you bought new tires?"

She shrugs. "Good question. But it's not your job to look after my car maintenance, anyway." She feels his body tense under her. Oh no, she's struck a nerve. She really doesn't want to fight with him today. Wishing she had kept her big mouth shut, she braces for an argument.

Ethan's jaw tenses and the nerve at his temple begins to twitch. "Would you fucking stop, please? Do you have to fight me at every turn? I'm concerned about your safety... not trying to take over your life."

At that, Olivia stiffens against him, bringing to his attention her obvious anxiety. Still annoyed with her answer, he makes a loud *tsk* sound in frustration. "Look." He lifts a key fob up in front of her face. "I ordered you, your very own key fob and I'm offering you the chance to drive the Hellcat for the day, full tank of gas. Are you going to pass on the opportunity?"

Relieved that an argument doesn't seem imminent, she tries to lighten the mood. "Hmmmm. And all I have to do is let you take my car to get the tire checked?"

"Well, no... there are a few more conditions."

"Of course there is." She smiles, knowing where this is going. "Like?"

"Like... you have to come to the new house to trade back later and have dinner with me."

She narrows her eyes at him suspiciously. "Are you cooking?"

"Yes."

She's surprised. "Can you cook?"

He raises his eyebrows with an insulted expression. "Yes."

She nods. "Alright then. Luckily, I like dinner. Is that all?"

"There was something else, let me think," he teases.

She raises her eyebrows and gives him a wicked little grin. "I'm listening."

"Oh, I remember... there are still a few boxes to unpack." He smiles.

Hmm, so that's the way it's going to be, huh? Two can play that game. Scowling at him, she grabs the key fob out of his hand. "Deal. I'll get you my keys." Getting to her feet, she heads into the house.

Once she's inside, he stares back at the birdhouse. A haggard breath escapes him, "Un-fucking believable."

"What?" she asks, returning with the spare keys.

Startled by her quick return, he gets to his feet. "Nothing."

Extending her arm, she holds out the keys. As he tries to take them, she pulls them back out of his reach. She laughs at his awkward attempt to grab them.

Ethan glares at her with an evil smirk that sends chills through her. *Oh Crap!* She didn't think that through, very well. She's on the edge of the porch and has no escape route. Grinning, Ethan's on her in an instant, forcing her back against the brick. *Holy Shit, the man is fast!*

Putting his palms against the wall, on either side of her head, he cages her in. Slowly and seductively, he moves forward, securing her there by pressing his hips in to her. His body is so solidly in place that there's no space between them.

The cool brick offers Olivia relief from the heat that's pulsing through her body and makes her stomach squeeze. When Ethan feels her clench her thighs together in excitement, his dick hardens in response. She lifts her chin willing him to kiss her throat.

Determined to teach him a lesson for his earlier teasing she puts a stop to his advances. "Down boy!" she says breathlessly. "Don't you have a tire to fix?" She tries to pull away but has nowhere to go.

Ethan laughs and then pulls away reluctantly. "We'll continue later, then. NO excuses."

"Pffft, I don't need an excuse, I don't believe that *sex* was part of our deal, only dinner and unpacking."

Ethan finds the way she challenges him refreshing, irresistible, and very, very sexy. He's not even concerned that his joke may have backfired on him. "We'll see about that. For now, you win round one," he chuckles as he walks away, humoring her.

Olivia is amused that Ethan thinks she could actually refuse him when he pulls out that authoritative tone. She's defenseless. She doesn't think he's actually figured that out, yet. She's thankful for that. When he does, she'll be in all sorts of trouble. Little does she know, he's already got her all figured out, he's just waiting for the right time.

Ethan holds out his hand. "Give me your keys."

Trying not to smile, she licks her lips as she extends her arm, hovering the keys over his hand. He tilts his head to the side, shooting her a warning look, which prompts her to drop them instantly.

"Thank you." Slapping her playfully on the ass, he makes her giggle, as she walks with him toward the lane. Ethan pulls his ringing phone out of his pocket and checks the display. "O'Connell."

Olivia smiles as he answers his phone, all-masculine like.

There's a quick change in demeanor as *business* Ethan makes an appearance. She can tell from the tone of the next few sentences that it's about the Artemis Project. "This can wait until tomorrow," Ethan stops walking, "because it's Sunday."

Olivia thinks she can hear laughter on the other end of the phone. She can tell by Ethan's expression, he's not impressed. But, how is that the fault of the person on the call? Ethan has admitted that he works 24/7. John McCabe is saddled with the same work hours because of it. "Call John in the morning. And if you want to keep your job, I wouldn't bother me again today, unless it's something really important."

Olivia feels a little intimidated. She doesn't think she'll ever get used to that side of him. Why is Sunday no longer a workday? What's changed? He's acting very strange today, indeed.

"Is there anything you need out of the car before I go?" He unlocks the door, waiting for her answer.

Olivia stares at his lips, remembering how good they feel against her skin and thinking about how delicious they tasted in her dream. She shrugs at his question. "I don't think so."

"So, I'll see you later? Around six, okay? I've set the GPS, all you have to do is hit the *go home* option and follow the directions." He pauses, now that could be a problem. "You can follow directions, can't you? I seem to remember that you have difficulty doing what you're told."

Olivia shakes her head, annoyed at his arrogance. "Pretty confident that I'd agree, weren't you?" Some things never change.

"I can be very persuasive." He flashes her that smile that makes her melt. "Have fun, but promise me you'll be careful. No stunt driving."

Olivia scrunches up her face and makes a clicking noise with her tongue. "I don't get to have any fun."

A questioning look washes over his face. "Are you feeling sick?"

"No, I feel fine. Why?" she asks curiously.

"Because the entire time you've been standing here talking to me, you've been rubbing your belly. I thought maybe you were feeling unwell."

Fear shoots through her as she realizes he's right. Damn him! This man doesn't miss a thing... EVER! She's standing there, thinking about her dream; mindlessly rubbing her hand on her stomach, as if she were soothing a pregnancy. She drops her hand to her side, feeling flushed and embarrassed. "I'm okay. Really."

"Alright," Ethan narrows his eyes, "I'm glad." He stares at her trying to figure out what just happened, then starts to chuckle, "Sometimes, you're the strangest girl!" He scratches his head. "I don't even want to know what that was all about."

Ethan looks back at her in the rearview window as he drives out the lane. She's still standing there with her hands over her face, covering it in shame. A very strange, but adorable girl, he thinks. Tonight, he's finally going to kiss those beautiful lips.

Chapter Thirty-One

When Olivia arrives at Ethan's house, she finds him in the driveway with the hood up on her car. Pulling up beside him, she's pleasantly surprised to find him shirtless. Looking up he smiles. "Did you enjoy your drive?" He wipes the grease off his hands with the old rag that's stuck in his back pocket.

"It was amazing!" she gushes, making Ethan chuckle. Leaning against the Challenger, she watches him check all her fluids and make sure everything's topped up. She smiles. It's such an endearing sight, and yet, completely sexy: him standing there naked from the waist up, wearing a pair of soft denim jeans, ripped at the knee. She has a compelling urge to strip him out of them, right here and now. She would, if his ass didn't look so perfect in them.

She jumps when he closes the hood with a hard slam. Wiping the sweat off his brow with the back of his forearm, he gives her that devilish Irish grin. He's dirty and sweaty and yet it doesn't matter, he's still so totally fuckable.

As if he can read her mind, he walks toward her. "You're looking at me with bedroom eyes, Miss James. Should we skip dinner and get straight to dessert?" He wipes his hands on the tattered rag and tucks it into the back pocket of his jeans.

"And miss your awesome cooking skills? Hell no!" She runs her tongue along her lips, trying to moisten them. Ethan oozes sexuality that's nowhere near subtle. *And can we talk about that tattoo!* The man is pure sex, all wrapped up beautifully in a well-hung, Irish package.

"I have so many *other* skills." He raises an eyebrow, giving her a slow simmering smile.

God she loves the way he flirts. "Yes, but I've seen those skills already." It's a good thing that he likes to be teased, because she loves to tease him.

Moving closer, the air becomes charged around them. "Baby, we haven't even scratched the surface, yet."

Olivia's stomach squeezes. *Geez, he's good.* She wonders if she'll ever be able to outplay him at this game. Something catches her eye and she focuses her attention on her car. Looking down, she notices a white marking on the front tire. She glances at the back tires and sees the same mark; then it hits her.

"You put new tires on my car?"

Shit. Busted! "No." He had hoped she wouldn't notice until after she got home.

Olivia glares at him, walking around her car checking all four tires.

"You're still a horrible liar, Ireland. Why do you even bother?" She shakes her head, completely flustered with the man.

"What do you mean *still?* I've never lied to you before," he says it with conviction, believing it's true.

Her eyebrows shoot up and she stares at him in amazement. "How about the time you told me that you didn't get into the bathtub with me, when I was sick?"

Fuck! Completely forgot. Ethan cringes and rubs his hand against the whiskers on his chin. "Is there anything I can say here, that won't get me into any more trouble?"

"Nope, and I think you're a total asshole for lying to me about it." *Whoa! Where did that come from?* She crosses her arms in front of her, taking on an angry stance.

Ethan pleads his case, with sincerity in those beautiful green eyes, "Olivia, I needed to get your fever down. You refused to get into the tub unless I did, too. I kept my shorts on… you had your panties on. Nothing happened. I thought you would feel uncomfortable about it. I figured that there was no harm in not mentioning it, since you didn't seem to remember anyway."

"But I did remember and when I asked you, you still lied. And now you're lying about having four brand new tires installed on my car? We need to have a serious talk about boundaries, Ethan," she scolds him, knowing it won't make a bit of difference. He'll always do whatever he wants. The man is incorrigible. It's hopeless to try to change him.

Swaggering his way over, he brings that beautiful, sweaty, rock hard chest close enough to touch. *Damn.* She seems to have lost her train of thought.

"Good idea. Let's have that conversation right after I shower, cook you dinner, and then fuck you until you're sore and too tired to be mad at me."

Olivia was totally wrong when she thought that his Irish accent couldn't get any sexier. *Gaaah!* "Stop it! I'm angry with you and it makes my panties wet when you say stuff like that."

She didn't mean to say that last part out loud. She wishes she could take it back once she sees the encouragement she's just given him. She tries to stay angry, but that chest just keeps on moving closer; his cock, now swelling inside his jeans, strains against the zipper. His smell is intoxicating, the rugged, salty, scent of his sweat and engine oil. Exhaling harshly, she tries to get a grip, but Ethan won't let her; he teases, keeping her right on the edge of arousal. He knows how to do it, so well.

"Well, maybe we should work in the reverse order then, Olivia. Let's start with the fucking."

Leaning his body against her, he presses his hard cock into her stomach. When he looks down into her eyes, warmth blooms between her legs. Her pulse takes off, shifting into third gear.

Not so fast, mister! She musters up every ounce of willpower she can, pushing him away. "Yuck, you're all sweaty. Go have a shower."

Grinning, he steps away. "I guess this round goes to you, as well. That's two today." He holds up two fingers and smirks. "I wouldn't count on anymore."

Olivia acknowledges his comment, knowing that when Ethan decides he needs to be inside her, there will be no stopping him. She changes gears. "What did you want me to unpack? I might as well start that while you're freshening up."

When Ethan leads her into the house, she's taken aback by how beautiful it is. It's meticulously decorated in a way that perfectly reflects Ethan, a stunning combination of the modern male and the romantic dreamer.

He smiles at her reaction as her eyes wander, taking everything in. "Ethan it's perfect."

"I was only joking about unpacking, there's only a few boxes of CDs and books left. I can do them later."

He hands her two remotes, one for the TV and the other for the stereo. "Make yourself at home. I'll be quick." He disappears upstairs and hops in the shower.

Olivia turns on the stereo and is about to make herself comfortable on the couch when her curiosity gets the better of her. She opens one of the boxes in the corner, in front of the bookshelf. Taking CDs out of the box, a few at a time, she looks at the covers. She tries to get a sense of who the man really is, as she puts them on the shelves. You can always tell by their music selection.

Olivia flips through an extremely eclectic selection of artists, everything from orchestral waltz music to Jason Derulo. Oh, yes... she blushes as she turns the case over to look at the song list. Jazz, Rap, music from the 20's and 50's, Hip Hop... Ethan has it all. She's not sure if that means he's well rounded and open minded, or if he's just a spaz who can't decide what he likes.

She snickers as she puts the last few in place, moving on to the next box. Unfolding the flaps, she finds a box of books. She wonders why he would still need the medical and business textbooks. Far be it for her to criticize anybody else's pack rat tendencies. The rest of the box contains hardcover books, extremely old in appearance. She takes them out one at a time, cautiously, since the covers and bindings appear to be extremely fragile.

She slides them carefully on a shelf at eye level, so they can be seen and appreciated. Curious, she skims through a few of them, still looking for clues to his taste. His collection mostly consists of classic novels and poetry; many of the authors she doesn't recognize other than John Keats, E.E. Cummings and Robert Browning. There is one last book in the bottom of the box, clearly wrapped by a detailed perfectionist. It must be extremely special to him.

Carefully unfolding the tissue paper, she reveals its brown leather cover. The name stamped in gold on the front cover is faded from age, but she can still make out the faint print, *Romeo and Juliet*. Brushing her fingers across the cover, she can feel the slight impressions from the stamped title.

Olivia gets that same unnerving feeling that she got when she saw the birdhouse. Her heart beats in slow motion as she gets the distinct feeling that this book too, is familiar to her somehow.

Goose bumps form on her skin and she has to remind herself to breathe. For the longest time she stands flipping through the pages, reading the ones that he's left strips of paper in, to mark his favorites parts. He would never dog-ear this precious treasure.

Tears come to her eyes as she peruses his selections. She's at a loss for an explanation as to why this book has made her feel so emotional. She knows one thing, for sure now; he's genuinely the romantic soul he seems to be. She's often dismissed that side of him as an act, but NO MAN would go through this much trouble and research, just to get girls into bed. Especially one, who could coax them there with nothing but his smile.

Freshly showered and dressed, Ethan stops midway down the stairs, watching as she thumbs delicately through the pages of the book. There are no words to describe the feelings that move through him at that moment. It's as if he's been waiting for her all of his life. Just like magic, one day she stepped right out of his dreams and into his world. He knows; **he absolutely knows,** without question, that they're meant to be together. The only problem is convincing Olivia. What he's about to show her will make it either easier, or so much worse. Olivia looks up to see him and closes the book, holding it to her chest. "This book is amazing," she says, emotionally.

"I thought so, too. I found it almost a year ago in a tiny little village in Ireland. It cost me next to nothing." He reaches for it. "Let me show you something." He flips it open, revealing the inside of the cover and hands it back to her to read. In faded black ink, on the inside of the cover someone has drawn the shape of a heart. Inside it is written, "EO'C + OJ forever."

Her eyes jerk up instantly to look at him. "I'm confused."

"That was written in it when I bought it."

"Get out of here, you're messing with me." She studies his face, looking for something in his expression that would indicate that he's joking.

"No, I'm not messing with you. I even had the ink carbon dated; the report is in the back of the book."

She flips to the end of the book and opens the paper that's tucked in the back cover. She looks up, surprised. "Early 1920's?" She flips back to the front cover, to look at it again, and traces her finger around the heart. *What the fuck is going on here: first the dreams, then the birdhouse and now this?*

"Some coincidence, huh?" Ethan takes the book out of her hands and closes it, watching her reaction as he puts it on the bookshelf.

"I'll say." She's pensive for a moment. "A pretty huge coincidence." This is the second time today she's had a gnawing feeling that he's hiding something.

Ethan takes her hand and leads her out to the backyard. "Come, it's time for dinner."

It's past dusk and she wonders why they're heading outside. "In the dark?"

"Not for long." Flipping a switch, the gazebo is illuminated by hundreds of white twinkle lights. She gasps when she sees it. The lights sparkle in the dark like fireflies. Ethan holds back the mesh doorway and lets her in.

Ethan has thought of everything. The small round bistro table is set with the most elegant dishes. A bottle of wine sits chilling in an ice bucket, on a sideboard nearby. Candles flicker in the center of the table.

Picking up a small remote, he presses a button. The air fills with the smooth sound of jazz. She's amazed at the time and thought he put into it. He returns her smile, as he pulls out her chair. Once she's seated, he pours her a glass of wine, and excuses himself for a moment.

Returning with two plates, he places them on the table and then sits across from her.

"When did you have time to cook?" she asks, surprised.

Ethan gives her that sexy boyish grin. "I can be very resourceful."

She stares at the plate in front of her: herbed chicken, roasted potatoes and asparagus.

"Ethan, it looks amazing." She picks up her cutlery and takes her first bite. "Mmmm, it is amazing. I'm sorry I ever doubted you."

When they finish eating, Ethan takes her by the hand and leads her to a couch against the back wall of the gazebo. It's clearly a piece of outdoor furniture but it looks comfortable and inviting, with lots of soft and cushy throw pillows. Turning off several strands of the little lights, Ethan leaves them with not much more than the soft glow of the candles. Sitting beside her, with his arm possessively wrapped around her shoulders, he keeps her warm.

"I love the picture on the fireplace mantel. I assume that's your family?"

"Yes, that was taken at Christmas. Christmas tradition is huge in my family. Every year my parents host a …" He pauses for a moment, not sure what word he's looking for. "Well, I'm not sure if it's called a *Ball* here, but they rent a ballroom and there's an orchestra and dancing."

"Really? It sounds wonderful, like the dream I had." She pauses. "Your sisters are very beautiful. It's hard being so far away from family." She tries to stop a frown from appearing on her face. "I know all about that."

"You're missing your sister?"

"Yes, very much."

"Can I ask about your parents? You never talk about them." He feels her body go tense, "You don't have to talk about it, if it makes you feel uncomfortable." Ethan kisses her temple, regretting that he brought it up.

Olivia reaches over and takes hold of his hand. Squeezing it, she takes a breath, trying to build up some courage.

"They were killed in a car accident almost seven years ago, now. There's nobody left but Megan and me. She married Rick almost a year after they died. I had a really hard time with that."

"I bet. I'm so sorry, Baby."

Olivia turns her body sideways. Lifting her legs, she settles them over his lap, bridging his thighs. Ethan feels a chill against his leg and looks down at her bare feet. "Where are your shoes, woman? Your feet are freezing!"

"I took them off during dinner. They were bugging me."

Ethan shakes his head, giving her that special O'Connell smirk: the one that's annoying and extremely sexy at the same time. The same one that's most likely going to get him into her pants.

Rubbing her feet, he tries to restore some warmth to them before moving his hands to rest on her thigh. Holding her there, he gently caresses her skin with his fingers, as if trying to erase her sorrow.

"How did your sister end up on the East Coast?"

"Rick's company closed their distribution center here. He was relocated to the East Coast office."

"Leaving you here alone?" Thinking about it makes him feel irritated.

Sensing the topic is about to spoil their romantic mood, Olivia decides to ease up on it.

"Not alone, Ethan. I have Scott and Rachel; they are family to me." She smiles, trying to distract him from his thoughts.

"And now you have me." He looks at her with an expression that very closely resembles a boyish innocence.

But how long does she have him for? Olivia presses her palm on the side of his cheek, holding him there. Her eyes lock with his in a long silent pause, acknowledging his sweet admission. In the past few days, she's seen a very different Ethan O'Connell. She no longer sees only the ruthless businessman but a whole softer, gentler side, a side that, until now, was hidden by his usual intensity.

Chapter Thirty-Two

A shiver moves through Olivia, making her avert her eyes. Spotting a guitar leaning in the corner, she smiles. Pointing at it, she asks, "Will you play something for me?"

Smiling, Ethan nods and turns off the stereo with the remote. Pulling a stool in front of her, he starts to strum on the strings.

Olivia gets comfortable on the couch, propping pillows around her and settling in. Her heart starts to throb when she recognizes Hedley's hit song 'Kiss You Inside Out.' Ethan's acoustic arrangement has a much slower melody and his voice caresses the words with tenderness. She can't take her eyes off him.

Ethan holds her gaze the entire time he serenades her, his love carried on the words that flow from his lips.

Olivia has heard the song a hundred times on the radio, but never really listened to the words. It's as if they were written specifically for her. Ethan's performance ignites something inside her that she thought she would never feel again. She fights the tears as moisture starts to cloud her vision, afraid that if she blinks it'll force them to fall. *Could this feeling be love?*

She closes her eyes as he sings those words and imagines being trapped beneath his kiss. Her blood pumps through her veins like molten lava. The sudden need to feel his body against her, overwhelms her.

Finishing his song, Ethan quickly returns the guitar to its stand. Catching a glimpse of Olivia in the candlelight, it's unmistakably clear to him that he's looking into both his past and his future. There's only her, no one else. Olivia takes his breath away so intensely, that he's not satisfied with just her body; he wants her heart, too. *Fuck the agreement.* He's been longing for her to look at him the way she is at this moment. It's a look of desire, passion, and adoration.

He's not going to screw things up tonight. He decides that he's going to worship her, the way she deserves to be worshipped by a man. Her soft brown curls fall seductively across her shoulders, perfectly framing her face. He's enchanted by the softness in her eyes, now wide with anticipation, as they look up at him through damp lashes. Her lips are soft, moist, and kissable. He'll no longer be denied them.

Sensing his need, Olivia gets to her feet as he moves toward her. The electricity in the air makes every nerve in her body tingle with the anticipation. No words are spoken as he wraps his arms around her. Their two bodies melt into one.

Bringing his hand to the side of her face Ethan pauses. His eyes lock to hers, as if he's searching for something in her gaze. He'd settle for anything: a clue, a hint, a silent confession of her love. When he finds what he's searching for in her riveting hazel eyes, he slides his hand through her hair. His fingers curl around the back of her neck, pulling her forward until their lips almost touch. Holding her there, he whispers against her lips, "I'm going to kiss you now. And you're going to let me."

His demand is met with tacit assent. Not wasting another second, he slants his mouth over hers. As their lips touch for the first time, in consensual desire, he entices her briefly with his warm, soft kiss. It's as all first kisses should be… soft, sincere and extremely sensual. Pulling away, he leaves her wanting more. Ethan's hands gently pull her hips against his, and then slide with desirous intent, around to her back.

His mouth hovers close, still tasting her on his lips. He waits for her response.

His intention sets off a torrent of emotions through her body. Raising her hand to the nape of his neck, her thumb gently brushes along the edge of his jaw. Moving to his lips slowly, her hesitation drives him wild. Finally, she presses against him and parts her lips, matching his movements, sliding along them in perfect unison.

Nipping at his bottom lip, she holds it gently between her teeth before breaking away and letting the suspense build between them. They're like teenagers kissing for the first time; figuring out how to please each other.

As the kisses deepen, with their building desire, Ethan opens his mouth wider, claiming her. Olivia responds, the first easy touch of her tongue making his cock swell painfully inside his jeans. Moaning, he closes his mouth around it and moves with a little more urgency.

Olivia recognizes his response and knows where it's leading. She prepares herself for the rough male aggression that comes with his need to be inside her. Tonight, however, there's no hostile takeover of control, just a sweet return of affection as they explore and learn how their mouths fit together.

Pulling away, Ethan gently brushes his thumb over her kiss-swollen lips as he releases her and takes a step backwards.

No! Her heart races; confused by the space that he's just put between them. Ethan takes the stereo remote out of his back pocket and turns on the music. Taking her hand, he guides her to the middle of the room. "Dance with me." He smiles, suspecting that she'd refuse him nothing at this moment. "Do you know how to waltz?"

"No," she looks up at him curiously. "Do you?"

"Yes, of course."

Of course he does! There's that damn smirk again. "Teach me?" she urges.

"Perhaps another time." He has other plans for tonight.

Olivia pouts as he fast-forwards the stereo, searching for a different song. When he finds the right one, he steps into her, wrapping his arms around her waist and sways her gently to the music. Their feet barely move but it doesn't matter; all she wants right now is to have his large masculine body wrapped around her. Her body craves him more than it ever has before. When she lifts her head, so she can look into his eyes, he kisses her repeatedly, making up for lost time.

"These lips are mine now," he says possessively, when he pulls his lips away. "Tell me they're mine. I want to hear you say it."

"Ethan," she protests, not wanting to encourage his possessive nature.

"Say it," his voice is soft, but it's still a command not to be ignored. He holds her chin so she can't look away.

Butterflies flutter around in her stomach as she looks, long and hard, into his meadow green eyes. "My lips belong to you."

Ethan rewards her with another kiss, rougher, more greedy. Tension coils deep inside her as arousal dampens her panties. Suddenly Ethan pulls away, looking at her with an expression she can't figure out. For the second time today, he looks like he wants to say something but he hesitates. *What's going on in his head?*

"Ethan?"

In one breath, he forces it out before he changes his mind, "Olivia, I know my temper is an issue for you. I should warn you that, I don't know what I'll do if I ever see the bastard, Noah Thompson, kiss you again."

It quickly becomes very clear to her; that look... it's his *inner turmoil.* Olivia's face flushes red at the thought of him witnessing Noah's kiss. Her heart prickles with an uncomfortable feeling.

"I just about lost my fucking mind last night watching him put his lips on you." His fingers dig possessively into the flesh of her hips.

Poor Ethan, she didn't set out to do anything to upset him. It just happened. It most certainly won't be happening ever again, after what Noah called her. If Ethan knew about that, he'd kill him for sure. The thought crosses her mind. Ethan kept his promise. Even after witnessing Noah kissing her, he controlled his temper. It couldn't have been easy for him. Maybe she really is important to him? The thought makes her stomach roll.

She can't bear to see the torment in his eyes. In a change of roles, Olivia needs to console him, reassure him; chase away his anxiety. "Shhhh." Running her hands over his shoulders and chest, she soothes away his tension. Whispering in his ear, she gently skims her mouth against the tender lobe, "My lips belong only to you."

Ethan relaxes, his shoulders softening as he loosens his grip on her. She pulls him in for a passionate kiss, wondering how she could have ever thought that *not* kissing him was a good idea. Possessing his lips with a scorching intensity, she makes him groan against her mouth.

Ethan lifts her off the ground, holding her tightly against his chest. When he sets her down, the expression on his face is no longer turmoil; it's something else... desire, passion... need.

Taking her by the hand, he leads her toward the house. *Yes! Now we're talking.* Olivia scoops up her shoes along the way, making him chuckle and shake his head. Ethan's phone rings, making her jump. Other than the sound of the crickets, it's the first time they've been interrupted all night.

"It's John, I better take this." Ethan frowns at the display and puts it on speaker.

"Of course." It's a welcome break for her libido.

"Hey, what's going on?" Ethan asks, concerned.

"Hey, sorry to bother you, but I have Nate Ross on the phone for you. I know you've been trying to touch base, so I thought you'd want to talk to him. I hope I'm not interrupting anything."

Olivia raises her eyebrows. "Nate Ross? As in lead singer of the group, Follow?" She's obviously impressed.

"Good evening, Olivia," John's not surprised at all that they're together.

"Hi, John." She smiles, batting her eyelashes.

Ethan rolls his eyes. "Yes, that Nate Ross. Will you excuse me for a minute?"

"Yes, I'm sorry, I should get going anyway."

Ethan grazes his thumb along her chin, "I'll only be a minute. Don't go anywhere." Heading up the stairs he puts his phone back at his ear, "John, go ahead and put Nate through now."

Olivia knows that the secrecy has to do with the grand opening. He's been very tight-lipped about his plans for the big night, and it's really quite annoying. She occupies her time by wandering around the room looking at his pictures. Picking up the photo of his family, she looks at it closely, thinking how wonderful it must be to have everyone together at Christmas.

It's getting late, and exhaustion starts to set in, making her eyes feel heavy. Ethan kept her awake the entire night. *Christ, the man has stamina.* Emotionally it's been a rough week; she just needs some time to recharge. Besides, work comes very early in the morning, so it's probably best that she just leaves now and avoids having to deal with him. She can send him a text when she gets home. He won't like it, but that's just tough.

Standing at the doorway, she slips her feet into her shoes, trying to make her get away. When she turns the doorknob and pulls, the door won't budge. Feeling the heat from his body behind her, she raises her eyes to find his hand flat against the door holding it shut. *Holy shit! How did he get there so quickly without making a sound?*

"Let me guess, in your other job you're a ninja?" she jokes, hoping he finds the humor in it.

"Right you are. Now that you know my secret, I'll have to keep you locked up in my bedroom to keep you from revealing my secret identity." With one hand still pressed against the door, he gently turns her to face him. Moving in close, he leans his forehead against hers. "You weren't going to leave without kissing me goodbye, were you?"

Ethan's voice is feathery soft and calming. Olivia lowers her eyes, saying nothing. Everything becomes so... still: quiet. She can hear every beat of his heart. Slowly raising her head, she rubs her nose against his. Tilting her head back, she searches for his mouth. When their lips meet, in a slow sweet gentle movement, she kisses him.

Wrapping his hands around her body, he holds her tightly. When Olivia can no longer bear the intimacy of the moment, she puts her hands to his chest, using the leverage to push away from his embrace.

"Everything okay, Princess?" He searches her eyes for a sign.

"Yes." She stares right into his big green eyes.

"Then, why are you sneaking out?"

"Because I knew you'd try and convince me to stay. Honestly, Ethan. I'm exhausted. Some sex fiend, who just can't seem to get enough, kept me awake all night last night."

A grin forms on one side of his mouth. "Mmmm... I hate when that happens to me."

She scowls at him. "Somehow, I doubt that."

He chuckles, "Okay, I won't stop you if you want to go home."

She breathes a sigh of relief, "Thank you. And we still have to have a talk about the tires."

Ethan edges forward, doing that sexy little thing he does: lowering his eyes, admiring her, from head to toe, in a slow perusal. Smirking and biting his lip as he goes, as if he has some very dirty, devious plans for her body. It makes her pulse jump every time.

"Why don't you just pretend that I'm the tire salesman?"

He doesn't have to finish his sentence, she knows what he's about to say. "Seriously, Ireland? That's not funny."

Ethan shrugs. "You shouldn't restrict your talent to fast food delivery men. Don't you believe in equal opportunity?" His smirk is infectious. "Tire salesmen need sex, too."

She tries not to laugh at him. "You're really annoying."

"So you've mentioned… several times." He runs his hands over her body. "I don't want to argue."

Olivia nods in agreement. She doesn't want to argue either.

"Then, if you insist on leaving, kiss me goodbye."

"First, tell me how you know Nate Ross."

"Hmm, are you withholding kisses unless I provide information?" His hands twist in her hair now, twirling it around his fingers.

"Yes, I guess I am." She bites her lip and waits, expecting him to protest.

"Nate and I met when he was in Scotland on tour. Now kiss me." He tugs her forward and smashes his mouth against hers. Annoyed at his sparse answer, her arms hang heavily at her side, refusing to return his embrace. His kiss softens as his mouth covers hers. Her body betrays her, bringing her hands up to his biceps, squeezing and caressing as she returns his kiss.

Somehow finding the restraint to ignore the raging hard-on in his pants, he takes her by the hand and walks her to her car. This day is not about the sex, it's about so much more; it's about the intimacy… the connection. Making sure she's buckled in safely, he closes the door. Just before she pulls away, she rolls down the window and asks, "One more kiss?"

Leaning down, he meets her lips through the window, gifting her with the hottest, make-your-knees-weak good-bye kiss. It's so hot; she almost reconsiders leaving. As he straightens, she puts the car into gear and starts to grin. "Hey, Ireland," she says out the open window. "Not that I'm bragging or anything, but I do believe I just won round three." She breaks into the cheekiest smile as she witnesses the look on his face.

"Well.Fuck.Me." He scratches his head and looks back at her beautiful smile. "Well played, Princess." A grin forms on his delicious, kissable lips, as Rachel would call them. She would be partly right. They are definitely more than delicious.

Chapter Thirty-Three

The air in the city is heavily burdened with smog on this humid summer morning. The traffic is at a stand still throughout the entire downtown core, yet Ethan sits in the Challenger unaffected by the mess around him. For the first time in many months he feels rested, recharged, even. He might even go as far as saying he feels *content*. He scans the radio stations looking for something that suits his mood. When he finds it, he sings at the top of his voice, confident that the closed, tinted windows of the Challenger hide him from view.

The phone rings, forcing him to turn down the volume before he hits the hands free button on the console. "Hello!"

"Hi?" John is a little shocked by Ethan's casual greeting. Usually by this time of the morning, he's worked himself into tyrant mode.

"Hey! How was your weekend? I trust you found a way to entertain our guest?" Ethan chuckles.

"It was a great weekend, Ethan. Thank you." John scratches his head suspiciously.

"I'm stuck in traffic. I'm still about twenty minutes out. What time is our first meeting?"

"Not until 10 a.m. You have plenty of time. I thought tomorrow night we could take Shannon to the restaurant for dinner. I'd like her to see it before she goes home."

"That sounds like a brilliant idea. Traffic's starting to move now. I'll see you in a few minutes."

John hangs up the phone and looks at Shannon with an uncomfortable look.

"What's wrong?" she asks, with concern. She'd be lying if she said she wasn't a little nervous about meeting Ethan in person. He has a reputation for being difficult, insensitive at times. Their reason for meeting today isn't under pleasant circumstances.

"Nothing. He's in a really good mood." John shrugs.

Shannon watches John's face, noting the uneasy look on it. He shuffles some stuff on his desk to make room for her to work there.

"That's good isn't it? Why do you look worried?"

"Ethan doesn't do *good moods* often, especially these days. It makes me nervous." Catching her watching him with wide eyes, he tries to put her at ease. "Don't worry. Everything will be fine this afternoon."

She nods her head. "I can handle it. You'll be there when I tell him, right?" Looking down at her briefcase, she fusses with the clasp, trying to hide her anxiety.

"Yes." Walking toward her, he puts his hand on top of hers, stilling her movements. Lifting it to his mouth, he kisses it gently, as he reaches over and pops open the clasp on the briefcase.

Shannon tries to smile at him. She wishes that their time together wasn't coming to an end. "I imagine the news will end his good mood."

John touches her chin with his thumb before brushing upward across her cheek. He doesn't care that anyone can walk in and see them. "Yes, I imagine it will." Her stark blue eyes mirror his own. He worries how a future together will be possible under his current employer. For now, he needs to concern himself with shielding her from the fallout that will come with this afternoon's news.

Taking a deep breath, Shannon presses her lips together tightly, reminding herself that she is used to dealing with tough clients. Ethan O'Connell is not the most difficult one she's had to deal with. Perhaps, it's his relationship with John that has made her feel more sensitive to the situation.

John looks at his watch. "I need to go and make sure he's ready for this meeting. You make yourself at home here in my office. Help yourself to whatever you need."

"Okay, I will." She watches him walk to the door. Feeling a little anxious, she calls his name, "John…"

Pausing, he turns to meet her worried look.

"Ethan's going to FREAK… isn't he?"

He frowns and nods his head in agreement. "Yes, but don't worry, Baby. I won't leave you to deal with him alone." He blows her a kiss as he pulls the door shut.

When John reaches Ethan's office, he finds him sifting through his emails. "Is there anything you need me to do in preparation for this meeting?" John asks, when Ethan acknowledges him.

"I don't think so. I've already reviewed the presentation we worked on last week. Everything looks good. The agenda went out ahead of time so things should run smoothly. There is one thing I'd like you to check into for me."

"Alright, what?"

"I'd like to know if we have any clients… or potential clients in Nova Scotia. I'm thinking about taking a trip out that way."

"I'll check into it and let you know."

Ethan stands and as he passes John, he grins and pats him on the back. "Let's get going, then."

John looks at Ethan suspiciously, shaking his head at his unexpected behavior. Picking up the stack of handouts and the laptop, he follows Ethan down the hall, reviewing and discussing the finer points of the presentation. Ethan's phone makes a beeping sound. He quickly checks to see what's going on and then looks at John. "The battery is almost dead, do you have a charger?"

"Not with me, but I know who does."

As they reach the reception area Hannah stands to greet them, adjusting her breasts as they approach. "Good morning, Mr. O'Connell," she says with a flirty smile.

"Good Morning, Hannah! I missed your beautiful smile when I arrived this morning."

She blushes as she sits down and gazes up at him. "I'm sorry I missed you, I must have just stepped away for a moment."

John flashes Ethan a look, which he completely ignores. Leaning against the desk, he continues flirting with her, "I was wondering if you might be able to charge my phone for me while I'm in my meeting?" He holds it out in front of him, showing her that the battery is almost dead.

"Of course!" she beams. "My phone uses the same charger." She reaches up and takes it out of his hand, making sure to touch him as she does. Her eyes never leave his. Glued to his, they glaze over with a hunger, as if she's been fasting and he's her next meal.

"Any calls that come through the switchboard for me you can forward to John."

"ANYTHING for you, Mr. O'Connell," her words purposely intended to send a seductive message.

John becomes concerned that Ethan seems to have no perception of the signals she's sending.

"Hannah, you're awesome." He winks at her. Putting his hand on top of hers, he gives it a little squeeze, not thinking twice about his actions. When they walk away from the desk, John leans in and expresses his concern.

"Do you think it's a good idea to encourage her like that?"

"Like what?"

"Flirting with her like that. It's a bad idea."

Ethan looks over his shoulder at her. Hannah leans forward, peeking at him around the corner of the desk. When their eyes meet, Ethan finally realizes what John is talking about.

"Oh shit! You're right. Sometimes I don't even realize I'm doing it."

"Well, you better dial it down, Prince Charming. If you're serious about Olivia at all, you had better start thinking about how she'd feel if she saw you flirting with another girl like that. Especially, Hannah."

Ethan stops dead in his tracks, looking at John as if he's just thrown a glass of water in his face to wake him up. "Christ, good point."

Olivia runs around her house, tearing it apart, looking for her phone. Sitting on the side of the couch, she runs her fingers through her hair in frustration. "Geez, not again." She worries that Ethan is going to think that she's doing it on purpose, as an excuse to see him. As if his ego needs to get any bigger. Deciding not to stress over it, she heads to work, excited over the news she has to share with Rachel.

Standing at the doorway, waiting for Rachel to acknowledge her, she can't hide her smile.

"What are you up to?" Rachel asks, when she finally looks up.

"I just wanted to let you know that Ethan's lips are definitely delicious and extremely kissable." She shifts her weight back and forth, far too excited to stand still.

"Get the fuck out of here! You finally kissed him?"

Olivia's eyes open wide, shocked at her reaction. "Rachel! You just said the 'F' word!" She's only heard Rachel use that word on very rare occasions.

"I knew those lips were sweet. Details... I want details!" She waves her hand summoning Olivia into her office.

Olivia laughs, "You won't believe the night he planned. He cooked dinner and he set up this beautiful gazebo outside with twinkle lights, candles, and music. Then, we danced." She glows as she recounts their evening for her best friend, making sure to include all the pertinent details. "He sang to me." Warmth washes over her at the memory.

"Are you kidding me?"

Olivia raises her eyebrows and smiles. "He almost has me convinced that he's not the arrogant, quick tempered, man slut that I thought he was."

"It sounds like a wonderful date. Scott used to do stuff like that for me," she reminisces for a moment, not realizing that Olivia's smile has faded into a frown and her brows furrowed.

"It wasn't a date," Olivia denies.

"Uh, it sure sounds like a date."

"Well, it wasn't," Olivia argues.

"Okay, if you insist. Who cares what you call it as long as there was awesome sex afterwards!" She wiggles her eyebrows at her.

Olivia develops a sour look on her face. "We didn't have sex last night. We just talked and danced... and kissed."

Rachel laughs, "It was definitely a date."

Olivia thinks about the night and closes her eyes, whispering under her breath, "Sneaky bastard!"

Rachel's smile is a mile wide as she tries to choke back her laughter.

"It's not funny," Olivia snorts.

"Come on, Liv. You have to admit it's *kind of* funny. He found a way to finally get you to go on a date with him and you didn't even realize it." She looks at Olivia's face and notices the chagrin. "You're not mad at him now, are you?"

Olivia takes a deep breath and lets it out all at once. "No, I'm not mad at him. It was a really nice night. I saw a side of him that I don't think many people get to see. He was sweet, gentle, and charming in a way that was... *genuine.*"

Rachel stares at her, stunned. "Oh, my God! You're falling for him."

Olivia is startled at the words. Her nerves spasm as if someone had just jumped out from behind the door and screamed 'boo!' "What? No!" Butterflies flutter through her veins with the realization. "He...I..." She silently concedes, looking down, ashamed. *Son of a bitch!*

Both girls stiffen as a deep voice speaks from the doorway, "Good morning, ladies, discussing your game plan for the day?"

Rachel looks at Olivia nervously, wondering if he heard any of the conversation. "Good morning, Mr. Dunn."

He looks between the two of them and then nods. "I was looking for Olivia." He passes a folder in her direction. She quickly stands to take it from him, flipping it open as she does.

Jeremiah Dunn, co-owner of Dunn & McLennan is short man, in his late fifties. The dark black rims of his glasses stand out harshly against his well-manicured white hair and beard. Unlike his business partner, he seldom wears suits to work. Casual slacks and sweaters are more in line with his *inner geek.* His rounded belly hinting that he spends much more time behind a computer than being active. As far as Olivia knows, there was never a Mrs. Dunn. She's wondered on several occasional about his sexual preference. Not that it matters; she enjoys working for him. As bosses go, he's patient and kind.

"I'd like you to go in and see this client today. They called me at home last night with some concerns. My notes are in the file."

Olivia nods as she reads through the papers. "Yes, sir. I'll look after it."

"Thank you, Olivia." He steps away from the door and stops, turning back to look at her. "There's something different about you today," he says with a smile. "You're absolutely glowing." Shoving his hands in his pockets, he scurries back up the hallway to his office in the south end of the building.

Olivia glances over at Rachel, absolutely horrified by his observation.

"Well, he's not wrong. You are glowing." Rachel shrugs.

Olivia frowns. "Now *I* feel like saying the 'F' word."

Rachel laughs and rolls her eyes. She holds her hand out, gesturing toward the file Olivia is holding. "What's going on?"

Olivia releases it to her and sits. Rachel quickly flips through the notes. She laughs once and glances up quickly. "Good luck with this one."

"Oh, don't worry. I already know how to fix it," Olivia says in a confident tone.

Rachel shakes her head. "Girlfriend, your brains are seriously wasted here," she says, handing the file back to her, "So, since you're going to be right downtown anyway are you going to drop in to see Ethan and have a nooner? I bet you're dying for him to spread you out across that huge mahogany desk."

"No! Oh my God, you can be crass sometimes." Olivia gives her a look of disgust to hide the real truth. She's fantasized about it many times, climbing up on that desk and spreading her legs in front of him while he sits in his chair, wearing a power suit and ruling over his empire.

Rachel glares at her, making a face that makes her feel that she's under close scrutiny. "This from someone who has sex with her boyfriend *anywhere* but in a bed?"

Olivia grunts her annoyance, "First... he's NOT my boyfriend." She ignores Rachel's eye roll. "And second, I'm fairly certain that you would never walk into Scott's office during the work day and let him lay you out on his desk."

Rachel stands in silence; a slow wicked grin starts to curl at the edge of her lips. Olivia's mouth drops. "Shut up! You did not."

"Laid out on it, bent over it…"

Olivia holds her hand up in the air, halting any further information from being shared. "Ew, I'm going to think about that every time I look at Scott, now. Thanks for the visual." She walks away, afraid to hear any more. "Oh, by the way I can't find my phone again. I think I might have left it at Ethan's house. I think I should stop by and see if it's in his car while I'm downtown. I just wanted to let you know, in case you're trying to reach me."

When she glances back over her shoulder, Rachel is smiling and shaking her head. "Drive safely downtown in that car of yours; especially, if you have no way to call for help if it breaks down again. As soon as you find your cell, please text me and let me know you're okay."

"Will do."

Olivia calls her client and arranges to meet him. Afterward, she dials Ethan's cell number to find out if he'll be in the office. It's odd that he doesn't answer, even odder that the call seems to get dropped, without going to voicemail. She dials the number two more times with the same results and scowls.

In the large empty foyer of Aurora Technologies, Ethan's phone buzzes to life on the corner of Hannah's desk. Curious, she peeks at the screen to see Olivia's name. Discreetly, she reaches over and hits the button, disconnecting it before the call can be directed to voicemail. Pleased with her interception, she does the same thing the next two times.

Olivia is ready to leave to meet with her client and still hasn't been able to reach Ethan. It must be an important meeting if he's turned off the ringer and ignoring her calls.

Rachel sticks her head in Olivia's office door. "Scott's not there," Rachel informs her. "He's out with a client, so he's not sure if Ethan is even in the office today."

"Oh, okay. Can I borrow your cell phone for a minute?" She uses Rachel's phone to send him a text. Surely, he'll check them when he's done whatever it is that he's doing. She tries not to have negative thoughts, reassuring herself several times that he's at work and a very busy man.

When Olivia's text message comes through, Hannah peeks around the corner to make sure no one is coming. When the coast is clear, she picks up the phone and deletes the text. Then, grinning mischievously, she quickly scrolls through the call log and deletes Olivia's missed calls.

A few moments later, the hallway fills with people leaving the conference room. John stops by to collect Ethan's phone, as Ethan walks along side one of the engineers. She frowns when walks past her, without even acknowledging her.

"We're going to be out of the office for a lunch meeting. We'll be back around 1:30," John says. "Thanks for charging the phone."

Hannah nods, her lack of eye contact, an angry dismissal, as she reaches for the ringing phone. "Aurora Technologies."

"Can I speak with Ethan O'Connell, please?" Olivia says, calling from a phone at her client's office.

When Hannah recognizes the voice on the other end of the phone, she leans forward to make sure that both John and Ethan are out of earshot.

"I'm sorry he's not available at the moment. Can I take a message for him?"

Her voice echoes through Olivia's ears like fingernails on a blackboard. "Uh, yes please. Can you let him know that Olivia James called? I'm trying to get a hold of him to tell him…"

"I'll let him know you called. Have a nice day." Hannah hangs up with no intention of giving Ethan the message.

When Olivia hears the dial tone, anger pulses through her body making her twitch. *Bitch!* Digging her keys out of her purse, she heads to the underground parking. When she reaches the street level, she sits waiting to turn left, to get back onto the highway and head toward home. Hannah has really grated on her nerves. Annoyed and angry, she checks her rearview mirror to make sure no one is behind her and quickly changes lanes, turning right to head into the city.

When Ethan and John return from lunch Ethan darts down the hallway to his office, avoiding eye contact with Hannah. John stops to check in and taps his fingers on her desk to get her attention. "Are there any messages for Ethan?"

Hannah shakes her head. "No. Nobody has been looking for him." She avoids eye contact, trying not to smirk.

"Is Miss Quinn still in my office?"

"Yes. She had a conference call so I ordered her in some lunch."

"Thank you, Hannah. I appreciate it."

When John opens his office door Shannon is sitting, looking through her notes. "Hey."

Shannon's face lights up when she sees him. "Hey!"

John's eyes become dark, looking apologetic as he presses his lips together in a hard line. "I'm afraid it's time."

Shannon frowns. "Okay, let's get it over with." Twisting her blonde hair, she clips it up on the top of her head. Taking a deep breath, she gathers her stuff and follows John into Ethan's office.

Ethan stands when they enter. Making his way around the desk, he extends his hand.

Shannon smiles as she shakes it. "It's really nice to finally meet you in person, Mr. O'Connell."

"Please, no need to be so formal today. Call me, Ethan. I trust that you had a pleasant weekend?"

Her face turns pink as she glances quickly at John. "Yes, thank you."

Ethan gestures toward the chairs. "Please, sit."

John pulls out a chair for her then winks, trying to break the tension and reassure her.

When Ethan settles in his chair, he leans back, waiting for Shannon to speak.

"We're making some headway with the investigation," she begins. "We've been able to find out that, later in the evening, Miss Keane showed up at Reese Wilson's apartment, expecting that he'd take her in but left angry when he refused."

Ethan's confused. "He refused?"

"Yes. She eventually ended up staying with her sister but later on that night... this is where it gets a little foggier... witnesses say that she was at McGuire's Bar at around 12 a.m."

Ethan scowls. "I was still there at the time. I would have seen her."

"Apparently, she wasn't there for long. We think that she arrived, saw you and then left. The interesting thing is that her car stayed on the property until the next morning. We have a copy of the parking ticket that was issued."

"So, if she left... who did she leave with?" Ethan asks.

"We know that it *wasn't* Reese Wilson. We have video evidence that he was at the gym on Park Street. Several of the regulars at the bar confirmed they saw her there, but nobody remembers seeing her leave with anyone. We're trying to get permission to view any of the traffic videos and security footage from outside the bar."

Getting nervous, Shannon pulls out a folder from underneath her paperwork and glances over at John. "Ethan, there's been a new development that complicates things." Standing, she walks to Ethan's side of the desk, and places a folder down in front of him. When she returns to her chair, she's too nervous to sit, so she stands holding the chair back for support. Ethan senses her anxiety and looks over at John, noting that he too, looks like he'd rather be anywhere but there. Picking up the folder, he reluctantly flips it open to read the documents inside.

All the way up in the elevator, Olivia is a bundle of nerves. She's not sure how she's going to manage keeping a civil tongue in her mouth. What she really wants to do is poke Hannah in the eye when she sees her. When the doors open, Olivia takes a deep breath and peeks out. There are plenty of people moving around in the foyer. Chasing one of them down the hallway, Hannah leaves the reception desk empty.

Olivia exits the elevator, blending in with the crowd. She zips down the hallway to the left unnoticed, heading toward Ethan's office. Most of the offices down this corridor are in darkness so she doesn't encounter anyone on the way. As she passes Scott's office, she notices that he's still not back. She shudders, thinking about her earlier conversation with Rachel.

Olivia hears voices as she nears Ethan's office. She slows down as she approaches the door, wondering if she should interrupt or just wait until they're done. When she's almost at the door, she stops, frozen, when she hears the intense tone of the conversation. Ethan's voice erupts loud and angry. She decides to stay out of sight, but close enough so she can hear what he's saying.

"PREGNANT? What the fuck do you mean PREGNANT?" His voice echoes through the hall. Olivia hears a woman's voice, but she's so calm and quiet, that she's barely audible.

A strange unidentifiable feeling pulses through Olivia's body. This is definitely not a conversation she wants to interrupt. Doing a U-turn, she heads back down the way she came. She only gets a few steps away when she stops, remembering that she needs her phone. *Shit! Shit! Shit!*

Turning back to the office, she stands at the edge of the doorway, hidden from view. She cringes as she hears the continuation of the conversation.

"I'm telling you, there's absolutely no way that it's mine," Ethan insists.

The woman says something else that Olivia can't make out.

"Well, then have it terminated," Ethan screams at her, "I'll get a court order if I have to."

Chapter Thirty-Four

Shocked at his suggestion, Olivia clasps her hand over her mouth.

The unfamiliar female voice grows a little stronger, "I'm afraid the pregnancy is too far along for that option, Ethan."

Ethan responds with a barrage of curse words. John's muscles tense as he weighs his loyalties; he's torn between his friend, who also happens to be his employer and the woman he loves.

Ethan's words spew from his mouth like poison. Having had just about enough of the way he's speaking to Shannon, John gets up to confront him. Swinging the door closed, he catches Olivia's reflection in the glass of the framed artwork on the adjacent wall. He leans his head out and finds her leaning to the right of the door. John is fairly certain, from the look on her face, that she's overheard the conversation.

Olivia hesitates, not sure how to react. Embarrassed, she steps into the doorway in front of him; her attendance is still hidden from the others in the office.

"Ethan," John says, trying to get his attention. When he doesn't stop his loud ranting John yells at him angrily, "ETHAN!"

Stunned at John's tone, Ethan turns his attention to where John's standing at the door.

"I'm sorry," John whispers to Olivia, as he moves to the side, revealing her in the doorway.

The red angry flush on Ethan's cheeks slowly drains, leaving him pale. "Olivia? What are doing here? Is everything okay?"

Olivia looks between Ethan and Shannon, her stomach churning; making her nauseous. Her heart is pounding so fast that she can't process what she's just heard, over the sound of the blood pumping through her ears. "Yes. Everything's fine."

"I… I think I dropped my phone in your car again." Unable to breathe, she starts to back up, nervously apologizing for interrupting, "I'm sorry. I'll just get it another time." Turning, she takes off down the hallway at an extremely quick pace, hoping that she doesn't pass out from lack of oxygen before she reaches the elevators. *Breathe…just breathe.*

Ethan puts his palm to his forehead, holding it a moment, before raking it backwards through his hair. "Fuck!" He heads to the door. "Olivia! Wait!"

John steps in front of him, halting his exit, "Ethan, you shouldn't go after her when you're this worked up. I'll go."

Ethan shakes his head. "No, I'll get her. You go and check my car for her phone."

Against his better judgment, John nods and backs off. "Okay. Are you good?"

Ethan hands John the key fob as he tries to push past him through the doorway.

Putting his hands on his chest, John stops him to verify his mindset. "ARE. YOU. GOOD?"

Ethan's tone is clipped. "Yes!"

"Good. I'm not sure how much of that conversation she heard, but she's obviously very upset."

Ethan glares at him, then impatiently shoulders past him into the hall. "Well, then get the hell out of my way, so I can catch up to her."

Down the hall, Scott has just dropped his briefcase on the desk and is about to sit down when he sees Olivia whiz past his office door. He squints and rubs his eyes, wondering if he's hallucinating. When he gets up to investigate, stepping out into the hallway, he collides with Ethan.

"Whoa!" Scott says, as they bounce off each other, "Was that Olivia? She looked upset."

"Yes."

"What the hell is going on?"

Ethan pushes him to the side so he can pass. "I'll fill you in later."

He hurries, almost catching up with her at the elevator. "Olivia, WAIT," he says in a commanding tone, watching the doors open as he approaches.

Olivia steps inside, frantically pushing the button to close the door. He reaches her just as the heavy metal doors start to close. "Whoa! Whoa! Whoa!" He lunges the last few inches and grabs the edge of the door, forcing it to reopen.

Swallowing hard, Olivia looks up into his stormy eyes. Despite John's efforts to calm him, he's still agitated. Watching her trying to close the elevator door only made it worse. The air is thick with angry tension as he gives her an icy stare. Stepping forward, he forces her to step back slowly, allowing him to enter.

Olivia can see the rise and fall of his chest as he struggles to catch his breath. As the doors start to close, Hannah is on her feet. Holding the phone receiver several inches from her ear, she watches in shock.

Olivia glares at her, her expression clearly sending Hannah a very unladylike message as the doors completely close.

Ethan stands still beside her, taking his time to catch his breath and calm himself. As the elevator starts to descend, the silence between them causes agonizing tension. Somewhere around the fifteenth floor, Ethan finally breaks the silence, barely turning to look at her. "How much did you hear?"

Fidgeting uncomfortably, she fixes her gaze at the wall on the opposite side of the elevator. "From the part where you're going to be a daddy."

Ethan squirms uncomfortably at the words. "And your first reaction was to run… without giving me a chance to explain?" He struggles to keep his voice calm.

"No further explanation is required. It's pretty clear." Stepping forward, she pounds the button for the underground parking level.

Ethan clenches his jaw tightly and presses the button for the ground floor.

"And I certainly wasn't going to stick around and listen to you continue to bully and berate the woman who's having your child!" Olivia bites out at him.

"The woman who…?" The nerve at his temple starts to jump. "You've got the wrong idea, Olivia." When the door opens on the ground floor, he tries to steer her out of the elevator but she puts on the brakes.

"Let go of me," she growls, as she pulls her arm away from him. "My car is in the underground parking. I'm leaving."

Ethan takes a deep breath in, his nostrils flaring, as he props his foot against the elevator door to stop it from closing. Ethan turns to her with a terrifying expression, grabbing her by her elbow; he yanks her roughly out of the elevator. "No, you're not! You're going to wait here for John and give me a chance to explain." Stumbling, she tries to keep up with his long angry steps as he drags her through the lobby.

Fear starts to grow in the pit of her stomach. "Ethan, please… slow down. People are starting to stare." She grimaces at the pain in her arm from his insanely tight grip.

It takes a moment for her words to reach him through the hazy cloud of anger. When he looks down at her, he's startled by the expression on her face. Glancing around at the people watching him nervously, he slows his steps and relaxes his grip on her arm. "Jesus… Olivia, I'm sorry." He grasps her hand, leading her to the small coffee shop in the corner of the lobby. Olivia protests, keeping her fingers stiff and straight in his hand, refusing to give in to him. Ethan looks down at her hand, hard and inflexible in his. With a worried expression, he turns his gaze to meet the coolness in her eyes.

Finding a table at the back of the room, he steers her toward it and pulls out one of the chairs for her. "We'll wait here for John to come with your cell." Pulling his phone out of his pocket, he texts John to let him know where they are.

Appalled and shocked at the abhorrent way he spoke to the woman in his office, Olivia considers making a huge scene. She feels a great deal of sympathy for that poor woman; knowing she's going to have a long difficult road ahead of her raising **his** child.

When Ethan looks up, she's standing. "Sit down. I'm going to get us a coffee, and then you're going to hear me out." When she doesn't comply, he commands it of her, "SIT DOWN!"

Glaring at him, she sits angrily against her will. Ethan starts toward the cashier and then stops to look at her. "And don't even think about leaving," he says watching her reaction.

Olivia looks away, her anger getting the best of her. She struggles to understand how the same sweet man, she spent time with last night, can become the insensitive, fire-breathing dragon she just witnessed upstairs.

Standing only a few feet away, Ethan finally understands the gravity of what's just happened and how it's affected her. Gone is his earlier placidity, as that old familiar feeling of angst washes over him. Afraid that he's going to lose her, anxiety pumps through his blood as he walks back to where she's sitting and crouches at her side.

"Olivia. Promise me you won't leave." He takes her hands in his and squeezes them, his tone softer, almost pleading. She refuses to make eye contact with him and it adds to his anguish. He gently caresses the back of his fingers across her cheek. "I'm so sorry. I know I'm an ass." Sliding his fingers under her chin, he gently turns her to face him. When she finally looks him in the eye, he leans forward pressing his lips against hers; trying to atone for his behavior.

Olivia stiffens, not sure how she feels about his kiss at the moment. The sickening memory of his reaction plays over in her mind. What if that had been her? Will he treat her the same way if she tells him something he doesn't want to hear? She doesn't return his kiss; her lips remain still and unwilling.

Ethan pulls away, frowning, and smoothes her hair behind her ears. "You're upset. You have every right to be. I don't deserve your kisses today." Leaning his forehead against hers, he says a silent prayer. "Please promise me that you won't leave. Just let me explain," he begs.

When he pulls away, the sadness in his eyes jabs at Olivia like a sharp knife to her heart. She replies with a quiet nod. As much as she'd like to walk away right now and never see him again, she can't. She knew from the very first day she saw him; that the moment he kissed her, there'd be no turning back. She's convinced that it's the reason he tries so hard to win her over; he somehow senses it as well.

"I'll be right back." Standing, Ethan kisses her on the top of head before making his way to the counter.

While he's waiting for his order, he makes a call. Olivia stares at him from across the room. *So, his phone is working.*

Ethan leans against the counter, watching for any sign that she might change her mind and bolt for the door. He needs to explain it to her, but he has no idea where to begin. Returning to the table, he pulls the adjacent chair around the table to sit beside her. He watches her face as she stares down at the cup of coffee he's placed in front of her. She fiddles with the lid, allowing it to distract her and avoiding his stare.

"Olivia, I'm sorry you found out like this. I would have told you. I just didn't want to lay all my ex-girlfriend baggage on you, right away."

She laughs once. *Baggage? He knows nothing about baggage.*

Ethan exhales harshly, preparing to begin. He takes her hand, holding it firmly when she tries to pull it away. "Olivia, that woman in my office is my lawyer."

Olivia looks at him surprised. "You knocked up your lawyer?"

Ethan makes a face. "No. She's not the one who's pregnant. It's a long story but I'll try to explain briefly. I had been living with a woman in Ireland for several months, when I suspected she was sleeping with someone else. When I confronted her, she admitted it. I asked her to leave, which she did, but when I cut her off financially things got ugly."

Olivia turns to face him now, listening intently. He looks so upset and sincere talking about it, she almost starts to feel a little sympathetic.

"She left me messages for weeks after I closed all her accounts, begging me to take her back. When I didn't return any of her calls, she decided to go public, going to the media with some pretty outrageous accusations."

"Oh, Ethan. I'm so sorry." Slowly, her anger turns to compassion. She just doesn't have it in her to pretend that she doesn't care. She'll just have to push her feelings behind that protective brick wall for now.

Shaking his head, Ethan looks into her eyes. Soothing himself, he squeezes her hand and rubs his thumb in circles in her palm. "Most of my friends still won't talk to me. My family supports me, but I can see in their eyes that they don't truly believe me when I say I didn't do the things she's accusing me of." He swirls his coffee around in the cup, thinking about the past several months. His attention drifts to unpleasant times.

"Ethan?"

Lifting his head, Ethan meets her softened gaze, and frowns. "The media frenzy was brutal. The company finally sent me to Canada to avoid any further negative publicity. Miss Quinn was hired, just in case I found myself in the position where I would need legal counsel. Turns out, they were right to do so. Just after I left for Canada, Jess went to the police and filed a complaint."

Olivia has completely pushed her anger to the back of her mind now. Her only thoughts, at the moment, are of consoling him. She doesn't even know yet, what he's being accused of. Really, dealing with his demons, has got to be much less painful than facing her own.

"Both John and Miss Quinn believe that every time she contacts me, it's because she wants money. When I refuse to respond, she does something drastic, trying to force me into contacting her. John thinks it's a form of blackmail. She'll just keep on trying to ruin me, until I take her back or pay her money to stop."

"So, she's the one who's pregnant?"

Ethan nods. "So she says." His voice gets desperate, "You've got to believe me, Olivia… if she's pregnant; it's not mine."

He really is clueless. Olivia rakes her hand through his hair. *This:* temper tantrums and pregnancies? This is easy. This is nothing compared to the secret she keeps guarded. She can deal with this. She brings her lips to his in a tender, reassuring kiss. Ethan relaxes into her touch, his soft and gentle lips accepting her kiss.

Olivia uses the pad of her thumb to wipe her lipstick from his mouth. Then, leaning back, she makes a sad face at him.

"Oh no, please… anything but the sad face." Ethan pulls his brows together.

"You think I'm upset because you knocked up your ex-girlfriend?"

"Allegedly," he adds.

"Whatever, Ethan. You think I'm upset because you *allegedly* knocked up your ex-girlfriend?"

"It's not the reason?" he asks surprised.

"Geez, Ireland, for someone so brilliant, you are incredibly dense sometimes. Unplanned pregnancies happen. It's not the end of the world, although it may feel like that to you, right now. Besides I would have no right to be upset about something that happened before we met." She stops, needing clarification, "Is your relationship with this woman finished? Or do you still have feelings for her?"

Ethan shakes his head. "The only feeling I have for her is hatred. I have no desire to ever see that woman ever again."

"Okay, I believe you. You're a smart boy, Ireland. I think you can figure out why I'm upset."

He looks at her confused for a moment then nods. "My temper?"

"Yup, your temper! What the hell was that?"

Ethan looks ashamed. "Liv, I've been trying really hard to keep it under control. When I heard that she's pregnant and claiming it's mine…" His nostrils flare as he pauses. "I know it's just another way she's schemed up to get money and… well… I lost it." He reaches for her, touching her hands, caressing her cheek, rubbing her knee; needing the warm tactile feel of her skin to calm himself.

"I've never felt as afraid as when I looked up and saw you there. I was so sure that you'd leave me, if you had overheard... and then you ran." He pauses, bringing her hand to his lips and kissing it. "I wouldn't blame you, if you didn't forgive me." Dark and hooded eyes don't hide his shame. He lowers his head, bowing to her in a humbled gesture; ripping her heart right out of her chest.

Olivia sighs heavily. That may explain his temper but it sure doesn't excuse it. She could never have had a conversation with Sam about his temper. But, Ethan isn't Sam. Something she has to keep reminding herself when dealing with her anxiety.

"Ethan, believe me, I can't believe I'm not heading for the hills, right now. I totally understand why it made you angry... but what really upset **me** was the way you were talking to that poor woman in your office. You should be ashamed of yourself, that was absolutely disgusting."

Ethan nods in agreement, surprising her by taking full ownership for his behavior. "You're right. I really fucked up. The way I acted was inexcusable. Please forgive me, Olivia."

The desperation and sincerity in his voice tugs at her heart. "It's her forgiveness you should be asking for, Ethan. Not mine." Although his anger often intimidates her, she knows that Ethan O'Connell is a gentle soul. There's nothing dark or evil about him. She knows that deep down. She's felt it all along. He's a good man with a quick temper. It's something she's going to have to come to terms with, if she intends to stay with him.

Ethan nods in agreement. "I promise to make it right." He searches her eyes for her acceptance. Lowering his head to stare at the floor, he silently thanks his Lord for sending him this angel. She'll save him from himself. He's certain of it.

In a reversal of roles, Olivia presses her finger under his chin and forces his gaze to hers. "Uh, you bet your ass you will, Mr. O'Connell."

Ethan stares at her, his heart pounding, as he falls in love with her, just a little bit more.

Olivia looks over his shoulder. "John's here."

John places her phone on the table in front of her. "You seem to have a problem keeping track of that thing."

Olivia wrinkles her nose. "Sorry, John."

He smiles. "No need to be."

"Ethan, I tried to call your cell several times, before I left the office, but you didn't answer."

Ethan looks at John and scowls. Taking his phone out of his pocket, he checks the incoming call log and finds nothing from her. "I don't have any missed calls from you this morning, Olivia."

John leans over his shoulder to look at the screen, furrowing his brow. "That's strange."

"I even sent a text message from Rachel's phone."

Ethan scrolls through messages, looking for that one as well, but comes up empty. "Really strange."

"You had it with you all morning?" John asks.

"Yeah, except when I left it with Hannah to charge." Instantly, he looks over to John with an alarmed expression. They exchange a knowing glance.

Olivia looks back and forth between them. "Speaking of Hannah, I even left a message for you with her, as well."

Ethan's jaw tenses as he continues to look straight at John.

"I checked with her after lunch, Ethan. She said she had no messages for you."

Under his breath, Ethan mumbles something in Gaelic, which Olivia assumes is not very nice. John interrupts, "Leave it with me to deal with. You're too upset."

Olivia continues to look back and forth between them. "I'm confused, what's going on?"

Ethan reaches over and picks up her phone, opens the contact list and makes a new entry. When he passes it back to her, he explains, "Olivia, I've just added John's cell number to your contacts. If you need *anything* or if you can't get a hold of me, I want you to call him."

Ethan looks at John. "You'll make her a priority. Anything she needs, you'll address as if the request has come directly from me."

John nods. "Yes, of course."

Olivia's eyes grow wide and she blushes. "Ethan! That's not necessary."

"The hell it's not! With everything else that's going on right now, I need to know that you're being looked after. I'll go fucking insane worrying about you, otherwise."

Olivia looks over at John, feeling embarrassed about being his new assignment. John looks calm, indifferent, not at all fazed by Ethan's request.

"Is there anything else?" John inquires.

"No, I'll walk her to her car and then be back up to my office shortly."

John nods. "Alright then, I'll go back up and check on Shannon." His face turns slightly red, as he thinks about Ethan's treatment of her.

Ethan picks up on his discontent, "Listen, John... about what I said to her up there..."

John stops him, "Not now, Ethan. Later... we're going to have a talk."

Ethan looks nervous and nods, holding up his hand halting the conversation. "I'd expect nothing less. I just wanted to say I'm sorry." He reaches across the table and grasps Olivia's hand, staring directly into her eyes. "If someone talked to *my girl* like that I would have murdered him on the spot."

Olivia looks up confused. *John and the lawyer are a couple?*

With a stoic expression, John makes his intentions very clear. "Oh, don't worry, O'Connell... You and I... we're going to come to a CLEAR understanding on how you'll treat Miss Quinn, from now on." Glancing over at Olivia, he gives her a quick wink to drive home the point that he made the day of their first meeting.

When Ethan nods his understanding, John turns and walks toward the elevator. Ethan looks at Olivia with wide eyes and panic on his face. "Well… Miss James, it was nice knowing you."

"Huh? What the heck are you talking about?"

"Apparently, I'm going to get another ass kicking from McCabe." Ethan's expression softens and he breaks into a chuckle.

"What?" She's surprised to hear that.

"He sparred with me a couple of weeks ago and sent me to the mat. He has one hell of a right hook." He grins, rubbing his jaw as he remembers the impact.

Why is he smiling about that? Men are so strange.

"Are you finished with your coffee?" Ethan looks at his watch, knowing that he has an appointment with important clients in his office soon.

"Yes," she says, still feeling a little edgy. She's certain that the added caffeine has made it worse. It's a strange combination of anxiety she's feeling. She's not sure if it's because of what just unfolded in front of her in Ethan's office, or the sight of him in that pale grey, Calvin Klein suit. The double-breasted jacket clings to his body perfectly, from his broad powerful shoulders to his well-toned waist. The sheen of the silvery tie catches her attention as it boldly stands out against his black dress shirt. Reminded of a scene in a book she once read, she rubs her wrists, imagining it tied around them, binding her, rendering her helpless against his sexual advances.

Heat shoots through her, from her head to her toes and back up again. *Oh, Dear God!* There couldn't be a more inappropriate time to have these thoughts. The past hour flashes through her mind at lightening speed: babies, abortions, lawyers, screaming, chasing, and dragging. She should be in her car, on the way home, never to speak with him again. Yet, when he extends his hand to her, she accepts it, locking her fingers together with his and making him grin.

"Stairs or elevator?" he asks.

"Stairs, I need the exercise." She's really hoping that it will help her burn off some of the sexual tension, so she can start to think more rationally.

Frowning, Ethan shakes his head at her remark. Leading her to the entrance to the stairwell, he's unaware of what's going on in her mind or her panties. When Olivia gets down the first section of stairs, a disturbing thought invades her brain, making her stop dead on the landing.

Ethan continues a few steps down, before he realizes she's no longer with him. He turns to her with a questioning expression.

Olivia's body has stiffened angrily and there's fury in her eyes.

"Olivia? You okay? What's wrong?" he asks alarmed. *What in the hell did I do now?* He watches as the tension pulls her shoulders upward, and her hands clench into fists at her sides.

"Gaaah! That BITCH deleted my messages off your phone!" She turns with an unexpected swiftness and heads back up the stairs.

He wondered when she'd figure it out. Watching her stomp her way back up to the first floor, he grows concerned, "Where are you going?"

"Where do you think I'm going?" she barks out angrily. "I'm going to grab that bitch by the ovaries and use them to rip her uterus out through her nose!"

Ethan laughs aloud. Panic sets in when he realizes that she's completely serious. *Oh shit!* He had better act quickly before she gets to the door. Taking the steps two at a time, he grabs her from behind, wrapping his arms around her waist in an attempt to stop her.

Jolting back as he grasps her, Olivia fights against him as rage spurs her on. *Christ, she's strong!* He lifts her, so that her feet are off the floor, causing her to lose traction. She fights him as he carries her back down to the landing and sets her down. Her body goes lax, as her feet hit the ground. Ethan nuzzles into her neck while she pushes at his hands, trying to unclasp them, "Let me go!"

"Oh, I don't think so, Princess. I'm not going to let you go up there when you're this upset."

"You're protecting her?" she says angrily, twisting her body trying to break free.

"No, I'm protecting *you*."

Something changes at that moment; a calmness sweeps across her. She's no longer angry, no longer thinking about the scene in his office. She no longer thinking about all the reasons she should walk away, never to see him again. Her fatalism prepares her for the realization that, whatever his shortcomings are, she's meant to be his. She's meant to surrender to him. Her body softens; then becomes tense in a whole different way.

Ethan feels it as it moves through her body. With one hand still banded around her waist, he moves the other to caress across her breasts, finding her nipples hardened in arousal.

His own pulse starts to race as he wraps himself around her. He thinks about lifting her skirt and taking her right here in the stairwell. His only hesitation is the danger of being caught. At the moment, he's not even sure if he cares. He wants her.

Feeling the movement in his pants, Olivia pushes herself back against his hips, rubbing the head of his cock between the cheeks of her ass. She smiles as she feels him respond, springing to life and hardening with his usual thickness. Licking her lips, she digs her heels in and tries to break free again, making him tighten his grip around her again.

"Stop it," he whispers into her ear. Ethan reads her body like it's one of his favorite books: knowing the plot... anticipating the outcome. He knows that she's excited. His control and her resistance are the source of her arousal. Ethan's lips form a wicked grin. "Seems you've got quite the nasty temper yourself, Baby Girl. Tell me, how long did you think you'd be able to keep that a secret?" Nibbling that tender spot on her shoulder, he makes her breathing stutter. He leans in close. "Jesus Christ, do you see the affect you have on me? I am so turned on right now," he growls, his voice saturated with sexual desire, as his rock hard erection pushes heavily into her back.

Biting at her lip, she holds back her smile. Locked firmly in his arms, she continues to play. The more she fights him, the harder he grows. The more he tries to restrain her, the wetter her panties get. It's so wrong but so incredibly arousing. He takes a couple of steps, overpowering her, pressing her body into the wall and holding her there. His chest expands as he breathes heavily against the back of her neck.

Ethan is a master at this game. When she teases him a little bit more, he presses harder into her. Dipping down, he rubs himself along her backside, drawing a low sensual growl from deep in his throat. His hands rub down her sides and curl around the hem of her skirt, dragging it upwards to expose her thighs. She tries to hide the amusement in her voice. "Apparently... holding me here against my will makes your dick hard, Mr. O'Connell."

Ethan smirks as his erection pulses and swells harder at her words. "Apparently," he admits. "It was THAT... and the way your dirty mouth talks about my dick." Breathing heavily against her ear, he glides his hand between her legs and into her damp panties. Her body keens as he presses his thumb against her very sensitive clit.

"There's something *wrong* with you." Moaning, Olivia surrenders to his hand. Her muscles are now exhausted from struggling with him.

Ethan laughs once, moving his lips down her neck. After brushing her hair to the side, he gently slides her top off her shoulder to expose her skin, kissing her there. "That's funny," he whispers, "because the only time I ever feel *right* is when I'm with you."

Chapter Thirty-Five

Loud, squeaky hinges echo through the stairwell. The heavy door swings open and footsteps bound toward them. Startled by the intrusion, Ethan eases away. Olivia turns to face him, her back now resting against the concrete wall. Standing sideways against her hip, he leans his forearm against the wall, hiding his arousal from the person approaching. Pretending to be engaged in nothing but a casual conversation, Olivia looks at him, appearing to be listening intently. Her gaze keeps dropping down to his lips; his warm, soft, delicious lips. Despite the acidity of the words they spoke in his office, she longs to have them pressed against hers; tasting him, kissing him. *For heavens sake hurry up and pass already!*

Rounding the corner of the landing, the intruder slows as he sees them, glancing at them awkwardly as he passes. Ethan nods a polite greeting, while Olivia avoids eye contact all together. When the door to the underground parking slams shut, she slides her hands into the space between his jacket and his body; running them from his abs to his hips and making his muscles tighten under her touch. Oh, how she wishes that his crisply ironed dress shirt didn't prevent her from touching his skin. She scrunches the fabric in her hands thinking about pulling it free from the waistband of his pants and getting underneath it. "Please… kiss me," she says, desperately.

Ethan grins, very eager to comply. Lowering his lips, he gently brushes across her mouth, growling in a dark, edgy voice, "I'm contemplating on doing more than just kissing you here." Sliding his fingers under her skirt, he lifts it well over her thighs. His palms smooth past her hips and over the rounded flesh of her bottom. In a quick movement, he pulls her forward, exhaling a long tortured breath. Skimming his hands along the edge of her panties, he tightens his fingers around the thin fabric. His wicked glare is full of sinful promises.

Olivia's pulse beats erratically, as she realizes his intentions are to rid her of them. "Do it!" she begs, encouraging his dick to jump and press harder against her. Straining against the pleated fabric of his pants, he tightens his grip on the delicate lace, seconds from ripping them away with a forceful tug.

The theme from "Rocky" blares out loudly in the enclosed space of the stairwell. Olivia frowns, completely frustrated. Growling his displeasure, Ethan leans his forehead against her, pulling the edge of her skirt back into place and straightening it. "John's new ring tone," Ethan confirms as he pulls it out of his pocket.

"Yeah? Yes, I know… I know… I said, I KNOW. Well, stall them a few minutes." He looks at Olivia and rolls his eyes. "Just make something up. Don't you have a list of excuses ready for these occasions? Well then, I'm obviously paying you too much money."

John loudly protests. Ethan winces, holding the phone away from his ear, making Olivia giggle.

Ethan smiles and winks at her. How does he do that? How does he make her completely forget about all the ugliness with such a small gesture?

"So let's recap shall we… *I'm* the boss, and *you're* the assistant. So assist me… by lying to them. I'll be there in a few minutes." He looks at his watch and then disconnects the call.

Olivia is holding her stomach, full out laughing when he turns his attention back to her. Ethan thinks it's the most beautiful sound in the world. "He's going to kick my ass later, anyway." He shrugs. "I figure, I might as well make it worth his while." He holds out his hand. "Come, I'm going to make sure you're safely locked in your car and then get back to work. Not that I'm going to be able to think about anything other than you for the rest of the day."

While he's being completely honest, there's something she needs to ask him, "Ethan?"

"Yeah?"

"Do you have any other baby mammas I should know about?"

Ethan's hand tightens around hers, painfully, forcing her to look up at him. He shakes his head. "None." He opens the car door and stands aside. "Well, at least none that have made themselves known to me."

Olivia stands with a worried expression on her face. "That's not funny, Ethan."

"I'm sorry, Babe. My bad." Grabbing her, he pulls her into him, crushing her against his chest. Lowering his lips, he possesses her in a greedy kiss. He curses when the LCD display of his phone lights up in the dim parking garage and "Rocky" plays again. Kissing her on the top of her head, he exhales heavily, "I have to go." Ethan hates the disappointed expression on her face. It would suit him if he never had to see it, EVER.

Olivia nods, giving him an understanding look. "I know."

Ethan secures her safely in her vehicle and sends her on her way. Olivia rolls down her window and calls to him as he walks away. "Hey, Ireland?"

He turns to look at her, walking backwards toward the stairwell door.

"Do I have a ringtone?" she asks curiously.

Grinning, Ethan ignores her question, taking another step backward.

"What is it?" Reaching over, she hits speed dial on her cell. When the call connects, Olly Mur's "Troublemaker" rings loudly from his pocket, echoing through the underground garage.

Ethan closes his eyes in regret. When he opens one eye to peek at her, she's staring at him with her mouth hanging open. "SERIOUSLY?" she yells with her arms crossed angrily in front of her.

Ethan laughs and continues to back away. Olivia tries hard to be angry with him, but his laugh is contagious. The sides of her mouth start to curl into a smile. Rolling her eyes, she shakes her head. Placing his hand to his mouth, Ethan blows her a kiss, then turns and jogs to the door.

On his way to John's office, Scott stops him in the middle of the hallway, concerned. "Is Olivia okay? She looked really upset."

Ethan nods, but it doesn't put Scott at ease. He places his hand firmly on Ethan's chest as he passes, stopping him. Ethan looks down at Scott's hand, then glances up to meet his irate expression.

"I believe my wife has already explained what will happen if you do anything to hurt Olivia."

Ethan raises his eyebrows, warning him that he's dangerously close to crossing the line. Pushing his hand away, he returns Scott's stare. "She's fine, Parker. And if you're looking to kick my ass today, you'll have to get in line." Shouldering past him, he opens the door to John's office, finding both him and Miss Quinn there.

"What did you tell the people from Bramtech?" he asks, standing in the doorway.

John stands. "I told them you were detained and I've sent them down to the executive lounge for coffee." He hesitates. "It's not like you to be late for an appointment."

Ethan purposely avoids the last statement. "Thank you, John. Could you give Miss Quinn and I a few moments alone to talk?"

John looks at Shannon nervously. She nods, indicating that she's comfortable with his request. "Okay. I'll go down to the lounge and bring your clients back to your office."

Ethan nods and closes the door behind him. Shannon meets his gaze when he turns to address her. Ethan's not sure where to start, but he's promised Olivia that he'd make things right and he intends to do so.

When John returns to his office, he hesitantly opens the door. He finds Shannon smiling and the two of them engaged in a casual conversation. Relief washes over him. "Ethan, I've taken Mr. Atwal and Miss Daniels to your office."

Ethan stands and buttons his suit jacket, nodding at John as he passes. "Thank you. You can join us when you're ready." Making his way to his office directly across the hall he stops, looking back at them with a warm smile, before he puts on his business face and opens the door.

Shannon lets out a loud breath and physically relaxes. Walking toward her, John runs his hand up her arm in a comforting gesture. "What happened?"

"He apologized."

John's face morphs into shock. "He what?"

Shannon nods her head. "Believe it. He apologized."

"Wow! Shae, you have no idea how *huge* that is for Ethan." John is flabbergasted.

"I think I understand just how huge that is. But that's not all." She watches him nervously, not sure how he'll react. "He's asked me to stay until after the grand opening of the bar, all expenses paid."

"That's two weeks from now." He blinks in disbelief.

"I know," she whispers.

John's hit with a lot of overwhelming emotions, all at the same time: suspicion, surprise and joy. Joy being the outward emotion he wants to convey to Shannon. But he's hesitated, just long enough, to make her feel insecure about his reaction; even when he wraps his arms around her and lifts her off the ground. When he touches her feet to the ground, she leans back so she can see his face. "John, I…I don't have to stay. That's a long time for you to be stuck with me. Just say that word if you need some space and I can go."

"Stuck with you? Are you kidding me?" He leans down and kisses her briefly, barely skimming her lips, when his cell phone vibrates in his pocket. He reads the message, sifts through a stack of folders on his desk, and pulls one out. "I'll be right back, Ethan needs this file."

Shannon nods, but she's still feeling uncomfortable with his answer. Reading it in her eyes, he puts down the file and rounds the desk to get to her. "Hey, what's wrong?"

"Nothing." She busies herself with the documents in front her, pretending that it doesn't affect her when he presses his body against her side.

"Shae? Talk to me. Do *you* want to stay?"

She stops what's she's doing, distracted by his hot breath against her ear.

Hesitantly, he reaches for her chin and turns her, searching her eyes. "Shannon? Answer me… do you want to stay?"

Shannon swallows hard as her breathing becomes shallow. Her body tingles in reaction to the muscular body pressing against her. "Yes."

She blushes and it makes him smile. "Good, because I really want you here with me."

She lets out a sigh of relief and closes her eyes, visibly relaxing.

Pressing his lips to her temple, John lingers there. "I'll call your hotel and arrange for them to check you out and have your stuff sent to my hotel. No point in having two rooms when you won't be there."

Shannon's eyes open in shock and she stiffens in his arms. She looks up into his eyes, loving him enough to give him an '*out*.' "Are you sure you want me to stay with you the whole time?"

Putting his hands on her hips, he pulls her into him. "Let me show you just how sure I am."

John lowers his lips to hers in a slow teasing kiss. Her hands snake up his arms to his shoulders and around his neck, holding him in place. He deepens that kiss, parting his lips and encouraging her with his tongue.

They don't even stop when Ethan bursts through the door. Ethan stops, frozen, and clears his throat, trying to interrupt them. "Ahem. I need that file, lover boy."

Without breaking his kiss, John reaches down to pick up the folder and holds it out in Ethan's direction.

Ethan chuckles lightly, taking it out of his hand. John continues to kiss and caress his woman, as if Ethan isn't even in the room. Feeling a little awkward, he shakes his head quickly to break his stare and then smiles. "Okay then, don't let me interrupt... " He salutes with two fingers. "Carry on!"

Ethan leaves, feeling warm and happy. He's not sure why, all of a sudden, he's become a romantic, sappy guy. A few months ago there was no room for disruptive women in his career. He wouldn't have tolerated that from John, either. But now, here they are... both of them distracted...enamored and totally consumed with thoughts of the warm tenderness of a loving woman. It's a huge contrast from his normal persona... Ethan O'Connell, badass executive.

Ethan is just wrapping up the meeting when John finally joins them. Mr. Atwal gets to his feet and shakes their hands before he leaves. Stacey Daniels however, remains seated... twirling her blonde hair and drawing out finished conversations. Leaning forward, Miss Daniels makes sure that Ethan gets a good look at her *assets*. When her breasts don't seem to get his attention, she sits back, crossing her legs; allowing her skirt to ride up high enough to expose her thighs and long, silk stocking covered legs.

John eyes Ethan nervously, knowing where this is going. John has seen it happen, all too often. Ethan, being Ethan, has always been receptive to their advances. He's flirted... schmoozed... and charmed them. John knows for a fact, that early in his career Ethan had bedded a few of his female business associates with the intention of "*firming up*" business deals. Not that John condoned it, but he certainly understood. He made every effort to discourage it, once Ethan hired him full time.

That doesn't seem to be the case today. Something seems a little *off*. He notices Ethan's somewhat uncomfortable expression and tense body language, an unusual behavior, since Miss Daniels is an incredibly sexy, young woman.

"I think we might be able to do business together." She smiles.

Ethan nods in agreement. "I think it makes good business sense." Ethan walks to the door, hoping that Miss Daniels will follow his lead and get on her way.

Stalling, she bites her lip. "I was wondering..."

Gliding over to where he's standing, she reaches up to touch his arm. "Maybe, we could discuss how our arrangement could be mutually beneficial... over dinner?" She squeezes his bicep as she takes an appreciative gaze at his chest.

Ethan glances over at John. Arrangement? Fuck he hates that word. When he hesitates in his reply, she finds a way to make him agree.

"After all, I am the swing vote on this deal with Bramtech," she reminds him.

Ethan's body tenses beneath her hand.

She traces little circles on his arm. "I'm staying downtown for a few nights and I'm bored out of my skull. I thought you could think of something for us to do."

"Us?" Ethan asks nervously. His male mind betrays him and he takes a long perusing look at her body.

She smiles when she notices. "Yes, silly, you and me. Later, my friends are coming to meet me downtown and you could take us to all the best nightclubs in the city." She bats her eyelashes and smiles, "Maybe, you could introduce my girls to some of your hot friends, so we can all have some fun?"

Ethan hesitates, feeling uncomfortable. He's never felt awkward in this situation before, but this is something he definitely doesn't want to do. All he wants to do is go home to Olivia and finish what they started in the stairwell.

"Miss Daniels, could you please excuse John and I for a moment while we check the schedule for this evening? Please make yourself comfortable, while you wait."

She grins hopefully. "Certainly, and call me, Stacey, please."

John opens the door and follows Ethan into the hall.

"In your office," Ethan directs.

Shannon is startled when the door swings open and she sees the look of distress on Ethan's face. He drops heavily into one of the chairs.

John sits beside him, with his phone in his hand and his schedule open, just to humor him. "Ethan you know there's nothing on the schedule tonight, right? You had me clear it earlier."

"Fuck, I know." Ethan leans his elbows on the edge of the desk, resting his head in his hands.

"What's going on?" Shannon asks, curiously.

"Miss Daniels would like Ethan to accompany her tonight for a night on the town," John informs her.

Shannon looks puzzled. "Is that a bad thing? I thought you two entertained clients all the time?"

John continues to field Shannon's questions while Ethan continues to struggle with his thoughts,

"Well, yes we do. But Miss Daniels has suggested that it would be wise for Ethan to '*entertain*' her this evening, as she has some leverage over the decision on whether they do business with us or not."

"OOOH!" Now she gets it.

Ethan lifts his head in disgust. "She expects me to prostitute myself out in return for her approval on our business proposal."

Now this is interesting. John leans back in the chair and stretches out his legs before crossing them at the ankles. "So, let me ask you a question, my friend. You've never had a problem with doing this in the past." He watches, as Ethan grows more uncomfortable. "In fact you've always rather enjoyed it. Stacey Daniels is an extremely sexy and desirable woman."

Shannon raises an unimpressed eyebrow at John's assessment.

Ethan had barely noticed her beauty. She's young and blonde and very well put together. The fact that her legs seemed to go on forever was the only thing that caught his attention, but other than that, he really felt no attraction to her. Where exactly is John going with this? Ethan stares straight ahead clenching his jaw.

"So, what's changed Ethan?" John presses him for an answer.

Ethan's surprised that John even has to ask him that question. "You know damn well what's changed, McCabe…Christ." He shakes his head at his audacity. "Olivia. Olivia has changed everything."

John grins. "I expected that's what you'd say."

"So then, why are you being such a dick?" He shoots him an extremely aggravated look.

"Because I wondered if *you* knew the reason why. So, it's simple then… go in there and tell her no. Tell her that you're madly in love with a wonderful woman and that you won't compromise that for a business deal. Whatever happens… happens. Worst case scenario, you don't get the business."

If it was only that simple, but it's not, this is a HUGE business deal. Ethan shakes his head, looking back and forth between John and Shannon. "Other options?"

Shannon leans forward. "What about accepting her invitation but inviting Olivia to join you?"

"Even better," John interrupts. "Shannon and I will join you, as well."

"I like that idea better. Call Scott and get him to round up a few of the guys from soccer. Get a few drinks into those boys and they should keep her and her friends *entertained* for the evening." Something on his phone momentarily distracts him. "Let's have dinner at that British pub beside the hotel I just invested in. It's close. Get the guys to meet us there around 8 p.m. There's plenty of stuff there to keep them busy. I'd like to avoid clubbing afterwards, if I can." He looks at his watch. "John, can you make the arrangements, and then let Stacey know what the plans are? I have to meet with Mike Johnson in a few minutes in the conference room."

John starts to grin. "You just don't want to go back in your office."

"You've got that right; first the pregnancy and now this. I'm afraid to go back into that office ever again."

He looks terrified and it amuses John. "What about Olivia?"

"I'll call her on my way to the conference room. I'll see if she can swing around, grab me a change of clothes, and meet me here around 6:30ish. Lets plan on dinner around 7?" Ethan is half way out the door and on his way down the hall, with his phone in his hand; trying to get away before John makes him deal with Stacey.

Ethan holds his phone to his ear and walks slowly as it rings. He laughs when she answers.

"Trouble Maker here! How can I help you?"

"Hey, Beautiful, I need a favor," he says, chuckling.

Olivia smiles. "Hmm, I'm not sure if I'm up to doing favors. I've had a very stressful day."

He knows that she's messing with him. There's a teasing element in her voice that he's come to recognize. "That's a shame. Do you want to tell me about it?" On his way past Mike's office, he stops at the door and waits until he gets his attention. "Give me fifteen minutes." When Mike acknowledges, Ethan continues toward the conference room, closing the door.

"It was horrible," she jests. "I was held captive in a stairwell by a sex craved lunatic."

Spinning the conference room chair to face the window, so he can see the city horizon, Ethan leans back, listening intently. Smiling. The playfulness in her tone makes him crave her with an overwhelming selfishness; he doesn't want to share her with anyone else tonight.

"It sounds horrible," amusement is heavy in his voice. Ethan plays along, thinking about those few brief moments when he held her captive and the intense feelings she stirred in him.

"It was horrible!" she exaggerates, imagining what this conversation must be doing to him right now. She smiles wickedly at how she fully intends to continue in spite of it.

"He touched me in very inappropriate places."

"I'll kill him for touching you," Ethan says, playing at being her protector. Though he's not really playing, he'd do anything to keep her safe.

"He held me against the wall so I couldn't move, and then rubbed himself against me. It was absolutely awful." She sits sideways on the couch lifting her feet up onto the cushion, getting comfortable.

"Sounds like it, Baby." Watching the dotted traffic move slowly through the city, Ethan tries to distract himself from the state of semi arousal in his pants.

"Can you believe that he was actually going to rip my panties so he could get to my naughty parts?" she says, holding back her laughter.

"Bastard!" he adds. Ethan loses the battle and begins to harden. His eyes watch the doorway, hoping no one enters until he can get himself under control.

"So, I was thinking…" she pauses, clears her throat, and tries to sound sincere, "I was thinking that I should take the stairs more often."

There's a brief pause as Ethan processes her joke. "Promise me that you'll never take the stairs without me."

"Oh, I promise." She tries to control her heightening arousal, as she considers just how close she was to being fucked in that stairwell.

"Jesus, stop it. I can't think straight when your voice gets like that."

"Like what?"

"All warm and soft, like you're purring," his voice is low and lustful. "Shit, I'm so screwed. I have a meeting in a few minutes. Now, all I can think about is all the different ways I'm going to fuck you."

She wonders if it's wrong that she's pleased about having such a powerful effect on him. His words are usually so sweet; carefully orchestrated to be romantic. Today is different; his words are raw and unfiltered. The way he speaks so blatantly about his sexual desires is such a total turn on, leading her mind to wander all sorts of directions.

"Jesus, I need you to do something for me and I don't have much time to explain."

"Sure. What's up?" She forces herself to focus.

"I really hope you don't have plans tonight." It wouldn't be a good thing if she did.

Olivia snickers, "Like that has ever made a difference to you."

He laughs, "True, but do you?"

Her voice gets a little more serious, "No, other than hoping that you would find a reason to stop by and finish what you started. I'm feeling a little… um… err… *restless*."

Ethan lets out a loud sigh; proof of his disappointment, "Something has come up. I have a client that I need to entertain tonight."

"Oh, well that's okay. I can always just… take care of things myself. It's not like I haven't done it for the past three years."

Ethan jumps to his feet, alarmed at her suggestion. "OH, HELL NO! Absolutely NOT!" he says with punctuated force.

"Whaaaat?" Olivia's jaw drops, shocked at his comment. He can't honestly think that he has a say in what she can and can't do with her own body? "SERIOUSLY, DUDE?"

"YES, I'm very serious! You won't ever touch yourself for pleasure again, unless *I* instruct you to do so." Ethan paces back and forth in front of the window. When Olivia starts to protest, he cuts her off short, "I'm sorry Baby, but you'll just have to stay *frustrated* until I can look after you myself."

He says it with enough authority that she thinks twice about defying him. There'd be hell to pay if he ever found out. Still, she has to bite her tongue to stop from arguing for the rights to her own body.

A sudden look of confusion washes over his face, "Wait… did you just call me Dude?"

Chapter Thirty-Six

Olivia holds back as long as she can. Finally, no longer able to contain it, she bursts out laughing. Ethan is only mildly amused but he starts to laugh himself, thankful for the break in the tension. Time's running out and he needs to have this conversation. "Olivia, I want you to come downtown and join us tonight for dinner."

"*Us?*" she asks, curiously.

"Yes. You, I, and Stacey Daniels… my client. John and Shannon are going to join us, as well. I know you've probably just got home and it's a long way back into the city… but I need you to be there, Baby. Will you come?"

Olivia doesn't need much coaxing. She's not going to pass up on the opportunity to see the great Ethan O'Connell schmooze a business client. She's been quite curious about what that entails, especially with the female clientele. "Sure," she answers enthusiastically. "What should I wear?"

"Nothing formal. Whatever you're comfortable in. Would you mind going by my house and grabbing me some clothes to change into and then meeting me here at work first?"

"No, I don't mind, but how am I going to get into your house? I somehow doubt you've left it unlocked."

"Go get the key chain I gave you."

Reaching for her purse, she digs through the accumulated junk in it. "Okay, I've got it, why?"

"Obviously, the key fob is for the Challenger. Do you see the single key with the green marker on it? That's the key to my house."

Olivia's heart races as she stares at it, feeling very overwhelmed by the gesture. "You gave me a key to your house?" Her voice is little more than a whisper.

"Well, yeah. Of course." It seemed like a very natural thing to do. "Take a cab into the office. I'll bring you home later."

"No, it's okay. I'd rather drive."

"Is there any point in me insisting you take a cab? " he asks, aggravated that she's always fighting him.

"Nope, so don't even bother. Is there something, in particular, you want me to bring you?"

"Jeans and a casual shirt, you decide." Ethan likes the idea of her picking out his clothes. It's something a real girlfriend would do; one that's in his life because they're interested in looking after him and his needs. Most of the women he had dated stayed with him because he demanded exclusivity while they were spending time with him. None of them would ever venture to engage in any domestic duties; it was beneath them. So his personal errands, et cetera, would fall on John. Regardless, he would always provide generously for the woman who was sharing his bed. He always had. But now, now he wants a woman who's in love with him for what he has in his heart, not in his bank account... or in his pants. He has never truly felt like he's had that before; never really cared until he laid eyes on Olivia.

"Okay." she pauses, "Is it safe for me to come up to the office?" She snickers, remembering how angry she was at Hannah earlier.

"There will be nobody here but you and me. I promise." The door opens and Mike walks in. "I have to go now. I'll see you soon. Text me when you're almost here and I'll meet you downstairs."

Olivia stares at the green key as she hangs up. How the hell did they get this far in the relationship? A lot of things have gone down today and it's an awful lot to try and process. No time to think now, she needs to get ready.

Rummaging through Ethan's closet is kind of exciting. She packs him her favorite black jeans; the ones that fit snugly over his backside, making her want to sink her teeth into his ass. She's not sure if the restaurant they're eating at is business casual or comfy informal. She grabs two different shirts and a pair of casual shoes that look worn enough to be comfortable, packing them in an athletic bag she finds at the foot of the bed.

On the way out the door, she notices that he's finished unpacking the rest of his stuff. Beside the jammed packed bookcase there's a rather old, antique looking birdcage. She didn't see it when she was there before. Maybe it was still packed in a box or possibly it's a new purchase? Noticing that it's empty, she wonders if he intends on getting himself a bird or if it's just for decoration. Huh. She'll have to remember to ask him about it.

Ethan meets her at the valet outside, nervously watching the shop across the street, and wondering if Eva Storm will make an appearance today. She has a tendency to pop out of nowhere and startle the shit out of him. Everything seems calm and clear; no crazy psychics in sight today. That's a good thing, since he has no idea how he'd explain her ramblings to Olivia, when he doesn't even understand them himself.

Sliding the bag off her shoulder, Ethan greets her with a passionate kiss. He protests the weight of the bag with a loud grunt.

Olivia shrugs an apology, "I wasn't sure what you needed, so I packed a few things." His eyes sparkle and a grin forms on his lips. He looks pleased about something but she's not sure what. She doesn't trust that smile at all. It's likely hiding some form of mischief.

Holding her hand firmly, he walks her through the lobby. When they step into the elevator, he wraps his arms around her waist, keeping her as close as possible, and stealing kisses every chance he can. As he promised, Hannah is nowhere to be found. Olivia smiles, thinking to herself. Life sure was a lot duller before Ethan O'Connell.

Ethan heads to the private washroom in his office with the bag. "You're awesome!" he hollers, looking through it.

"What was that? I'm awesome? Could you repeat that? I'm not sure I heard you properly?"

His laughter is muffled by the sound of running water.

Wandering around his desk, Olivia nosily looks through his stuff. Suddenly, she remembers about the empty birdcage. "Hey, Ethan?"

"Yeah?"

"I noticed the empty birdcage at your house this afternoon. Is that new?"

"No, I brought that with me from Ireland. I've had it since I was a child."

"Oh, that's so sad," she says, teasing him. "Most kids make up imaginary friends to keep them company but you had to create an imaginary pet?"

Sticking his head out the door, he scowls at her. "Funny girl! There was a bird in there. It got out when I moved to Scott's. Lost forever now." He pouts; it's the sweetest thing she's ever seen. Man, oh, man! She thought she cornered the market on sexy pouty faces.

Ethan exits the bathroom, dressed in the black jeans and plaid cotton shirt over a soft grey T-shirt. God, he even makes the casual layered look seem sexy.

Olivia continues to explore his desk, not even ashamed when she's caught doing so. Mischievously, she smiles at him when he realizes what she's doing. Crossing his arms in disapproval, he shakes his head. "Don't mess with my stuff, Woman!"

When her stomach grumbles loudly, it makes him chuckle. It's a common thing for him to laugh these days. The fact that he can do so after today's events is a miracle.

Olivia rolls her eyes. "Oh please, like you've never heard my stomach grumble before." She takes a slow breath in, enjoying his cologne. "Maybe we could just stay here," she suggests. The devil is in her smile, as she backs up against his desk, beckoning him to join her with her finger.

Ethan swaggers to the desk, pressing into her so that the edge digs into the back of her thighs. Looking at his watch, he frowns. "Sorry, Sweetheart. We need to be on our way. I promise I'll take care of you the minute we get home."

Ethan runs his finger across Olivia's pouting lip. "God, I can't stand it when you're disappointed, Baby." He presses his lips to hers, starting her engine running all over again. Abruptly, he moves his mouth away. "Is it that bad for you?" he asks with concern.

"I'll live, I suppose." She stares at him boldly.

"You aren't the only one worked up." Looking down at her breasts, he lifts his hand to palm one. Rolling her nipple between his fingers, she responds. Ethan reclaims her lips, making her moan into her mouth. Her body tenses, clenching with the touch of his hands. Suddenly, he pulls himself away. Looking conflicted, he heads across the room to lock the door.

"What are you doing?"

"I'm going to take care of you before we go."

Yes! Oh wait… No! "We'll be late," she reminds him.

"I don't care," Ethan answers without hesitation, his eyes taking on a look of determination.

"Well, I care! I don't want you to be pissy, all night, because I made you late, Mr. Intolerant to Tardiness." Having witnessed his anxiety over being just "on time," on a few occasions, she has a very valid concern. It's no wonder John didn't have a list of excuses prepared this afternoon. Ethan is ALWAYS early. Hmmm…she ponders for a moment; this is the second time *today* that he's been willing to be late for an appointment, in favor of being with her. That's almost as huge as giving her a house key. She watches him turn the lock on the door, checking to make sure it's secure. She takes a deep breath, feeling a little overwhelmed at how quickly things are moving again.

"It will definitely piss me off knowing that I've left you uncared for. I'll be thinking about it all night. I like control, Olivia. However, I'm not a sadist. It gives me no pleasure knowing my woman has unmet needs." He makes his way over to the windows. "Lose the pants," he says closing the blinds.

"Excuse me?" Olivia stands still, not moving.

"I don't like to repeat myself. Do it… *now!*" There's enough authority in his command that she unzips them, without hesitation; letting them slide off her hips, as he watches from across the room.

His eyes burn into her, studying her intently, as they hit the floor and she steps out of them. There's something unnerving about standing in a room under the gaze of a gorgeous man, while wearing nothing, but a pair of black silk panties, from the waist down. Her skin starts to tingle as cool air flows around her, making her wish she could cover herself up.

Wearing a very smug grin, he's pleased at how she submits to his command, "Now your top. Take it off, too." Knowing that she **will** obey him, he takes a few steps closer. "I was just going to take care of you down here..." Smoothing his hands over her panties, he runs them down between her legs. "Now that I see you like this... I want to see more."

There's something edgy in his voice. It makes Olivia's stomach tighten, twisting in knots. She pulls her shirt off over her head, dropping it to the floor.

The soft swells of her breasts spill out over the edges of the matching bra, teasing him, begging for his mouth. "Fuck," he growls. He reaches for them, roughly grasping the round sensitive flesh.

Despite the fire starting deep inside her, goose bumps start to show on her arms. Ethan smoothes his hands up and down her sides, trying to warm them away, but she continues to shiver.

"Lay down on the couch, Baby. The desk is too hard and cold. I want you to be comfortable."

Momentarily disappointed, about not living out her fantasy of being ravaged on his desk, she's thankful for the soft, warm leather underneath her. When he walks toward her, with that confident, commanding swagger, her stomach bottoms out. Roller coasters are less exciting than being alone with this man.

"You're so beautiful." Sitting down beside her, Ethan studies her expression; twirling her hair around his fingers, "You look nervous. It's not the first time we've been intimate." Running his hands along her leg, he makes her pulse quicken. Parting her lips to breathe through her mouth, Olivia tries to ease oxygen into her lungs.

"I love the reactions I get from you." Moving his hand up her thigh, he begins to explore her body, his touch brushing fire across her skin. Tipping her chin, he claims her lips in one hell of a possessive kiss; adding to the intensity as he parts them to slip his tongue inside. When Olivia shudders in anticipation, her response gives him great pleasure. He pulls his lips away to look at her face, intrigued by her reaction to him tonight. It's driving him wild, feeding into his inner caveman. "Why do you look so nervous? Tell me."

Olivia stares into his eyes, trying to focus her thoughts. It's hard to think with the intense thrumming of her pulse. "I never know what you're going to do. One day you're all love songs and twinkle lights... the next day you're all about ripping panties and fucking. I don't know what to expect."

Ethan's shoulders tense. Leaning forward, he rests his nose against her forehead, nuzzling for a moment. He needs to know the answer but he's afraid to hear the truth. "Do you think I could ever hurt you?"

"No, I'm not frightened," she says confidently.

"So you're nervousness is from suspense, then? You're excited?"

Olivia can feel the relief roll through his body.

"Yes." She squeezes her thighs together, growing impatient for him to touch her.

"I'm not gonna lie. I like that." He brushes his cheek down hers, moving his mouth to her ear he whispers. "Do you trust me to look after your needs?" Sucking her earlobe into his mouth, he nips it with his teeth.

"Yes," she moans.

Ethan slides his hand between her thighs, gently prying them apart. "Good, because that's my job now. Only mine." Skimming his hand over the outside of her panties, he slides them to the side. Arching her back, she adjusts her hips, allowing him better access. He grows hard as the tips of his fingers glide over the slick folds. She's smooth as silk.

"I like how wet you get for me." Lightly grazing over her opening, he uses his fingers to gather moisture. Gliding over the rest of her, he spreads it around; making sure she's completely slick and ready. When his fingers find their way to her clit they dance over it delicately, tormenting her by denying her the heavier touch that she's craving.

"Please, Ethan," begging through panting breaths, she arches her back; trying to press the pad of his index finger more firmly against the swelling, sensitive knot of nerves.

Ethan lets out a low guttural growl, rubbing in small circles. Gradually increasing the pressure, he makes her body tremble under his touch; every so often, driving her crazy when he lowers his finger and teases it across her opening.

Olivia's body twitches, desperately wanting release. But he seems intent in making her wait, as if it's some kind of a game he's playing to keep her frustrated as long as humanly possible. *I thought he wasn't a sadist?*

"Ethan!" she complains. "Just how late are you intending to be for dinner tonight? Because at this rate we're going to be *very* late."

Ethan grins, placing kisses along the edge of her jaw. "At the moment, I wouldn't care if we didn't make it at all."

Right on cue "Rocky" interrupts them. Reaching for his phone, Olivia stops him with a firm grip on his wrist. "Don't even think about it. I've got it this time, you keep on doing what you're doing." She reaches for his phone, smiling. Ethan is eager to hear how this conversation will go.

"Mr. O'Connell's office," she says in her best secretary's voice.

Ethan grins, trailing kisses down her neck as he heads for her breasts.

"Hi, John. I'm afraid Ethan can't come to the phone right now. There is some last minute business he's tending to."

Listening in, he unintentionally slows his movements, the phone conversation commanding his attention.

Olivia puts her hand over the phone trying to mute the speaker. "Hey!" she says, waiting for him to look at her. "Union rules… you don't get a break, yet. Stop slacking off and get back to work."

"Sorry," Ethan chuckles against the breast that's in his mouth; immediately resuming his previous mission with renewed determination.

"Okay, John. I'll let him know that Miss Daniels will be there in twenty minutes." She gasps as Ethan hits a very sensitive spot, causing a pause in the conversation. "Fine, John, I understand. I'll make sure he gets on his way right now." Frustration is evident in her voice, causing Ethan to look up. "Forget about it, Ethan. We need to leave now." With a disappointed breath, she pushes his hand away.

Ethan moves his hand back to where it was. "I'm not going anywhere, until I'm done."

"It's okay, really." She tries to get to her feet only to be yanked back down into Ethan's strong arms.

"It's anything **but** okay. I'm not leaving you hanging twice in one day. Don't even suggest it." He continues to nibble and nip along her neck.

Olivia battles the feelings stirring between her legs, knowing that she has to get him back on track and out the door.

"Ethan, we have to be there in twenty minutes. We don't have time."

"Plenty of time, Baby, it's only a few blocks down." His hands continue to explore her body. "It only takes ten minutes to walk there."

She tries to pull away from him so she can see his face. "Are you saying you think you can get the job done in ten minutes?" she asks, amused.

Ethan smirks, running his hands over her breasts, giving her nipple a firm tug. "No, Olivia. I'm saying I *have* ten minutes to get the job done… but I'm going to get it done in five."

Olivia laughs, "Yeah… that's not going to happen, but I admire your confidence."

He leans his lips against hers and kisses her repeatedly. "Care to bet on it?" he asks between kisses.

She accepts his challenge, not believing there's a chance in hell that he can pull it off. "You're on. What's the reward?"

"If you win, you can decide on how you want the next round to play out." He bites her bottom lip and holds it between his teeth.

"Ouch!" She grimaces as she pulls away. "*Anything*? Do I have to decide now?"

"No, you don't have to decide now. It doesn't even have to be next time. You can play that chip anytime it suits you. And yes, *anything*. I can't imagine that there's anything you desire that I wouldn't do for you." He runs his fingers through her hair, wrapping it around his hand and tugging on it playfully, pulling her head back. "Sexual or otherwise," he clarifies, as he lowers his mouth to her neck nibbling at it. "We were made for each other, you and I."

Olivia came to that same conclusion in the stairs earlier today; but the hot nibbling of his lips across her shoulder, makes her body burn with a powerful desire. "What if you win?" she asks hesitantly, knowing all too well the filthy mood that he's in.

Ethan takes a brief pensive moment and then his face lights up. "You give up anal. I decide when and how."

Olivia panics, putting both hands on his chest, pushing him away. "Hell, no!"

Ethan grabs her hands and pulls them aside, laughing. "Come on, Baby," he pleads. "Have you ever tried it?"

"I came close to doing it once and it was very painful." She pulls her hands out of his grip.

Wrapping his arms around her, he pulls her onto his lap. "Then he didn't know what he was doing. It can be uncomfortable at first, but it will start to feel good. I promise, I'll take care of you properly."

There's a sincerity and tenderness in his voice; for some reason, his normally pale green eyes are sparkling like emeralds. She has to force her gaze away from him, shaking her head no.

"No way. Pick something else." She doesn't feel bad in the least about the disappointment on his face; she's just not going there.

Raking his hand through his hair, his face contorts in thought. Then, a slow wicked grin starts to curl at the corners of his mouth.

"What?" she asks cautiously; afraid of the thoughts he's having.

"Blow job," he says, a little too calmly.

"That's it? Not much of a prize. What's the catch?" she asks, suspiciously.

"You have to swallow."

"You're joking, right?" She closes her eyes and lowers her face, covering it with her hands, certain that she hears him laugh out loud.

"Baby, I'm sure you've heard this before, but guys *never* joke about blow jobs."

She thinks about the little fantasy she had this afternoon, her hands bound with his tie, him in complete control and her helpless. The night they formed their agreement, he had expressed his desire for dominance and submission. He hasn't even tried to take her there. *What's up with that?* If she wins that's exactly what she wants. The thought of it makes her clench her legs together.

Feeling her reaction he leans so he can see her face, raising his eyebrows in a quizzical gesture. "Would you rather reconsider the other offer?"

"Nooooo!"

Ethan gets impatient. "Tick, Tock, Miss James. We're running out of time. Current offer on the table is a blowjob, complete with all the bells and whistles. Do we have a deal?"

Gah! "Fine, we have a deal," she blurts out.

Ethan smiles, running his thumb across her lips; imagining them wrapped around his dick. "You're going to swallow?" He makes sure there's no misunderstanding about what he expects.

"Yes," she says, in disgust. "You're such a pig."

He chuckles, "Say it out loud. I want to hear you say it."

She shakes her head, not believing that she's agreeing to this. "If you make me orgasm in five minutes."

"Or less," he interrupts.

She rolls her eyes, "If you make me orgasm in five minutes **or less**, I'll give you a blow job."

"And?"

"AND I'll swallow." She crosses his arms in front of her like an angry child.

"Fuck, you're adorable… and pouting won't get you out of it either, so don't even try," he warns.

"Dammit! I was going to give that a try," she admits.

Ethan laughs, "Yes, well like I've mentioned several times. I know you a lot better than you think." He tips his watch so she can see it. "Check the time. Are you ready?"

"Jesus, Ireland, I've been ready since this afternoon. Get on with it!"

In a split second, Olivia is looking up at the ceiling with Ethan between her legs. What the? One moment she's sitting on his lap, the next she's flat on her back. She has no idea how he maneuvered her position that quickly. Maybe he really is a ninja.

Moving his lips over hers, Ethan engages her in the challenge; his hands quickly grasping the sides of her panties and slides them down. Taking her breasts in his mouth, one at a time, he sucks hard, drawing a loud moan from her.

Ethan slides his hand between her legs. This time, he wastes no time in pressing firmly against her clit in a rhythm meant to get her there quickly; and it's working. Already, she can feel the waves of pleasure starting to build, coiling tighter. When he pushes his finger into her, thrusting in and out, she pushes her hips forward trying to press herself harder against his hand. Forcefully, he pushes her legs further apart, lowering his body between them, anxious to get his mouth on her. The first few long, wet strokes with his tongue prime her for what's to come.

Starting at her knees he trails kisses; licking and nibbling back up her legs. Slowly and deliberately, he grazes his prickly two-day growth of beard along her thigh, leaving a trail of pink-chaffed skin as he goes. It stings a little, but oh, how she's fantasized about it. She's not disappointed. The rough chaffing of his stubble, followed by his warm soft lips, sets off a frenzy of sensations through her body. The tension builds at her core, aching for a quick release. *Oh! My God, he's actually going to do it in five.*

Small pleasured moans escape her throat, alerting him that she's getting close. Ethan bends her knees, pushing them wider apart to give himself a better angle. Licking with heavy pressure on her clit, he feels it swell, becoming slicker against his tongue. Olivia can't lay still any longer, her body twitching and jumping against his mouth.

Grinning with satisfaction, Ethan knows it's time to close the deal and win the bet. Sliding his fingers across her pussy he draws the wetness down toward her backside, massaging across sensitive nerve endings. She opens her mouth, as he rims gently around the tight muscles of her bottom, wanting to protest but unable to speak. His other hand starts to work his fingers into her dripping pussy, angling them to hit just the right spot; pumping them hard and relentlessly.

Closing his mouth around her clit, he massages it one last time with his tongue before he draws in heavily, sucking it hard. Her body starts to tremble, waves of pleasure start to spread through her, When he pushes his finger, with just the right amount of pressure, against the tight ring of her anus; her response is nuclear! Her climax shoots through her body; shocking her system with an overload of sensations. Olivia screams out his name as she completely unravels, shuddering against his mouth. It seems like forever, before the waves of her orgasm start to fade.

Ethan lifts his head from between her legs and looks at his watch. "You lose," he chuckles, as he holds his forearm up so she can see it.

Raising her head, she glances at the time and groans, "Crap!"

Ethan moves from between her legs and helps her to sit up. "But, I wouldn't exactly call that a loss, Baby," Olivia pants, as he settles beside her.

Moving toward her mouth, he kisses her. "No, I suppose it wasn't. I still get my blow job, though." He starts to get up, but pauses, giving her that silly boyish grin.

"What?" she asks, suspiciously.

Ethan shrugs. "I like it when you call me Baby. You don't do it often."

Well fuck, if that isn't the most adorable thing he's ever said. He confounds her sometimes with the contrast between his tender admissions and his filthy mouth. Oh, and it's a wicked, wicked mouth at that.

"We better get on our way. I hope I can walk."

"I'll carry you if you need me to." Straightening out his clothing, he runs his fingers through his hair.

"I think I'm okay." Getting to her feet, she makes her way into the bathroom. Joining her at the vanity, he wraps his arms around her middle, nuzzling against her neck. Looking at their reflection in the mirror, he stares for a long while, pleased at how perfect they look together. She smiles shaking her head in awe. "Really? Four minutes and twenty-eight seconds?"

Ethan starts to laugh, "Well, I'd like to take credit for my superlative oral skills. But honestly, Sweetheart, you were so worked up, a stiff wind on the walk to the restaurant would have set you off."

Olivia laughs at the truth in his statement. "You are sooo right about that." She pauses and her expression morphs into annoyance. "Wait a minute… you knew that and you still let me take that bet?" She watches him in the mirror as his shoulders shake with laugher. Her jaw drops; not amused with him at all.

"A bet is a bet," pulling away smiling, he pats her playfully on the bottom. "You finish cleaning up and I'll let John know we're just leaving now. I'll tell him that negotiations took longer than expected."

Olivia shoots him daggers with her eyes. "Oh my God! I could strangle you sometimes!"

Ethan ducks as she throws a towel at him. He laughs heartily, quickly retreating into his office and safely out of her throwing range.

Chapter Thirty-Seven

As Ethan promised, it's only a few blocks and a very short walk to where they're meeting for dinner. The sun slowly becomes lost behind the highrise buildings of the downtown core, making it feel a little chillier than normal for a summer evening. For some reason, Ethan's mood mirrors the dark, cool air. He's been pretty quiet since they left the office. He's kept a noticeable foot of space between them as they walk, proof that something is on his mind. Keeping his usual quick pace, Olivia feels like she's almost running to keep up with him and his much larger strides. Shivering, she stops in the middle of the sidewalk to zip up her hoodie. Ethan is several steps ahead before he notices and stops to wait.

"Are you okay?" she asks, when she catches up with him. "Something is stressing you. Is it because we're late?"

Ethan growls in frustration, knowing that he needs to come clean, but not wanting to. "No, not because of that." He looks away from her for a moment, expelling an anxious breath, before looking down into her eyes. "It's just that…" He stops again, looking even more anxious.

Olivia becomes nervous. "Just say it, whatever it is." She searches his face for some kind of clue.

"This client is expecting me to keep her *entertained* tonight. I need her to be happy, going into her next board meeting and that means that I may have to be somewhat *attentive* to her tonight." Getting really uncomfortable talking about it, he scrubs his hand over his face. "I just want to let you know, before we get in there, that I have no interest in this woman. Whatever you might see tonight… it's only business. The only thing I'm interested in… is the business deal." He looks at her, desperately needing her acknowledgement.

"Okay, I get it. I'm not going to have your undivided attention tonight."

He turns to start walking again, this time holding her hand snugly in his. "I'm not happy about it. Not one fucking bit. I just wanted to let you know what's going on. I didn't want your girl brain to kick into overdrive once we get there. I'm entertaining a client and that's all."

Olivia knows that he entertains clients all the time. She's at a loss to understand why this one seems to be causing him so much anxiety. Obviously, he's not telling her the whole story. Not wanting to add to his stress, she gives him a reassuring smile, squeezing his hand tightly.

"Okay, so let's get it over with, so we can get back home and you can collect on your bet."

Ethan gives her a quick smile, but his forehead is still creased with dread. It's not quite the response she was hoping for but she smiles anyway.

"Just promise to trust me. No matter what happens tonight, there can't be any ripping out of anybody's uterus." There's a small hint of stress in his voice.

Oh… she gets it now. He's worried that she's going to get jealous and make a scene. She's quick to tease, catching him off guard, "How about a karate chop to the ovaries? Is that allowed?"

"No, that would be frowned upon, as well." Slightly amused, his mood starts to lighten a little.

"Spin kick to the taco?" She looks at him with a mischievous grin, watching his face contort into different expressions.

Ethan tries to work through what she means by 'taco'. Understanding flashes in his eyes and he responds with a light chuckle, "Uh… No."

There, that's much better. She finally gets him to smile.

There's a coat of arms on the window of the old English pub. A British flag hangs lazily on a short staff, just outside the front door. It looks like a small, intimate place from the outside.

"You know, it's times like this when I'm *absolutely* certain you're trying to drive me crazy… and enjoying every minute of it."

"Possibly." Giving him a wry smile, she glances up into his gorgeous green eyes. "Please, stop stressing, Ethan. I get it. Really, I do. Jealous friend… NOT COOL. I entertain clients from time to time, so I know what's expected." Ethan's body stiffens beside her; stopping abruptly he makes her jolt backward.

"Ethan? What the hell?"

Raking his hand through his hair, he holds the back of his head, his expression as if he had just received some horrible news. Olivia looks at him, quizzically, waiting for an explanation. "Ethan?"

"Jesus, don't tell me that shit. I can't think about you trying to secure business from some douche bag, who wants to get into your pants. I'll go insane."

Whoa! There's a lot implied in that statement. She's not sure she wants to know the answer, but she forces herself to ask, "Is the woman we're having dinner with expecting to get into your pants?"

Swallowing hard, he looks away, focusing on the doorway. Pulling the knob he opens the door, gesturing for her to go in, completely ignoring her question.

"Okay, obviously, the answer is yes." Anxiety prickles through her when she looks into his eyes, noticing something dark and unfamiliar in them.

"Mr. O'Connell! It's so nice to see you!" George, the manager, greets Ethan with a handshake, speaking with him casually like an old friend. "Your friends are here. They're sitting in the bar watching the game, but I have made available your favorite table when you are ready to eat. Come, I'll show you the way."

"It's okay, George. I know my way, thank you." As Ethan leads her through the restaurant, she understands why he likes this place. It's much larger inside than it appears from the street. It has all the charm of an authentic British pub. Well, not that she's ever been in one, but she imagines this is what one would look like. Pool tables are lined up along the far side and dartboards along the other. In the bar there are several big screen TV's playing all the popular overseas sports: cricket, soccer (or football as Ethan calls it) and rugby.

As they near the bar, Olivia can see that John is in the company of two beautiful blonde women. Ethan drops his hand from the small of her back as they get closer to them. Olivia notices how one of the women leans softly into John's side. She assumes that she's the woman that was in Ethan's office. She didn't get a good look at her this afternoon but she's stunning in a classy, feminine way. Olivia wishes that she had it in her to look like that.

John immediately introduces them, "Olivia, this is, Shannon Quinn."

"My lawyer," Ethan adds.

"Not tonight, buddy. Tonight, Shannon is my girlfriend and nothing else. You keep your ass out of trouble. Got it?" He grins at him, but it's a warning hidden in jest for sure.

Ethan smiles. "I'll do my best, but trouble seems to stalk me."

Olivia shakes Shannon's hand, trying to ignore the awkwardness of the afternoon events. She notices the other blonde swooping in to stand at Ethan's side. Olivia immediately hates her; from her blonde hair and perfect complexion, to the long slender legs that go on forever, disappearing underneath an obscenely short dress. Those '*come fuck me stilettos*' bring her sparkling blue eyes conveniently to Ethan's eye level, and her ruby lips within a dangerous range of his. Olivia smiles, feeling a little satisfaction at the slight swell of this woman's small breasts. Ethan would never be happy with those little things. Olivia turns toward them, waiting for an introduction, which Ethan neglects. Wow, he's totally off his game tonight. Taking a step forward, she takes matters into her own hands and gives her a polite smile. "Hi!"

Ethan realizes that he needs to make the introduction. "I'm sorry, Olivia. This is Stacey Daniels from Bramtech Industries. Stacey this is my friend, Olivia James."

Friend? What the? Something jabs sharply at Olivia's heart. Odd, since she had used the word *friend* to describe herself on the walk over; but there's something upsetting about *his* lack of acknowledgment, all of a sudden. Olivia tries not to look annoyed as Stacey gives her a quick, once over evaluation, from head to toe, sizing her up and obviously finding no threat. She doesn't even extend her hand in greeting but merely offers an insincere, "Hello" instead. Turning her attention back to Ethan, Stacey reaches up and touches his arm.

"I'm sorry we're a tad late," Ethan apologizes.

He's just made a huge mistake. He had a moment of anxiety over the possible loss of business when he saw Stacey, and his brain misfired. It's too late to make amends, now.

Olivia tries to come to his rescue. "Totally my fault," she adds, trying to steer the blame away from him. "I kept him waiting."

Stacey nods at her, making no effort to hide that she's not pleased, at all, about Olivia being there. In fact, a few times she gives her a look that makes Olivia wonder if she's trying to make her disappear with her mind. After a few awkward minutes of trying to engage Stacey in friendly small talk, she finally gives up. *What a Bitch!* Ethan glances at her, his expression sending her a silent apology. Sensing the awkward moment between the two women Shannon tries to intervene.

"John, didn't you say another one of your colleagues is joining us this evening?"

"Yes, actually. He should be here shortly." John's thankful that Shannon is well attuned to the situation. Ethan looks at him for an explanation. "Carter Brant took an earlier flight. He just checked into the hotel and he's on his way here to join us for dinner."

Ethan nods, directing the conversation solely to Stacey, he explains, "Carter is the sales manager at our office in Australia. He'll be here for a few weeks while we work out a new business plan."

Olivia feels the anger start to niggle at her as she watches him engage Stacey in a conversation that doesn't include her. Ethan rests his hand on the edge of the bar and Stacey immediately situates herself into the crook of his arm. Leaning her ear into his mouth, she pretends that she needs to be closer to hear what he's saying. *And he's falling for that? Jerk!*

"My ears are burnin' so they must be talkin' bout me."

Olivia tenses at the sound of the sexy Australian accent behind her, standing alarmingly close, and practically whispering in her ear. She glances back at his towering six foot two height; meeting the smile of a sun kissed god.

He steps to her side and extends his hand. "Carter Brant."

Olivia reaches for his hand and smiles. He's the most strikingly handsome man she has ever met; with his movie star good looks, bronzed skin and totally buff body. Wavy, sun-bleached blonde hair is brushed back and styled. His chiseled face and strong jaw line, framed by well-manicured sideburns. His eyes remind her of the pictures that she's seen of the Caribbean ocean: crisp, clear and brilliantly blue.

"Olivia James," she answers, feeling her cheeks flush in his presence.

Carter grins at her reaction, prolonging the release of her hand. When she looks up, Ethan is glaring at them. Her heart thumps quickly in her chest as he abandons Stacey at the bar and starts toward them.

"Carter." He holds out his hand for a brief shake; then a quick man hug. "Good to see you. How was your flight?"

"Brutal, as usual," Carter complains. "Thank God for my long-standing membership to the *Mile High Club*," he jokes.

"I thought you were travelling alone?" Ethan looks past him for a companion.

"I am." He raises his eyebrows and smirks. "There's never a shortage of eager participants on those long flights."

Olivia's a little embarrassed. Have they forgotten that she's standing right there? Or maybe, they just don't care that she knows about his casual manwhore escapades in the airplane washroom with random women? Hell, he's so beautiful that she might even consider it. Her mind drifts off for a moment on a little Australian vacation. The sound of Ethan's voice pulls her back to reality.

"Olivia?"

"Yes, sorry, what did you say?"

Ethan flashes her a look, as if to say *what the hell is wrong with you?* "I said, if you're ready we'll head to the table and order dinner now."

"Oh, okay."

Olivia's about to make her way to the table when Stacey flanks in from the side, taking Ethan's arm. Olivia walks behind them, trying not to let it bother her that he's chosen to escort his client, instead of her, to the table. She repeats his words in her mind; *He's only interested in the business.*

Carter places his hand gently on Olivia's back, guiding her through the bar toward the table. John and Shannon are already sitting. Stacey strategically insists that Ethan slides in around the back of the booth, closing him off from any unwanted distractions or communication from anyone, but her.

Shannon looks over at Olivia, with regret in her eyes, wishing she could do something to reassure her that Ethan is only doing what he thinks he needs to for the sake of the business.

Looking at them, snuggled closely together on the bench seat, Olivia can't hide the hurt look on her face. Carter's large hand is still pressed firmly against her back, making her feel warm. She looks at the two empty chairs, side by side, on the far side of the table. "I guess you're stuck with me," she says, apologetically.

Carter's brilliant blue eyes sparkle in the light of the chandelier that hangs centered over the table. He pulls out her chair and smiles. "I wouldn't consider that unpleasant." After making sure that she's seated and comfortable, he settles beside her.

Ethan briefly glares at Carter again, looking extremely agitated. *What is his problem?*

Feeling awkward, the time drags on painfully slow for Olivia. She fakes interest in the small talk at the table. Through polite conversation, she discovers that Carter's accent is a little more polished than she expected because he spent his younger years in boarding schools in the U.S. before, finally, choosing a university in London. That's where he met Ethan. They shared a 'flat' while they attended school with two other friends, Landon Scott who is the sales manager for Aurora Tech's division in South Africa and Reese Wilson. Carter only offers that Reese is in Ireland, but he hasn't seen him in some time. Olivia wonders why discussing Reese makes Carter look so uncomfortable. Obviously, there's a story there.

Glancing over at Ethan, she thinks how incredible it is that he's a man with such devotion to his friends. It impresses her that he hired two of them to head up important positions in his empire. She assumes that in return he'll always have their loyalty.

The boys eventually end up talking to Stacey about the benefits of the Bramtech proposal, leaving Olivia to feel even more out of place. Thank God for Shannon, who takes the opportunity to engage Olivia in conversation about her career and her interests. Olivia already knows that she and Shannon will be great friends. What's not to like? She's beautiful, kind and extremely intelligent, but not in a geeky way. Olivia downplays her own intelligence most of the time; not wanting it to define who she is. But Shannon; she makes being an intelligent woman very sexy.

As hard as she tries not to glance across the table, she can't help it. Every few moments, her eyes take a quick peek to see what's going on between Ethan and Stacey. Slipping into his normal charming self, Ethan listens attentively; flirting in his special way that has the potential to get any woman addicted to him. Olivia knows that it's his nature. He just has this way of drawing women to him, making them eager to rid themselves of their panties. Let's face it; he's one hell of a sexy man, to begin with. When his voice gets thick and heavy with that Irish accent, he could make any woman come on command, a fact that he has proven to Olivia many times.

Olivia tries to ignore the jealousy starting to claw at her insides like a wildcat. It only makes it worse when the waitress returns to the table. She learns that Ethan, at some point, had ordered some kind of pink, frozen drink garnished with strawberries and a little umbrella for Stacey and two fingers of Johnny Walker Black for himself. *He's going to drink now, too?* Tension starts to creep through her muscles, alerting Carter of her anxiety and prompting him to lean over and whisper in her ear.

"You look like you need a drink yourself, is everything okay?"

It makes her sad that Carter is more interested in looking after her needs than Ethan is tonight. In fact, the only time Ethan even acknowledges her is when Carter is a little too attentive. Every time he touches her or gets too close, she can feel Ethan shoot daggers at Carter with his eyes.

"Yes," she whispers back. "Would you order me…" she hesitates, trying to make a decision. She needs something strong, that's for sure. "Anything with vodka in it," she says, shrugging indecisively.

"Of course." Carter's smile would light up even the darkest stormy evening. She wonders if Aurora Tech hires anything but gorgeous men. She'd love to be a fly on the wall during the interview process, that's for sure.

Olivia fumbles with the zipper on her purse trying to retrieve her beeping phone. Losing the battle, her hand slips and she drops it on the floor, upside down, making things spill out. Everyone looks at her as she mutters a quiet curse. Sliding her chair back, she disappears under the table.

Crouching, she turns her purse right side up and gathers up her things. Something on the other side of the table catches her attention. Looking up, she sees Stacey's dress hitched as high as it can go, just barely covering her crotch. Unable to contain her curiosity she takes another look; praying that she can see some evidence that she's wearing underwear. She's just about to look away, in disgust, when Stacey slides her hand down Ethan's leg, caressing it as she goes up and down. She stops at his groin, her fingers curling around the inside of his thigh, her thumb gently rubbing against him. *Oh My God!*

Carter bends down to see if he can help and looks over to see what's caught her attention. Noting the look of utter heartbreak on Olivia's face, he touches her arm, trying to distract her by passing her the lipstick that had rolled a few feet away.

Olivia looks at him with a forced smile. "Thank you," she whispers.

Getting to his feet, Carter offers her his hand and pulls her to stand. He squeezes her hand, giving her a sympathetic look. Olivia's eyes instantly glance to the opposite side of the table.

Ethan looks at her with a flash of regret then turns away, unable to look her in the eye. He holds his water glass tightly in both hands, looking like he could crush it under the force. His conversation with Stacey continues calmly, as if nothing is wrong. *What an asshole!*

"Excuse me for a moment," Olivia says to Carter. "I need to freshen up a little." Carter nods politely, moving her chair out.

Olivia thinks about how messed up things are, right now. Carter has stepped in as her date for the evening; but just a short while ago, Ethan had her spread wide and writhing in pleasure in his office. Now, Ethan is being fondled under the table by another woman. Her anxiety starts to build. She has to concentrate hard on her breathing in order to control the panic attack that's threatening to make an appearance. It's her own fault, she thinks. She wanted to make sure 'blondie' knew what the score was the minute she saw her, but then Ethan introduced her as a friend; putting distance between them. Was he lying about only being interested in the business? She's so confused.

Stacey rambles on about her friends and the clubs they want to check out later on and how much fun it's going to be. *Just shut the hell up, already!* From where they're sitting, John and Shannon have a clear view of what's going on between Stacey and Ethan. Shannon glances over to see the look on Olivia's face as she walks away.

Stopping, Olivia turns to speak, "Carter, whatever you order me, make it a double."

Carter grins. "My kind of girl."

Ethan watches her leave the room with a very stoic expression. He glances over at Carter, who returns his stare, not feeling at all intimidated by him. Carter shakes his head in disapproval as he returns to his seat.

"Is there something you wanna say to me, Brant?" Ethan growls angrily, causing John to tense in preparation for a showdown.

Carter pauses a brief moment, giving it consideration; thinking the better of it, he refuses to take the bait. "Not at the moment. No."

Chapter Thirty-Eight

Shannon frowns when John breathes out in relief. "This is getting out of hand," she whispers. "You need to talk to him and put an end to this. I'll go make sure Olivia's okay."

"Good idea." John stands and gives Shannon a brief kiss as she gets to her feet.

Ethan's not sure just how much more of this he can take. He knows that Olivia has seen where Stacey's hand is; he's certain that it was Stacey's intention for her to see it. Is any business worth this? Worth losing the only woman he has ever loved? Seeing the pained looked on her face when she stood up? Then, there's Carter… Carter fucking Brant! He'll kill him if he doesn't keep his hands off Olivia.

Olivia is splashing cold water on her face when Shannon reaches the ladies room. "Are you okay, Sweetie?"

Olivia forces a smile. "Yes, I'm fine I guess. I'm just not sure why I'm here."

Shannon sighs, "Well, we all thought that if you came with Ethan tonight, Stacey would understand that you two were together and she'd back off."

Olivia finds it hard to remain calm when her jealousy starts to bubble to the surface. "Well, exactly how was she supposed to get that impression when he introduces me as a friend, ignores me, and doesn't discourage her from putting her sleazy hands all over him?"

Shannon puts her arms around her and gives her a reassuring hug. "I know, Sweetie, we're all a little confused about that. I don't know what he's told you about what's going on back home, but trust me when I tell you that he's had a rough year in his personal life. Today's news certainly didn't help any. My guess is that he panicked, fearful that he's going to mess up his business career, too."

Olivia shakes her head. "Seems to me that he didn't set the record straight because he doesn't want to."

"No, don't think that. You should have seen him after he spoke with Stacey this afternoon. John says he's never seen him that upset about entertaining a client. He was so worried, in fact, that he got in touch with Carter and asked him to join us, thinking that he might just charm Stacey away." Shannon lets out a small feminine sigh, "But he seems to be more interested in *you*. Things are all backward."

Frowning, Olivia lets out a drawn out breath. "Maybe I should just leave."

Shannon gives her a very serious look. "Olivia… Ethan is stressed enough tonight. If you left, he would lose it for sure. And I'd be very careful with Carter, honey. It might not look like Ethan's paying attention, but he's watching you two like a hawk. I know it sucks, but let's just try to get through this evening without incident."

Olivia shrugs. "I won't make a scene. Apparently, that's all everybody's concerned about. Heaven forbid anybody upset the great Ethan O'Connell! And as far as Stacey is concerned, he's free to be with her if he wants. I don't really care. That's not the kind of relationship we have."

"Sweetie, if we were in court, you would never be able to convince a jury of that. It's in your eyes. You're in love with him."

Olivia says nothing, her face flushing pink. Shaking her head, she tries to deny it but Shannon just smiles at her. "That wasn't very convincing, at all. Let's get back to the table."

John and Ethan are returning from the front of the restaurant, just as the girls get back. John makes eye contact with Shannon and nods his head once, sending her a silent acknowledgement that he's indeed had a few words with Ethan. Reaching the table at the same time, Ethan and Olivia end up toe to toe. Refusing to look up at him, Olivia waits for him to move. Ethan discretely reaches for her hand, giving it a squeeze. The chill of his fingers against her hot palm is a shock that makes her nipples go taut. When electricity passes through his touch, a shiver moves through her body. How can he still affect her so intensely?

"Everything okay?" he asks, quietly.

She tries to get to her chair, still refusing to look at him.

"Yes, just fine. Excuse me."

Rubbing his hand up and down her arm a few times, he warms it against her skin; wishing that she knew just how much he wants to take her in his arms and kiss her. He has nobody to blame but himself if she never kisses him again. This has been one fucked up day. Stepping aside, he lets his hand delicately brush along her back, while she passes.

The touch is agony. A reminder of what's been missing all night. She hadn't really noticed before, just how often he touches her when they're together.

Every little touch of his hands, his soft lips, his warm body brushing against her…
all taken for granted until, right now.

It's like that feeling she gets when she forgets to put on her favorite ring,
the one that she wears faithfully every day. The entire day feels a little skewed, like
something just isn't right. Feeling anxious every time she looks down and thinks
that she's lost it. She just doesn't feel complete without it. That's how she feels
about the lack of Ethan's touches tonight: incomplete. Panicked at the loss,
hoping… *praying*, actually, that once they get home she'll find them again; if she
can just get through this dinner.

She waves off Carter as he starts to stand. When she sits, tuning into the
conversation, she quickly realizes that Stacey has engaged him on the deep and
intellectually stimulating topic of… *kangaroos*. Olivia looks over at Ethan, who's
looking back at her trying to keep a straight face. Stacey turns to Carter with a very
serious expression and asks, "Have you ever boxed a kangaroo?"

Olivia doesn't hear his answer as she swipes her hand over her face, trying
to hide her snickering. She feels Carter's arm wrap around the back of her chair as
he leans into her ear and whispers, "Thank Christ, you're back. After only ten
minutes of brilliant conversation, I can safely say that she must have slept her way
to the top."

Unable to control herself, Olivia snorts. Carter chuckles, and looks up to
catch Ethan's stare. Recognizing it as a silent warning, he straightens in his seat
and removes his arm from Olivia's shoulder.

When dinner is finally over, they mingle between the bar and the billiards
room. The silence is broken, by a shrill scream, as Stacey runs like she's on fire
toward the front of the restaurant to greet her friends. One by one, they file into
the restaurant wearing short skirts and stilettos with their perfect hair and
schoolgirl giggling.

Olivia watches them in horror from the bar. "Dear God help us, the rest
of the Barbie girls are here. Bartender… two tequila shots and hurry!"

Carter chuckles and takes one of the shot glasses out of her hand. After
clinking them together, they raise them, simultaneously and throw them back.

"Whew!" Olivia's eyes slightly water from the burn in her throat. "Hey,
Carter, let me ask you a question. Would you let any of those girls join your *Mile
High Club*?"

"Hell, no!"

"Not even Stacey?"

He makes a face. "Even I have standards." Leaning in, he whispers in her
ear, "I don't want you to think poorly of me… that whole story… not true. But
don't tell the blokes that, they worship me for it." He flashes her his best playboy
smile.

Olivia laughs, "Hey? Where's O'Connell? I haven't seen him for awhile."

Carter puts both shot glasses on the bar, indicating to the bartender that he wants two more. "I think he's playing darts with John." Passing her another shot, he laughs at her sour face when she downs it.

"Bleh! I don't think I can do any more of those." She shudders.

"One more," Carter insists, waving at the bartender. "And a glass of red wine," he adds, as Shannon makes her way to join them.

Hearing a familiar voice, Olivia looks up to see the boys from Dufferin County announcing their arrival, in their normal rowdy manner. Her face lights up. "Pete! Danny! Oh my GOD... Brandon? I haven't seen you in forever!" After greeting them with warm friendly hugs, she introduces them to Carter and Shannon. Danny spots Stacey and her friends immediately on the other side of the bar. "Olivia, please tell me that those are the girls we're here to hang out with tonight."

Rolling her eyes, she looks over at Carter's smile. "Yup, they're all yours."

Having heard the ruckus, Ethan makes his way to the bar. Welcoming the boys, he buys them a round of drinks. They exchange a few rude comments about the girls, chuckling and slapping each other on the back, as if they have just won an unexpected lottery. When Ethan takes the boys over to introduce them, Stacey quickly positions herself at his side; letting them know that she's already spoken for.

Olivia tenses and breathes deeply in and out, calming herself; trying to remember if bitch slapping was on the list of things that would be frowned on. Ethan rounds everyone up and steers them through the bar toward the pool tables. On the way past he stops.

"The boys are going to play a game of pool, as they call it, and the girls are going to watch," he says to Olivia.

She makes a face, unsure what his intentions are for stopping to share that information with her. At the moment she doesn't really care, she's had just about enough of *Ethan O'Connell* and way too much tequila. "Awww. The girls are going to watch? How cute is that?" she says sarcastically. "I suppose the poor things are too delicate to play." She keeps her eyes focused on Ethan, her stare; sassy and unwavering. "It's such a shame because I'm sure everyone in the bar would love the view of camel toe when they lean over to shoot."

Carter bursts out laughing. Shannon chokes on her wine, quickly holding a cocktail napkin over her mouth. With a boldness already fueled by tequila, Olivia picks up her shot glass and tosses its contents deep into the back of her throat, letting it wash down effortlessly. Slamming the glass down hard on the bar, she gives him a smile that impolitely says, *piss off !*

Ethan stares at her, his jaw clenched and his lips pressed in a hard line. Turning to his right, he establishes eye contact with Shannon, knowing that it's a far better idea to let her deal with her. "Shannon, Please take Olivia down to the pool tables, so Carter and I can have a talk."

Olivia raises her eyebrows. "You can't be serious? You're dismissing me?" She laughs at his nerve.

Shannon nods and takes Olivia by the arm, knowing this is not the time to defy him.

"Come on, Sweetie. The boys need to talk. We can wait for them down there." Olivia protests but Shannon is a lot stronger than she looks. She steers Olivia through the bar. Swaying slightly, compliments of her good friend Jose Cuervo.

Carter sits on the barstool, waiting until the girls are out of earshot. "What's up, Boss?" He knows, full well, the conversation that's about to take place.

"Keep your hands off my girl, Carter," Ethan says harshly.

Carter gets defensive, furrowing his brow; he speaks to his old friend, with much more casual Aussie slang after several rounds of tequila. "Don't chuck a spaz, Ethan. I haven't had my hands on your girl. She was firmly attached to your dick all through dinner. Find it hard to believe you didn't notice, mate,"

"I'm talking about Olivia." Ethan's anger starts to build.

"Olivia? Huh, it's not like you to be so greedy. Since when do you play two girls at the same time?"

"I'm not playing Stacey," Ethan insists, his muscles starting to tense and tighten with anxiety.

"Could have fooled me. And let me tell you, you most certainly haven't fooled Olivia. I have to say, mate, I'm a little shocked."

"At what exactly?" Ethan crosses his arms in front of him, widening his stance.

"Making a Sheila, who's obviously in love with you, watch another girl manhandle your junk at the dinner table. That's a little cruel, don't you think? I don't want to judge you, mate; but it was a dick thing to do. I've only just met Olivia, but I already know that she's the kind of Sheila that deserves a lot more respect than that."

Ethan stops for a moment. Horrified at what Carter has just said. He looks over to the pool tables, catching Olivia watching him. She quickly looks away when she realizes she's been caught. He rakes his hands through his hair in frustration. Carter is right. He should have put a stop to it immediately when it happened. How did he let things get so messed up? Ethan's face looks tortured, physically pained; and Carter knows right away. "Oh shit. You're serious about Olivia?"

Ethan nods. "Yes, I think I'm in love with her." He corrects himself, "I *know*… I know I'm in love with her."

"Then, what's going on with Stacey? Don't tell me nothing. I have eyes."

Ethan closes his eyes and shakes his head. "She's just a client who's made it very clear about the only way I'm going to get her approval on our proposal." He curses at the thought.

The bartender looks up at the cursing and Ethan orders another scotch. Lifting himself on to the stool beside Carter, he looks at his friend and frowns. "Jessica's pregnant," he confesses, loosening up with the booze. "She says it's mine. I just found out today."

Carter is shocked. "Fuck, that's rough. I'm sorry."

Ethan takes a mouthful of scotch and sets his glass down. "I'm pretty sure it's not mine. But she's contacted my lawyers, saying it is. She's looking for financial support during the pregnancy and after."

"I always hated that bitch!" Carter confesses.

Ethan gets angry. "Jesus Christ… apparently, John did as well. Why the fuck didn't anybody say anything to me at the time?"

Carter shrugs. "Would you have listened?"

Ethan answers into his glass as another mouthful flows smoothly over his tongue. "Probably not, she had magnificent tits." They both chuckle a little, clinking glasses in recognition of that fact.

"What are you going to do now?" Carter asks, ordering a beer.

"Paternity test, first and foremost."

"Good plan. Does Olivia know?"

"She knows about the pregnancy, but she doesn't know about the other stuff."

"It's none of my business, Ethan, but since you just bitched me out for not speaking up about Jessica, I'm going to tell you that I think you need to tell Olivia everything."

"I want to," Ethan says, swirling what's left of his scotch in the bottom of his glass. "But her last boyfriend was abusive, Carter. I'm afraid if I tell her what I'm being accused of, she'll leave me."

"Ah, but you know you can't keep it a secret for long. Better you come clean now and find out if your relationship is strong enough to withstand it. Yeah? Jess is going to fight you tooth and nail. Eventually, Olivia is going to find out. It should come from you, before that happens."

Ethan nods. "You're right, but not just yet. I'll find the right time after the grand opening." He stops and puts his hands over his face. "If she's even talking to me still. Christ, Carter… what I've put her through today… it's really fucked up."

"Only you can fix it, O'Connell. Get your shit sorted."

Ethan rubs his eyes; they're getting heavy under the effects of alcohol. "You're right. John just hauled my ass outside and told me the exact same thing."

"Smart man, that John. So what's the plan for the evening?"

Ethan looks over at the crowd of guests at the pool tables. "It looks like they're all getting along really well. So, I'm hoping I can send everyone off to the club and I can take Olivia home and try to set things right."

"All right then, mate," he says sliding off his stool. "Let's make that happen."

Ethan gets to his feet. There's one more thing on his mind. He reaches over, grasping Carter's arm.

"I'm not joking. If you so much as get close enough to breathe on her, I'll kill you."

"Ok, Boss. I've got it."

"And Carter... don't buy her anymore shots. She's pretty feisty when she's sober but from what I've just seen, if she keeps drinking tequila, she'll have my balls by the end of the night."

Carter laughs, "Yeah, I think you're right about that. But she's fucking brilliant!"

Ethan grins, "That's why I love her. But, I'm rather fond of my balls, as well."

Chapter Thirty-Nine

Carter gives his friend some serious advice. "Ethan, fuck the business, mate. It's not worth it, if you lose her."

Ethan raises an eyebrow. "Who are you and what have you done with the real Carter Brant?"

Carter chuckles, "I know, I guess old age is starting to mellow me out. Lately I find myself wanting that kind of love. I think about settling down with the right woman; one I want to make babies with and come home to at the end of the day. A beautiful woman to love, cherish, and to share the rest of my life with. I'm getting tired of the jet setting playboy routine."

Ethan shakes his head, exhaling a reassured breath, "Thank God, it isn't just me. I felt that way the moment I saw Olivia."

"No, it's not just you, mate. Amazing what the love of a beautiful woman does to a man."

"No kidding. Olivia has brought me to my knees several times, and I don't think she even realizes how much I love her."

"Well, you need to change that, before she gets away."

Ethan nods in agreement, watching her from across the room. Olivia looks over at him every few moments; looking away when he catches her.

Ethan makes his way toward her, like a man on a mission. Olivia gets nervous when she sees him advancing at such a rapid pace. He doesn't take his eyes off her for a second. Watching the scene unfold, Stacey rushes toward him, trying to intercept, but he ignores her; focusing only on Olivia.

Just a few feet from where Olivia is chatting with Shannon there's a door to a small room that provides a little privacy. When Ethan finally reaches her, he grabs her hand.

"Come with me." He tugs her away without waiting for a response, denying her the right of refusal. Pushing open the door, he pulls her inside, spinning her around while he closes it.

"Ethan? You're starting to freak me out a little bit." Olivia begins to feel nervous and she fights her natural flight response.

"I know you're pissed at me."

"No, I'm not," she begins to argue.

"Don't lie to me. You're pissed about Stacey. I don't blame you. I asked for your trust and then I let you down."

"Why would I be upset Ethan? I'm *just your friend,* remember?"

Ethan grunts, desperately, wishing he could gain back control of this day. "I'm sorry I said that. I'm not sure why I did." He's amazed at how one mistake can fuck up everything.

"Well... it's true. We're *not* dating," she quickly retorts.

"NO?" Then what do you call it?" There's a deep rumble of anger in his voice.

Olivia chooses her words very carefully, "An agreement."

"I see. Still insistent on that ridiculous fucking agreement?" Ethan's nostrils flare as he fights to remain calm.

"Yes." Olivia crosses her arms, resolute in her defense.

Ethan raises an eyebrow. "We spend almost all of our time together; going out to dinner, hanging out at home watching TV... making love. Often, I might add." Ethan advances, backing her up against the door. "Baby, in any country around the world, that's dating."

Ethan makes his point and it infuriates her. This close to him, she can smell the strong scent of alcohol on his breath. "Okay," she concedes, wary of antagonizing him further.

"Okay?" Ethan watches her with cautious eyes, surprised that she's given in that easy.

"I guess we're dating," she shrugs, "but not exclusive."

"What the hell does that mean?" he yells.

Olivia's stomach bottoms out at his harsh tone. That Irish temper is definitely making an appearance. She assumes that the fact that he's been drinking is going to make it a whole lot worse.

"Well, it means that we go out on dates and all those other things you mentioned. HOWEVER, it's not a *committed* relationship. You're free to see other people, if you want to. It was what we agreed to, Ethan."

"What if it's not what I want?" he challenges.

Olivia shrugs. It's not what she wants either. It's been three years since Sam left her for dead. She seriously doubts that she'll ever be able to love or trust again.

"Things are different between us now, neither of us wants to see anybody else," Ethan growls, in a dangerously low tone.

Olivia laughs, mockingly. "Says the man who just allowed a business client to feel him up before he even bought her dinner. Tell me, how far would that have gone if I *wasn't* here tonight? Would you have slept with her? Maybe snuck her into this room and fucked her right here? It would have been easy since she isn't wearing any underwear!"

Olivia stops, noting that Ethan isn't surprised by the news.

"Oh my God, you know that she isn't wearing any?" Her pulse becomes explosive, rushing so angrily through her ears she can barely hear herself think. "You discovered that for yourself at the table, didn't you?"

Ethan doesn't answer, but it's obvious by the rise and fall of his taut chest. She lifts her hands to cover her face for a moment then drops them to her side, shaking her head. "You know what, by all means if that's what you want... you can have her! I'll get Carter to take me home."

Ethan's cold look becomes glacial; a sign that he's seriously pissed off.

Olivia gasps, as she's pinned against the door by six feet of very edgy, extremely angry, Irish alpha male. His muscles are like hard slabs of steel against her. "What are you doing?"

"Kiss me." It's a sharp command she shouldn't ignore.

"NO!" In complete contradiction to her words, Olivia stares at his lips in anticipation, her leg jiggling anxiously.

Ignoring her refusal, Ethan lowers his mouth and claims her. She hates that she wants him to kiss her right now. She doesn't want to *want* it, but she desperately needs his reassurance.

Ethan's approach is tender, despite the anger that vibrates through his body. Raising his hands, he holds the side of her cheeks. When his lips brush softly against hers, it incites a flash of heat that rushes through her body. Pulling her forward, his mouth moves with desire, making her moan against his lips.

Grabbing her wrists, he pulls them over her head, holding them there. Pressing them firmly against the wall, he makes her body respond to the promise of his possession.

Parting his lips, he slips inside her for a soft meeting of tongues. She tastes the lingering fruity taste of the scotch, as he licks and teases; deepening his kiss until she's so lost in it that she can't think of anything else. This is what she's been longing for all night; a long, sensual kiss, the soothing caress of his tongue; his exchange of breath

When he releases her wrists, she runs her hands through his hair. Olivia holds him against her mouth, afraid to let him go. When he breaks that kiss, he leaves her feeling dazed and light headed, weak in the knees.

"I don't want her. I want you. If you ever doubt how I really feel about you... think about that kiss." Leaning in, he nuzzles her nose then moves in for one last kiss; so sweet, so delicious.

"Are we okay?" He smoothes his hands over her cheek, her hair, her shoulders… everywhere he can touch her. It's the only way he seems to be able to soothe his anxiety these days.

Olivia's brain is numb. She blinks excessively, trying to re-focus. "She's just a client, right?" She desperately wants to believe him.

Ethan nods. "Yes, and I intend to make sure, the minute we go back through this door, that she knows that I'm not available to anyone but you."

When he swings the door open, Olivia's face turns red as everybody turns to stare. Reaching down, Ethan takes her hand, and guides her across the room toward Carter. Planting himself on one of the tall stools, Ethan widens his knees and pulls Olivia between them. He gives her a long sensual kiss on the lips as her chest lands against him.

Carter and Ethan give each other a little fist bump, behind her back. She glances to the side, meeting with Carter's smile. He nods, winking at her, genuinely happy for his friend. But, there's something in his eyes, something that tells a different story: one that she'll keep to herself for now.

Olivia turns in his arms, meeting with the angry glare of the group of women on the other side of the table. All of them listening attentively to Stacey and looking over at her with disgust. When she tenses, Ethan locks his muscular biceps around her, keeping her tucked firmly between his knees. Sliding his cheek against hers, he whispers into her ear, "Just ignore them."

"It reminds me of the night we met," she whispers back.

"Really? Why?" he asks, curiously.

"When you rescued me from the chair of death."

Ethan leans to the side so he can look at her face, shaking his head and looking confused.

"Really, Ireland? All the women were seething in jealousy when you helped me up and held me in your arms. They gave me the stink eye the rest of the night."

"I had no idea," Ethan says, surprised.

"Oh, pulleeze! They had been drooling over you for weeks, from what Rachel tells me."

"Huh, no kidding? I never knew." Grinning, he tightens his arms around her and trails his lips across her neck. "The only woman I ever noticed at that field was *you*." He lifts his eyes to look at Carter's impressed expression.

"Smooth," Carter mouths.

Olivia relaxes in Ethan's arms. "You make it increasingly difficult to be angry with you, you know." She leans into him, determined not to take his touches for granted any more.

"That's good for me, right?" Ethan asks, with his lips pressed against her shoulder.

Feeling his heated breath against her skin, Olivia sighs, "Yes. But it's really getting annoying." She spots Shannon and John kissing over in the corner.

"Shannon said that you're letting her stay a few more weeks, so she can spend more time with John."

"Did she? Well, I thought I was letting her stay so I can keep an eye on her while she works on my case. I don't trust lawyers, especially the women."

"Again… you're not a very good liar, Ethan." She turns her head and kisses him, pulling away just a little. "I take it back… you're not a huge jackass."

Ethan raises his brows in surprise. "Oh? I don't remember you calling me that."

Olivia grins. "Oh, I did, and several other *less* lady like things, actually. Some I'm sure Stacey and her friends will have to look up on dictionary.com. I doubt any of them even own a book."

Ethan and Carter chuckle, "You're definitely my kind of girl," Carter announces. Ethan stops dead and glares at him.

"Just saying, Boss. So don't fuck it up," Carter warns.

"Uh Oh," Olivia says, as Stacey makes her way toward them.

Walking right up to them, Stacey addresses Ethan, as if Olivia isn't even there. "The girls want to go over to 'EUPHORIA' and do some dancing."

Olivia tries to move toward Carter to get out of the way, but Ethan grabs her hips, holding her against him.

"Sure, if that's what you want to do. It's only a few doors down. I'll have John call over and get you on the VIP list." Ethan waves John over. "Carter, have the tab charged to your room and then submit it with your expenses."

"Sure thing, mate."

Stacey stands staring at Ethan with an unimpressed expression. "You're not coming?"

"No, it's been a long day and I think I'm going to get on my way."

She crosses her arms in anger. "You can kiss my endorsement goodbye if you don't go."

Ethan anxiously scrubs his hand over his stubble. Olivia can feel the tension in his body. She shrugs, trying to put him at ease. "It's okay with me if we go for awhile."

Ethan gives her an apologetic look. He's going to have to buy her something really special to make up for all her concessions this evening; not to mention dealing with his temper. Oh, and there's that whole pregnancy thing that she seems remarkably calm about… Dragging her out of the elevator… And what happened under the table. Oh, Christ! What happened under the table! He has no idea what kind of gift could ever wipe that slate clean. She's right; he's a HUGE jackass.

Stacey storms back across the room to her friends, her heels clicking heavily on the floor as she goes. Ethan meets John halfway across the room to discuss plans. Shannon wanders over to Olivia and Carter. "What's going on?"

"Barbie wants to go dancing and she's insisting that Ethan goes, too." Olivia rolls her eyes.

"Wow! She doesn't discourage easily does she?" "Apparently not, so I hope you have comfortable dancing shoes on." Olivia looks down at Shannon's feet.

"Oh, I don't think John and I will go."

"You have to go," Olivia says panicked, "Ethan won't go unless I do. And I'm not setting foot in that place with the Barbie girls, unless you go with me to make sure I don't scratch out their eyes."

Carter laughs, raising his beer bottle in a salute. "Well, you ladies have fun."

Olivia sneers at him, "Not so fast, Crocodile Dundee. You're going, too. Ethan is going to need you there." She narrows her eyes at him, giving him a warning that makes him reconsider.

"Fine, I'll go," he says, giving in reluctantly. There's no way he wants to be on the wrong side of Olivia's threats.

"Go where?" Ethan asks as he returns.

"To Euphoria with us," Olivia answers for him.

Ethan looks over at Carter, noting the strangest look on his face. "Awesome, I'd feel better if you were there. Nice of you to offer."

Both Shannon and Olivia start to snicker and look away. Ethan looks back at Carter, confused. "Oh, I didn't offer," he explains. "I'm going because your girlfriend here, told me I have to. And quite frankly, mate, I'm afraid of what she'll do to me if I refuse."

Olivia tries to look innocent, batting her eyelashes at him. Ethan grins and shakes his head. "Wise decision, my friend."

The room erupts into a barrage of girlie giggles. Ethan glances over at them. "John has already gone over to make the arrangements. We'll walk over whenever the girls are ready."

Thirty minutes passes by. Ethan paces, going out of his mind. "Jesus Christ, how long does it take to *freshen up*?" he asks, looking back and forth between Shannon and Olivia for an answer. Olivia shrugs.

Finally, the girls file out of the restroom and make their way to the front door. Pete and Brandon abandon a drunken argument over something ridiculous and straighten up; thrilled to escort such hot women.

Stacey firmly grasps Ethan's arm and starts to walk. Feeling uncomfortable, Ethan looks over his shoulder at Olivia.

"It's okay," she says, putting him at ease.

The lights in the city are bright against the black veil of night. The sparkle of the stars remind Olivia of the shimmery twinkle lights that Ethan had strung on the gazebo yesterday, for their *date*. She wonders if there will ever be another night like that one, one where she doesn't want to strangle him.

Chapter Forty

Standing between the lovely lawyer and the sassy IT consultant, Carter mans up, presenting his arms for them.

"Ladies? Shall we?" The girls smile at each other and accept his offer, one on each arm. Ethan peeks over his shoulder several times on the short walk, making Carter chuckle.

John is waiting outside the nightclub, on the ground floor of a prestigious hotel in Toronto's famous entertainment district. Shannon glows when she sees him. Olivia would have never guessed that there's close to ten years difference in their ages. Shannon is wise and mature beyond her years; John's style and fit body in no way reflects his age.

The minute Stacey leaves Ethan's side, Olivia finds renewed confidence and steps up, reclaiming his hand. He grins at her possessiveness and leans in for a kiss. Looking around, Olivia realizes that there's a strict dress code in effect and Ethan is wearing jeans.

"Ethan, I don't think they're going to let us in, we're not dressed properly."

Ethan kisses her on the forehead, as if to say, *aren't you cute for worrying.* "Trust me, they'll let us in."

The line of patrons standing outside, hoping to get in, extends down the street and around the corner, on a Monday night, nonetheless. Looking doubtful, Olivia follows him to the door. Stopping, while Ethan deals with the security at the door, Olivia glances over at Carter and shrugs. An amused grin crosses his lips. "You didn't know that he's part owner?"

Olivia's body straightens and her eyes open wide. "Of the nightclub?" she says, in shock.

Ethan turns to take her hand, smirking at the conversation he's overheard. "No, Baby, of the hotel."

Bypassing the lineup, they head right to the second floor VIP lounge. There's barely room to move on the dance floor. Olivia holds his hand tightly, following him through the crowd and silently taking everything in: the bright neon signs, the flashing lights, and the vibrating bass of the speakers.

After a few drinks, Olivia watches the dance crowd from the balcony of the second story VIP lounge. Ethan returns from the bar and brushes up against her. "I like that look," he says, reaching for her and pulling her into his arms.

"What look?"

"*That* look, the one that says that I've done something to impress you."

"You're a very successful and accomplished business man, Ethan. I can't figure out why on earth you're so concerned about what I think."

He brushes her hair away from her face, rubbing his fingertips across her cheek. "You're the only person whose opinion I do care about. Everybody else can go to hell."

Clearing his throat to signal his entry, Carter joins them on the balcony. "Sorry to interrupt but I've been sent over to inform you that Stacey wants to dance, now," he points at Ethan and smiles, apologetically, "*with you.*"

Ethan takes a frustrated breath. Heading to the dance floor, Ethan is careful to stay close to Olivia. She rolls her eyes and shakes her head as Stacey continues to try to capture Ethan's attention.

A very popular dance song by Usher comes on. Everyone explodes into his or her best hip-hop moves. Carter joins them, not surprising Olivia at all with his accomplished dance moves. She can't keep track of the number of female heads that turn in his direction. It's as if every vagina in the place has GPS and the destination is set to six feet two inches of Australian hottie, who's built like a linebacker. If the old saying is true about the size of a man's feet… well then, Carter is hung like a horse. He's succeeded in getting the attention of every woman in the place, except for Stacey, who still has her GPS set on a trip to Ireland. SO NOT HAPPENING, BITCH!

Olivia is shocked at how forward some girls can be. Carter has never met any of them before, and yet there they are, rubbing up against him and grinding their asses into him like cats in heat. Geez! Carter moves with great skill and rhythm, making sure no one is left out. Looks familiar. Obviously, both he and Ethan perfected their dance moves while attending university together. She doubts that either of them ever went home alone. What woman wouldn't be curious to find out if they could move as good in bed as they do on the dance floor? Glancing over in Ethan's direction, she notices Stacey watching Carter. She's looking him over very thoroughly, actually. Thank God! Olivia finally sees a shimmer of hope and dances over to Carter.

"Carter!" she screams in his ear. "Stacey is watching you."

Carter looks over and catches Stacey staring.

"So?"

"She's checking you out. Please… please… please….go over and dance with her and give Ethan a break."

The music changes to a slow jam. Before Olivia can get to him, Stacey has her arms around Ethan, pressing her body against him, swaying. Olivia stands still in the middle of the floor. "Fuck," she whispers.

Carter walks Olivia off to the side and stands against the wall, watching. Within seconds, he's flocked by a group of girls, who are infatuated with his blue eyes and accent. He turns down several invitations to dance, but they distract him with their flirting.

Olivia can't take her eyes off Ethan. He clearly looks uncomfortable, trying to keep space between them. Only a few moments in to the dance, Ethan's movements appear to get lazy. Olivia can tell that he's starting to feel the effects of the several scotches he's had.

She watches from across the room as his body becomes heavy and his dancing begins to slow. Stacey settles in to the slower pace. Leaning against Ethan's chest, she buries her face into his neck, wrapping her arms completely around him and tightly squeezing his butt.

Fireworks go off in Olivia's brain. Jealousy claws at her like a wildcat on steroids! She shoots out toward the dance floor with the intention of doing bodily harm. Suddenly, she's stopped dead by a pair of strong arms.

"Whoa! Where are you going?" Carter's voice echoes in her ear.

"I'm going to peel that SKANK off MY MAN!" Olivia says through clenched teeth.

Carter chuckles, "Oh no you're not, at least not while you look like you want to stab someone."

Worried, Ethan watches Olivia through the crowd, understanding why she's clearly upset. When Carter drags her back toward the wall, he sends him a look to say, *thanks*. Carter nods his acknowledgement.

Olivia is literally trembling with anger. Carter spends the next few minutes to settle her. Then, the loyalty that Olivia assumed Ethan would always have from his friends suddenly becomes evident in Carter's next move.

"Listen, you just stay here. Okay? I'll look after it." Needing liquid encouragement, he drains his glass in one gulp.

"Carter? What are you going to do?" she asks, worried.

He pinches her chin and smiles. "You look absolutely miserable and I can't take it anymore. I'm going to do what I should have done back at the other bar. I'm going to suck it up and take one for the team."

Olivia lets out a heavy sigh of relief, "Thank you, Carter. You're a good friend."

"Yes, I am. And you're going to owe me one. A *huge* one, I might add." He grins.

"Anything, I promise."

He nods his head. "Alright, let's get on with it. Order me another drink. I'm going to need it."

Carter makes his way onto the dance floor. Tapping Ethan on the shoulder, he asks to cut in. Stacey glances over at Olivia with hatred in her eyes. Geez, what is it that this woman just doesn't understand?

Relieved, Ethan grabs Olivia by the hand and hurries her upstairs. Alone in the VIP lounge, he gives in to his needs. Pressing her against the wall, he kisses her roughly, like he means it. He doesn't stop until she pulls away, needing air. "Can we go now?" she begs.

"Absolutely."

Olivia's surprised by the look of concern on John's face when Ethan steps away to get a glass of water. Shannon shrugs, clearly not understanding his concern, either.

John pulls out his phone and dials. "Hi Sarah, it's John McCabe. I'm fine, thanks. Listen, Mr. O'Connell is going to need a room tonight. Can you get one ready for him right away? Thank you. I'll be right there."

John recognizes something in Ethan's look that tells him that he's about to surpass his limit. Who, other than John, would know that?

"Sit, until I get back," John says to him.

Looking exhausted, Ethan takes a seat in one of the large chairs and refills his water glass.

When John steps out of the room, Shannon takes Olivia's hand. "Come here, I want to show you something." She pulls her out on the balcony overlooking the dance floor. "Have a look," she says, nodding in direction of the back of the room.

It's dark and the flashing lights make it hard to see. "What exactly am I looking for?"

"Carter. Look straight past the bar and to the right. Against the wall."

Olivia tries to focus and follows the line of people down the wall. Finally, she sees him, recognizing him only by his height and clothing. His back is to them and his face is hidden in the darkness. "Okay, I found him."

"And?"

"And what?" Olivia watches intently, getting only quick glimpses as the lights pulse off and on. When she gets a really good look, her mouth widens in shock. "Who is he kissing?"

Shannon starts to smile. "Stacey!" She looks behind her to make sure nobody is listening. "A few minutes ago he had her in the corner under the stairs. It was dark but I'm pretty sure her legs were wrapped around his waist."

"Oh, my God! What do you think they were doing?" Olivia looks shocked, but deep down inside she's pretty impressed with Carter right now.

"I'm pretty sure they *weren't* dancing." Shannon grins.

"Well, he said he was going to take one for the team," Olivia laughs. "Ethan's lucky to have such a good friend."

Shannon looks at her and raises her eyebrows. "I think we both know that he did it for you, not Ethan."

Olivia says nothing, but knows that there's more than a little truth to that. She and Shannon became instant friends when they met; the same was true for her and Carter. Although, she was sure from the moment they sat down for dinner that Carter was hoping for more than that. She's seen it in his eyes, more than a few times tonight.

When John returns, Ethan is napping in the chair. He opens his eyes as John taps his shoulder. John hands him a hotel key card. "Here, there's a room ready upstairs for you. Carter is looking after Stacey."

Ethan looks at the girls suspiciously when they start to snicker. Ignoring them, John continues, "Shae and I will make sure everyone else gets home safe. Go and get some sleep. It's been a crap day. I'll have one of your suits sent over in the morning."

Ethan slaps him on the shoulder. "Thank you, John." Holding out his hand to Olivia, he waits for her to join him.

She looks stunned for a moment. She hadn't thought about what would happen at the end of the night. Her car is at the office, but she certainly shouldn't be driving. Ethan would never permit her to take a cab all the way back to Dufferin County at this hour of the morning, not even if she went back with the three boys. She takes a deep breath and takes his hand. "I guess I'm staying."

"Of course you are." He frowns at her, wondering about her ridiculous statement.

On the journey from the club to the hotel room, Ethan's mood shifts away from the warm, fuzzy feeling brought on by the alcohol. Ethan becomes quiet, pensive, moving into that downward spiral that creeps into sadness as the buzz wears off. Lost too deep in thought, Olivia fears. She can tell there's a lot going on in his mind.

The situation feels way too familiar to her, causing anxiety to rumble around inside her. As Ethan fumbles with the key card, fear overtakes her. "What's wrong?" he asks, concerned when he notices the tears forming in her eyes.

"I don't think I can stay," she says anxiously. With Sam, a night of drinking was always followed by depression that quickly morphed into violence; that anger was always directed at her. It's not something she wants to tell Ethan about in his current alcohol haze. How does she make him understand?

Ethan is disheartened. "Please don't go. I don't think I could bear it if you left me tonight." His eyes are hooded, heavy. His speech starts to slow.

He hasn't given her any reason to believe that he's dangerous when he's like this, but he's nowhere near the state of mind that will allow him to comprehend how terrified she is, right now.

"Please stay," he begs with a sad, desperate voice. "I just need to be close to you. I just need to know that things are *okay* between us."

Poor Ethan, Olivia's been so caught up in her own whirlwind of emotions today; she hasn't thought about how hard everything has been on him. She can see that now in his face. His eyes are lost and hollow, searching for a sign of forgiveness, acceptance, and unconditional love. There's no way she could leave him alone tonight. She just doesn't have it in her. When she nods her consent, she hears him exhale a heavily weighted breath as she walks into the room.

Ethan locks the door behind them and strips down to his boxers. Swaying a little, he makes his way into the bathroom and closes the door.

Olivia uses the opportunity to quickly get undressed down to her panties. Grabbing the t-shirt he's discarded on the floor, she pulls it on over her head. Near the end of her relationship with Sam, this was where things always went terribly wrong. Her heart starts racing, making her consider getting out of there as fast as she can. She tries to put it out of her mind but all she can think about is how, after a night of drinking, she'd be roughly dragged to the edge of the bed and her body used as an outlet for Sam's anger.

Can she possibly bring herself to sleep in the same bed with Ethan tonight? Their *first time* in a bed together? In fact, the first time she would be in a bed with any man after her last night with Sam.

Olivia digs really deep for the trust she needs in Ethan and finds it. She's already under the covers when he returns. Holding her breath, she nervously waiting to see what comes next.

Ethan stands at the side of the bed, staring at the tension in her shoulders, and her hands firmly fisted in front of her, grasping the blanket. He's sober enough to remember the look on her face when he opened the door. The fear there is not far removed from her eyes. He sits on the side of the bed, thinking for a long period of time, before he lies back against the pillow, swinging his feet in under the covers. Clinging to the furthest edge of the king size bed, he makes no effort to touch her at all. He lays there in silence; his arms stretched up over his head. "I'm sorry, Liv."

Olivia rolls, turning away from him. The calm, gentle sound of his voice helps her to relax. "You don't have to apologize."

His voice is heavy with emotion.

His voice is heavy with emotion. "Yes, I do. I was a complete bastard today."

"A lot of things went on today. We got through them, that's all that matters." She can hear the angst in his voice and desperately needs to prevent him from getting wound up.

Ethan suddenly has the need to talk through what's going on in his head. "Everything is so fucked up. I feel like my life is veering out of control. All my friends are angry with me over this Jessica thing. My father hasn't talked to me since the first newspaper report. My sisters are trying to be supportive but I can see the disappointment in my mother's eyes when she looks at me." Raw emotion eats away at him.

When Ethan gets quiet and despondent, Olivia turns to face him with the sudden, overwhelming need to console him. He looks forlorn and lost. She wiggles close to him so she can touch him, stroking his hair and soothing him. He can hardly bring himself to look at her, let alone acknowledge her touch.

Fighting the urge to reach for her, Ethan lowers his arms to his sides and then remains completely still, his biceps hard and tense.

Moving her head against his pillow, she lowers her lips to his shoulder and presses them against the dark ink of his tattoo. "Ethan, everything is going to be okay, Baby. Get some sleep, we can talk tomorrow."

Taking a deep breath in, he holds it, his eyes look cloudy and heavy, his expression dejected. His voice cracks when he speaks, "I… I didn't think this day could get any worse, then Carter showed up… and I saw that look in his eyes when he saw you."

"I'm not interested in Carter, Ethan," she clarifies. She needs to console him, hold him, just as much, if not more than he needs to be held. "Come here," she says, beckoning him into her arms.

Ethan closes the space between them, pressing his body against her, letting her surround him with her softness.

"I'm sorry," he whispers against her neck. "After everything that happened today, after Stacey… fuck… and I didn't stop her…" He tenses and takes a few sharp breaths. "If you leave me… I deserve it."

Olivia's emotional level is through the roof from her own sobering. "Shhh, Baby. I'm not going anywhere. Everything is going to be all right. Please go to sleep now, okay?" If she can just get him to relax enough to sleep it off, he'll be fine in the morning. She knows that he probably won't remember anything anyway. Sam never remembered the hurtful things he said or did the next morning.

Wrapping the blanket around them, Olivia presses her warm lips to the top of his head. He lies heavily against her chest, his cheek rubbing gently on the skin just above her breasts. He wants to hold her but he hesitates, bringing his hand to her hip then letting it slide down, twisting the edge of her t-shirt around his fingers.

Ethan shakes his head slightly, a result of his continuing internal struggle. "Without you, the only thing I have left is my career and I can't seem to get that right these days, either," he says in a pained voice. Nuzzling his face against her skin, he sighs. Finally, unable to restrain himself any longer, he wraps his arms around her, holding on tightly.

There's a long silence; the only sound in the room is Ethan's breathing. Olivia can hardly stand to think about the pain he's feeling; she's experiencing it as if it's her own. And in some ways, it is. Feeling his breath stutter against her chest, she continues to hold him close, rubbing her hands across his body, trying to hug all the hurt away. That's all he needs right now, to be held and to know that she cares. Ethan O'Connell would never let anyone see his pain. It would make him appear weak. He's the kind of man who looks after everyone else in his life. She doubts that anybody has ever looked after him. She's going to change that, right now.

"Olivia?" Ethan's voice is slow and raspy; a clear sign that sleep is near. "Yes?"

"I was angry that you said we should see other people. But I understand why, now."

"Ethan, stop." Tonight was proof that she'd go insane if he was to date anybody else. She doesn't want to share him. She wants to be his only girl.

Before she can get the words out, he speaks, "I realize now, that it's because you could never love me. I mean… how could you? I'm a complete and utter fuckup." His voice is strained. Full of emotion, his heart is under an overwhelming heaviness. He barely gets the words out, then takes a deep breath in, his chest heaving a few times as he does.

Feeling like this is all her fault, Olivia's heart shatters into a million pieces. With all her insecurities and stupid rules, she's made a strong confident man feel like a failure. It takes her a moment to swallow her own emotions before she can tell him how she feels. "Ethan, nothing could be further from the truth." She pauses, nervous about her confession, "I am yours. I know that now. And I don't want you to see anyone else. I want you to be mine."

Ethan lets out a long, hot breath against her chest, tightening his hold on her. She feels the tension ease out of his shoulders as the anxiety leaves his body. No words are spoken. After some time, his breathing softens into a slow rhythm against her chest and she realizes that he's drifted into sleep.

Tracing her fingers along the strong line of his jaw, she brings her lips to his, intending to give him a kiss. Her heart skips a beat when her fingers brush across his cheek. Pulling back a little, she can see him in the faint light trailing in from the window. His eyes are closed, and his lashes are wet. Fallen tears have left salty trails as they travelled down his cheeks and dampened his skin. Gently, she wipes away the moisture with her thumb, erasing the evidence of his vulnerability.

Olivia's eyes well up with tears as she presses her lips to his cheek, his forehead, his nose, then landing on his lips she whispers, "I love you."

Chapter Forty-One

Delicate lace in a pale, pastel pink covers the long flowing ball gown she's wearing. It skims seductively against the soft silk lining, making it feel warm and creamy against her skin as she moves across the ballroom. As always, he's with her, his strong arms keeping her in hold. His body guides her across the floor, commanding her movements. She trusts him to lead her, to partner her; she'll follow without question. Her feet glide confidently around the room, stepping in perfect time with his. The orchestra plays a slow waltz as he dances her across the black and white marble tiles, with little effort. There's an intuitive feel to his movements, as if they've danced together forever.

She feels content, her soul filled with an ethereal beauty. She positively glows; her aura an overwhelming beacon of her femininity. In this dream, she still can't identify this man, his features hidden in the darkness of the room. Sometimes she's certain it's Ethan, other times she's not sure at all. She doesn't need to know what he looks like to know that he's her soul mate; her reason for existing. She can't imagine that there are any stronger feelings than the happiness she experiences in his arms, in this place, in this time.

Quicker then a flash storm, a wicked darkness surrounds her. She's pulled from his arms and dragged away into a cold dark frightening place. Reaching for him, she tries to stop her free-fall into her nightmare but she can't hold on. Blinking rapidly, she tries to focus but she can't see anything clearly. Her vision is blurry and distorted. Her body begins to shake violently; whether from the cold or the fear, it doesn't matter. Heaviness presses against her body, pinning her with an invisible force and ready to consume her. She can't move, can't breathe, she struggles at first to fight it, but the thought of existing without him is unbearable.

A strange moment of peace washes over her body as she stops fighting and surrenders to the darkness. Confusion takes over her thoughts as moonlight passes through the murky water. Suddenly she feels like she's floating, suspended in time and motion, feather light, unrestrained… free from pain… and lifeless.

Jolting from her sleep, Olivia gasps and sits straight up, her pulse jumping at a dangerous rate. The unfamiliar room only heightens her distress, until she hears his voice as he reaches for her in the darkness.

"Olivia? Are you awake?" Ethan's hand brushes her hair away from her face and across her cheek. "You were having a nightmare. Are you okay?" Wrapping his arms around her, he pulls her closer to him.

Olivia concentrates on breathing, trying to expel the poisonous images from her mind. She turns to look at his worried expression. "Yes, I'm okay."

Exhaling harshly, he leans back against the headboard, pulling her into his arms. Cradling her head in the hollow of his shoulder, he holds her tightly against him, feeling her heart still beating violently against his chest. "You scared the shit out of me, woman!" he says, taking his own calming breath. Brushing her face softly against his neck, she can tell by the rapid twitching of his pulse, that he's telling the truth. She startled him out of a sound sleep to witness... only God knows what that was.

"I'm sorry," she whispers.

"Do you remember what it was about?" He folds her into his body and presses his lips to her forehead.

"I'm not sure. I couldn't breathe. It felt like I was drowning or suffocating." She blinks her eyes rapidly, afraid that if she's still dreaming the darkness will come for her again. Wrapping her arms around him tightly, she makes sure that nothing could break her hold. "It was terrifying."

"Hey." Kissing her on the top of the head, he tightens his own grip. "It's okay. I'm here. I won't let anybody hurt you." His hand smoothes through her hair and then, just as he has done a hundred times before, he rakes his fingers through the silky strands, moving it away from her face. His fingertips skim across her scalp, discovering the raised ridges of scar tissue. His heart thumps hard against his chest. He repeatedly traces the long line of healed skin beneath gentle touches, wanting so badly to erase the scars, so she'd never have a reminder of what that asshole did to her. Rage boils deep in his core and deeper. He'll kill him, no question, if their paths ever cross.

Olivia's tension slowly recedes as her body melts into his. Holding his jaw in her palm, she peeks up at him through eyes so trusting and loving. She lets go of every fear: every inhibition She lets him discover her scars; something she's never let anyone do. Even though she's yet to share with him the details of that evening, she can tell by the rise and fall of his chest and the slight tension in his shoulders that he knows at whose hand she received them. Despite being obviously troubled about it, there's so much love in the tender way his hands brush across her that she knows his touch is her cure for the pain and the nightmares.

With the fear from her recent nightmare completely abated, she searches for his lips, needing him to kiss away the bad memories. When he lowers his mouth to bring them together, her warm breath burns like fire against his skin.

They fit perfectly together when they kiss, like two pieces of a puzzle; each of them the perfect shape to fit into the other. He falls into place, his mouth against hers, hesitating… holding back. If he kissed her right now, he wouldn't stop and he fears that she's in too vulnerable of a state after her nightmare.

Olivia can't stand it any longer. Running her hands through his hair, she twists it around her fingers and presses her lips against him. For the briefest of moments, he doesn't return her kiss, still unsure that this is the right thing to do. He starts to pull away. "Liv…"

Olivia grasps at him, desperate and pleading. "Ethan, please kiss me. I need you right now."

Her confession lights the fire deep down in his soul. Ethan brings his lips back to hers for a gentle kiss before whispering, "What do you need, Baby? Tell me. I need to hear you say it."

"You. I need you. I need you to make love to me." Her hands trail down his stomach feeling the warmth of his skin and tracing the ridges that separate tensed muscles and making his body respond.

Just as she has asked him to, he kisses her. Every brush of his lips, every stroke of his tongue creates a whole new kind of connection. One forged at a raw, emotional level. It's deep, it's moving, and so powerfully saturated with love that it seals the cracks in her heart where hope and trust have, for so long, been leaking out.

His approach changes from a soft, tender gentleness to a toe curling *need to have you now* hunger, as his desire grows in intensity. Easing her back, he lowers her down and presses her into the mattress with his heavy body.

Olivia tugs at the waistband of his boxers, sliding them down below his thighs. Reaching down, he quickly strips them the rest of the way off. Then, with skilled swiftness, he rids her of his t-shirt. His hands move to her breasts, kneading them and surrounding them with the warmth of his touch. She arches her back in response, pressing her breasts into him as he teases her nipples into taut nubs. Moving his mouth from one tender breast to the other, he licks and sucks them with varied pressure.

When Ethan slides his hand down her stomach and underneath her panties, she inhales sharply. His hand skims over her, finding her swollen, excited, and very ready for him. Rubbing his cock against her thigh, he moans into her breast. When he glides his fingers over her folds, Olivia clenches and raises her hips making his cock grow even harder.

Olivia's hands move down his sides, exploring his body. She tries to pull him closer, wanting to feel the weight of his body on top of her. Ethan's breathing gets heavy and shallow. He pulls his mouth away from her breast with one last hard suck, making her cry out as he leans back onto his knees. The darkness hides his eyes but she knows that he's staring at her, watching her; taking in every inch of her body through the filtered moonlight.

"You're the most beautiful woman I've ever seen."

When Olivia whispers his name, her voice translates her desire and need. On a mission to fulfill that need, Ethan moves between her legs. Starting at her stomach, he trails his lips downward, licking and nibbling at tender skin and jumping nerves. As he kisses his way to her hip, his hands skim along the top of her panties, slowly sliding them down.

Ethan gives her a subtle nudge, needing her to lift her bottom so he can remove them. But Olivia's mind is focused on the pleasure building inside her. Becoming impatient, he nips the tender flesh of her hip with his teeth, making her gasp. When she bucks her hips upward in shock, he strips her panties down and pulls them off. Tossing them to the floor, he climbs her like a predator; using his knee to force her legs wider.

His forearms brace his body on either side of her head, controlling his height over her, while she adjusts her position beneath him. When he lowers himself on top of her, he claims her mouth. Hungrily possessing her lips, he takes one greedy kiss after another. The feel of her underneath him, skin on skin, drives him wild. He knows he's not going to last long.

He rubs his cock against her entrance causing her to squirm in anticipation. When she opens wider to accommodate the width of his hips and invites him in, he growls. Reaching for her wrists, he pulls her arms up over her head and holds them there.

Olivia's heart pounds, her heated blood pulsing through her body in a rapid boil. Exhaling sharply, Ethan presses her palms flat beneath his and locks their fingers together.

Lifting his hips, he teases her, dragging his rigid cock across her throbbing clit, one more time, before pressing into her with one hard push. Inhaling deeply, Olivia holds her breath; knowing that he's not yet completely inside her. He becomes perfectly still for a moment, relishing every moment of her squeezing him as tight as a fist. Kissing her, licking at her mouth and teasing her tongue, he tightens his grip on her hands, securing her for what's to come. He slowly slides out, almost all the way. In one languid thrust forward, he pushes all the way inside her, balls deep. The walls of her pussy strain at his size, making her moan at the burning fullness. She clenches around him, amazed at how she's able to completely take him in. It's the most magnificent feeling in the world.

Completely inside her, Ethan rolls his hips slowly, pushing in and pulling out in a lazy rhythm. Taking his time. "Jesus Christ, you feel so good around me," he whispers.

Meeting his movement on the downward strokes, she lifts her hips, hooking her legs around him. His pace quickens, his thrusting becoming harder as his head falls to rest on her neck. The sound of his hips pounding against her thighs echoes in the room. Ethan releases her hands. Free from his hold, Olivia's hands grasp his sides, desperate to touch him. Digging her fingers into his flesh, she pulls him forward.

Moving his forearms to either side of her, he uses them to leverage his body as he continues to thrust in and out, driving them both closer to release. Feeling his control waning, Ethan groans against her skin, "I'm not going to last much longer, Baby. What do you need to get there? I don't want to leave you behind."

Olivia pants, her body on the edge, as his constant delivery of pressure, in exactly the right spot, promises her own quick release. "I'm right there," she moans.

Ethan sets a punishing rhythm, moving faster and harder. His body tenses as it collides with hers. As he feels the ripples of her orgasm start to overtake her, he completely unravels, cursing at the intensity of his release. Olivia screams out his name. With one last thrust he pulses inside her, filling her with a steady, seemingly endless stream of his seed. It's like nothing he has ever experienced with anyone else. Only with Olivia has he ever felt emotion this raw, this impassioned, this out of control.

When their breathing settles back into a normal rhythm he adjusts his weight, allowing himself to slowly withdraw and slide to her side. His hands never leave her body, always touching, tenderly caressing her skin, as if he's assuring himself that this isn't a dream. Brushing the slightly damp hair from her forehead, he brings his lips back to hers in a sweet kiss.

Olivia winces at the stiffness already setting in. She moans as she slips her feet over the side of the bed and sits up.

"I'm going to be sore tomorrow."

"I'm so sorry, are you okay?"

Turning to look at him sprawled out buck-naked across the bed, she teases him, "Sorry for what, exactly? The best sex I've ever had in my life? Yeah, you should be real sorry for that." She smiles, her body feeling tired and heavy as she makes her way into the bathroom.

She grunts as she bends over to grab the t-shirt from the floor and pulls it on over her head.

Ethan grins and lies back, stretching out across the entire bed. Folding his hands behind his head, he thinks about how easy it is for him to lose himself in her. The bathroom door swings open and the bright light behind her makes him squint. Standing with her arms crossed, she looks really angry. "REALLY?" she says, scowling at him.

Ethan sits up, concerned. "What's wrong?"

Lifting the edge of the t-shirt, she reveals his teeth marks on her hip. "You couldn't have just asked me to take them off?" She shakes her head, not amused at all.

Ethan grins, admiring his little love bite. "Where's the fun in that?" A dirty little smirk forms at the corner of his mouth. He pats the spot on the bed next to him. "Come back to bed and I'll kiss it better."

"Don't you think we should get some sleep? We both have to work tomorrow."

Ethan sighs and gets to his feet. Reaching the doorway, he presses his naked body against her and gives her a kiss. "You're right, we should get some rest." He rubs his hand over her hip, frowning when she winces. "Go get into bed, I won't be long." In a moment of thought, he turns back to her, looking unsure. "Don't leave, okay?"

Olivia nods, confused at why he'd think that. "Okay." As if she would leave now that she's finally admitted that she belongs to him.

When Ethan returns, he joins her under the covers, pressing his chest against her back and wrapping his arms around her. "I like this," he whispers in her ear.

"You like what?"

"I like you… in my bed, staying with me."

Olivia sighs drowsily, "Me, too." The feel of his naked body pressing against her is distracting. "Ethan? Where are your boxers?"

"On the floor. I don't need them," he yawns loudly.

"You don't have any problems with being naked, do you?" Olivia smiles, remembering how freely he stripped down to nothing at the soccer field.

"No, not really. Especially around you." Ethan presses his hips against her backside and his body starts to respond.

Olivia looks at him over her shoulder. "Would you please control that thing and go to sleep?"

Ethan nibbles on the base of her neck. "I don't want to sleep. I want to stay up all night and watch you. It's like having an angel sleeping next to me. I'm afraid if I close my eyes you'll disappear."

Olivia's heart thumps against her chest. "Hush now, I'm not going anywhere. Please go to sleep."

"Okay, but just so you know. I'm not letting you go. Not even for a second. I'm going to hold you in my arms all night long and *that* will most definitely make my cock hard. So you'll just have to deal."

Chapter Forty-Two

When Olivia opens her eyes a few hours later, she's covered in over 200 pounds of an extremely warm, incredibly muscular, Irish blanket. Ethan wasn't kidding; his legs twist around her, pressing his rock hard erection against the small of her back. He shares her pillow, his arms draped heavily over her middle and anchoring her to his body. Olivia smiles at the incredible feeling of him around her. What woman wouldn't want to wake up every morning wrapped in Ethan O'Connell? Suddenly she hears the sound that woke her.

"Ethan, you're phone is ringing," she says sleepily. No response. Nothing. How the hell can he sleep through that? She nudges him with her elbow. "Ethan, your phone."

He exhales his warm breath softly against her neck. "Hmmm? What time is it?" He releases her and rolls onto his back, stretching as he yawns.

She looks over at the blue glowing light of the alarm clock. "It's 5 a.m."

"Shit!" Ethan bolts straight upward, grabbing his phone. "O'Connell. Good morning, sir. I'm sorry; I had stepped into the other room for a moment."

He looks at Olivia with an expression that slightly resembles panic. Picking his boxers up off the floor, he tries to step into them, using one hand to pull them up while holding his phone to his ear. Olivia chuckles, watching him try to maneuver into them and listening curiously to the conversation.

"Friday? Yes, sir, I can have it to you before next Friday. It outlines my plan to increase our presence in international markets. I think there are some huge opportunities in Australia and South Africa. Carter Brant is here with me now. I'll be working with him myself, over the next week, to nail down a business plan. Yes, sir, he's the right man for the job, you won't be disappointed. Landon Scott will be on point in South Africa, I haven't decided yet if I should go there to work with him. We can go over the presentation when I'm back at the end of the month. I like Canada just fine, but I'm looking forward to coming home. Yes. I have no doubt that Miss Quinn will get to the bottom of it. Yes. Okay. Have your assistant send the dates to John and I'll make sure to attend. Thank you, sir, you have a good day, as well."

Olivia is dumbfounded and it shows on her face.

"The BIG boss," Ethan explains after he hangs up. "It's already mid morning over there."

"Oh, I haven't really thought about you having a boss."

"One day, I plan on being the BIG BOSS, if I haven't screwed that up already." Ethan sits on the side of the bed and pulls her into his lap.

That's not the part that interests her. "You're going back to Ireland?" she asks, trying not to sound upset.

"Yes, after the grand opening of the restaurant. There are a few events that I'm expected to attend, as well as some personal things I need to tend to." His head snaps up, suddenly wide-awake with the realization that he'll be away from her for a very long time. He doesn't like that idea at all. "We can talk about it later,"

There's a long dramatic pause. Olivia had never thought to ask him if he'd be in Canada permanently. "Are you coming back?"

Noticing her angst, Ethan rakes his fingers through her hair, playing with the soft curly strands. "Of course, I'll only be gone for about a month."

A month! Her stomach does a flip-flop and no matter how good of an actress she is, she's certain that he can see the horror on her face. WTF? She finally gives in to him and agrees to be in a relationship and he's leaving?

"You don't look very happy about that." He's glad that she doesn't seem to like the idea any more than he does.

"I just didn't know you were going. It's a long time, that's all."

"Yes, it is." He nods. He'd ask her to go with him, but he already knows that she won't. Rachel has told him that Olivia refuses to take vacation from work.

When his phone rings again he grabs for it, scowling as he looks at the display. "Oh, this can't be good." He lifts Olivia off his knee and sets her on the bed beside him.

"Mom? Is everything alright?"

"No, not really Ethan."

"Madison? Why are you at Mom's house? Is she okay?" Ethan gets to his feet and paces the floor.

"Yes, Mom is fine. Ethan, Jess phoned here this morning."

"SHE WHAT?"

"Why didn't you tell us?"

"Because I only found out yesterday. My lawyers are dealing with it. Maddie, there's no way that baby is mine. You believe me, right?"

"She says it is."

"I know. We're trying to arrange for a paternity test when I get home. Who else knows about it?"

"Everyone."

"Fuck." He scrubs his hand across the bristles on his jaw.

"Kaylie is here, she wants to talk to you." Madison hands the phone to an extremely upset Kaylie.

"Hi," she says, sniffling.

"Hey, don't listen to what everyone is saying, Kaylie. It's not true. Everything's going to be okay." Taking a deep breath, Ethan looks over at Olivia's sympathetic smile. "Kaylie, you're killing me. Don't cry, Sweetheart."

He hears a muffled voice in the background and then the sound of Kaylie breaking down into a hard sob.

"You're a right asshole, you know that?" Comes the voice of an extremely angry Irish woman.

"McKenna? Jesus Christ… are you all there?"

"Yes, and Mom wants to talk to you."

"McKenna, wait… don't put Mom on the phone. I don't want to talk to her, right now."

"Ethan," his mother says dryly into the phone.

"Hi, Mom." Ethan closes his eyes, his shoulders slouching in defeat.

"What are your plans, Son?"

"Mom, I'm dealing with it. I'm going to be home in a couple of weeks, and then we'll do the tests to confirm that it's not mine."

"You sound pretty sure that it's not yours."

"I'm positive it's not mine, Mom. I was very careful. I think it's Reese's."

Whoa! Reese Wilson? Olivia tries to hide the look of shock on her face as her stomach bottoms out. No wonder Carter looked uncomfortable when she asked questions about Reese at dinner. Reese is the man that Ethan's ex was sleeping with while they were together! The reason he left her. She cheated on him with his best friend? Her heart dips, understanding his heartbreak. For Pete's sake, what's wrong with some women?

"Well, you listen to me ***Ethan Joseph O'Connell***… if it turns out that this child is yours you ***will*** make sure they're both properly looked after. Nothing short of that will be acceptable, Son," Anna O'Connell's voice is stern, as she lays down her expectations.

Ethan stands up tall and stiff responding to her tone. "Of course, Mom. Does Dad know?"

"Yes, boy… You can't keep a secret like that in this town."

Ethan becomes agitated. "No, I guess not. Can everyone just believe me this time? Is that too much to ask?"

"Of course we believe you. I never trusted that woman, she always seemed right crazy to me."

Ethan curses under his breath, "Well, I had no idea that there was an '*I hate Jessica Club*' until after I left her."

"Just get home and look after your business, Ethan. This is difficult for all of us, Son."

"I will, Mom. I'll be there in a couple of weeks. Is Kaylie okay?"

"She'll be fine. She's been very emotional the past couple of days. I think she's on her period."

Ethan cringes. "MOM! I don't want to know that stuff!"

"I love you, Ethan. No matter what."

"I love you, too, Mom. Can you put McKenna back on the phone?"

Olivia sits on the side of the bed listening to the conversation, as Ethan paces back and forth in front of her. Reaching out she grabs his hand, making him stop and look at her. Giving him a reassuring smile, she lifts his hand to her mouth, kissing it to show her support.

After a few moments, McKenna comes back to the phone. "What do you want, dick?"

"Nice mouth, McKenna. I hope Mom's not in the room. Listen, I need you to handle this with Dad."

"Not a chance. Grow some balls and come home and talk to him yourself."

"McKenna, I'm not asking. I'm telling. When you get to the office, you need to tell him the truth. Jess is only looking for ways to get money from me, and he should NOT give her any if she contacts him. Be pissed at me if you want, but you will do that one thing for me."

"Fine."

"Thank you, McKenna. I really miss you guys."

"Madison and Kaylie miss you," she says sharply.

"And you? Don't you miss me?"

"Not really. You're a pain in the arse."

Ethan chuckles, "So I'm told, on a regular basis; by a lot of people actually." He glances over at Olivia's smirk. She can't hear the other end of the conversation, but he's sure she knows what was said. "Thank you for looking after everyone while I'm gone, McKenna. I love you."

A few moments pass before she breaks the silence. "I love you, too," she says in a softer voice. "But, Ethan, I'm telling you if you don't get this Jessica thing under control soon, I'm going to take things into my own hands and there will be bloodshed."

"McKenna, don't do anything stupid. We need to let the lawyers handle it. Okay?"

"Whatever! I had better go. Ian has called me at least a dozen times this morning wanting to know where I am."

"Well then, you better get into the office. You'll handle Dad, yeah? You're the only one he'll listen to."

McKenna sighs, "It's exhausting covering your ass all the time."

"I'm sure it is," Ethan chuckles, "I'll check in with you later." Disconnecting the call, he looks down at Olivia with a look of despair. "I don't suppose I have to explain that call, do I?"

Shaking her head, Olivia tugs on his hand, pulling him back down onto the bed, and stretches out beside him. Leaning against the headboard, Ethan makes a call.

"Hi, Shannon. I'm sorry, I know it's early."

Olivia watches him on the phone, staring at his bare chest and the muscular breadth of his shoulders. She doesn't know what it is about that tattoo that does it for her, but her insides squeeze every time she sees it. *Whew! Did it just get hot in here?* She should probably try to go back to sleep for another hour or two but she's wide-awake and her mind is racing with naughty thoughts.

"I've just received a call from my family."

Poor Ethan. She wishes she could give his mind a break from everything that's going on. He has all these problems already crammed in his brain and he isn't even dressed for the day yet. An idea strikes her.

"Jessica has contacted them this morning about the pregnancy."

No time like the present to settle up on debts. In a flash, Olivia's sitting on top of him, straddling his legs. He's not the only one that can move quickly when he wants to. Ethan gives her a quizzical look. "There must be something we can do. Can we get some kind of a court order to stop her from contacting my family?"

Olivia grins as she pulls down the waistband of his boxers, uncovering his incredible cock. Ethan raises his eyebrows as she takes it in hand, rubbing it from base to tip, and making it spring to life.

Completely focused on Olivia, he puts his hand over the speaker. "What are you doing?" he whispers.

She grins as she strokes him with a firm hand up the heavy shaft, and then back down again. "A bet's a bet, right?"

Ethan hardens swiftly with her touch, making him anxious. "Thank you, Shannon. Let me know when I get to the office later." With his gaze still locked onto Olivia's, he ends his call.

Ethan adjusts his position, giving her better access. Olivia wastes no time, grabbing his boxers, she pulls them all the way off, and quickly moving between his legs. Reaching down, he twists her hair around his hand; pulling on it gently and making her look up at him. "You don't have to do this."

Olivia licks her lips. "Oh, I'm sure I'd never hear the end of it if I backed out of a bet, so you just try and stop me."

He grins. "Right then, if you insist… have at it." He releases her hair, letting it fall softly around her face.

His leg muscles twitch as she holds him firmly and slides him into her mouth. He groans as she moves her head up and down, closing her mouth around him. She presses hard along his shaft with the flattened edge of her tongue. Wrapping her hand around the base, she licks all the way up the hard length of him. When she reaches the end, she closes her lips tightly around the head, sucking and swirling her tongue around it. She hears his sharp intake of breath as her soft curls brush across the bare skin of his thighs.

Pushing his hips upward, it takes everything he has to resist the urge to take over and fuck her mouth, fast and hard. Looking up at him through the fallen strands of hair, she can see the precise moment that his mind empties of all thoughts, except for his pleasure. The pleasure *she* is giving him.

Ethan's stomach tightens as the pleasure builds inside him, climbing faster with every stroke of her tongue, every downward thrust of her mouth. He's so damn close already.

He pushes his hair to the side, tucking it behind her ear so he can see her face and watch her soft, warm mouth slide down his cock. "Beautiful," he whispers. "So beautiful."

Olivia's even more determined to rock his world. Locking her gaze to his, she slides her mouth down taking him in as far as she can. After pausing, and taking a quick breath, she relaxes the muscles in her throat. Widening her mouth she takes him in even deeper, to the furthest spot, deep within her throat. All the while, her hazel eyes remain locked to the green of his. Pleasure surges through him, his balls pulling tight and taking him by surprise as he explodes in her mouth, giving her no warning.

She's unprepared when the first hot spurt hits the back of her throat. He curses then groans, his hands tangling in her hair. He's so deep that she can barely swallow around him. He continues to come in what seems like an endless climax; she struggles to keep up. Gasping slightly she tries to swallow without choking, her eyes beginning to water. He hadn't meant for that to happen at all. He pulls back, trying to slide out of her mouth and give her space to breath.

Olivia stops him from withdrawing; determined to follow through with her promise and lick clean every drop that he can give her. She releases him only when he begins to soften in her mouth.

Ethan reaches down with both hands, grasping her by the ribs and pulls her up onto his lap. Olivia clears her throat a few times, coughing lightly. He holds her tightly against his chest and wipes the moisture from her eyes

"I'm so sorry, Baby. I had no intentions of making you go through with that. But you looked up at me with those eyes and your sweet lips wrapped around my dick… and I… It just happened so fast. I couldn't talk. I couldn't stop it."

Olivia rests her head against his chest; extremely pleased that she was responsible for making Ethan O'Connell lose control for a change. She wishes she had thought to look at the clock since she's certain that she had beaten his record of four minutes twenty-eight seconds.

"My God, you're amazing." He presses his lips to the top of her head. "It's barely even 5:30 a.m. and you'd do that for me? Even after you woke up to the shit storm that's *my life* these days?"

"I meant to distract you from it all, even if it was for just a few minutes." Running her hand up and down his bicep, she squeezes it, when he flexes, her hand barely even circling half way around the thickset muscle.

Lifting her chin so he can see into her eyes, he lowers his lips for a kiss. "My sweet, sweet girl. You are far better than I deserve."

Olivia smiles, tracing the black ink of his tattoo. "You're naked again."

"That happens a lot when I'm around you." Running his hands down her sides and sliding them underneath her, he cups her bottom and gives it a firm squeeze. "I need to have a shower."

He lifts her swinging his legs over the side of the bed, getting to his feet. She squeals, wrapping her arms and legs around him to stop from falling. "Ethan! Put me down!"

"What? You're not going to join me?"

"Nooooo! Don't think I don't know that it's a trap to get me naked, so you can ravage my body again."

He laughs as he stands her on her feet. "Damn, I've become too predictable."

"I'm too tired to fight you off in my sleep deprived state."

"Well, that's disappointing. It turns me on when you fight it."

"I've noticed," she says with a sly grin. "That's so incredibly wrong."

Ethan reaches for her and she ducks just out of reach. "Oh no you don't. I'm exhausted. Go! Shower alone."

He teases her with that *'come and get me'* smile. "Okay, but I'll leave the door unlocked in case you change your mind."

Chapter Forty-Three

After a long hot shower, Ethan returns to the room, wrapped in a towel.

"John had a suit sent over." Olivia extends her hand so he can slip the clothes hanger off her finger.

"Thanks, Love." Ethan's brow furrows as he takes it from her. His playful tone is gone in a flash and there's no mistaking the hint of anger in his expression. "Tell me you didn't answer the door dressed like that!"

Oh! Ooops. Her heartbeat picks up a little. "Well, yes but..." Looking into his eyes, she knows that there's no excuse that he'll find acceptable.

Ethan starts to lose his temper, exhaling harshly and cursing. "You didn't..." His frustration is evident in his voice. Rubbing his forehead, he pauses to take a breath, rethinking his approach.

"Olivia, I don't know how the other guys in your life felt about you exposing your body to other men... but it's NOT OKAY with me. The thought of another man seeing you half dressed infuriates me."

The man has incredible *nerve!* "Yeah? Well, the sight of another woman's hand on your dick didn't do too much for me, either!" she spouts angrily. She crosses her arms in front of her, not thinking about the consequences of taking the conversation there.

Ethan takes a deep breath and closes his eyes, swallowing his anger. "I deserve that. Believe me, nothing like that will ever happen again."

Olivia's not quite sure how to respond without sounding like a jealous lunatic. She says nothing and looks away.

Ethan shakes his head. "Don't turn away. Look at me," he demands, trying to keep the anger out of his voice.

Olivia drags her eyes back to his and bites her lip.

"I don't feel any less possessive of your body than you do of mine. Could you at least try to be mindful of that?" Ethan stands staring, waiting for an answer. He becomes frustrated when she replies with a nod.

"Words," he snips impatiently.

Heat flashes through her as she finds herself submitting to his authoritative voice. God she hates that his dominant tone gets her blood simmering; yet it does, every time without fail.

"I'm sorry, I'll be more mindful." She jiggles her leg, resentful that he's somehow dismissed *her* anger, and once again, she finds herself doing the apologizing.

Ethan swings his suit over his shoulder; the hanger hooked around one finger. "Good." He leans forward, kissing her on the lips before beginning to get dressed.

Olivia looks down at the pile of clothes on the floor. Since she hadn't planned to stay, she didn't pack a bag for herself. Stepping into her pants, she pulls them over her hips and zips them up. Tugging her shirt on over her head, she climbs into the huge chair in the corner. Watching Ethan get dressed on the other side of the room, she feels that tightness in her stomach that spreads outward, making her feel tingly. She stares, unashamed, as he pulls up his pants and then slides his arms into the crisp white dress shirt. Mercy sakes, the man is gorgeous.

Ethan O'Connell is a man at odds with himself on every level. He dresses in the finest tailored suits, conveying his perfect *'everything is under control'* badass, business executive persona; a complete contradiction to his self-proclaimed *'my life is a shit storm'* reality.

There doesn't seem to be any middle ground for him. Everything about him toggles from one extreme to the other without notice; including his personality. It's like two sides of the same coin, keeping Olivia on her toes because she never knows which side will land facing up.

Tails… ruled by his Irish temper; his primal urge to protect what's his and keep safe those he loves. It's what keeps him focused and engaged. Dark, mysterious, and dangerous at times, it's what's responsible for his drive and success.

Heads… ruled by his Irish heart; his playful and loving personality, blessing him with his romantic and quixotic nature. It gives him the overwhelming need to nurture and care for others, while neglecting his own emotional needs. It fills his life with light, hope, and laughter, making him the most loyal lover and friend.

Olivia's not entirely sure which side of the coin rules his sense of humor or his sexual nature, although at times, they both seem to be heavily rooted on the dark side. That thought makes her smile. On both accounts, he's most certainly met his match in her.

Ethan straightens and then flattens his tie, dark turquoise against the crisp white shirt and the charcoal vest of his suit. Perfection.

"Olivia?"

"Huh?" she says, momentarily lost deep in thought.

Ethan smirks. "I said… you're giving me that look again. Should I bother doing up my belt?"

She gives it some serious thought. That feeling in her stomach starts to squeeze tightly again, waking up the butterflies and sending delicious little pulses of heat through her body. Walking over to him, she presses up against him, wrapping her arms around his neck. Ethan's hands come up to hold her hips, making her smile playfully. Her eyes skirt down the length of his body taking a good, long, appreciative look. "I can't decide if you're hotter when you're completely naked or when you're completely dressed."

Gently tightening the grip on her hips, Ethan sways her, smirking proudly. "You think I'm hot?"

"Oh yeah! Super hot!" She runs her fingers through the hair at the back of his neck, amused at how he seems to be humbled by the suggestion. "Sizzling, as a matter of fact."

Ethan raises his eyebrows. "Sizzling? That's good right?"

"Yes, that's good." Laughing, Olivia licks her lips before brushing them against his. Tightening his grip, he pulls her close, claiming her mouth. They curse in unison, when Ethan's cell interrupts again. "Well, at least we know it's not John," she says, noting the unfamiliar ring tone.

"Sorry, Baby, my day starts early and picks up speed as it goes." Pulling away, he brushes his fingertips along her cheek and answers the call.

"O'Connell."

How does he make his own name sound so sexy? Moving to the desk, Olivia checks her purse, making sure she has everything before they leave.

"Bonjour mon ami. Je suis entrain de partir pour le bureau."

Olivia stops and looks up. Damn! Only Ethan O'Connell can take *sizzling* and turn it up a notch. Something she didn't even know was possible before meeting him.

Ethan catches her staring and smiles. "Listen, I'll ring you in an hour." Ethan throws his discarded clothes into the bag that John sent over, while continuing his conversation.

"Sure, but why are we speaking English? I thought you wanted me to help you keep your French in practice," Landon Scott asks, with a heavy French accent.

"Because I'm not alone and it's impolite." Ethan zips up the bag and takes it to the door, stopping to kiss Olivia on the way. It's one of those cheesy exaggerated kisses, the kind that makes a loud '*muah*' sound as he pulls away. Olivia bites her lip, glad that his playful mood has returned.

"What the hell was that? Are you kissing me goodbye, Ethan? I didn't know you switched teams, big guy," Landon teases.

"As if I'd kiss you, you ugly fucker." Ethan laughs. "I'll ring you later, Landon. I need to escort a very beautiful woman to her car."

Olivia smiles as he tucks her hair behind her ear and kisses her again. "Landon Scott from South Africa?" she whispers, as he pulls away. Ethan winks and nods his head.

"Okay, I was just checking in. I heard that you were having more problems with Jess."

Ethan holds his hand out to Olivia as he opens the door. "That's an understatement. Call Carter, he can fill you in."

Feeling his pockets before he closes the door, he checks to make sure he has everything: his watch, his wallet, and his keys. "I'm just heading into the office."

"You already told him that," Olivia says impatiently.

Ethan looks at her with a suspicious kind of surprise as he disconnects his call and tucks his phone into his pocket.

"What?" she asks, annoyed at the strange look he's giving her.

"Yes, I did, but I didn't know you understood what I said."

"Well, I told you my French was a little rusty but I can pick out words here and there. So you best not ever talk about me, thinking I won't know." Her grin spreads wider and she gives him a little hip bump.

"Good to know." He quickly reads a text message, and then shoves his phone back in his pocket. "John sent a car. It's waiting downstairs."

It's a short drive to the office and Ethan makes sure Olivia gets safely to her car. "Are you going to work? Or are you going to go home and get some sleep?" Wrapping his arms around her middle, he pulls her close for one last cuddle.

"I don't know, I guess I'll text Rachel when I get close to town and see what's going on."

He reaches up, holding her chin. "Wait until you get home before you text her, yeah? Don't be doing that shit while you're driving, it's not safe."

Olivia's would be annoyed that he warns her about her safety, as if she's a child without any common sense, but there's something calming about his concern today. His worry is a welcome acknowledgement of how much he cares for her. Now that she's agreed to forget about the agreement, it's either going to get better or so much worse.

Chuckling when she rolls her eyes, Ethan opens her car door, making sure she's safe and secure. When she rolls the window down, he leans in for one last kiss. "I'll call you later," he says between little love pecks.

Olivia yawns against his mouth and then laughs. "Totally your fault."

"My fault? Now wait a minute… who woke up in the middle of the night and needed some loving?" He raises his eyebrows at her when she tries to look innocent. "Yeah, thought so. It was you."

Olivia pouts. "Hey, I had a nightmare, and I needed my knight in shining armor."

"Well, far be it from me to refuse a damsel in distress." Ethan looks up when he hears his name. Turning, he searches the garage and finds Scott approaching.

"Hi, Liv," Scott says, surprised to see her. "Are you coming… or going?" he asks, looking at his watch.

"Hey." She smiles. "Don't worry. I'm going."

"Drive safe. Traffic is brutal today." Scott looks over at Ethan. "We have an account update with the rest of the team in ten minutes. Are you going to be late?"

"No, Olivia's on her way. I was just saying goodbye." Leaning down, Ethan peeks in the window. "Have you got your phone, Love? In case you have any problems?"

That's the second time he's called her that today. Her heart beats at the sound of it spoken with his Irish brogue. *Love.* How dreamy. Reaching down she pulls it out of her purse and holds it up for him to see.

Having a clear look at the call display, Ethan frowns. "Looks like Noah is pretty anxious to talk to you, is there something I should know?"

Scott leans in to look at the screen and shakes his head.

"What?" Olivia says surprised. Turning the screen, he shows her that there are several text messages and missed calls from Noah; some from last night and one already this morning. Sighing, she takes her phone out of his hand and proceeds to delete them.

Ethan watches her erase all the messages from her phone without reading them. "Have you talked to him since Saturday?"

She shakes her head. "He keeps sending messages but I delete them. I don't really care what he has to say."

Scott interrupts, "Ethan, we need to go."

"Okay." He caresses his thumb across her cheek, knowing that she's obviously upset about what happened. "We'll talk later." He gives her a reassuring smile and sneaks in one last kiss before Scott drags him away. If the truth were known, Ethan's happy Noah has fucked up big time. He'd be even happier if he were out of the picture all together. He doesn't like him one bit and trusts him even less than that around Olivia.

Olivia drives toward the exit feeling content. As she passes from the dim light of the parking structure into the bright sunlight on the street, someone steps in front of her car. "Holy Shit!" Slamming on the brakes, she makes the tires squeal. When she opens her eyes and looks up, the thin figure steps out of the blinding sunlight into the shadow of the garage. Olivia's eyes try to adjust to the light and focus on the blurry figure; her hands shaking and her breathing ragged from the fright.

"Are you nuts lady? I could have killed you!" Olivia screams.

Unfazed by Olivia's anger, the little, silver haired psychic saunters to her open window, glaring at her. "It's happening," she says in an eerie tone. "*You* are the key to his anger."

Feeling more edgy than ever, Olivia almost hyperventilates. Blowing air through her mouth, she consciously tries to regain control over her breathing and her racing heart. "Excuse me?"

The psychic takes on a serious and hardened look. "You need to know child. YOU are the *happening* that finally ends his turmoil. All his struggles, his anger... will come to an end with *you*!"

Olivia feels nauseous. "What the hell do you mean *I am the happening?* Who's struggle do I end?" The thought makes her blood run cold. "Is Sam coming back for me?"

Eva starts to back away slowly, an unnerving look on her face.

"Wait!" Olivia pleads.

"Provide closure to the one who deceived you and the pain will end. New life will welcome you. You must trust the one who guards your soul."

The one who guards her soul? Olivia opens the car door and gets out, but Eva continues to back up toward the street and into the bright sunlight.

"Please! Wait!" Olivia shields her eyes as they adjust to the intense brightness of the sun, but it's too late. She's vanished. Olivia looks right and left but the frail woman is nowhere to be seen. Her eyes flash across the street to the small shop just in time to see the door swing shut. *How the ever-loving hell?*

Chapter Forty-Four

A car horn beeps impatiently behind her, waiting to exit.

"Sorry!" Rushing back she gets in her car and exits onto the street. The drive home seems to take forever and she nearly works herself into an anxiety attack on the way. She tries to contort the psychic's words into several different interpretations, trying to make it fit a better outcome. But by the time she gets home, she's convinced herself that she's just been warned that Sam's coming back to kill her.

Climbing into the shower, she hopes that the hot water will massage away some of the tension, but it doesn't help. Maybe she just needs some sleep? Lying on the bed she wraps her arms around her pillow and tries to relax, but her racing mind won't settle long enough for sleep to set in. The longer she lies there, the more her thoughts start to dwell on the past day's events. Her muscles grow tighter, tenser.

Finally, she throws off the blanket and gets dressed. She's not going to get any sleep and thinking about *the day of destruction* will only drive her completely insane. She might as well go to work and keep her mind busy.

By late afternoon, she's haggard; her mind is bouncing all over the place. Looking out her office window she sees Noah walking through the parking lot, heading to the front door. Horrified, Olivia gets to her feet and finds Rachel standing at the door.

"You saw him?" Rachel asks.

"Yes. Can you make up some excuse about being on a conference call or something?" Olivia's eyes plead for her help.

"Okay, but you know you're going to have to face him at some point. It doesn't look like he's going to give up and eventually, Ethan is going to find out."

"Ugh, that'll get ugly." Olivia sighs, "I just can't deal with him today, Rach. Can you please just get rid of him?"

Rachel nods her head. It's no secret that she'd like to get rid of Noah permanently. "Yes, of course."

As Olivia closes the door, she hears Rachel say, "Noah, what a nice surprise. I'm afraid Olivia isn't available this afternoon. She's on an important conference call. She could be hours."

Olivia's phone rings making her jump out of her skin. "Hey."

"Hi. Are you okay? You sound a little *off.*"

"I'm exhausted, Ethan," she explains, purposely leaving out the part about Noah tracking her down at work.

"Me, too. Are you up for dinner? John wants to take Shannon to the restaurant. I thought that since you two seemed to hit it off last night that she might enjoy your company, instead of sitting around listening to John and I fake our way through polite conversation."

Olivia laughs. "I agree that would be painful. I'll go, but it needs to be an early evening."

"Sounds good to me. Our last meeting is at four p.m. then I'm taking off. We can eat around six, if that's okay. Shall I pick you up?"

"No, I'll drive myself." She feels relief, watching out the window as Noah walk to his car and drives away. Ethan yawns loudly and it makes her laugh.

"Your fault," he chuckles into the phone.

"Fine! It's my fault. But it was worth it. Right?"

"Absofuckinglutely!" he whispers into the phone.

Rachel startles her as she swings open the door to her office and gives her the thumbs up on the Noah situation. Boy, is she edgy this afternoon.

"I have to go. I'll see you tonight." Hanging up, Olivia looks over at Rachel, who's still standing in the doorway with her arms crossed and giving her *that look.*

"What?"

"You look like crap, James. Are you going to tell me what happened last night?"

"Nothing," she yawns, as she says it. Rachel raises her eyebrows in disbelief. "Okay, something. I stayed the night with Ethan in a hotel downtown. Did you know he owns a hotel?"

"You spent the night with Ethan? In a hotel, that he owns? In a BED?"

Olivia grins. "Well, he's part owner of the hotel, but yes… in a BED."

"So I'm guessing you look like crap because you didn't do much sleeping," she laughs.

"Something like that," Olivia replies blushing.

"Well, what the heck are you doing here? Go home and sleep! I'll cover for you. The day is almost over anyway."

"Thank you, Rachel" She quickly retrieves her keys out of her purse. "I'm exhausted and we're going to dinner at six with John and his girlfriend, Shannon."

"Wow, look at you. For three years, I couldn't get you out of that house. Ethan shows up and all of a sudden you're never home."

Olivia worries, feeling guilty that her friend is starting to feel a little left out. "I'm sorry, Rach. I guess I've been busy lately."

Rachel holds her hands up, halting her. "Don't say another word. You don't need to apologize to me. I'm so happy that you're out and doing stuff, again. Actually, now that I'm not constantly worrying about you, Scott and I have been doing a lot of... you know? Rekindling the romance. I'd forgotten just how sexy that man is, once we got all caught up in our careers and grown up life."

Olivia frowns. "I didn't know I was the reason you two had drifted apart."

"You aren't. You were just a convenient excuse. Now go home and get some sleep."

A few hours later, Olivia pulls the Mustang into the parking lot of her old favorite restaurant, soon to be re-opened as "Ireland's." She loves it, loves that it's the nickname that she had given him after Rachel's messed up drunken introduction. *Loves him.* Thank God, she was able to get a few hours sleep when she got home.

She's just getting out of the car when Ethan pulls up in the Challenger, screeching to a halt in the spot reserved for him. When he gets out of the car, he watches her make her way across the parking lot. His stomach squeezes. He feels the air around him charge with energy as she approaches him. Lord have mercy! Her smile could stop traffic. It's safe to say that he has it bad for Olivia James. He doesn't think that feeling will ever go away. *Love her.*

"You look well rested. Got some sleep, did you?" Smiling, he leans down to brush his lips on her cheek in greeting.

"Yes, did you?"

"A little. But not very well without you beside me," he admits, as he reaches down to grasp her hand.

"Aw, you missed me?"

"I did. Even though you didn't let me do much sleeping last night."

"Complaining? Am I too much for you?" She flashes him a challenging grin.

"Nope. Maybe bragging a little." His lips start to curl into a cheeky smile as he opens the door for her. "John and Shannon are already here."

As they walk toward the table, Shannon greets Olivia with a big hug and a huge smile. "I'm so glad you came."

John and Ethan glance at each other quickly and acknowledge the instant friendship between the girls. It's not anything they've discussed, it's just known at this moment that their lives will be a lot less stressful if there's harmony between the two women who will be their companions.

Sliding into the booth, they fall easily into comfortable conversation. Ethan holds Olivia's hand the entire time, tracing soothing patterns on the back of it with his thumb. She steals a few sideways glances at him, enjoying his attention and the sparkle in his eyes when he laughs; such a contrast from last night.

When the waitress arrives at the table and refills the water glasses, Ethan picks his up and quickly chugs it down. Olivia raises her brows at him and smiles. "A bit dehydrated, Baby?"

"Just a tad," he says, putting down his glass so she can refill it. "We're ready to order," he says to Cindy, the cute waitress with the ponytail. Olivia is the last to order, she's gone over the menu several times. Closing it and handing it to the waitress, she finally makes a choice. "I'll have a small chef salad, dressing on the side please."

Ethan gets the server's attention. "No tomatoes in that salad, Cindy."

Cindy makes a note. "Sure, Mr. O'Connell, I'll let them know."

Olivia looks at him impressed.

"What?" he asks, "I pay attention, sometimes."

"You're only having a plain salad for dinner? That's not very much food. Aren't you going to be starving?" Shannon asks.

Olivia responds in a manner that's very matter of fact, but she gives Ethan the devil's smile. "No, I'll be fine. I had enough protein this morning to hold me over… *for days.*"

With his water glass pressed to his lips, he's stunned at her comment. Swallowing too quickly, he chokes as it goes down the wrong way.

"Are you okay?" Concerned at how red his face is, she gently pats him on the back until he stops coughing.

"Yes, I'm fine," Nobody else at the table is any the wiser, but Ethan shakes his head and tries to hide his smile.

Shannon has a thought. "Ethan, did you tell Olivia about the Bramtech deal?"

Remembering that they ditched Stacey with Carter, without even saying good-bye, Olivia gets a little nervous. "What about it?" she asks curiously.

Ethan squeezes her hand. "They came by the office this afternoon and signed the papers."

Olivia is surprised. "Really? I thought they had until next week to decide?"

"They did, but they came in today and said they had made a decision and were ready to sign."

"Ethan, that's great news!" Olivia's glad that's over with so he can stop stressing. "So…. was Stacey there? How was she?" She quickly glances at Shannon who's trying to hide a smile.

Ethan makes a face, trying to figure out what's going on between the two girls. "Yes, she was there. She was in a really good mood, actually. She looked…" There is a pregnant pause as he thinks of the right word.

"Satisfied?" Shannon adds, not able to hold back her grin any longer.

"Yeah! She did. Didn't she?" Ethan agrees looking at John to see if he concurs.

Shannon and Olivia start to snicker. Ethan looks between them both and then back over to John who shrugs. Shannon puts her hand over her mouth trying to stop her laughter. Olivia can't even look at her as she tries to regain her composure. Ethan tilts his head and waits, looking for an explanation. "What did I miss?" he finally asks.

"Wow, you really did have a lot to drink, didn't you?" Shannon asks.

"Shannon," John warns, trying to steer her away from that conversation.

"Well, it does get a bit fuzzy after we ended up at Euphoria," Ethan admits, looking confused and wondering what the hell happened.

Olivia looks over at him, still trying to pull herself together. "Let's just say that you need to give Carter a *big raise*, and leave it at that."

"Carter?" Ethan looks at her as if she has three heads and then turns to John. "Come to think of it, where was Carter today? I didn't see him."

"He sent a message and said he wouldn't be in today. He didn't say why," John replies, hoping that Ethan will drop it.

"He probably needed time to recover," Olivia adds, still struggling to hold back her laughter.

"Really? What did he get into last night?" Ethan wonders.

"Stacey," Olivia says under her breath. Shannon snorts, breaking into a fit of uncontrollable laughter. Olivia follows holding her stomach.

"Huh?" Ethan looks over at John, completely frustrated. "Do you have any idea what they're laughing at?"

"No clue," John lies, deciding that it's one of those details that Ethan just doesn't need to know. If Carter wants to tell him, he'll leave it up to him.

"Well, I was drinking. What's your excuse then?"

"I don't have one," John nods in the direction of the girls, "but I think it's pretty clear that we should keep these two away from each other."

Ethan watches Olivia wipe the tears from her eyes as she pulls herself together. "No kidding." He shakes his head, tired of trying to figure them out.

After dinner, they order coffee and relax; listening to the live band that Ethan had booked for the evening. Starting to feel really tired, Olivia yawns, and rests her head on his shoulder. Leaning his head in toward her, Ethan rests his cheek on the top of her head.

"I like these guys. They're pretty good." She nods her head to the beat of the music.

"I agree," Shannon says. "So, what plans do you have for the grand opening, Ethan? John won't tell me a thing."

Olivia grins. "Good luck, he won't tell me a thing either. It's a giant secret, apparently."

Ethan laughs. "I thought women loved surprises?"

"NOOOOO!" both girls say in unison.

Ethan looks at John. "They're starting to frighten me, now." John nods his head in agreement.

"Well, I have a few bands scheduled to play live. Ones you may know. And my friends are coming from Ireland. They have a band and play mostly local pubs. I thought I'd like to incorporate a little bit of home."

"That sounds really nice," Olivia says. "I am looking forward to meeting your friends."

This time, both John and Ethan laugh. "Trust me. If I can find a way to keep you away from these guys, I definitely will. Although, I'm not sure if there's any point, since you'll just ignore me anyway."

Olivia leans back to look up at him with her brows lowered. "Well, now I'm just more curious why meeting these guys has kicked your ICF into overdrive."

"ICF?" Shannon asks curiously.

"Inner Control Freak." Olivia looks up to meet Ethan's scowl. Grinning, she offers up her lips for a kiss. He hesitates for a bit, still a little annoyed. Finally, he sighs and lowers his lips to hers, brushing them with a brief kiss, and then quickly moves away. But Olivia's not having that; she raises her hand, reaching for the back of his neck, and firmly pulls him forward for a longer, sizzling lip lock. Trailing her hand down his chest and across his stomach, she reaches down to brush along his thigh; making his muscles tighten and the front of his pants start to bulge.

Pulling away, she smiles, lightly pressing her mouth to his ear and whispers, "I think there might be something we need to discuss in your office, Mr. O'Connell."

Chapter Forty-Five

For the next few days, everybody is extremely busy. Shannon is busy trying to get a judge to sign an order preventing Jessica from talking to the media. John is up to his ears in grand opening arrangements. Rachel and Scott are busy rekindling their romance. Ethan and Carter spend hours, behind locked boardroom doors, hammering out a business plan for Australia. And Olivia? Well, she's taken on a very challenging client at work.

The events of the past week are starting to wear her down. Her current client is difficult beyond all reasonable measures, and for the first time ever, she feels like throwing her hands up in defeat. Then, there are the nightmares. Since the psychic warned her about Sam, they happen every time she closes her eyes. It's hard to cope with difficult days at the best of times; it's damn near impossible when you don't get any sleep. It wouldn't take much to push her over the edge; into that anxiety attack that's been threatening all week.

"Hey, Beautiful."

Olivia smiles for the first time today. "Hey."

"I've missed you the past couple of days."

"You've talked to me every day, Ethan," she laughs.

"I know, but I want to see you. Join us for dinner tonight."

Hearing his charming Irish voice makes her miss his smile even more. She thinks about it for a minute. "I don't think so. I really wouldn't be good company."

"What's wrong?" he asks, with concern.

On the edge of tears, she fights to prevent an emotional response. "I'm just really stressed."

"Well, then I won't go to dinner. I'll come to your place and we can talk."

"No!" she insists, pulling herself together. "You go to dinner. I just need to go home and try to get some sleep. If you come over that won't happen."

"I'm more than capable of exercising self control, Olivia," Ethan says, annoyed.

"Yeah, but I'm not and I have a bruise on my stomach from Tuesday night to prove it."

Ethan groans. Why did she have to mention Tuesday night? He still has a lot of work to do today and he can't afford to be distracted. Despite the efforts to stay focused, his mind now wanders to what happened behind locked doors in the restaurant office; the sight of her bent over the edge of his desk, the feel of her body underneath him as he slid into her from behind.

"You'd be impressed," she says with a half giggle. "It's in the perfect shape of your stapler."

Ethan frowns. "Why didn't you say something if you were uncomfortable?"

"Because at the time I didn't care, I just needed you deep inside me."

He quietly curses. "Do you know what it does to me when you say things like that?" he whispers into the phone.

"I think I might have an idea," she teases. "Seriously though, you go to dinner. I need some downtime."

"Olivia, I want to see you tonight." He's not prepared to give in this time.

"Ethan, please stop."

"No. I want to see you."

She sighs, "You'll live."

"Are you sure? I haven't seen you in so long, it feels like I might die."

"It's been two days! You'll be fine. Since when are you such a drama king?"

"Since I haven't been able to kiss you or touch you for two days," he says, with a low raspy growl in his voice. "You're all I can think about."

Ethan O'Connell knows the meaning of perseverance and he drives her crazy with it. Two hours of emails and several sad face texts later, Olivia gives in and dials his cell phone.

"Okay, Ireland. I give up! I'll come by on my way home and say hello."

Ethan's mood lightens. "Really?"

"Really. But I'm not staying for dinner, and no funny stuff from you. Got it?" She knows that he'll do everything he can to stop her from leaving.

"Promise," he says, a happier tone returning to his voice.

When Ethan sees Olivia walking toward the table, he gets to his feet, reaching her in a few quick strides. Throwing his arms around her, he lifts her into the air; squeezing her before letting her slide slowly down his body. When her feet touch the floor, his mouth swoops down for a kiss, and then another.

"Wow!" When he finally lets her up for air, she fans cool air over her face with her hand. Shannon gives her that knowing girlie smile.

After ushering her into the seat against the wall, Ethan slides in beside her so she can't escape.

She looks at him with a warning in her eyes. "I'm not staying."

Ethan tries to look innocent. "I know."

"Then, why do I feel like I'm being corralled?" Before he can say anything, the waitress places a plate of pasta topped with roasted chicken in front of her. She looks at it, sighs and looks at Ethan with her brows raised.

"What? I ordered you dinner. You have to eat right?" He turns away, glancing at her sideways, waiting for her reaction. When he catches her rolling her eyes at Shannon, with a small smile on her lips, he takes a breath and relaxes.

Olivia hasn't eaten much in the past few days; she should be starving but she isn't. She begins to wonder if today's harassment, about joining him for dinner, is because Rachel has tattled on her again. She manages a few mouthfuls but food right now isn't really appealing.

"Eat," Ethan encourages, his patience starting to wear thin.

She looks up at him, catching something in his expression. *Yup. Fucking Rachel!* She plays with the chicken a bit, cutting it into smaller pieces and moving it around on her plate.

Ethan's well aware of what's going on. "Don't think you're going anywhere until I'm satisfied that you've had a decent meal." He says it in that *'don't even try that bullshit with me'* tone. Olivia looks up at Shannon for support.

"And don't bother looking over at Shannon; she's not going to rescue you from me. You need to eat. I'll feed you like a fucking child if I have to."

Olivia's jaw drops. *You have got to be kidding me!* She looks over at Shannon and John in total embarrassment. Picking up her fork, she stabs it angrily into a piece of chicken. She glares at Ethan as she shoves it in her mouth. He can't help but smirk at the look on her face. He imagines she would much prefer to jab that fork straight into his chest instead. "Brilliant!" he chuckles, "I'll sleep better knowing you're not going to die of malnutrition today." The words are no sooner out of his mouth when he realizes his hand is about to be pierced by her fork. Moving it just in time, the tines miss his hand, hitting heavily down on the table.

"Christ, woman! You're ornery when you're hungry!" he says startled.

John smiles and Shannon lets out a little giggle. Eventually Olivia smiles, too. Managing to eat several more mouthfuls, she actually starts to feel a lot better. She would never admit that to Ethan.

"I need to go shopping for a dress for the grand opening." Shannon says, turning to John.

"Why don't you take Olivia with you and have a girlie day. I'm pretty sure there's no time in my schedule for shopping."

Shannon frowns. "Fine, your loss. No change room sex for you."

John grins. "My loss, indeed."

Ethan looks at Olivia with a sly smile and a raised eyebrow.

"You're not getting change room sex, either." She pats him on the thigh to comfort him when he looks disappointed.

"I have no idea where to go, Olivia. Will you go shopping with me?" Shannon asks.

"Sure."

"That's a great idea, buy something for yourself to wear, as well," Ethan suggests.

"Uh, I'm wearing my black dress remember?"

"Yes, I remember that dress. It's quite sexy." He winks at her. "But why don't you buy something new?"

"Because I don't have the money, right now." She starts to feel a little anxious.

"Oh, right." Ethan digs into his back pocket and takes out his wallet. "I almost forgot." Flipping it open, he pulls out a card. "Here, this is for you."

Olivia leans forward and reads the name on the credit card he's placed down in front of her, "Olivia James - EOC Holdings and Enterprises."

She looks at him confused. "What is this?"

"It's a credit card, from my personal company. I had you added to the account so you can use it whenever you need to."

Olivia is dumbfounded. "Why would you do that?"

"Because I want you to have whatever you need." He's confused at her resistance. *Women like to shop, right?*

She feels the tension run up her spine and into her shoulders. "I can buy the things I need on my own," she says defensively.

"I know, but I'll feel better knowing that you have it if you need it."

"Ethan…" she starts to argue, but he holds his hand up to halt her.

"Olivia, just put the damn card in your wallet and don't argue with me about it," his voice is hard and authoritative. She quickly does as she's told, the tension starting to wind tighter inside her.

"When do you want to go shopping?" Shannon asks.

"Next week, maybe. I'm kind of up to my ass in alligators, right now." Olivia tries to shake off her annoyance with Ethan, but it isn't easy.

The four of them laugh at how absurd that saying is. "It sounds like something Carter would say," Ethan jokes.

"Speaking of Carter," Olivia says turning to John. "Please tell me that Stacey and her friends are not on the guest list for the grand opening."

Ethan asks what Stacey has to do with Carter, getting really annoyed when she ignores him.

"Just let it go," John advises him.

"Oh, my God, that would be horrible if they showed up." Shannon looks at John for confirmation. "Are they on the list?"

"No, I don't believe so." John tries to recall if her name was there or not.

"That's good," she says looking over at Olivia. "I wouldn't have been as polite as you, if some girl was all over John like that."

Olivia's heartbeat starts to race, as the thought of that night claws at her from the inside.

Ethan tenses a little.

"Shannon," John warns her, trying to evade the topic for the second time.

"I mean, you held it together, amazingly well, for being in such a new relationship," she says to Olivia.

"We aren't in a relationship," Ethan corrects.

That's when, for Olivia, it all starts to come crashing down around her. Her head snaps toward him in shock. *What the fuck?* Shannon looks to Olivia for an explanation. "Excuse me?"

"Olivia's rules," Ethan continues to explain. "We're not in a committed relationship. We're both free to date other people."

It hits Olivia hard when she figures it out. He was already asleep when she told him that she didn't want him to see anybody else, that she belonged only to him… and that she was in *love* with him. She finally finds the nerve to admit how she feels, and he was out cold, under the influence of too much alcohol. Great… just great!

Anxiety turns to anger and she needs to get away from him. "Excuse me, please. I need to get out." Sliding over on the bench seat, she nudges him, encouraging him to move.

He's alarmed at her expression. "Olivia?"

"Please, Ethan. Let me out." Her eyes dart nervously around the room looking for a place to retreat to. She needs a few moments, while she calms down. Ethan looks over at John trying to figure out what's going on.

Shannon watches the tears start to form in Olivia's eyes and knows that she needs a moment. "Ethan, I think you should let her out."

He acknowledges Shannon, looking more than a little lost. "Of course." Sliding over, he stands up, letting her move out from behind the table and get to her feet. When he sits back down, Olivia turns, looking down at him. She's careful not to raise her voice and make a scene. "There's a blonde in the bar that's been staring at you for the last hour. Maybe you should ask her out. Blondes with long legs seem to be your type."

Ethan is confused. "What?" He looks past her into the bar to see what she's talking about. Sure as hell, there's a pretty blonde, sitting in the corner staring at him. She smiles when he makes eye contact, holding his gaze for a few moments before looking away.

"I know," Olivia continues angrily. "Why don't you ask her to be your date for the grand opening? Since you seem to be okay with dating other people, now."

Stunned, Ethan scratches his forehead, his voice showing his frustration, "What the? You're mad? Why are you mad? This is your arrangement, not mine,"

"I'm curious, do you remember anything that happened after we went up to the hotel room?" She looks over at Shannon and John, not caring any more what they think.

"Honestly, Liv? I remember getting in the elevator and then waking up when you had your nightmare."

She nods her head. *She was right!* "Awesome! Well, nothing important happened in between, so it doesn't really matter, anyway."

She's just about to turn and walk away when the new club manager joins them. "Hey, guys, everything ok?"

"Yes, we're fine," Ethan says in a calmer voice.

"Great. Ethan, I left some invoices on your desk to be paid."

"Thank you, Brad. I'll look after it tomorrow."

"Thanks. Olivia, I'm glad I've run into you."

"Oh? Why's that?" she asks curiously.

"There's a guy that keeps coming in looking for you. He's been here three or four times in the past week."

"What guy?" Ethan asks, getting to his feet.

"He never leaves his name, just inquires if she's here and then leaves."

"That's strange," Shannon adds.

"What did he look like?" Olivia asks nervously.

"Tall, maybe six-two or taller. Stud earrings; short black hair. He was a big guy."

Olivia gasps. Fear starts to ripple through her bloodstream like ice water, making her shiver and turn pale. Watching the horror on her face, Ethan starts to walk Brad toward the front desk. He gives him instructions on informing the staff to immediately ask for his ID and call the police if he shows up again. Under no uncertain terms are they to let this guy in the door.

Olivia struggles to breathe. Her heart races so quickly, she can feel it pounding in the back of her throat. She presses her hands to her forehead and closes her eyes. Everything gets fuzzy for a moment.

"Olivia?" Shannon calls out, "John, something's wrong!" She tries to climb over him to get to Olivia but she's stuck where she is. "Olivia?" she says louder, as John slides over to get out. She vaguely hears Shannon's voice as she's swallowed by her anxiety attack. Forgetting to breathe, she fades into blackness as she passes out, her body melting to the floor, as if she were suddenly boneless. John reaches for her as he gets to his feet, but he's is too late.

Shannon screams for Ethan. Cursing, he crosses the room in a few long strides to get to her. "Olivia?" He takes her pulse and then checks her pupils.

"Is she okay?" Shannon asks concerned.

"Yes, it looks like she's just fainted." He lifts her into his arms. "Let's get her to my office."

When Olivia opens her eyes, she finds herself lying on the couch in Ethan's office, with Shannon sitting on the edge beside her and holding a cool cloth on her forehead. It takes a moment but her eyes finally focus.

"Ethan, she's awake," Shannon says.

The light is bright and Olivia squints until Ethan's tall figure stands in front of her blocking it. Shannon gets up to leave the room.

Ethan sits beside Olivia on the couch.

"Hey," he says softly.

"Hey," she answers, feeling more than a little out of sorts.

Shannon returns with a cool cloth. "I'll go wait outside with John."

Ethan dabs the cloth on her forehead. "Do you want a drink of water?"

"Yes, please." Holding out is hand; he helps her to sit up and then passes her the glass. "You feeling better?"

"Yes. Thank you."

Ethan gets to his feet. "Good!" Dragging his desk chair, he moves it beside the couch, the wheels screeching across the tiled floor like fingernails on a chalkboard. Sitting down he crosses his legs so that his ankle rests on the opposite knee. "Now you can tell me what that was all about."

"I guess I haven't had enough sleep. I felt dizzy."

Ethan presses his lips together and takes a deep breath. "Um. Medical school... remember?" he says, referring to himself. "Shall we start again? Without the bullshit this time?"

Feeling embarrassed Olivia stares at him, not knowing what to say.

"Okay," Ethan says, tired of waiting for her to explain. "I'll go first. How about you tell me how long you've been having anxiety attacks? And before you try to tell me that's not what that was, please remember that I work with the emergency medical team. I've seen thousands of anxiety related panic attacks. So, just save us both a lot of time and tell me what brought this one on."

She fidgets uncomfortably. "Everything. Everything just sort of came crashing down on me all at once."

"Like?"

"Noah, on Saturday night."

"I swear to Christ, Olivia. If you lied about him hurting you, I..." He tries to keep the anger out of his voice but it doesn't work. She sits up straight, alarmed at his tone, trying to reassure him.

"Ethan, No! I was telling the truth about that, but he said some pretty horrible stuff."

"Like what?"

"Well, he kind of called me a... tease. He accused me of leading me on. But he was really crude and vicious about it."

"Fucking Noah Thompson, I knew there was a reason I hated him from the first time I met him."

"Then, I found out the reason Scott and Rachel haven't been getting along is because of me."

"What? Did Rachel say that?"

"Well, not in so many words, but she said that because they were so busy worrying about me, they stopped looking after each other's needs."

"That is NOT your fault. Go on," he encourages.

"Hannah." She decides not to tell him about the conversation that took place in the women's washroom.

"She's a non-issue. I've told you that before," he dismisses it, as if there isn't anything to be concerned about, as far as he's concerned.

She takes a deep breath. "The whole thing with Stacey." Her bottom lip starts to quiver.

Ethan's heart cracks. "Baby. I wish I could erase that day. I would give anything to go back and make things right."

"I know."

"Will you ever forgive me?"

"I have forgiven you, Ethan. I just need a little time to forget."

He nods accepting her request. "Anything else?"

Olivia can't stop herself, suddenly needing to purge. "I have an extremely difficult client, who's stressing me right out. Nothing I do or suggest is good enough. I don't know how to handle him and it's freaking me out." She sniffs. "Then, there's the nightmares."

"You're still having those?" Ethan asks concerned.

She nods her head.

"So, when was the last time you got a decent night's sleep?"

She shrugs, her eyes starting to feel heavy.

"Okay, eating properly and sleep; first two things on the agenda. Got it?"

"Yes."

"Do you know who the guy is that's been coming in and looking for you?"

"It sounds like Sam," she says his name with no emotion, her eyes don't even blink for several moments. She dare not mention the psychic's prediction to Ethan. He'd lose his mind.

"He's out of jail? Shouldn't someone have notified you?" Concern flashes across his face.

Olivia looks down, ashamed, and then peeks up at him under her lashes. "He never went to jail, Ethan. I never pressed charges."

She hears his sharp intake of breath and looks up, bracing herself for his censure. He says nothing, his eyes gentle and his expression softens; he looks almost sad… like he feels sorry for her. "So, what happened at the hotel?" He changes the subject, for fear he'll lose his mind if he continues to think about Sam.

"What do you mean?" She wonders where this is going. Is he talking about Carter and Stacey? Or what happened in the hotel room, when he wept in her arms just before falling asleep?

"You asked me if I remember what happened at the hotel. Obviously, something happened that I should remember."

She shrugs. He shows his frustration with her avoidance by letting his hands drop heavily on his thighs. He persists, not ready to give up. "At the Lions Head Pub, after dinner, when we were talking, you insisted that you and I were in a noncommitted relationship." He stares at her, locking her eyes to his. "Then, tonight you got angry when I brought up that arrangement."

He stops to watch her reaction. "Did something change at the hotel?"

Breaking away from his gaze, she looks down, twisting her hands into knots in her lap, but doesn't answer.

It's eating away at him, the anxiety becoming more evident in his tone, as he continues pressing her for answers. "Olivia, is there something you need to tell me? I feel like shit for not remembering, since it's obviously something that's upsetting you."

Swallowing hard, she begins to feel like she's back to square one. Maybe it's for the best that he doesn't remember. She feels, once again, that it would be a mistake to trust her heart to anyone. "No, nothing happened."

Ethan knows that she's being dishonest with him, again. *Fucking alcohol and stubborn women!* "Olivia, is this really what you want? Do you still want for us to be in a noncommitted relationship?"

His tone is sharp and she looks up at him, trying to gauge his anger.

Something jabs sharply into her heart. "Yes, that's what I want."

"You want us to see other people?" It's almost said in ridicule as he shakes his head.

She nods again.

Sighing, his heart sinks. He rubs his hand over his face as he exhales his disappointment. "I don't believe you. Why won't you just tell me the truth?" he finally pleads.

She looks up at him, dying inside but not making a sound, squashing all those useless, troublesome feelings back down into the dungeon. She can't speak.

"Fuck it! I give up. I won't bring it up again," he growls in utter frustration. "How are you feeling? Are you good?"

Nodding, she finds every ounce of strength she has to choke back the urge to break into tears. "I'm good," she assures him.

"Let's just get you home and into bed. I'm going to stay with you tonight and make sure you're safe, so you can get a good night sleep."

She looks up at him wanting to say something and stops when she sees the determination in his eyes.

"Don't even think about protesting," his voice is stern with command.

Chapter Forty-Six

Olivia says almost nothing on the way back to her house. She would have refused Ethan's offer to stay if she wasn't feeling so unsettled. It was upsetting to hear that some guy, whose description resembles Sam, has been looking for her. She admits that if she had any doubt about the validity of the psychic's ramblings, they have been laid to rest now. Sam is obviously back.

Ethan drops his bag at the bottom of the stairs and looks around the room. "Why don't you put the kettle on while I check the windows and doors?" When she nods and heads for the kitchen, he starts with the basement.

Olivia holds the kettle under the tap, filling it with water. Her mind wanders in a million directions. Suddenly her head snaps up with a disturbing thought. "Ethan!" Her voice is panicked, prompting him to come up the stairs quickly.

"What's wrong?" he asks, concerned.

"Don't yell at me, okay?"

He gives her a questioning look. "Okay, what's going on?"

Rubbing her hand on her forehead, she blows out an anxious breath.

"Liv??"

Olivia wrinkles her nose, feeling embarrassed. "After Sam... I didn't change the locks."

Stunned, his eyes open wide and he blinks them rapidly. "Are you kidding me?"

She shakes her head. "By the time I got out of the hospital, he had already left town. It never occurred to me that he would come back."

"So, you're telling me that he has keys to the house?"

"Yes." She nervously waits for his reaction.

"Fuck!" Without hesitation, Ethan gets his phone out of his pocket and searches for a locksmith online. "Hi, I need emergency service. Two new door locks. Whatever is the most secure. How soon can you be here?" There's a pause in the conversation and Ethan looks at his watch.

Feeling overwhelmed, Olivia moves toward him, pressing into his body. His arm wraps securely around her.

When the kettle whistles, he releases her. "Go sit down while I get us some tea."

"I can do it."

Ethan waves her off. "I've got it. You go find us something to watch while we wait for the locksmith." When he returns with tea, he finds her waiting on the couch, looking exhausted. The moment he sits beside her she climbs onto his lap and snuggles against him, finding refuge in his strong arms. In a matter of moments, her anxiety has dissipated and the sleep that has eluded her for days, comfortably settles in. She barely even stirs when Ethan lifts her off his lap and lays her on the couch so he can answer the door.

In less than an hour, both the front and back door locks are replaced. Ethan feels a load of weight fall from his chest as he turns the stronger, more effective deadbolt on the front door. While Olivia is still sleeping peacefully, he goes room to room, checking that all the windows are closed and locked. When he returns to Olivia, she lazily opens her eyes to look up at him and smiles. She looks so beautiful in that moment, that his breath sticks in his throat as he looks down at her. "We're all secured now." He holds out his hand for her. "Let's go have a shower and then get to bed."

When she takes his hand, he leads her up the stairs. Olivia retrieves towels from the hall closet, while Ethan turns on the taps, allowing the water to adjust to the right temperature. He's just stepping into the shower when she returns. She stops in the doorway to admire the magnificent sight of his naked body. The dark ink of his tattoo is just as sexy on the back of his shoulder as it is from the front. She quickly slips out of her clothes and climbs in with him. Stepping back, Ethan allows her to get under the warm spray of the water. He picks up the body wash, squeezing some onto the cloth, and gently scrubs it across her body, working up a soft bubbly lather. She breathes slow and deep, completely relaxing under his touch.

"I love taking care of you," he whispers. "There's no greater pleasure in my life then when you let me."

Leaning back against him, she lets the water wash away the lather. His hands retrace his previous movements, caressing her with tenderness. "When you're like this with me... when you're not trying to find ways to push me away, and you surrender, letting me in... I feel it right down to the furthest depths of my soul. It's a gift. It gives me hope."

Olivia turns in his arms and then smoothes the drops of water from his face. He leans his cheek into the palm of her hand, wanting to prolong her touch. Standing on her tiptoes, she waits until he lowers his chin, bringing his lips closer to hers. Moved by his confession, she gives him another gift, in the form of a sweet and sensual kiss. As her lips move from tenderness into a deeper, smoldering passion, Ethan pulls away.

"Stop," he whispers. "This isn't where I intended to lead you. We don't have to go there tonight. I just want you to trust me; feel safe with me. I want to look after you in all things, not just sexually."

She looks up into those beautiful green eyes and wipes the wet strands of hair from his forehead. The warm spray of water on her back creates a mist around them. Damn him, saying those romantic things and confusing her; making her regret not telling him the words she spoke at the hotel. He gets her heart all mixed up in things that her head is clearly struggling to deny. She doesn't say a word, just gazes at him and sighs.

Ethan wraps her in a towel and helps her step out of the shower. He gathers up his stuff and then follows her into the bedroom. When he gets there, she's standing, frozen, at the side of her bed. Her calm relaxed body, now brittle and tense. Instinctively, he moves to protect her, wrapping his arms around her from behind. "Tell me what's wrong," he pleads.

Olivia takes a few sharp breaths in then shakes her head. "I don't think I can stay in here tonight."

"We can go back to my place," he offers, waiting out her long pause.

"No," Olivia takes a deep breath and closes her eyes. "It's okay. I can do this. I'm just being stupid."

Ethan spins her around so he can see her face. "You are NOT stupid. You've had a very stressful week, ending in one hell of an anxiety attack. Maybe tonight is not the right night to take on the demons in this room. Yeah? How about tonight we stay in the spare room instead?"

Pressing his lips to the top of her head, he lingers there until she relaxes in his arms and takes a calming breath.

"I think I can handle that."

Leading her down the hall to the spare room, he waits for her to get under the covers before turning off the lights and sliding in beside her. "Liv?"

"Hmmm," she replies, sleepily.

"You okay? You're still awfully tense."

"Yes, I'm okay. I'm sorry." She regrets that her past still haunts her. It's just not fair to Ethan.

"Can I ask you a question?" He has to ask. He needs to know.

She feels him tense slightly and braces herself for what's about to come. "Yes."

"Is it being in the bed or being *with me* in the bed that freaks you out?"

Olivia knew, eventually, that they'd have to have this conversation. The tension in her body is overwhelming. She realizes that the only liberating factor is probably admission. Taking a deep breath, she indulges him. "Both, actually."

Ethan tightens his grip around her waist.

"I've not been with anyone since Sam, so being in this situation is a little unnerving on its own, but sometimes sleeping in a bed, even alone, brings back horrible memories." She's glad for the fact that he can't see her face.

"You were okay at the hotel." Rubbing his cheek against her temple he tries to work through the logic of her reactions.

"Yes, it would have appeared so, until I had the nightmare."

"Good point," he acknowledges.

"Sometimes I have to take things *one night* at a time. Other times I have to take them *one hour* at a time. Things are getting better for me, but truthfully, Ethan, sleeping in *that* bed frightens me at the best of times. The thought of anyone else sleeping in it with me absolutely terrifies me."

Ethan thinks about the scars on her scalp and the look on her face when Brad described the man looking for her. He has to know what happened. He *needs* to hear it from her. Before he can talk himself out of it, the question is out of his mouth, "What happened with you and Sam? How did you end up where you did?"

"Ethan," she tries to stop him.

"I need to know, you've told me that you don't want to be in a committed relationship with me. If I have to comply with that rule then I need to know why it exists."

Olivia adjusts her position, uncomfortably, taking in a breath. "I'm not sure where to start?"

"Did he break your heart?" He moves his muscular chest against her back and rests his chin against her shoulder.

"No, not really. I thought I loved him, in the beginning. What has Rachel told you? And don't lie to me and say nothing."

"She only told me that he hurt you. That you were in the hospital for several days." He's glad that she remains facing away from him. She would know for sure that he's lying if she could see his face.

"Well, I guess that's the short version of the story but you're obviously not satisfied with that."

"No, I'm not."

She sighs, "Ethan, when I first met Sam I had just been dumped by the man I thought I was going to spend the rest of my life with. I was feeling very vulnerable. Sam was strong and in control. I found that very attractive for all the wrong reasons."

"So, it was a rebound? An innocent, heartbroken girl falling for the bad boy?"

"Yes, sort of, but I was far from innocent... and I wasn't heartbroken... just broken." Pausing, she chooses her words very carefully. She keeps her back to him, feeling that it affords her a small sliver of anonymity. "It was with Sam that I discovered how much I find true freedom in my submission." She hesitates, finding it difficult to say. "But Sam, he liked it a little *too rough,* sometimes."

Ethan's jaw clenches against her shoulder, but he says nothing.

"We were happy at first. It wasn't long before he told me he loved me and then something changed in him. He got quiet, withdrawn. The more depressed he became, the more he drank. The more he drank... the more violent he became." Olivia's voice becomes callous, as she forces herself to remain free of emotion. Best to just get it all out in the open now.

"Over time it escalated until I couldn't hide the bruises anymore and I knew that I had to break it off. That was the day he crossed the line."

"He hit you?" The thought of that infuriates him. He can't stand the thought of any man laying his hands on her. His angst only gets worse when he thinks about his problems in Ireland. Now more than ever, he's worried that when Olivia finds out he'll lose her forever.

"Ethan... he hit me on a regular basis, but that night... he beat the shit out of me. He left me barely able to breathe, choking on my own blood," Olivia's voice is calm and cold, barely acknowledging the horrific nature of what happened. "Sometimes, I'm sure that he didn't intend to leave me alive that day."

"Jesus Christ, Olivia!" Ethan feels like he's just taken a sharp knife to the heart. There's nothing he can say to make things right. He'll kill the bastard when he finds him. If he's back in town, he fully intends to find him. Taking several calming breaths, Ethan gently caresses his hands across her skin, realizing that he's doing it more to soothe himself than her. "I know you didn't press charges but what happened to him after?"

"While I was still in the hospital, he left town with a girl that he was apparently seeing at the time. I haven't seen or heard from him since. I don't know where they went or where they are now."

There's silence between them for a moment, and as hard as Olivia tries not to, she starts to become upset. "Ethan, I don't want to talk about it anymore today. Okay?"

Pressing his lips against her shoulder, he nuzzles his face into her neck. His hands rub and squeeze along her upper arm. "Okay, Baby, we'll table it."

Her heart starts to race and she feels a shiver of fear wash over her. "Ethan?"

"Yes."

"I need you to hold me." On the edge of tears, she lays in the dark facing the wall; her body so tense that her muscles are starting to ache.

Ethan reaches his arm over her and adjusts his position. "Come here." Pulling her backward, he rolls her to face him. His hand sweeps through her hair as she tucks her head in under his chin.

Wrapping her arms around him, she holds him tight. She stops the tears from falling, but he can still feel her pain in the rigid muscles of her body and her shallow breaths.

They fall asleep that way, Olivia held safe in his loving embrace, not moving or waking the entire night. It's the most peaceful rest she's had in three years.

Olivia is pulled from sleep by the vibrating of her cell phone. Reaching for it blindly, in the muted light of the sunrise that's filtered through the window, she finally finds it. "Hello?" she whispers into it, trying not to disturb Ethan.

"Hey, Baby Sister!" Megan says, with love and warmth in her voice.

"Hi, Meg!" Olivia's amazed at how tuned in her sister has always been to her emotions, even from the Atlantic coast. Gently prying herself out of Ethan's arms, she rolls to her side away from him trying not to wake him.

Despite her efforts he senses the moment she leaves his arms. Opening his eyes, he stretches beside her, listening for a moment before he gets up to use the bathroom.

"Is everything okay?" Megan asks, trying not to sound suspicious.

"Everything's fine. How are the kids?" Olivia feels so much more settled now.

"They're a handful but I couldn't imagine my life without them."

Ethan returns after having rid himself of both his shorts and his boxers, and climbs back into bed. Sliding under the covers, he rolls over so that he's at Olivia's back.

"Well, that's a good thing since you can't return them," Olivia teases. Her breath hitches at the feel of his warm body moving in closer.

Kissing her shoulder, Ethan works his way up to her neck. His lips linger just behind her ear; so close that he can hear her call.

"Whoa!" she says under her breath, as she feels his naked body melt into her. Pressing his hips forward he rubs his dick along the seam of her ass.

"Well, I can always send them to live with their Aunt Olivia," Megan says laughing.

Olivia's body starts to respond to his hot breath against her ear. Sliding his hands around her, he slips under her shirt, caressing her breasts. When he lowers his mouth, gliding his tongue across her neck, she becomes speechless for a moment.

"Tell Ethan I said good morning."

"Oh, my God!" Olivia says, shocked. "How did you know he was here?"

"Are you kidding me? You're practically moaning into the phone."

Ethan laughs against her neck and then brings his mouth back up to her ear. "Good morning, Megan."

Olivia tips the phone slightly so that the speaker is between them.

"You better be looking after my little sister," Megan warns.

Ethan grins and gives Olivia's sensitive nipple a firm tug, making her clench and press back against him. "I'm doing my very best," he says. "But, your sister is extremely stubborn."

Meghan scoffs, "Ha! That's an understatement."

"Hey!" Olivia protests, "No fair ganging up on me."

"I'm sorry, Baby. Let me make it up to you." Sliding his hand from her breast, down the sensitive twitching nerves of her stomach, he gets underneath the waistband of her pajama pants. Yanking them down to her hips, he finds her already wet and ready for him.

"Oh my!" Olivia squirms, trying to press her swollen clit against the palm of his hand, encouraging him into an erection that's so hard it could drill through cement.

"Ummmm. I think that's my cue to say good-bye," Megan says uncomfortably.

Olivia has to concentrate hard to find her voice. "Okay Meg. I love you." Ethan hits just the right spot making her moan into the phone. "I'll talk to you later," she says through panting breaths.

"Geez, thanks, you guys! Now I'm all worked up. I'm going to go wake up Rick, and he won't know what hit him. If I get pregnant again, I'm going to kill you both," she threatens, as she hangs up.

Olivia lets her phone drop out of her hand. Ethan flips her onto her back, out of her pants, and is pushing her legs apart with his knee before it even hits the floor.

"I can't wait… need to be inside you," he mutters as he lowers himself on top of her. Entering her with one smooth movement, he makes her gasp with his thick penetration. He stills for a moment, taking a breath, and withdraws, leaving only the swollen head of his cock inside her. Despite his own urgency, he has the presence of mind to make sure that he's not hurting her. Sliding back in slowly, he tests her acceptance, waiting for her reaction. When he's certain that she's able to take him, he begins to thrust into her with an insurmountable desire.

Olivia groans, helpless against his sudden rough possession. Feeling heat pulse straight to her core, the tension coils low in her groin, already aching for release. Jesus, what the man does to her.

Thrusting steadily upwards, Ethan repeatedly hits her g-spot with a heavy pounding pressure. She quickly starts to unravel, calling out his name as pleasure blooms inside her and spreads outward. Her body shudders, as she tightens around him, squeezing his cock.

Driving into her one last time, his hips jerk forward as he comes. The feel of his pelvis slamming hard against her makes him moan with the gratification of his own hard release. For the longest time afterward, Ethan stays inside her, throbbing. Trying to calm his breathing, he rolls to his side taking her with him; relieving the heavy weight of his body on hers. "Well, somebody's eager this morning," she laughs.

Smiling, Ethan brings his lips to hers for a kiss. "I'm eager for every morning that begins with me hard as stone and deep inside you."

"I think I could get used to waking up like that," she says, sighing against his neck. She protests the emptiness she feels with his withdrawal, as he slowly moves away from her.

Kissing down her throat, he lifts her t-shirt, and licks his way down her stomach. Stopping at the sight of the bruise on her stomach, he gently runs his fingertips over it, sweeping them across to her opposite hip where he can still see the faint marks from his teeth.

Ethan's shoulders tense. "Am I too rough with you, Princess?"

"No, Ethan, I'd say from the mind numbing orgasms and how quickly you make me come that you are just rough enough."

"I'm sorry, I didn't mean to hurt you. I just wanted to get your attention. Here let me kiss it better." Olivia draws in a deep breath as he brushes a kiss across the healing skin.

"Oh, you got my attention all right. I damn near came apart when you did it."

"Really?" Ethan says intrigued. "That's interesting." He pulls her shirt back down over her stomach and lays his head on it. "It sounds wrong to say it out loud, but I like seeing my mark on you. It pleases me to know that you'll think of me, every time you feel how sore you are."

"Gee, that's romantic. I don't recall reading that in Romeo and Juliet," she teases.

Grinning, he lifts his head to look at her. "No? Are you sure?" Moving his body to the head of the bed, he lays his cheek beside her on the pillow, wrapping his arms around her and whispering in her ear, "I think we may have traumatized your sister."

Olivia grins and tries to hold back a snicker. When Ethan starts to chuckle, she bursts into laughter. God he loves that sound. He'd do anything to hear it more often.

Chapter Forty-Seven

For the rest of the week, Ethan and Olivia spend every moment together doing the things that couples do. Although, Olivia continues to deny that they're a couple. Ethan does his best to ignore the times when she catches a pretty girl looking at him and reminds him that he's free to date other girls, if that's what he wants. He tries to put her at ease by reminding her, irrefutably, that she's the only girl that he wants. He knows that the events of the past week have left her feeling unsettled and insecure. However, by Friday, under the weight of a few stressful workdays it's starting to grind on his nerves.

Obsessed with the possibility that Sam might be back in town, he has Shannon trying to track him down, leaving his personal investigation to the team in Ireland. In addition to everything else; Carter, just barely, made his presentation deadline. He's spends all his time holed up in his hotel room brooding about something. He even turns down Ethan's invitation to go a few rounds at the gym; an opportunity that he would normally be eager for.

After Ethan has burnt off some of his frustration in the ring, he walks the few blocks to Carter's hotel. He stands waiting in the hallway for a long time. "Open the door, you dick. I know you're in there." he says, banging on the door again. Finally, the deadbolt turns and the door swings open. Ethan looks around the room and then back at Carter, waiting for an explanation.

"What are you doing here?" Carter asks, annoyed at the intrusion.

"I came to see what the hell is wrong is you."

"Nothing is wrong." Well, nothing that he could share with Ethan.

"Really? It's not like you to pass up an opportunity to take a few swings at me. I'm not leaving until you tell me."

"Fine," Carter grunts. "Let me get my shoes and we can go down to The Lion's Head for a beer."

Two beers in, Carter is still not giving away any information that would give Ethan a clue to his odd behavior. Feeling uncomfortable about the real reason that he's feeling off balance, Carter tries to avoid Ethan's questions, all together. Instead, he occupies himself with a woman sitting at a corner table on the other side of the bar. He's seen her there almost every night since he arrived, but for some reason he can't seem to take his eyes off her tonight. Several times during their conversation, he looks past Ethan to see what she's doing.

Ethan finally turns completely in his seat to see what has him so captivated. She's a beautiful woman, probably five foot eleven in those heels, with soft, feminine curves to her body. Her long blonde hair is swept away from her face and fastened on top of her head. Even from across the bar her raspberry lips look soft and delicious, but they're nothing in comparison to the intensity of her blue eyes, sparkling like sapphires.

Ethan whistles, "Fuck man, is that what's got you so twisted?"

"What? No!" Carter denies it. Then, realizing that he can't tell his friend the truth about the woman he's fallen in love with, he decides that maybe the beautiful blonde would be a good diversion for his questions.

"Lying bastard." Ethan tips his beer glass against his lips. "Have you talked to her?"

Carter glances over at her and then back to Ethan. "No, what's the point. I'm going home in a week."

"Did you just ask me what the point is? The point is you're still *here* for a week. What the fuck is wrong with you? I seriously think you need a good shag."

Carter tenses. There's only one girl that he's interested in right now and he can't have her. However, Ethan may have a point. He wasn't attracted to Stacey at all; his being with her was more *duty* than pleasure. Maybe this beautiful girl would take the edge off; distract him until he leaves for home and is half way around the world from the source of his affliction.

"Are you going to sulk for the rest of the week? Or are you going to talk to her?"

"That depends, are you going to be an annoying dickhole for the rest of the week?"

Ethan laughs, "Okay, not another word, I swear."

"Thanks, mate, I appreciate it." Carter gets up and makes his way to the bathroom at the back of the bar. Taking advantage of the opportunity, Ethan walks straight over to her. She watches him cross the floor and smiles when he stops at her table.

"Hi!" she says in a friendly manner.

"Hello, He holds his hand out and she promptly shakes it. "Ethan O'Connell."

"Katherine Ryan," she says, as she releases his hand.

"Ah," There's a glimmer in Ethan's eyes, "Ryan is a good old Irish name. Are you from Ireland?"

She laughs, "Maybe many generations back, but I was born in Canada and so were my parents and grandparents."

"Shame, I'm feeling a little homesick and it would be nice to find someone from home to talk to."

"Sorry, I can't help you with that."

There's something in her eyes that's sensual… almost erotic, like she's hiding some very dark naughty desires. Her smile is in complete contrast: warm and friendly. She's a beautiful woman in every aspect, but those eyes… wow! Ethan understands Carter's attraction.

Carter returns to his seat and glares at Ethan from across the room.

"How about your friend, is he Irish?" she asks curiously.

"Carter? No, he's from Australia." She stares at Carter, unable to tear away her gaze. "Australia? No kidding?"

"No kidding, he's only here for another week and then he's heading home."

"Oh." Picking up her purse, she digs through one of the compartments. Pulling out one of her business cards, she writes something on it, and then hands it to Ethan. "Why don't you give your friend my number? I'm here on an extended work project, so I won't be going home for a long time. Tell him to call me. Maybe we could keep each other company next week." She peeks up at Ethan, her face turning a little red.

Ethan grins as he turns over the card to see her phone number and her name. *Kate.*

"I'll give this to him, Kate."

She grins and lets out a little laugh. "I won't be offended if he doesn't call. He's been here every night this week. I catch him staring but he doesn't seem to be a very chatty kind of guy."

Ethan grins. "Well, that's not usually the case, trust me. I believe that your beauty has left him speechless. I can't say I blame him; any man would feel unworthy of your attention."

Blushing, she looks over at Carter and smiles.

Carter can't stand to watch what's going on. He turns to face the opposite direction, trying not to lose his mind right now. Ethan has never been able to resist a beautiful woman, but this is too much. Olivia is head over heels in love with him, and he's over there flirting with another woman. Carter wants to kill him right now. He silently vows that if O'Connell does anything to break Olivia's heart, he absolutely will. Fuck the friendship. Nervously jiggling his leg on the rung of the bar stool, he repeatedly taps the drink coaster on the hard edge of the bar. When he can't stand it anymore and turns with the intentions of confronting him, Ethan is standing behind him.

"Whoa! Relax buddy, it looks like that vein in your forehead is about to explode."

"What the fuck, Ethan?"

"I did it for you." Ethan slides the card toward him with her name and number side up. "In case you change your mind. Just so you know, I didn't ask for it. She was asking questions about you. She said she's here on an extended work project and that maybe you could keep each other company next week. Oh, and she said she noticed that you've been here every night this week, and wondered why you haven't stopped to chat with her."

Carter is vaguely aware that Ethan is still talking to him as he settles their bar tab. He's not sure that he's interested, but he picks up the card and slides it into his wallet anyway. Ethan would never let it go and he wants to avoid any more speculation, on Ethan's part, about why he's been brooding. Maybe he should just go over there, say hello, and keep Ethan off his back. When they stand to leave, Carter glances at her table but she's gone.

On the way back to the hotel, the boys fall back into their familiar male banter. They're insulting each other and making obscene comments at just about everything. Suddenly something Ethan says sparks Carter's curiosity.

"What do you mean Olivia doesn't want to be in a committed relationship?" *Is his friend absolutely nuts?* A beautiful, intelligent, amazing woman like, Olivia James, and he's not staking his claim? If it were Carter, he'd do everything in his power to make sure she belonged *only* to him. He'd claim her for his own and NEVER let her go. Olivia is one of those girls you come across once in a lifetime: the kind you marry, have babies with, and grow old together. You'd have to be a complete idiot to let one of those girls slip through your fingers.

Ethan shakes his head in frustration. "She's still a little freaked out, Carter. She's just learning how to trust again. I only made it worse the other night."

"Are you kidding me, mate? You agreed to a noncommitted relationship? YOU? The Ethan O'Connell who, in university, demanded that the girls you brought back to the flat agreed to submit complete control to you? If I remember correctly, exclusivity was part of that deal. Well, except for those girls that you and Reese…" Carter stops, deciding it's wise to refrain from finishing his sentence. He glances over at Ethan who looks pissed that he almost brought it up.

"Things have changed since university. And for the record I am in *complete* control of my relationship," Ethan assures him.

Carter laughs. "You're fucked, mate. I've met Olivia remember?"

Ethan gives him an annoyed look. "She's not the kind of girl to be dominated in all areas of her life, Carter. I don't think I would love her so much if she were. Trust me when I tell you that she submits in the bedroom. It's the one area that she does allow me complete control."

"Obviously, that's the one place that you still need it," Carter says, shaking his head.

"She can call it a noncommitted relationship if she wants. It's completely irrelevant, since I have no intention of seeing any other girls."

"And have you considered that the agreement also gives her permission to see other guys and there's nothing you can do about it if she does?"

"Oh there's plenty I can do about it." Ethan is feeling extremely possessive and the thought makes him angry.

"Are you willing to share her, mate?"

Ethan's face turns red as his anger starts to boil. "Fuck, no!"

Carter shakes his head. "That's what I thought. Think about it, Ethan. Once again, you've left the door open for assholes like Reese to get their foot inside."

That comment cuts straight into Ethan's heart. "Fuck you, Brant!"

Carter stops in his tracks and turns to face him. "Sorry. But you needed to hear it. Like I told you the other night, Ethan, that girl loves you. Get your shit sorted out, treat her right, and don't fuck it up, because there will always be some prick waiting for a chance with a girl like Olivia."

Ethan drives back to his office, beyond distracted by his conversation with Carter. Especially since he had the nerve to bring up Reese. He would have never believed it possible that his friend was capable of such a betrayal. But, Jessica and Reese proved to him that there are some things that can't be protected, not even by loyalty, women being one of them.

Pulling into the underground parking, his jaw clenches when he finds Eva Storm standing in her favorite place, in the middle of his parking spot. "What the hell?" He edges forward slowly, herding her off to the side so he can park. What does this crazy woman want? He's definitely not in the mood for this today. He needs to put a stop to this insanity. Growling, he gets out of the car and slams the door. "What is it that you want from me?"

Eva stands firm, not intimidated at all. "You and your heart are a little out of step. Your souls need to realign themselves, and then you'll be where you need to be. I'm here to help you." Reaching for his hand, she quickly flips it over and studies his palm, tracing several of the lines with her finger and looking pleased at something she reads there. "Ah, you've been dreaming, haven't you, lad? You know other things you can't explain."

Skeptical and still not yet ready to accept what she's saying as the truth, he pulls his hand away. "She's having the same dreams."

Smiling at his glower, she begins to back away. "Whatever souls are made of, yours and hers are made the same."

Ethan recognizes the famous quote. "That's Emily Bronte." He's read her work several times. Rubbing his hands through his hair, he considers what's she's saying. "She's much more stubborn than I am."

Backing into darkness, Eva is no longer visible to him, but her voice calls out one last time, "Without her, you'll never find balance in your world. It's time for you both to believe."

Ethan tries to restore some normalcy to his day by sorting through some files on his desk. Opening his bottom drawer to store them, he looks down to see Olivia's panties. He had forgotten about them. They've been in there since she left them behind at the bar, a souvenir of the first night of their agreement. He remembers it like it was yesterday. He had been so rough with her that night, a fact that he regretted often. That thought is always in the back of his mind when they're together. He has to restrain himself, at times, from the things that he'd really like to do to her. Although, she said she had similar desires, he fears that if he takes her there, he runs the risk of losing control and pushing her further than her limits.

Grasping the soft material in his hand, he pulls them out of the drawer and holds them up, remembering how beautiful she was that night. The memory of pressing her up against his office door and lifting the bottom of her dress so he could get his hands on them, stirs arousal in him. His enjoyment, however, is short lived as he shudders, imagining some other guy helping her out of them. He curses, his chest pulling tight as he thinks about Carter's earlier words and acknowledges that he's right. He can't allow this agreement to continue any longer. He needs her all to himself. What was he thinking when he agreed to a noncommitted relationship? Did he really put himself in this position because he was obsessed with having her and it was the only way? Christ, what this woman has done to him. He's never felt this out of control in his life. He hates it! Eva Storm just may be on to something; his head and his heart are definitely out of sync. He needs to get things under control, restore the natural order of things. *Realign their souls.*

All the way home, Ethan stresses over how he's going to approach the subject with her. He has the notion to just tell her straight out that he'll no longer accept it. He knows her too well. If he deals with it using his dominate side, she'll likely bolt, leaving his ass and ruining any chance of them being together. No. It's too risky; he needs to find a way to convince her that she doesn't want this agreement, either. A way that makes her think that stopping this nonsense is *her* idea.

Think, O'Connell. How are you going to do that?

Chapter Forty-Eight

Rachel! Of course! He dials the phone.

"Hey, what are you up to?" he asks, when Scott answers.

"Working on my *honey do* list," he laughs. "Do you want to come rescue me?"

"Not a chance. I need to talk to your wife."

"Oh, that can't be good. Are you sure?" Scott chuckles while he walks the phone to Rachel.

"Yeah, I need to ask her a question," Ethan's tone turns serious.

Scott gives Rachel a concerned look when he hands her the phone. "It's Ethan."

"Hey! What's up? Don't tell me that you miss my cooking?"

"Umm… of course I do!"

He lies and she knows it. Nobody would miss her cooking, it's dreadful. Looking at Scott, she wrinkles her nose in a playful gesture.

"Listen, Rachel, I need to talk to you about Olivia." He can't hide angst in his voice

Immediately, Rachel starts to worry. "Is everything okay?"

"Yes… No," he growls in frustration. "Yes, Olivia is fine, but I need your advice on something."

Rachel shrugs when Scott gives her a questioning look. "Okay, well, why don't you come by the house? We're just going to eat dinner."

"Thanks, Rach, I'm just coming up the street."

Ethan lets himself in and searches out Rachel in the kitchen. She heads toward him for a hug. Sensing the tension in his shoulders, she gives him a little extra squeeze in acknowledgment. She frowns at him when she pulls away. "Let me get you a beer. Dinner is almost ready."

The basement door swings open and Scott joins them. Popping the cap off a beer, he passes it to Ethan. While the boys set the table, Rachel serves up pot roast with roasted potatoes and carrots. Ladling the gravy into the gravy boat, she makes a face at Scott.

"Lumpy again?" He tries to hide his amusement, but he has a huge smile on his face.

"Yes," she says, pouting in disappointment.

Scott joins her at the stove. Taking the ladle out of her hand, he scoops one big spoonful into the gravy boat. "That's okay, Sweetheart. I like your lumps." He leans over and gives her a kiss on the nose.

When dinner is finished Scott soaks up the last bit of lumpy gravy with a buttered dinner roll and turns to Ethan. "So, out with it. There's obviously trouble in paradise." Popping the last bit of the bun into his mouth, he licks his fingers.

Rachel shakes her head. "Nice table manners, Honey."

"That's why you married me, isn't it, Baby?"

"Yes, I do believe you're right… I was attracted to your table manners and your huge…um… errr… appetite." She grins from ear to ear as she turns to look at Ethan. "So, what did you want to talk about?"

"Olivia. I just don't understand her."

Scott laughs, "She's a woman. You're not supposed to understand her." He ducks quickly to avoid the cork out of the wine bottle that Rachel tosses at his head.

Ethan rolls his eyes. "And why are they always throwing shit? Seems I'm always dodging projectiles aimed at my head!"

"Tell me about it. I feel bad for you. Olivia, understandably, has one hell of an arm. I'm lucky this one…" he nods in Rachel's direction, "throws like a girl."

The comment about Olivia piques Ethan's curiosity, but Rachel interrupts before he has a chance to inquire further. "Did she do something in particular that's upsetting you? Help me out here."

"Did she tell you about last night?

"No, I was out of the office all day."

"She joined us for dinner last night."

Scott immediately interrupts, "That bitch!"

Rachel is not amused, "Okay, you need to go and wash the dishes or fix something before I hurt you."

Scott knows he had best take her advice. He can't help but smirk as he starts to clear the dishes.

"Sorry," she apologizes on her husband's behalf.

"Funny boy, that one." He looks over at Scott, who can obviously hear everything that's being said. "As I was saying, Olivia had an anxiety attack after dinner. Passed out."

"Oh my God! She told me she hasn't had one of those in months."

"Well, there is a lot going on right now. I guess it caught up with her. She finally told me about Sam."

Rachel is shocked. "Everything? About Sam? Are you serious?"

"Well, almost everything, I'm sure you can figure out which part she left out. I didn't press her about it."

"Oh, my God, Ethan, that's still HUGE!"

"Well, yes, I thought so too, at first, but now I feel like we aren't really getting anywhere."

"Why?"

"Because she's still going on about us seeing other people."

"What? That's ridiculous!" Rachel is certain that he's just misunderstood. He is a man after all. "What *exactly* did she say?"

"She agreed that she and I have been going on dates, and therefore we are logically *dating*." He pauses to take a sip of wine. "Then, she tells me that we are *not* in a *committed relationship*. That we're both free to date other people."

"OMG! She's nuts!" Rachel shakes her head. "It just goes to show you how powerful that kind of abuse is, when it affects someone with her IQ, so harshly. The only explanation is that she's making such ridiculous decisions to protect herself. She could be running her own multimillion-dollar company instead of fixing everybody's mess at Dunn and McLellan, but NOOOO! He fucked up her head, but good."

Ethan looks at her with a questioning brow and Rachel explains. "Oh, you don't know?" She shakes her head. "Of course, you don't know. It's not as if she'd tell you something like that. Olivia's IQ is 139." She sees Ethan trying to work out what the means in his head. His eyebrows shoot up in surprise.

"I know right?" Rachel says. "She was considering a partnership offer at one of the largest Greater Toronto IT support firms. After this thing with Sam… she turned it down. She wouldn't even meet with them to discuss it further."

"I'm going to kill that bastard when I get my hands on him." Ethan means to keep his promise.

"You're going have to wait your turn," Rachel advises, "So, what happened that made her panic enough to insist that you see other people?"

"My instincts tell me that she's been feeling a little insecure since the client dinner. Understandably, so."

"Yes, that's exactly what it is. I heard about that, what the hell were you thinking?"

"I wasn't, obviously. Now, if there's a pretty girl anywhere we go, she points her out to me and tells me that it's okay for me to ask her out. That we agreed to see other people."

"Oh, Ethan, you don't believe that she wants that, do you?"

"Well, it's bloody hard not to, when she keeps saying repeatedly. I want to believe that she has feelings for me."

Rachel notices the frustration in his voice. "Ethan, she has feelings for you. Strong ones. I've never seen her this happy and _you_ are the reason."

"I want to believe that and I don't want to see anybody else."

"Trust me, if you went out on a date with another girl, she would freak!" Ethan looks up from his wine glass.

"That would sure teach her a lesson wouldn't it?" Rachel stares at him with a devious grin.

"Are you suggesting that I actually take someone else out on a date?" The thought is shocking at first.

"Well, it's one way to force her to admit how she feels about you. I bet if she finds out that you've asked someone out on a date, she'll immediately insist on a committed relationship."

After giving it more thought, it sounds to Ethan like it could be a good solution to his problem.

The sound of clanging pots and pans in the kitchen stops instantly. Scott sticks his head around the corner. "Would you like my opinion?"

"NO!!!" Rachel yells.

"I think it's a bad idea," he offers, despite her objection.

Rachel dismisses him. "Just wash the dishes, Honey!"

Ethan considers Scott's opinion for a minute. "But, if she does get upset, then maybe, I can convince her to forget all this nonsense." Clearly, he's talked himself into it.

"Bad idea, brother!" Scott chirps from the kitchen.

Just as Rachel has done, Ethan decides to ignore Scott's advice. "Right, so who do I ask?"

As the dishes hit the rinse water, they faintly hear Scott grumble under his breath, "Dumb ass!"

"What about the girl at your office that's always throwing herself at you?" Rachel offers. Ethan flashes her a confused look. "You know… the one with the REALLY big... ummm... *personality*!" She uses her hands to gesture enormous breasts as she says it.

"Ah! The receptionist, Hannah." He laughs at Rachel's description. "I have no idea how to get in touch with her at home and I don't think it would be appropriate to ask her out at the office." Before either of them can speak again, Scott walks out of the kitchen with his phone in hand. Clicking open the contact list, he hits "H" and hands it to Ethan. Instantly, Hannah's name and number flash up on screen.

As he turns to walk away, Rachel hollers after him, "Excuse me? Why do you have that bimbo's phone number?"

Scott smirks and keeps walking. "Sorry I can't hear you, dear... I'm washing the dishes and minding my own business."

Ethan glances over at Rachel, feeling a little awkward. She snaps at him, "Well? What are you waiting for? Get the number and then give me the phone."

Intractable *Souls*

Ethan takes out his phone and carefully creates a new contact entry for Hannah, double-checking the number before he hands the phone to Rachel. She immediately hits the delete button, muttering a few not nice things. Scott walks back into the room drying his hands on a towel. She looks at him with an unapologetic look on her face. "Oops, sorry, Scott... I accidentally erased her number."

Scott takes the phone out of her hand and leans down to give her a kiss. He loves that his wife is jealous. When Rachel stands to leave the table, he wraps his arms around her in a loving embrace. Annoyed at him, she tries to push him away but he refuses to let her go. Surrendering into a long sensual kiss, she knows she can't stay mad at him.

"Well, I think that's my signal to leave," Ethan laughs, as he heads for the front door.

Arriving home, Ethan turns on the TV and sits on the couch, thinking long and hard. Reaching into his pocket, he takes out his phone. This somehow doesn't feel like the right thing to do. It could turn out to be more of an explosion than a realigning of souls. His anxiety level is through the roof as he takes a deep breath and dials the phone.

"Hello?" the voice on the other side answers.

"Hi, is this Hannah?"

She would recognize his voice anywhere. "Mr. O'Connell?" A nervous excitement fills her.

He closes his eyes and takes a deep breath. "We're not at the office, Hannah. Please call me Ethan."

"Okay, Ethan. What's up?"

"I was wondering if you wanted to have dinner with me tomorrow night at my restaurant, maybe stay for a little dancing?"

"I'd really like that!" She jumps up and down in celebration, trying not to show her excitement in her tone.

"Great! I'll pick you up around eight? If that's okay?"

"Actually, Ethan I have a late class tomorrow. Would it be okay if I just met you there?"

"Of course, that would be fine." Ethan is surprised that Hannah is continuing her education. "What class are you taking?" he asks, curiosity overtaking him.

"Zumba," she says feeling very proud.

Ethan almost chuckles; of course, it's a Zumba class.

"That's brilliant." Suddenly he feels awkward. "Well, I'll see you tomorrow then. Oh, and, Hannah... we should be discreet around the office, yeah? Don't mention it to anyone."

"I won't. I'm looking forward to it, Mr.... Ethan. Good night."

He sends Rachel a quick confirmation by text.

From Ethan: All done. Meeting Hannah at the bar 2moro at 8

Guilty feelings start to overwhelm him now, and watching TV doesn't make it go away. When the phone rings, it makes him jump. He answers with unintentional brevity, forgetting that he's not at work, "Yes."

"Hi!"

"Olivia, hey." Her voice sounds so sweet that the feelings of guilt twist in his gut like a knife. He missed her today. He decides it's a bad idea to tell her that, when he's about to tell her that he's going on a date with another girl.

They chat for a few brief moments about the events of their day. For the first time ever, Olivia senses a coolness in him. She feels something shift between them as the conversation starts to slow and become awkward. Then, she says it. A hundred times, he's waited for her to reciprocate this feeling and she's always held back.

"Ethan… I miss you tonight. I thought you might find a reason to stop by."

Of all nights for her to admit it, why tonight?

She grows nervous with the pause in the conversation, her women's intuition confirming that something's wrong. "Ethan? Is everything okay?"

Fuck! Fuck! Fuck! "Yes, I'm just tired. I'm planning on going to bed early tonight."

He's hiding something and it makes her feel off balance. "Oh, of course. I'm sorry I'm keeping you up, you must be exhausted." There's another long silence proving that something definitely isn't right.

"Ethan, please tell me what's going on."

He braces himself, wishing that he never agreed to this. Maybe he doesn't have to tell her. "Olivia, I know I said I wouldn't bring it up, again." He swallows hard and tenses, the muscles in his shoulders becoming tight, pulling upwards.

"What? Just tell me." She prepares herself for the worst.

"Are you sure that you want us to see other people? Are you **absolutely** sure?" He holds his breath, praying that she's changed her mind. He'd love nothing better than to phone Hannah and call the whole thing off. Then, he'd drive over to Olivia's house and sink himself deep inside her, claiming her as his own: *ONLY FOR HIM.*

Olivia is caught off guard by his question. She hesitates, thinking hard about her answer. She panics, stuck between what she really wants and what her head says she needs. "I guess so." She's confused, and not sure why she's suddenly feeling unsettled.

Ethan loses it and anger vibrates in his voice, "Not good enough, you better damn well be sure. Do you want a relationship with me? Yes or No!" *Why is this woman so fucking stubborn?*

"Ethan?" There's something in her voice. Fear? Anger? Confusion?

He can't hold it in anymore. "I have a date tomorrow," he blurts it out, almost choking on the words.

Olivia is stunned. She told him to see other people but she wasn't quite prepared for it. The words affect her like a blow to the stomach, making her feel physically ill.

There's silence on her end of the phone. Ethan's anger sinks into remorse. *What has he done?* "Olivia?"

"Sorry, I'm still here. I was... doing something." That was a sad excuse but she needed an explanation for her lack of response. "So you have a date? Nice. Have a great time." She's been preparing herself for the inevitable, since the day she met him. Apparently, today is that day; she refuses to show him her pain.

This is a huge mistake. "Olivia," Before he can get another word out she interrupts.

"Good night, Ethan."

Hanging up, Olivia stands perfectly still, unable to move, unable to process what just happened. The weight of it pressing down on her so heavily that her heart struggles to beat against it. When she looks up at the red painted wood of Noah's front door, she has no idea how she got there. With unshed tears burning her eyes, she swallows hard as she bangs on the door; urgent... panicked.

When Noah whips the door open briskly to see what the bloody hell is going on, he stops frozen at the sight of her. "Liv?"

She says nothing, she can't say anything; her words are just... gone. Blinking, tears start to trickle down her cheeks. Noah's heart sinks as he quickly stands aside. "Don't stand out there, come in." It takes her a moment to move, but as she passes him in the threshold of the door she notices that he's barefoot and shirtless.

She stares at the light smattering of dark hair on his chest that trails down his abs and then disappears, unable to process even the smallest coherent thought. He's wearing nothing but a pair of jeans, casually unzipped, revealing that he's not wearing any boxers either. Obviously, he's just pulled them on to open the door.

"Olivia? What's wrong?"

Her chin starts to quiver and she shakes her head, trying desperately to find her voice.

"Fuck," Noah says in desperation, running his hands through his hair. "Give me a minute, okay?"

When she doesn't answer, he bends his knees to look into her eyes. "Olivia? Give me a minute. Don't go anywhere. Okay?"

Nodding her head, she silently agrees, watching him take the stairs to the second floor, two at a time. A few minutes later, she hears a door close and the clicking sound of heels across the hall floor. She's obviously interrupted something.

Looking up, she sees the leggy blonde make her way angrily down the stairs, pulling her sweater around her and tying it at the waist. She stops at the landing when she sees Olivia, and then turns to flash an icy glare at Noah as he follows behind her.

Reaching the bottom of the stairs, she stares at Olivia, looking like there's something she'd like to say. Noah gently grasps her by the elbow and ushers her toward the door. Olivia can tell she's furious by the heavy thumping of her feet on the floor. When Noah leans in to kiss the blonde goodbye, she pushes him away. "I'll call you tomorrow," he promises. Raising his arm to touch her, she steps back out of his reach, slamming the door behind her.

Olivia gives him an apologetic look.

"Don't give it another thought. She'll get over it," he assures her. "She's crazy about me." Pausing, he leans back against the wall. "You know, I've been trying to get a hold of you all week to apologize."

She finally finds her voice, although it's small and shaky. She barely recognizes it as her own. "I know."

"So, does you being here mean that you've forgiven me?"

Olivia nods.

"Thank God!" He holds his hand over his heart, the corners of his lips curling up in a slight smile. Olivia can't smile back; she takes in a couple of shallow breaths, tears welling up in her eyes again.

Noah frowns. "Hey, what's with all the tears tonight? Are you going to tell me what's going on?"

She sniffs a couple of times, wiping the moisture from her eyes.

"Let me guess. That asshole O'Connell did something to upset you?"

Hearing his name is all it takes to make the tears fall again. Noah reaches for her and pulls her into his arms, sheltering her against his chest. "Shhhh. I've got you. Fucking O'Connell, I knew there was a reason I hated that prick from the first time we met."

Olivia's tears turn into a hard uncontrollable sob against his chest. Noah's heart hurts as he holds her tighter, completely wrapping his big body around her in a protective cocoon. His mouth rests warmly on the top of her head. "Jesus. What the fuck did he do to you, Baby Girl?"

Chapter Forty-Nine

For the first time in weeks, Olivia hasn't heard from Ethan. She's not even sure if she's happy about that or not. Keeping her office door closed, she hopes that no one will bother her, since she's not feeling like any company today. Eating lunch at her desk, she throws herself into her work, trying to keep her mind busy.

When Rachel gets back into the office after her meeting, she peeks through the glass door trying to get her attention. When that fails, she opens the door and intrudes. "Time to go home, James!"

"Already?" Olivia picks up her cell phone to look at the time. An entire day has gone by and not one text from him. Her heart feels heavy, but she has nobody to blame but herself.

Rachel grows tired of waiting for her to offer the information. "Is everything okay between you and Ethan?"

"Yes, fine. Why?" Olivia tries hard not to let it show on her face.

Rachel is annoyed that Olivia is keeping secrets from her, AGAIN. She's absolutely going to call her out on it. "I heard a rumor that he has a date tonight."

Hearing Rachel say it aloud makes Olivia suck in a deep breath. "That's not a rumor. He told me that himself last night." She avoids Rachel's glare while putting away some files and tidying her desk.

"And... you're okay with that?"

"What am I supposed to do about it?" she asks annoyed.

"Ummm, how about tell him that you love him and that you don't want him to date anyone else?" Rachel crosses her arms in front of her and widens her stance, growing angry.

"Why would I do that?" Olivia feels her eyes start to tear up again. She fights it with everything she has. "We both know it's only a matter of time before he leaves anyway. Besides, Noah and I worked things out last night."

Rachel's mouth drops open in shock. "You did not!"

"Yes, we did." Picking up her purse, Olivia pushes past her in the doorway. Rachel lets her go, horrified by what she just heard. This is all her fault. She convinced Ethan that this is a good idea. Now, it would appear that she's sent Olivia running right back into the arms of Noah Thompson.

All the way home from the city, Ethan is looking at his phone, hoping that Olivia messages him. She's all he can think about. He didn't get a damn thing done today. All she has to do is send one message, asking him not to go, but that message never comes. When it's almost 8 p.m., he dabs on a little cologne and jumps into the Challenger.

Rachel immediately waves him over when he enters the restaurant.

"Did you see Olivia today?" he asks her, anxiously.

"Yes," Rachel hesitates, not certain that she wants to be the one to tell him.

Scott interrupts, "Ethan, please don't do this."

"I can't handle it anymore, Scotty. Always guessing, never knowing for sure how she feels. Does she love me as much as I love her? Does she see us together in the future?" Ethan's stomach bottoms out. "I can't stand the thought of her being with another man, and I'm sure as hell not sharing her." A slight twist of nausea washes over him as he realizes what it is that he's admitting. He can't stay with her unless she belongs only to him. This could be the end.

"Then just talk to her, but don't do this. This is wrong." Scott's getting angry now. "This is cruel, after everything she's been through. I understand you're frustrated... but this?"

Ethan thinks for a moment, knowing there's truth in what Scott's saying. Running his hands through his hair, he pauses with his hands on the top of his head. Why does she mess up his thoughts and cloud his judgment? Women!

"What do John and Carter think about your plan?" Scott asks curiously.

"They don't know. I didn't tell them."

Scott raises a brow. "Exactly! You didn't tell them because you know this is wrong and they wouldn't approve."

Ethan glances over at Rachel and she gives him an apologetic smile.

"I'm sorry Ethan, but now that I've had time to think about it, Scott's right."

Scott glances at her from the side. "You think? Here's something to think about, my darling wife, I will definitely be dealing with you when we get home." He tries to hide a grin when she wrinkles up her face and winces.

Ethan frowns and his brow creases. "Jesus. What am I doing? You're right, I can't do this to her. I'm going to call the whole thing off."

"Don't look now, but it's too late! Your date is here." Rachel nods her head toward the door.

Ethan turns to see Hannah in the tightest dress he has ever seen. "Lord have mercy," he murmurs. "It's a miracle that such a small amount of fabric can hold such enormous breasts."

"Holy crap!" Rachel says aloud. "I hope nobody gets hurt if those things escape!"

Scott pinches her. "Ouch!"

He raises an eyebrow at her in warning when she turns to give him a dirty look.

"What do I do?" Ethan asks Scott.

"Jesus, for a brilliant business man, you know fuck all about relationships. You should at least buy her a drink before you break her heart and send her packing."

"Very funny."

"I'm not kidding, don't even sit at a table, just bring her into the bar, buy her a drink and explain it to her. The truth. Then go to Olivia; tell her that you lied about having a date, to make her jealous. Then get down on your fucking knees and beg for forgiveness."

Ethan raises a brow at him.

"Trust me, five years of marriage. I know what I'm talking about."

Ethan looks to Rachel, who throws her hands up in the air. "Don't look at me, I'm deferring to my husband from now on."

Ethan nods. "Okay." He heads toward the door to greet Hannah with a forced smile.

Rachel picks up her phones and dials. "Who are you calling?" Scott asks.

"Olivia, who else?" She gives him an annoyed look. "I think she's ignoring me." She looks at the display as if it personally offended her.

"Poor thing is probably devastated," he surmises.

Looking up at Scott, Rachel is overcome with a horrible guilt. "This was a horrible idea! Why didn't you stop us?"

Scott glares at her shaking his head and biting his tongue.

Back at the house, Olivia is putting on mascara in the hall mirror. When the phone rings again, she answers it knowing that Rachel will just continue to redial until she does.

"Hi," Rachel says, expecting to find Olivia in a fragile state of mind.

"Hey!"

"So, how are you?"

"I'm okay."

"Why didn't you answer earlier?"

"I'm getting ready."

"Ready for what?"

"To go to the restaurant, I'll be there in a few minutes."

"Oh! Shit!" Rachel says loudly.

Olivia holds the phone away from her ear a few inches. "Excuse me? What's wrong with you?"

"Honey, please don't come in here tonight. It's not a good idea."

"Rachel. It's okay. I know Ethan will be there with his date."

"Olivia there's something you need to know about that."

A car pulls up out front of the orange brick townhouse and beeps its horn. "I have to go. I'll see you in a few minutes." She gives Rachel a taste of her own medicine and hangs up.

When Rachel gets dial tone, she panics. As Ethan ushers Hannah back into the bar his cell phone rings and he excuses himself. "Order a drink," he offers. "I have to take this call and I'll be right back."

"Wait, Ethan!" Rachel yells after him as he heads to his office.

"What's going on?" Scotts asks, concerned.

"Olivia is on her way here, Scott. He has to get Hannah out of here before she shows up."

Scott looks at his watch. "Okay, let's give him a minute."

"No! He needs to do it NOW! She'll be here any minute."

"All right! I'll go and let him know." His voice fades as he moves to the other side of the room. Rachel barely makes out something about... not being in this mess if they had listened to him in the first place.

She frowns; she knows her husband is right and she's so thankful for his patience. Growing up she often felt socially inept, but then that's bound to happen under her circumstances. There were never any adult role models who cared about her. At times, it feels like her moral compass just can't seem to lock onto magnetic north. Olivia's parents loved Rachel as one of their own: taking her in, supporting, and guiding her. Directly within the loving arms of the James family, she almost started to feel *normal*. She didn't get enough time with them before they were taken away from her, as well.

Assuming that the horn blast means that he isn't coming to the door, Olivia walks out front to meet him. It feels odd when he doesn't get out of the car to open her door, but it doesn't surprise her.

"You look beautiful tonight." He takes a long look as she slides in and pulls her door closed.

She forces a smile. "Thank you, Noah."

They say very little on the short drive to the restaurant. Noah picks up on her tension. When he parks, he turns to look at her. "Are you okay?"

"I have to tell you that I'm having second thoughts." She nervously bites at her fingernails, avoiding his eyes.

"We talked about this last night. Everything will be fine." He tries to reassure her.

Anxiety pulses through her veins. "I'm so sorry. I can't ask you to do this." She panics as she undoes her seat belt, reaching for the door handle. Swinging it open, she starts to get out. "I'll call a cab to take me home."

"Wait!" Grabbing her arm, he stops her. "If you're not going to go in, then I'll take you home. You're not calling a cab."

"Thank you, Noah." Relief rushes over her quickly.

"But, I have a confession to make first."

She pulls her leg back inside the car and closes the door. "What?" Turning to look at him, she sees something dark and troubling in his eyes.

"Tonight is not only about letting O'Connell know that you're not going to stay at home and cry, while he's out with other women."

Olivia narrows her eyes, as he seems to struggle with whether to continue or not.

"You know that Ethan and I don't get along very well."

"Yes, which is why this is an even worse idea."

"That's why I suggested we do it. I can't think of any better way to get even with him for that shot he took at me, than to show up with you here tonight. It'll kill him and I like the idea of it."

She turns to look at him. "Are you nuts? You know he's going to hit you again, right?"

Noah smiles. "You let me worry about him, Baby. Nobody messes with me or my girl."

"Noah!" She scolds. "I made it very clear last night that nothing will ever happen between us. We'll always be *just friends*."

"I know, but you'll always be my girl."

Letting out a heavy sigh, Olivia flips down the visor to check her make up in the mirror. "I'm going straight to hell." She shakes her head, showing her discontent. "Okay, let's get this over with."

Glancing up at Noah, she exhales a nervous breath.

"Are you ready?" He asks as he holds opens the restaurant door.

"Here goes nothing." She tries to shake off the nerves.

Leaning down, Noah speaks quietly into her ear, "Stick with me, Baby. I know exactly how to make him squirm."

Feeling impatient, Hannah calls over the waitress. Rachel desperately tries to get Cindy's attention to wave her off, but she isn't paying attention. When Ethan finally shoots out of his office, he sees them on their way to a table. He tries to get to them as quickly as he can, but it's too late. Even at his quick sprint, they're already at the booth by the time he reaches them. "Hannah," he calls, wanting to discourage her from sitting.

Poison shoots through Olivia's veins as she hears his voice call out *that* name. She had no idea who he was seeing tonight, but she was absolutely **not** prepared for that. Noah recognizes Hannah immediately. Quickly stepping up behind Olivia, he wraps his arms around her middle, giving her a reassuring squeeze. Her body tenses against him. He's pretty sure that she's holding her breath. Pressing his lips to the top of her head, he holds them there. "I'm so sorry, Sweetheart. I know how much that must hurt."

When she finally finds the strength to look over, Ethan is standing frozen in the aisle, staring at her and Noah, his hands fisted at his sides. Her gaze locks to his, she tries to remember to breathe. It feels like somebody has just dropped an elephant on her chest.

Hannah, as usual, looks spectacular, immediately making Olivia feel even more inadequate. Noah rocks her gently in his arms, trying to soothe her. Dropping his mouth to her ear he whispers, "Breathe, Baby. If that's the kind of girl he's looking for, then you are way out of his league. He doesn't deserve you."

Scott taps Rachel on the shoulder, directing her attention to the door. Rachel looks at Olivia, then at Noah, and then over to Ethan. "Oh shit! We're in big trouble." They helplessly watch the scene unfold from the bar.

"Fuck!" Scott says, "This is going to get ugly. Where the hell are McCabe and Brant?" Taking his phone out of his pocket, he sends a few quick text messages.

Olivia takes a very deep breath. Letting it out slowly, she forces herself to smile and raise her hand to give Ethan a small wave hello. Nodding slightly, Ethan glares at Noah with murder in his eyes, trying to talk himself out of walking over and killing him.

Meanwhile, Hannah has made herself comfortable in the booth. "Ethan?" She looks to see what he's staring at. When she sees Olivia, a slow, wicked grin forms on her lips. Ethan sits; resigning to the fact that he's now on an official date with Hannah and that bastard, Noah Thompson, has his hands all over the woman he loves.

As Noah and Olivia are shown to a table in the same section, the hostess looks very confused as she glances over at Ethan with another girl.

Suddenly it's too much. Olivia can't fight back the tears that are welling up in her eyes. "Noah, I can't do this. I can't stand to see him with her."

She tries to pull away to leave but Noah takes hold of her arm, halting her in mid stride. "Hey. Relax. We're just going to have dinner. It will be fine, trust me."

To make things worse, they're seated at a table directly across from Ethan and Hannah, with a perfect view of everything going on. Hannah wiggles over as close as she can to Ethan, thrusting her humongous breasts at him. Olivia tries not to make eye contact, but she can't help it. When she does Hannah playfully feeds him the skewered cherry from her drink, making sure that Olivia knows that he's with her tonight.

Olivia can't believe her eyes. Why Hannah? She wishes it were anybody but her. Well, actually, that's not true. She wouldn't be too happy to see Stacey, either. Olivia tries to pull herself together, but a single tear escapes and trickles down her cheek.

Noah frowns as he brushes it away with the pad of his thumb. "Don't let him see you cry."

Dinner drags on forever, drawing out Olivia's torture. When the DJ starts to play music, the bar starts to become busier, providing a bit of a distraction. Feeling Ethan's eyes on her, she looks up to meet the heat of his stare. She feels a little bit of satisfaction in that he doesn't look like he's having a good time at all.

Rachel catches her attention and nods in the direction of the restroom. She leaves Noah for a welcome conversation with her best friend. Ethan's eyes follow Olivia across the room. Then they flash back to Noah, who's leaning back against the booth with a great sense of victory and an evil smirk.

Hannah excuses herself, leaving the table. Noah watches as her boobs sway back and forth, like heavy pendulums, as she struggles to walk in her stylish stilettos. He chuckles, shaking his head, and then looks back at Ethan. "Nice!" he says sarcastically. "She looks just like *your* type."

Ethan clenches his jaw as his muscles tighten. He'd like nothing better than to flatten Noah, right here and now, but he made a promise to Olivia. Another plan then, getting to his feet, he heads over to the waitress station. He grins mischievously as he punches in his password and spends a few moments on the computer billing system.

Once inside the bathroom, Rachel can't wait to get a few things off her chest. "What the hell are you thinking bringing Noah here?" she yells.

Olivia is feeling more than a little annoyed at the question. "Why wouldn't I bring him here?"

"Let me see… ummm… because Ethan is going to kill him. Does that sound like a good reason?"

"Stop it, Rachel," Olivia says angrily. "Ethan obviously doesn't care whom I'm here with. He has his own date."

"Yes, he does," Hannah says, standing just inside the doorway. "And, it's about time you realize, once and for all, that you could never make a man like Ethan O'Connell happy."

Here we go again! Olivia folds her arms in front of her and waits for the humiliation.

"Excuse me?" Rachel says disgustedly. "I wasn't talking to you."

"No, but you and your friend, were talking **about** me." She gives Olivia the once over. "Honey, you shouldn't be surprised that he stopped asking you out. I offered you the number for my personal trainer months ago. You should have taken it."

Rachel gasps! Her jaw dropping as her head snaps in Olivia's direction. "Is she the reason you haven't been eating?" Her expression quickly changes to anger. Olivia doesn't have to answer, it's written all over her face. "What a Bitch!" Rachel is about to throw down.

"Oh, please," Hannah says, as she turns to ridicule Olivia. "Even if you did ditch that extra… what? Forty pounds? How long do you think you could keep him happy? I'm thinking a few months tops, before he gets bored and starts looking for a woman that's much more interesting."

Rachel starts toward her but Olivia grabs her. "Just let it go, Rach. She's right."

"To hell with that, she's NOT right. Ethan is in love with you, always has been. He's only here with her tonight because you're too freaking stubborn to admit you feel the same way."

Hannah laughs, "That's hilarious! Ethan in love with *her?*"

Rachel lurches forward but Olivia holds tighter. "You better walk back to your table right now, or they're going to have to take you out of here in an ambulance."

"Rachel? Honey? Is everything okay in there?" Scott stands with his foot on the edge of the door, holding it open just enough so he can hear her answer.

"Not really, Scott."

"Well, Sweetheart… everybody out here by the pool tables can hear you."

Olivia finally lets go of her arm. Rachel takes a deep breath and her tone becomes calmer.

"Okay, we're coming out now."

Hannah gleams as they walk past her. "Off you go ladies, back to the trailer park."

They're almost at the door when Olivia looks back at Hannah, wishing she had something to say. As usual, dealing with Hannah has left her feeling insecure and self-conscious, stripped bare to a painful level of vulnerability.

Hannah has to get one last jab in. "Honestly, honey, at least your friend has trapped some poor sucker already. If you're not going to lose some weight then at least stop buying your clothes at the second hand store. Or is that where you're looking for men to date now?"

Rachel turns, fully prepared to put an end to it. Scott grabs her from one side and Olivia pushes her from the other, until she's all the way out the door. Storming through the restaurant, she heads straight toward Ethan. Scott turns to Olivia. "Are you okay?"

She nods her head. She's really not, but she needs him to deal with Rachel.

"Okay good, because I think O'Connell's in danger. I better catch up to her."

"Go!" Olivia says, encouraging him to intervene.

Scott takes off at a quick jog and Olivia looks up to see Cindy standing a few feet away with a few shots of tequila. Walking over, she picks them up, one in each hand and downs them. "Please add those to Mr. O'Connell's bill tonight, Cindy." Emptying both glasses, she puts them rim down on the tray.

Cindy crinkles her noise and sighs as she turns to go back to the bar to refill her order. "Okay, but I have to tell you, I'm starting to miss my old job. It was nice and boring. I've never seen this much drama in my life, until I started here."

Olivia feels bad now. "I'm sorry."

"Oh, it's okay. They can wait a few minutes for new ones. Are *you* okay?"

Olivia continues to walk with Cindy back to the bar, letting out a big sigh.

"That bad huh? Did you two break up?" She glances over at the table where her boss is sitting with another woman.

Olivia laughs once. Apparently, everybody considered them a couple anyway. She wasn't even doing a good job of fooling herself. "Yeah, I guess so."

"So, what's all the excitement tonight?"

Olivia cringes, as she says it, "Revenge dates. Old Crush versus Office Whore: The death match. In the same restaurant."

"Oh! No! Are you kidding me? That chick comes in on a regular basis to see if he's here. If he's not here, she orders water and then leaves."

"That doesn't surprise me, at all."

"EW! She works with him?" Cindy suddenly realizes that's what Olivia said. "What is he thinking taking her on a date?"

Olivia jumps as Noah's voice approaches from behind. "Olivia? Is everything okay?"

"Noah. Yes, I'm sorry I was on my way back to the table but then I got side tracked by these two tequilas... and." Realizing that she's rambling, she stops herself and then looks up to find him chuckling at her.

"It's okay. Parker's wife came through there like a bat out of hell, grabbed O'Connell by the ear and was dragging him out of the booth by the time Parker got to her. He had to pick her up and throw her over his shoulder and take her outside to cool off. It was the funniest damn thing I've ever seen. I don't know what happened, so when you didn't come back right away I was concerned."

"Oh my God, Noah! That bitch cornered us in the bathroom and if you knew the things she said, you'd understand why Rachel was so angry."

"I could hear some of it when I was serving drinks over at the pool tables. It wasn't very nice at all," Cindy adds. Noah glances over at Cindy and smiles, making her blush. Olivia narrows her eyes at the reaction.

"I'm sorry, have you two met? Noah this is, Cindy. Cindy this is my friend, Noah Thompson."

"It's nice to meet you." He extends his hand and gives her an appreciative look.

Cindy dries her hands on her apron, takes his hand in hers and holds it. "Likewise."

She blushes again and looks between Noah and Olivia. "So, you two are just friends?"

Noah chuckles and his eyes sparkle a little. "Yes, Olivia and I are completely head over heels in friendship with each other. Have been for years."

Cindy glances over at Olivia who nods her head in agreement. "He's only on a date with me tonight to drive your boss nuts. They hate each other."

"Hate's a strong word, Olivia." Noah doesn't want to give Cindy the wrong idea.

Olivia puts her hands on her hips and scowls at him.

Noah laughs. "Okay, you're right. I hate him. But do you know what I do like? Dessert! And I ordered us some." He grins like a young child. "After you, my beautiful friend."

Olivia rolls her eyes as she starts to walk toward the table. Noah hesitates for a minute and then turns back toward Cindy with a very charming smile. "So, tonight I'm a little busy torturing your boss, in hopes that his head will explode in a jealous rage. Maybe another night you and I could have dessert together?"

Cindy blushes again and smiles. "Sure, that would be nice."

Noah grins from ear to ear. "Awesome, I know where to find you when I'm done, but for now I have to get back to my evil plan." He rubs his hands together like a cartoon villain. When he turns around to walk away, Olivia is standing, looking unimpressed with her arms crossed and her eyebrows raised. "I can let you out of this gig, right now, if you want."

"Ah! Well that's very kind of you, but as much as I'd like to spend time with the lovely Cindy tonight, I'm not quite finished fucking with O'Connell." He glances at Cindy over his shoulder and winks, leaving her smiling.

As they return to the table, their waitress arrives with a warm brownie right out of the oven, smelling absolutely sinful. There is a dollop of vanilla ice cream slowly melting on top. Placing it in front Olivia, she hands her two spoons. Noah slides over beside her and puts his arm around her. Taking one of the spoons out of her hand, he scoops up a small piece of brownie and directs it toward her mouth. He stares at her lips, waiting for her to open them so he can feed her, and smirking at her hesitation. "Come on, Baby."

She rolls her eyes and opens her mouth, letting him gently place the spoon on her tongue. Closing her lips around it, she moans when he slowly slides the spoon out of her mouth, leaving the chocolate treasure behind. She licks the chocolate off her lips seductively. Running the pad of his finger across her mouth, Noah collects the chocolate that she missed and then holds his finger to her closed lips.

Olivia talks really low, "Are you sure you wouldn't rather eat more of your brownie first, because if I lick your finger… you're going to get punched."

Noah shrugs. "Bring it on."

Olivia parts her lips, opening just enough for him to push his finger in. Using her tongue, she licks the rest of the chocolate off it.

Rachel's mouth hangs open as she watches.

"What's going on?" Scott isn't sure he wants to know.

"Oh, this is not a good thing. Ethan is barely keeping his shit together, over there, and Noah just turned the heat up a notch."

When Olivia looks over at Ethan, he's staring right at them and he's livid. She can feel the anger vibrating off his body from across the room. Hannah is trying desperately to regain his attention, but it's a lost cause. She flashes a look at Rachel who makes a face at her. More than a few minutes pass; Ethan hasn't broken his stare, nor has he acknowledged Hannah, even once.

In utter frustration, Hannah moves to the edge of the bench and picks up her purse. "Well, thank you for dinner, Ethan. But I need to go now." Standing, she moves around the table. "Don't bother seeing me out," she says in a snarky voice. "And don't bother calling me again."

Noah and Olivia both watch as Hannah stomps to the front of the restaurant and leaves.

"I can't believe she just left," Olivia whispers, looking over at Rachel.

"I can't believe he hasn't seemed to notice she's gone," Noah chuckles. Then, his face takes on a very serious look. "I think things just got very **REAL** for Mr. O'Connell. Are you ready?"

"For what?" She's curious about his change of expression.

"He's on his way over here."

Chapter Fifty

Olivia tenses and turns slightly in her seat, focusing on Noah. She resists the urge to look over her shoulder as Ethan walks over to their table and stops. She knows that he's there. She can feel his energy. It's been that way since the first day they met. Noah acknowledges him with a nod. "Ethan."

The DJ starts up a song. Noah wipes his mouth with a napkin, tossing it on the table. Grabbing Olivia's hand, he slides out of the booth taking her with him. "Excuse us, my date has promised me a dance."

Bumping him purposely, as he passes, Ethan clenches his fist readying himself for a fight. As Noah drags her by her hand, Olivia looks Ethan straight in the eye and whispers, "Don't."

Ethan's eyes are dark, intense. "What are you doing with this guy?" he asks angrily. Clenching his jaw tightly, the nerve at his temple starts to jump with an angry tick. His Irish temper boils very close to the surface.

Noah keeps moving, with Olivia trailing behind him. Turning, she looks for Ethan and finds him standing, motionless in the same spot; fists still clenched.

Reaching the dance floor, Noah spins her around until she's facing him. He wraps his arms around her, starting to move with the rhythm of the music. At first, there's an appropriate amount of space between them. As they turn and move with the music, Noah smoothly reels her in, closer and closer, until their bodies are touching.

Olivia can't help but watch for Ethan, her eyes darting across the room. She finally sees him taking a seat at the bar between Rachel and Scott. Anxiety winds tight inside her when the bartender hands him a shot glass and a bottle of scotch. Apparently, Johnnie Walker Black is the mind numbing booze of choice for Ethan O'Connell.

Now that she knows where Ethan is, she relaxes a little in Noah's arms. Noah is a good dancer, but not quite as good as Ethan is. Her body certainly doesn't react with the same molten heat as when she's close to Ireland. Noah's hands move from her hips to her back, pulling her closer. "You smell very nice," he whispers.

"Thank you, it's Ethan's favorite…" Stopping her thoughts, she groans, "Why did I say that? He drives me nuts, that man."

"Olivia, please forgive me for saying so, and I can't believe that I'm going to say this… but it seems to me that you love the guy."

Shocked, Olivia pulls back so she can see his face. "WHAT?"

Smoothing her hair behind her ear, he moves his lips to press against her forehead. "Don't get me wrong, I absolutely despise the bastard, but he's changed something in you. You glow when you look at him. Even tonight, I can tell when you're thinking about him, I can see it in your eyes. Question is… why are you fighting it?"

"I guess, I just don't understand what a man like him would see in a girl like me." She shrugs. "Then, Hannah said that a girl like me would never be able to make him happy in the end… and I know she's probably right. So, why put myself through that only to have him break my heart."

"Sweetheart, if that happened, and I'm not saying that it would… it couldn't possibly be as painful as what you two are putting each other through, right now."

"It almost sounds like you're trying to sell me on him."

"No! Don't get me wrong, I still think you should kick him to the curb and date me instead."

Olivia leans back and raises her eyebrows. "You're not going to try and convince me that we should give it a try after you just asked out another girl during our date?"

Noah tilts his head to the side, and then a charming grin starts to curl at the sides of his mouth. "That's a NO then?"

Olivia laughs and shakes her head. "That's a HELL NO!"

Spinning her around so that she's facing the bar, he continues to sway with her from behind. "Look at him. He's absolutely miserable. THAT… is a man in love. Why wouldn't he be? You are the most amazing, brilliant, and beautiful woman. The kind of woman *every* man fantasizes about."

Olivia blushes. "You've been very nice to me tonight."

"It's easy to be nice to you, Olivia. Really, it is." He smiles as he continues to sway her with the music then gently spins her back around so they're dancing chest to chest.

Olivia watches over his shoulder. Ethan downs another shot, banging the shot glass down so hard, it breaks. Rachel and Scott exchange tense looks.

"Noah… Ethan is getting really angry," Olivia frowns. "I'm sorry, Noah, but I think we should leave before he loses it."

"I can handle Ethan," he assures her. When he starts to lower his mouth to hers, she faintly hears Rachel scream out Scott's name. As Noah brushes the smallest of kisses across her lips, she feels him being abruptly ripped away. Opening her eyes, she sees Ethan standing nose to nose with Noah, engaging him in a standoff, in the middle of the dance floor. His hands are twisted in the material of Noah's shirt, holding him. Noah grins at him, which only stokes his fire.

"Something wrong, O'Connell?"

Noah's ghost of a grin taunts Ethan into something that closely resembles rage. "I've told you before to stay away from her, Thompson."

"Okay, guys, let's just calm down." Scott tries to diffuse the situation but he fears he's a few warriors short for this battle. Where the fuck are Brant and McCabe? "Ethan, you need to walk away."

Olivia starts to get a little freaked out. When has Ethan warned Noah to stay away from her? "Ethan!" She tries to get his attention, knowing that he's a few scotches past being rational.

"I hope veterinarians have good dental plans, because I'm going to knock out all of your teeth," Ethan growls, as he pushes against Noah's chest. Scott grabs him by the shoulder and tries to pull him away but Ethan shakes him off, taking another step toward Noah. Noah holds his ground, making Ethan bump hard against his chest. The restaurant security team has joined them. When they see that it's the boss causing the ruckus they hold back and wait.

Watching the aggressive pushing and shoving take place between these two uber alpha males is threatening to coax poor Olivia right into another anxiety attack. Rachel stands at her side, rubbing her back gently, trying to soothe her while they watch helplessly. "Scott, just put an end to this!" she snarls.

"I'm trying to, Honey," Scott's voice is strained as he physically tries to pry them apart. Looking over at the burly security detail, he scowls. "A little help here, fellas?"

Olivia holds her palms to her forehead and tries to take in long slow breaths. Struggling to hold back the tears that are forming in her eyes, she takes a step forward, pressing herself against Ethan's side. "Ethan," she says calmly. When he doesn't respond she tries again a little louder, "ETHAN!"

Glancing over at her, nostrils flaring, he establishes eye contact. He lets go of Noah's shirt when he sees the tears in her eyes. The fear on her face makes him feel much more concerned for her, than his anger for Noah. "Are you okay?"

"Of course she's okay, O'Connell. She's with me." Ethan tenses again.

"Stop it, Noah!" Olivia warns. "Ethan, please. I'm not okay. You two are freaking me out. And… you made me a promise."

Ethan stares at her, recognizing the signs of her anxiety. He did promise her. "You're fucking lucky, Thompson," he growls, as he takes a step back. Scott quickly steps in between them and then ushers Ethan back into the bar.

He has barely sat down, when Noah walks past and grins at him, taunting him again. Ethan's on his feet in a flash; heading after him. Better prepared this time, Scott steps in front of him, putting both hands on his chest, stopping him in his tracks. "Sit down, buddy."

Ethan looks over Scott's shoulder and tries to push past him. Scott stands firm. "Ethan, I'm not kidding. Sit down! You started this and it back fired on you, so you're just going to have to deal with it."

Cursing, Ethan lets out a ragged breath and returns to his stool at the bar.

"Where the fuck are Brant and McCabe?" Feeling a little desperate, Scott pulls out his cell phone, checking it again.

Olivia is one big ball of anxiety now; Noah senses it in her body. Massaging her shoulders gently only seems to make it worse. "Are you okay?" He's concerned now, finally realizing that this whole thing is having a more serious effect on her than he thought it would.

"No! You guys stress me out."

"He sure is wound tight, right now. I told you he loves you."

"Oh that's right, that's why he asked Hannah big boobs out on a date!" She frowns.

"Well, I think I understand why he did that. I think he was trying to prove a point. I think he was trying to prove to you that you really don't want him to see anybody else. So, was he right about that?"

She shrugs her shoulders. "Is it okay if we call it a night? I'm exhausted."

Noah sighs deeply, "Of course. I'll see to the bill."

"I'm just going to say goodbye to Rachel."

It isn't easy ignoring Ethan when he's only a few feet away, but she does. Barely holding it together, she gives Rachel a hug, trying to avoid his unnerving stare. Suddenly Noah's voice echoes across the room, growing louder with his escalating anger. Standing alert, she tries to hear what's being said.

"$300? Just what the fuck was in that brownie?" He screams at the waitress. "Even *special* brownies wouldn't cost that much. Fucking O'Connell!"

Olivia looks over at him suspiciously. "Ethan? What the hell did you do?"

Looking mighty pleased with himself, Ethan turns away avoiding eye contact. He says absolutely nothing as he tips his glass to his lips.

When Noah starts to scream at the poor waitress again, Olivia grabs Cindy by the arm. "I need your help." Dragging her toward the table, she shoots Ethan a nasty look as she passes. "You're an asshole, Ireland."

When Olivia is far enough out of the room, Rachel turns to look at him. "Did you really charge him $300 for a brownie?"

Ethan nods, trying to hold back his laughter.

"Nice! I'm impressed!" Rachel nods her head in acknowledgement.

Once Olivia and Cindy have gotten the bill sorted out, Olivia starts toward the bar and notices Ethan is no longer there. She puts her hand on Rachel's shoulder to get her attention.

"Hey girl! Are you leaving finally?"

"Yes, this was a bad idea and I really want it to be over with." She frowns. "Where's Ethan?"

Rachel opens her eyes wide. "Um, well Scott suggested he go outside and get some air."

"Is he still angry?"

Rachel laughs, "That's an understatement! Seething is more like it."

"Oh, just great."

Noah waits for her at the front door, holding it open for her. Walking out into the cool evening air, she shivers. Ethan is parked right out front, leaning against the hood of his car waiting for her. Standing when he sees them come out, he begins to walk toward them, making Olivia nervous. She glances at Noah. "Please, don't get into a fight."

He smiles at her but doesn't answer.

"Noah?"

"Okay, I promise I won't start anything."

When Ethan reaches them, he ignores Noah all together. "Olivia, can I talk to you for a minute?" He stands in front of her, stopping her from passing. "Please."

Noah isn't impressed, but he waits for her cue. "It's okay, Noah. Can you give us a few minutes?"

Noah locks his eyes to Ethan's, giving him a silent warning. "I'll go get the car," he finally says, as he walks away leaving them alone.

"Ethan, please don't make a scene." The cool breeze makes her shiver again, prompting him to take off his jacket and wrap it around her shoulders.

"I just want to talk to you." She can hear the distress in his voice. "Can I drive you home so we can talk? Please."

Noah pulls up beside them. Getting out, he waits at the passenger door for her.

Oh hell no! He'll lose it, if she gets in Thompson's car. "Olivia. We need to talk," his voice is low and desperate. Something in his eyes traps her there, stopping her from leaving. She thinks on it a long time before walking over to where Noah's waiting. Ethan paces, muttering in Gaelic while he waits.

"What's going on?" Noah doesn't like the look on her face.

"Would it be extremely horrible if I let Ethan take me home?"

"Do you think that's a good idea?" Noah asks with concern. "He still looks really angry."

"You're the one who made him angry, he's not mad at me." Her tone has a little bite to it. She quickly apologizes, "I'm sorry, Noah. I'm just... he won't hurt me. He just wants to talk and I guess you're right... maybe I do love him."

Noah shrugs. "Well, if that's what you want, then my job here is done. Any chance I can get a good night kiss?"

"That would *not* be a good idea," she says, rolling her eyes.

Glancing over, he catches Ethan's glare. "Yeah, you're probably right and now that I realize just how much he loves you, I feel a little guilty for yanking his chain tonight. Listen, Olivia, if ever there's a time that he doesn't treat you right, you give me a call… I'll kick his ass. I promise that I'll take good care of you, if you give me the chance."

"I believe you. Thank you so much for tonight. I think this was the worst date I've ever been on." She gives him a small smile.

"What are you talking about worst date? I got a dessert date with the beautiful Cindy. You figured out that you're in love with a tightly wound Irishman. It's a win-win situation, right?"

Olivia wraps her arms around his middle giving him a friendly hug, knowing that Ethan hasn't taken his eyes off her for a minute. When Noah drives away, she walks back to where Ethan is waiting at the Challenger with the passenger door open. Smelling his cologne on his jacket, she inhales deeply, wrapping it tighter around herself as he closes her door. Getting behind the wheel, Ethan drives toward the road; he then suddenly pulls into a spot at the back of the parking lot away from everyone.

Consumed by jealousy and fueled by his anger, he puts it in park, taking his hands off the steering wheel. They sit in silence for quite some time. Ethan's body rigid and tense as he stares straight ahead. His silence is tormenting her; making her wish he would say something… anything. It's not his style to keep this still. Why is he so quiet? She's just about to plead him to just get it over with when he turns toward her, finally breaking the silence.

"Are you warm enough?"

What? She looks at him trying to gauge what's going on in his head. "Yes, thank you." Growing nervous, she fidgets with the sleeves on his jacket.

As Ethan does, his tone goes from quiet and concerned, to angry and combative, without warning. "Olivia, tell me you didn't kiss him goodbye."

She's startled at his change in tone. "Not this again, Ethan." The frustration makes her want to scream. In the faint illumination of the parking lot light, she can see his jaw tense and his rapid pulse thrumming in his neck. "Why do you insist on asking me these kinds of questions? Why do you care who I'm kissing?"

"Because I'm jealous!" His loud voice is evidence of his rising anger. "You had to know that seeing him touch you was going to push me over the edge!" His eyes open wide and brows rise. "Are you happy now?"

"Why would I be happy about that?" she says, feeling defensive.

He turns in his seat shifting himself sideways so that he can see her. "I can't handle seeing you with that guy. I don't want you to see him, ever again."

She laughs at his ridiculous statement. "Well, you have a lot of nerve!" She feels her own temper start to flare now. "I do believe that it was *you* who asked Hannah on a date first."

Ethan's expression takes on a hard edge. "I only did it because you told me to date other women!" His tone threatens to engage her in a full-blown screaming match. "That's all you've talked about for two days."

"Well, you didn't waste any time did you? But then, she practically throws herself at you every day." Raising her voice, Olivia has no intentions of backing down this time.

"And how many times has Noah tried to get into your panties?" Staring at her with steely eyes, the muscles in his jaw clench, his nostrils flaring as he tries to hold back his anger. "What was I supposed to do? I figured you really must want me to do it, you just kept pushing."

"I never pushed you to see other women!" *Or did she?* Olivia can feel herself getting antsy. As her natural flight response starts to kick in, she battles the urge to run.

"Yes, you did!" Ethan erupts, "Jesus, woman!" His arms flail angrily as he speaks.

"Ethan, I said you *could* date other women if you wanted to… not that I wanted you to!" She can't look at him anymore. Her eyes drop to watch her hands fidgeting frantically; twisting at the cuffs of his jacket.

Furious, he bangs his hand down hard on the console making Olivia jump. "How am I supposed to know what you want?" The angrier he gets the stronger his accent is. She has to concentrate hard in order to understand some of what he's trying to say. "You tell me it's okay to date other women and point them out to me for two days. Then when I ask someone out, you're upset because you don't *want* me to see other women?" After running his hands through his hair, he leans his head back against the headrest. "I can't fucking win! Then, you show up here tonight with that jackass?"

"Well, if you didn't get drunk and pass out on me at the hotel, maybe you would have remembered that I agreed to be your girlfriend that night," she blurts it out; then watches the uncontrollable rage flash across his face.

"I knew you were fucking lying to me about that night!" he says through gritted teeth. "Why? Why didn't you just tell me when I asked you? We could have avoided this whole fucking mess."

Startled by the intensity of his outburst, she slowly retracts towards the door; further out of his reach… just in case. Ethan stops and forces himself to take a calming breath. He struggles with himself, but he just can't let it go. "What a surprise. You don't have an answer?" His ability to control his rage is declining. "I can't stand it anymore, Olivia. You get into my head and I can't think straight. I knew the very first time I saw you that we're meant to be together. I can't stand the thought of you being with another man. I've explained to you before that I'm the kind of man who needs to be in control. Every second of every day, I fight against my desires for you, and look at all the fucked up shit that's gone on in the last week because of it. Well, from now on we do things my way. Starting with this *'seeing other people'* garbage. That shit stops and it stops, right now!"

Olivia locks her eyes to his, her breathing starting to come at a quicker pace. There's something in her expression that he can't read until she speaks, "Why do you have to fight your desires because of me?"

Fuck. He takes another calming breath, letting it out slowly.

"Ethan? Answer me. I knew exactly what I was getting myself into with you. We discussed it at the beginning, how things would be. How sex would be. You've been holding back and I want to know why." She doesn't look away, no longer feeling intimidated. For once Ethan hesitates, not wanting to answer.

"Rachel told you *everything* that happened, didn't she?"

"Olivia ..." he starts.

"So, is that why you won't do those things we talked about? Dominance, false resistance, submission."

"Olivia. There's nothing wrong with the sex that you and I have." His jaw tenses as he tries to keep his voice calm. "It's pretty fucking amazing."

"You're deflecting."

"How can I possibly take you there after what happened to you?" he growls out in frustration.

Olivia gets angry. "Damn it, Ireland! See? That's why I didn't want to tell you about it. I told you that you would treat me differently, if you knew."

Rage can no longer be contained and he yells his frustration, "Different how? By caring about your physical and emotional well-being? Damn right! There's nothing more important to me than that. And yet, despite how hard I try to put you at ease, you keep yourself so closed off to me that we can't seem to move forward together. Things would be fine if you would just stop fighting me. I could make you happy... I know that I'm what you need. There's no question that I'm the one you want. But you're so damn... **Intractable.**"

Olivia sits still, not moving, not blinking. His harrowing words hit her hard. The few moments of absolute silence that follow them are daunting. "You think I'm *that* difficult?" She can't hide the hurt in her voice.

Ethan calms his tone but he's still aggravated. "Yes... more than stubborn. Like a precious metal from some other fucking planet that won't be shaped."

She sits pensively, her hands stilled in her lap. "Rigid," she whispers sadly.

Ethan continues, not even noticing that she's given up and no longer fighting. "You won't just let things happen, it's like you try to calculate every little thing that can go wrong and then avoid everything that would put you on that path."

He's right, that's exactly what she does. She can't even begin to defend herself.

"Life shouldn't be lived that way, Olivia. You should jump in with both feet and experience it. Life is not a straight line... it has *bends* in it. You have to learn how to bend."

The message would have been much better received, if not growled at her in anger. Tears form in her eyes as her emotions turn to sadness. "Well then, I understand why you'd prefer to be with the pretty blonde with all the boobage. She certainly seems to be more... *bendable*." Her voice cracks as her insecurities take control of her. She's been dreading this day; the day she can no longer restrain the tears.

Ethan still has no idea why she feels so threatened by Hannah. Realizing how damaging his words have been, he softens his approach. "How could you possibly think that I would rather be with Hannah? Haven't I proven to you, time and again, that it's *YOU* that I want? God knows why... you're the most difficult woman I've ever met." He shakes his head, rubbing his hand along the whiskers on his jaw. "When I'm with you, I feel like our souls are tangled together and we're not meant to be apart. Don't even suggest that you don't feel the same. How can you question something THAT strong?"

She says nothing, and it makes him angrier. Sighing, he continues to fight hard enough for the both of them.

"Has it ever occurred to you that I'm scared, too? This is new to me. I've never felt like this before either, and you don't make it easy on me. I have to weigh every word before it comes out of my mouth, every action, and every movement has to be carefully considered. I fight my own nature because I'm terrified that I'll scare you away. Please stop running. Let me love you... we'll figure it out together."

Olivia wishes she could believe him, but how? How long could he be happy with her? How long would it be before another Stacey or Hannah comes along and gets his attention? "Why her, Ethan? Of all the girls that fall all over you, why did it have to be her?"

The guilt hits him right in the stomach, harder than one of McCabe's punches. "Olivia."

"Every night I go to bed," she interrupts. "And I worry that all those things she said to me a few weeks ago and again tonight are true." Tears well up in her eyes and she fights them with everything she has.

"What did she say to you, Olivia? Tell me." There isn't a word to describe the emotion he feels when he sees the tears in her eyes. "Please, don't cry. For fuck's sake, just tell me what she said," he pleads. "How many times do I have to beg that of you?" He reaches for her hand, tortured by seeing her so upset. He gets a sharp pain in his heart when she pulls away, moving closer to the door.

Sniffling, she sits forward and drops his jacket off her shoulders and onto the seat then pulls away from him, wiping her tears with the back of her hand.

Ethan becomes distressed. "Olivia, what are you doing?" He recognizes her response. She's going to run. Pulling on the handle, she opens the door, swinging her legs out and standing. "I'm walking home."

"Don't you dare walk away, we're not finished talking about this," he commands. Jumping out of the car, he quickly rounds the hood and gets to her side. Continuing to walk toward the road, she completely ignores him. Desperate, he grabs her arm from behind, stopping her in mid-step and forcing her to turn around and look at him. "You have to know there's not a chance in hell that I'm letting you walk anywhere alone at this time of night. Get your ass in the car!" he yells.

Looking down at her elbow, where he has a firm hold on her, anger starts to pulse through her blood like a jolt of electricity. When she lifts her gaze, Ethan sees, for the very first time, unsettled anger in her eyes. Finding the strength to challenge his authority, she glares at him with a cold, dark look of fury.

Frightened by what he sees in her expression, Ethan releases her immediately. His hand drops heavily to his side. A stabbing pain pierces his chest, straight into his heart. He doesn't ever want to see that expression on her face again. His anxiety is evident in the rise and fall of his chest as he desperately considers how to stop her from leaving.

"Olivia," whispering in a gentle, nonthreatening tone, he tries to persuade her to stay. "Be reasonable. I'm sorry. No more yelling, we'll just talk. Please, just get in the car."

She takes a step back, not once looking away from his eyes.

"Olivia, wait." He reaches for her again.

She stops him with an arctic stare. Stepping back, she moves further out of his reach.

Turning, she moves away at a brisk pace, leaving him frozen where he stands and watching her disappear. Her voice trails off into the cool dark veil of night, "Go fuck yourself, Ireland!"

The story continues...

Book 2 of the Bound4Ireland Series

When the one you want, is undeniably the one you need…
put aside your fears and believe.

Coming Winter 2015

Book 3 of the Bound4Ireland Series

When he's everything she needs, and she's the only one he wants…
All things are possible, when you believe.

Tricia
Daniels

How to find me!

Author.Tricia.Daniels@outlook.com
Twitter: @TDanielsAuthor
Td Blog spot: triciadanielsbooks.blogspot.ca
Facebook: Author Tricia Daniels
TSU: Tdaniels
Amazon Author: triciadanielsamazonauthor
Goodreads: Author Tricia Daniels
Pinterest.authortriciadan
Tumblr: triciadaniels

Romance Eh, Canadian Style Blog:
romancecanadianstyle.blogspot.ca